beyond the
Summerland

THE BINDING OF THE BLADE

BY L. B. GRAHAM

Beyond the Summerland

BOOK 1
THE
BINDING
of the
BLADE

beyond the Summerland

L. B. GRAHAM

P&R
PUBLISHING
P.O. BOX 817 • PHILLIPSBURG • NEW JERSEY 08865-0817

Page design by Tobias Design
Typesetting by Michelle Feaster

Printed in the United States of America

Library of Congress Cataloging-in-Publication Data

Graham, L. B. (Lowell B.), 1971–
    Beyond the Summerland / L. B. Graham.
        p.   cm.—(The binding of the blade ; bk. 1)
    Summary: Joraiem and other young members of Novaana, the ruling class of men, train in Summerland to rule Kirthanin and to defend it against the evil schemes of Malek.
    ISBN 0-87552-720-5
    [1. Fantasy.] I. Title.

PZ7.G7527Be 2004
[Fic]—dc22

                                                     2003067184

For Jo, who loves me

CONTENTS

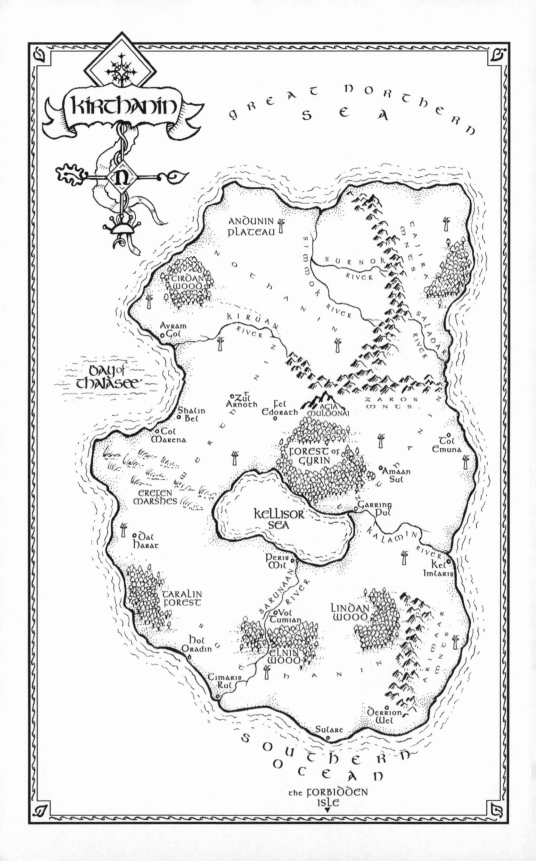

PROLOGUE
MALEK'S GIFT

ANDUNIN CRADLED THE HEAD of his son, his only son, in his lap. Slowly his fingers brushed back the dark hair from the boy's eyes. The blood on his own fingertips left damp smears on the smooth skin of Tarlin's forehead. A wind like Andunin had never felt before sliced through his soggy cloak as the rain fell cold and hard. Water slipped down his face under the curls of his thick grey beard and fell from his chin upon Tarlin's face and neck. His hands, trembling from the cold, brushed Tarlin's eyelids closed.

In the distance a group of armed men stood around a pile of bodies, slowly but steadily dragging more and more of the slain to the growing mound, but Andunin hardly noticed them. What did he care who else had died? The plight of some foolish merchant or farmer, or even one of the Novaana who had joined in a band of like fools to oppose his army, was no longer of any consequence to him. His son was dead.

The howling of the wind faded, and for just a moment Andunin thought that he could hear music. Just a few notes, faint and distant, echoed in his mind. What was the song? He could not remember it, but he was filled with the certainty that it was very important that he remember. He had sung the song a hundred, maybe a thousand times before, but still it eluded him. He didn't seem to be able to think of anything. The fine black hair in matted clumps under his fingers and the pale cold skin beneath it obscured all else in his memory. There had been a song, of that he was sure, and somewhere, just beyond the edges of his consciousness, that song was playing. If only he could squeeze everything else out and hear it. If only he could forget the endless marches, the bitter battles, and the sudden, fateful, fatal blow.

Suddenly it was there—a single note at first, then the beginning of a melody. His eyes flickered shut.

Andunin strolled through the field. The grass that had been a brilliant green when he left was now rimmed with brown. Much longer without rain and the summer harvest would be less than the early signs had promised. Even so, while a drier than expected summer would be disappointing, the yield of Andunin's land would be far short of disastrous. Any man who owned as much land as Andunin—in fact, any man who owned or worked the land at all—knew it was foolish to think that some seasons would not be difficult and some harvests not disappointing. For every year that the land produced an abundant yield, there was one, sometimes two, in which the final output was moderate if not lean. To allow such realities to rule one's spirits or emotions was to be broken by the land, and Andunin was not a man to be broken by anything.

Davras appeared over the rise leading the sleek, chestnut gelding Andunin had given to Tarlin for his birthday. Tarlin sat proudly, if cautiously, upon the horse's back. Andunin smiled as recognition suddenly showed itself in Tarlin's face.

"Dad! You're back!"

"That I am, son," Andunin answered as Tarlin hastily dismounted and ran across the field to him. Andunin stooped and picked up his ten-year-old son, then swung him around and around. "Oh," he groaned, "you've grown in the last month, I can tell."

"How were the meetings, Dad?" Tarlin asked when finally he had come to rest against his father's chest. "Were there many dragons?"

"There are always dragons when the Novaana meet, Tarlin, plenty of dragons."

"Was Sulmandir there?" Tarlin asked with a reverent whisper.

"No, son, Sulmandir wasn't there this time."

"Oh," Tarlin said, obviously disappointed. The next moment his face brightened, though, as he added, "I thought about naming my horse Sulmandir, Dad, but it didn't seem right. Guess what I did name him."

"I don't know, Tarlin, what did you name him?"

"Minladir. Davras says that means 'friend of the dragon.'"

"Indeed it does, Tarlin. It is a good name." Andunin set Tarlin down and greeted Davras as he caught up with them at last. "Allfather's blessing upon you, Davras. My thanks for your many pains taken with Tarlin."

"And upon you, Master Andunin, I assure you I took no pain from my service with Tarlin, none whatsoever," Davras replied with a slight bow. "How was the Assembly?"

"As such things go, it was all right. The number of the Novaana seems always to grow, and with growth everything takes longer. Consensus isn't as easy to attain as it once was. Just thinking about it hurts my head." Andunin laughed as they all turned back toward the house. "I wonder," Andunin continued, "if the Twelve ever take so much time to make decisions."

"Why don't you ask Malek the next time he comes, Dad?"

Andunin threw his head back and laughed. He roared until his sides ached and tears began to stream down his face.

"Ask Malek," he gasped when he had gathered his breath, "that is priceless."

He stooped and took Tarlin in his arms. "I have missed you, my son, very much. You give mirth to my heart, but I am afraid that I cannot ask Malek."

"Why not?"

"Because the Twelve are Allfather's representatives, here to rule Kirthanin on Allfather's behalf," Andunin replied. "They do not consult with men about their business. What's more, if any man even considered posing such a question to one of the Twelve, it would not be to Malek." He wiped the tears from his face and suddenly grew sober. He grasped Tarlin by his arms. "It is important that you learn from me, as I learned from my father, the appropriate way to approach any of the Titans. The first rule is to treat them with almost as much respect as you would treat Allfather if you could see and talk to him in the flesh. They do not look it when they come among us, but the Twelve are powerful beyond imagination."

"Are they as powerful as Sulmandir?"

"They are even more powerful than the Father of Dragons, as hard as it may be for you to believe that."

"Father, are you afraid of Malek?"

The question surprised Andunin. "No, I wouldn't say that I am afraid, exactl, he said as he lifted Tarlin onto Minladir's back. The Twelve are servants of Allfather as are we. They guide and direct us. However, prudence demands we treat them with respect. At any rate, I was just thinking out loud. I have no real desire to know anything other than what the Twelve wish to tell me. Besides, we are not likely to see Malek again until after the harvest has come and gone, if then."

As they approached the house, a massive golden form soared over the trees that lined Andunin's fields to the south. The beating wings of the dragon sent powerful gusts of wind that bent back the ripening grain and blew Andunin's hair about his face. The dragon gripped a moderate sized garrion in his talons, perhaps large enough for a dozen men.

"Sulmandir! It's Sulmandir, Dad!" Tarlin yelled with excitement.

"No, Tarlin, it isn't Sulmandir," Andunin answered.

"But he's gold," Tarlin protested.

"Yes, I know it's hard. All of Sulmandir's children appear golden. Only Sulmandir is *completely* golden. If you look closely at this dragon's scales, Tarlin, you will see that they have a bluish gleam as well. Can you see?"

Tarlin squinted at the dragon as it passed to their left. "I think so, but I'm not sure."

"It takes time to be able to see, son. I was older than you before I could tell from a distance which dragons were blue, which green, and which red. I'll tell you a secret, though. If you get close enough, there is another clear color marker on any dragon. Look at the nails on his talons. The skin beneath the nails always tells you what color the dragon really is. Still, before you know it, you'll be able to tell by the color of the scales, even if far away."

As they watched, the dragon wheeled before them in the sun, and the light reflected blue-gold off of its sleek and powerful body. "I saw the blue, Dad, I saw it!" Tarlin called out.

"Good," his father replied as the dragon passed almost directly above them and disappeared to the north. A dragon tower and garrion field lay in that direction. "We had better get home quickly so we can warn your mother that we may have guests."

Andunin's house was spacious and comfortable, even if it could not rival the remarkable three-and four-storied homes of some of the Novaana further south. Andunin helped Tarlin down from Minladir's back and mounted the horse himself. "Tarlin, hurry now and tell Mother that I am off to greet our guest—or guests. I'll be back shortly. Davras, saddle as many horses as you can quickly and follow me to the tower. If one or more of the Twelve have come, it would be best not to keep them waiting."

Andunin spurred Minladir on and was soon racing along the narrow road that ran through the trees north of the house.

As Andunin entered the large empty field that surrounded the dragon tower, he saw the open garrion resting on the ground beside the tower. His eyes traced the slender line of the tower up into the dazzling sky. As he squinted, he thought he saw a massive golden wing extend beyond the gyre and then retract. Looking back from the tower to the garrion, he approached it slowly, wondering who waited within.

As he prepared to dismount Minladir, a tall figure stepped from the shadows of the garrion, pausing momentarily so that only his silhouette was visible, before stepping into the bright sunlight. He was a little taller than Andunin, standing almost a full hand over a span high, and powerfully built. Indeed, he projected such an image of strength that it often took some time for those meeting him for the first time to realize he was also quite handsome. He was dressed all in blue with a silver insignia of a great hammer upon his chest. A long white cape swept the floor of the garrion as he stepped into the grass of the field, and thick brown hair fell down upon broad shoulders, curling slightly at its ends. His sharp blue eyes gazed out from a face that reminded Andunin of the solidity of iron despite the slight smile that traced his lips.

"Malek," Andunin began, dropping from Minladir and taking a knee before the Titan in human form before him, "I did not expect you at this time of year. I was not prepared to greet you appropriately. I am sorry. My servant, Davras, is on his way with a horse. Forgive the delay."

"Andunin," Malek began with a voice that was simultaneously soft and powerful. "Do not worry yourself. I am well aware of the unusual nature of my visit. I did not expect that you would be prepared to greet me. I am reasonable, after all."

After saying each syllable of the word "reasonable" slowly, as though savoring them, Malek threw his head back and laughed. Andunin looked in wonder. In the many years he had known Malek, he had never heard such laughter. It was as if Malek had told a joke that only he could understand. When he had finished laughing at his own apparent hilarity, Malek placed his hand upon Andunin's shoulder and gazed into Andunin's eyes. Andunin saw a spark in them that he had never before seen in the eyes of any living thing. Though his recent claim to Tarlin still lingered in his mind, he felt wary and frightened. He had never thought before this moment that this kind of fear was possible before one of the Twelve, but he felt it now.

"I am reasonable," Malek continued, "and I know that you are reasonable as well. Yes, Andunin, you are reasonable and valiant and wise, which is why I have come to you. There is much that must be said. I have, shall we say, an offer to make, unlike any that has ever passed between one of the Twelve and mortal man."

Andunin, who had started to stroke Minladir as though to soothe him, realized just then that his hand was shaking slightly. "I come to you with the promise of a new world," Malek continued. "A new dawn for Kirthanin is coming. Indeed, in one sense it has come already, and I have come to you, Andunin, to explain what part you are going to play in it all—to offer you something you would never imagine."

At that moment, Davras emerged from the woods, riding hard with four horses in tow. Malek looked beyond Andunin at the approaching horses and continued, "Of this I have more to say, but not tonight. Let us enjoy the fine evening that lies before us and the beautiful Nolthanin stars. Take me to that lovely wife of yours, Andunin, and we will feast tonight as we have so often before. Even now she prepares the feast, does she not?"

"She does," Andunin replied. "It has been hastily prepared, but Cilana is remarkable even on short notice."

"I doubt it not," Malek replied.

Davras arrived and soon Malek was seated on Nothrimar, a pale white stallion of exceptional size and strength that he had ridden many times before. Malek spurred the great horse and led the way at a gallop back south across the field and into the woods.

The following day a steady rain fell throughout the morning. Andunin watched it through the window, knowing he should feel grateful, but the uneasiness and uncertainty that Malek's arrival had created hung heavily upon him.

Malek sat and told stories of the Twelve and of life in Avalione, the blessed city, to a fascinated Tarlin, who knew enough to know that he was bearing witness to a rare thing. The Twelve did not speak often of life upon Agia Muldonai, the Holy Mountain, especially Malek. Though Malek was the contact between the Council of Twelve and Andunin and the other Novaana of the far north, he seldom spoke of anything other than human affairs. Today, though, he spoke of the great temple to Allfather, located in the center of the city, and the Crystal Fountain in the temple courtyard. The water of the Fountain was as clear as glass, the purest water in all Kirthanin. Since the dawn of time, streams and rivers from the Fountain had flowed through the center of Avalione and down the slopes of the Holy Mountain itself. Eventually the waters poured from a waterfall near the base of the mountain into a pool that drained by way of a subterranean cavern beneath the mountain. The Fountain tapped the waters of the great deep and was said to be the fountainhead of all the lesser waters of

Kirthanin, but Malek did not speak of that today. Rather, he spoke with a whispered awe of the glory of the blessed city and the beauty of the Crystal Fountain.

When at last the morning rain had passed and the midday meal was over, Malek turned to Andunin and said, "Time is pressing. Let us ride and speak together."

Little more than an hour later, Andunin found himself astride his own horse, Folnik, riding quietly beside Malek and Nothrimar through the hills beyond the dragon tower. Eventually they came upon a small tributary of the Simmok River. Malek dismounted and led Nothrimar to the water to drink. As Andunin watched Malek, today swathed in a great dark blue cloak, he felt for the second time the ripple of anxiety that had pierced him the previous day. He felt it more deeply with each passing moment.

Malek turned from the water, and Andunin saw an eerie light glowing in his pale blue, almost luminescent eyes. "Andunin," he began, "a great change is coming to Kirthanin, and I have come to reveal to you the role that you will play in it."

"Yes, my Lord," Andunin replied in a trembling voice, dismounting from Folnik and leading him also to water.

"The old order is passing away and a new order will soon begin. The Council of Twelve has served its time, but it no longer satisfies the needs of the land. The Novaana have served their time, but they no longer satisfy the needs of the men of Kirthanin. The time has come for me to assume my rightful place, not as first among the Twelve, but as ruler of all Kirthanin. It is also time for the unwieldy council of the Novaana to yield its authority to the rule of a mortal king, a king who will receive his crown, of course, from me. I have decided that this king shall be you."

Andunin stroked the smooth back of Folnik, who greedily drank the cool water. Andunin tried not to look at Malek, but the intensity of Malek's gaze drew him back. "You speak of rebellion." The words slipped softly but firmly from his mouth.

Rage leapt quickly into Malek's eyes but subsided just as quickly. "I speak of revolution. I speak of the good giving way to the better. The land cries out for leadership. Do you not feel it? I was first among my brothers, and I assert the right of that position to be their leader and the ruler of all living things. You are a good and capable leader too. Do you not feel frustration with the inability of the Assembly to act quickly and decisively? The land would benefit from a benevolent king with your talent and wisdom." He paused and peered more intently into Andunin's eyes. "Not only would Kirthanin benefit, but so would you and your son. The throne, of course, would pass to Tarlin after you.

"Look at the river, Andunin, and learn from it the nature of all that Allfather has created. Do you see the large rock along the far bank, how it is curved and smooth where the river bends? As strong as the rock is, the superior strength of the water has molded and shaped it. So it is in all things. With time the weak gives way to the strong. The weak plant bends under the force of the strong wind, and the weak branch snaps when the strong hand breaks it off to make it fuel for the fire. This is good and right. As it is in all nature, so it is among the Twelve and among the Novaana. This is not rebellion against Allfather; it is the fulfillment of the only future imaginable for his creation."

Malek clenched his hands and the veins on his forearm bulged as far up as Andunin could see before disappearing into his cloak. He stood beside the water, no longer looking at Andunin but past him, as though gazing at something far beyond him in the south. "Why should I continue to share the power and position that I am better suited to wield and control alone? It should have been mine from the beginning. I have long wanted it to be mine, and soon it will be."

Andunin squatted and lifted a handful of cool water to his lips. The water ran down the inside of his arm and wet the sleeves of his cloak. There was too much to process. He had only ever spoken with Malek about the will of the Twelve for Nolthanin and all the Novaana. Now Malek spoke of things he had never even dreamt. Malek spoke of them as though they were not only good and right, but as though they were inevitable. Andunin splashed water in his face. The future, his own and his son's, hung in the balance.

He looked up at Malek, who had known him since he kicked in his mother's womb. He didn't want to displease Malek, but his plan sounded like rebellion, whatever twist Malek put on it. He had indeed been frustrated by the Assembly, but he had never desired the power to rule it. And yet, the prospect of that power was not entirely undesirable. He knew that he could rule well, and with careful training, so could Tarlin.

Malek fixed his gaze once more on Andunin. "In effect, I am already the true ruler of Kirthanin. I am the greatest of Allfather's creations and chief of the Titans. If I revealed myself to you as I truly am, you would tremble before me like a blade of parched grass before the whirlwind. The sight of my glory and majesty would rend your mind in two. Even the streets of the blessed city, Avalione, built as it is upon the immovable ground of Agia Muldonai, trembles under the weight of my footsteps. Apart from the Twelve, only Sulmandir has ever beheld my splendor and not fallen on his face in fear, and that is only because the golden dragon was created by Allfather to behold us as we are without awe. I will rule all. I am the strongest. Why should you not rule as my lieutenant, as chief of all my human servants?" Malek stooped beside Andunin until his face was just slightly above, and he peered into Andunin's eyes. "I assure you, I will find someone to receive the throne that I offer if you do not. It would be most foolish to decline."

As Andunin looked into Malek's face, he understood that the price of refusal would be total. The spark he had seen in Malek's eyes burned now a full fire, fierce and strong. Those eyes laid the future bare before him. A great storm approached, and there would be no safe place in which to take shelter.

"I am only one man, and even with the whole clan behind me, even all Nolthanin, we could never impose our will on the rest of the Assembly of the Novaana and Kirthanin. And you, Malek, though I do not doubt you are even more powerful than I can imagine, how could you stand against all the Titans at once?"

"Leave the Titans to me, Andunin," Malek smiled. "I am no fool. I would not have come to you if the success of my plan was not assured. As for you, I will approach others to join us, though it will be clear that you are first among all men who follow me. Even so, that is not why all Kirthanin will bow before you. No indeed. Kirthanin will give way before you, because I will give you a gift that will set you apart from all men. I will give you a gift that will make you the lord of men. I will give you instruments of war, tools that have been designed to take life, to kill those who would oppose us. I will forge these with my own hand for this purpose, that you might rule mankind on my behalf."

That evening Andunin stood between Folnik and Nothrimar, holding their reins. The smooth walls of the great dragon tower rose before him into the darkening sky. Great streaks of pink and orange light swirled across the treetops and the side of the tower itself. On the ground, the heavy door of the garrion swung closed and latched with a clang that echoed to the far reaches of the field. As Andunin gazed into the sky, the head of the dragon appeared above the edge of the tower roof. The eyes of the dragon surveyed the ground as two massive wings opened on either side, measuring at least eight or nine spans from tip to tip. For a moment they simply stretched outward and still more outward, until they finally held taut at their fullest extension. Then the dragon leapt from the side of the tower and swooped into the air, its powerful wings fanning the warm summer air into Andunin's face. The dragon began to rise, circling the upper reaches of the tower in an ever widening arc above the gyre from which it had leapt. It circled upward and upward until it at last seemed just a large bird framed in shadow against the clouds. Then the head of the dragon dipped, and he began to dive. Around and around it swung, moving steadily downward in a great elliptical orbit around the stone tower. As it finally neared the ground, its trajectory carried it several times almost the whole length of the field, but even so it made its circuit with terrific speed. On the final round he slowed his great wings to a gentle rhythmic beat, and the great talons of his claws locked upon the T-bar of the garrion and lifted it into the sky. The dragon shot across the field, elevating to a comfortable distance above the trees, and in a moment, he had disappeared beyond the horizon.

As the last golden gleam of the dragon's scales disappeared in the fading sun, the deepening darkness comforted Andunin. He felt as never before an overwhelming desire to hide. He mounted Folnik and slowly walked the horse through twilight to the path that led home. Soon the even greater shadow of the forest enveloped him, and he pressed Folnik to run with Nothrimar following close behind.

As he drew near to the house, the stars of the northern constellations emerged from behind the passing cloud cover. Even though it was difficult to see this far north, Andunin could see the cluster of stars that made up the topmost section of Alazare's Staff. Further north, but off to the east, the outline of Balimere's Mirror was also clear, indeed exceptionally so. The dimmer outline of the mirror, usually hard to make out from this distance, could be traced around the twin stars that framed Balimere's Eyes. And, of course, almost directly overhead, the bright stars of Malek's Hammer looked down upon him.

Malek. Andunin wondered what Alazare and Balimere, or any of the Twelve would have thought of Malek's plan. Perhaps they already knew. Would Malek even consider the changes he was proposing without the cooperation of Alazare, second only to Malek in power and wisdom? And what about Balimere, the most beloved of the Titans, blindingly beautiful and full of laughter? Could Malek hope to succeed in ruling man if he did not gain the favor of man's chief patron and provider? All acknowledged the leadership of Malek, but rarely had Andunin ever heard anyone speak of love for him. Come to think of it, Andunin had never heard anyone speak of love for Malek. He just wasn't thought of in those terms.

And beyond the Twelve, what of the dragons and Great Bear? Andunin would have gratefully sought Kiraseth's advice if he were still alive. The Father of the Great Bear had been renowned even among his own kind for his wisdom and insight. It was often said that on the day of creation, after Allfather had created the Twelve and imbued them with all their wisdom and might, he then created the three great creatures of earth: the dragons, the Great Bear, and man. To each he had given a special gift. To the dragons he had given unparalleled physical strength and might. To the Great Bear he had given great wisdom. To mankind he had given beauty and creativity, a dexterity and ability to make objects of industry and art.

Of course, the generalization was limited, as all are. Dragons did not lack for wisdom or, for that matter, their own form of beauty and creativity. Little under the heavens could compare with the beauty and majesty of a dragon in flight, its great wings reflecting gold in the bright Kirthanin sun. And the

Great Bear, among all the creatures who walked the earth, were foremost in strength. Even men, at times, could exhibit both wisdom and might. What's more, the proverb did not take into consideration the claims of many who had sailed the deep waters far and wide, that in some of the lands in and beyond the Southern Ocean, other creations of Allfather walked the earth, the likes of which had never been seen in Kirthanin. Andunin had grown up with the stories, but living within a day's ride of the Great Northern Sea made all such tales of places in or beyond the Southern Ocean seem unreal.

Even so, like many of the old sayings, this one expressed a kernel of truth, and Andunin did not doubt that the counsel of Kiraseth would have been of great help to him. Malek's offer did not feel right. Had Allfather decreed that the time of the Council of Twelve and the Assembly of the Novaana had passed, surely this would have been made clear to the Council and through them to the Assembly. Furthermore, why had Malek come alone and at such an unusual time? Why had the Titan taken him aside with promises of power and threats of punishment for refusal to comply? The Titans had never used their might to intimidate men before, at least not that Andunin knew. His own father had always taught him that the Twelve were to be obeyed and served without question, but such humility was borne out of proper respect, not fear of reprisal.

Most puzzling and troubling was the offer of tools designed to kill. "Instruments of war," Malek had called them. Malek, Master of the Forge, was no doubt capable of such a creation, but it was clearly contradictory to Allfather's will. Shedding the blood of any living animal was strictly forbidden. It wasn't that Allfather disallowed meat; in addition to the fruit of the ground, Allfather had given his blessing to the eating of any of the ignorant animals that walked the earth, but it was not given to man to kill them. In due season, all animals, like all men, reached their appointed time and died. When an animal was found dead in a wood or field, it was considered a gift from Allfather's hand. Thus man always gave thanks to the hand of Allfather, who had created life and sustained it. To be given instruments designed to shed blood, and human blood at that, was a terrifying thought. What might have prompted such an idea in Malek's mind, Andunin could not imagine. This grim truth plagued Andunin's thoughts—if Malek was capable of conceiving and creating these weapons, he was capable of anything.

Davras appeared from the house and took the reins to Nothrimar, then he waited while Andunin dismounted Folnik. Davras led both horses away through the darkness toward the stable. Andunin followed him with his eyes for a moment, watching the shadows cast by Davras's lantern swing gently from side to side. Turning toward the house, Andunin stepped onto the wide veranda that encircled it, hesitated, then turned toward the back. There, where the land fell away from the house into the apple grove that his great-grandfather had planted over one hundred years before, he sat on the edge of the smooth wooden porch.

What to do? That was really the only question that mattered now. Malek's plan might indeed represent rebellion against Allfather, perhaps even rebellion against some or most of the Twelve, but would that matter in the end? Andunin did not desire to join in a rebellion, but neither did he desire to be the first of Malek's enemies to die. If he joined Malek, he might well find himself on the losing side of an insurrection and paying a terrible price. But if he did not join Malek, would anyone be able to save him and his son from Malek's hand? Surely none of the Twelve alone could stand against Malek. At least if he sided with Malek, there was hope that he would live, and Tarlin too. Did he have the right to place Tarlin's life in immediate danger? Did he have the right not to? Could any choice he made at this point be the right one, or had all meaningful choice already been taken from him?

Perhaps he could at least try to approach another one of the other Titans about the matter, a prospect that just the day before had seemed laughably absurd. But how, and which one? How could he know which would be safe? Surely Malek was not alone in his plan. At least some of the Twelve must have given Malek their consent. It was even possible, though unlikely, that Malek had convinced them all to join him. Perhaps it was Allfather's will for Kirthanin that they do so. Certainly Malek had implied that this was the outworking of Allfather's own design.

Andunin's head shook almost involuntarily. It was inconceivable. If the thought of all the Titans joining Malek in this plan seemed unlikely, then the idea that it was Allfather's will was even more preposterous. Andunin could not imagine that the gleam of power and rage in Malek's eyes were from Allfather.

Would Allfather protect Andunin from Malek's wrath if he refused to submit? He knew no stories of Allfather intervening directly in the affairs of Kirthanin before. Could he risk defying Malek in the hope that he would do so now? Andunin couldn't guess.

The risk seemed too great. Surely Malek would not undertake such a war if he was not convinced he could win, and how could he win if Allfather intervened directly? If Malek believed Allfather would not concern himself with Malek's actions, Andunin had no choice but to assume he was on his own. He hadn't asked for this, but he was here. He needed to act prudently to protect himself and his son.

The back door swung open, and light from within flooded out. Tarlin stood there blinking in the doorway, allowing his eyes to adjust to the darkness. He stepped out of the light and reached for his father. Andunin met his embrace and caught him up, pulling him to himself.

"Mom let me wait up for you, Dad," Tarlin began, "but she told me I had to come out and tell you goodnight now."

"How did she know I was here?"

"I saw Davras taking the horses to the stable and told her, and she said you'd be sitting back here."

Andunin laughed. "Mother knows me well."

"Is Malek gone, Dad?"

"Yes, Tarlin, he's gone."

"Will he bring Sulmandir when he comes back?"

"I don't know," Andunin answered, but as he did, he felt quite certain he did know. Adjusting Tarlin's place in his lap he looked his son in the eye. "I haven't had a chance to tell you properly since I returned, Tarlin, but I love you very much. You know that, don't you?"

"Yes, Dad."

"Good," Andunin replied. "With all the excitement last night, we didn't have time to sing our song. Should we now?"

"Yes, please," Tarlin answered, barely containing his excitement.

"Let me see, then," Andunin began. "How does it go? Oh, I think I remember, it goes like this . . ."

Hey bora, hey nora,
I knew a girl named Dora,
Hey bida, hey nida,
I knew a girl named Lida . . .

"No, Dad. It doesn't go like that." Tarlin laughed, gently pulling his father's hair.

"Oh, well how does it go? Would you start it for me?"

"No, Dad, you start it! You always start it."

Andunin closed his eyes. The melody began to ripple through his mind. He opened his lips and found that he was singing.

Peace, my son, and lay you down,
The sun has gone away.
Wake and find the dawn at hand,
Tomorrow is today—
Tomorrow is today.

When they had sung the song several times together, Andunin kissed his son and watched him retreat into the house. As the door closed once more, leaving him fully in the dark, he saw a vision. It was brief, yet vivid. In his mind's eye he beheld a grand hall, unlike any he had ever seen. In the middle of that hall, he could see a throne, ornate and grand. Around the throne stood the Novaana, hundreds if not thousands of them, bowing in honor and allegiance. Upon the throne sat Tarlin, crowned.

The image lingered even when he closed his eyes. Opening them again, he found the picture still pressing upon him. He rose and walked from the house into the open space behind it, peering into the sky. There it was still, though fading, visible in the heavens. Then, as quickly as it had come, it was gone, leaving him to wonder where it had come from and what it had meant. *A crown for Tarlin means a crown for me.*

A cold wind blew in off of the Great Northern Sea. Today the often tempestuous waves barely rippled as they lapped the stony beach. A flock of gulls swept across the horizon and came to rest in the water. As far as the eye could see, gray skies covered the cold, dark waters. What lay beyond these shores? Strange lands and creatures, as rumored in the Southern Ocean? Or nothing but endless water, as the ancient sailors claimed?

"Father?" The sound of Tarlin's deep voice snapped Andunin out of his reverie. He turned from the waters and looked at his son astride Minladir. How much the child had grown in these seven years past. The wiry frame of a little boy had been replaced by the muscular body of a man. Andunin had long since conceded his son's superior speed and agility. He had tried to prepare Tarlin for what would follow this day, but Andunin had been limited by his own need of preparation. What would follow was as much a mystery to Andunin as it was to Tarlin. Yet Andunin knew Tarlin would need to be hard if a throne was one day to be his, hard like no other seventeen-year-old had ever needed to be. As Andunin looked at the grim determination and cold concentration in Tarlin's gray-green eyes, he knew he had succeeded. The laughter of childhood was gone, long since replaced by eyes that reminded him, well, of Malek.

"Father," Tarlin repeated, "Let me come with you to the cave."

"No, we've been over this."

"You shouldn't go alone. You may need me."

Andunin waved his son to silence. "Tarlin, you will not come, because I will not need you. Whether test or trap, if Malek betrays me, there will be absolutely nothing you can do except perish with me, and in my dying moments I would know that my only son was dead or soon to die and my line had failed. If Malek deals truthfully, then I will bring back the weapons he has prepared and the secret of their making."

Tarlin looked out over the sea, avoiding his father's eyes. Andunin understood his frustration and helplessness. How many days had he felt exactly the same way these last seven years? And yet, what was he to do? Sometimes a man's destiny chose him rather than the other way around. All one could do was make peace with the road set before him. "Son, if I have not returned by nightfall, head to the Simmok ford, and I will find you there. If on the second night I have not come, return home and take your mother and sisters away. Where you take them does not matter. If Malek has determined to destroy us, it will little matter where you go, but you will need to be strong for the others." He managed a reassuring smile for Tarlin. "Even so, I don't think you need worry. If Malek wanted to kill me, he could have killed me before now. He means to rule, and I mean us to rule with him. I will return. Farewell."

"Farewell, Father," Tarlin replied, riding up beside his father and clasping Andunin's arm in his. "With you rides the honor of our family and our people. With you rides, rides . . ."

"There is nothing more to be said. What was the custom of our fathers and forefathers has changed. You can no longer send with me the blessing of Allfather. That is all there is to say."

Andunin wheeled Folnik and rode swiftly down the beach toward the west. Glancing over his shoulder only once, he watched Tarlin retreat from his exposed position at the water's edge into the scattered trees. They would afford some shelter from the first drops of the rain beginning to fall, and, perhaps, from unseen but watchful eyes.

Andunin hesitated at the cave's yawning mouth. He glanced back over his shoulder at Folnik, calmly grazing around the tree to which Andunin had tied him. Again Andunin listened. The quiet lapping of the slight waves upon the beach reached his ears, and perhaps the barest whisper of a gentle wind, but nothing more. Andunin could see no garrion, no dragon, no horse, no sign at all that anyone else was here. This was the appointed day and the appointed hour. But what if Malek wasn't here? Perhaps something had delayed him. Andunin's mind raced. What if Malek's plans had been unmasked, his rebellion unveiled? Maybe the remaining Twelve had confronted and detained him. Maybe Allfather himself had rebuked or even punished Malek for his mad conspiracy. Andunin felt a mixture of hope and disappointment. He feared what lay ahead, but the image of Tarlin upon a regal throne was seared inside his memory.

Then Andunin heard it, a deep, metallic ring echoing from the depths of the cave. It was the sound of a blacksmith at his forge. It was the sound of hammer on anvil, folding and re-folding molten metal. It was the sound of Malek, Master of the Forge, shaping for Andunin and Tarlin and all who followed them, weapons of war. It was the sound of Andunin's doom.

Andunin stepped into the cave. The passageway that led from the opening chamber curved slightly down and away from the Great Northern Sea. In a matter of moments, the light from outside was completely lost, and the darkness of the earth would have been complete if not for the presence of odd, iridescent rocks that marked the center of the tunnel floor every five spans or so. Andunin had never seen anything like them, but their glow provided enough light for him to make out the passageway and obstacles.

As Andunin walked, the sound of hammer on metal came ringing again from somewhere deep in the recesses of the cave. Over and over the clashing call echoed along the corridor like a beacon summoning Andunin to his destiny. Then, just like that, the sound disappeared, and the cave was quiet.

Eventually the slight curve of the passageway straightened, and the gentle slope became a steep drop, so steep that at times Andunin had to turn sideways and place his hands on the ground behind him to avoid falling. Even so, Andunin slipped and slid twice. The second time he fell until his precipitous drop was interrupted by the floor of a small room.

Andunin stood and brushed himself off. Several of the glowing rocks surrounded him, embedded in the walls far above his head. The room was perhaps fifteen spans long and ten spans wide. Looking back the direction he had come, Andunin did not relish the thought of returning up that steep slope, especially if he was to carry Malek's promised gift.

A sheep bleated. Turning toward the cry, Andunin saw a doorway at the far end of the chamber. He quickly passed through and found himself in an enormous cavern. A great orange glow emanated from a massive stone forge on the far side of the room. Beside the forge stood Malek, his massive arm wielding a great, shiny hammer.

Malek seemed completely oblivious to Andunin, his eyes focused on the long slender blade that he was shaping. His left hand controlled long, sturdy black tongs, with which he deftly manipulated the steel. The hammer fell on it again and again in rhythmic strokes, working up and down the length of the blade. Malek's bare, muscular arm flashed up and down. For a moment Andunin closed his eyes. The sound! The sound was almost deafening, filling the great chamber, pulsing and loud. Then, the ringing stopped.

Andunin opened his eyes. They readjusted slowly to the glowing forge. Malek watched him now. He laid both hammer and tongs down and stepped back from his work. "You have come in good time."

Andunin could not tell, but as he approached Malek, he could have sworn that something like a smile passed over Malek's face, like a solitary wisp of cloud quickly passing through an empty sky. Malek continued, "The sword that I have just completed is too hot to touch yet, but I have something else to give you first."

Malek motioned for Andunin to come around the forge. Andunin hesitated but did not stop. He could not stop. He felt drawn, compelled to follow Malek's instructions. If death lay beyond the forge, Andunin could not stop it. The hot surface radiated waves of heat as he rounded it, coming to the place where Malek stood. There, leaning against the wall, was a long, smooth wooden shaft. Bolted to the end of the shaft was a jagged blade, perhaps three hands in length. The blade was dark and bore the single engraved emblem of a silver hammer.

"This is Ruun Harak. It is a spear. The sword you saw me making has a cutting edge along both sides and is handy for fighting at close quarters. This is a weapon, though, with which you can strike a fatal blow long before your foe is close enough to harm you. Andunin, with enough of these, no number of farmers armed with scythes or hay forks will be able to stop you and your men. You will cut down your enemies like wheat."

Andunin gazed at the long, cruel blade. He had no doubt that being punctured by that jagged edge would indeed prove fatal. Graphic images of blood pouring from gaping, open wounds flooded his mind. His stomach felt queasy. It was not the first time he had considered what Malek's killing tools would do. His dreams had been full of blood and death, the cutting and ripping of human flesh. But now that he beheld with his own eyes a blade created specifically for that purpose, he felt the waking reality of all those dark nightmares.

"Here," Malek said softly as he stepped toward Andunin. "Take it in your hand. Feel it for yourself."

Andunin's hands closed around the smooth shaft. The wood was firm and strong. If not for the blade at the end, it might have been any of a dozen winnowing forks or harvesting tools that he kept in his barn at home. But this was no farming instrument. There were no simple wooden pieces fastened at the end, nor a dull sickle blade forever in need of sharpening.

"How does it feel, Andunin?"

"Strange," he replied, "very strange."

Malek laughed. The sound of his laughter reverberated through the chamber as his hammering had. "Of course it feels strange; no human hand has ever grasped its like before. It will feel strange until you learn how to use it."

Malek's face grew sober. "You must practice using Ruun Harak before you wield it in combat, Andunin. You may spar carefully with others, but that will not be enough. You will all need to practice making use of your weapons to finish your enemy. All stages of warfare will be strange to you, but you must be as comfortable as you can in making the killing blow. Hesitation at the wrong time could be fatal. I would suggest that you give all of your men a chance to use their weapons on real flesh and bone before they ever see battle."

Andunin gazed from the spear to its maker. "What are you suggesting?"

"I am suggesting that you practice killing. It may save your life."

Malek disappeared for a moment around the side of the forge, and when he re-emerged, he was leading a dirty white lamb. The creature trembled as it followed him, alternating between compliance and resistance to Malek's tugging.

"I cannot say that he volunteered, exactly, but here is your first opportunity to use your gift. Strike, Andunin, and feel in your heart the quickening wonder of what it means to have power over life and death."

Andunin gazed at the lamb, which had raised its head and was looking from Malek to Andunin and back again. It seemed vaguely aware of the danger of the hot forge and shied away from it. It seemed totally unaware, however, of the danger posed by Ruun Harak.

Andunin looked from the lamb to the spear and then back again. He had honored the prohibition of Allfather all his life, never shedding the blood of any living thing. How could he slaughter the innocent creature that stood before him? Andunin shuddered; if he followed Malek there would be more than sheep ahead. If he wanted to secure the throne of Kirthanin for Tarlin, he would have to kill. If he could not kill the lamb, what would he do when a man stood before him, just as innocent and undeserving of death? No, it had to be done. The lamb had to be sacrificed. He raised the spear, which trembled in his hand, then plunged it deep into the lamb's side.

The lamb uttered a stunned cry, then proceeded to stumble and fall with the spear still sticking out from its side. Andunin wrenched Ruun Harak free, eyes riveted to the bleeding wound on the dying animal. Steadily, the wool turned a deep crimson.

Andunin raised Ruun Harak and gazed at the jagged blade. Against the almost black metal, the blood was at first hard to see. But it was there, flowing in a zig-zag pattern down the blade toward the wooden handle. Slowly, small rivulets started to stain Ruun Harak's shaft. *So that is what it feels like to kill.*

Malek placed his hand upon Andunin's shoulder. "In addition to Ruun Harak and the sword, I have readied a dozen or so other blades for war. I have hid them in a copse of trees not far from the entrance of the cave. Take them with you today. Also, and far more importantly, I will show you how they were made and train your blacksmiths myself. The appointed time is drawing near. In less than a year it will be time to strike. You must prepare your men. You must teach them what it means to kill."

Malek's words echoed in Andunin's mind as the raindrops continued to fall. He gazed once more at the blood on Tarlin's face, blood that had splattered there from the open wound on his chest. He had taught Tarlin what it meant to kill, and Tarlin had killed many. He had fought as hard and as bravely as any, despite the ruin of Malek's plan and all Malek had promised them. Ruin was all that Malek had succeeded in bringing to himself, to Andunin, and to all Kirthanin. Andunin had known this for weeks, but now he cradled the ruin in his hands and felt its cold totality.

And yet Andunin knew that it was he who had led his son to this bloody death. Tarlin had followed him, not Malek, never questioning, never complaining, and certainly never accusing. Now Andunin bore the blame and the guilt for his son's death as well as for his own sin. He sighed as he stroked his son's face. So many wrong turns, so many mistakes. The guilt lay heavy upon him, a burden he could neither carry nor lay down.

He looked through the steady rain at Minladir, standing head down a few feet away. The horse waited patiently for the steadying hand of his master. On the ground, between Minladir and him, lay Ruun Harak. He leaned over, careful not to let Tarlin's head touch the soaking ground. He pulled the spear to himself. He wanted to curse the blade and all it represented, but instead he only gazed upon it. The handle felt comfortable in his hand. He had grown used to its feel. He held the blade up above his head and watched the water from the rain stream down its length.

He could not curse it, for he did not hate it. Even now, as he considered the consequences of following Malek, he did not want to let Ruun Harak go. Hard as it was to even acknowledge it, the spear had become part of him. Ruun Harak brought fear, and fear brought power. No, even now, as Andunin kissed Tarlin's forehead, the cold, wet flesh still dear to his touch, he knew that despite the terrible price he had paid for such power, he would never willingly put Ruun Harak down again.

Clutching the spear, Andunin closed his eyes and sang the song that had been a lullaby but was now a dirge.

Peace, my son, and lay you down,
The sun has gone away.
Wake and find the dawn at hand,
Tomorrow is today—
Tomorrow is today.

SUMMERLAND

1

JORAIEM'S BOW

JORAIEM ANDIRA LOOKED UP from the footprint, large and deep and frighteningly clear in the sand, and turned his head to survey the water. The dark green waves rolled in half a span high before breaking on the beach. Several gulls flew above the water, their shadows gliding across the deep that pulsed with an incessant power that always filled Joraiem with wonder and awe. He loved the ocean, but since childhood he had nearly always felt foreboding when near it, as though some dark destiny lay waiting for him beneath the surface of the restless waves.

The foreboding that Joraiem felt today, however, could hardly be attributed to some vague childhood sense of misgiving. He stood and turned to his friend Evrim, who was looking down at the footprint Joraiem had been studying. Evrim was tall and lean, and though generally quiet and reflective, his tight-lipped grimace was unusually inscrutable even for him. He looked at Joraiem and raised his eyebrows just the smallest bit, as if to say he still had no answers to the question before them.

Joraiem nodded, acknowledging his friend's deference. He'd known from the beginning that the decision would ultimately fall to him. Joraiem was one of the Novaana, and at times like these he was expected to lead. Though he still struggled to trust his own decisions, he had been raised from birth by his mother and father to lead, and he was learning to accept the responsibility. Usually, though, his choices did not involve life or death consequences.

Joraiem ran his fingers through his short blond hair, scratching his head. His mother laughed at him whenever she saw him do this. She said it was the only remnant of childhood left in her son. She meant it as a compliment, but her words embarrassed Joraiem all the same. For all his manhood, he would not deny that he was nervous now. Evrim was as skilled with both bow and sword as any of the young men of Dal Harat, and just about as good as any of the older ones as well. Joraiem was himself widely heralded as the best bowman Dal Harat had seen in several generations. Even Monias, Joraiem's father, admitted he had never seen his son's equal. But then again, Joraiem and Evrim had learned their weapons in competitions and games. This was neither.

Though he knew it would be exactly where it had been, he looked again at the sun, which hung low above the waters. An hour to darkness, maybe two—was that enough time? That was the critical question. All hope for success lay in catching the Malekim before night fell. Few would dare to hunt one of the Voiceless in the full light of day; only a fool would consider hunting one in the dark. As Joraiem gazed at the footprint once more, he found himself deciding, for there was no time left to debate.

"If we follow," he said without looking up, "we may not catch him before dark."

"I know," Evrim answered.

"He is one of the Voiceless. I have to follow." Joraiem continued as he turned to Evrim, who slowly nodded. "You don't have to come. You could wait here for the rest. I'm sure they'll be here before too long."

Evrim mounted his horse in reply. "I'm coming."

Joraiem mounted as well, running his hands along Erador's smooth neck, and moments later they were riding hard along the beach, following the tracks. As he rode, Joraiem considered what a day it had been. Tomorrow he was to leave for Sulare, so he had expected a big day, but never a day like this.

Earlier that morning, the rising sun had found Joraiem, as it often did, already far from home. Joraiem thought of the rolling hills that extended east and north of Dal Harat in the direction of the Kellisor Sea as his own private training ground. His feet followed instinctively the path they had worn each morning in the grass as he ran the private race with himself that he had been running with himself since he was a child.

"Why do you run on your own in the hills like that?" Evrim had once asked. "There is no one chasing you. You are not playing a game. Why do it?"

"Because I enjoy it."

"Enjoy it? Don't you get tired?"

"Eventually. Dad says that it is a mistake to train the body only to be strong. Endurance and self-discipline are just as important. That is why I run."

His father did not run with him anymore. In part it was because Monias had become more involved in the affairs of the Novaana, not just in Suthanin, but in all Kirthanin. He had become an important man within the Assembly. Joraiem also understood that his father did not run with him because he struggled to keep up. At fifty-two, Monias shied away from few physical challenges. The problem was that Joraiem had become almost fanatical in his training and could run for hours without growing weary.

As he rounded the hill on his left this morning, the sun, which had remained more or less ahead and to the right to that point, began to slip behind him. His feet turned him again toward home. The familiarity of the way freed him to think of other things, and there was much on his mind about the prospect of leaving Dal Harat the next day for Sulare. If he was honest, though, his preoccupation had little to do with leaving Dal Harat. He had known since childhood the day of this departure was coming. The distraction, rather, was caused by the idea of leaving Alina Tomian. He was unsure of how he felt about her, and even more unsure of what to do about it.

There was no doubt about how Alina's twin sister, Aleta, felt about Joraiem. She had tortured him with unwanted affection for almost ten years. He remembered well the cool summer evening when he was thirteen years old that she had announced her decision to marry him one day. The whole village had gathered to celebrate the rites of Midsummer and to seek Allfather's blessing at the Mound in the town square. Afterward, of course, villagers and farmers for miles around had danced and sang until the early morning. Joraiem had been sitting on the roof of the Morsats' butcher's shop, his favorite spot for watching the festivities, when a loud voice from below had distracted him. Looking down he had seen Aleta and Alina, eleven-year-old twins who had lived in Dal Harat for less than a year, looking up at him. Joraiem did not know either well, but he knew them both well enough to know it was Aleta who had called him. Aleta could barely keep her mouth shut on any occasion, whereas he had never even seen Alina open hers.

"Jor-y," Aleta called, using a nickname he despised. "Come down and dance with me!"

Joraiem had responded by scrambling over the ridge of the roof away from the well-lit front so that he could lie flat on the shadowed back. Aleta was not to be so easily defeated, however, and soon Joraiem heard her calling from the back of the house as well.

"I'm going to marry you one day, Jor-y, whether you like it or not!" For almost a quarter of an hour she had tortured him with this refrain. Only then did she move away, but she didn't move very far. She sat with her sister watching the Morsats' roof like a windhover watching a field mouse. Joraiem lay still against the roof in the darkness for most of the night. When at last he had been able to get down, he figured that the ordeal was over and the whole incident would soon blow over. Nine and a half years later, Aleta Tomian remained as confident as ever that Joraiem was her husband-to-be.

But even while Joraiem was equally confident that this would never happen, he felt confused about Aleta's sister. Alina was rarely far from Aleta's side and had borne silent witness to her sister's unflagging pursuit of Joraiem. The few times Joraiem had seen her around Dal Harat without Aleta, she had been unwilling to converse with him at any length, taking the first and quickest chance to get away. Joraiem assumed that Alina did not like him, perhaps because he had held Aleta at arm's length for so long. He had assumed this until a cool day early in Fall Rise the previous year, just six months ago.

On that day, Joraiem had been to the village to have his brother's horse reshoed. On his way out of town Aleta had accosted him. Hollering for him from across the street, she had walked with determination to cut him off before he passed through the town gate. While she had stood there gushing on and on about things that Joraiem forgot as soon as he heard them, if he heard them at all, he had looked over her shoulder at Alina and found her eyes locked on him. Alina blushed at being caught staring and quickly turned away, almost running across the street. Aleta was herself so stunned by her sister's unusual and hasty retreat that she left off with her discourse in midstream and followed her.

Alina's eyes had betrayed affection mixed with sadness. Yet, as Joraiem headed home, he found himself in deep confusion over the encounter. What did her stare mean, and how should he deal with it?

As Joraiem ran, his comfortable stride formed a gentle rhythm for his thoughts. Alina had mostly avoided him since, though at times he noticed her observing him from a distance. He had searched his own heart a thousand times since that day. Did he really return Alina's apparent feelings for him? Most of the time he felt sure he did. He would see her in the village walking with her sister and would long to sneak up beside her and pull her away so they could talk in private. Sometimes, though, he doubted his own heart. He would see her and want to disappear, to hide from them both. He was certain about what he did not feel for Aleta, but he didn't know for sure what he did feel for Alina.

He wondered if it even mattered. Tomorrow he would leave for Sulare. Ten months he would be gone, and it would be Full Winter before he returned. Ten months was a long time. He'd never been away from Dal Harat for anywhere close to that long. Would Alina still care for him when he returned? Did she even care about him now? They'd never spoken, and it was certainly possible that he had read into her look his own desire.

Even beside all that, who would he be when he returned? Monias always spoke of his own trip to the Summerland as a time of transformation. What would his time in Sulare be like? Would he change as his own father claimed he had changed during his visit? Would anything be the same again? There were many questions but little time. Tomorrow was the first day of Spring Rise, and he was leaving home. That was all he knew for sure.

When Joraiem finished his run and entered the house, he found the whole family gathered around the breakfast table. His father, Monias, sat at the head of the table moderating the family meal. Bustling around the table was Joraiem's mother, Elsora, her long golden hair wound tightly upon her head in a bun. Joraiem thought of the style as her "working look," as she always let her hair down when the busy morning time had passed.

On the left side of the table sat Kyril, Joraiem's only sister. At seventeen, she was just a year shy of marriageable age. Joraiem at times felt guilty that he would not be around to be a big brother to her in this important year of preparation for adulthood. Even though his father joked about never letting any man take his daughter away, Joraiem knew it was quite possible that he would return from Sulare in ten months to find her promised. She was sweet and beautiful and had been admired by many for years, and he could sense already the established single men of Dal Harat and surrounding areas positioning themselves to be attractive suitors both to Kyril and to Monias. Joraiem's one comfort was that both had high standards, and finding someone who pleased them equally might take some time.

Opposite Kyril sat Brenim, Joraiem's twelve-year-old brother. Whereas Joraiem clearly resembled his mother, Brenim was almost a perfect replica of his father. Joraiem remembered vividly the night Monias brought Brenim out of the birthing room. "This is your baby brother," he had said as he showed him to Joraiem. Then he had said, "I am forty and a father, Allfather's name be praised." Brenim had been Joraiem's shadow for the last twelve years, and he knew that while Brenim pretended not to be upset that he was going away, he, perhaps most of all, was dreading the following day.

"Joraiem, stop lurking in the doorway and come in," his father said without looking up from the table. "It is already Second Hour, and we have nearly finished without you."

"Yes, Father," Joraiem replied as he entered and took his seat beside Brenim.

"Did you have a good run?" Elsora asked her daily question as she placed a tray of hot rolls, fresh from the oven, upon the table.

"Yes, Mother," he answered as he grabbed a roll. "Though it was sad in a way. I'll miss the hills. Father says Sulare is flat. I don't know how I will be able to get a decent run the whole time I am gone."

Monias smiled. "The Summerland always surprises, Joraiem. Don't be so sure that your trip and training will be easy. Indeed, I will pray that Allfather will give you the strength for whatever he has in store for you and the others who will gather with you." Joraiem winked at Kyril, mouthing his father's well-worn phrase as he did. "You would be wise to do the same. Just be faithful to your duty and trust the rest to Allfather."

"I will, Dad. As for me, I will pray for you, Kyril, that Allfather will watch over and protect you in a special way this year. I'm sorry I won't be able to myself."

Kyril smiled at her brother. "You don't need to be sorry, Joraiem. It can't be helped. You must do what is before you to do, as I will have to in seven years. Besides, Father and Brenim will be here to look after me."

"That's right," Monias replied, "We'll look after her, won't we, Brenim?"

Brenim nodded but didn't speak. In fact, he looked almost to be on the brink of tears. Joraiem put his arm around his brother and asked, "I've saved this afternoon especially for you. What would you like to do?"

"You know what I'd like to do," Brenim replied quietly.

Joraiem looked at Monias, who sat considering, then nodded, adding out loud, "But don't even think about going in!

It's more than enough to get close enough to see it. Be careful and keep your distance."

"Will you take me?" Brenim asked.

"Yes," Joraiem answered, "provided that you listen to what I tell you."

"Before you two go off on this foolish venture," Elsora interjected, addressing her sons but looking at her husband, "remember that you promised to pick up my order from the Morsats' this morning. If you're going to get to Dal Harat and back in time to go, you'll need to move quickly."

"But not," Monias said before anyone at the table could rise, "before we pray. It is the last morning we can linger a moment at the table together."

They bowed their heads and stretched out their arms to join hands. "Allfather, give us strength to do your will and keep your commands, until the Mountain be cleansed and the Fountain flow again."

"Until the Fountain flow again," they echoed.

After a moment, Monias at last looked up. "While Brenim helps Kyril clear the table and prepare the horses, I want half an hour with you, Joraiem. Let's shoot together one more time."

Joraiem retrieved his bow and walked around behind the house to the range where his father had taught him how to shoot. Monias was waiting there with Suruna, his bow. Suruna meant "sure one" in the language of the Mountain and was, in Joraiem's experience, every bit as reliable as its name implied. It had been in their family for hundreds of years, and family legend claimed that it had been used at the end of the Second Age against Malek's armies when he invaded Kirthanin from the Forbidden Isle and took Agia Muldonai. Joraiem had used many bows, but never had he fired one with the power and accuracy of Suruna. When he used Suruna, he felt as though he could hit any target at any distance.

"Are you ready, Father, or should I shoot first?" Joraiem asked as he approached.

"I am not shooting today."

Joraiem, who was preparing to string his bow, paused. He looked at Monias, who sat watching him with Suruna across his lap. "Should I sit, too?"

"I said that I am not shooting. You are. That is, I would like you to. I will watch and talk."

"Of course," Joraiem strung his bow and began to shoot. Halfway through his quiver, he turned again to his father, who still had not spoken, and waited. Monias watched him intently.

"What is it, Father?"

"Many things, I suppose. Sending you to Sulare is not exactly as I had expected. I knew it would be a bittersweet day when pride in your achievements and sadness at your departure would mingle in my heart. I anticipated the excitement I would feel for you, even the curiosity as I wondered if it would be for you all that it was for me." Monias paused here, looking down, "I just didn't foresee the worry and the anxiety that grows in my heart."

Joraiem set his bow down and sat beside his father, looking down the length of the range as Monias was. "Is it the Black Wolf?"

"Yes, that and other things."

"Are you worried more will come?"

Monias looked at Joraiem and shrugged his shoulders just slightly. "I don't know, Joraiem. Perhaps. I just don't know what to make of it. Since Malek retreated into the Mountain, Black Wolves have rarely been seen anywhere but near Agia Muldonai. What one would be doing here, so far from its home and so close to us, I just can't figure out. It is an ill omen."

"But he is dead."

"He is, dead and gone and burned to ash. But the scent of

Malek lingers behind. I smell it in the air. I feel it in my blood and my bones."

Joraiem didn't know what to say, so he remained silent. He had seen his father's disquiet of late, his growing tendency to separate himself, deep in thought, from the world around him. But he had been no more inclined to reveal what was troubling him.

He continued, "The Assembly worries me, Joraiem. It has grown complacent. We talk of the need for vigilance and unity, yet we spend less and less time speaking of Kirthanin's universal needs and more and more time bickering over petty trade disputes and regional squabbles. I fear we won't be ready."

Monias put his hand on Joraiem's shoulder and peered into his eyes. "What you do tomorrow, Son, is of the utmost importance. You must know and you must trust those with whom you will serve in the Assembly. Even that may not be enough. I thought when I left Sulare that the Novaana I met there would never allow the uglier side of regional pride to eclipse our better judgment and commitment to each other, but there are days when I wonder how strong our bonds really are. Above all else, seek to forge those bonds."

"I will," Joraiem answered, gripped by the urgency he read in his father's eyes. He was not used to this intensity in his usually placid father.

Monias seemed to relax, patted Joraiem gently on the shoulder, and smiled. "I know you will. You have always done your best at whatever lay before you. I'm sorry if I worried you just now. I have tried not to burden you with too much information before you were ready for it, but perhaps we should have spoken more of these things than we have. Of Malek and his servants, especially. It always seemed so much more important that you know of Allfather and our cause for hope.

Hope is a delicate thing, and the darkness of fear can easily overwhelm it. Very easily. But when I feel close to being overwhelmed, I go back to Valzaan's words. Remember the promise he brought from Allfather at the beginning of the Third Age.

> *On that day, the Fountain will flow again.*
> *The Mountain will be cleansed*
> *And all will be made new.*
> *All instruments of war will be destroyed.*
> *They will be unmade;*
> *They will be reforged.*
> *Recast as implements of peace, as plows*
> *These blades will work and till*
> *The ground forevermore.*
> *No one will ever harm or kill again,*
> *And Peace will be restored*
> *On All My Holy Mountain.*

"Hold on to hope, Joraiem. Even when darkness seems overwhelming. Hold onto hope. The Fountain will flow again, and the Mountain will be cleansed. And, yes, sometime between now and then, Malek will come forth again. We may not know how he can be stopped, but he has failed twice already now, so we must trust Allfather to show us a way."

"Perhaps when Malek comes Valzaan will show us how."

"Perhaps, though Valzaan has not been seen among men in my lifetime. Maybe he will appear again when we have need of him, or perhaps Allfather will raise up another prophet to do what must be done. Who can say?" His father sighed and clapped a hand over Joraiem's knee. "Anyway, enough talk of the future. For all we know we will neither one live to see Malek's third attempt. Almost a thousand years after he descended into Agia Muldonai, we still wait. Let us talk of happier things, of Sulare. We have spoken of it many times, have we not?"

"We have."

Monias laughed. "You are gracious. I know I have prattled on about the Summerland since you were a boy. I find myself hardly able to imagine that the day for your departure has come. Sometimes, even now, when I close my eyes I see Sulare as I first saw it twenty-eight years ago, when I was not much older than you are now.

"Though I spoke just now of the political import of Sulare, there is more at stake in this journey than that. More happens there than the forging of regional alliances and diplomatic ties. In the Summerland, boys become men and girls become women. In the Summerland, you find out who you really are. You will return when Full Winter is upon us, but you will not be the same. You will be more than just older; you will be more aware of your true self." Monias paused, smiling. "When I think of Sulare, the first image that comes to my mind is the figure of your mother standing beside the water with her golden hair streaming behind her. Sometimes I wonder if I distort the importance of Sulare because of her, but truthfully, I don't think I do. Even if I had not met her there, I still believe that my time in the Summerland would have been just as important. Aside from everything else, I do not know who I would be today had I not been there."

Monias stood and faced his son. "There is much that I would send with you, but you must travel light, for the journey is long. This I do give you, though, take it and use it in time of need."

Monias handed Suruna to Joraiem, who took it in stunned silence. He ran his fingers along the smooth wood and felt the carefully carved handle. He could not believe what his father was doing. "But, Father, I am not ready for this."

"Nonsense, you are more ready than I ever was. You are already better with bow and arrow than any man I have ever known. Allfather has given you a great gift, and there is no reason why you should not also have a great bow. Suruna has never failed me, and I trust and pray that she will never fail you. Besides, I will not be with you to celebrate your twenty-third birthday. Accept this now as your gift for that day. Now finish your quiver, retrieve your arrows, and let's get back to the house. You have an errand to run for your mother, and a promise to your brother to keep."

Joraiem and Brenim had just passed through Dal Harat's main gate when a tall, slender figure appeared coming down the street toward them. It was Evrim Minluan, approaching gracefully and virtually without noise, catlike as always. Joraiem considered Evrim his best friend, and rarely did Joraiem appear in Dal Harat without Evrim somehow appearing too. Joraiem had wondered at times if Evrim kept a lookout for him from one of the village rooftops, or if he had some mystical ability to sense his presence.

"Joraiem," he began as they drew closer together, "you'd better be careful unless you want to spend your last day trapped in town. Aleta is not far away." Evrim gave a slight nod in the direction from which he had just come.

"Thanks for the warning, but I won't be long. Brenim and I are just on our way to the Morsats', then we'll head home."

"Preparations for tonight?"

"I think so. Knowing Mother, she'll make enough food to feed a dragon. You'll be there?"

Evrim smiled. "On dragon's wings. You know I will."

"Joraiem!" a voice called loudly from up the street.

Joraiem did not need to look to know who had summoned him. "It would appear that peace is not to be my lot today."

Evrim waved Brenim to his side, saying, "I'll take Brenim with me to Kernan's. I think he is finishing the gate today. We'll come back for you later."

Joraiem nodded. "Take the cart too, if you don't mind." He knew that, unlike some of his other friends, who derived a perverse pleasure in the torture Aleta's presence inflicted on him, Evrim was only trying to help. His friend understood how hard it was for him to be around Aleta, and he was grateful Evrim was taking Brenim away.

He turned to face Aleta, and seeing Alina with her, found that he no longer feared her approach. In fact, he was surprised to realize that his dread had been replaced by anticipation. He knew Alina would not speak, perhaps not even make eye contact, but he desired to have her near him all the same.

"Joraiem," Aleta began as soon as she was close enough to clasp his arm in her hands, "I am so glad to see you. You have been, as usual, often on my mind, and there is much I'd like to tell you. I would love to give you a proper send off, to say good-bye in my own way, but as I'm sure you understand very well, the party tonight simply will not do. I'm not saying that the party isn't going to be wonderful, or that it isn't important. Quite the contrary, I think that it is great for you to have a chance to bid farewell to the village, but there will be too many people for me to have either the time or the opportunity to say what I would like."

"Well, Aleta, we've been talking about my going for a while now. I think I understand how you feel about it."

Aleta sighed, "Yes, yes, I know. I've probably become quite predictable to you, but I can't help it. Until you realize how perfect we are for each other, I'm just going to have to keep repeating myself. Even so, I want you to know I'll seek Allfather's blessing for you every day that you are gone, as I have these many years and as I will until the Fountain flows again or you get some sense, whichever comes first. I will think of you always, and most importantly, I will wait patiently and faithfully for your return. I know you have important things to do down there, so I don't want you to think for a moment that I don't understand. I do. I understand very well that as one of the Novaana, you are an important man with important tasks ahead of him. My one and only desire in life is to support you and stand by you in all you need to do. Make no mistake about it, I will not stand in your way."

"I appreciate your understanding, Aleta."

To Joraiem's amazement, Aleta fell silent. She appeared at first to be considering her move, but then, without saying a word or even saying farewell, she simply turned around and began walking away. Joraiem looked after her, stunned. Even Alina, who had been pretending to watch the clouds drifting by in the distance, stared after her sister. Though surprised, Joraiem was also relieved. It seemed to him that everything that could be said had already been said—many times.

Then Joraiem realized that perhaps for the first time in all the years he had known them, Aleta had left without waiting for Alina to follow. The fact that he and Alina now stood alone together also seemed just then to dawn on Alina. She turned slowly from watching her sister and looked nervously at him. He grabbed his chance.

"Alina, I need a moment with you before you go." He was surprised to find his voice relatively stable.

"Why?" she answered, eyeing him warily.

"Just to talk a little bit. Are you coming tonight?"

Alina looked back up the street. "Yes."

"Could I talk to you then?"

"Not tonight. Whatever it is, Aleta is right about tonight not being the time. She'll be there, and so will lots of other people. Perhaps when you've returned . . ."

"No, I need to talk to you before I go."

Alina glanced back over her shoulder again, shifting her stance awkwardly. "All right, when?"

"I'm to meet Evrim at the east bridge by Third Hour tomorrow. I could always leave home a little earlier. Could you meet me somewhere nearby in the morning? Would that be all right?"

She nodded slowly, "Yes."

"Will you be able to get away?"

"I'll find a way. Where?"

"Alina! Aren't you coming?" Joraiem looked up and saw Aleta at the other end of the street. She had turned back toward them and now stood waiting. She did not look pleased.

Alina started to back up the street in the direction of her sister as though drawn, her nervousness now turning to distress.

"The rock on the east side of the stream. You know, the one down in the woods where we all used to go a few years ago, remember?"

Alina nodded, "Yes, I'll be there by half past Second Hour." She turned and ran up the street toward her sister.

Joraiem sat on the carved bench behind the Morsats' butcher's shop, glad for the partial warmth afforded by the sun, which had almost reached its pinnacle in the late morning sky. Mistress Morsat had remembered just as he was about to leave that she needed to give him one more thing and had gone to fetch it. Having already loaded the cart for the return trip, he let his thoughts drift. He wondered what exactly to say to Alina. He wondered how she would get away from Aleta's watchful eyes. He even wondered where Evrim and Brenim were. Surely they weren't still at the blacksmith's. Even though Kernan had a soft spot for Evrim, he was more than a little secretive about his work. He disliked interruptions as a rule and rarely allowed visitors for long.

His thoughts wandered back to Alina. He regretted not doing something dramatic and passionate. He should have taken her arm as she started to move away. He should have asked her to come alone tonight. He should have kissed her right there in the street. What did he care about Aleta? He'd made himself clear enough to her. At this moment he felt the strong desire to be with Alina, to listen to her tender voice without fear of intrusion.

"Here we go, Joraiem," Mistress Morsat called out as she emerged from the shop. "I made you a special going-away treat. Now I know it may smell a little unusual, but it's supposed to. This is a Morsat specialty. Years ago, Creen and I invented our own little secret blend of salt and seasoning for keeping meat from spoiling on long trips. A sailor friend of ours used to buy this by the wagonload. I thought that you could use some for your journey. It's a long way to Sulare."

"Thank you very much, Mistress Morsat, but Father didn't authorize me to spend any extra today."

"Don't you worry about that, Joraiem. This is a present from us."

As she was speaking, Creen came out and stood beside his wife. Master Morsat was short, thin, and without a single hair on his head or face. His wife, by contrast, was a little bit taller, more than a little bit wider, and had a head full of curly red hair. They were an unusual looking pair, but apart from his family, he would miss no one in Dal Harat more than them.

Joraiem gave Mistress Morsat a hug and took Creen's hand. "Thank you very much. I will miss you both terribly."

"We'll miss you," they echoed, looking pleased. "Farewell."

"Goodbye," Joraiem called as he carried their gift around front to the cart.

Evrim and Brenim were waiting for him by the horse. "Evrim is coming with us," Brenim said when he saw Joraiem. "I asked him if he wanted to go with us to the dragon tower."

"That's great, but we're going to be pressed for time unless we get out of Dal Harat soon. Do you need to go home for anything, or can you come with us now?"

"I'm ready. Lead on."

"All right then. Brenim, let's get home, pack some lunch for the ride, and get on the way."

Joraiem gazed at the dragon tower that rose above the thick cluster of trees on the northern side of the road. They had ridden hard and made good time, arriving with most of the afternoon still before them. Now they sat in awe of the majestic structure, their horses panting hard. Though each of them had been this close to it before, few people ever really found themselves at ease around a dragon tower. It wasn't just the imposing form of these monuments, which hinted of a greater time, a more resplendent age, and thrusted the ancient dragon gyres into the heavens. Nor was it their endurance through the darkest ages of Kirthanin's past, when almost everything else gave way. It had more to do with the thought of the dragons that had once dwelt within them, and beyond that, the legend that Grendolai still did.

"Joraiem," Brenim started again, "I still don't see why we can't just cut through the trees directly."

"I have told you already why we can't."

"You don't really think anything lives in there, do you?"

Joraiem turned toward his brother and looked him in the eye. "I believe the Grendolai were real. Are they still alive after all these years? I don't know. But I don't think the old stories lie when they speak of them as utterly terrifying. If it is true that Malek used them to assault all the dragon towers when he returned from the Forbidden Isle, they must have been."

"The end of the Second Age was a thousand years ago."

"I know, Brenim, but how do we know whether any have survived? What is the life span of a Grendolai? Some of the stories say that both Malek and Vulsutyr trembled at the sight of the Grendolai when they emerged from the fire of their birth."

"I don't think the Fire Giant or Malek would have trembled for anything, except maybe Sulmandir," Brenim said.

"Maybe not," Joraiem said, "but I don't think I'd like, for the sake of a shortcut, to discover that the Grendolai are alive and the stories have not been exaggerated. If you want to see the tower up close, we will go the long way around and approach through the clearing on the western side."

They circled the trees until they came upon the broad, grassy lane that led up to the western side of the dragon tower. The grass was waist high and brushed against their legs as they rode. Joraiem knew that others from Dal Harat as well as some of the coastal villages both north and south came to the tower from time to time, but this road had not been used recently.

About fifteen spans from the tower, the lane opened into a wide clearing, which encompassed the tower. They dismounted by the southern edge of the lane and tied their horses to a small poplar tree. Joraiem slung his quiver onto his back and strung Suruna. Evrim buckled a short sword around his waist. None of them spoke.

Joraiem started out toward the dragon tower, angling slightly south and east of the single door in its base. Evrim and Brenim followed single file as they waded through the thick, dried overgrowth. After the constant rhythm of their horses' footfall and the wind of the ride, the clearing felt abnormally still and quiet. The swish of the high grass and the distant sound of birds calling to one another were all that they could hear.

Just short of the tower wall, Joraiem stopped. Sheltering his eyes with his hand, he tilted his head back and peered up the side of the tower into the sky. The wall seemed to run more or less straight up, perhaps slightly inward, as it shot into the sky. Then, as it seemed to rise into the clouds, it flared outward like a birdbath of enormous proportions. The wide, circular platform that marked the top of the dragon tower was the gyre.

"How far up do you think it goes?" Brenim asked quietly.

"A hundred spans, maybe," Evrim replied.

"More," Joraiem added. "I think it's more."

Joraiem walked the last few spans to the wall and touched the masonry of the tower. The large dark stones were cool and smooth, though a careful examination revealed some broken stones. It didn't look to Joraiem like deterioration that the wear of time would have caused, but Joraiem didn't know what could have gouged such chunks out of a massive structure that had stood for so long.

"Father says these were built during the First Age," Brenim said, joining him, "before Malek's Rebellion. Do you think it is possible?"

"Of course it's possible," Joraiem replied. "Father wouldn't have told us if he didn't know it was true. The towers were made by men and Great Bear with the help of the Titans, even Malek. That is why they still stand. They were built with Allfather's blessing and with the Council of Twelve wielding Allfather's power. Dad says that whatever else comes and goes in Kirthanin, these will remain, like Avalione on Agia Muldonai."

Brenim started around the wall toward the door. "Where do you think you're going?" Joraiem asked.

"I'm going to see if we can open the door."

"No you're not. You're not going to touch that door."

"Why not?"

"Did you hear nothing that I said on the way here? It is forbidden. Even if it wasn't forbidden and I wasn't responsible to Mother and Father for you, you have no idea what lies on the other side of that door. None of us do."

Brenim stopped walking but turned his back on Joraiem as though he wasn't there. Leaning over and searching through the grass, Brenim picked up a small stone. Turning back suddenly, he threw the stone as hard as he could at the door. When it struck, a hollow thud rang through the clearing as the stone bounced off and fell into the grass.

"What are you doing?" Joraiem started, the anger clear in his voice, but before he could continue, the sight and sound of a dark form rising from a crouching position near one of the trees behind them silenced him. It started running at great speed toward the road. They each froze as the creature flashed out of the trees and across the lane not ten spans behind their horses. The creature crossed the road, darted across the open ground, and disappeared into the trees on the other side, heading away from dragon tower.

"A Malekim!" Joraiem gasped. His legs began to work again and he ran back to their horses as quickly as he could. Evrim and Brenim followed. When the horses were untied and mounted, Joraiem addressed Brenim. "Listen to me very carefully. I must follow the Malekim. You cannot, so don't waste my time with objections. Your foolishness has done enough here already. Go with Evrim back to the house as quickly as you can, and bring back Father and anyone else you can find."

"I'm going with you," Evrim said with resolution.

"You need to take Brenim back."

"I can find my own way."

"Joraiem, Brenim *can* find his own way. The Malekim is headed north and west, and unless he doubles back and slips past us, we'll be between him and Dal Harat. Brenim will be fine. If anyone needs help, it's you."

Joraiem wasn't pleased. The Voiceless that they had seen was indeed headed away from Dal Harat, but how did Joraiem know he was the only one about? Though it seemed impossible that even one would be here, why not two? Still, if he waited to win this argument, he'd never pick up the trail of the

Malekim. The Voiceless were large, but from what he had just seen, also very fast, and his only hope to keep up was to pick up that trail now. "Fine. Brenim, go back the way you came, but no shortcuts, unless you want to find yourself under the hammer! Stick to the road. We've all just learned a valuable lesson about what may lurk among the trees."

Brenim didn't answer, but started back the way they had come. Joraiem watched him for a second, then spurred his horse toward the brush where the Malekim had disappeared. He turned to Evrim, "First a Black Wolf, and now this. What next?"

"I don't know."

Joraiem peered into the thick undergrowth. He could only imagine what Monias would say when he learned of this, if Joraiem lived to tell him. He looked down at Suruna, which he still held at his side. *It looks like I may need you earlier than we expected,* he thought, touching the smooth, cool wood as though needing reassurance of its solidity.

"Come on," he said to Evrim, looking up. "Let's go."

2

RETURN TO THE FIRE

JORAIEM AND EVRIM RELENTLESSLY tracked the
Malekim into the afternoon. They had no opportunity to discuss the pressing questions raised by the presence of one of
Malek's children so far southwest of the Mountain. Equally as
perplexing as the Malekim's presence was the Malekim's
flight. They had by no means anticipated the encounter, and
Joraiem knew the Voiceless could have torn them all apart if it
had desired. Instead, it had run, and as much as Joraiem knew
his duty was to prevent it from getting away, he was almost ter-
rified to catch up.

The Malekim was moving at a tremendous speed. Indeed,
despite his size, his trail was not always easy to follow, and Joraiem had to admit that without Evrim, he would have lost it
long ago.

Evrim had displayed his mastery of the hunt just six weeks
prior, when the Black Wolf had come mysteriously to the vicin-
ity of Dal Harat. On three successive nights, the men of the vil-

lage had gone out after the wolf and returned frustrated and tired. On the fourth evening, shortly before twilight, Evrim picked up the wolf's trail and led the men all night in its pursuit. By the time morning broke, the wolf had been cornered and killed as Evrim all but collapsed with exhaustion. Evrim had been given his due; the people of the village now claimed that he could track a day-old moth trail through a meadow. His triumph brought hope to the gloom that had descended over the village in the wake of the Black Wolf's appearance.

If the Black Wolf was a dangerous quarry, how much more so was one of the Voiceless, created by Malek to rival the Great Bear? Joraiem knew he was no physical match for the creature. For its part, the Malekim had stayed under the protective cover of the woods as long as possible, no doubt realizing that while men on foot were no match for his speed, pursuit on horseback put him at risk. So the Malekim kept to dense growth that slowed down horse and rider. In this way he had moved steadily west and slightly north toward the coast. Eventually, the Malekim ran out of trees and broke across an open field, which brought him either by design or by accident to the beach. Confronted with the ocean, the creature had turned north along the sand.

Joraiem rode with Evrim beside him, galloping up the beach in the hope that at last, with no low-hanging branches or precipitous hills to negotiate, he would be able to close on the Malekim. He had wondered beside the first footprint about the wisdom of the pursuit, feeling very much like a mouse chasing the cat. Now the hunt had begun to feel desperate. Joraiem thought maybe the water hindered the Malekim's escape, and if Joraiem felt that way, perhaps the Malekim did too. If it felt cornered, there was no telling what it might do. All Joraiem knew was that their hope for success depended entirely on getting a clean shot with the one and only cyranic arrow he carried. If he fired and missed, then they had no means to kill the Malekim short of hand-to-hand combat, and there was little hope they could prevail in that.

While daunted by the prospect of facing the Malekim with only one cyranis-coated arrow, Joraiem knew things could be worse; many of the men in Dal Harat did not routinely carry any. In fact, Joraiem had given Monias a hard time when he had insisted that Joraiem do so.

"It's useless, Father," he could hear himself say. "Cyranic arrows aren't used for anything but Malekim, which I've never encountered and probably never will. I have less room for arrows I can use, and I can't draw an arrow and shoot without first checking to make sure it isn't the poisoned one."

"You'll have to live with those minor frustrations, Joraiem, and you will carry the arrow. I pray that Allfather will never place you in a situation where you need it, but it might save your life if you do. When a cyranic arrow punctures a Malekim hide, the poison hardens his blood immediately, just as it would your blood if you even cut your finger with it. For that reason you must always wrap the arrowhead in leather, and you must never remove the wrap unless in great need. It is one of the many unfortunate necessities of life in this dangerous world. You had better get used to it."

He had gotten used to it and at this moment was very glad. He barely even noticed anymore the solitary arrow with its bright red fletching, held to the side of his quiver by a leather strap that he had made himself. With the cyranic arrow secured, he never removed it from the quiver by accident. It sat there waiting, the deadly poison coated upon the hard, slender, iron point of the arrow. Even the point was specially designed to puncture the thick gray hide of the Malekim, for the cyranis could not work unless the arrow penetrated far enough for the poison to enter the bloodstream.

One arrow, though, meant one chance. The sun had already dropped considerably since he had paused to examine the footprint in the sand. The trail they followed remained unswerving, the footprints revealing the Malekim's long, even strides. *Does he not get tired? How can he maintain this pace for so long?* Even if Joriaem hated the creature, the runner in him could admire its power and stamina.

Then he saw it, a dark shape ahead of them running along the beach, its great hulking form silhouetted by the low hanging sun. He looked over his left shoulder at Evrim to see if he had glimpsed it too. Evrim nodded to Joraiem and pressed his horse forward. Joraiem reached down beside him as he rode and began to loosen the straps that held Suruna, though he did not try to hold the weapon now. He was an excellent shot, but even he would not risk his one chance to kill the Malekim while galloping at full speed on horseback. He would need to get into position to take the shot. How he would do that, he didn't know.

Ahead the beach began to curve out to sea. The Malekim followed the line of the beach. Although the curvature of the sand would soon have the Voiceless running almost perpendicular to the rest of the mainland, Joraiem knew that the distance was still too great, even for Suruna. A shot at this distance across the open water at a fast moving target would be extremely difficult, and he could not afford to trust his success to luck. As the horses approached the place where the beach began its curve, Joraiem slowed, scanning the land just beyond the curve carefully.

"Do you recognize this place, Evrim?"

"I'm not sure, why?"

"The dunes, straight ahead, they remind me of the dunes that the Belin brothers used to take us to when we were little, remember?"

"Yes. Do you think it's them?"

"Could be. If so, this may be our chance. We've got an hour at the most, then it will be dark. If we are where I think we are, then the beach is going to turn back north after this curve, and then once more back inland. If we pass directly ahead and through the dunes, we should pick it up on the way back in. If we can cut through quickly enough, I may get my shot."

Evrim signaled his understanding by plunging up the bank, straight ahead and through the dunes. Joraiem followed closely behind.

Joraiem dropped from his horse and stood beside Evrim. Ahead through the dunes he could see the open water. They had reached the place where the beach curved back inland. They couldn't risk having their horses give them away, so they would have to be left behind. Evrim took his sword, and Joraiem grabbed Suruna and his quiver.

Their feet sunk deep in the loose sand as they ran, both instinctively heading for the large dune just above the bank that overlooked the beach. Resting against the dune, Joraiem peered around it to get a better look at the beach below.

He could see nothing moving in either direction. Straight ahead the beach came out of its curve and resumed its journey north. He could see neither the Malekim nor any signs that the Malekim had been there. Either they had succeeded in cutting it off, or something had gone wrong. If the Malekim didn't shortly appear, it would soon be dark, and they'd have lost him.

The prospect of a Malekim lurking in the coming darkness was more than a little alarming. Perhaps sensing that they no longer followed, the Malekim might have doubled back. Perhaps it had turned into the dunes, realizing that the geography of the beach might put him at risk. Maybe the Malekim would indeed appear, not in front of them on the beach, but behind them. Maybe the hunters had already become the hunted.

Joraiem glanced back through the dunes at the horses. He wiped the sweat that was now streaming down his brow with the sleeve of his shirt. Evrim leaned against the dune next to him, looking with expectation at Joraiem. Evrim's face didn't seem to contain any nervousness at all. Of course, Evrim wasn't the one who'd have to take the shot. Joraiem strung Suruna and then stole another glance down the beach. Still nothing. Where was it?

"Keep an eye on the dunes behind us," Joraiem said as he unstrapped the cyranic arrow and began carefully to remove the leather cover that protected the deadly point. Delicately he laid the arrow upon Suruna, nocking it firmly but gently. He used his left forefinger to clamp it down tight, so that there would be no danger of losing control of the precious and deadly point.

He looked down the empty beach once more. They would have to pull back. The sun had finally touched the distant horizon, and the waves reflected its twilight rays. They could not risk being caught here.

Just as Joraiem began to turn to Evrim for his thoughts on their dilemma, the Silent One appeared, still moving at an impressive speed. Even from a distance, Joraiem could see the great cloud of sand that followed it like a whirlwind. The ninety-span gap between them was cut to eighty spans, then seventy. Joraiem slid his fingers into position, preparing for his shot and whispering a prayer to Allfather.

With only forty spans left, Joraiem stepped out from behind the dune and took aim with Suruna. The Malekim, seeing Joraiem, momentarily paused, then accelerated and swerved toward the ridge in a desperate race to reach Joraiem before he could shoot. Joraiem held his ground and at twenty spans, let the poisoned arrow fly.

The arrow struck the Silent One squarely in the chest, and the cyranis-tipped point sunk deep. The Malekim's pace continued unabated for a few steps, then suddenly the creature dropped away from the bank toward the water, losing its balance. It slowed to a halt and tottered, like a tree about to fall. The Voiceless dropped to his knees in the sand, his arms at his sides and his eyes staring straight ahead, and did not rise again.

Joraiem gazed down at the body of the Malekim, silent in death as in life. Of course, he didn't know for sure that the Voiceless was dead. He had never killed a Malekim before. Everything he'd ever shot had either been inanimate or food for the table. He had never killed simply to destroy, and even though he knew this had been a necessity, it was a difficult thought to swallow.

He reached back into his quiver and removed another arrow. He nocked it and readied Suruna, should the Malekim be alive after all. He started to descend the steep slope of loose sand and dropped onto the more firmly packed beach less than ten spans from the body.

"Joraiem, wait," Evrim called as he also dropped from the bank behind him. "Let me. What good is your bow up close?"

Joraiem looked at the sword in his friend's hand and nodded. "Approach him from the side. If he stirs, I'll put an arrow through his neck."

Evrim walked deliberately along the bank on his left until he was a little past and behind the motionless body. He circled behind it as Joraiem, who had been slowly sliding closer from the front, stopped and took careful aim at the Silent One's neck.

Evrim moved in until he was within reach, and with a mighty swing, his sword flashed through the weakening rays of twilight and struck the Malekim on the neck. The blow bounced off of the thick gray hide without even leaving a mark. Evrim swung again, this time even harder, and again failed to penetrate. He looked at Joraiem in wonder.

"I'm glad you're a good shot. If you'd missed, we'd be dead now."

"I guess we would be," Joraiem replied without taking his eye off his target. His hand remained steady on Suruna, but he felt shaken, and the full gravity of the moment just past came crashing in on him.

Evrim swung his sword again, and this time it made a small cut in the neck of the Malekim. Again he swung, and the cut widened. Over and over he wrenched the sword free, pulled back, and swung. Eventually, Evrim opened a gaping wound, and with a few more swings he severed the head completely. With the last blow it tumbled from the lifeless body and rolled across the sand toward the surf.

Joraiem approached the corpse. Even on its knees, the Silent One was almost as tall as Joraiem. The wound on the neck was oozing what must have been the Malekim's hardened blood. Joraiem estimated that two minutes at most had passed since the cyranic arrow had struck the creature. How remarkable it was that the recently severed arteries pumped so little blood from the exposed wound. What bubbled from it now was hardly like blood at all. Rather, it rolled down the side of the neck like tree sap, slowly spreading toward both shoulders like the creeping shadow of a thundercloud that gradually covers the sky.

From the body, Joraiem turned his attention to the head, the face of which lay about a span away covered with a thin layer of sand. It rested on its left ear, facing inland, avoiding even in death the last rays of the sun it so despised. The wide eyes that appeared to gaze on the rest of its body seemed filled with a cold and fearful rage. Joraiem was glad he had not had to look into them before he shot—they were most unnerving, a window into a heart ruled by hatred of Allfather's servants.

"Joraiem."

He turned. Evrim was carefully wiping the little Malekim

blood that had oozed onto his sword off the blade with a cloth. "You'll need to burn that with the body," Joraiem said.

"I know," Evrim nodded. As he finished wiping he draped the cloth across the Malekim's neck. Returning his sword to its scabbard, he continued. "What do you think it was doing by the dragon tower?"

Joraiem shook his head. "I don't know. I've been wondering that all afternoon. There are a lot of possibilities. None make much sense, and all are disturbing."

"They're more than disturbing."

"It could be that the Malekim just happened to be there. The dragon tower is visible from a great distance, and it may have been using the tower to navigate the woods. Our encounter could have been purely coincidental."

"Or perhaps he was out scouting for Malek. Why else would a single Malekim be so far from Agia Muldonai? Why did he run away instead of charging us? He could have killed us all."

"I know," Joraiem nodded, finally removing the arrow from Suruna and returning it to his quiver. "Though maybe he wasn't ready for us either. He may not have been a scout, you know. It's possible that he was a messenger."

"A messenger? To whom?"

"Maybe not to whom, but to what? He may have been sent to the tower."

"Why?"

Joraiem shrugged. "We really don't know anything about the dragon towers. Maybe Malek uses them as outposts for the Voiceless. They'd be perfect. Everyone is frightened of them because of the stories of the Grendolai. What if the Grendolai aren't real, or are all dead, but Malek uses fear of them to protect some secret?"

"Or maybe the Grendolai are real, and Malek keeps in touch with them through Malekim messengers."

Joraiem scratched his head, then realized what he was doing and self-consciously removed his fingers from his hair. Evrim was right. The possibilities were more than just disturbing—they were ominous. "There is another possibility, you know."

"What's that?"

"The Malekim might have been there because we were."

"Because we were there, why? What would a Malekim want with us?"

"Maybe it had nothing to do with who we are. Maybe it only had to do with where we were. Maybe he had been tracking us."

Evrim stared at Joraiem closely, "Do you think there's a connection to the Black Wolf?"

"All I know for sure is that he was there and now he's here." Joraiem glanced out over the water. "The sun will be completely down in a matter of minutes, and we need to burn this body. Let's get back to the horses, grab the lanterns, and start collecting the wood. I don't want to be here all night."

"Neither do I," Evrim answered. "I promised a friend I'd go to his going away party."

The last rays of light falling across the dunes cast long elliptical shadows across the sand. They mounted their horses quickly and pressed them east through the dunes and inland. Before long the dunes gave way to a wide-open space that extended for several hundred spans up to the edge of a moderately dense wood. A rough, sparse grass grew knee-high in the sandy soil.

By the time they had gathered a full load of wood and started back toward the beach, a host of stars twinkled above them in the cloudless sky. It was the last day of Winter Wane, so the thinnest sliver of moon was visible. Returning to the body of the Malekim, they deposited their wood in a pile in the sand.

"I think we are going to need more," Joraiem said.

"We are," Evrim answered.

They rode back up the embankment into the dunes, but sound of voices and the glimmer of lights distracted them from their mission. They halted where they were, listening.

"It's probably a party from Dal Harat," Joraiem said, urging his horse back toward the voices. A few moments later, they found themselves face to face with Monias and seven other men of the village on horseback and carrying lanterns. Monias dropped to the sand.

"You are well," he said with a trembling voice as he clasped Joraiem to himself. "Allfather be praised."

Joraiem found himself struggling to hold his emotions in check as he stood in the brisk night air. A deep relief that his father was there beside him now overwhelmed him.

"It's dead. We left his body on the beach beyond these dunes. We were returning inland to finish gathering wood for his pyre when we saw your lanterns among the dunes."

"Are you sure the Silent One is dead?"

"Yes."

"Joraiem shot him with a cyranic arrow," Evrim joined in. "Then, to be sure, I cut his head off."

Monias, keeping his hold on Joraiem, looked at Evrim. "Well done, both of you. There is one less Malekim in the world tonight, one more of the Voiceless among the lifeless. We must finish the task as Allfather wills it. Let's gather the wood quickly and return to the beach. We must be sure nothing is left of this accursed child of Malek."

The men of Dal Harat who had come with Monias rode up beside Evrim and Joraiem and greeted them. Creen Morsat was first. "You are dragon-hearted and no mistake," he said with a smile on his face.

The others followed his example, each with a look of awe in their eyes that Joraiem found disconcerting. Not only were they his elders, but most were more than twice his age. As a little boy, Joraiem had bounced on Gralos Bren's knee, and Palin Baanir was older than his own father. He did not know how to respond.

"We are grateful for your praise, but we only did our duty."

"Did your duty?" Gralos replied. "Maybe so, for we are all sworn to oppose Malek and his creatures, but few men in these parts are ever called upon to do what you have done, and few would be prepared if they were."

"Let's hope that no one else from Dal Harat ever faces the choice," Palin added quietly, "for I fear most would turn and run away rather than follow after."

"It isn't 'ever' that I'm worried about," Monias interrupted. "Malekim usually move in groups, so I'd just as soon dispose of this body and head back to Dal Harat."

After Monias had organized the wood retrieval, he pulled Joraiem aside. "Let them go and let Evrim go with them. He can guide them back to the body. Take me to it now, and tell me everything that has happened—everything."

As they headed back through the dunes, Joraiem felt himself beginning to relax for the first time since the dragon tower. Even knowing that the Malekim was dead had failed to dissipate Joraiem's anxiety. But now, as he narrated in detail everything that had happened that day, from the discovery of the Voiceless to its death, calm returned. Even the concern about the possibility of other Malekim nearby didn't have the same power to cause fear now that his father was with him.

Joraiem brought Monias to the place where he had stood when he took the fatal shot. Despite the stars, which glimmered on the water, the Malekim's body was not easy to see at first. The Malekim's gray hide provided little contrast with the sand of the beach. Even so, Joraiem was able to pick out the still form and point it out to his father.

"This is where I stood, and that is where he fell."

Monias looked quietly down the sandy bank to the fallen foe. His placed his hand on Joraiem's shoulder. "It was a good shot, son. You have done well. Suruna was well given today. I have intended to give you Suruna the day before you left for Sulare since you were a child. I had no idea how soon it would be of use. The timing was not an accident or coincidence. All-father is good."

They scrambled down the bank and walked across the beach toward the body. Even though Joraiem knew the creature was dead, he found himself approaching warily. Monias, though, didn't seem tentative at all. He walked up to the head-less form, circling it before stopping again in front of it. "Where is the head?"

"There," Joraiem pointed.

Monias walked over to the place where the Malekim's head rested in the sand. Much to Joraiem's surprise, Monias picked it up by the wiry black hair that grew in patches on its scalp.

"Although I feel an urge to heave this accursed thing into the deep, it must be burned along with the rest." Monias walked swiftly back, the head swinging from his hand like a lantern. When he was a few feet from the body he let go, and it flew in a slight arc over the legs of the Malekim that were extended behind the body, landing in the sand not far from the rest of it.

As Joraiem watched all this, he realized that part of his surprise sprang from the fact that he had not yet dared to touch the Malekim himself. He hadn't consciously avoided it, but neither had he seriously considered the idea. Curiosity now moved him to step closer and place his hand on the Malekim's shoulder. The grey hide was thick and rough, resembling the texture of mud that has been completely dried, cracked, and then fired by an unrelenting sun. He ran his hand down the arm and wondered at the coarse feel beneath his fingertips. There was no question that what he felt reminded him more of an animal hide than human skin, but even then it didn't feel much like any animal he'd ever skinned.

"Fascinating creatures in their own right," Monias said.

"Yes," Joraiem replied. "That hide is remarkable. The first few swings of Evrim's sword didn't cut it at all."

"No, it wouldn't have. Ordinary sword blades are not of much use against Malekim. Still, for all its might and strength, this Malekim died today because it wasn't invincible. No living thing is."

Joraiem looked at the red fletching of the cyranic arrow, still buried up to mid-shaft in the Malekim's chest. He had indeed exploited his enemy's weakness, but he knew very well that the smallest of mistakes would have changed his victory into defeat. "Father, what if there are more nearby?"

"Even though I said there might be, I doubt this one would have allowed you to hunt him for so long if he'd had friends close at hand."

"But what if there are more in the area, even if they weren't close enough to be of aid today? What if this one was an advance scout and more are coming? Dal Harat could be in trouble. You and Mother, Kyril, and Brenim could all be in danger. Maybe I should delay my departure for Sulare."

"Absolutely not!" Monias's vigor surprised Joraiem. "You will go as planned. Not only is it the law that you appear at Sulare by the first day of Spring Wane, but there is no good reason why you should stay behind. Even if trouble does lie ahead for Dal Harat, what would your staying change?"

"I could help to fight the Malekim, if there are more on their way."

"I have no doubt you could, but there are many men in Dal Harat who can use a bow. If a small number of Malekim or

Black Wolves come, we can defend ourselves against them even without you. If a large army of any kind marched on Dal Harat, though, there would be nothing we could do, even if we had you and a dozen more as skilled with their bows as you are."

Joraiem wanted to object but he thought of nothing.

"What if you had known this morning that a Malekim was as close to Dal Harat as this one was?" Monias continued. "Would you have decided not to go to the dragon tower so you could stay home to guard the house and your family? If so, you would have missed your opportunity to kill it. Allfather used you to kill this creature, not because you were the only one who could, but because you were where you were supposed to be, where He wanted you to be. It may be hard to go, but going is more important, even than Dal Harat. Go, as you have planned, and leave us in Allfather's merciful hands."

It did not take long to get the fire started once Evrim and the others returned. Moving the Malekim onto the pyre was another thing altogether. They rocked him back and forth in the sand until they had enough momentum to tumble him over altogether. The horizontal body was a little easier to lift, but only slightly so, and it took six of them to maneuver it onto the pyre. Monias followed them and rested the creature's head in the crook of his bent legs.

They stood in a semicircle on the dune side of the pyre and watched the flames begin to run up the wood and singe the Malekim's limbs. The smell of roasting flesh began to billow out with the smoke. Even so they did not move, but stood watching the fire increasingly devour their offering. When the body was fully ablaze, Monias broke the silence.

Child of Malek, born in flame,
Return to the fire from whence you came.

Return to the darkness, return to the earth,
You have no part in the second birth.

The ritual completed, the men quickly ascended the embankment and mounted their horses to return to Dal Harat. As they started into the dunes, Joraiem halted, turning back for a final look. The waves swelled and surged and rolled, just as they had, but where not long ago the peaceful light of the stars had danced across the surface, the red-orange glow of the fire now rose from the beach and cast flickering shadows across the water. It was the last peaceful thing this particular Malekim would disrupt.

Monias led the way back toward Dal Harat, riding hard through the starlit night. Much of the trip was a blur to Joraiem, for whom the events of the day swirled and tumbled in his mind incoherently. Weariness seeped up through his tired body and clouded his thinking until he was able to do little more than focus on the road ahead.

First Watch had passed by the time they finally reached the Andira home, where torches and lanterns blazed. Most of Dal Harat was gathered there. When word of the Malekim had spread throughout the village, even those who had not planned to attend came out to wait together. They came to support Elsora and to avoid being alone at home after such news.

As Monias and the others arrived, silence fell on the waiting families and friends. The entire village gathered around to hear what Monias had to say. "The Malekim is dead, and we have all returned safely—Allfather be praised!"

A great cheer erupted. For several minutes, as the men dismounted and found themselves overwhelmed with hugs and handshakes, the crowd pressed in around them. Soon, a cry went up for Joraiem and Evrim to tell their story. Before long, the whole village had taken seats at the tables as Joraiem recounted the story of their day from the dragon tower to the Malekim's funeral pyre.

Joraiem had barely finished narrating the story before the first question came from somewhere near the back of the gathered assembly. "What's going on, Monias? Six weeks ago it was a Black Wolf, today a Malekim. What's happening?"

"What if there are more still out there?"

Murmurs and echoes rippled through the gathering as Monias climbed onto one of the tables and raised his hands. "I understand your concerns and share them, but we have no reason to believe that we are in any more danger."

"How do you know?" a couple of voices called out.

"I don't know for sure."

"What are you going to do about it? We need help from the Assembly."

The murmurs grew louder. Monias had to wait for the chatter to die down before he could make himself heard. "I will send a message with Joraiem to a friend of mine from the Assembly in Peris Mil. I also suggest that the Village Council meet tomorrow to discuss the matter further. For now, that is all we can do. I would invite you in the meantime to enjoy our hospitality as much as you are able."

Joraiem could see in the faces of those around him, that the fears of many had not been allayed. Even so, the villagers returned to their eating and drinking, and soon the sound of laughter from various tables helped diffuse the general gloom. Joraiem seized his opportunity to satisfy his ravenous appetite and slake his thirst. When he had, he turned his attention to finding Alina. He spotted her at last, at a table near the side of the house. Aleta was also there, a few spans away, apparently engrossed in a conversation with her mother. He hadn't looked for Alina with any clear plan other than to see her, but now seeing her, he knew he had to speak to her. He had to be near her. It was worth the risk of being caught by Aleta.

He stepped out of the circle of tables and began to walk swiftly around the perimeter of the gathering. A couple times he had to pretend not to notice someone trying to get his attention, but before long he was only a table away from Alina. He slowed to approach her, then froze. Aleta had returned to the table with her mother and taken a seat just the other side of Alina. Before Joraiem could decide what to do, he heard his father calling out.

He looked back at the main table across the circle and saw Monias beside Kyril. He called again, "If I could have your attention please, I'd like Joraiem to come forward."

The crowd grew quiet and Joraiem stepped out of the shadows. Several of those seated nearby appeared startled by his sudden appearance. Walking across the circle to his father, he looked back over his shoulder and found both Aleta and Alina watching him carefully. He had a sinking feeling he wouldn't get another chance at Alina tonight.

"Thank you all for coming," Monias began as Joraiem took his place beside him. "As you all know, Elsora and I planned this evening as a going-away party. Despite all the excitement today, this is still a going-away party."

Some people applauded, while others pretended to boo. "You can't send our hero away!" someone called jokingly from across the circle. Laughter rippled through the gathering.

"I'm sorry," Monias smiled, "but it must be this way. However, to mark the occasion, Kyril helped me to compose a brief song in honor of Joraiem, which we'd like to sing for you. After today's events, though, some of the verses didn't seem appropriate anymore, so, with the help of a few of you, we've made some hasty revisions. Some parts are still a bit rough, and as you all know, only too well, I'm not the best of pipers, so please bear with us."

Monias's pipe squeaked as he played the introduction to

the song, and he had to pause to regain his composure as most of the village laughed, he most of all. After a moment, he was ready to try again, and this time he made it through without mistake. Kyril began to sing.

One summer's morn a child was born
His beauty all could see,
His mother wept
His father leapt
"His name shall be Joraiem!"

His eyes were blue a lovely hue
His hair was fairest gold,
And on his face
Allfather's grace
Taught us to love Joraiem!

He learned the bow and time would show
The skill that he possessed,
His form was pure
His aim was sure
A master shot, Joraiem!

And then there came what was no game
A Malekim appeared,
A fearful fate
This child of hate
To meet this day, Joraiem!

The hunt was long his heart was strong
He followed to the sea,
And there his foe
Nowhere could go
He had to face Joraiem!

There on the sand he took his stand
He held Suruna true,
The arrow flew
The Voiceless slew
Felled by the man Joraiem!

Then he was free there by the sea
The Silent One was dead,
They built a pyre
And set the fire
And watched it burn, Joraiem!

At break of day he will away
To do what he must do,
He'll travel far
So here we are
To say farewell, Joraiem!

Where'ere you go this should you know
You are a part of us,
So though we part
We're in your heart
Forevermore, Joraiem!

As Kyril and Monias took their bow, someone called from the crowd, "Again!" A few more voices joined in calling for a second performance, and Monias looked at Kyril, who nodded her assent. The crowd quieted and Monias lifted his pipe to his lips again.

"Aoooooo!" Rather than the rich melody of pipes, a long, lonely howl cut through the still night. A chill rippled through Joraiem as the gathered villagers flew into an uproar. Pressing in toward the center of the circle of tables, the people pushed together in a confused mass. In the chaos, a few tables were overturned, and a small fire in the grass started by a lantern had to be extinguished.

"Please!" Monias shouted, trying to be heard over the din, "Don't panic! A single wolf isn't going to hurt us."

"How do you know there is only one?"

"Look, if we stay calm, everyone will be fine. Gather all the lanterns and torches you can find and head back to the village. Women and children and those who came on foot should stay in the center, but stick together! If you live out of town, stay in the village tonight and don't go home until daylight. If this is indeed another Black Wolf, we will hunt him down like we did the last one."

It didn't take long for the villagers to organize themselves. Most were on horseback, and the few that weren't huddled tightly together in the middle of the crowd. Soon they were ready to go, waiting only for Creen Morsat and Gralos Bren, who were still talking quietly to Monias.

As Evrim sat on his horse, holding a torch, Kyril approached on the ground and touched his hand, while Joraiem stood some distance away with Elsora.

"Kyril," he said, surprised.

"I wanted to apologize for leaving you out of the song. I know you played an important part in killing the Malekim, but the song was originally all about Joraiem and there wasn't enough time to change it to include you. Sorry."

"I understand. Don't worry about it."

"Be careful, Evrim."

"I will."

Creen and Gralos mounted their horses and rode to the front of the group. As they started forward, Monias called after them, "Allfather be with you." A few called out the usual reply, "And with you." Soon the villagers had moved out of sight, and both the sound of their voices and the light of their lanterns and torches faded away.

Joraiem stood in the doorway of the house. The rest of the family had gone to their rooms, but as he stood gazing out over the mess the rest of the family would have to clean up tomorrow, his thoughts kept straying to Alina. He didn't like the thought of her out there while the Black Wolf was too.

"Joraiem?"

He turned to see Monias across the room, candle in hand. "I thought you were in bed."

"I will be soon, and so should you. You begin a long journey tomorrow."

"I'm still not sure I should go."

"I know." Monias moved across the room until he stood behind Joraiem. "I can't tell you that I know what is going on here. I don't know what Malek could be concerned with in Dal Harat, but I can't deny it is getting harder to see recent events as coincidence. All I know for sure is that I need you to be faithful to your responsibility and to go to Sulare as planned. More watchful eyes than yours are looking after us."

Joraiem turned, closing the door, and walked with his father toward the bedrooms. "I will do what is necessary."

"I know you will. And, if I didn't say it earlier, let me say it now: I am very proud of what you have done today. I'll probably be boasting about it all over Dal Harat until you get back."

"Goodnight," Joraiem said, hugging his father.

"Goodnight."

Despite his great weariness, Joraiem did not go to sleep right away. He was worried Alina might not be able to meet him in the morning now and equally worried that he wouldn't know what to say if she did. He tried to organize his thoughts, but he didn't seem to be able to focus long enough to come up with anything coherent. Eventually, he just gave up.

Joraiem felt the swish of the high grass as he walked down the overgrown lane to the dragon tower. The afternoon sun glared down into the clearing, and even the tower's dark masonry gleamed with light. As he stepped into the wide circular clearing, he realized that he had not brought his horse. He wore his quiver and held Suruna, but other than those he had nothing with him.

He searched the trees on his side of the tower but saw nothing in the wooded shadows. He turned back to the tower and started across the opening toward the door. He knew it was foolish to enter a dragon tower, but he felt he must. The enormous iron door was a span wide and two spans high, large enough to accommodate a Great Bear. He reached for the door's enormous iron ring.

A flash of wings flapping up out of the high brown grass caught his eye. When he turned he saw a windhover rising into the sky and circling the Tower. He moved back from the wall so he could follow its flight with his eyes, but it soon wheeled out over the trees westward and disappeared heading toward the sea.

As he returned his attention to the dragon tower door, a Malekim sprang up out of the grass right beside him. Its eyes glistened with rage as it knocked Joraiem through the air with the back of his arm. Joraiem flew backward into the door, his shoulder erupting in pain as it slammed against the door's great ring. As Joraiem staggered to his feet, he saw that he was alone in the clearing. There was, though, a clear trail through the high grass back down the open lane. He tightened his grip on Suruna and, using his other hand to hold his quiver, began to run.

He ran and ran through the high grass and the dense woods, all the time following the trail of the Malekim before him. Despite the pain in his shoulder, it felt good to run. Suddenly he broke out of the trees and onto the beach and continued the chase to the place where the beach curved out to sea. He didn't even pause but headed instinctively up the bank and through the dunes. He was soon standing on the embankment on the other side, holding Suruna ready. The Malekim appeared around the curve and accelerated up the beach. Joraiem waited for it to cut the distance between them in half, then let the arrow fly.

As his fingers released the bowstring, he realized his mistake. Alina was walking slowly toward him with a smile. He watched the arrow rip through the air and screamed as it headed straight for her. She disappeared. Relief swept over him as the arrow passed through the place where she had been standing.

The arrow continued to fly down the length of the beach, and as Joraiem watched it, he saw a white-haired figure in green come around the bend. The man carried a long staff with a King Falcon engraved on the top. A real windhover like the one from the tower flew in circles around his head, and as the old man turned the corner, he reached out his hand and plucked the arrow from the air. Holding it by the shaft, he continued to walk toward Joraiem, who stood amazed.

Though he didn't appear to be moving quickly, the old man covered the distance between them rapidly. His flowing green robe was tied with a simple white belt. A plain white sash draped around his neck hung below his waist on both sides. His hair was wild, unruly, and white as snow. What struck Joraiem, though, upon closer examination, was that the man was obviously blind. A translucent white film, which only barely revealed the color beneath, covered his eyes.

"How did you catch the arrow?"

The old man smiled as he handed it back to Joraiem. "Such things are easier to do in dreams than in real life."

Joraiem thought as the old man spoke that his voice was both full of authority and kind. "I am dreaming?"

"You are, but you will soon wake."

"Who are you?"

Again the old man smiled, "The answer to that and other

questions will come soon." He closed his eyes, lifting his face to the sky. "I can feel change coming. Allfather is on the move!"

Facing Joraiem again, he added, "That might also mean Malek is on the move as well. For now, though, sleep well, and when you go tomorrow, know that you go at Allfather's bidding to do His will with His blessing."

The man disappeared and for a moment Joraiem stared upon an empty beach, but only for a moment. The scene soon faded, and he woke to find the first rays of dawn shining through his window.

3

REVELATIONS

JORAIEM BENT DOWN FROM Erador to kiss his mother's forehead. "Don't fear for me, Mother, I can take care of myself."

"I know," she said, running her fingers through Joraiem's hair.

Kyril approached as Joraiem sat back up, "Don't worry, Brother, I'll protect the things you've left behind from Brenim."

"Ha," Brenim scoffed. "Who'd want any of that junk?"

"Junk, eh?" Joraiem smiled. "Then I guess you won't be wanting my old bow."

Brenim's eyes grew wide. "You mean you'd give it to me?"

"Sure. I'm taking Suruna with me. I don't need two bows. Do you want it?"

"Yes!"

"It's in its usual place. Go on and get it."

Brenim tore off toward the house. Monias watched him go, then walked over beside Erador. "Remember in Peris Mil to find Tal Kuvarin. Tell him what has happened here and pass on my message. Answer his questions as best you can."

"I will, Father."

Stepping in close to the horse, Monias patted his son on the leg. "And you, Son, don't fear for us. The hope of Dal Harat and the hope of Kirthanin rides with you. Whatever Malek is up to here, his ultimate designs are no great mystery. To frustrate them, we will have to be strong, and to be strong, we will have to be united. Focus on that, and your journey will be a success."

Monias stepped back as Brenim returned from the house with Joraiem's old bow held up over his head. "Thanks, Joraiem!" he called out.

Joraiem waved. "You're welcome! Use it well." Turning toward the road, he looked back over his shoulder once more. "Allfather's blessings be upon you."

"And on you," they called after him as he galloped away.

The morning was beautiful, and the soft warmth of the early sun was just what Joraiem needed after the long night. He pushed away thoughts of the previous day's adventure and of the howl that ended his party. He would have plenty of time along the road to Sulare to consider what had happened. What he needed now was time to think about what he would say to Alina.

His feelings no longer confused him. Somewhere between his brief encounter with her in Dal Harat and the moment he had spotted her late last night, sitting by herself at the table, that question had been settled. He craved Alina's company, wanting nothing more than to be with her. Monias had told him once that perhaps at its most basic, love was essentially a hunger to be with someone. If that was true, then love was the best way he knew to describe his feelings for Alina.

But what right did he have to tell Alina that he thought he

loved her and then ride off to Sulare? Whatever her reaction might be, it would be hard for her to hear him and then watch him go. It wasn't her fault that he had taken so long to sort out his feelings. Still, he wasn't sure what other options there were. He had to go, and he didn't think he could leave for ten months without telling her. All the same, anything short of a declaration of intent would make talk of love on the morning of his departure awkward and out of place.

Joraiem slowed to a stop. He understood at last why all the approaches to Alina he had sampled in his mind had felt wrong. They either explained the depth of his feelings inade-quately, or they trifled with hers by holding back the proposal they should lead to. It was clear now what had been lacking and what choice he had to make. Either he needed to conceal from Alina the full depth of his desire until he could follow through on its implications, or he needed to leave her with a serious proposal and his commitment to marry her when he re-turned and could arrange appropriate terms with her father.

Despite the magnitude of the realization, it brought him a wonderful sense of relief. It was comforting simply to know the desires of his heart, to be able to remove the shroud of mystery. He spurred his horse on and raced the rest of the way to the southern gate of Dal Harat.

As he approached the village, he departed from the main road and took a smaller path that skirted the southeast perimeter and joined the major east-west road by Dal Harat's east gate. This road ran all the way to the ocean in the west. To the east, it ran south of the Kellisor Sea all the way to Peris Mil and the mighty Barunaan River.

Joraiem was reluctant to promise himself to Alina without talking to Monias first. It wasn't because he didn't have the right; he was of age and completely entitled to marry the woman of his choosing. Even so, it felt strange that he might propose marriage to Alina, a girl his family had known for years, when he had not even mentioned the possibility to his parents. Even if he asked her to, it might be impossible for Alina to keep the proposal a secret from her own father if other proposals were made while he was gone. If she told him, then Monias would surely find out.

The thought that other proposals might come frightened him. If he didn't declare the full extent of his feelings, it was possible that Alina would accept the proposal of another, unaware of how he truly felt. Still, though possible, it could be avoidable. He could conceal the full depth of his love for her while making it clear that he desired to be with her very much. Perhaps that would be sufficient to convince her to wait for his return. Maybe he could even ask that she wait so they could take some time together to sort all this out. After all, if he had seen in her eyes what he thought he had seen, then she might be as eager for that return as he.

Despite the possibility that he might get Alina to wait for him without having to offer his pledge, he felt uneasy. Did he have a right to ask her to do anything without giving a true account of himself? This was the fundamental question and he had no more time to contemplate it. The rock where he was to meet Alina lay just through the trees on his left, down by a small stream.

The rock jutted out over the gently flowing stream, beneath the pleasant shade of many trees. The rock also marked one of the only good swimming holes in the entire stream. The youth of Dal Harat often assembled on hot summer evenings for a swim, then rested on the rock as they cooled off. Other times, they simply sat together at dusk and talked until late in the night when they were sleepy or family curfews called them home.

As Joraiem approached, he recalled a particular evening when he went to the stream for a swim during summer harvest. He was planning to meet Evrim, but when he reached the rock he found no one. The stream was too inviting to wait, so he waded into the cool water until Evrim should come. As he floated on his back, he saw the branches around the rock rustle. He stood, putting his feet on the bottom and lifting his head out of the water to call his friend.

It was Alina, and she was alone. Joraiem, who had drifted to the far bank and a little downstream, watched quietly as Alina sat down and dangled her feet in the water. She put her hands down behind her and leaned back, staring dreamily upstream at nothing in particular. Though he was completely decent—everyone knew that both boys and girls came to this spot at all hours of the day—Joraiem felt awkward for not alerting Alina to his presence. At the same time, he was reluctant to call out. Alina never stayed anywhere he was if Aleta wasn't with her. As he watched her sitting there, he knew she would leave as soon as he called out to her, and he did not want her to go. In the end, he waded a little closer and did his best to get her attention without startling her. Despite this, she was obviously caught off guard and embarrassed. She stood hastily, and after making some excuse about being late for something, she disappeared into the woods.

Now, as Joraiem stepped out of the trees into the open space just above the rock, he saw Alina sitting in that same place once more. It was only the first day of Spring Rise and the weather was still cool, so she wore a thick gray cloak over her dress. Her long brown hair hung midway down her back, and as he approached her, she ran her right hand through it and turned back to look at him. She smiled nervously. "It's strange, meeting here again after all this time."

"I was just thinking about that too. It would have been nice that day to have talked to you."

A trace of sadness flashed through her bright green eyes. "That was a long time ago."

He crossed the rock to where she sat and slipped off his riding boots so he could dangle his feet in the water beside hers. "It's ice cold!" he shouted as he pulled his feet back out.

Alina laughed at him. "It is not."

"It is so, it's freezing!" he said, gingerly dropping them back in.

"Don't tell me the big Malekim hunter can't handle a little cold water," she said with a grin.

"Ouch," he said, pretending to be hurt. "And here I thought we were going to have a nice conversation."

"Did you?" Alina asked, growing serious and turning away from him.

Momentarily unsure how to respond, Joraiem soon recovered enough to say to her quietly, "I had hoped we would, anyway."

"Then let's do," she answered earnestly. "Let's have a nice conversation, no matter what."

"Sure, did you think that we wouldn't?"

Alina gazed across the stream. "I didn't want to assume that I knew how this would go. People can get themselves into trouble when they think they know what someone else is thinking or feeling, and I didn't want to do that." She turned toward him. "Let's just agree that we'll have a nice talk. I would hate it if we parted on bad terms."

A plea filled her eyes and her voice. For his part, Joraiem was surprised that he wasn't reeling from being caught off guard. Instead, he felt he understood the source of her anxiety, and he wanted to alleviate it as fully as he could.

"I understand, Alina," he answered. "I agree completely. The last thing I want to do is part on bad terms. On the other hand, it would be wonderful to have pleasant memories of this morning and of you to take with me."

He smiled, thinking he had surely put her fears at rest, but she still looked uneasy, perhaps even worried. Joraiem was at a loss.

"I've often wished we could have a chance to talk without Aleta around," he finally said.

"She does make it hard."

"How did you manage to leave her behind today?"

Alina blushed. "I learned many years ago that Aleta has no patience for bird watching. She thought I was crazy to go out today after what happened last night and almost came with me. Thankfully she didn't, but I feel awful about lying to her. Still, this was important."

"I'm glad you think so," Joraiem said. "It's important to me too. Perhaps I should just get right to the point—"

"Yes, we should," Alina cut him off. "If you don't mind, Joraiem, I think I should speak first."

"All right," Joraiem said, a little surprised.

"I've been wanting to clarify something for a while, and I'd like to tell you about something else that I don't think you're aware of."

"All right," Joraiem said, laughing quietly.

"What's funny?"

"Nothing's really funny, I guess, except that it feels like we keep saying almost exactly what the other is going to say. I've got something I'd like to clarify, and there is something else I'd like to tell you about, but go ahead."

Alina hesitated, but then fixed her eyes on Joraiem's. "About six months ago you were talking to Aleta. I forgot myself and was sort of staring at you, and then you looked at me and caught me. I was embarrassed and left straight away. Do you remember?"

"Of course. That's one of the things I wanted to talk to you about."

"I thought you might, but let me say first that I'm sorry about what happened and about not explaining myself to you."

"Sorry? Why? I'm glad it happened. I think it helped me to understand you better. If it wasn't for that day, I might not have come this morning. I don't think explaining was necessary."

"Yes, Joraiem, it was and is. I think things have gotten horribly mixed up because of that day. It should never have happened, but after it did, I should have corrected it."

"What are you talking about?"

"Joraiem, what do you think that look told you?"

"Well, for one thing, it told me you didn't hate me. I'd always thought that you wouldn't talk to me because you didn't like me, but it seemed pretty clear then that you weren't looking at me with dislike."

"I wasn't, but what else did it tell you?"

Joraiem stopped himself from saying in plain words what he really thought he'd seen in her eyes. "I guess it told me that you had avoided me not because you hated me, but because you were interested in me yourself."

"That's what I thought. That's why I should have explained sooner."

"Hold on, Alina, what are you saying? Are you saying I didn't see what I saw? I saw affection, maybe even love. Look, if you're worried that I don't return your feelings, don't, because I do. That's why I'm here. I wanted to tell you before I left how much I care for you."

"Joraiem, stop. I know what you think you saw, and you were partially right, but you've jumped to the wrong conclusion. I do care for you. I have since the day we met. Aleta knew I liked you. That's why she decided that Midsummer night to tell you she liked you. We'd had a big argument that day, and it started as a way to hurt me. But, somewhere along the way, it stopped being a game for her and started to be real. You need to understand, though, that even though I cared deeply for you and hoped for many years you would care for me too, I gave up on that years ago."

"Why?"

"Why? Because you never showed any interest in me, that's why. I know that most of the time you avoided me because you were avoiding Aleta, but there were opportunities to pursue me along the way, and you didn't."

"Alina, how could I? You never even let me say hello to you without rushing off."

"Of course I rushed off! I was smitten. I could hardly stay calm when Aleta would corner you, even though I knew you wouldn't talk to me. But Joraiem, what does that matter? As far as I knew, you were only being polite. Saying hello whenever you see me walking down the street in Dal Harat doesn't qualify as pursuit."

"Maybe not, but how could I know you'd be interested in me pursuing you, when from all I could see, you couldn't stand to be around me?"

"Why did you need to know I'd be interested? If you were interested, you would have told me without needing to know how I'd respond. Aleta certainly hasn't needed encouragement from you to make herself clear."

"I'm not like Aleta."

Alina sighed. "I know you aren't like her, and I didn't want you to be. I just hoped that you would one day be able to see past her and see me. I knew she drives you crazy; everybody can see that. She's loud and pushy. I thought that if I wasn't anything like her, you might eventually notice I was different, that I was more of what you were looking for. I wanted you to have a passion for me the way I felt a passion for you, but when I came of age and you still hadn't shown any signs of interest, I decided it was finally time to accept that it wasn't going to happen."

"But it has happened! Look, I'm sorry that I didn't pursue you. I'm sorry that all this time I didn't understand the real reason why you avoided me, but it's all right now. Don't you see? I see you the way you've always wanted me to see you. I feel the passion! I wasn't sure how much of this to tell you today, but given what you've said, I think you have a right to know. I love you, Alina. I really do."

"Oh, Joraiem," she said, "this is even worse than I imagined it would be."

Alina buried her face in her hands and started to cry. Joraiem could only stare at her in confusion. "Alina, why isn't this a wonderful thing?"

Alina did not look up but spoke through her sobs, "Because I am promised to someone else!"

Alina continued to sob into her hands as Joraiem sat stunned. He fumbled for something coherent to say but failed completely. He stood and walked to the other side of the rock. The once-peaceful silence of the cool morning now felt oppressive. He ran his fingers through his hair and scratched his head. This was a nightmare, in some ways far more terrible than the sudden appearance of a Malekim.

"Joraiem," Alina called quietly to him, her voice regaining some of its composure, "I'm sorry to have to tell you this way."

He closed his eyes at the sound of her voice. "I don't understand how this could be."

"It was only just formalized with my father a week ago. There is to be a celebration of the engagement near the middle of Spring Rise. The invitations go out tomorrow."

"That's not what I mean. I mean how could you accept the proposal of another when you love me?"

"I did love you, Joraiem, and I still care about you, but I can't really say that I love you anymore, not that way."

"How could you love me for years and years and then not love me?"

"It didn't just happen all of a sudden. Love is something that can be fed or starved, and when I decided my heart couldn't take the waiting and the feeling of rejection anymore, I started to starve my feelings toward you. I stopped allowing myself to daydream of you. I stopped nurturing the affection I felt for you. I know all this must sound horrible and cold, but I thought it was necessary to protect my own heart. I didn't want to be alone all my life, and I realized that if you weren't going to love me, I needed to be free to love someone else."

"Then you're saying you love this other man?"

"Yes, of course I do. I wouldn't have accepted his proposal if I didn't. I've known for almost a year that he wanted to marry me, and I've known for nearly as long that I would accept. He's waited to formalize the arrangement until he knew my family better and knew how to approach my father. That's why we've only just entered into the marriage contract."

"Almost a year? Alina, how can you say you've loved this man for almost a year when I saw what I saw just six months ago? I saw it in your eyes as plainly as I can see you now. Are you sure you don't still love me, even if you've pushed it away?"

"Perhaps you saw some regret that day for what I had once hoped would be, but I think that while you saw affection and concern, you saw pity more than love."

"Pity?"

"Yes, pity. Just because I no longer love you doesn't mean I can't feel sorry for you."

"Why feel sorry for me? Because of Aleta?"

"No, not because of Aleta. Despite the annoyance, I think there is a certain comfort for you in your encounters with her. You know exactly how you feel when she's around, and I don't think that's often true for you. I've pitied you most when I've seen the uncertainty in your heart that you think you conceal. I pity you because I see all the wonderful gifts that you have, and at the same time I see your own struggle to understand who you really are and what you really want. I remember thinking just before you looked at me that if things had been different, I would have loved to bring light to some of those dark places."

Joraiem walked back across the rock to where Alina was sitting and stooped beside her. He wasn't sure exactly what he'd say, but he was desperate now. If he didn't try something, anything, then Alina would be gone, and he'd return to find her married. "Alina, please," he began softly, "there must be something I can say that will convince you to reconsider. Surely we shouldn't miss our chance to be together just because the timing was off? Life isn't that cruel. You say you don't love me anymore, but surely you can see that at least some of that love is still alive inside you. Why else would you feel for me when you saw my pain?"

"Joraiem, you mustn't say these things. It isn't right! I told you I am promised. My father has entered into a contract. I love another!"

"Do you?"

"I do! He is the only one other than you that I have ever loved, and just because I loved you first doesn't mean I don't truly love him."

"But if I had returned your love sooner, he would never have mattered to you."

"Please stop this. Why are you trying to shame me and dishonor my family? It is beneath you."

"Beneath me? Alina, I love you! I'd do anything for you. I didn't come here to ask you to dishonor yourself or your family, but to tell you that I love you and I want to marry you! This wouldn't be the first time a marriage contract was broken. It has happened before, and life did not end for those who broke it. We could still be very happy together. When I come back we could marry right away and eventually the scandal would disappear. Your engagement hasn't even been publicly announced yet."

"No!" Alina stood and began backing away from him toward the woods. "I am sorry for your pain, but I won't listen to this anymore. You have no right to even suggest these things. We're not meant to be. I accepted this long ago. It was hard, but I accepted it. So can you." She turned and ran into the trees.

"Alina, wait," Joraiem called. "Don't go like this!"

"I'm sorry, Joraiem, I can't . . ."

"At least let me tell you goodbye!" he called into the still swinging branches.

There was no answer, and after a few moments of watching and listening for any sign of her return, Joraiem collapsed on the rock.

Joraiem did not know how long he lay there. He was lying flat upon his back with his eyes clamped tightly shut. The words and images in his mind swirled. He switched back and forth between examining the conversation just past and his whole history with Alina. His mind combed through as many memories of her as he could recall, looking for something that he could not define. It was as if he was trying to find that single moment when he had lost what he had not known until now he wanted.

Suddenly all the frantic searching in his mind stopped, replaced by a single vivid picture of Alina sitting on the edge of the rock. Her feet dangled in the water, slowly kicking, and her hair fell over her shoulders and down her back. She turned to look at him and he saw the care and affection in her eyes. Now he saw the pity too.

"Joraiem," a voice called from somewhere above him on the ridge where the path lay. He didn't move. He wasn't even sure that he could move. The voice, this time closer, called his name again. It was a familiar voice, and just as it was dawning on Joraiem who it was, he felt a hand touch his shoulder.

"Are you all right?"

"Evrim?" Joraiem said as he opened his eyes.

"Yes," Evrim answered, "and I repeat, are you all right?"

Joraiem sat up but didn't answer the question. "How did you find me here?"

"I was waiting at the east gate, wondering where in the world you were, when Alina came by not half an hour ago."

"What did she say?"

"Only that I'd find you here."

"Oh."

Joraiem stood, but made no move to say any more. "Joraiem, what's going on?"

"Nothing."

"Nothing. You're more than an hour late, lying on a rock with your eyes shut, right where she said you would be. What's more, even though she was trying to hide it, she had plainly been crying. Is that what you mean by nothing?"

"You're right. It's not nothing, but nothing is what I have to say right now. Let's just go and maybe we can talk about it later."

He retraced his steps to where he had left Erador, mounted, and they rode briskly along the narrow path that brought them back to the main road. Pausing briefly at the east gate, Joraiem took one final look back at Dal Harat. This morning he had thought he would not be able to bear leaving the village, but now he wondered if in ten months he would be able to bear returning. He wheeled away from the village and began to gallop along the road that led to Peris Mil.

Joraiem and Evrim rode hard all morning. Fortunately, there was no market in Dal Harat that day and little traffic along the road. The pair only saw one other traveler, a bald, older man with a small empty wagon headed toward the village. Joraiem blew by the wagon at full speed without so much as a nod of acknowledgment. The startled horse tried to step sideways off the road, and it was all the man could do to keep him from pulling the wagon over. Behind him, Joraiem heard Evrim give a customary greeting awkwardly. An angry grunt was all Joraiem heard in reply as Evrim apologized for Joraiem and quickly pushed ahead to catch up with him.

Joraiem rode on without pause or second thought. Anger

rippled through him—anger aimed at almost everything and everyone. He felt angry at Alina for never giving him a chance to know her heart before she abandoned her love for him. Why did girls always think a guy could just magically know what they wanted? Aleta had told him over and over in unbearable detail how she felt for him; why couldn't Alina have made her case just once?

And Aleta, he was furious with her. How dare she! Her spiteful little joke so long ago had led to this whole mess. If she hadn't made his life so difficult, he wouldn't have avoided the two of them so much. If he hadn't been so preoccupied with dealing with her, maybe he would have noticed Alina as a woman sooner. Aleta's selfish little game had cost him his chance at happiness with Alina, and that he would not forgive. If Aleta thought to receive a warm, or even polite reception when he returned, she was in for a rude awakening. He would end once and for all any hopes she might still harbor the very moment he saw her again.

Joraiem was even angry at Alina's betrothed. Who was this person who had swooped in and taken her heart? He had forgotten to ask Alina his name. Was it someone he knew? How could he return to live peaceably as a neighbor to this man who had stolen his love? He would find a way to make this man pay. Whoever it was, he would learn the folly of offending one of the Novaana.

Though he was slower to acknowledge it, he was angry at Allfather too. If yesterday was evidence, as Monias had put it, of Allfather's special care and protection of his people, what was today? If Alina and Joraiem were "not meant to be" as she claimed, who had willed that? If Allfather guided the lives of men, as he had been taught to believe, how could any of this happen without His blessing?

He pressed forward even harder and for a time forced all thought from his mind. The wind ripped through his hair, and the countryside that he had intended to enjoy on this pleasant ride with Evrim passed him in a blur. He couldn't put the leagues between himself and Dal Harat fast enough.

As time passed, though, the swirling rage inside began to subside. It was easy for him to be angry at everyone else, but what about himself? Alina was right that he had not shown interest in her. If he could consider it unfair to seek her pledge without giving his, how could he insist she open her heart to him with no sign that it would be received? And even though it still seemed that what Aleta had done to Alina was in one way unspeakably cruel, that was really a matter between the two of them. Alina seemed convinced that for some time Aleta's advances had been genuine, so at least Aleta had possessed the courage to communicate her real feelings even without much hope of their being returned in kind. That was certainly more than Joraiem could say for himself. Furthermore, whoever Alina's future husband was, how could Joraiem blame him for loving the same girl that he loved? How could he blame him for seeing in her the beauty that he saw himself? And how could he blame Allfather for his own mistakes? Joraiem had avoided dealing with his own feelings, not because Allfather forced him to, but because he didn't want to be faced with their complications. He liked trying to keep life simple, and he had always thought that it would be imprudent to even consider love before his trip to Sulare. He had chosen to avoid the issue, found that it couldn't be avoided, and now bore the consequences of that choice.

He was suddenly aware that sadness had replaced his anger, and without the adrenaline of his rage, he now felt weary. He slowed his horse to a walk and felt the animal's relief almost immediately as it labored to breathe normally. He looked at the sky and saw that the sun was well past its zenith. Sixth Hour had come and gone, and he estimated that it was now approaching Eighth Hour. Hunger gnawed at him, and he motioned to Evrim, who was a few paces behind, that it was time to stop for lunch.

Joraiem and Evrim didn't speak during lunch, and when they were through eating, Joraiem lay back in the soft grass and stared into the sky. A few thick white clouds floated high above, and he wondered if they bore the promise of rain. There'd been little rain in Winter Wane, and Spring Rise was often a wet month. With few inns along the way, his trip to Peris Mil—and beyond it, Sulare—had the potential to be wet and uncomfortable much of the way.

He rolled over on his side and leaned on his elbow, looking at Evrim, who sat cross-legged with his back against the trunk of a small tree. He was looking back down the road in the direction that they had come, probably more to avoid looking at Joraiem than anything else. Joraiem didn't think Evrim was angry, though it was possible. More likely, though, Evrim understood something important had happened and that Joraiem wouldn't talk about it until he was ready.

"Sorry I left you waiting this morning," Joraiem said.

"That's all right," Evrim answered, turning toward him.

"I'm also sorry I barked at you when you found me."

"That's all right too."

Joraiem sat up and brushed bits of grass and dirt off of his cloak. "When I told you I'd be at the east gate by third hour, I hadn't yet made plans to meet Alina. That came up more or less at the last minute."

Evrim looked carefully at Joraiem. "You don't have to talk about it. I don't need any explanations."

"I appreciate that, but I'm going to be on the road a long time, and I need to talk to someone about it. I'm just glad it's you, because I know you can keep a secret."

"I won't tell anybody anything you don't want them to know."

"I know." Joraiem hesitated for a moment, considering how to proceed, then continued abruptly, "I met with Alina this morning because I needed to tell her I love her."

Evrim, who rarely betrayed much of what he was thinking, let his eyes go wide and his mouth drop open. Joraiem continued, "It's been awhile since we last talked about Alina, so I know this is a surprise. I've been confused myself about how I felt, so I haven't felt like talking about it. I'm sorry about not telling you more."

"You told her you love her?"

"Yes."

"Then I think I understand what happened this morning."

"What do you mean?"

"Well, Alina is promised. You must not have known."

"No I didn't. How did you know?"

"It isn't really a secret. They've been seen around Dal Harat together a lot recently, so most people who know her saw the proposal coming. I heard yesterday before I saw you and Brenim that it was official."

"You knew yesterday she was promised, and you've known for a long time that she was moving that way?" Joraiem felt the rage wash back over him. "Why didn't you tell me?"

Evrim looked startled again. He had only seen his friend this vehement once or twice before; this was the first time he was the target. "Our little adventure yesterday sort of drove the news from my mind."

"And the fact that she was on her way to engagement? What drove that from your mind? Didn't you think I might have been interested? If I'd known even a few weeks ago, before the contract was formalized, I could have told her how I felt. I might have had a chance."

"You haven't mentioned her in at least a year—"

"If I'd known she was about to accept a marriage contract, maybe I'd have understood what I needed to do sooner. I've been trying to figure out how I felt for a long time. Why didn't you tell me any of this?"

It was Evrim's turn to be angry, and it showed clearly in his voice as he answered Joraiem as vehemently as he'd been addressed. "Why are you mad at me? How was I to know that you were interested in what you would normally call the village gossip? You've never been interested in it before, so why should I have thought you'd care now?"

"Because it was never about Alina before."

"So what? I didn't know you were still interested in her. If I'd known I would have told you. Besides, I didn't know you were unaware. Most people knew."

"I didn't know."

"Is that my fault?"

Joraiem didn't answer. "Is it?"

"No," Joraiem said after a long pause, "it isn't."

Joraiem lay back in the grass and covered his eyes. In the midst of his swirling thoughts, a question occurred to him. "What's his name? I don't know who he is."

"I don't think you know him, but his name is Radin Marigan. He's got a farm about an hour northeast of Dal Harat."

"Radin Marigan," Joraiem repeated, as if trying to measure the man by his name. "What's he like?"

"I don't really know him," Evrim answered. "He's older than we are, maybe five years or so. He's always been nice to me, but he doesn't say much. You know me, though, I'm not much for conversation, so it may be me more than him."

"Does she seem happy when she's with him?"

"Look, Joraiem, I don't know how to—"

"Does she look happy? You know, does she smile, laugh?"

"Yeah, she does."

Joraiem stood, untied his horse, and mounted. He sat staring back down the road to Dal Harat, as Evrim also mounted.

Eventually Joraiem turned back at Evrim. "I guess there isn't any more to say about that."

Evrim shrugged.

"Sorry about shouting at you," Joraiem continued. "You didn't do anything wrong."

"I'm sorry too."

"Thanks. Like I said, I'm glad you're here. Let's go."

It was just about dark when they stopped to camp for the night. Despite the late start, their furious pace early in the day had made up for the lost time, and they had arrived at last at the Water Stone they had hoped to reach by nightfall. It jutted out of the ground almost twenty spans into the sky and was perhaps twice that wide, its sides scored with winding grooves by the many rivulets that must have streamed down it during the First Age. Monias said there were many Water Stones around Kirthanin, but this was the only one Joraiem had ever seen. Overnight trips to the Water Stone had long been a rite of passage of sorts for the youth of Dal Harat, and Evrim and Joraiem had made that journey together when they were fourteen. They had agreed several weeks ago that this was the point they would make for today, since it seemed appropriate that they should relive that happy time on their last day together before Joraiem continued toward Sulare. As Joraiem stood with Evrim at the base of the great stone and surveyed the scene that held so many good memories for them, he felt sad that their plan to relive that experience had been ruined by his encounter with Alina. He knew that Evrim had been looking forward to this trip as much as he had, so he determined not to let his own inner turmoil dominate the rest of the evening.

As they sat around the fire for their evening meal, he worked hard to get Evrim to reminisce with him about their first trip to the Water Stone, but though at first it seemed to work, Evrim was increasingly reluctant to talk. At last he stopped trying to direct the conversation at all, and Evrim seemed content to let it go.

After a while, Joraiem broke the silence. "I know that I haven't been a good traveling companion today. Sorry about that."

"You don't need to keep apologizing."

"You're not mad?"

"No."

"No?"

"No, I'm not mad. It's just that the more you've talked about the way things were, the more I've become depressed about tomorrow."

"What do you mean?"

"I mean the more you remind me how good things were, the more I don't want them to change, and they will."

"It's just ten months—it isn't forever."

"How do you know?"

"Evrim," Joraiem laughed, "I'll be back next winter."

"I hope so, but I don't know so. Neither do you. There's a big world out there, and you're of age. You can do what you want. You're one of the Novaana too. Maybe you'll make new friends and want to see new places."

"Where did this come from? We've talked about my going before, but you've never mentioned any of this."

"I know, but I keep feeling like this is more of a goodbye than we think it is."

"Okay, I'll admit that after this morning the thought of coming back is less appealing than it was, but everything I know is still here. My family is here. You're here. Anyway, where would I go? I wouldn't worry about it. I've never thought about staying away; it's hard enough to think about going in the first place."

"I thought you wanted to go."

"I've always wanted to see Sulare, you know, 'the Summerland,' but I'm not that excited about meeting the other Novaana. Monias keeps telling me how important it is, but I don't know them and they don't know me. What if we don't like each other? I'll probably be dying to get home."

"You always underestimate yourself. You'll make lots of friends."

"I might, but that doesn't mean I won't come home when the time comes. Even if I make friends there, they won't replace my friends here."

"I'm glad of that, which brings me to something else I need to say to you."

"What's that?"

"Well, it made sense yesterday for me to talk to you about this tonight, but after this morning, I'm not sure."

"Is it about Alina?"

"No."

"Why hesitate then?"

"Because it's a bit awkward by itself, and I don't want to complicate what you're already dealing with."

"Evrim, you're making it worse."

Evrim stared into the fire for a moment.

"I wanted you to know, that even though you'll be gone, I'll still be looking in at the house. You know, seeing how everybody is, especially Kyril."

"Especially Kyril," Joraiem echoed, looking closely at Evrim. "You mean you'll be looking after her since I won't be around this year, like a brother."

"That might be one way of looking at it, but it isn't exactly what I mean."

"Evrim, are you telling me you're interested in my sister?"

"That's what I'm telling you."

"Since when?"

"I don't know, since a little while ago. I guess it just happened."

"And Kyril, what does she think? Does she know?"

"She knows."

"Well," Joraiem said, scratching his head. "I'm beginning to wonder if I really know anybody or notice anything going on around me. Does my father know?"

"I think he has a pretty good idea. I don't know what he thinks about it, but I've noticed him watching me talk to her at times."

"Evrim, how serious is all this? Kyril comes of age this summer. You aren't thinking about doing anything foolish, are you?"

"I don't know about doing anything foolish, but I am pretty serious. I've felt this way a while, and I think that when she's of age, she should know—that is, unless you disapprove. I won't say anything until you get back if you don't want me to."

"You want my permission to ask her to marry you?"

"Yes."

"My father is the only one who must agree to the contract."

"I know, but I wanted your permission too."

Joraiem laughed. "My, what a day! I realize that I love Alina, find out she's promised to someone else, then learn that my best friend wants to ask my sister to marry him while I'm away."

"You see, I thought this might be awkward."

"Evrim, don't worry. I'm surprised, sure, but this is great. My best friend marrying my sister sounds pretty good to me. I wouldn't worry about her if she was with you."

Evrim exhaled as if he'd been holding his breath. "I'd hoped you would approve."

"Absolutely. Its just a shock, but by all means, return to Dal Harat tomorrow with my blessing. If Monias and Kyril accept your terms, I'll support the marriage completely. Will you wait for me to come back to get married?"

"Of course, if you'll come back when you're supposed to."

"I'll be there by the start of Full Winter. That's a promise."

4

PERIS MIL

THE NEXT MORNING A distant rumbling in the north woke Joraiem and Evrim just before dawn. When the pale morning light began to push back the shadows of the night, they noticed ominous grey clouds that stretched from horizon to horizon. The previous day had been by no means hot, but the chill wind that blew around them now was colder even than the night had been. Joraiem had no doubt that they were both in for a wet day of riding.

Even so, a lighter mood prevailed, and both talked and laughed freely together for the first time since they had left Dal Harat. Joraiem still felt keenly the ache of yesterday's loss, but he was heartened by the change that had come over his friend since disclosing his intentions toward Kyril. Evrim was happy to the point of being giddy, something Joraiem had never seen in him before. Joraiem gazed at the look of delight resting on Evrim's face and wondered if that was what he had looked like as he galloped toward his meeting with Alina the morning before. But he resisted the temptation to focus on the disparity between his own state and Evrim's. There would be time enough along the lonely road ahead to mourn his loss. For now it was soothing to see another basking in the glow of what still might be.

When they reluctantly acknowledged that it was past time to be on their way, they packed up their things and prepared to ride. It was strange for Joraiem to think that today Evrim was heading back to Dal Harat while he would be heading away. Until now Joraiem always had some point of contact with the familiar, which kept the feeling of complete separation at bay. In a few moments, though, Evrim would be lost from sight.

"It's been a wild couple of days," Joraiem said.

"It has indeed."

"Can you believe we hunted the Malekim only two days ago? After yesterday, the events of the day before feel like a dream. I hope today is a lot less interesting; I don't think I can take a third eventful day in a row."

"Unless you think getting soaked is eventful, this will probably be just the boring day you're after."

"I wouldn't have minded boring and dry, but I guess I'll have to take what I'm given."

"We both will."

"True, but at least you know that when this day is over, you'll be able to crawl into your own warm bed."

"There have to be some advantages to not being one of the Novaana," Evrim said, grinning.

"I can think of a few more, just in case you're wondering," Joraiem replied with a laugh.

Evrim placed his saddlebag on his horse and drew from it a carefully wrapped bundle. Walking over to the place where Joraiem was standing, he placed the bundle in Joraiem's hands. "Look," he started, "I had all kinds of things I thought about saying this morning, but most of the important things that needed to be said we covered last night. I want you to know, though, that your friendship is about the most important thing to me there is. So, I'd be honored if you took this with you to Sulare. If you were carrying it, I'd feel in a way like I was going with you."

Joraiem took the bundle in his hand. It felt as though he held little more than cloth. He unwrapped it carefully. Inside lay a silver pendant in the shape of a quarter moon strung on a long, fine chain that ran through a hole in the top. Joraiem looked up in wonder at his friend.

"Evrim, I can't take this."

"Sure you can."

"This was your father's. Even you don't wear it."

"Not yet. When you come back I will."

"But why? I have nothing to give you."

"You already have. Last night you were willing to trust me with your sister, and I hope that in time she'll accept me as a husband. I wanted to send something along with you as a promise that I'll take care of her."

Joraiem felt the cool, smooth silver between his fingers. It was a simple but elegant piece of craftsmanship. He slipped the chain over his head and dropped the pendant inside his shirt. "I will take care of it until I can return it to you."

"Farewell then, Joraiem."

"Farewell, Evrim. Allfather's blessing be upon you."

"And on you. We will watch for you in Full Winter."

Just as Joraiem prepared to answer, lightning flashed out of the dark northern sky. A few seconds later, a thick rumble of thunder echoed about them.

"Sounds like Malek himself is at the forge," Joraiem said when the thunder had died away.

"Yes, but it isn't the thunder that worries me," Evrim answered. "Here comes the rain!"

As Evrim spoke great drops of rain began falling all around them. They pounded the hard soil and splashed off of the Water Stone. Joraiem tilted his face to the sky and felt the sting of the drops on his skin. "Allfather sees how I am feeling today," he said. "He has sent this storm to sympathize with me."

"Then I will be on my way home and trust that his sympathy is blowing east with you."

Joraiem smiled. "Ride well, Evrim."

"Ride well, Joraiem."

Evrim wheeled around and was off toward Dal Harat. Joraiem watched him go, then began to pull up his hood. He looked again to the sky, stopped, and pulled it back down. Soon he was speeding down the road with the wind and rain in his face, his short blond hair matted to his head.

For ten days the spring rains poured. Each morning the dawn revealed a bleak grey sky, and each night the darkness concealed it. Day and night, though, the rain fell. Sometimes it came hard and fast as it did the morning Evrim turned back to Dal Harat. Other days the rain was slow and sure, falling at the same steady rate for hours on end. Joraiem was wet continuously. Even the few times he found adequate shelter for the night, he never dried out completely before morning came and he had to continue in the soaking rain.

Even so, Joraiem found the constant presence of rain and gloom strangely welcome. He was vaguely aware that had he been in any other frame of mind, the interminable movement from one sunless day to the next would have been oppressive. In the aftermath of the episodes with the Malekim and Alina, however, it was not so. Allfather had seen his turmoil and pain and summoned the clouds to enshroud him in their darkness.

At first he thought it strange that his memories of hunting the Malekim were not more happy; after all, he had killed the foul creature and earned the admiration and gratitude of his family and friends. Why then was the experience in retrospect not more pleasing? Why did the images of the long pursuit that came to his mind unbidden while awake and asleep not fill him with more pride and joy?

He came to see his misgiving as a sense of loss, an awareness that the peace and safety surrounding his home village had been shattered that day. The crack made in the villagers' confidence by the arrival of the Black Wolf had been splayed open by the appearance of the Silent One. Joraiem knew it would never be restored. Of course, he had known bad things could happen to people in Dal Harat. He fingered the slender silver moon against his chest and thought of Evrim's father. During a summer drought almost fifteen years ago, a fire swept across the Minluan's farm. Evrim's father rushed into the barn to try to save Evrim's older sister, who was inside. He was struck by a burning rafter when the roof collapsed. Both died in the fire. What had happened to Evrim's father and sister had been an accident. Accidents happened anywhere. Malekim and Black Wolves, though, if they belonged anywhere in Kirthanin, belonged far away, near Agia Muldonai and their master. They did not belong in Suthanin, and certainly not near Dal Harat.

On its own, the disquiet Joraiem felt about the Malekim and the Wolf would have been enough, but these concerns lingered on the margin of Joraiem's consciousness, while Alina remained at the center. The second night after leaving Evrim, Joraiem had dreamed that when he returned to Dal Harat, he found Alina waiting to greet him. Her face glowed with love and joy as she explained that though she had initially rejected Joraiem's suggestion that she break the contract with Radin, she had realized later that Joraiem was right. She truly loved him and always would. Of course Radin had been disappointed, but because he loved her, he didn't want to make her unhappy by marrying her, nor disgrace her by pressing his claim with her father. He graciously agreed to void the contract by mutual consent, which now freed her to marry Joraiem. When Joraiem understood at last what she was saying, he took her in his arms and pulled her off the ground with a hug. He could feel her hair against his face as she rested her head on his shoulder. It felt so real that for several moments after he awoke, he wasn't aware he had been dreaming.

Reality crashed down on him, but the damage of the dream was done. He now found it impossible to dismiss the possibility that Alina might be free to marry him when he returned. After all, had there not been times in his own life when he had at first rejected a suggestion only to embrace it upon further reflection? The thought that there was even a slim chance he might find her waiting for him was in one sense more torturous than the thought that there was none. What if he harbored hope for ten months only to find that she was long since married when he returned? How great would his despair be then?

He needed to force himself not to hope. He needed through sheer willpower to prevent his heart from clinging to any equally unlikely scenarios. In this the rain was a blessing, because the chill and discomfort kept him anchored in reality.

Even so, Joraiem welcomed the morning of the twelfth day of Spring Rise, because it brought with it a clearing sky and his first glimpse of the sun since the Water Stone. Joraiem felt heartened by the simple fact that the rain had ended and the sun had risen. He did not suddenly feel happy, but the morning sun reminded him that eventually even the darkest of storms pass, and that was the first genuinely hopeful thought that had come to him since he had watched Alina slip away into the trees.

After the first deluge, the spring rains became an intermittent backdrop to his journey east to Peris Mil. The land about him was beautiful and green, and it grew more so as the rains fell. Though few trees graced the way, the scenery was not dull as the road wound over and around many hills both large and small.

Habitations were even more infrequent than trees, though occasionally Joraiem passed places where smaller lanes deviated from the main road, some headed south, but most headed north toward the Kellisor Sea. Joraiem knew that many fishing villages on the southern coast of the Kellisor Sea sometimes used the road to transport goods to the larger markets of Peris Mil, though most trade between the town and coastal villages on the sea traveled by boat up and down the Barunaan River.

As the end of Spring Rise approached, Joraiem noticed an increase in the number of smaller roads branching off from the main road, both north and south. That, along with the fact that it was not uncommon for him to meet multiple travelers most days, told him that he was not far from Peris Mil. This meant he was nearly halfway to Sulare, and soon his road would turn almost due south on the eastern shore of the Barunaan.

Joraiem had never been to Peris Mil, but Monias said it was at least three times as large as Dal Harat, which seemed to Joraiem very large indeed. Even so, Monias assured him that Peris Mil was a small place compared to the great cities of Kirthanin like Shalin Bel, which lay north of Dal Harat in Werthanin. Such talk of relative size was almost meaningless to Joraiem, however, who had seen few places outside of Dal Harat, none of them much larger.

On the evening of the twenty-fifth day of Spring Rise, Joraiem was beginning to look for a place to camp when in the distance he saw the outline of a great tree rising into the sky. Straining through the dusk to make out its shape, Joraiem realized this tree must be either of great size or far nearer than it appeared. His curiosity aroused, Joraiem pressed on to see if he could reach it before dark.

He soon discovered it wasn't one great tree but two, almost exactly the same size, standing on either side of a broad lane that stretched southward into the distance. By now light had all but abandoned the sky, but Joraiem could still make out the dark form of two dense hedges that ran beyond the trees along either side of the lane as far as he could see. Thick, identical posts elaborately carved with running foxes stood beneath each of the two trees. Joraiem dismounted and moved in for a closer look. The carvings, like the posts, were mirror images of one another. Connected to the post on his right was a large iron gate, completely open and tied at the far end to a smaller post beside the hedge. Joraiem stepped back from the entrance to the other side of the main road. He looked back along the road in the direction he had come and then along the road in the direction he was headed. In both directions the road was every bit as bare as it had been. He looked again at the remarkable sight before him. As the slim waning moon and the many stars of the southern sky cast their dim light, the extensive branches of the two great trees rose dark and powerful before him.

Joraiem needed to settle on a place to camp. He was uneasy sleeping near this entrance, not knowing what it was or where it went, so he walked his horse along the outside of the hedge on the western side of the lane until he was well off the main road. It was almost certainly an unnecessary precaution, but Monias had always taught him to err on the side of caution in unfamiliar circumstances. As Joraiem lay down beside the hedge, he felt confident that he was well-hidden from view.

Joraiem woke with the morning sun, sat up, and stretched. He stood beside the dense green hedge, which was just a little taller than he was, and looked back toward the road. Much to his surprise, he saw a cart rolling slowly by, driven by a man with a great black beard and thick curly hair. The man was looking right at Joraiem, and when he saw that Joraiem had seen him, he smiled and waved. Not sure what else to do, Joraiem raised his hand and waved back.

The cart rolled past the first tree and disappeared. Joraiem thought about going after the driver to find out where he was, but though the man had seemed friendly enough, Joraiem decided against it. If he was heading toward Peris Mil at that pace, Joraiem would surely overtake him by midday, even if he did take time for breakfast. So he did.

When he'd finished, Joraiem rode back down the hedge to the main road. He took a second look at the trees, the gate, and the lane in the daylight and found them just as curious as they had been the night before. He would certainly ask the man in the cart about this place.

Joraiem had not gone far when he began to pass houses on both sides of the road. Sometimes three and four houses appeared, clustered together. Frequently a man or woman or children were out and about, and invariably he received a smile and a wave from those who saw him. He realized he must be on the outskirts of Peris Mil and that the bearded man was likely already about his business in the town.

It turned out that Joraiem was right, at least about being near Peris Mil. He'd only been riding about an hour when he reached the western gate. As he passed through it, he was overwhelmed by the number of people walking and riding in its streets, and by the way so many houses and shops were packed so tightly together. Children dashed in and out of the crowds, and though the other riders and cart drivers didn't seem to notice them, he was worried that he might ride into one of them. He dismounted from Erador and walked. He walked for a long time along many different streets, trying to take in the scale of the town. He saw not one but several blacksmiths, not one but several butcher's shops, not one but several inns. The sides of the streets were lined with stalls and wagons full of fruit, corn, bread, cloaks and tunics, leather goods, brightly colored quilts and dresses, and much more. Joraiem walked and stared, amazed at the variety of merchants and the quantity of goods for sale.

Eventually, he found himself at the town square, which also exceeded the proportions of the one in his home village. The town square of Dal Harat would have fit several times into this one, and the Mound of Peris Mil dwarfed the Mound at home. Not only was it larger, but Joraiem could see it boasted terraced steps, so that whoever was chosen to ascend it on feast days could climb with relative ease.

Joraiem pushed eastward through the town, noticing that many of the streets now seemed to slope downward. He understood why when the street he was on suddenly emptied out onto a broad landing beside an even broader stretch of water. Joraiem knew he was looking at the mighty Barunaan River, which flowed from the Kellisor Sea north of Peris Mil all the way to the Southern Ocean. He could make out the far bank of the river, which was a good distance away, and he understood now the awe with which those who had seen the river spoke of it.

A tinge of nausea, that familiar foreboding, swept over him as he gazed across the water. He forced himself to look away, disappointed. He had hoped the Barunaan would be different.

Looking up and down the landing, he saw many boats loading and unloading. In some places men operated what appeared to be mechanical arms of some sort. These swung from the landing out over the boats, where workers hooked large crates to the end of the arm so they could be lifted off and swung back onto dry land. Joraiem was fascinated by all that he saw but soon turned back into the heart of the town to look for an inn. He had promised himself when he left Dal Harat that he would treat himself to a comfortable room and a real bed when he reached Peris Mil, and now that he had at least surveyed the town, he looked forward to getting that room and seeing that bed.

Joraiem settled on one called The Winter's Moon, which faced the town square. The Winter's Moon was a two-story inn that was newly painted and appeared clean and well kept. Stepping inside, Joraiem found the public room was well lit and comfortable, though no one was using it at that early hour.

A small bell hung beside the entrance to the public room, and Joraiem pulled the cord to ring it. Soon after, a slender woman with partially grey hair pulled back from her face appeared through the door on the opposite side of the room. She looked tired but smiled as she saw Joraiem waiting patiently by the bell.

"What can I do for you?" she asked as she drew nearer.

"I'm looking for a room for the night," Joraiem answered. "Are there any available?"

"There are indeed. How many nights do you need it?"

"Just one."

"Just passing through, are you?" she asked, still smiling.

"Yes, I'm afraid so, though it looks like there is much to see and do here."

"I suppose there is if you haven't been here before. Where are you coming from?"

"Dal Harat."

"Dal Harat! That is a long way. How long have you been on the road?"

"Since the start of Spring Rise."

"Mercy," the woman exclaimed as she looked at him. "And did it rain out there as much as it did here?"

"Well, I don't know how much it has rained here, but it rained a lot out there."

"Then I guess you'll be glad to have a roof over your head and a warm bed to sleep in. Come with me and I'll give you the best I have available. I'll have my stable boy tend to your horse. I'm Mistress Doran, and if there is anything you need, just let me know."

"My name is Joraiem Andira, and the only thing I can think of that I might need while I'm here is a good hot lunch, a supper, and breakfast in the morning."

"That I can arrange. This way."

Joraiem followed Mistress Doran to a room at the front of the inn that afforded a pleasant view of the town square. A young tree grew beside the window, and the midmorning light shone through and around its light green leaves. After finding out what Joraiem would like a little later for lunch, Mistress Doran left him alone in his room. Joraiem laid his pack on the floor in the corner and sat on the bed. It felt amazingly soft, and he felt instant regret that he would only be able to enjoy it for a single night. At least he was nearly halfway to Sulare, and there he would have a bed again on a regular basis. For now, though, he lay back simply to take pleasure in the comfort of the mattress.

Joraiem woke to a soft, persistent knock at his door. Though momentarily disoriented, he soon realized what had happened and answered the door. Mistress Doran stood in the hall looking apologetic.

"I didn't know if I should wake you," she began. "It was hard to know whether sleep or the hot lunch would be more important to you, so I compromised and let you sleep an extra hour."

"An extra hour?"

"Yes, when you didn't answer my knock the first time, I decided to give you an extra hour."

"When was that?"

"Sixth Hour."

"Sixth Hour! I've slept from midmorning to Seventh Hour?"

"Yes, but unless you have urgent business in town today, there's no harm done. I've kept your lunch warming on the stove, so when you're ready, come and I'll serve it."

"I'm ready," Joraiem answered. He followed her to a small table in the public room near the kitchen door. The lunch was nothing fancy, but it was good. Mistress Doran brought out a large bowl of piping hot stew, full of potatoes and carrots and peas and lots of beef. Thick slices of fresh bread with butter and cheese were heaped on a plate on the side. A tall mug sat beside a tall pitcher of cool cider for washing it all down. When he had hungrily devoured it all, she brought a second serving of the stew, and Joraiem gratefully finished that as well.

With lunch over, he began to think of what he needed to do before morning. The supplies he had brought from Dal Harat, including the Morsat's gift, were almost completely gone, so he would need to purchase more food for the next leg of the journey. He would also see a local blacksmith about a new shoe or two for his horse. Other than that, all he needed to do was find this member of the Assembly that his father had directed him to see.

Joraiem found Mistress Doran in the kitchen, talking to the stable boy. He excused himself for interrupting and asked where he could find Tal Kuvarin.

"Master Kuvarin? Do you know him?"

"My father does."

"Where did you say you were headed again?"

"I didn't say, but I'm on my way to Sulare."

Mistress Doran nodded, looking more closely at him. He could see her taking note of his well-cut riding tunic, which, though a little worn from the travel, was of superior quality. "Master Kuvarin lives a little less than an hour west of town. You probably passed his place on the way in. You can't miss it; the avenue that runs to his house leaves the road at the foot of two enormous trees and is lined with thick hedges."

Joraiem nodded. "I do remember that place. Very well." He wondered if his face betrayed embarassment. "Thank you, I'll just get my horse and head back out that way."

"There's no need to do that. Master Kuvarin will almost certainly be in town today. He comes in most market days. At this time of the afternoon you'll probably find him by the river. He owns several of the buildings on the quay. Just head down that way, and when you get there ask anyone at the dock for him. They'll steer you in the right direction."

When Joraiem returned to the landing by the river, it was midafternoon, and the flurry of activity he'd witnessed that morning had settled down considerably. Nevertheless, Joraiem had little trouble finding someone to direct him to Master Kuvarin, and after a few moments, he found himself approaching a large, plain-looking warehouse well south of the place where he had entered the landing.

The warehouse's large double doors were wide open, and the enormous interior space seemed almost completely dark and empty. Joraiem could make out a smaller open door on the opposite side of the warehouse, from which a small amount of light spilled into the larger room. Joraiem, hesitant to enter without being invited, called out from where he stood. "Hello? Is anyone here?"

There was no answer. Joraiem looked around but saw only a few dock workers well down the landing, paying no attention to him. Joraiem stepped into the warehouse and began to cross through to the second doorway. As he drew near, he could make out most of the smaller room. Seated at a table with a mug before him was a plainly dressed man with short grey hair, who appeared to Joraiem to be a bit older than Monias, perhaps in his early sixties. He was sitting back in his chair, talking to someone just out of Joraiem's view. Stacks of paper covered the table and even parts of the floor.

Joraiem called out once more, "Hello?"

The man who had been seated stood quickly and stepped to the doorway to see who had called. "Yes?" he answered.

Joraiem stepped into the small section of the warehouse that the light from the inner room lit so the man could see him clearly. "I called from outside on the dock, but no one answered, so I came in."

"I see that, young man, I see that. Come all the way in then." The man in the doorway smiled, stepping back from the door to allow Joraiem to enter. "What can I do for you?"

Joraiem took the invitation to step into the room and was about to speak when he noticed the second person in the room. The thick curly hair and great black beard were unmistakable.

"Well, well," the cart driver said. "This is the very fellow I was telling you about earlier, Tal."

Joraiem blushed and turned to the grey-haired man who had taken his seat again. "Master Kuvarin?" he asked tentatively.

"I am Master Kuvarin, and you must be the young man who took shelter beneath my hedge last night."

"I'm sorry about trespassing."

Master Kuvarin and the cart driver both laughed. Joraiem felt his blush deepen. When he had regained his composure, Master Kuvarin answered, "No offense taken. You are welcome to sleep anywhere you wish on my property, but had you known the danger you were in last night, I doubt you would have stopped there."

"Danger?"

"I'm afraid so."

"What danger?"

"Last night, Garin here, tracked a most dangerous predator across my fields and killed the creature near my hedge, thankfully, or you might have had a most unpleasant awakening. What's your name, and what brings you to Peris Mil and to me?"

"My name is Joraiem Andira, and I am passing through Peris Mil on my way to Sulare. I have come because my father sent me to see you."

"Joraiem Andira!" Master Kuvarin exclaimed, the smile disappearing from his face. "Well then, I am doubly glad you didn't meet an unfortunate end outside my house last night, or what would I have told Monias? Goodness, Joraiem, why didn't you come up to the house?"

"I didn't know it was your house."

"Garin, it seems I am even more indebted to you than I thought."

Joraiem turned and took a closer look at the man Master Kuvarin called Garin. He was short and stout, thickly built from head to toe. His hands and face were rough, like those of a man who knows hard work and spends most of his time outside. His eyes were kind, though, almost merry, peering out from beneath bushy eyebrows that were almost as curly and thick as the man's beard and hair.

"I thank you also, Master Garin," Joraiem added, receiving a nod in return. "What kind of predator was it?"

Garin looked at Master Kuvarin, who said, "It's all right, Garin, you can tell him."

"It was a Black Wolf."

"A Black Wolf?" Joraiem replied. "Another one?"

Again Kuvarin and Garin exchanged looks. "What do you mean another one?" Kuvarin asked.

Joraiem quickly told Master Kuvarin and Garin about the Black Wolf and the Malekim killed recently near Dal Harat, and about the howl that ended his going away party. Master Kuvarin asked a few pointed questions about each incident, then rose from his chair, facing Joraiem.

"Joraiem, what has Monias told you about Black Wolves?"

"Well, I know what most people know, that the Black Wolves first appeared in Kirthanin when Malek invaded from the Forbidden Isle at the end of the Second Age. I know they are the accursed children of Rucaran. I also know that few have been seen during the Third Age, but that there are probably many living under Agia Muldonai who will come out with Malek when he emerges to make his third attempt at conquest. Why?"

Kuvarin did not answer but stood and, motioning to Joraiem to follow, walked out of the room into the warehouse. He carried with him a lantern that had been hanging by the door, and went to the double doors that opened onto the dock. Rather than going out, though, he closed and barred the doors. He then walked to the corner farthest from both the main entrance and the small interior office they'd just been in. As they approached, the lantern revealed an old cart, the same one that Garin had been driving that morning. A large tarp covered the back.

"Are you sure this is a good idea, Tal?" Garin asked.

Kuvarin nodded. "Joraiem is on his way to Sulare, and he'll learn more there than I will tell him." Turning to Joraiem he added, "Traditionally, most of the Novaana let their children learn about things like this during their sojourn in Sulare. I imagine Monias never expected that you'd see what you have seen before you had a chance to go there. Still, with an object lesson so close at hand, let me show you something. Did you see the Black Wolf killed near Dal Harat?"

"No, Monias took possession of the body as soon as it was dead and burned it with no one around."

"I'm sure he did, though you would have had a right as one of the Novaana to see its destruction. Monias probably needed to make sure the body was burned completely and quickly. Black Wolves are disquieting enough without their gruesome ends being displayed for all to see. Look."

Kuvarin pulled back the tarp that covered the cart and raised the lantern. Joraiem looked in, and what he saw revolted him. Whatever had once been in there, it certainly didn't resemble a wolf anymore. He saw large strips of black fur and the remains of a wolf's head with large jagged teeth. But in and around the wolf's remains, hundreds of dark worms squirmed and writhed, seeking shelter from the light of the lantern.

"You are looking at something few living men have seen," Master Kuvarin continued. "When a Black Wolf dies, it is eaten away in less than a day by worms that come from inside of it. I can't tell you exactly how it works, but somehow the death of the wolf triggers the release or hatching of the worms. They awaken with a voracious appetite and gorge themselves on the organs, the flesh, and even the bones and fur of the wolf. By the time they are finished, they have eaten so much that they die and soon decompose. So it is that no trace is ever left of a Black Wolf's death."

"If they disappear on their own, why must they be burned?"

"Joraiem, the Novaana do more than just govern, they safeguard man and man's memory. We have kept full knowledge of the Black Wolves alive, but we protect those we govern from the fear they inspire. One of Malek's chief weapons is fear, and we do what we can to counteract it. It is enough for the people of Kirthanin to know whom the Black Wolves and Malekim serve without being dismayed by the details of their creation or destruction."

"Master Kuvarin, why would a Black Wolf and a Malekim be near Dal Harat?" Joraiem asked. "What could they want with us?"

Kuvarin shook his head. "I don't know, Joraiem. Garin and I were wondering the same thing about Peris Mil. Neither Black Wolves nor Malekim wander aimlessly. They go only where they are sent. Still, I wouldn't jump to any conclusions yet. It may be that Malek has some particular interest in Dal Harat, but the appearance of these creatures is far from conclusive evidence that he has some dark purpose there."

"What will you do now?" Joraiem said, looking back at what was left of the wolf.

"I had Garin bring the Black Wolf here, because I had never seen one before and wanted to see if the accounts of their passing is true. By rights I should have had it burned, like Monias did, but I never was as good at stifling my curiosity for duty's sake." Master Kuvarin smiled again at Joraiem.

"As for what I will do about this news from Dal Harat," he continued, "that is another matter. But it is not one that should burden you. The Summerland is a wonderful place. Ride on and enjoy its wonder. Leave the worries of this world to other men. Soon enough they will be your responsibility, but not yet. Now let's leave these wretched things to their fate and go somewhere a bit more cheery."

That place a bit more cheery turned out to be a small table by the waterside. After the dark warehouse and the darker business within, the sun seemed exceptionally bright. Garin excused himself to take care of business in town. Joraiem sat with Master Kuvarin, drinking some of the best ale he'd ever tasted and listening to stories of the Assembly and Monias's role in it. Joraiem soon realized that though his father might be younger, Kuvarin respected Monias very much. It fascinated him to see his dad through the eyes of one of his Assembly peers.

Their conversation quickly turned to Sulare, and when it did, Joraiem saw in Kuvarin the same distant look of longing that often appeared in Monias's eyes when speaking of it. "Such a simple idea, yet so wise," Master Kuvarin said, taking another drink. "Every seven years, all the Novaana between the ages of eighteen and twenty-five, gathered together in one place. A chance to get to know those who will be your peers in the Assembly in a beautiful and peaceful place. A chance to form friendships with them as people, and to see them as they are, not just as representatives from a rival region or city. I sometimes wonder if any of that wisdom and foresight remains in the Assembly."

Kuvarin looked down and was silent, and when he spoke again it was not of Sulare or the Assembly but of the journey before Joraiem. If one was going to travel near or along the Barunaan in Full Spring, Kuvarin said, one must understand some pretty important things about the river. Kuvarin also gave Joraiem the name of a butcher and a blacksmith who would be more than happy to take care of his needs before morning. So, with the sun showing Tenth Hour was almost come, Kuvarin walked with Joraiem back to the street that would take him to The Winter's Moon.

"Now Joraiem, promise me that on your way back through Peris Mil you will come stay with me at the house."

"I would like that."

"Good, then I will not be embarrassed about my failure to welcome you when next I see Monias. I assure you that you will be well taken care of."

"That sounds great, and thank you for your help today."

"You are more than welcome. Be sure to tell anyone you have dealings with between here and the ferry that I have sent you personally. Most people around Peris Mil would treat you just fine anyway." Kuvarin paused at this, and Joraiem thought he could see a distinct twinkle in his eye. "But let's be sure you get their best."

Joraiem soon understood the twinkle, because neither the blacksmith nor the butcher would accept any payment for their goods or services after Joraiem mentioned Kuvarin's name. The butcher packed him a wide variety of meats, some for the first few days out that would spoil if left too long, and others guaranteed to retain their flavor for weeks. The blacksmith replaced all four shoes and wouldn't hear of having Joraiem wait while he did the work. He promised to return the horse to The Winter's Moon personally as soon as the work was finished. At both places, Joraiem protested that he could pay, but the men grew very animated at this and insisted they couldn't possibly take any money from him. In the end, Joraiem returned to The Winter's Moon just before dark with everything he needed for the next morning and more, all free of charge.

Inside the public room he found several people already eating their suppers. The smell of chicken roasted in herbs wafted across the room as he walked in, and he looked hungrily at the generous bowls of green beans and roasted potatoes on the various tables. Under normal conditions, having so large a lunch so late in the afternoon would have greatly diminished Joraiem's appetite, but after so long on the road, the smell of freshly cooked hot food was almost more than he could stand.

A young girl of perhaps fourteen walked around to the tables, filling mugs from a large pitcher she carried. Joraiem asked her where Mistress Doran was, but she wasn't sure. The girl thought she had seen the mistress heading out back, but that had been at least ten minutes ago.

Joraiem made his way into the empty kitchen. The back door stood ajar, probably to let the cool spring breeze into the hot kitchen. Joraiem was about to return to the public room to wait when he heard raised voices coming from outside.

He crossed to the door and peered out. The small courtyard between the inn and the stable was empty, but he could see Mistress Doran standing at the gate that led to the side alley. She seemed engaged in vigorous conversation, and from the angle at which she was holding her head, it appeared she was talking to someone very tall.

Joraiem stepped softly into the dark courtyard. He had no reason to suspect that Mistress Doran was in danger, but he couldn't tell if the conversation was friendly. As he slipped closer along the outer wall of the courtyard, he began to distinguish the silhouette of a man in the alley. He was tall, well over a span, and his long hair touched his broad shoulders. The man turned to gesture down the alleyway, and Joraiem almost gasped out loud as the light revealed massive scars on the right side of the man's face. Joraiem could not imagine such wounds open and raw. Several vertical slashes ran lengthways from the bottom of his cheek up the side of his face and disappeared under his hairline. Somehow, the man's eye was still intact, even though one of the big gashes ran right up to the socket and then continued on the other side.

Joraiem stood still, transfixed by the ghastly sight, until suddenly the man turned and walked off down the alleyway. Mistress Doran put the latch on the gate and turned to head inside, stopping short when she saw Joraiem.

"Master Joraiem," she said, a bit startled. "I didn't expect to find you there standing in the dark."

"I've just returned and was coming to make arrangements for supper. Who was that? Is everything all right?"

"Yes." She hesitated. "I think so. He was just a traveler like you, looking to make lodging arrangements, but he wanted some special accommodations that The Winter's Moon just couldn't provide. He wasn't pleased about it, but I think he understood."

"There's no trouble?"

Mistress Doran turned and glanced over her shoulder at the alley, "No, I hope and think not."

"I hope not too. He looked, well, a bit rough."

"Yes, those awful scars. I consider myself a pretty good judge of faces, and my first instinct was to think that despite appearances, he was pretty safe. But he does have the look of one who could be quite dangerous if he chose to be, doesn't he?" Joraiem wasn't sure he shared Mistress Doran's opinion of the man's safety, but the smell of roast chicken soon put those thoughts from his mind.

5

HAIL AND WELL MET

WHEN JORAIEM'S EYES FLICKERED open, they quickly adjusted to the darkness. Several stars lined the night sky, except where the shadow of the hedge above him obscured them from view. He contemplated sitting up, but it felt quite comfortable just to lie there, indeed, unusually comfortable. Suddenly, a deep uneasiness swept over him. He was being watched.

He rolled onto his side and looked up the hedge line. At first he couldn't see anything, but gradually he made out a sleek dark form moving stealthily along the hedge, protected from the moon and starlight. He felt around for Suruna, but couldn't find her. Looking quickly around, he realized his horse was nowhere to be seen either. Turning back, he was sure he could make out two silvery eyes watching him. He started to get to his feet slowly. His only chance was to run for the great tree at the end of the hedge and hope that the lower branches were low enough for him.

The shadowy form began to move quickly, and suddenly

both Joraiem and his hunter were running. The soft padding of swift footfalls drew closer, and Joraiem realized he wasn't going to make it. He turned to face his pursuer, and the Black Wolf sprang. Huge paws struck him squarely in the chest, knocking him through the air and onto the ground. As he fell he could feel the hot, foul breath of the creature fill his nostrils. His head struck something hard.

When he could open his eyes again, he looked up, expecting to find the open jaws of his adversary above him. Instead, he was staring directly at the moon, which hung bright and full and shimmering above him. Whatever his body was lying on, it was hard and cool, and he shifted to get a better look. He soon realized that he was atop the Water Stone only a day's ride from Dal Harat. He didn't understand how he had come there, but as he looked around and found no sign of the Black Wolf, he accepted the change as a welcome miracle.

"You do choose some fascinating places to visit when you sleep," a voice spoke from behind him.

Turning, he saw the same blind old man who had appeared in his dream before leaving Dal Harat. He was sitting with his long white sash draped over his green clothes and with his shock of long white hair standing out from his head on all sides. A windhover, perhaps the same one as before, though it looked larger, sat perched attentively beside him as well. "Am I dreaming?" Joraiem asked.

"You are, but why you would leave a comfortable bed in Peris Mil for this place is beyond me. I am no stranger to the wild, but even I know the value of a good night's sleep on a long journey."

Joraiem started to speak but the old man interrupted him.

"There will be time for that and other questions later," he said as he stood, his long green cloak flowing in the stiff breeze. "I am waiting for you and the others, but I have come to tell you this. I can sense that Allfather has placed among you some extraordinary gifts, but if I can sense it, then Malek can too. Beware!"

Sitting up on the edge of the bed, Joraiem stared out the window of his room at The Winter's Moon. Though he couldn't remember them all, he knew that strange dreams had troubled him all night. The last of them remained quite clear, however, and the relief of waking to find himself not cornered by a Black Wolf was mitigated by the parting words of the old man. They echoed in his mind, and as he scanned the empty town square in the first light of day, he wondered if there was anything or anyone here for him to "Beware!"

He lay back on the bed. What had the old man meant, and what should he make of his second appearance in his dreams? Had Joraiem fabricated him out of the depths of his imagination, or could the man be real? Though he could not explain how the man could appear, seemingly at will, in his dreams, Joraiem felt sure that the man was real. If real, though, what did his message mean?

The first time Joraiem dreamt of him, he had said something about the time being near, but what time was that? Now he spoke of gifts and of Malek's ability to sense them, but what gifts, and who did he mean by "the others"? Did the old man speak of Dal Harat? Was there something special about the people of his home village that had drawn Malek's attention? If so, then they continued to be in danger. He felt an urge to warn Monias of the old man's message. He knew, though, that if he did, he would never reach Sulare, which would be disobeying the law and disappointing his father. Monias had made himself clear that whatever danger may or may not come to Dal Harat, Joraiem was to go. He tried to assure himself that if the old man's message had been about Dal Harat, then presumably he could also warn someone in the village the same way he had warned Joraiem.

But what if the others the man had spoken of did not refer to Dal Harat? What then? Could he mean the other Novaana on their way to Sulare? Was that what he meant when he said he was waiting for them? If so, then perhaps the Black Wolves and the Malekim were stalking him. Maybe this Black Wolf slain by Garin had come to Peris Mil looking for him. Perhaps his family and friends would be safe now that he had left. But what about him would draw anyone's attention, let alone the attention of these dark creatures or their master?

Joraiem sat up again. That was plainly ridiculous. There was nothing extraordinary about him, certainly nothing that would set him apart as a threat to Malek. Whatever the old man had meant, it couldn't have been that. He would heed the man's warning and be careful, for he still had a long way to go, but until the message was made clearer, there wasn't much more he could do.

Joraiem dressed and slipped out of his room to get breakfast before leaving for the Barunaan Ferry south of Peris Mil. The rest of those staying at the inn must have still been asleep, because he found only Mistress Doran stirring, and she was at work in the kitchen. She greeted Joraiem cheerfully, asking how he had slept.

"Very well," he answered, feeling like a liar, but it wasn't entirely false. His sleep had been unbroken if restless, and that was more than he could say for many of his nights on the road so far.

"You'd mentioned wanting to get an early start for the ferry this morning," Mistress Doran began, "so I've got your breakfast all ready. Go ahead and have a seat in the public room. I'll be there in a moment."

Joraiem sat at the small table by the kitchen door where he had eaten lunch the day before. As he settled in, a loud noise from behind startled him. He stood quickly, knocking over his seat, whirling around. As he turned, he saw the front door standing wide open. He moved cautiously across the room to the door and peered out into the street. He could see no one. As he began to close the door, Mistress Doran entered the room.

"What happened?" she asked, looking at Joraiem by the door.

"I'm not sure. I was sitting at the table and heard the door swing open, but when I turned to look, no one was there."

"My apologies, Master Joraiem. It's my fault. I often open the door just a bit in the morning to let some fresh air in, especially in springtime. Sometimes the wind pushes it open or pulls it to. I'm sorry it startled you."

"That's all right. I just wasn't expecting it." Joraiem picked up his chair and took his seat again, feeling his face blush.

Mistress Doran went back into the kitchen while Joraiem ate. The basketful of rolls and sizable plate of fried eggs and sausage reminded him of the large family breakfasts that his mother usually prepared. Maybe it was the real breakfast after sleeping in a real bed, or maybe it was the uncertainty he felt about home after his troubling sleep, but for the first time since he had left Dal Harat almost a month before, Joraiem was homesick.

After breakfast, he returned briefly to his room to gather the few things he had left there. Suruna rested in the corner, and his pack sat on the floor beside it. Looking one final time at the still quiet town square out the window, he turned from the room and gently pulled the door closed.

He found Mistress Doran in the small courtyard between the inn and its stable. "Well, Master Joraiem, I believe everything is ready. You remember how to get to the ferry?"

"I go out through the south gate and take the road that heads left at the first fork. After that, the road to the ferry stays within view of the Barunaan most of the time, so if I can't see the river on my left, I've gone the wrong way."

"That's it," she said, smiling.

"Well, I think I'll be fine. Thanks for being such a good hostess," Joraiem said, pulling a small drawstring purse from the inside pocket of his cloak. "You said a room for the night and three hot meals would be three silver pieces. Here they are. It was well worth it."

As Joraiem held out the money, Mistress Doran shook her head, holding up her hand to refuse the coins. "There's no need for that," she said. "Your stay was on the house."

"On the house, why? Did Master Kuvarin speak to you?"

"He came by on his way out of town yesterday while you were still out. Any friend of Master Kuvarin's is a friend of The Winter's Moon."

"I can appreciate that, Mistress Doran, but I ate three large meals and used one of your nicest rooms. Surely even a friend can pay for another's expenses on his behalf?"

"There's no need. Save your silver for the road. Take this as a gift, not just from me, but from Master Kuvarin and all of us at Peris Mil."

"I'm not sure what to say, but thank you."

"You're welcome. I hope you have a safe trip."

"So do I, and I hope that Allfather's blessing will rest on you and The Winter's Moon for many years to come."

Joraiem mounted Erador and led him through the gate into the alleyway beside the inn. There were few people out and about yet, so he wasn't as hesitant to ride through town as he had been the day before. He soon found the large street that Mistress Doran said ran more or less directly to the south gate.

Even without all the commotion of the previous day, Peris Mil still awed him. Perhaps especially in these quiet morning hours, the town's size impressed him. Without the people crowding around him, his focus was drawn to the buildings themselves, some more than two stories tall. They were painted all kinds of colors, some bright and garish, others simple and subtle. At one point, after cresting a small hill, he stopped and looked around him. Houses and shops and inns and other buildings extended almost as far as his eye could see in each direction. He would tell Evrim when he returned to Dal Harat, of course, but he wouldn't really comprehend it, even as Joraiem hadn't before coming. Some things simply needed to be seen and experienced to be truly understood.

Passing through the southern gate of Peris Mil, Joraiem was struck by the beauty of the early morning sun reflecting on the waters of the Barunaan on his left. The light danced across the rolling waves of the river. Joraiem felt drawn to the splendor of the sight, but even as he did, he felt the old foreboding that washed over him whenever he neared a large body of water. He wondered how he would fare when he reached the ferry.

Joraiem slipped from Erador's back and tied him loosely to a small tree on the opposite side of the road. He scrambled down the bank to the river's edge and knelt beside the water. Here the river didn't seem to move with the same force as the central current. He dipped his fingers into the cold water to scoop a handful up to his mouth for a drink.

As the water passed his lips, a strange feeling seized his body. He shook suddenly and violently, and a powerful and lifelike vision came to him in a blinding flash. He saw before him a large and beautiful beach. The deep blue waves rolled in steadily as large thick clouds drifted across the horizon. The early morning sun rose on his left, and its rays glowed across the ocean's surface. Then, without warning, the peace was shattered by a sharp pain in his stomach. In the vision he sunk to his knees on the sand, and his eyes lost sight of the water as they were drawn to the growing blood stain in the sand below him. The pain in his stomach was excruciating, and he pressed against the worst place to make it stop. Blood flowed warm and steady between his fingers, oozing down the back of his hand and across his wrist until it dropped from his arm, making a smaller, second stain. The pain gradually receded, until it seemed at a great distance. His eyes began to dim and he felt himself toppling over. He heard his lips whisper a strange word, then his head struck the sand.

Joraiem splashed into the river, stood with a gasp and spat out the water. He stumbled backward to the river's edge as he clasped at his stomach wildly. He looked down to see if he was bleeding but saw nothing, even though he could still faintly feel the pain of the wound. His hands moved to his face in search of clinging grains of sand. He blinked a few times and concentrated on breathing normally, as he stood dripping on the shore.

He stared at the water. It was probably a coincidence that the vision had come at the same time that he took a drink, but he wanted to be sure. He was going to be traveling across and then along this river for a long time, and he needed to know what was going on. He crouched tentatively, scooping up some water. It was cold in his hand and appeared inviting, but he released it and watched it fall back into the river.

He headed back to the bank and started to climb, but stopped midway. *This is silly. I can't live in fear of my primary source of drinking water for the next month.* He turned back to the Barunaan, knelt on one knee, and plunged both hands into the river. Without hesitation he raised the water to his lips and took a long deep drink. He closed his eyes in anticipation but felt nothing except the refreshing taste of cold water.

He looked at the river. The images had been so potent. They had appeared to him not with the shadowy unreality of dream, but with the startling clarity of memory. Still, they couldn't be images even from distant memory, for only one word could describe the experience in the vision—it had felt like death.

He felt his head. Perhaps he had a fever. Maybe all those days in the rain had made him sick. Or maybe his sickness wasn't physical at all. As he climbed the bank, a new thought came to him. Perhaps he was beginning to lose his sanity. He had twice seen a bizarre old man in his sleep, and now a vision of his own death had come to him while awake. Joraiem had heard of people who'd lost their grip on reality, people who'd started to see things that weren't real as though they were. When he was younger, a man in Dal Harat had lost his senses that way. Though the man's family tried to take care of him, he had grown worse, until one morning they awoke to find him gone. They found him at last in a ditch, all but dead from exposure, murmuring incessantly about needing to hide from the watching stars. It had been the middle of a hot summer afternoon.

Joraiem didn't feel like he was going mad, but would he know it if it were happening? As he remounted Erador, he thought suddenly of Alina. He wanted to confide in her about the dreams and the vision. He laughed bitterly at the thought. He would never be able to confide in Alina about anything. She would be married when he returned, and his display at their parting would ensure that she kept her distance. He felt the pang of regret that he had felt many times since leaving, and he pushed his fears of madness away. *Mad men don't feel embarrassed about their shameful behavior.* He galloped off down the road.

The road south from Peris Mil eventually began to pull away from the Barunaan, but even though he traveled toward the fork for some time with the river out of sight, it was never out of mind. What struck him the most as he traveled this road was how much less inhabited it was compared to the road west of town. Some of this barrenness he had expected, after listening to Master Kuvarin describe the power of the river in flood stage. Still, the almost immediate disappearance of homes and people was a stark contrast to the well-populated west road and the busy town itself. He felt he had stepped back into the wild.

He found the fork, took the road that headed left, and was soon back within view of the Barunaan. This stretch was perhaps the most beautiful he had seen since leaving home. The total absence of trees on the bank opened a completely clear view of the river, while the opposite side of the road was thickly wooded. In the late afternoon this early in the spring, he would have had a cool ride beneath the shade of those trees, but with the sun still low in the east, the road remained pleasantly sunny and warm.

Joraiem did not pay much attention to the road as he gazed at the rolling water. Erador could be trusted to navigate such an easy road without direction, so he was surprised when he pulled up short and reared back on his hind legs, almost throwing Joraiem to the ground. Joraiem fought to control him, scanning the road for an explanation.

Joraiem found himself staring at an enormous tiger, lying maybe ten spans away, partially in the tall grass between the road and river and partially on the road itself. Joraiem held Erador as still as he could, but he could feel its panic as it stepped sideways away from the tiger.

"Easy," he whispered.

For his part, the tiger did not look terribly interested in either the horse or rider, though he was clearly watching them. Only a few seconds after Joraiem spotted him, the tiger yawned, opening his immense mouth to reveal a truly impressive set of teeth. This was almost too much for poor Erador, who started backing up, despite all Joraiem did to stop him.

When at last he had him under control, Joraiem considered the impasse. The only road that he knew led to the ferry was this one, but he doubted he would get even a step farther as long as that tiger was there. He hated the thought of shooting the animal for no reason other than the fact that it was lying in his way, but his options seemed limited. Perhaps he could scare the tiger away by throwing rocks, but it would turn out to be a foolish gamble if he did little more than make the tiger mad.

He waited and watched. Slowly, he untied Suruna from the place where he had it fastened to his pack. Stringing a large bow like Suruna on horseback was difficult but not impossible, and soon Joraiem had the bow strung and an arrow nocked. He was trying to decide where to aim when a voice called from the river's edge.

"Hold your arrow!" the voice yelled, quickly adding, "Koshti, here!"

In a flash the tiger had disappeared through the high grass down the bank, which was steep enough along this stretch to make the very bottom invisible from the road. The tiger's rapid disappearance did little to alleviate Joraiem's concern; it could easily reappear just as quickly, and a moving tiger would be more challenging to hit than a stationary one.

Joraiem sat still, holding Suruna ready. As he scanned the tall grass at the top of the bank, a hand waving a shirt appeared. "If you put the bow away, I'll come up to talk to you."

"Where is the tiger?" Joraiem replied.

"He's here with me, and he won't hurt you. Put the bow down?"

Joraiem slowly lowered Suruna, keeping the arrow on the bowstring as he rested the bow across his lap. From that position, he could ready the bow and fire a reasonably accurate shot in seconds.

The hand waving the shirt disappeared, and slowly a head emerged above the grass. Joraiem recognized the scarred face of the man at The Winter's Moon the previous night. His dark hair was dripping wet and clung to his neck, and a broad smile softened his appearance. He came up the bank holding his shirt and a very long sword in a dark sheath in one hand and a pair of boots in the other. His arms and chest were thickly muscled, and he exuded power as he walked, his long dark pants clinging to his legs.

As he neared Joraiem, still smiling, he tossed the shirt over his shoulder, shifted the sword to his other hand as he dropped his boots and reached out his right hand. "Aljeron Balinor, at your service," he said.

"Joraiem Andira, at yours," Joraiem answered as he took the man's hand, trying to match his solid grip.

"Hail and well met, Joraiem Andira. This," he added, "is Koshti, my battle brother." He whistled again and the tiger leapt up the bank and came up beside him.

"Battle brother?" Joraiem asked. With the tiger only a few feet away, he was beginning to appreciate just how big he really was. Erador sidestepped nervously, showing that he too was getting a closer look than he desired.

"Yes. We are closely connected, Koshti and I," Aljeron answered. He stroked the top of Koshti's head and the tiger sat down beside him. "It is a difficult thing to explain, because it's so rare, but my grandfather, who's a well-respected lore master, says that in the First Age such relationships were much more common."

"Where are you from?" Joraiem asked, dismounting, but still stroking his horse's side.

"Shalin Bel."

"Shalin Bel! That's a long way from Peris Mil," Joraiem answered. "What brings you here?"

"I'm on my way south."

"So am I," Joraiem replied, taking a closer look at Aljeron. Joraiem was sure Aljeron was older than he. He had thought initially Aljeron was several years older, but looking again at his face, Joraiem wondered if the scarring hadn't given him the wrong first impression.

"Where are you from?" Aljeron asked.

"Dal Harat. It isn't a big city like Shalin Bel, so you probably haven't heard of it."

"I have though," Aljeron answered. "Dal Harat isn't that far from Shalin Bel, though the marshes make direct travel by land difficult. Where are you headed?"

"Sulare."

"I knew it!" Aljeron exclaimed, giving Joraiem a big slap on his back. If it were possible, his smile grew even bigger. "So am I, and don't ask me how, but when I saw you sitting there, I had this strong feeling you were headed to Sulare too. Why don't you travel with us?"

"Us? You mean you and Koshti?"

"Yes and no. I consider Koshti part of us, but I meant all of us. I've been traveling with five others from Werthanin."

"Where are they?"

"They spent the night in Peris Mil. I wanted to stay too—it's been a long time since I had a good night's sleep in a real bed—but no one would stable Koshti."

Joraiem nodded. "No, I guess not." The previous night's exchange between Aljeron and Mistress Doran made more sense now.

Aljeron shrugged his shoulders. "I try to explain that Koshti is no harm to anyone, but most people won't trust a stranger with a tiger, especially if he has a face like mine!" Aljeron laughed.

"So, where did you stay?"

"In those woods over there. Koshti is in the most danger in places where men don't know us. I have to stay close to him to make sure that well-meaning strangers like yourself don't put an arrow through Koshti's throat, which, by the way, might have been a big mistake. I'm not sure a single arrow would take Koshti down. If you'd hit him, he would've been really angry."

"You may be right," Joraiem answered, looking at the tiger that must have been over a span and a half long. He still thought that a well-placed arrow from Suruna would have dropped him, but he was glad he wouldn't need to find out.

"So," Aljeron continued, "will you ride with us?"

"Sure, are the rest of your company on horseback?"

"Of course. We wouldn't have made it this far on foot."

"And you, do you ride on Koshti?"

Aljeron threw his head back and laughed, giving Joraiem a firm slap on the back again. "Mercy, no. I have no doubt that he would bear me on his back in time of need, but it would be a frightening ride. I haven't seen a horse that can keep up with Koshti, and without a saddle, I'm not sure how long I could hang on."

"Where is your horse, then?"

"He's with the others in Peris Mil. I've no idea when my companions will be along. I urged them to get an early start, but if Mindarin has any say in the matter, they'll stop frequently so she can shop for a new hat or dress or something."

"There are girls in your company?"

"Yes, two, though Bryar prefers the company of the men to Mindarin. Would traveling with women be a problem?"

"No, I didn't mean that," Joraiem said, blushing. "I just haven't traveled long distances before, really, and I hadn't thought about traveling in mixed company."

"You must join us now that we've met. You might as well start putting up with us now, since you'll have to for six months at Sulare."

"Are you sure the others won't mind? I mean, they may not feel comfortable having along someone they don't know that well."

"That won't be a problem. We didn't even know each other that well before we left. Our parents arranged it so we would travel together. They said it would be safer, and that by the time we got to Sulare we would know each other well enough to represent Werthanin as a unified land."

"Sounds like a good idea."

"For the most part, only they didn't count on the fact that it has also given us plenty of time to start getting on one another's nerves."

"Oh. Has it been an unpleasant trip?"

"Not really," Aljeron answered, "though we have our share of strong and conflicting personalities. You'll figure it out before long. Anyway, no need to dwell on that. Why don't you come rest with me in the sun by the river as we wait for the others? You can tie your horse just inside the tree line over there."

Joraiem did, and soon he was sitting at the water's edge, talking to his new companion. It was odd to have a conversation with a man who was stroking the head of a tiger, but gradually he adjusted to Koshti's presence. Aljeron suggested Joraiem stroke Koshti's soft fur, which he did gently but not for long. Joraiem felt it wise to take his time getting to know the tiger.

It soon became clear that for Aljeron, knowing Joraiem was a Novaana on his way to Sulare guaranteed his trustworthiness. Aljeron talked to him as though they'd known each other for years, never showing anything less than full acceptance. He didn't seem to mind that Joraiem was from a small village, even though Aljeron was from one of the great cities of Kirthanin. Nor did it apparently bother him that Joraiem was from Suthanin, though some from Werthanin and Enthanin looked down on the Suthanin "southlanders," as they were sometimes called. Even when Aljeron, a few months shy of his twenty-fifth birthday, learned that Joraiem was more than two years younger, he still expressed genuine pleasure in Joraiem's willingness to join them.

Joraiem also noticed that though Aljeron's face was terribly scarred, it communicated kindness and good humor more than anything else. Joraiem did not doubt for a moment that he was no physical match for Aljeron, who was taller, larger, and more muscular, and yet Aljeron carried himself with a gentle, even humble demeanor. It didn't take long before he found himself at ease beside his new acquaintance, even if his face was dramatically scarred and his best friend appeared to be a rather large tiger. Before he knew it, they were both talking of home and laughing about the way their fathers had given identical advice on the importance of Sulare. That was at least one thing they had in common.

A few hours passed, and soon the sun hung almost directly above them. Joraiem guessed it was past Fifth Hour, and he almost wished he hadn't bothered getting such an early start. He was glad to have had these hours with Aljeron, though, because it would be easier to meet the rest of the group now.

Koshti, who had been resting beside Aljeron as though asleep, raised his head and turned to look back up the bank. Aljeron sprang to his feet and scrambled most of the way up to the road. He lay flat against the bank and peered back up the road.

Joraiem joined him. "What is it?" he asked, surprised.

"Someone is coming," Aljeron said. "Perhaps the others, perhaps not. Until I know Koshti is safe, I need to be careful."

"I can't hear anything," Joraiem said in awe.

"Neither can I," Aljeron answered.

"Then how do you know?"

"Koshti knows."

Joraiem lay still beside Aljeron, and shortly he heard what seemed to be multiple horses coming along the road. Aljeron smiled, and Joraiem shook his head. "That's amazing. Does he hear them or smell them?"

"I don't know, but he's never wrong."

The sound grew closer, and moments later a group of five

travelers appeared around the bend. Aljeron jumped up onto the road and waved his arms. He whistled and Koshti sprang up the bank, passing through the air not far from Joraiem.

"Hello at last!" Aljeron shouted. "I was wondering if you'd decided to go home."

"Someone couldn't decide which outfit to be seen in to-day," said the rider at the front of the small group. He was also dark haired, though not nearly as tall as Aljeron and thin by comparison.

"Who's this?" the man said.

"Some stray, no doubt," said a well-dressed young woman, who rode up beside the first speaker. She wore a light black cloak over silk scarlet pants with a matching shirt. Her light brown hair fell in curls over her face, which was very pretty, though it struck Joraiem as cold and unfriendly. "Aljeron is always picking up strays, isn't he? He's probably forgotten we're on a serious expedition. And as for you, Rulalin, even though I know it is hard for you, try not to be so rude. The delay was only partially my fault. If you had bothered to check the horses last night before bed, then we might have known before we were leaving town that my horse needed a new shoe."

"Peace, Mindarin," Aljeron interrupted. "Joraiem is no stray. He is also on his way to Sulare, and I've asked him to join us."

The woman named Mindarin didn't seem impressed, but the remainder of the group came closer to have a better look at him. Meanwhile, the man Mindarin had called Rulalin slid off his horse and extended his hand to Joraiem.

"Glad to meet you," he said. "I'm Rulalin Tarasir."

"Joraiem Andira. The pleasure is mine," Joraiem answered.

The rest of the group also dismounted, and introductions were made. Kelvan was short and stocky, and his quiet manner reminded Joraiem of Evrim. The other boy was named Elyas and didn't appear to be old enough to be in this group at all.

As Joraiem later found out, he had only turned eighteen a month ago. His older sister, Bryar, had short blond hair, much the same shade as Joraiem's, and wore a brown cloak and riding pants, both well made and durable.

When the group was finally ready to ride, Rulalin called Aljeron up front almost immediately, and Joraiem found himself riding at the back beside Elyas, who was friendly and eager to chat. Elyas was more than willing to do all the talking and happily summarized their trip to that point, gradually making the order of age and authority clear. Though at first Rulalin had chafed at it, Aljeron was the consensus leader, partially because he was oldest, but mostly because he was easier to get along with. Elyas hastened to explain that Rulalin wasn't difficult, normally, but he did have some dramatic mood swings. At any rate, Aljeron's leadership had become less difficult for Rulalin to accept when he realized Aljeron would confer with him about most of the decisions anyway.

The next oldest and most assertive of the others was Mindarin, who, as it turned out, was the closest in age to Joraiem. She had turned twenty-two a week before arriving in Peris Mil, and had spent the day complaining that her husband hadn't sent along a present for her to open. Yes, Elyas explained, she was married. Though most Novaana chose to wait until after their time in Sulare to marry, even if that would mean being of age for several years first, Mindarin had decided to marry anyway. At the age of nineteen, she'd married a prominent merchant, more than a few years her senior, who was not a Novaana by birth but was quite well off. Bringing spouses to Sulare was not common, and at any rate Mindarin's husband was a successful man who could not afford to leave his business unattended for almost a year. According to some, Elyas said, his decision to stay hadn't grieved Mindarin too much, though Elyas was quick to say he didn't presume to know the truth of the matter.

Kelvan and Bryar came next, as both were twenty. Neither Kelvan nor Bryar had much to say most of the time, so most of the decisions were made by Aljeron and Rulalin, with or despite the vocal input of Mindarin. Elyas added with a laugh that he always had a lot to say, but since he was only eighteen, no one listened much.

Elyas speculated that Mindarin would be unhappy to discover that Joraiem was older than she. Up until now, she had acted as though the group were defined by the "older" three and the "younger" three, but now Joraiem's arrival dropped her a notch in the pecking order. Though Elyas insisted this was a good thing, insisting that Mindarin needed a little bringing down, Joraiem wasn't quite so sure. She'd been less than friendly already, and he wasn't sure he wanted to spend the next four weeks on the road with her if she was going to be actively resentful.

As if sensing Joraiem's anxiety, Elyas added, "Don't worry about Mindarin. Let her feel important once in a while and she'll be fine. Besides, you look like a man who knows how to handle a woman."

Joraiem looked at Elyas, not knowing quite what to say. After a moment, he turned away and shook his head. "Elyas, you have no idea how wrong you are."

It was almost Seventh Hour when they reached the ferry. An older man sat in the sun at a small table with a younger man, not much older than they. Both had midlength, unkempt beards and the look of those who had taken a bit too much to drink the night before. The ferry didn't look a whole lot better. Though a large boat, it looked like its best years of service were well behind it.

As they came to a halt, the older man addressed them without rising from his chair. "Looking to use the ferry?"

"If the ferry is still capable of use," Mindarin retorted.

"She does just fine," the old man answered. "She took twice your number plus horses and a couple of full carts across just a week ago, so don't you worry about her."

"There are seven of us with horses," Aljeron said, "and one other passenger who's not yet arrived. How much will it be?"

Joraiem watched the old man size them up. His eyes appeared to take in all at once the good horses, fine saddles, and Mindarin's expensive clothes. He exchanged glances with the younger man, "It'll cost you fifteen pieces of silver, one each for you, for your horses, and for the extra passenger. When are we expecting him?"

"He'll be along directly," Aljeron answered.

"We'll not pay fifteen silver pieces to hire that dilapidated old ferry," Rulalin said with indignation, half to Aljeron and half to the man.

"Rulalin," Aljeron said, cutting in over the start of the ferryman's objection. "We'll pay what the man asks us to pay."

"Four pieces of silver will be sufficient," Joraiem said firmly in the silence that followed. All eyes turned to him, but he fixed his eyes on the ferryman. "Master Kuvarin said that the cost of passage for man and horse is a single bronze penny. Four silver pieces will more than cover the seven of us, our horses, and the additional passenger. Or is Master Kuvarin a liar?"

The older man turned to the younger for support, but found little as the other was doing his best to look as though he wasn't really there. The man turned back to them, and finding by now the look even on Aljeron's face to be less than friendly, he quickly nodded and said, "Four silver pieces will be fine. I'll ready the ferry, or should we wait until your friend arrives?"

"That won't be necessary," Aljeron said, then whistled loudly. Koshti, who had spent much of the afternoon shadowing the group in the trees—Elyas had explained that this was an accommodation for the horses—sprang out of the trees and raced to Aljeron's side. The older man stepped back and the younger leapt from his seat, all but knocking over the little table.

"You have to be kidding," the younger man said, speaking for the first time. "You don't really think we're going to take that creature on the ferry, do you?"

Joraiem watched Aljeron's eyes narrow. "You will take him on the Ferry. I assure you there will be no danger if you do. I can't offer the same assurance if you refuse."

Again the two men looked at one another, then they looked back at Aljeron. His face didn't reflect anger so much as resolute conviction that they would do as he said. However much they had drunk the previous night, this was also clear to them. They looked at Koshti, then walked away toward the ferry without a word.

While they readied the boat, Aljeron approached Joraiem. Before he could say anything, though, Joraiem jumped in. "I wasn't questioning your authority, Aljeron. It's clear you're the leader of this group. But I promised Master Kuvarin I wouldn't let these men take advantage of me. He said they had caused problems before."

Aljeron smiled, "I'm not angry. That was great, thanks. A good leader accepts help whenever he can get it. I didn't agree to the price because I thought it was fair, I just didn't want Rulalin starting trouble. You handled that well."

"So did you—about Koshti I mean."

"Thanks," Aljeron said, turning to go, then turning back. "I have to say, Joraiem, that I'm really glad you agreed to travel with us. I can tell already that we'll be friends. We are well met today indeed!"

The crossing of the Barunaan was not as bad as Joraiem had feared. He experienced no cold sweats or visions of impending doom. Once the ferry was underway, he found a seat by one of the rails and tried to think as little as possible about the water. The others stood or leaned against the side and watched the water collide with the side of the boat, sending spray into the air. The only other passenger that appeared worried was Koshti, who picked a spot in the middle of the deck, lay down, and didn't move a muscle after the ferry launched.

Joraiem's skepticism of the ferry itself proved to be unwarranted, for despite the occasional creaking of the deck, it showed no signs of being anything less than sturdy. The ferrymen avoided all of them, especially Koshti, and they applied themselves to guiding the boat. The ferry soon reached the far shore, and all quickly disembarked. Soon it was underway again, returning to the Peris Mil side. The ferrymen never looked back.

The group turned the horses free to graze beside the river while everyone sat alongside the road for lunch, though it was now Eighth Hour. Having crossed the Barunaan seemed to trigger levity among them. They all seemed to share an understanding that they'd reached an important milestone. Even Mindarin seemed more relaxed, and the edge in the tone of her voice faded. In fact, all through the meal she was exceptionally polite to all, though she seemed to make fun of Aljeron with some reference to Shalin Bel he didn't quite understand. All the Werthanim thought it was pretty funny, however, and even Aljeron smiled.

While they ate, Joraiem said little, unless he was directly addressed. He wanted to make the most of his first opportunity to observe his new companions interact. As Elyas had hinted, neither Kelvan nor Bryar talked much, although they communicated with each other plenty. Several times Joraiem thought he saw them giving hand signals to one another when they thought no one was looking. Just after one of these exchanges, Bryar caught Joraiem watching. She blushed and looked away. There were no more signals, which Joraiem found all the more conspicuous in their sudden absence.

After the meal, Aljeron suggested that Elyas sing, and several of the others echoed the request. "What should I sing?" Elyas asked.

"Any one of those silly songs you're always singing," Aljeron answered.

"All right," Elyas said, "a silly song it is." He stood before them with his back to the river and began to sing.

> *Old Farmer Bean*
> *Was never clean*
> *Much to his wife's dismay.*
> *And though she cried*
> *He never tried*
> *To wash the dirt away.*

> *He smelled of bog,*
> *He smelled of hog,*
> *He smelled of barn and field.*
> *She offered gain*
> *She threatened pain*
> *But he would never yield.*

> *And then one day*
> *She got her way,*
> *Her husband came home clean.*
> *The smell was gone*
> *New clothes were on*
> *A different Farmer Bean.*

> *So now she sighs*
> *And wipes her eyes*

Recalling yesterday,
And she is sad
She called it bad
And wished the smell away.

There was laughter all the way through, but when Elyas finished there was much applause as well. He gave a bow and took a seat.

"Thanks for that reminder of the fickleness of women," Rulalin said.

"Thanks for that reminder of the folly in thinking that washing the dirt off a man will improve him," Mindarin snapped.

"I suppose it's good to see that even though we've crossed the Barunaan, things haven't changed too much," Aljeron sighed. He stood. "We should press on before dark. Gather your things."

6

IN THE WAKING WORLD

T HE ROAD SOUTH FROM the Barunaan Ferry was wide and smooth, a remnant of an age when people traveled more freely and roamed farther from home. In those days—before Malek tempted Andunin and the people of Nolthanin to their ruin in the First Age, and before the War of Division paved the way for Malek's return from the Forbidden Isle in the Second—trade flourished on and along the wide Barunaan. In some places, the remains of small river towns and pieces of piers and docks were still visible from the road. For the most part, though, no towns of any size or significance remained along the entire Barunaan River from the Kellisor Sea and Peris Mil in the north to the city of Cimaris Rul at its mouth on the Southern Ocean.

The one major exception to this was the village of Vol Tumian, which lay about midway between Cimaris Rul and Peris Mil. The primary function of the town was to serve as a stopping point for river traffic, so almost half the town was dedicated to its large quay. Those who didn't work on the docks worked in some capacity to accommodate the merchants, tradesmen, and boatmen that passed through. No fewer than five inns thrived within walking distance of the river, most of them full almost nightly, except during Full Winter when traffic along the Barunaan dwindled. The actual population of Vol Tumian was smaller than that of Dal Harat, but on any given day, twice as many people walked its streets.

The most direct route to Sulare would have taken Aljeron, Joraiem, and the others inland toward the Elnin Wood before reaching Vol Tumian, but for the most part, the group was willing to go out of its way to stay one more night in the comfort of civilization. Only Aljeron objected. "Why spend two extra days on the road for one night in a bed?" he reasoned.

Though both Joraiem and Rulalin were willing to bypass Vol Tumian, Mindarin's sharp tongue won her way. She claimed Aljeron didn't want to go because he knew he'd have to spend another night on his own with Koshti while they enjoyed real shelter. It wasn't fair to keep the rest of them from enjoying the comfort of society just because he couldn't. Though he insisted this wasn't true, he stopped arguing and put it up for a vote. With Joraiem and Rulalin abstaining, the other four voted against Aljeron.

They arrived in Vol Tumian on the eleventh day of Full Spring. The town was not like Peris Mil, and not just because it was smaller. It didn't have the same pleasant feel. The buildings were run down and the people were rougher in their appearance and slower to give a friendly smile. Since Aljeron had decided not even to bother coming into the town, Rulalin and Joraiem led the way in. They rode side by side, with Mindarin and Bryar behind them and Kelvan and Elyas in the back. It wasn't that they expected to find trouble, but given their experience at the ferry, it seemed prudent to be cautious.

The nicest looking of the inns was completely full, and

even Mindarin's best attempts at flattering the tired-looking, middle-aged man who reluctantly claimed to be the innkeeper couldn't make it otherwise. When she realized she wasn't going to get anywhere with him, she started to give him quite a tongue-lashing, but Rulalin stepped in and all but dragged her from the premises.

"Let me go," she said vehemently as they found themselves once again in the street. Her strident tone attracted the attention of a few passers-by in the crowd, but the lack of anything more interesting than simple bickering failed to keep their attention.

"Mindarin, have you forgotten completely how to treat someone with dignity and respect?" Rulalin said calmly but firmly. "These people aren't your servants. If the inn is full, it's full."

Mindarin stood up in Rulalin's face, her eyes glaring. Her fists were clenched and trembling. Joraiem had seen her lose her temper in the last couple weeks, but he had never seen her this furious. "Don't ever touch me again! Ever! Not you, Rulalin. Of all people, not you. You don't have the right. Do you understand?"

"That isn't the point, you—"

"Do you understand?" she said again, louder.

Rulalin, now looking very uncomfortable, quickly said, "I understand, now stop yelling."

Mindarin wheeled away from them all, leading her horse. Rulalin shrugged his shoulders and didn't even look at the rest when he said, "Come on, we can't let her wander around here on her own."

At the next inn, Rulalin did the talking, and when it was clear that this one was also full, Mindarin silently exited and the others followed. The same scene was repeated at the third one, and they began to wonder if their detour would be for nothing.

"If we don't find a place to stay tonight, Aljeron won't let us forget it," Elyas said.

"There are still two inns left," Kelvan answered.

"They look wretched," Mindarin said, speaking for the first time since her argument with Rulalin. "I suppose all we can do is check the one that is less filthy looking than the other."

The inn that earned the distinction of being "less filthy" was called The Rusty Anchor, though it was hard to make out exactly what the picture on the sign above the entrance was supposed to be—certainly it bore little resemblance to anything like an anchor, rusty or otherwise. Inside, a remarkably thin woman greeted them, if coughing in their faces could be considered a greeting.

"I have room for four," she said when they inquired about rooms.

"As you can see, there are six of us," Rulalin replied. "Do you think you might be able to find room for us all?"

The woman looked coldly at Rulalin. "I have two rooms with room for four total. Do you want them or not?"

They agreed to take the rooms. Mindarin and Bryar would share one, and Elyas and Kelvan the other, though Rulalin felt Joraiem should be one of the ones to remain to watch over the rest.

"We're younger than you, Rulalin," Bryar said, "but we're not children. We'll be all right with Elyas and Kelvan."

When the others were settled, Joraiem and Rulalin set out for the only remaining inn, a small place in evident disrepair south of the main village. The faded white paint on the outside of the inn was mostly discolored with dirt and grime, and the windows were so dark as to be virtually opaque. No sign hung from the dangling sign-pole chains, but a small piece of board that read "Tumian Inn" was nailed above the door.

The interior did not disappoint. The potent smell of fish that permeated the public room was so strong that both Rulalin and Joraiem all but choked as they entered. As Joraiem's eyes adjusted to the darkness, a few dim wall lamps revealed a hodgepodge of tables and chairs. In a few places, there were no tables at all, just ramshackle benches made of lumber set on rocks of roughly equal size.

Despite the shabby appearance and unpleasant odor, there were several guests about, most of them rough-looking in their worn jackets and faded pants. Joraiem knew the clothes he and Rulalin wore—Rulalin's black coat with gold embroidery around the cuffs and collar especially—stood out, and he reconsidered even asking about a room. The place where they had agreed to meet Aljeron in the morning looked like a comfortable enough place to camp, but Rulalin rang the bell by the door before he could suggest they go. The innkeeper appeared from the kitchen, and to Joraiem's surprise, she turned out to be a short stout woman who looked for all the world as though she were as happy as could be.

"Good afternoon, young masters," she said. "Welcome to the Tumian Inn. Are you looking for a drink? Dinner? A place to stay?"

"All of them," Rulalin answered. "Do you have rooms available?"

"I have two, but if you wouldn't mind sharing, I'd like to keep the other open in case it is needed later on."

"That would be fine."

"Good, then follow me."

The room was small and sparse, containing only two single beds. The lone window looked south from the inn toward a small cluster of trees about fifteen spans from the river. Joraiem and Rulalin set their things on the beds and headed back to the public room.

Though it didn't look very promising, dinner at the Tumian Inn tasted better than either of them expected. Given the intense smell of fish that filled the place, Joraiem was not surprised to see that fish was the main course, but he didn't recognize what kind of fish it was. He assumed it must be something found only in rivers or perhaps only in the Barunaan, for he had never seen its like in Dal Harat, where fresh fish from the coast came often.

Afterward, Rulalin suggested they go for a walk. Joraiem readily agreed, eager to escape the dim public room for the cool night air. They strolled outside into the fading light of the warm spring day and agreed that walking back toward Vol Tumian was not a good idea. They took a path that ran south along the river.

"It's strange to think that Full Spring is almost half over," Rulalin began. "It was still Winter Wane when we left home."

"It is strange. Much of what I associate with springtime is tied to specific places, and without being there to witness the changes in those places and things, it hasn't always felt as though Spring were real."

"I know what you mean. We've watched trees and flowers bloom along the way, but they aren't the same trees and flowers that I've grown up watching bloom. I've seen streams fill with water from the spring rains, but they aren't the same streams. The signs of spring are the same in a general way, but they lack the familiarity of home."

Joraiem nodded. "I guess it's good that Sulare is equally strange for us all. We will share in the unfamiliarity, and no one will have the advantage of feeling at home."

"I think you're right."

"I keep wondering what it will be like when it's over," Joraiem said. "I wonder if it'll be hard to leave, or if we'll be eager to get home."

Rulalin walked with his head down as though carefully considering his opinion. "That will probably differ for each of us. Some may have reason to want to get home, while others may have reason not to."

Joraiem watched Rulalin, who seemed on the brink of adding something else, but he said no more. Joraiem wondered what he had been about to say, but, uncomfortable with the new silence, he tried to change the topic. "One thing is for sure, if bad weather comes early, the trip home will be uncomfortable. I think I'd be glad to have our room at the Tumian Inn then, and I'll be really glad to take shelter in Peris Mil before striking west toward Dal Harat. It will probably be even harder for you. I should be able to make it home by Full Winter, but you'll likely still be on the road."

"Very possible," Rulalin said, but Joraiem could tell his mind was on something else.

"What's on your mind?" Joraiem asked, surprising himself with his uncharacteristic boldness.

Rulalin's answer added to the surprise. "Have you ever been in love, Joraiem?"

Rulalin looked closely at Joraiem as he asked the question, and Joraiem blushed as an image of Alina came immediately to mind. "Yes, I have."

"What happened?" Rulalin asked, his eyes searching Joraiem's face.

"Nothing," Joraiem answered, looking away. "When I finally figured out how I really felt, I discovered she was promised to someone else."

Rulalin stopped walking and grabbed Joraiem's upper arm tightly with his right hand. A strange light glowed in his eyes. "So you understand what it is to love from a distance, when the object of your love is inaccessible?"

"Yes," Joraiem said, a bit taken aback by Rulalin's transformation. "I suppose I do."

As quickly as the change had come, Rulalin seemed to realize how tightly he was grabbing Joraiem and released his arm. The fire that blazed in his eyes receded, and he sighed as he turned off the path toward the river's edge. As Joraiem stepped off the path to follow him, foreboding rushed over him. He paused with his foot in midair, and it took a concentrated effort to make it come down in the grass beside the path. He felt queasy as he pushed himself the eight or nine steps it took to reach Rulalin, and by the time he reached his friend, he was almost dizzy.

Rulalin, though, did not turn to look, for which Joraiem was grateful. He didn't want to have to explain the beads of sweat that were rolling down his forehead.

"For over eight years I have felt the pain of a love so strong it overwhelms me," Rulalin began without turning from the water. "I have no control over its passion, nor have I yet had any hope of its satisfaction. At times, I have feared it would consume me utterly."

Joraiem felt unsteady. He stepped back to a rock that was a little too small to make a comfortable seat but was a welcome support at the moment.

"You aren't referring to Mindarin, are you?" Joraiem asked nervously, wondering if the question was too indelicate for this vulnerable moment.

Joraiem was relieved when Rulalin turned to look at him and laughed, shaking his head. He walked over and sat on the ground by the stone, leaning back on his hands. "No, I do not speak of Mindarin. Why?"

"At times, like earlier today, I've wondered. The intensity of your arguments suggests there might be a story behind your difficulties."

"Difficulties? You are polite. Mindarin hates me, and for that reason, well, I guess I don't much care for her either."

"Why does she hate you?"

"Because I didn't love her."

Joraiem looked at Rulalin's face as he spoke. He was calm and matter-of-fact, devoid of the powerful emotions that had swept across him moments ago. "I assume then that at some stage she loved you?"

"She did. Mindarin's family lives outside a small town a few hours east of Shalin Bel, where Aljeron is from. I come from Fel Edorath, several weeks east of Shalin Bel toward Agia Muldonai. Though Fel Edorath is every bit as great as Shalin Bel, it is close to the Mountain, and those who live there know what it is to be under the shadow of Malek. For that reason, when the Novaana of Werthanin assemble each year, they gather in Shalin Bel. Many times, my father has taken me as his eldest child on the journey to Shalin Bel, and Mindarin's family has often given us shelter on the way. Four years ago, when I passed through with my father in summer, she declared openly what I had feared, that she loved me."

"Why did you fear it?"

"Because I couldn't love her. I loved another. I tried to tell her that, but as you've seen, she has quite a temper. She's hated me ever since. Even after she married her merchant husband, her hatred continued. At first I felt sorry for her, because I know what it is to love and be held at a distance from the object of that love. I know what it is like to feel the ache of deep longing. But I have long since grown weary of her antipathy. I am not to blame because I love another."

Joraiem's thoughts turned to Alina. He knew that what Rulalin said was true. He was not to blame for loving another, even as Alina was not to blame. He sighed and hung his head, wishing once more that he could change his parting words to her.

Rulalin picked up a small rock and threw it into the river. The splash snapped Joraiem out of his reverie.

"So, why is there no hope of satisfying your love?"

"I didn't say there was no hope. I said I hadn't had a chance *yet*. I have waited years to have that chance, and every step that takes me closer to Sulare takes me closer to that opportunity, closer to her."

"She is one of the Novaana gathering at Sulare?"

"She is indeed. Her name is Wylla, and she is no ordinary

Novaana. As you know, the Novaana of Enthanin chose a king to lead them during the War of Division at the end of the Second Age, and though there was talk of abandoning the monarchy at the start of the Third Age, they did not. The last king, Pedrone Someris, died eight years ago. When we heard the news, my father and I made the long journey across the Kellisor Sea to Enthanin, all the way to the majestic city of Amaan Sul, to pay our respects to his widow, Marella.

"She welcomed us, and we stayed for a month at her home, which is truly like one of the palaces of old. I first saw Wylla beside the great fountain of the palace courtyard, dressed in black for her mourning. Her hair was long and black as night. Her eyes, though, were bright as the stars, radiating light and loveliness. When they looked on me, I knew that I loved her. When I saw her face, I knew what it was to see beauty unveiled. I saw her sadness and grief and felt sympathy for her loss, but I could not pity her. She was too magnificent to be pitied. I saw in her already the attributes of a queen, for as the eldest child of Pedrone and Marella, she is heir to the throne, though she has twin younger brothers. I longed to be with her. I knew that if I were to marry her, I would have to forfeit my rights as eldest son in my family and go to be with her in Enthanin to be consort to the queen, but it would be a small price to pay to live in her presence.

"During my stay we spent many hours together. I knew that it was not appropriate to speak of love in her time of grieving, so I restrained myself. The whole month I kept from her my burning passion, never hinting at how she had seared my heart.

"Our friendship grew, so when the time came for my father and I to leave, we met one last time. She was sad at the prospect of my departure, for I had helped to comfort her. In a moment of weakness and poor judgment, thinking that her sadness might mean more, I spoke of my love for her. It was a mistake. Her heart was still consumed with her father's death. She was not ready for me to open my heart to her, and I think the depth and degree of my feelings overwhelmed her. She did not reject me outright, and we parted politely, but I knew that I had overreached.

"Wylla is a few weeks younger than I, so I knew we would meet again in Sulare, and I have waited patiently. I have waited for my chance to redeem myself and to prove that what I felt was real love, not an infatuation of youth. I have waited to show her the firm constancy of my heart."

"Have you not seen her since?"

"No."

"Have you sent word to her, or had word from her?"

"No."

Joraiem looked with amazement at Rulalin. No wonder he came across as a mystery, full of intensity. He seemed so calm now, but Joraiem had glimpsed the fire that burned in his heart. How he could keep it burning for so many years without any contact with Wylla was beyond him. He thought of Alina, and asked, "How do you know that you will not find her married or engaged or in love with someone else?"

"I don't know, but that is beyond my control. I have only known what I must do to be worthy of her. I have not pursued any other woman or allowed any other into my heart. If that makes me cold as Mindarin says I am, so be it. I had to be able to come before Wylla and tell her that nothing had changed, that nothing was different."

"What will you do when you see her?"

"I will say hello. We have six months together in Sulare. I will not speak too soon this time. I will first earn her forgiveness for my inconsiderate words, then I will earn her respect and hopefully her love. It is my great hope that when I leave Sulare, I will leave as her escort and return with her to Amaan Sul to be married."

Joraiem slid off the rock, which had become quite uncomfortable, and settled in the grass beside Rulalin. He gazed out over the Barunaan, dreaming again of Alina. He envied Rulalin's hope that the fulfillment of his dreams might still lie ahead. "It must be exciting to think about getting to Sulare, to think about seeing her again."

"It is, and yet there is also fear. I've lived with the dream so long, it has come to be a comfort by itself. Now the time comes when I will either have the dream or lose it entirely."

"It's an awful thing to lose that dream," Joraiem answered softly, "and I hope you don't."

Rulalin turned to Joraiem. "I'm sorry, I didn't mean to open an old wound. How long since you lost yours?"

"A month and a half."

Rulalin looked puzzled, "A month and a half?"

"I didn't declare myself until the morning I left, and it was then that I found she was already lost to me."

Rulalin put his hand gently on his shoulder. "I am sorry. It looks like I'm not the only one who has made this journey with swirling emotions in my heart. I'm glad we've spoken. Perhaps we can support one another in the months ahead."

"I would be happy to do whatever I can."

"As would I," he smiled. "It is always good to find a trustworthy friend."

"Who else knows this about you and Wylla?"

Rulalin's face darkened. "Everyone in our group knows some of it. I made the mistake of trying to explain Wylla to Mindarin, and she has not forgotten. The others have pieced together the main idea from a few pointed comments she has made."

"Do you think she will make trouble for you?"

"I don't know, but Mindarin's spite will be wasted on Wylla. She would need to be subtle to really poison Wylla against me, and I don't think Mindarin knows much about subtlety."

"No, it doesn't seem so," Joraiem agreed.

"Well," Rulalin said, standing, "Thanks for listening to my story, and for being willing to help me bear this burden. I'll pray that Allfather helps you to carry yours. Perhaps He'll even provide relief for you in Sulare. Wylla may not be the only beautiful girl there, you know."

Joraiem, who had stood as well, scratched his head. "I don't think I need any more confusion about women right now."

"Perhaps not, but you might want to wait until we get to Sulare to decide. I've heard that in the Summerland, almost anything can happen."

Their night in the Tumian Inn was uneventful, and in the morning they met the others outside The Rusty Anchor and headed out of town to meet Aljeron. He did not show any evidence of being angry or upset about the detour; instead, he hailed them warmly, listening attentively to their stories. As it turned out, The Rusty Anchor hadn't been a whole lot nicer than the Tumian Inn, and none of the four who stayed there had gotten much sleep, as a pair of dogs had howled outside all night.

The day was sunny and clear, and they made good time as they left the Barunaan behind. By evening, they had rejoined the road that ran southeast from above Vol Tumian to Sulare, and that night they camped on the edge of Elnin Wood. When the morning came, they followed the road into the forest and walked in wonder among giant trees with enormous trunks and branches, the lowest of which were four and five spans off the ground. The light of day only partially filtered through the distant canopy of leaves, and the high branches left the forest floor open. Joraiem felt as if he were walking through a vast but dimly lit hall full of thick columns placed at uneven intervals.

On their second and third day of travel in the wood, Joraiem felt increasingly as though they were being watched. He noticed too that the whole company had grown more subdued. The wonder they'd felt at the magnificence of the trees was gradually replaced by a curiosity about what might live in the deeps of the forest on either side of the road. Even Koshti seemed to hold himself warily as he glided along the trees near the road.

Their third night was restless. They huddled close around the fire and took turns keeping watch. Even when he wasn't on duty, Aljeron sat most of the night with his back against a fallen branch as thick as a fallen tree, listening in the dark. All had a strong sense of something near them, but Aljeron declared he felt responsible for the safety of the group.

Morning arrived without any mishap, and though it was Midspring, when their families and friends would be observing the Mound rites and celebrating the feast day, the thought that occupied their minds was to get out of the forest as quickly as possible. They eagerly set out in hope that they would reach the end of the wood before nightfall. Lunchtime passed and as the afternoon dragged on, their spirits began to sink with the sun. Twilight was almost upon them.

Then, without warning, Koshti leapt out of the trees and onto the road, tearing ahead. Aljeron spurred his horse to follow and quickly realized what had lured Koshti out of the shadows. He turned back to the others. "Come!" he shouted. "There is light ahead!"

They all pushed their horses then, and soon they, too, saw the orange glow of sunset falling more clearly on the road ahead. The great trees began to thin, until finally the group emerged from the woods completely. They quietly reined in their horses and stared.

The southern edge of Elnin Wood looked out over a wide expanse of flat land, covered with a kind of wild grain. Before them the road sloped gently downward toward the plain and ran as far as the eye could see through its midst. The open land south of the Kellisor Sea that Joraiem had passed through had been green and hilly, but this seemed wholly level and bright yellow under the evening sun.

The golden plain would have covered the whole horizon, if not for the enormous structure on their right, well west of the road. It stood between them and the Barunaan, though certainly the river had to be much further beyond it, perhaps even several days beyond. In the middle of the broad yellow land, the dark and imposing form drew all eyes to itself. "A dragon tower," Aljeron said.

Joraiem's mind filled with images as he stared at this tower, which was virtually identical to the one he had left behind. He saw Evrim and Brenim walking with him through the tall grass. He saw the Malekim running through the trees and across the open lane. He even saw the picture from his dream of his hand reaching for the dragon tower door.

"Do we go on, or do we camp here for the night?" Aljeron asked.

"Why would we camp here?" Elyas asked. "Let's get as far from these woods as we can. They're beginning to spook me."

Bryar and Kelvan nodded, and Mindarin added, "Here, here."

Aljeron looked at Rulalin and Joraiem. Rulalin shrugged, "I don't know. Normally, I'd say it was foolish to go on. We don't have much light left, and what will we do for a place to camp out there? We have no idea how far the road runs through that stuff, so we may well have a few nights without shelter of any kind. Normally, it would make sense to stay right here, but that's normally. It may not be logical, but I understand what Elyas is saying."

"Joraiem?" Aljeron asked.

"I also hear what Elyas is saying, but I say we stay right here. It's true that I felt something odd in those woods, but I'm not sure it was bad, if you know what I mean. I felt uneasy, but not scared. I think we'll be perfectly safe here. If we go on, not only will we have to camp on the road or possibly in some of that grain, we won't be able to have a fire."

"Why not?" Mindarin asked.

"Look at it," Joraiem replied. "As far as the eye can see, tall golden-brown vegetation. What would we use for fuel? Are we going to carry wood from here? What's more, the last several days have been dry. Are we willing to risk setting that whole field ablaze while we're in it? Besides, I'd feel a whole lot better if we started out in the morning, when we knew we could put that dragon tower behind us in the light of day."

"Why?" Aljeron asked.

"You're not worried about stories of Grendolai," Elyas said, "are you?"

"No, though I wouldn't discount them. I'm worried about Malekim."

"Malekim?" Rulalin said. "Why?"

Joraiem sighed. "I know that Malekim are a constant threat near the Holy Mountain, and I've heard you speak of fights and encounters with them near Fel Edorath. Dal Harat is not Fel Edorath. Malekim shouldn't be that far south and west of Agia Muldonai, but the day before I left home, my friend Evrim and I hunted one."

Elyas and Kelvan looked at Joraiem with admiration, while Aljeron and Rulalin sat stone-faced. Aljeron scratched his scarred cheek and looked out across the plain at the dragon tower. "What is the connection between the dragon tower and the Malekim?"

"I'm not sure, but that's where we encountered it. We were at the dragon tower about midway between Dal Harat and the coast when we found him. There may be no connection, but I wouldn't want to find out down there that dragon towers were some kind of shelter or refuge for Malekim far from the mountain." The "Beware!" of the strange man in green echoed in Joraiem's mind, but he didn't dare mention that his caution was based in part on the admonition of a mysterious blind man from his dreams.

"This is ridiculous," Mindarin said. "So what if we can't have a fire? So what if we might need to camp in the open? We've done without fire or shelter before. Let's get away from these trees. The dragon tower is far west of here and more than likely abandoned."

"Maybe," Aljeron said, "but we camp here. I was against starting out so late in the day with little light, and Rulalin and Joraiem have both confirmed my caution in their own way."

"Let's put it to a vote," Mindarin said, looking to the others for support.

"No vote this time," Aljeron said firmly. "It is decided. If you're worried about the forest, sleep on the far side of the fire."

"Small consolation that will be if something comes out of the trees in the dark and kills us all."

"Well, at least you'll die last," Aljeron said dryly as he dropped from his horse. The others did the same until even Mindarin begrudgingly settled in for the night.

Despite the occasional grumble, when the darkness fell and the moon shone eerily off the dragon tower in the distance, all were glad to be huddled around their bright fire. The trees still caused some uneasiness, but being out of their midst did much to minimize it. The broad, open expanse that stretched before them also counteracted the feeling of being trapped.

As the darkness grew, a fluttering cloud of glowing green Azaruul butterflies hovered above the plain below them, and Joraiem gazed out over the beautiful sight. There were thousands, and one even flew near the fire and alighted on Joraiem's hand, its delicate wings temporarily still. At such close range, Joraiem could see how the bright green rim framed its pale, translucent wings. Its brief respite past, the Azaruul flew off into the nighttime sky.

They decided to have a watch again, and Joraiem and Aljeron took the first shift. They talked about a number of things, but mostly Aljeron wanted to know about the Malekim that Joraiem had hunted with Evrim. He pursued a detailed account of the whole adventure. As Joraiem told the story, he saw in Aljeron's eyes a smoldering hate he had not seen before. Aljeron nodded with satisfaction as Joraiem narrated the specifics of the creature's death and beheading, and when Joraiem described the burning of the body, Aljeron chanted along with him the words that Monias had spoken over the pyre:

Child of Malek, born in flame,
Return to the fire from whence you came.
Return to the darkness, return to the earth,
You have no part in the second birth.

When Joraiem had finished, Aljeron stared into the fire, absorbed in thought. His right hand clutched his sword as he ran the fingers of his left along the long, dark blade. When it was clear that no more questions were coming, Joraiem asked, "Why the interest in the Malekim?"

Aljeron shrugged his shoulders and continued to stare. "No special reason. Like all servants of Allfather, I hate the Malekim and love to hear of their death."

"Have you encountered any?"

"Yes," Aljeron answered. "More than once."

"What happened?"

At first Aljeron did not answer. He lifted a cup of lukewarm water and took a slow drink. "I first encountered one of the Malekim when I was a young boy, and the memory is evil to me. Since then, I've taught them to know that even though I'm only a man, they should fear me."

Joraiem could see the fire's flame reflected in Aljeron's eyes. It struck Joraiem that words like these from almost anyone else would have come across as the vain boasting of a foolish man, for who would claim that he was able to strike fear in the Voiceless?

And yet, as Joraiem looked at Aljeron's face, he believed his friend. Aljeron was physically imposing, though humble and gentle, and Joraiem could easily believe that Aljeron would make a fearful enemy. It struck him that there was in this a clear parallel between Aljeron and Koshti, his "battle brother." Both were physically daunting, but neither was aggressive, though he knew Koshti hunted often at night for food. Still, despite Koshti's passive, sometimes even playful carriage, Joraiem never doubted that when stirred he, too, would be a frightful enemy.

Joraiem sensed their conversation about Malekim should be left where it was, for the time being anyway. Perhaps in Sulare they would explore the matter more closely. Indeed, he expected that if he was going to learn more about Black Wolves there, as Master Kuvarin had suggested, then certainly the Malekim would also be a topic of much discussion, and maybe Aljeron would speak further then.

Aljeron woke Rulalin about midway through Second Watch, and he and Joraiem both went to bed. For a long time, though, Joraiem could not sleep. He lay beside the fire staring at the stars and moon above the dragon tower. One thing that had remained constant in his journey were the southern constellations, and he was grateful that even in Sulare he would have their company. Tonight, though, he found his attention continually drawn away from the stars to the tower, unable to put it out of his mind.

He rolled onto his stomach to gaze at it, resting his chin on his hands. He wasn't surprised at the fascination the tower held for him; as it had for Brenim, the towers tapped the curiosity and imaginations of most young men. What surprised him was the fact that as he stared at it, an image of the blind man kept coming before him. Why? What was the connection?

Joraiem rolled over, turning his back to the dragon tower. He didn't want to think about it or his dreams any more. Both presented mysteries with no apparent solutions, and he didn't want to deal with them. He wanted to sleep.

When he woke, the moon had almost dropped below the trees, and a sleepy Elyas sat at the fire nodding by a snoring Kelvan. A movement just beyond the tree line caught Joraiem's eye, and he sat up straight. Elyas's head jerked up at the same time, and he whispered to Joraiem, "What is it?"

Keeping his eyes on the trees, Joraiem motioned to Elyas to be quiet and reached for Suruna. Several minutes passed, and Joraiem relaxed his grip on the bow. Whatever he had seen wasn't there now. He turned to Elyas, "It was nothing, don't worry about it."

Elyas did not look convinced, and he remained focused on the trees as Joraiem lay back down. It was odd, Joraiem thought, that he wasn't more concerned, but his intuition told him that whatever might be out there wasn't dangerous to them. It might watch, but it didn't threaten. He wondered what it might be and how long it had been watching them. He wondered if it lived in the woods or if it had followed them in. He wondered if it would follow them out. All of those questions were intriguing, but he was nagged by one in particular: What would it cost him and the others if his intuition was wrong? He pushed the question from his mind and kept it at bay long enough to fall asleep again.

Joraiem woke with Rulalin's hand upon his shoulder, shaking him. "Wake up and have some breakfast before we go."

He yawned and stretched, sitting up facing south across

the broad plain. It was a beautiful scene. The early morning sun was rising on his left, and the sea of golden grain gleamed in its light. A strong breeze rippled across the field, sending waves across the horizon. Even the dragon tower looked inviting. For a brief moment, Joraiem felt as though he was seeing it the way it might have been seen in the First or Second Age, before it had become a symbol of dread. He saw the magnificence of the tower and could almost imagine a great golden dragon circling it in the sky above. What must it have been like to live then, in an age of wonders, an age of peace?

When they were ready to go, Aljeron took the lead with Koshti beside him. The road dipped steadily downhill from the edge of the wood to the plain below, and as they neared the bottom, Joraiem looked over his shoulder for a final glance at the great forest. He understood the relief his companions had voiced about leaving it to travel under the warm spring sun, but he felt strangely as though he was leaving a place of refuge.

By late morning, the waist- to shoulder-high grain on both sides of the road was all they could see in any direction, except the dragon tower, which continued to loom large in the distance to their right. Though they made good time along the smooth and easy road, the dragon tower always appeared to be ahead of them. It was a testament to the true size of the tower that it had been so clearly visible from the edge of the wood.

Soon after they stopped for a brief lunch, the road across the plain began to swing slightly west. When it straightened out again, it seemed to Joraiem that they were now headed more or less due south. It also appeared to Joraiem that they were gaining on the tower, and he guessed they would be past it by nightfall.

In the late afternoon, when they appeared to be more or less even with the dragon tower, Koshti broke off the road and ran into the tall grain. From his vantage point on Erador, Joraiem could see the swath Koshti was cutting in a diagonal south and west. He and Rulalin rode up next to Aljeron from the back of the group, and all three strained to see where the tiger was headed. "What do you think he's doing?" Joraiem asked.

Aljeron shook his head. "He must have sensed something, but I can't imagine what. He's gone so far already. Unless the road starts bending west, I'll lose sight of him soon."

The road did not bend west and before long, none of them could see any trace of Koshti. "What do you want to do?" Rulalin asked.

"Keep going," Aljeron said. "I didn't sense danger when he headed off, but even so, Koshti can take care of himself. He'll be able to find me when he decides to return."

So the group continued forward for another hour or more, until at last they came to the first real variety in the landscape they had encountered all day. The ground on their right began to slope up in the direction of the dragon tower, which finally appeared to be just behind them to the west. Appearing suddenly in the midst of this rise was a narrow road heading up the sloping ground toward the tower.

The entrance to this lane was overgrown, and they might not have seen it at all if not for the stones that lined the place where it intersected the main road. The group dismounted to pull back some of the grain that obscured these stones and found more thick, flat paving stones.

"What do you make of that?" Rulalin asked, looking puzzled.

"It looks like a stone-paved road that leads to the dragon tower," Aljeron said.

"It looks like that because it is that," Mindarin muttered.

"It may have been laid about the time the tower was built," Joraiem said. "Look at the stones. They resemble the kind used in the tower. If they are the same, this road might have been here for thousands of years."

They stood silently, looking at the dark stones that stretched between the crowding grain on either side. In places it sprouted from between cracks and gaps in the road itself. Joraiem stooped to feel one. It was smooth and cool to the touch, and it had the same feel as the wall of the dragon tower near Dal Harat.

The sound of a hoof on stone in the distance caught their attention.

"Did you all hear that?" Elyas asked.

"Yes," Aljeron answered, "now be quiet so we can listen." The sound came again, and it soon became clear that at least one horse was moving through the grain in their direction. Everyone returned to their horses and mounted to get a better view. Someone was coming.

"What should we do?" Rulalin asked. "Wait here, or head down the road to meet them?"

"Maybe we should hide until we can see who it is," Mindarin hastily added.

"There are seven of us, Mindarin, and as far as I can tell, there is only one horse approaching," Aljeron said calmly. "I say we ride up the stone road to meet him."

Aljeron led his horse onto the stone road, and the others followed him in single file. As they drew nearer to the rider and could see him better, Joraiem found his heart beginning to beat faster. Even from a distance, the white hair stood out against the golden grain, and the green cloak and white sash were likewise clearly visible.

When the rider was finally close enough to be seen in detail by them all, Joraiem heard gasps and muttering around him. He realized that the man's startling appearance was probably new to them, and those blind eyes were just as striking in real life as they had been in his dreams. Aljeron suddenly called out for Koshti, for they could all see the tiger now walking calmly beside the rider. He sprang forward and came running to Aljeron.

The blind old man stopped the tall white horse that he was riding and addressed Aljeron. "It is a remarkable gift, you know. I haven't felt a bond so strong between man and animal in a long, long time."

"How did you know?" Aljeron began.

"I know many things," the old man smiled. As he did, a windhover appeared from somewhere high in the sky above them and settled with wings flapping on his shoulder.

The group looked at one another in wonder, but Joraiem urged his horse forward. The old man cocked his head at the sound of the movement, and soon his sightless eyes were pointed at the place where Joraiem now sat. "What would you have me tell you, young master?" the old man asked kindly.

"Your name," Joraiem said with surprising calmness.

The old man laughed. "I have been known by many names, but you may call me Valzaan."

7

THE ROAD TO SULARE

"VALZAAN," JORAIEM WHISPERED UNDER his breath. As he repeated the name, he began to feel dizzy. He reached out instinctively to steady himself. Something was happening to him.

Joraiem's eyes fluttered shut. When he opened them again, he could feel that something was different. He looked over his shoulder at Aljeron, who was the closest to him. Aljeron was motionless, as though his body had become completely stiff. Koshti was like his battle brother, still as stone. In fact, none of them were moving. Even the grain that surrounded them in every direction, though stooped as if bent by the wind, did not seem to be moving at all.

Joraiem rubbed his eyes and looked again. No change. He turned back to the old man who called himself Valzaan. He sat quietly, stroking the neck of the immobile Erador.

"What's going on?" Joraiem asked

"You are experiencing *torrim redara,* or in the common

tongue, slow time," the man answered, appearing to gaze at
Joraiem intently, though of course he could not be. "In a moment, everything will continue as it was, and your friends will
not realize that anything has happened, because for them it
will not have happened. You, however, will have complete recall of everything that is said or done."

"How can it be?"

"It is a gift that prophets have."

"A prophet?" Joraiem answered, confused. "You mean
you've done this? But why have you slowed time for everyone
but me? Is it because of my dreams?"

"No, at least not like you think. Nor have I done anything
to you, Joraiem. Allfather has not granted me the power to
slow time for others, but when I saw that you were entering *torrim redara* yourself, I decided that it might be good for me to
come with you."

"Entering myself? What do you mean? I blinked. And how
do you know my name?"

The blind man laughed, and his body shook with his
laughter. As Joraiem listened to the reverberating sound, he
realized just how silent as well as still the world had been. "Did
you not hear me? I am Valzaan! Why do you marvel that I
know your name? I have been a prophet of Allfather longer
than any man remembers. I know only what Allfather has chosen to reveal, but even so, what I know I could not explain to
you in full, not even if you had a lifetime to learn it."

Joraiem tried to comprehend what was happening. If indeed this man was Valzaan as he claimed, then he could believe him capable of slowing time. Valzaan was a legend
among legends. But he claimed he had done nothing, that he
had followed Joraiem into this bizarre place. What was happening?

As if reading his mind, Valzaan continued. "As I said, I felt
you entering slow time, so I decided to follow. Since this is

your first time, I thought you might like some guidance. I have seen others enter for the first time unaware. It can be disconcerting."

"Disconcerting, indeed!" Joraiem answered. "But even if it is as you say, how could I enter slow time on my own? You said this is a gift that prophets have."

"That is what I said."

Joraiem waited for him to continue, but he didn't. "Well?"

"Well what? What do you not understand?"

"How I'm here! You are here because you're a prophet. I'm not a prophet, so how am I here?"

"How do you know you aren't a prophet?"

Joraiem's mind reeled. Valzaan or not, this man was playing tricks with his mind. "I'm not a prophet because I can't be. I'm just an ordinary man!"

Valzaan shook his head and sighed, then mumbled under his breath as though addressing himself, "Why do even the most clear-sighted fail to see themselves rightly?" Speaking louder, he continued, "Allfather chooses who will be His prophets, and He chooses whomever He likes, that I can assure you. He could make your horse His prophet if He wanted to. You may be ordinary, you may not be, but it is the power of Allfather that makes a prophet. Who you were before He called you has nothing to do with it."

Joraiem started to feel dizzy again, and his vision began to blur. This time he was not quick to steady himself, and he felt himself sliding sideways. Valzaan reached out and caught his arm, keeping him from falling on the ground. He could hear Valzaan speaking again, "You are slipping back into real time. It would be wise to keep this to yourself for now. I will speak to you about it when I can."

Joraiem blinked again, and when he opened his eyes, the first thing he felt was the wind against his cheek. The grain bobbed in the field beyond him, and he could hear the stunned whispers of his friends behind him repeating Valzaan's name as he had done. Despite the narrowness of the path, Aljeron pushed his horse forward, past Joraiem. "Do you mean to say that you are *the* Valzaan?"

"I'm not sure what you mean by *the* Valzaan, but if you mean, am I Valzaan the prophet, about whom you have heard many tales, some of them true, then the answer is yes."

Again whispers and murmurs spread throughout the group. The old man certainly seemed to be serious. His long white hair stood out from his head at all angles, and those eerie white eyes appeared to be staring at them all. The windhover sat contentedly on his shoulder. He certainly had the look of a legend.

Aljeron moved his horse further forward, stopping beside Valzaan's. "Forgive me, Master Valzaan, I'm unsure how to properly greet you. I don't wish to offend by addressing you incorrectly or failing to extend the right arm of fellowship. I am Aljeron Balinor, and we are all children of the Novaana bound for Sulare. You are most welcome among us, and we would be honored if you would join us on our way."

"He is not welcome to join us," Mindarin exclaimed. "Are you insane? This man must be out of his mind to make such an outrageous claim."

"Mindarin! Hold you tongue," Aljeron began before the old man interrupted him.

"You would do well, young mistress, to follow the example of wiser heads and address a prophet of Allfather with respect," Valzaan answered calmly but firmly. "I am not crazy."

"Then you are a liar, so don't patronize me," she snapped. Addressing Aljeron she continued adamantly, "We have enough worries of our own without taking this old fool—"

"Enough!" proclaimed Valzaan, the command echoing across the silent plain. None of them dared to move or make any sound. "I have not traveled these many leagues and revealed myself to you to be greeted as a liar and a fool. Even if I were a madman, deprived of sanity and sense, my many years alone should have merited a gentler reception from you than this, and mercy rather than mockery should have been your response. But I am not a madman, and as a prophet of Allfather your insults and insolence are an offense not only against me but Him. Therefore you will be silent! No sound will you make until the morning of the third day. I have spoken!"

All stared at Mindarin, whose mouth opened but made no sound. Her face blushed as she moved her lips to no avail. She cupped both her hands over her mouth and started to cry.

Valzaan pushed his horse between Aljeron and Joraiem and stopped it in front of her. He reached out and touched her, gently pulling her hands away from her mouth. She stared at him, frightened. "Do not fear me, Mindarin Orlene, daughter of Garek Elathien. All of Allfather's dealings with His servants, even those involving discipline, are intended for their good. This is mercy, even if difficult, for you will find wisdom should you accept His rebuke and acknowledge your fault."

Mindarin pulled her hands free of Valzaan and covered her whole face as she cried with noiseless sobs. She turned her horse away and rode back toward the main road, riding in the grain to avoid the others behind her.

Aljeron spoke to Valzaan. "Forgive us. Mindarin is often quick to speak and slow to learn."

"There is nothing to forgive," Valzaan replied. "You are all old enough to bear responsibility for your own actions. I do not hold against you the fault of another. As for Mindarin, Allfather's dealings with her are His own. She is headstrong, but if she learns to control her tongue, her strength could be used for much good. She will learn."

"Master Valzaan," Rulalin said, hesitantly. "You speak of Mindarin as though you know her, even calling her by name. Do you know her? Do you know us?"

"Indeed I do, Master Rulalin. I know all of you, after a fashion. I've said already that I have come to meet you. Allfather has sent me to go with you to Sulare, so I hope you meant what you said, Aljeron, about wanting me to come with you along the way."

"It would be a great honor," Aljeron answered.

"Good, then I will ride with you the rest of the way. Two weeks are left before Spring Wane, and we will need most of that time for the journey. There will be time for questions later, but if we ride hard now, we can reach the edge of this plain tonight."

They did ride hard. For a blind old man, Valzaan was quite an able rider. He rode silent and intent between Aljeron and Rulalin at the head of the company as they thundered down the road through the golden grain. Valzaan's great white horse hardly seemed to labor, keeping a smooth and even gait, and a careful observer could see the windhover gliding in the sky far above them. A little behind followed Kelvan, Elyas, and Bryar, while Mindarin rode on her own behind them. Joraiem had dropped back to the very rear, though it hadn't been easy. When first they had returned to the main road, Mindarin had kept right out of everyone's way, carefully avoiding eye contact. It soon became apparent that Mindarin intended to lag a comfortable distance behind the others. So, as Joraiem kept dropping back, Mindarin kept slowing as well, until they were both well behind and almost out of sight of the others.

After jockeying back and forth for the last position for a while, Mindarin grew frustrated with Joraiem's persistence and spurred her horse forward. Though she couldn't express her displeasure verbally, there was no mistaking her body language and the burning glare in her eyes as she pushed past him.

Joraiem was not unsympathetic. Ordinarily, he would have quite happily allowed her to drop behind, understanding her embarrassment and wanting to give her the room she desired. But his brief exchange with Valzaan in *torrim redara* had filled him with a compelling desire to be alone. He was afraid that the others might see in his eyes some evidence of what had happened and perhaps ask questions. He didn't even want to face his own questions now, let alone theirs.

He did not doubt Valzaan's identity, though he had struggled to come to terms with it. That left Joraiem in an awkward place when it came to grasping their conversation. Valzaan's words could not be doubted, for it was surely impossible for a prophet of Allfather to lie. Valzaan had not said explicitly that Joraiem was a prophet, but he had said that slow time was a gift from Allfather to prophets. He had also said that Joraiem had gone there on his own, so what other conclusion remained?

And yet, Joraiem found such a conclusion absurd. How could he be a prophet? Had he not shown a remarkable lack of insight even into his own heart regarding Alina? Could a prophet of Allfather be so far in the dark, or would a prophet of Allfather have made such a fool of himself?

Joraiem squirmed uncomfortably in his saddle. He glanced up into the bright afternoon sky and watched the fluid grace of the windhover. He was deliberately avoiding the obvious, trying to cloud the issue. Valzaan had been perfectly clear that who one was when Allfather called didn't matter; He chose His prophets. Joraiem's embarrassing episode with Alina was not relevant. One question, however, was: If Allfather had put His hand upon Joraiem to make him a prophet, why? That was the question he needed to ask Valzaan when opportunity allowed.

That opportunity did not come as quickly as Joraiem would have liked. By dusk the edge of the field was within sight and the company pressed on even as the sun slowly sank and disappeared. The stars appeared, sparkling, and the waning moon rose. At last the road led them out from the broad plain and into more open terrain, but they were all so tired that they dismounted and began to set up camp with hardly a glance at their new surroundings.

When the fire was ready, dinner was the first order of business, and after eating hastily, Mindarin buried herself in her bedroll at the farthest point from the fire she thought safe. Meanwhile, the others ate in silence, sneaking curious glances at Valzaan and having to remind themselves from time to time that the prophet was blind. At first only Aljeron and Rulalin dared address him, but as they observed his openness and amiable manner, gradually their reserve gave way to their natural inquisitiveness. They plied Valzaan with questions about past, present, and future, though Valzaan never answered these last, unless it was to point to prophecies spoken long ago that were known to all.

Joraiem sat, watching and listening, the one question he longed to ask dancing continuously through his mind. Why me? What have I been chosen for? He looked behind them at the vast field no longer golden under the silvery light of the moon and stars. The dragon tower that had dominated his thoughts the previous night lay essentially out of sight, though Joraiem imagined that its dark outline was dimly visible on the far horizon.

Second Watch was half over by the time Aljeron put an end to the discussion. "It's late, and we need some sleep. There'll be plenty of time between here and Sulare to ask Valzaan questions."

Joraiem thought he could hear reluctance in Aljeron's voice. He looked at Valzaan's face as the prophet remained seated, facing the fire while the others prepared for sleep. The light of the fire glowed in his eyes, and Joraiem's memory flashed back to earlier that day. It hadn't registered clearly at the time, but as Valzaan had silenced Mindarin, something had appeared in the prophet's eyes, much like the glow of this fire. He knew it didn't make a lot of sense, the appearance of flame reflected in Valzaan's eyes in broad daylight in the middle of a field of grain, but he was sure he had seen it. He would ask Valzaan about that, too, after he dealt with his more pressing business.

Valzaan stretched and stood, retrieving a blanket from his saddle pack. Joraiem watched as he took the blanket and, rather than using it as a covering, compressed it into a ball and put it under his head for a pillow. He lay down on his back beside the fire. If he hadn't known better, Joraiem would have thought he was lying that way to be able to watch the stars.

Aljeron approached Joraiem and said, "You don't seem to be in a hurry to get to bed; would you be willing to take the first watch?"

"Sure."

"Great, I'm exhausted. Wake me when you're ready."

Joraiem nodded. He sat quietly by the fire, staring into it for a long time. He wasn't sure how long he sat there, but the fire was little more than a small pile of glowing embers by the time he woke Aljeron. He lay down and gradually slipped into darkness.

The next day began as the previous day had ended. The company rode at a good pace with Joraiem bringing up the rear and Mindarin not far ahead of him. When they stopped for lunch, though, Mindarin didn't separate from the others as completely as she had at breakfast that morning. She sat on her own but didn't turn her back on the group, and when she was finished she didn't walk off to wait at a distance. Joraiem also noticed that during the afternoon she rode closer to those ahead of her than she had been, forcing Joraiem also to move closer so that his lingering behind wouldn't raise questions. When they stopped for the night, she sat in the circle around the fire, and as another round of questions and answers began with Valzaan, she remained where she was.

Joraiem offered to take the first watch again, but Aljeron insisted he go to bed. As it had turned out, Joraiem had kept watch on his own for more than three hours the previous night, and in truth he was grateful for the gift of a complete night's sleep. His questions remained, but even they couldn't keep him awake. He slept soundly and did not dream.

The sun was just peeking over the horizon when he woke, and for a moment he lay still, watching the first rays of dawn creep across the sky. Stretching, he sat up and looked around at the others, still asleep around the remains of their fire. As they moved further south and as Spring Wane drew closer, the mornings were not as cold, and so keeping the fire had become less pressing. Even so, with thoughts of breakfast on his mind, Joraiem arose and fanned the still glowing embers to resurrect the fire.

As he did, he realized not all were still asleep. Sitting side by side on a fallen tree at a distance, facing the rising sun, were Valzaan and Mindarin. Joraiem couldn't hear them, but it was evident that they were talking.

"The morning of the third day," Joraiem muttered to himself.

"What was that?" Aljeron said with a yawn as he sat up.

Joraiem turned to him, and when he had Aljeron's attention, he nodded in the pair's direction, adding, "It seems as though Mindarin has returned to the world of the vocal."

Aljeron lifted himself to get a better look, and when he had seen them, he looked with surprise at Joraiem. "What do you think they're talking about?"

Joraiem shrugged. "We may never know, but I bet she'll be a bit more careful today."

Mindarin's private conversation was not the last surprise of the morning. By the time she returned to the fire with Valzaan, the others were all awake and finishing their breakfasts. As Valzaan took a seat and was served by Elyas, Mindarin remained standing where she was.

"There is something I'd like to say to you all," Mindarin began, her voice quiet but even. All eyes but Valzaan's turned to her. "I know that I've been difficult, and I want to apologize. I also want to ask you to forgive me. I will try to be better from now on."

They were all quick to accept Mindarin's apology, though Rulalin didn't seem as eager as the others to assure her that it hadn't really been that bad. Before they were through, Mindarin was actually in tears, but this time she stayed with them.

Mindarin did not ride alone that day but rather moved back and forth among them all. While Joraiem brought up the rear for the third straight day, he watched as Mindarin maneuvered her horse to ride beside each of them one by one. After riding a long time beside Rulalin, she even dropped back until she was beside him.

"Joraiem, do you mind if I ride with you for a while?" she asked.

"Of course not."

"It's clear you've wanted to be alone these last few days, so I won't be long. I don't want to intrude."

"It's clear, is it?"

"Pretty clear," she laughed. "Did you think no one would notice?"

Joraiem blushed. "I thought that with Valzaan's arrival and . . ." He hesitated, looking at her and turning even redder.

"And with my situation?"

"Yes, I hoped it wouldn't be so noticeable."

"Perhaps the men haven't noticed. Men don't seem to notice a lot of things, though by now you would think even they might be catching on. Three days is a bit of a giveaway."

Joraiem didn't reply. He was growing a little uncomfortable with the direction of the conversation. To his relief, she continued on a different line. "I wanted to apologize personally for the way I've treated you. From the moment you joined us I've been pretty unfriendly, and you didn't deserve it. I'm sorry. Would you forgive me?"

Joraiem looked closely at her face. There was no hint of insincerity. "I forgive you, Mindarin. I have no reason not to."

"Good," she said again, smiling warmly, and for the first time since they had met that day outside Peris Mil, Joraiem thought that Mindarin actually looked quite lovely. "Perhaps we will be friends then."

"I would be honored to be your friend."

"So formal," she said with a laugh. "I would be honored," she added, imitating him. "Have you always talked to women like this?"

Joraiem blushed again. "Yes, especially married ones."

For a moment, the smile disappeared from her face and a cloud passed over it. Joraiem started to wonder if he'd said something wrong, but the smile returned. "I appreciate your desire to be respectful, but as we are going to be spending six months together, you really don't have to be so formal. My husband wouldn't mind."

Joraiem nodded, and Mindarin pushed her horse forward to rejoin the group. He wondered as she moved away if he should move up too. He didn't want anyone else to pursue the issue of why he had been riding alone. He didn't feel much like participating in any small talk, but it was becoming clear that Valzaan wasn't going to drop behind the others to talk to him. He wasn't sure how he was going to get the prophet on his own to talk, but he felt that the time to end his self-imposed exile had come. He spurred his horse on and before long found himself beside Aljeron, Rulalin, and Valzaan. No words were exchanged as he joined them, but Aljeron turned his head and smiled as he came alongside. It felt strangely comforting to be back, and for the first time since Valzaan's arrival, Joraiem found himself riding, not with questions of his identity or Valzaan's troubling words, but with thoughts of home and Alina.

That night the fire was almost a merry place. They camped beside a lovely copse of tall trees with golden bark and enormous green leaves. A refreshing warm breeze blew in from the west, and the change in Mindarin had produced a ripple effect of good will among the company. The discussion revolved less around specific questions for Valzaan as the travelers chatted about their hopes and expectations for Sulare. They talked as late into the night as their travel-weary bodies would allow.

A flash of light startled Joraiem. He opened his eyes. He rubbed them and peered into the night sky at the stars that sparkled there. The flash had seemed high above, but as he looked now he could not see anything out of the ordinary. Suddenly, a shooting star blazed into view and cut a swath of intense light across the heavens. Joraiem's eyes followed the path of the shooting star as it passed overhead, but the shadow of something tall and dark arose to block his view. Wondering what it could be, he sat up.

"Another dragon tower!" Joraiem exclaimed with a hushed whisper.

"Yes it is," a voice answered from beside him. "As I have pointed out before, you choose some interesting places to visit in your sleep."

Joraiem turned to face Valzaan, who stood surrounded by tall stalks of golden grain, the windhover on his shoulder. "This is a dream?"

"Yes."

"Are you real?"

"Of course I'm real," Valzaan answered. "Who do you think you're talking too? A figment of your imagination?"

"That makes as much sense as anything else." Joraiem stood, stretching as he did. "If you're real, how are you here in my dream?"

"Dreaming is a form of seeing, and you will come to understand, Joraiem, that as a prophet, you have been given the ability to see extraordinary things."

"I'm not sure what that means or how it explains your presence."

"I cannot see what the sun reveals in broad daylight, but sometimes I can see other things. I have seen things that were taking place far beyond the horizon, things below the earth and things deep under the surface of the sea. I have seen things that did not take place until many years later. I have seen things that are coming but have not yet come to be. As I slept tonight I saw this place, the stars shining down upon it as the dry grain rustled in the warm breeze. I saw the first shooting star flash through the sky and saw you here below the dragon tower opening your eyes. Seeing you here, I came to meet you. That is all I can tell you."

"Valzaan, I don't understand. You said that I chose this place, but how did I choose it? I just thought I was waking up. I thought I'd find myself with the others around the fire, but here I am. Am I really here? If so, how did I travel all this way in my sleep?"

"You are only here in spirit. Your body remains beside the fire, as does mine. As for how or why you chose this place, I cannot answer your question. As you grow in your awareness of your gifts, you will become more conscious of what you are able to see and why. You will not find yourself in places like this or in *torrim redara* without knowing how you came there or why, but control will take time. I came here following you; why you came here I cannot say."

Joraiem looked around him at the field of grain and the dragon tower that rose beside them into the sky. "Am I really a prophet?" he asked quietly.

Valzaan walked up beside him and placed his hand on his shoulder. "That may be a larger question than I can answer. To be a prophet means more than simply to be gifted with prophetic abilities. To be a prophet means to be called to speak the words of Allfather to His people. To be a prophet means that one is willing to go where he is sent and to do what he is sent to do. I can see that Allfather has placed His hand on you and gifted you, but I cannot see how you will respond or what you will do."

"Then I don't have to be a prophet if I don't want to be? I have a choice?"

"You have a choice, but it is not what you think it is. You can never go back to what you would call normal life. Allfather has called you to something else. Your choice is to be faithful to Allfather and answer His call, or to refuse to serve in the way you have been called to serve. There is no third option. You must serve Allfather on His terms, not yours. But, lest you think you're an exception, know that this is true for all. Allfather calls us to serve, and it is His right to choose the manner of our service. To serve Allfather in any capacity is an honor."

Another shooting star streaked across the sky, and Joraiem gazed up at its beautiful light quietly. He didn't know what he should say. He'd wanted get answers from Valzaan, but the more the prophet spoke, the less Joraiem wanted to hear.

"So what do I do now?"

"We'll be in Sulare soon, and once we're there, we'll be able to talk about it more. For now you don't need to do anything, just—"

Valzaan spun away from Joraiem and stared into the dark field of grain. The starlight seemed faint after the intense light of the shooting stars. Joraiem stared in the direction that Valzaan gazed, but he couldn't see anything.

"What is it?"

"Black Wolves. I feel them. We are not alone."

Joraiem looked harder and the ripple of grain in several places soon became evident. Many dark forms were moving at great speed through the field. "How did they get into my dream?" Joraiem asked, feeling in vain on his back for Suruna.

"They are not in your dream. They are approaching the fire where we lie asleep. Allfather has sent us warning! Awake!"

Joraiem's first motions after waking beside the fire were clumsy and slow. He felt as though he'd been pulled forcibly out of a deep and heavy sleep. He looked around and found everyone asleep, even Rulalin, who had been taking the first watch. He struggled to make his legs respond to his mind's urgent request that they move. He scrambled to Erador, and soon had Suruna and his quiver in hand. He wished he could be sure Erador would remain steady despite the approaching wolves; it would be nice to have the advantage of his height and speed.

Whatever else remained sketchy and unclear after that, he never forgot what he saw when he turned back to the circle. A wave of light swept out from the fire, which blazed in an almost completely straight line up into the sky as far as the eye could see. The fire seemed to roll up and down from the earth to the heavens in a great column of flame. Illuminated in its light was the figure of Valzaan, standing with arms outstretched behind the column, facing north.

The others were well and truly awake now, staggering to their feet and rubbing their eyes in the intensity of the light. Joraiem ran back to them and began to quickly explain their situation. "Black Wolves are approaching. Grab your weapons!"

"Black Wolves?" Aljeron asked, a cold grimace stealing over his tired face. "Where?"

"From the north," Valzaan answered. "They are running with great speed and will soon be upon us."

Aljeron looked at Joraiem as he readied Suruna. Turning to the others he cried, "Children of Werthanin, arm yourselves!"

They ran in a staggered line to the horses, returning to the column of fire with both their horses and their weapons. Elyas and Bryar had bows, Mindarin and Kelvan long hunting knives, and Rulalin and Aljeron swords. Rulalin's sword was much like the one that Monias kept wrapped under his bed at home. Aljeron's sword, though, was unique in Joraiem's experience. The hilt was smooth and bare, while dark mysterious runes ran up both sides of the blade. In any hand but Aljeron's it would have seemed abnormally large and awkward, but Aljeron wielded it masterfully. Aljeron noticed Joraiem's close attention and a grim, slow smile formed on his mouth. Shadows from the rolling fire behind him danced across his scarred face and Aljeron held his blade toward Joraiem.

"Bow and blade, let us fight side by side!" Aljeron exclaimed, and a strange delight echoed in his voice.

Joraiem held Suruna out and tapped Aljeron's sword. "Bow and blade."

Aljeron smiled but soon turned toward Valzaan, who had not moved. As Joraiem also looked at him, he was again struck by the appearance of rolling flame reflected in the prophet's eyes. This time the appearance of flame was even more pronounced. There was something else too: Valzaan seemed shadowy, as though he had faded while standing there. Joraiem almost thought he could see the outline of the distant trees through his body.

"Do the Black Wolves fear the fire?" Aljeron asked.

"No, but they prefer to hunt in darkness," the prophet answered. "They rarely attack in daylight unless driven by great need. I don't know that the light will stop them, but they may come more cautiously and be more vulnerable."

"What should we do?"

"Stand your ground. Even now they are circling around the edge of the light."

At this the company began to watch carefully in all directions, and slowly they retreated as far as the horses and the ferocious heat on their backs would allow. Only Koshti moved outside the ring, pacing furiously back and forth, growling in first one direction then another.

The seconds became minutes. Sweat flowed freely down Joraiem's face, and he had to keep wiping it away from his eyes. He couldn't see anything in the darkness beyond the light of Valzaan's fire, but he could feel the wolves. In his ears he heard their panting, and he seemed to feel their hot breath against his face. They were there for him; he knew they were.

"Hear me, children of Rucaran, come not into the light of this circle. I am Valzaan! Death alone waits for you here! You were spawned in darkness and in darkness you run, but I am filled with Allfather's light. If you approach me you will know His wrath!"

As Valzaan cried these final words, he quickly turned his head to look behind him and without moving anything else, whipped one of his hands in the direction that he faced. For a moment it seemed to Joraiem that Valzaan flickered, almost disappearing, but then an explosion of fire took place near the perimeter of the light and several sudden, short howls sent shivers through Joraiem's body.

"I have spoken!" Valzaan cried again.

Several streaks of black broke into the ring of light, and Joraiem loosed an arrow into the side of one while another nearby burst into flame. A third streak appeared as a blur in his peripheral vision and suddenly a large paw ripped through the sleeve of his shirt and spun him around. As he fell to the ground, he saw Aljeron's sword slicing the Black Wolf in two. Part of the body landed on him and spilled its warm blood on his face and hair, and Joraiem pushed it off. By the time he had regained his feet, the encounter was over.

A handful of wolves lay dead near them, and several more lay burned out beyond where the perimeter of light had been.

The fire had returned to normal and Valzaan sat wearily beside it. "Are they all dead?" Aljeron asked.

"Those that were nearby," the prophet answered.

"There are more?"

"There are always more."

"What now?"

"Gather the bodies to burn, then sleep if you can."

Mindarin sat with Joraiem beside the fire, wiping off his face and tending his arm. The cuts were deep, but according to Valzaan, clean. That was fortunate, for he said the infections that came from a Black Wolf wound could be fatal. Mindarin tore what remained of Joraiem's shirt into strips and bandaged the wound. It was uncomfortable, of course, but even with the pain and the alarm at having been attacked, Joraim found that sleep came quickly.

In the morning they mounted in silence, weary but eager to be underway. Joraiem sat astride Erador in a daze, his arm aching. His mind kept going back to the dream of the dragon tower. How had he seen the dark forms moving through the grain? How had he sensed the presence of the wolves? What if Valzaan hadn't been there? Would he have sensed them in time? Surely his companions would have been ripped to pieces as they slept if he hadn't.

The next several days passed uneventfully. They rode, ate and slept, a sobriety settling on them all in the wake of the attack. The weather grew warmer and the land greener, but none of it completely dispelled the residual gloom of that harrowing night.

Almost a week later, on the twenty-fourth day of Full Spring, while they were stopped for lunch, he took Valzaan aside. "How much farther do you think we have?"

"Sulare is perhaps five days from here, should we keep up our present pace and avoid any trouble."

"Good, I think we are ready for a more enduring rest. Have you seen any more wolves in your sleep?"

Valzaan shook his head. "I've not sensed them since that night." The prophet massaged his temples, the first sign Joraiem had noticed that he might experience fatigue or weariness like the rest of them.

"Does that mean they're gone?"

"I don't know. I think that if some were close I would know, but they could be following at a distance."

"Had you sensed them before that night?"

"I have been involved with Black Wolves on many occasions."

"I mean recently. Had you felt them before we met you by the dragon tower?"

"No. Why do you ask?"

Joraiem shrugged his shoulders. "I'm not sure, but I think the wolves may have been following us for a while. One was killed near Peris Mil the night before I came there, and all through Elnin Wood the group had a feeling of unease, as though we were being watched. I didn't think we were in danger, but I fear that I was mistaken, badly mistaken."

Valzaan looked carefully at Joraiem. "Your intuition told you that you were safe within the trees?"

"Yes."

"Good. You were absolutely right. I can't say where the wolves came from or how long they have been following you, but I can tell you with certainty that they did not pass through Elnin Wood with you. You have not been safer since you left your own doorstep than you would have been in there."

"How can you be so sure?"

"Because you passed within a day's ride of the Elnindraal."

"Elnindraal? You mean that there are Great Bear in that wood?"

"There are indeed."

"And they were watching us?"

"I have no doubt of it. You were probably shadowed by a company of Great Bear from the moment you entered the wood until the moment you left."

"How could so many large creatures follow us through the wood undetected?"

"The Great Bear may be large, but they are masters of the wild. Their stealth is unrivaled. Even Koshti would have struggled to find one had he left you, though he would not have done so, for surely he knew that what lay beyond the trees was more than he could handle."

"I wonder why they didn't come speak to us. If we were safe there, they knew we were friendly. Why not come and talk?"

Valzaan shook his head. "You should not wonder. The Great Bear have a long memory, and the betrayal of Corindel is not forgotten. They do not carry a grudge, but it has been many years since they emerged freely from their draals and conversed with men on the road. They would have shadowed you to make sure you did not wander from the road in the direction of El-nindraal, but they would not have revealed themselves to you except in great need. No pack of Black Wolves would ever have entered Elnin Wood in pursuit of you. They would have either fallen upon you before you reached the wood, or circled round the western side between the wood and the Barunaan."

"Then I was right after all."

Valzaan laughed, and the sound was soothing though Joraiem felt his face color slightly. "You were indeed. Does it still surprise you?"

"No, I suppose it doesn't. Even then I felt strangely sure that we were safe."

"And you were, though here we are not. We should be on our way again."

The next day the company was halted midmorning by the stunning sight of a grove of snow trees in full bloom. Joraiem had seen individual snow trees around Dal Harat, but he'd never seen so many in one place, nor had he seen any so magnificent. These before him had branches thickly interlaced far above the ground with millions of small white blossoms all over them. The gentle spring breeze rippled through the tree-tops sending "snow showers" of petals swirling, as though a blizzard had just blown in across the warm Suthanin landscape.

The party dismounted and walked in among the snow trees. Joraiem felt the soft silky flowers falling upon his face. Their scent was light and sweet, like honeysuckle. He reached his good arm up above his head to catch some petals as they fell, and a small pile accumulated in his cupped palm.

"If only real snow could be caught and captured in such a pleasant way, without melting and sliding through your fingertips," a soft voice said from behind him.

He turned, surprised, and saw a beautiful woman, silky white petals resting in her long black hair and covering the shoulders of her light blue cloak. The cloak had silver clasps down the front, a high collar, fine silver embroidery running down the left side, and a single silver pin on the right side displaying a bright star. The color of the cloak highlighted the clear blue eyes that gazed at him from the most beautiful face he had ever seen. He lowered his outstretched hand and ran it through his hair, scratching his head, spilling petals as he did so all over his face and chest.

The woman smiled as he held back a sneeze from a couple of petals that momentarily rested on his nose. Heat rose to his cheeks, and he quickly brushed most of the excess flowers from his head and body as he spoke, "My name is Joraiem Andira, who are you?"

"I am Wylla Someris."

8

THE SUMMERLAND

JORAIEM SWALLOWED. WYLLA. HERE, then, was the answer to Rulalin's riddle, the heir to the Enthanin throne, and she was every bit as beautiful as Rulalin had suggested. He could understand now, standing here with her beneath the snow trees, the enchantment Rulalin had fallen under all those years ago.

"Wylla Someris? The Enthanin heir?" he managed to say. "Surely you aren't out here on your own."

"My brothers are here too, with our horses. How do you know who I am?"

"I am traveling to Sulare with some of the Werthanin Novaana, and I've heard of you from them."

"Ah," she said, nodding. "And you are one of these Werthanin Novaana?"

"No, I'm from Dal Harat, a small village in northwestern Suthanin."

"Well, Joraiem Andira of Dal Harat, I am pleased to make your acquaintance."

"And I am pleased to make yours," he answered, extending his injured right arm and accepting her outstretched hand gingerly.

Seeing now the bandage, she stepped closer to take a look. "What happened to your arm?"

"Black Wolves, a week ago."

"Black Wolves!" she said, looking with amazement at him. "You were attacked on the road?"

"We were, but I was the only one hurt. We were fortunate to have Valzaan with us."

"Valzaan? The prophet? With every word your story becomes more and more incredible. If you are telling the truth, this sounds like a most extraordinary journey you've had. Is Valzaan still with you?"

"Yes, he is going to Sulare with us."

"I must meet him. Will you take me to the rest of your number?"

"Gladly, we are . . ."

"Wylla?"

They turned. Beneath one of the snow trees stood Rulalin. "Rulalin?" Wylla asked. "Is that you?"

"It is, though I can't believe you're here," he said, looking from Wylla to Joraiem, who stood awkwardly beside her.

"It has been a long time," Wylla said with a smile, but it seemed to Joraiem that there was sadness in her eyes.

"Yes," Rulalin answered. "It has been long, but I'm so glad we've come across you on the road. Are Pedraal and Pedraan with you?"

"They are."

"Is that all in your company?"

"Yes."

"Take me to them, and I will introduce you all to our party."

"Good," she said, turning to lead them through the trees, but not before she paused, touching Joraiem's wounded arm.

"We will speak more of your wound and your journey later, Joraiem Andira. It sounds like a story I'd love to hear."

She smiled as she started away. Joraiem scratched his head again and felt his ears burn red as Rulalin brushed past him to follow Wylla through the falling flowers.

Wylla's twin brothers, Pedraal and Pedraan, though just barely nineteen, were already exceptionally large men. Though shorter than Joraiem, their chests were bigger and their backs broader than Aljeron's. They greeted both Rulalin and Joraiem with warmth, and soon all three of the Someris family had been introduced to the others. Even though they were from the royal family of Enthanin, they were very friendly and duly awed at meeting Valzaan. The introductions made, the group decided to eat an early lunch together, and they tarried beside the grove of snow trees exchanging tales of the road.

Soon, though, it was time to go, and they took to the road again, now a party of eleven. Several times over the next few days, Joraiem found himself in the pleasant but awkward position of riding beside Wylla, and while he enjoyed their conversations, he was keenly aware of Rulalin's watchful eye. So, while he didn't avoid her exactly, he made a point of sticking near Aljeron or Valzaan, occasionally seeking out the twins to speak with them of Amaan Sul and Enthanin.

At last, on the evening of the twenty-eighth day of Full Spring, Valzaan announced that he thought they would reach Sulare the following day.

"Tomorrow!" Elyas exclaimed. "We're finally there!"

The others were equally excited, and even Joraiem found himself drifting off to sleep with the scattered images of Sulare from Monias's stories circling round his head. The Summerland. He would see it for himself at last.

The following day they eagerly arose and pressed forward, hardly stopping for lunch when the time came. The level ground, covered with lush green grass, stretched from one horizon to the next, and as the afternoon passed they could all feel a change in the air.

"Can you smell it?" Aljeron asked with laughter in his voice. "Salt!"

Wylla replied, her face beaming, "It's glorious, isn't it?"

"We must be close now," Rulalin added, taking in a deep breath. "What do you think, Valzaan? Will we reach Sulare before nightfall?"

Valzaan sat motionless upon his horse, his face tilted upward as though looking into the sky. Following his apparent gaze, Joraiem saw the windhover. It was circling in the sky above them as they were halted on the road.

A smile crossed Valzaan's face, and he turned to the others. "The causeway lies not far ahead. We will not only be in Sulare before nightfall, we will be there in time for supper!"

Valzaan spurred his horse forward and the others fell in behind him. They thundered along the road in a tight pack behind the prophet, his long white hair flowing in the wind. Gradually the green of the land ahead of them gave way to a blue that rippled in the stiff breeze. As they drew nearer, they could see the water more clearly. It was not the Southern Ocean, but a great channel that had been cut in the Second Age. The channel ran west and eventually south in a long sweeping arc from a great sheltered harbor just east of Sulare. The effect of the channel was to make Sulare approachable by land in only two places. The first was a long causeway that crossed the channel from the north, and it was this main entrance that the company now approached. The second was a stone bridge that crossed the channel within sight of the place where it rejoined the Southern Ocean west of Sulare. The bridge made traffic between Sulare and Cimaris Rul at the mouth of the Barunaan possible.

As they approached the channel, Joraiem gazed in wonder.

Monias had spoken so often of his own first glimpse of Sulare, that Joraiem was quite unprepared for his own emotion as he approached it himself. The rolling waters of the wide channel flowed swiftly along from the east to the west. He had not expected it to be so wide.

"Men made this waterway?" he asked in awe as they paused before riding onto the causeway.

"Yes, men made this," Valzaan answered. "The channel was conceived by men and dug with help from the Great Bear. It was and still remains an impressive feat."

"I'll say," Aljeron answered. "It must be a hundred spans across."

"More," Valzaan said.

As the others charged behind Valzaan onto the causeway, Joraiem hesitated on its brink. He had been more than two weeks away from the Barunaan, and though he had of course realized that he would be near water during his time in Sulare, the channel brought this reality abruptly home. The deep blue water rolled swiftly toward the solid causeway, some of it swirling in eddies as it hit the east side. There must have been a passage or passages beneath the causeway, though, because the water continued its flow on the west side. However the causeway had been constructed, Joraiem looked at it with deep misgiving. As he thought about the water flowing on either side of him and even somewhere down below him, he felt the old queasiness return. He looked straight ahead at the rest of his company, by now almost on the other side, and taking a deep breath, spurred Erador forward.

As he galloped across, he didn't dare to turn his head either to the right or the left, but he was peripherally aware of the water that surrounded him. The sun shone brightly above him and the blue of the Full Spring sky sparkled and glistened in the reflection of the water. Suddenly it felt very hot, and he gripped his reins tightly as he tried to keep himself from slipping to the side. He blinked and quickly wiped the sweat that had begun to flow from his brow.

Mercifully, it did not take long for him to cross the channel and catch up to the others, who had slowed to a moderate trot. As he came up to them, he heard Valzaan begin to speak, his rich, melodious voice sounding both clear and far away at the same time.

"We stand on wondrous ground. Since the fall of Malek and the defilement of Agia Muldonai, Sulare has been a haven of beauty in a broken world. Here the temperate breezes of the Southern Ocean blow year round, and few who stay even for a little while can leave without sorrow. Here the earth yields willingly its harvest, and every imaginable fruit-bearing tree prospers. Here the waters teem with life, and even the leviathans still swim within view of the shore.

"From the early days of the Second Age, when dragon and Great Bear and man sought to prepare for the possibility of Malek's return from the Forbidden Isle, Sulare has been a symbol of hope. The great channel was dug for defense, and the Summerland became a living sentry, keeping watch lest Malek should steal upon Kirthanin unawares. Almost every day, the sails of the ships that patrolled the waters could be seen rippling in the wind as the ships sailed into or out of the harbor, tirelessly performing their mission. During the day, the courtyard of the Great Hall rang constantly with the sound of men learning to wield the weapons Malek had made for Andunin, so that never again would Kirthanin be defenseless.

"At night, though, the Great Hall would be filled with music, as the light of a thousand torches illuminated it from one end to the other and from the floor to the very top of the dome. The sound of laughter and singing could be heard by the sentries who stood guard along the coast, keeping watch over the moonlit waters, their purpose kept firm by the constant reminder of what they guarded."

Valzaan's voice, which had grown excited as he spoke of Sulare's beauty and wonder, shifted, and the enthusiasm disappeared as he continued. "But even the Summerland was not immune from the evil of the War of Division. When war began to ripple throughout the land, gradually the soldiers and sailors that had lived so many generations here in peace began to slip away, each to his own ancestral home. The music disappeared and the light was dimmed as fewer and fewer remained, a small remnant of those who had once inhabited this place. Only a handful of ships came and went, and these manned by so few as to be incapable of anything save a few meager patrols. To walk Sulare in those days was like walking the streets of a village that had been ravaged by plague or pestilence, and men who had known it alive and well wept.

"Then Malek came, and the worst fears and nightmares of all were realized. Wave after wave of ships landed, filled not only with Andunin's descendants but with the giants and their father, Vulsutyr, as well as the spawn of Malek. The Voiceless poured from the ships like a flood, along with Rucaran the Great and his offspring. The few that remained here were slaughtered as the wave passed over Sulare and inland. Behind the armies of Malek, comprised of men, Malekim, Black Wolves and Vulsutyrim, came the Grendolai. Sulare was abandoned for a short while, dark and cold, bereft of all but dust and decay."

Valzaan turned back northward for a moment, and the eyes of the rest followed him. "But, after the tide turned and Vulsutyr was slain by Sulmandir at the foot of the Holy Mountain, and when Malek retreated with what remained of his army to the caverns beneath it, men returned to Sulare. Here, it was decided," the prophet continued, turning back to face Sulare, "that this would be the meeting place every seven years of Kirthanin's young Novaana. Here, where once had thrived a community of people from every corner of Suthanin,

Werthanin, and Enthanin, a new Summerland would be established. Sulare would again be a symbol of hope, but this time it would be a symbol of hope that civil war would never again divide Kirthanin.

"So far, that vision has been realized. The prophecies warn, however, that before Allfather brings healing and restoration to Agia Muldonai, and before He cleanses Avalione and the Crystal Fountain, Malek will try a third time for mastery of all things. The Summerland will face trouble and turmoil again. When it was foretold after Malek's first fall that twice more he would bring war, it was also said that the last time, the very waters of the sea would obey him and fight for him. If this be so, then I cannot imagine how Sulare will escape his wrath."

"What does it mean, that the waters of the sea will fight for him?" Joraiem asked while the others sat hushed.

Valzaan shrugged. "The prophecy I know. Its fulfillment, well, that remains a mystery."

"Do you think Malek will come forth again in our lifetime?" Aljeron asked, staring back north in the direction of Agia Muldonai.

Again Valzaan shrugged. "There are times when I sense that we stand on the cusp of the final scene of Kirthanin history, when Malek will issue forth from Agia Muldonai and bring war and quite possibly ruin to every corner of this world. But it has pleased Allfather to grant me years almost beyond reckoning, and I do not always know how to gauge my own sense of time. What seems to me to be near may be tomorrow, or next year, or a hundred years from now."

"Well I hope it's a hundred years and not tomorrow," Elyas said.

Valzaan laughed. "And well you should. Malek has twice made his assault on Kirthanin, and twice he has almost succeeded. The second attempt was so terrible that even to speak of it brings shadows across my heart. If the third is as bad or worse, as I fear it will be, then I shudder to think of it."

The company shifted uncomfortably in their saddles. Valzaan seemed lost in thought but soon snapped out of his reverie, beginning again with a sigh. "Forgive me, all. I had only intended to introduce you appropriately to one of the true wonders of our world, I didn't mean to cast shadows across you this fine spring day. Let us enjoy the light while we can, for we will all have to deal with the darkness when it comes. Let's experience the splendor of Sulare in time of peace."

Valzaan rode forward and again the company fell in behind him. The wide green fields along either side of the road were dotted with wildflowers, purple and yellow and pink and blue. Soon the group approached and passed through groves of trees, most in leaf without fruit, though some were heavy with spring harvests. Joraiem was astonished not only at the abundant yields of many of the trees, but also with the variety.

In some places, the trees grew right up to the side of the road, casting a pleasant shade along their way. The warm spring sun had been by no means harsh, but the shadows reduced the glare as it dropped low in the west. The beautiful sea breeze, the refreshing shade of the groves, and the bounty that surrounded them made Joraiem wonder if the causeway they had crossed had in fact been a bridge into another world, a world of fulfilled longing and infinite blessing. He repented in his heart that he had ever rolled his eyes when Monias would begin to speak of Sulare with that far-off look in his eyes. He could see and smell and even feel the wonder of the place, the dreamlike and even ethereal peace that emanated from it. He knew without doubt why this land had for so many years carried the evocative appellation, Summerland.

The thick trees parted to reveal an enormous Water Stone rising up beside the road. The company slowed to admire the great rock as it jutted up out of the earth into the sky. Joraiem recognized upon it the same winding grooves, carved by years of flowing water, that marked the Water Stone a day's ride from Dal Harat. "Tell us, Valzaan," he said, turning to the prophet, "what were the Water Stones once like?"

"They were remarkable. When Allfather opened the great deep to create the Crystal Fountain in Avalione, powerful underground springs broke out all over the world and pushed up massive stones like this from far below the surface of the land. The water that lifted them bored through them and poured in rivers down their sides. Many believe they were fed by water that flowed out of the great deep through the Fountain and back down under the Holy Mountain. The channels cut by that water in the rock flowed night and day with clear, clean water throughout the First Age. After Malek defiled Avalione, and the Crystal Fountain stopped flowing, the waters of the Water Stones slowed and stopped. For many years, traces of the great streams that once came from the Stones remained, but no longer. You will not even find them damp anymore unless it has recently rained. But that will change! Allfather will restore all things, and the Fountain will flow again. I believe that when it does, the Water Stones will flow again as well."

Joraiem gazed at the Water Stone, large and majestic, towering above them. He tried to envision water shooting out of the top and flowing in all directions down the side, but it was hard to picture. He turned away and found Wylla, sitting on her horse, smiling at him. He smiled too, then tried to focus on the road as they continued forward into more trees.

Not long after, they emerged almost suddenly back into the open, only to be faced this time with rows of buildings encircling a large and magnificent dome. They slowed to a walk as they passed the first of the smaller buildings, a simple white structure with large open windows on every side so that the wind blew straight through it. Large wooden shutters above the windows were propped open with long wooden poles. With no one in sight, they continued to follow Valzaan toward the great domed hall, passing several similar buildings along the way. Joraiem was struck by the feeling of openness they conveyed, not only because of the many large open windows, but also because of their lack of furniture. In some there were small tables, but most had only pallets of straw or hay on the floor.

After passing through several "rings" of smaller buildings, they entered a large open space between the lesser buildings and what Joraiem had guessed must be the Great Hall. It was a simple if majestic structure. Towering white walls covered with intricate but not ornate carved designs of all varieties rose many spans into the sky, where they were capped by a large dome. Bright yellow vines with broad yellow leaves stretched high up the walls and reflected the late afternoon sun. Around the hall, at some distance from the building itself, a slow moving stream surrounded a series of cultivated gardens. Well around to the south, Joraiem could see a large white stone bridge that crossed over the stream, and it was toward this bridge that Valzaan led them.

They rode beside the stream, parallel to the western side of the Great Hall. The stream itself was clear and bright, except where the evening sun cast their shadows across it. Eventually they rounded the bend that led them along the southern edge of the grounds and toward the bridge, and as they continued ahead, Joraiem looked right and gasped. The rings of houses through which they had passed did not continue all the way around the southern side of the Great Hall, for a great, wide avenue ran from the white bridge straight ahead for a long way until it seemed to empty into the Southern Ocean itself. A great expanse of blue lay in the distance, offset by the white of the houses in either direction along the horizon, and the green grass that grew along the avenue all the way down. It was a marvelous view, and Joraiem looked in wonder, knowing that he was seeing the southernmost tip of all Kirthanin.

There wasn't time, though, to think any more about it, for they had soon arrived at the bridge. As they turned to cross over it, Joraiem noticed a lone man standing on the far end. He was tall and had a neatly trimmed grey beard and grey hair, though his head was mostly bald. He wore a loose flowing jacket over simple white pants and a white shirt. The only ornament of any kind upon him was a silver medallion that hung upon his chest.

"I was but a boy when last you were in Sulare, Valzaan," the man said as the prophet bowed toward him. "Whatever has brought you back, be it good or ill, you are most welcome here again. Indeed, so are all of you after your long journeys. Welcome to the Summerland."

"Thank you, Master Berin, it's good to be back. With your permission we will cross and enter the Great Hall."

Berin nodded. "Enter, and find rest from your labors, prophet of Allfather. For a season, lay aside the burdens you carry and stay awhile among us. All of you, enter in peace, and may peace dwell here with you."

With that, Valzaan rode across the stone bridge and dismounted. Following his example, they all crossed and dropped to their feet, and for Joraiem it seemed even more gratifying than usual to be through with riding for the day, perhaps because after so many weeks of riding, he had arrived at last. No, it was more than that. For the first time in a long while he noticed the absence of worry, concern, or turmoil. Gone were the fears of Black Wolves, the questions about what it meant to be a prophet, the thoughts of Alina, the anxieties that he had perhaps left Evrim and his family in danger. All had been replaced by the calm assurance that this was a place of peace.

Berin took Valzaan's extended hand and shook it warmly, and then Valzaan stood by his side. Neither Valzaan nor Berin spoke or moved, and in the end, Aljeron stepped forward and introduced himself.

"I'm Aljeron Balinor of Werthanin, and I am honored to be here, Master Berin."

"Welcome, Aljeron Balinor, the blessing of Allfather rest upon you," Berin answered as he took Aljeron's hand. Looking at Koshti, he added, "And welcome to your companion. It's been long since battle brothers like him rested here, but he is most welcome."

"His name is Koshti. On his behalf, thank you for your welcome."

One by one, everyone introduced themselves to Berin, and one by one he greeted them all with the same words. After the six from Werthanin, Wylla, and her brothers, Joraiem stepped forward. "I'm Joraiem Andira of Suthanin."

"Welcome Joraiem Andira of Suthanin. May Allfather's blessing rest upon you. It's good to see Werthanim, Enthanim, and Suthanim traveling in one company. The road has begun to bring you all together already. As long as peace remains among us, Malek will find Kirthanin united against his dark designs."

He motioned them to follow him toward the Great Hall as several young men approached from behind Master Berin and took the reins of their horses. "Come, the stables await your tired horses, and a feast awaits you. Your companions are here already. Come and meet them."

As they followed Master Berin through the grounds of the Great Hall, Joraiem looked with more attention at the immaculate gardens. Flowers of all colors and varieties grew in artistically designed beds fifty spans in either direction from the main road that led from the bridge to the Great Hall. Weaving in and out of these, were paths made of chalky white and grey gravel. Green bowers of twisted vines rose intermittently throughout this great network of flowers and paths, and carved wooden benches rested in their shade. He was reminded, as he looked at these, of the stories his father liked to tell of meeting his mother here. He had once heard Monias whisper to her that he would like to stroke her hair and kiss her once more beneath the moon in the gardens of Sulare. As the evening sun bathed the garden in a dusky twilight, he understood how love could be nurtured in this place and why lovers, having once been here together, would want to come back.

All musings about the gardens of Sulare disappeared when they entered the Great Hall. The interior was dominated by the splendor of a great fountain that stood in the middle of the floor beneath the dome. Its waters leapt perhaps ten spans into the air before cascading downward into a series of terraced pools. The outermost pools were at floor level, and the innermost were some three to five spans above them. A series of beautifully carved ladders led from one pool to the next, and several children were swimming and frolicking in them.

For someone who had never seen the great fountain of Sulare before, it was very impressive. Even so, Joraiem had scarcely taken in the fountain when his eyes were drawn above its waters to the top of the dome. Well above the fountain, at the dome's peak, a large hole had been cut in the very center of the roof. Through that hole now streamed the late evening sun. Late as it was, the sunlight coming from the west glowed a vibrant orange, and the whole eastern side of the dome was ablaze with the colors of sunset. The western half was also alight, but with the lesser glow of hundreds of torches. The shadows of manmade lights on that side danced along the white walls and roof of the dome, while all such shadows on the eastern side were drowned out by the radiant light of the sunset. In the very center, the topmost spray of the fountain reached just high enough to be illuminated by the slanted rays of light from the outside, and for just a moment every drop seemed to sparkle with a divine glimmer before splashing down into the pools.

The open design of the Great Hall was simple enough. The space between the front door and the fountain was a large empty area often used for various exercises and training, Master Berin explained, and for refuge from storms. Farther back, to both the right and left of the fountain, tables were arranged haphazardly, both sides easily accessed by the servers who issued up from a short but wide stairwell on the far side of the fountain. A vast network of kitchens and other storage rooms lay beneath the ground, where it was cooler. No matter where Joraiem stood in the hall, he felt as though he was in a large clearing, with echoes of talking and songs and laughter floating throughout the room.

Large tapestries spaced in even incrememnts around the hall adorned the great white walls. As Joraiem surveyed them, even from a distance he was impressed by the craftsmanship. Some depicted peaceful scenes of tranquil domestic life: ships sailing on calm, blue waters, groves of fruit trees with magnificent yields of fruit and bright green leaves, children running in the mad excitement of a game, and more. Some of the tapestries, though, depicted disturbing images of war: Sulmandir with wings spread, claws raised, and jaws open, descending upon a giant, perhaps Vulsutyr himself; hordes of Malekim swarming across a beach and standing over the bodies of slain men; the grim black faces of howling wolves assaulting a small but ferocious company of Great Bear; and more, including one depicting in dark shadows the arrival of the Grendolai.

On the far side of the fountain, beyond the tables, there were many more chairs, grouped in various formations. On one side was a series of semicircular rows facing a small dais with a table and podium on it; in another place, a circle of chairs. In still another place a square had been formed by wooden tables with chairs around the outside. Joraiem wondered if this was where they would be trained. *I will soon find out.*

All this Joraiem took in with his first few glances, though much of how the hall functioned and why would not become clear for weeks to come. Master Berin did not pause at the entryway long, though everyone except Valzaan was all but immobilized by the grandeur of the sight. Soon, Berin was shepherding them toward a cluster of people sitting at tables close to the right side of the fountain. As they drew nearer, Joraiem noticed that those sitting at these tables were all roughly their age and were intently watching them, especially Koshti, approach.

Master Berin introduced the seven Novaana who were seated. From Suthanin, there were three: siblings Darias and Calissa were from Kel Imlarin in northeastern Suthanin, not far from the Enthanin border. Also from Suthanin was a girl from Cimaris Rul named Nyan. Joraiem noticed how different his fellow Suthanim appeared from one another. Nyan wore the white, billowy clothes of the Suthanim from the deep, warm south. Her brown hair hung just above her shoulders. Darias and Calissa wore the colorful dress of Suthanim from the east. Even Calissa's blond hair was decorated with a scarlet string that wound itself in and out of her long braid. Darias wore a deep blue coat over his light grey pants, and a wide yellow sash was tied around his waist. To Joraiem, these three were visible reminders of Suthanin's diversity. Though less populous, Suthanin was larger than either Werthanin or Enthanin, and the scattered habitations were virtually independent.

Even so, Joraiem found a certain comfort in meeting more Suthanim. Though the Werthanim had taken him in for the most part with real friendliness, they shared many words, phrases, and even jokes that he didn't understand. In truth, he knew Aljeron and Rulalin and the other Werthanim better than these three, but something about their slight but expressive smiles reminded him of home.

"I am Joraiem Andira, from Dal Harat, and it is good to meet each of you," Joraiem said when he had an opportunity to address them all. "It is good to finally meet some of my Suthanim brothers and sisters among the Novaana."

Darias nodded in agreement. "Welcome, Joraiem. My father has spoken of your father, I think. It's good to meet you."

"How long have you been here?" Joraiem asked them.

"Calissa and I arrived three days ago. We were the first. Nyan came in yesterday."

"The ride from Cimaris Rul is not long," Nyan said. "It only took me a handful of days."

"Did you come alone?" Joraiem asked, a bit surprised.

"She didn't," Calissa answered, her eyes glowing with excitement as she spoke. "A rather handsome young man was seen kissing her farewell."

"You'll learn, Joraiem," Darias began, shaking his head while Nyan colored, "that Calissa has an almost insatiable appetite for gossip. Beware."

Joraiem turned from his fellow Suthanim to meet the other four, whom Berin had introduced as part of the contingent from Enthanin. The eldest of these was a shy, slender girl named Karalin, who came from a village a few hours from Amaan Sul that Joraiem had never heard of. She was slightly crippled in her left ankle, and so appeared always to be leaning as she stood. Even so, she moved gracefully.

Next in age below Karalin, who, save for Wylla was the oldest of the Enthanim, was a grim young man named Saegan. Saegan came from Tol Emuna, a fortress city of some renown in the far northeastern rocky highlands of Enthanin, not far from the deserted ruins of several ancient Nolthanin towns. Saegan wore durable attire of simple grey, and his brown eyes peered out from his unkempt hair that hung haphazardly across his face. Though he lacked the stature of Aljeron, Joraiem had the feeling that he was someone cut from the same cloth, hardy and intense.

The last two Enthanim were two young cousins who could barely be separated. Valia and Tarin lived southwest of Amaan Sul, not far from the Kellisor Sea. They had come down the Barunaan, accompanied by trusted friends of their fathers, two brothers who knew many river captains who traded from the Southern Ocean to the Kellisor Sea.

After the introductions had all been made, Berin urged them to sit so that the feast could continue. They complied happily, and the hungry travelers fell voraciously on the plentiful supper. The serving men and women placed platters of bread and cheese and great bowls of ripe fruit upon the tables. They also brought up from the kitchens great quantities of roasted fish, shellfish, and even great eels. Though Joraiem was slow at first to try some of the more exotic selections, he found that everything he tasted was good and so dared to be more adventurous than he would normally have been.

As they ate, the groups shared tales of their travels, and while many interesting stories were told, none was more exciting than the attack of the Black Wolves on Valzaan, Joraiem, and the Werthanim. Joraiem blushed when asked to tell about what it was like to take down one of the Black Wolves and to be wounded by another. He did as he was asked, but he was briefer with the tale than many wished.

When the dishes were cleared away, the Novaana relaxed around several small tables and the edge of the fountain itself, talking in many different groups. As Joraiem leaned back against the side of one of the fountain pools, looking up through the opening in the dome at the night sky, Wylla came and sat beside him. She lifted the edge of his sleeve and peeked at his arm.

"The wound looks like it has healed nicely."

"Yes, I was fortunate."

"You were the only one hurt; I'm not sure how fortunate that is."

"True, but it could have been worse. Aljeron was there when I needed him."

"Yes, though it sounds like you were the one who actually took a wolf down before it could hurt anyone."

"Valzaan took care of most of them."

"Sure, but he's a prophet after all."

She smiled. Joraiem, who had been hard pressed to look at anything but Wylla, looked down as she spoke, hoping his face hadn't betrayed anything at her words. When he looked up at last, she was still smiling at him.

"What is it?" she asked.

"Nothing," Joraiem began, blushing. He looked away and caught sight of Rulalin, who had been sitting with Aljeron and Wylla's brothers, watching them with a blank, unreadable expression.

"If you'll excuse me," Joraiem said, standing, nodding to Wylla and moving toward the three Suthanim who were talking at another table. He sat and joined in their conversation, but though he forced himself to focus on it, he couldn't shake the distinct feeling that he was being watched.

The weariness of the day crept over Joraiem. Above the fountain, the light of a thousand stars shone down through a waning-moon sky and sparkled in the fountain's ever-flowing cascades. The sight was so lovely that he could not understand the feeling of overwhelming sorrow that stole over him and cast a great shadow across his heart.

The feeling did not disappear as the group began to disperse. They walked together through the Hall and out into the garden, then down to the bridge across the stream that surrounded the grounds. There, Berin bid them good night. The women followed a stout lady named Merya and the men followed her husband, a white-haired man named Falin. Falin and Merya, Darias told Joraiem as they crossed the bridge, were the chief stewards of the Great Hall and the surrounding guesthouses. They oversaw all the stewards who lived and worked in Sulare with their families. A small but vibrant community of sailors and stewards lived east of the Great Hall in the direction of the large sheltered harbor, which was still home to a few ships.

Falin led the men down the great lane that headed toward the Southern Ocean, eventually turning right and bringing them to a few houses like those they had passed on the way in. Falin lit torches inside the front door of three of them and, after giving them a few terse instructions about the morning, disappeared back up the lane.

"Where's Valzaan?" Elyas asked.

"He stayed behind with Berin," Aljeron answered.

"I can't believe you traveled with Valzaan," Darias said in wonder. "What was it like?"

"It was a bit overwhelming at first," Aljeron replied, "but he is so gracious you could almost forget who he is. Almost."

"How could you forget?" Darias asked. "That would be like forgetting that Agia Muldonai is Malek's home."

"Agia Muldonai is not Malek's home," Saegan said, his voice both quiet and emphatic. "The Holy Mountain will never be his."

Joraiem realized that this was the first thing Saegan had said all night. He studied Saegan, but the Enthanim's hard face betrayed no hint of emotion.

"I didn't mean that," Darias said. "I just meant that forgetting who Valzaan is while he's right there beside you would be like looking at Agia Muldonai and forgetting that Malek lived there."

"It isn't a bad analogy," Rulalin said. "When you live close to the Mountain, you don't forget that Malek is there, like we never really forgot it was Valzaan riding with us, but you do eventually make an uneasy peace with the circumstances of life. It's how you cope."

Joraiem yawned, suddenly and loudly. The sound startled the others, who were contemplating these sobering images. The serious mood was broken, and all of them, even Joraiem, laughed together.

Darias explained Berin's sleeping arrangements, which were, like everything in Sulare, subsumed under the larger goal of fostering unity. They were always to sleep in small groups, and those groups were to change every few days. This way, it was hoped, none of them would be content simply to make friends with only one or two others.

Dividing into three groups took no time at all. Rulalin asked Pedraal and Pedraan if they'd like to share one of the houses, while Darias invited Joraiem to sleep in with Saegan and him, who had been paired together a few nights now. That left Elyas, Kelvan, and Aljeron, who wasted no time bidding the other groups "good night." Soon their lamps and candles were extinguished, and only the light of the stars and thin crescent moon shone in through the large open windows.

For a long time Joraiem lay there, unable to sleep. The heaviness that had descended upon him earlier in the evening weighed on him more and more. He tossed and turned until he thought he was going to go mad. Rising, he slipped into his cloak and walked quietly out of the house and back to the avenue that led from the ocean to the Great Hall.

The night was perfectly clear, and the starlight that he had observed above the fountain in the Great Hall was every bit as brilliant as it had appeared earlier in the evening. He stood for a moment on the avenue, looking alternately toward the Great Hall and down toward the ocean. He wasn't exactly eager to stand beside the ocean again, but he felt a pull within to head that direction. Too tired to try to understand why, he began to walk that way.

The avenue emptied out onto a broad white beach, the sand soft and cool beneath Joraiem's bare feet. The sensation of the grains slipping between his toes was the first comforting thing he had experienced all night. The breeze that rippled across the water also whispered solace as it gently caressed him. How odd in this strange dark night of his soul, to find comfort and reprieve here beside the mysterious waters of the Southern Ocean. He braced himself for some manifestation of his enduring fear, but it did not come.

The memory of the evening he shot the Malekim came vividly before him. Soon, his mind overflowed with images of that night and the following morning. He saw them all, Evrim, his family, his friends, and Alina. Alina! How long until she was married? He couldn't remember if she had said when the wedding was; perhaps it had happened already. Alina. What he would give to stand beside her at the stream again and bid her farewell with tenderness and dignity. What he would give to take back his desperate and ignoble words. What he would give even now to beg her to forgive him, to remove his shame. What he would give, just to see her face.

And then, in that moment, the storm inside him broke. The dark clouds that covered him burst, and tears began to pour out of him. As he dropped to his hands and knees in the sand, his whole body shook with the force of his sobbing. Though his groans were inarticulate, he could hear the word "farewell" echoing in his mind.

When the tears had passed, he rose again without brushing off the sand and walked slowly toward the water, waiting again for any sign at all of his old trepidation. Still, it didn't come. Perhaps it was gone, washed away with his tears to trouble him no more. Perhaps tonight Allfather had granted him a rare reprieve. Perhaps it would return if he allowed himself to touch the water.

He looked down at the waves, silently slipping up the beach in wide arcs of foam. He stopped just beyond their reach and looked. What was the harm? Even if the sinking feeling did return, it couldn't hurt him. He thought of the disconcerting vision that had come to him beside the Barunaan, how real it had seemed. He wasn't exactly anxious to experience that again.

Still, he was going to be here for six months. He couldn't avoid the water all that time. He might as well face it first tonight, when no one else was up, and see if he would faint or fall. He lifted his foot, suspending it for a moment in midair, then placed it in the water.

The water was cool and soothing. He waited, but nothing happened. He stepped farther forward and soon stood knee-deep in the water. It felt strange and wonderful. The water rolled in one moment, then the tide pulled it back past his feet and ankles, the sand beneath his feet slipping away with each successive wave. He walked farther out until he was waist-deep, then chest-deep. He felt unbelievably elated. The darkness that had threatened to envelop him just moments ago was gone, left somewhere behind him in the sand.

It occurred to him, though, that wading so far into the water on his own was not wise. What if he should suddenly be overcome by a spell or vision as before and collapse in the water? Who would save him then? But he dismissed the fear as soon as it appeared. He pushed off the bottom and lay on his back, gently moving his arms in an arc to keep himself afloat. If he were to die this night in this water, so be it, but he felt as though he could float here forever. He stared up at the beautiful nighttime sky, relaxing as he bobbed up and down. Eventually, he closed his eyes and let his thoughts drift. He saw himself as a boy, running through the hills around Dal Harat in the light of the morning sun. He felt the elation of the adrenaline as he ran and soaked up the sunlight on his face.

Suddenly, Joraiem sat up in the water and tried to touch bottom but couldn't. He looked behind him and saw that the shore was far away and the avenue nowhere in sight. For a moment, fear gripped him. How long had he been floating? How far out was he? He started to swim toward shore. He had never been much of a swimmer, but he was capable enough to move with some efficiency through the water. Eventually, he found himself close enough to touch bottom, and he started to walk, reaching the dry ground at last.

He pulled off his shirt and wrung it out by hand. When he'd dried it as best he could, he used it to towel the excess water off his face, chest, and back. He wrung it out again and draped it over his shoulder, then started walking back up the beach. He wasn't sure what time it was, but morning couldn't be far away. Both the deep sorrow and the strange joy that he had experienced that night were gone, replaced by a physical weariness that pulled him back up the avenue toward the small cluster of houses where the others were. Each step was a trial, as he wanted little more than to lie down where he was and sleep. He had never known such weariness, and he doubted very much that he would be able to get up in a few hours for breakfast. He couldn't recall much at all of what had happened that day; it all seemed so long ago. He found and entered the house where Darias and Saegan slept soundly, slipped out of his semi-dry clothes and into his bed, and was soon asleep.

9

TENDING THE FIRE

WHEN JORAIEM WOKE, his whole body was damp from sweat. The room in which he was sleeping was dark and stuffy. It gradually dawned on him that all the large windows were covered by the wooden shutters. The front door was also closed, denying both the ocean breeze and the light that glowed around the edges of the shutters full access to the room.

He looked about the small house, but the others were gone. Standing, he walked over to the window that faced the water and pushed the shutter out and up until he could secure it in the open position. Instantly, light and fresh air flooded the room. He opened the shutters on all four sides and stretched as he surveyed the outside world.

The sun was high above, Fifth Hour at least. The shutters of the other two houses were also open, and so far as Joraiem could tell, both houses were empty. After a month of traveling in a group, this was the first morning since before Peris Mil that he had awakened without being surrounded by others. At times along the way he had found himself wishing for a little solitude, but now that the others were nowhere to be seen, he felt strangely lonely. He wasn't sure whether he was grateful they had let him sleep or irritated they had left him behind.

Joraiem dressed quickly and stepped out of the house. He made his way down the narrow worn path to the wide avenue and stood once more at the crossroads. A quick glance at the ocean brought the events of the previous evening before him, but more than that, it brought him a distant tinge of fear. It was swift and sudden and then gone, but Joraiem did not doubt what it had been. So much for thoughts of freedom from the foreboding.

Joraiem started up the broad avenue toward the Great Hall, which rose before him in the distance. Aside from the occasional path that led to a group of houses, the land on either side of the path was wide open and green with thick, coarse grass. The closer he drew to the Great Hall, the more dense and frequent these clusters of houses became, so that as he neared the bridge that crossed the stream into the gardens around the Hall, the numerous houses on either side appeared to have networks of streets like normal towns instead of narrow dirt paths.

He crossed over into the gardens and continued up the avenue toward the Great Hall. As he walked, he became gradually aware of dark smoke rising from the other side of the dome. From where he was, he couldn't tell if it was rising off the Great Hall itself, or from someplace on the far side. Either way, Joraiem was alarmed.

He started around the outside of the Great Hall to the right, which seemed to be the side from which the smoke was rising. Though he had not yet seen this side of the Great Hall, it was much like the other. The immaculate gardens lay in beautiful patterns around the tall white walls covered with that same yellow creeper.

Eventually, Joraiem went far enough around to see the smoke, rising not from the dome, but as far as he could tell, from the ground next to it. He couldn't see any flames or bushes on fire, but something had to be burning there to be sending up so much smoke. He started to jog toward it.

As he drew closer, he noticed a figure sitting in the tall bower not ten spans from him on his right. He paused for a moment, taking his eyes off of the smoke for the first time, and looked at the person in the bower. Wylla. Her long black hair fell over her shoulders, and she watched him carefully with her clear blue eyes. For a moment, Joraiem lost track of the question he had been about to ask. He ran his hand through his hair, scratching his head, and looked back over his shoulder, as if to see what he had been about in the first place. Seeing the smoke, he turned back to her.

"Sorry to bother you, Wylla, but it looks as if there is a fire over there. Do you know where anyone is who could help me get some water to it?"

Wylla, who was sitting comfortably in the shade, looked back at Joraiem with a bemused smile. "I'm sorry, but I don't."

Joraiem stood there, wondering what to do. He knew he should continue on toward the fire, but he was having trouble regaining his sense of purpose.

Before he could do or say anything, Wylla added, "You know, I'm not sure I would be that concerned about it if I were you."

Joraiem stole another glance over his shoulder at the thick black smoke, and looked back at her. "Why not? A fire in the Great Hall would be terrible."

"Oh it would be," Wylla replied earnestly, rising from her seat and stepping out into the sunlight. In the light, she was dazzling, and as she walked toward him, around a small flowerbed filled with dainty blue blossoms, he noted that even her graceful footsteps were beautiful.

"I'm sorry," Joraiem said, feeling himself blushing a bit, "I didn't catch the last part of what you said."

Wylla pointed past him in the direction of the smoke. "It's the smoke that comes from the ovens down below the Great Hall, and it comes out through a series of grates in the ground by the wall over there."

Joraiem turned and looked more carefully. Knowing what to look for, he quickly caught sight of one of the large grates beside the wall from which the smoke was rising. He blushed again as he thought about how stupid he must look and tried to think of something to say. Nothing came to mind.

Wylla, who was now standing just a span or so away from him, also looking at the rising smoke, said gently, "It certainly would be easy to mistake that smoke for a fire, though, especially at a distance."

Joraiem turned to her, grateful for her kindness but eager to change the topic. "I'm afraid I've missed breakfast. Where are all the others?"

"Most of them are on a little tour with Master Berin."

"Why aren't you with them?"

"I was, but this was as far as I got. I walked out of the Great Hall into this splendid morning, and I decided that I had six months to learn my way around. I've done nothing but ride and walk and journey for ages. I just wanted to sit in this beautiful place and enjoy some peace this morning."

"Yes," Joraiem said, "it is beautiful here. I'm sorry I intruded."

"Oh no," Wylla said, reaching out and gently squeezing his hand. "Don't be. Your company is pleasant. There's no intrusion."

When she let his hand go, he raised it and scratched his head, at a loss for words. She smiled, and then reached up and took hold of Evrim's pendant, which Joraiem had forgotten today in his rush to tuck under his shirt. "What's this? It's beautiful."

"A gift."

"Ah," Wylla said examining the delicate moon. "Something to remember your beloved by?"

"No, I haven't got one, a beloved I mean," Joraiem stumbled. "It's from my best friend."

"Oh," Wylla said. "What's his name?"

"Evrim."

"Evrim, I like that name."

Joraiem was trying to think of something to say when Wylla looked over his shoulder, letting go of the pendant. "I think the others are returning."

Joraiem turned and looked. Coming over the bridge at the front of the group were Wylla's twin brothers, Pedraal and Pedraan.

"Your brothers look so much different than you do," Joraiem said half to himself, and he was almost surprised when Wylla replied.

"They have our father's build, medium height but broad and powerful, and yet they have our mother's hair, golden and thick. I, on the other hand, have my mother's build but my father's hair, black and fine. Those curls, though, no one knows where they came from." She laughed lightly.

"Which of them is older?"

"Pedraal. He is half an hour older than Pedraan. It isn't much, but that half hour makes a difference to them."

As they drew nearer, Master Berin addressed them. "We are hungry from our walk. I hope the two of you can live with an early lunch."

"That would be great," Joraiem said, his stomach grumbling.

"Yes," Wylla added, smiling at Joraiem's enthusiasm, "an early lunch is fine."

When they had eaten, Master Berin led the Novaana to the far side of the Great Hall, where they took seats in one of the semi-circular arrangements Joraiem had noticed the day before. Master Berin and Valzaan sat behind a small wooden table on the dais, and the assembly grew quiet as Master Berin rose to speak.

"On behalf of the Assembly of the Novaana, I formally welcome you to Sulare. May Allfather's blessing rest upon you all."

As Master Berin gave them a slight bow, a cheer went up among them. Joraim knew most of them had been many months on their way, and it was especially exciting to hear not only a welcome, but words that hinted of beginnings. As Joraiem had been primed by Monias, he expected they, too, had all been primed by their parents, grandparents, older siblings, aunts, and uncles for the wonder of the Summerland. Now the long marches, wet nights, and obstacles overcome began to fade from memory as they envisioned the possibilities of tomorrow. They were really there, and the sojourn they had waited for all their lives was about to begin.

When the cheer had settled, Master Berin continued. "It's important from the beginning that you remember why you are here. The War of Division decimated Kirthanin. Even if Malek hadn't taken advantage of the situation to invade at the end of the Second Age, the effects of the war alone would have been disastrous. Cities were ravaged, years of harvests lost, and bridges and roads lay in shambles. Even more difficult to overcome would have been the mistrust among the nations that had been created and reinforced time and again.

"Of course, Malek did come, and he brought with him unimaginable terrors that covered the land with fear and death. Without the aid of Sulmandir and the dragons, and without the Great Bear clans, we would surely have been swept away. But after his victory over Vulsutyr, Sulmandir withdrew from this world, most likely to die from wounds received in his struggle against the Fire Giant. The rest of Sulmandir's children also withdrew, mourning their great father, and seldom do they venture forth from their high and hidden lairs to hold commerce with the world of men."

Master Berin turned to Valzaan, and for a moment stood silent. Almost reluctantly, he turned back to face them again. "One day, perhaps not far away, Malek will come forward again. We cannot rely on the aid of the dragons, without whose strength we have never faced our enemy. What's more, the Great Bear, scourge of the Malekim, have also withdrawn from human society. Though they realize that Corindel's betrayal was not the work of all men, most of the Great Bear have followed the example of the dragons and isolated themselves, minding their own affairs. There are those who believe that in time of need they will stand beside us in battle once again, but there are also those who believe they will remain within the strength of their draals until the end.

"What is truly the case, only the future will reveal. What cannot be doubted, though, is that any division among the people of Kirthanin could be fatally and finally exploited by Malek. We must make sure that doesn't happen. We must make sure that our full strength is always held in reserve— even then it may not be enough. Whether it is or not isn't even ultimately the point. If it is our fate to pay the final price for Andunin's ancient sin, then such is the will of Allfather, and we will face that day when it comes. Until that day, however, we will do all that we can to oppose Malek's designs. For you that is simple. You will learn to work together, to care for one another, and even to consider the good of those seated around you as more important than your own. In peace and unity, we will find strength."

The Novaanas' earlier signs of excitement had been subdued by the weightiness of the moment. Joraiem glanced at the somber faces of his companions, noting especially the sharp glint in Aljeron's eyes as he stared ahead, fingering the long jagged scars on his right cheek.

Master Berin continued. "Tomorrow's worries can wait until tomorrow, but tomorrow's needs call us to use today wisely. I urge you then, to make the most of the time granted to you. The six months that lie before us will pass quickly. You will soon find yourself setting out on your respective journeys home. Who will you be then? How strong will be the bonds you have forged with one another? How firm will be the foundation you have laid for Kirthanin's future? Those are questions only you can answer. We will do our best to help you, your instructors and I, but we cannot decide your fates for you."

Again Master Berin paused, this time apparently lost in a world of thoughts suggested by his own comments. Joraiem looked around him, noticing that most of the others were doing the same. They were taking stock of each other. Who were these other Novaana, roughly their own age, with whom they would live and breathe, eat and sleep? As children they had dreamed of these boys and girls scattered across the face of Kirthanin who would one day be men and women in Sulare with them, just as they knew they'd be men and women when the time came. Now the time was here. Now they were here. And so too were these mysterious others. They looked around them, scanning the faces, perhaps speculating the histories of the lives that would be so intertwined with their own, not only here but in the Assembly thereafter.

Joraiem noticed Wylla looking his direction. Soon, though, he realized she wasn't looking at him but at something beyond him. Curious, he slowly turned his head.

Two older men had slipped up along the wall of the Great Hall and were leaning against it about ten spans away, watching the assembled gathering intently. The man nearest the group appeared to be in his sixties, perhaps older. He was completely bald, with a closely trimmed white beard. He was colorfully dressed, with light blue, loose flowing pants and a thin yellow shirt, but what really stood out about him was his complexion. He was dark skinned, his face deeply tanned by the sun to a deep brown. Joraiem thought that it must have taken a lifetime of exposure to the hot south Suthanin sun to create a complexion like that.

The man next to him was not quite as old, perhaps fifty. He was taller than the first man, with shoulder-length russet-red hair, some of which hung in long braids well below the rest. He was wiry but not exactly thin or slight. His clothes were simple: matching shirt and pants, light grey. What Joraiem noticed immediately about him, however, was the long sword that hung strapped to his waist. Though many of the Novaana had brought weapons with them, it was quite unusual to see a Kirthanin man armed indoors among others. As far as Joraiem knew, it was generally understood throughout Kirthanin that while one might take bow and arrow, even sword and dagger, on the road or on the hunt, these ought to be left outside the house of one's host, though among good friends exceptions to this rule could be made. This man, though, stood just ten spans away with a sword as long as Aljeron's hanging from his side. The anomaly reminded Joraiem that they had stepped for a short time out of the mainstream of Kirthanin life. Things in Sulare were different, and only time would tell how so.

He turned back carefully, not wanting to betray to either of the new arrivals that he had been stealing a look. This time Wylla was looking at him. When she saw that he had noticed her, she smiled. It was a simple, indeed friendly, smile, but Joraiem was caught off guard and felt his face grow hot. He gave her a polite nod and then tried to occupy himself with anything or anyone else. His eyes landed on Rulalin, seated ahead of him and a little to his left, looking at him with curious and reflective eyes. Master Berin started to address them once more. Rulalin, too, nodded slightly at Joraiem, then turned back around toward the front to listen to Master Berin.

"I want to introduce you to two of the men who will be working closely with you while you are here." The two men Joraiem had observed by the wall approached and stood beside Master Berin. Master Berin placed his hand on the younger of the men, the one with the sword, and said, "This is Caan, our combat instructor. He will be your teacher in all things military. He is not only a master of strategy, well-schooled in the military history of Kirthanin, he is accomplished with almost any weapon you can imagine."

Caan stepped forward and bowed slightly before them, his long braids hanging down on either side of his head. When he rose from his bow, he stepped back to his original position, not saying a word.

"This is Ulmindos," Master Berin continued while the older man stepped forward and raised his hand with a smile. "Ulmindos is high captain of the ships of Sulare. While our once magnificent fleet has dwindled to only four ships, the expertise of our sailors has not diminished. Ulmindos, like his fathers before him, is one of the ocean-born. He will teach you all that mankind knows about the waters of the deep and the stars of the heavens."

Ulmindos, like Caan, bowed before them and then stepped back silently. Master Berin continued, "There is something you should all note about the three of us who will be your principal instructors while you are here, for I too will be your teacher, primarily in the areas of Kirthanin history, custom, and diplomacy. We are all from different lands. Though I have lived here most of my life, I was born in a small village, almost exactly midway between Fel Edorath and Shalin Bel, so I am Werthanim by birth. Ulmindos, as you would guess since he is one of the ocean-born, is from southern Suthanin. Caan grew up not far from Amaan Sul and learned to fight within view of Agia Muldonai, so he is Enthanim. We are children of the three great lands of Kirthanin, serving together in harmony because we are united in purpose. We share a love for Allfather, a loathing of Malek, and a longing that Kirthanin will hold together until Allfather will restore all things. We are, I hope, an example of what we desire all of you to be when you leave here—friends. May Allfather grant you the understanding of one another that he has granted us.

"Finally, I'd like to formally introduce you as a group to Valzaan, prophet of Allfather. You met Valzaan last night, but I didn't know then that his intent was to remain with us during the time of your training here. It would seem that Allfather has placed, for a while, Valzaan's path beside yours. Though Caan, Ulmindos, and myself will be your formal teachers, Valzaan should be regarded as equal in authority and just as deserving of respect as the rest of us, if not more so."

Valzaan stood, and like Caan and Ulmindos, bowed in their direction. "I'm aware that my presence here has already raised questions among you," Valzaan began. "I know my reputation—after all, I lived it." Valzaan smiled and a ripple of laughter spread throughout the room. "Still, I wanted to address you as soon as I could to assure you that you know as much about my coming as I do. When Allfather calls me to a task, He rarely explains why. I've come to understand that His instructions are opportunities to demonstrate my trust in Him and to obey without question. So, I have journeyed here from a place, very far away, where it had been my intent to rest for a season. What I am to do, now that I am here, I don't know. This will not answer all of your questions, but it's as much as I can tell you. Still, let me add one thing; the task that Master Berin has described, which is even now set before you, could not be more serious. I have beheld the power of Malek with my own eyes on many occasions, and it is fearful. Even so, you should pursue your training and your study and your fellowship here with all earnestness and with real hope, not because you are stronger than he is, because you are not. Rather, you should move forward in the certain knowledge that Allfather is as superior to Malek as Malek is to you. In that truth, and in that alone, all our hopes lie."

Joraiem had considered the room quiet and somber before; he hadn't realized how much more so it could become. Mixed with the gravity of Valzaan's words was an apprehension that Joraiem did not doubt was all his own. Why had Allfather called him to be a prophet? Why had Allfather brought Valzaan here? Why were Black Wolves in Dal Harat, Peris Mil, and on the road to Sulare? He felt a chill. He scanned his companions. They too had been summoned to this place by right of birth, but had any of them received the summons he had received? Did any of them carry the weight that he carried? Did any of them have a secret like his?

Caan led the group of young Novaana down toward the ocean along the wide avenue. A little after the cluster of houses in which the men had slept the night before, Caan turned off of the avenue on the other side and took them along a winding dirt path that ran almost parallel to the water on its right and into some trees. The trees were some of the first non-fruit trees that Joraiem had seen since crossing into Sulare. Further, as they passed into their midst, he realized how few trees there were among the buildings that surrounded the Great Hall. Here, however, though they were not exactly dense, the trees were plentiful on either side, ultimately blocking their view of both the ocean and the Great Hall. Eventually, they reached a large, wide-open ring, surrounded by long benches. Caan motioned to them to take seats, which they did, while he strode into the center of the ring.

Standing in the middle, not having spoken a word to any of them, he unbuckled the great sword that hung around his waist and dropped it to the ground. "Is there anyone here who thinks he could hit me with this sword?"

Caan gazed around the circle, and after a moment, so did Joraiem. He wasn't sure where this was headed, but he didn't think he wanted to be the one to answer the question. Apparently the others didn't either.

Caan spoke again, "I meant exactly what I said, no tricks. Who among you thinks you could come out here, pick up this sword, and hit me with it?"

Pedraan laughed and said, "I can hit you with it!"

Caan clapped a few times loudly and waved Pedraan on. "Come on then, come pick it up and strike me."

Pedraan rose, a bit more hesitant than his voice had made him sound. He walked into the center of the ring and picked up the big sword, which remained in the sheath. He started to move toward Caan.

"Take the sword out of the sheath. I am the enemy, and you don't approach the enemy unprepared."

Pedraan stopped. "I don't think I should—"

"I didn't ask you to think about it! Take the sword out of the sheath and try to strike me with it. I'm waiting."

Pedraan drew the sword and stepped toward Caan. As he drew near, Pedraan raised the sword, and with a sudden surge forward, he swung it in a half-hearted arc in Caan's direction. Caan easily sidestepped the stroke, and when it had gone safely past him, he stepped back toward Pedraan and delivered a strike with his open hand to Pedraan's elbow, which echoed across the clearing with a crack. Pedraan grunted with pain and dropped the sword as he clasped his elbow. Caan stepped quickly in front of him and scooped up the sword. His face betrayed no emotion, while Pedraan looked both bewildered and annoyed.

"I know it was a strange request and that you did not strike as hard as you could out of a wish to protect me, but I had told you I was the enemy and to strike." Caan spoke gently and put his hand on Pedraan's shoulder. "You will need to learn both that I am to be obeyed and that you need to trust my judgment. Even had you moved faster, you would not have hit me. You will learn soon enough the skill that would have enabled you to do so, but you do not have it yet. Return to your seat."

Turning and striding toward the benches where the rest sat watching, he started again. "The key to combat is neither strength nor speed, though both of these things are assets. Success in combat starts with timing and balance. These are the essentials. Greatness as a warrior begins with wisdom and agility. Everything else is secondary." He paced like a restless animal. "If you know when and how to move and are nimble enough to do it, you have won more than half the battle. This is why even you, ladies, will be trained. It is not our desire that any of you should ever have to fight in battle, but we would not have you be defenseless. We will train you how to fight, so that in time of need, you will know what to do."

"Now," Caan continued, pausing before them, "let's try our exercise again. I'd like another volunteer."

Again, no one was immediately forthcoming. Caan still held his sword in his hand, and after waiting a few moments, he stepped toward Aljeron. "You look old enough to have had some experience with a sword. How about you?"

With these last words, Caan raised the point of the sword about halfway off of the ground and pointed it haphazardly in Aljeron's direction, but by no means in a threatening manner. The lack of serious threat didn't matter to Koshti, who had been lying in the grass beside Aljeron's bench. However, the moment the sword point started to rise off of the ground and toward Aljeron, the tiger sprang up and leapt onto the surprised Caan, knocking him to the ground. Koshti kept one of his great paws on Caan's chest and unleashed a savage growl that chilled Joraiem's blood.

"Koshti! No!" Aljeron cried, leaping from his bench and pulling on Koshti to restrain him. Soon Aljeron had pulled the tiger off of Caan, who quickly rolled to the side and regained his feet, looking remarkably calm considering what had just taken place.

"I'm sorry, Master Caan," Aljeron began, "but Koshti thought you meant to threaten me. Once he knows you are a friend, it won't happen again."

Caan laughed. "It's quite all right. It was a shock, to be sure, but your friend has proven my point much better than I could have. As quick and strong as he is, it was his agility and timing that made his strike so effective. He moved with perfect balance, his speed and power harnessed to a specific end. Learn to move even a little like him, and you will all be greatly feared."

After supper that night, a loud and boisterous affair reflecting the emotional wave the Novaana had been riding all day, Master Berin invited them all down to the beach for a bonfire. It was customary for the new arrivals to hold a vigil on the last night of Full Spring on the shore of the Southern Ocean. The purpose was for all to be reminded tangibly by the rolling waves, which in their journey through the great deep had washed up more than once on the distant shore of the Forbidden Isle, that Malek, though now far north in the Holy Mountain, was still an imminent threat.

Despite the sober purpose, the night was not intended to be morose or solemn, since "tending the fire," as the vigil was called, was also symbolic of their coming of age and their assumption of responsibility. When they returned home in six months, they would all be eligible to attend meetings of the Assembly. Practically speaking, though, only the eldest among them would go, since twenty-five was generally considered the appropriate age to be formally recognized there for the first time. This meant that only Aljeron, Rulalin, and Wylla would soon take up duties there. Even so, by virtue of being in Sulare, all had stepped across a threshold. When they returned, even the eldest among them, who had been treated as men and women for many years now, would be seen differently by their families and communities. They knew this, and although quietly awed by this fact, they shared a communal excitement over it.

And so when the dinner was over, they filed out of the Great Hall behind Master Berin and Valzaan, carrying great torches that flickered in the steady ocean breezes. They talked and laughed as they walked to the beach, turning right and heading west, parallel to the water. In a short time they reached a place where a great fire was already burning under the watchful eyes of Falin. Ulmindos and Caan were also present, sitting cross-legged on the far side of the fire, talking quietly.

They sat around the fire, the size of which prevented Joraiem from seeing or hearing those on the opposite side. Accordingly, conversations broke out in small groups around the circle. As the night grew late, however, the fire died down until it was possible for all to see and hear one another without strain.

The waning moon had been barely visible for several days, and tonight it was wholly absent from the distant sky, though the stars were bright and clear. Tomorrow was the first day of Spring Wane, but despite the increasing warmth and length of days, the nights were still cold, and they huddled closer to the fire. As the separate conversations around the fire began to dwindle, the generally quiet Saegan asked Valzaan a question.

"Master Valzaan, would you tell the story of Corindel? The real story? My father and my uncles avoid it, telling me that it is the story of our shame, like the story of Andunin. But I want to know why the Great Bear that once walked the streets of Tol Emuna in the days before Corindel walk it no longer. If I'm ever to be a leader of our people, I want to know our shame, all of it, so that I can approach in penitence and contrition the only allies we can hope to have in the coming war. I know enough of our history to know that today Master Berin understated our peril. Without help we will surely fall before Malek, unless he has grown weaker since he retreated to the Holy Mountain, and that is a vain hope. With the Great Bear, we may fail. Without them, there is no question of it."

Master Berin stirred as though to speak, but Valzaan laid his hand gently on his arm. "What you say is likely true," Valzaan said. "Allfather has granted me no vision of the Great Bear's future, and though I still have some dealings among them, I do not speak of what is past. Out of respect for me they would discuss it if I pressed them, but out of respect for them I do not. At times, I feel as though nothing can heal this rift. At other times, I feel as though the love of Great Bear for men, through the long years of separation, has grown even stronger than it was before. I feel these things at times in my bones, but still I have no word from Allfather. Those pages of the future are wholly dark, and my thoughts and feelings on the matter are as speculative as your own.

"As for the story of Corindel, I will tell it, but not tonight. Your father and uncles are right to say it is the story of our shame, in one sense even greater than the shame of Andunin. Malek sought Andunin out and tempted him to his ruin, but Corindel sought out Malek, ignoring the clear warning of Allfather that I gave him concerning the foolishness of the quest. Allfather had revealed beyond question that Corindel's assault could not succeed. Though hatred of Malek drove him on, and though he never could have imagined the evil that would come from his choice, still, all that followed his defiance of Allfather must be laid at his feet. I don't hesitate to tell the story because of its shame, for you are right to desire to know it, but tonight we tend the fire. Tonight we lay aside stories of

Malek's victories and our defeat. There will be another time to speak of Corindel."

Saegan nodded toward Valzaan in deference. "As you wish."

"Is there no other story you would have me tell?"

"I'll leave that choice to another."

Before anyone could speak, Valzaan said, "I am not unwilling to tell a story, but there is a story I should like to hear from Aljeron, if he would be willing."

"From me?" Aljeron said in surprise.

"Yes, from you."

"What story could I tell that you don't know?"

Valzaan laughed. "There are many. Your entire life is a story, though I'm not inquiring about that. I would like to know how you discovered Koshti was your battle brother."

A murmur of approval rippled through the circle, as many nodded their heads at this idea, including Aljeron's companions from Werthanin. Aljeron gazed at the fire and rubbed Koshti's head, as the tiger lay contentedly beside him.

"I don't know why you shouldn't know, but the events surrounding our second meeting if not the first are somewhat personal. I'll tell you if you wish, but I'm not sure how interesting it would be to anyone but me."

"I'm sure Aelwyn would love to know," Mindarin said teasingly.

"Who's Aelwyn?" Calissa asked eagerly, while her brother Darias looked at Joraiem and rolled his eyes.

"Aelwyn is my sister," Mindarin said.

"Yes, her eight-year-old sister," Rulalin added.

"She may only be eight, but she's a great admirer of Aljeron. Only ten years more and she'll be of age." Mindarin giggled as she spoke, her voice dripping with mischief.

Valzaan put an end to the playful exchange. "My request was made out of curiosity about your bond, which is as strong as I've ever seen between man and beast. Even though battle brothers are rare these days, this hasn't always been the case, and meeting you has raised a few questions for me. I thought your story might answer them. Perhaps another time would be more appropriate."

Aljeron shook his head. "I'm not sure I have many answers, since I don't understand myself everything that happened, but the story is easy enough to tell."

The embers in the fire crackled as Joraiem leaned forward and Aljeron began.

"About a week south of the Nolthanin border, in the north central plains of Werthanin, is a small village called Nol Rumar. My aunt and uncle and three cousins, all boys, all older than me, live there. Once I had four cousins, but the youngest, Merwyn, was killed when he was sixteen, as my story will relate.

"It was in the summer, almost thirteen years ago, when I first encountered Koshti near Nol Rumar. I was eleven years old and had accompanied my family on a visit to see my cousins, who treated me like a little brother.

"On this particular day in late Summer Wane, a big feast day was planned for the village. What was being celebrated I don't remember. All I recall is everyone in Nol Rumar looking forward to a day of eating and drinking, dancing and singing. My cousins were likewise excited, mostly because the day promised to showcase the girls of Nol Rumar. Each of my cousins, except Merwyn, who like me was not yet overly excited by such things, had picked out a girl of the village that they would ask to dance. The morning of the feast day, they went to a stream outside Nol Rumar to bathe, and we tagged along.

"As with all things my cousins did together, the simple bath soon became a brawl. My cousins were splashing and dunking and throwing one another around in the water. After being thrown more than once completely out of the water, I allowed myself to float to a safe distance downstream where I could watch the battle in peace. While I sat, bent over in the water to keep warm in the early morning air, I heard a rustling in the undergrowth beneath the trees.

"I couldn't see what had caused the sound. I figured it had been a bird or small animal of some sort, but as I was turning my attention back to my cousins, I heard the sound again. This time I heard a pained whimper as well, so I scrambled up onto the bank to see what was there. I tiptoed across the rocky soil toward the sound. I had to brush some brown, gnarled, woody vines out of my way, but when I had gone about fifteen spans, I stopped dead in my tracks. I could see a young tiger, clearly not full grown, but also clearly not a cub anymore. He lay on his side, and I could see the shaft of an arrow protruding from his ribs.

"I approached him cautiously, and he looked at me with something between rage and terror in his eyes. I talked softly to him as I stooped, well to the rear and far enough away that his side was just barely in reach. I tried to stroke his fur near the arrow gently, but he thrashed suddenly out with his hind leg and cut me along my bare arm. Seriously wounded as he was, I knew he would prevent me from helping him unless I had some help of my own.

"It didn't take me long to gain the attention of my cousins, and soon all five of us stood around him. Merwyn's oldest brother examined the puncture wound while the other two took a few of the woody vines and immobilized the tiger's paws. My cousin pronounced the wound fatal and advised that we kill the animal quickly lest his death be long and painful.

"I protested so loudly and vigorously that, to my surprise, my cousins deferred to me and said I could try to tend him if I desired, but they would not help me. I asked Merwyn to stay with me and watch over him, and I think he was torn. In the end, the lure of the celebration and feast was too strong. I begged him to bring me any salves or medicines that his mother might have, as well as an old bowl or dish I could use to give the tiger water, and he agreed. Within the hour, he brought me a large bowl, a jar full of a potent ointment, and an old shirt of his to use as a bandage if I could remove the arrow.

"I tended the tiger all day, trying to sooth its fears of me as well as its pain. I brought him water from the brook, which he lapped up quickly if awkwardly while tied down on his side, all the time keeping his eyes trained on me. If I moved too close to the arrow, he would lift his head as far as he could and growl at me until I moved away. It went like this most of the morning, until at last I spoke firmly to him, explaining that unless he allowed me to remove the arrow and treat the wound, he would die.

"That was the first time that I realized something strange was going on. He looked at me for a moment as though considering what I had said, and then laid his head on the ground and closed his eyes. I couldn't believe what I was seeing, but I slid closer all the same, waiting for him to growl as he had done all morning. He did not. At last I was in position, right beside him, and I prepared to remove the arrow. I placed my left hand on his side with my thumb on one side of the arrow and my fingers on the other, and with a strong, steady tug, I pulled the arrow out as smoothly as I could. It must have been excruciating, but the tiger barely whimpered. I immediately washed the wound with a bowl of fresh water, then I applied some ointment. There was a lot of bleeding initially, but the medicine helped the blood to clot. I applied more ointment later in the afternoon, then once more as it began to grow dark. I had been with the tiger all day, and I knew I had done all I could. I tore the shirt into two long strips and bandaged the tiger's side as best I could. When I had given him another drink, I untied the vines. Despite his complacent behavior, I was a bit concerned about what he might do once free. So, I stepped back quickly as he stood up. I needn't have been afraid, however, because he wasn't interested in getting me so much as getting away, or at least that was how it seemed, because he moved as quickly as his wound would allow him into the cover of the thick trees.

"I watched him go, then headed across the stream and back to Nol Rumar. It was almost completely dark when I arrived, but the celebration was still going strong. The music played and the dancers whirled, but after a few moments of watching I turned to go. I just didn't feel like participating.

"Four days later I returned with my family to Shalin Bel. I hadn't seen him again, though I'd felt once or twice that if I would just go back into the woods, he would come to me. It was a strange feeling that I didn't quite understand.

"We did not return to Nol Rumar until Full Autumn three years later. Full Autumn can be quite cool that far north, and it certainly was that year. It wasn't cold enough, though, to stop Merwyn and me, along with two of his older brothers, from planning an expedition toward the ancient Nolthanin border. We would be traveling in wild and desolate land, and neither my father nor my uncle were crazy about the idea. But they couldn't object too strenuously since both had journeyed that way before when they were our age.

"The four of us packed up and headed out for two weeks of hiking. We planned to reach the Ciruan River, which marked the boundary of Werthanin, cross it somewhere where the current wasn't too strong to set foot in Nolthanin, then come back the way we had come. Countless groups of young men had undertaken the same mission at least once, including my older cousins.

"The first four days went well, and we made good time on a hunter's path that was for the most part in disuse. On the fifth day, though, we ran into trouble. The day started out rainy and overcast and only got worse. By evening, we were soaked to the bone, and a dense fog had settled in. We were trying to figure out what we would do to camp for the evening when they came.

"They were a pair of Malekim, who fell upon us as we were stopping for the night. What happened next is not entirely clear to me, except that I remember my two older cousins trying desperately to distract the Voiceless that had grabbed Merwyn and was crushing him in its great arms. I think he died almost instantly, and so I don't think that he felt much pain, mercifully. It is my cousins' opinion, at least, that Merwyn was dead before the Malekim proceeded to rip him to pieces, and I hope it's true. I don't know, because I soon found myself running desperately through the fog, trying to escape the second Malekim.

"I was not successful. After stumbling several times, I finally emerged into an open area where the fog was not so dense. When I paused for a moment to get my bearings, the Malekim leapt out of the fog and knocked me to the ground. I waited with my eyes closed for the death blow, but it didn't come. When I looked, I saw the Malekim take its short sword, perhaps half a span long, and jab it into the dirt beside my head. Then he knelt, one great knee on each of my arms, and stared at me with malice and hatred. He took one thick, black fingernail—a claw really—and dug it into my face right under my hair. The Voiceless applied pressure until it seemed to scrape my bone. I have never thought of myself as weak, but the pain was so intense that I screamed like a baby. I had only recently turned fifteen, and nothing in my wildest dreams had prepared me for that kind of pain. He proceeded to rip my face open, all the way down to my jaw. He then took two fingers and pressed them in on either side of the first cut, and ripped down my face again, this time all but gouging out my eye. For a moment, my left eye flickered open, and I saw him preparing to do the same on the left side of my face, when suddenly, an orange streak flew above my head and knocked him off of me.

"I rolled over, lifting my aching face half a hand off the ground, watching with fascination as the same tiger I had met those three years before sank his massive jaws into the Malekim's throat, ripping a gaping wound through the thick hide. The Voiceless cannot scream, but I saw the agony flare in his eyes. He freed himself with a mighty effort and hobbled off into the fog. The tiger made as though to pursue him, but came swiftly back to me.

"He stood over me, looking tenderly, I thought, at my horribly gashed face, and he began to lick me. Though his tongue was warm and wet and the saliva stung at first, I realized that he was washing my wound. I lay still as he licked both dirt and blood clean.

"When he was finished, I slowly rose to my feet and followed him through the fog, holding onto his fur. It felt like hours that we walked, my face throbbing, though I doubt it was that long. Soon, the fog lifted and I could see the night sky, the quarter moon newly risen over the horizon. The tiger led me to a small cave where my older cousins were huddled, both wounded but alive. When they saw me, they approached with fear and wonder. I wasn't sure what to say, and in the end, all I said was, 'This is Koshti, my battle brother.'"

Aljeron finished speaking, and the rest of the circle sat quietly. Valzaan nodded his head. "Thank you. I'm sure that is not an easy tale for you to tell. Still, I have learned much from it, and perhaps we may speak further about it later if you are willing."

Aljeron nodded, but said nothing.

The remainder of the night passed uneventfully. More stories were told, but Joraiem found none as engrossing as Aljeron's, and Aljeron himself did not speak again. Joraiem kept an eye on him, hoping to attract his attention so he could nod or in some way show his support and friendship, but Aljeron merely sat, stroking Koshti's fur and staring into the fire.

10

FOOTFALLS

SPRING WANE PASSED QUICKLY and became Summer Rise, which in turn passed and brought Full Summer. Master Berin, Ulmindos, and Caan worked the assembled Novaana steadily and hard, but not without opportunities for relaxation. Even so, Joraiem found the days and weeks slipping by quickly, as every day seemed to hold half a dozen different experiences designed to inform, to train, to equip and ultimately to unite them.

For the most part, the group seemed to come together well. As far as Joraiem could tell, each was well intentioned in pursuing their common goal, and to a point, that had been enough to get things off to a good start. The reality of differences in personality, temperament, and background did show itself from time to time, enough to remind them why they were there. While general good will was sufficient to keep things peaceful, it was soon clear some bonds of true friendship would be forged only by hard work.

Early on, Joraiem had thought the friendship that was going to be most difficult for him was that with Saegan, who was actually the male closest to him in age. The comraderie he'd established with the Werthanim on the road continued in Sulare. The three Suthanim, for their part, looked to him as their leader, as he was the eldest. Darias went even further, treating Joraiem like an older brother. Of the seven Enthanim, the young cousins, Tarin and Valia, were nice to everyone, even if that consisted mostly of blushing and giggling around the men. Both Wylla and Karalin, the oldest of the gathered Novaana women, were gracious to all, and the twins, Pedraal and Pedraan, had taken to Joraiem from the moment they met him by the grove of snow trees. In fact, Joraiem had become something of a common link to all the men younger than he, except Saegan.

It took Joraiem a while to figure out why things developed the way they did, but he eventually began to understand what had put him in that role. Aljeron, despite being warm and friendly, was held in awe by all the younger men. Not only was he the eldest and a natural leader, but the presence of Koshti, plus Aljeron's size and strength, set him apart. While the younger men admired and liked him, they found it hard to see him as a peer. Rulalin also remained distant from most of the younger men, but that distance was due more to Rulalin's mood swings than awe. While he could be likeable, Rulalin could also withdraw almost instantly and completely from them all, and during those times, he was prone to treat the younger men as nuisances. So, while he was respected for his age, his skill in combat, and his capable mind, Rulalin did not have the same influence Aljeron did.

Then there was Joraiem, also capable and skilled, but seen by the others as one of them. They might come to him for help with something they were learning, but they also came to him just to talk and laugh and spend time together. He began to feel like a bridge, connecting the younger men with the older.

What had made that job difficult at first was Saegan. Saegan quickly established himself in the training sessions with Master Caan as a formidable opponent in all areas of skill. Aljeron was the best of them all, but Saegan made him work the hardest. With everything they did, no matter who was naturally gifted or already skilled, Saegan soon became the dominant challenger. Even Joraiem, who was the best archer among them, realized that Saegan had the best eye among the rest and had made the most progress in mastering the bow.

For all of this Joraiem admired Saegan, and from early on he tried to befriend him. Saegan, however, normally quiet and reserved, seemed even more reticent than usual to be engaged by him. For the whole first month Joraiem failed in all attempts to break through the barrier, but early on in Summer Rise, Joraiem spent three successive nights sharing one of the open houses with Saegan alone. The first two nights, Saegan reluctantly talked to Joraiem when necessary but avoided meaningful discussion. On the third night, though, Saegan's whole demeanor changed. He was both open and friendly, even talkative, and since that night, Joraiem had ceased to worry about that relationship. He didn't know what had happened, and he didn't ask, accepting the change gratefully. Saegan remained quiet and reserved, but the barrier was gone.

And so Joraiem started to think that he would have relatively smooth sailing with the group. He soon realized his mistake. As Summer Rise progressed, three things increasingly troubled him. First, Rulalin's initially subtle and occasional overtures to Wylla were becoming more frequent and more overt. More to the point, it was increasingly clear that Wylla was not interested in Rulalin the same way, and Rulalin's mood swings were growing more frequent and more severe. He could sense desperation growing in Rulalin as Full Summer approached; a third of their stay together in Sulare had passed, and he was no closer to winning Wylla's heart than he had been when he arrived. In fact, he was probably further away.

Second, he began to notice that though Wylla was truly one of the most gracious people he had ever met, she did seem to be developing a favorite among the men—him. He had never quite overcome his awkwardness around her, and every time they spoke, he felt nervous and hesitant. This did not surprise him. Wylla was beautiful, and her beauty only grew in his eyes over time. Still, he couldn't deny the warning signs that his feelings involved more than simple awkwardness around a pretty girl. The first was the realization that Alina had almost disappeared from his waking thoughts. Occasionally he still dreamed of her, but those dreams were rarer and less traumatic than they once had been. Another warning sign was the way Pedraal and Pedraan had started to act. One day, after talking briefly to Wylla on the walk back from a training session, Joraiem had noticed Pedraal whispering to Pedraan as they were looking his way and laughing. To make matters worse, when Pedraal saw that Joraiem was looking at him, he winked. Joraiem almost tripped and fell in his haste to turn away.

Joraiem felt the urge to push all of this away, to ignore the increasing distraction that Wylla was becoming, to deny the insinuations he thought he was seeing in Pedraal and Pedraan, but he knew he couldn't because of the third thing that troubled him: Rulalin's marked withdrawal from their friendship. Without accusations, angry words, or physical blows, Rulalin had severed any meaningful connection they had established. He was polite, respectful, even gracious, but wholly closed to dialogue of any depth. During their weeks on the road, Joraiem had shared Rulalin's confidence. That had continued during their first few weeks in Sulare, but by mid-Spring Wane, it had started to disappear. Now it was completely gone, and as the sun rose on the third day of Full Summer, Joraiem lay wondering what he was going to do about Rulalin, about Wylla, and even about his own confused feelings.

Eventually Joraiem rose, though the light of morning was still but a scant glimmer on the horizon. Dressing quietly, he slipped out of the little house he was sharing that week with Pedraal and Kelvan, both of whom were still sleeping soundly. Walking down to the edge of the beach, he yawned and stretched before setting off on a jog along the shore. He hadn't thought that running in the morning in Sulare would be either as difficult or as beautiful as running in hills near Dal Harat, but he had been wrong. Running along the edge of the sand was challenging, despite the flat terrain, and the Southern Ocean presented a backdrop every bit as beautiful as the hills near his home.

Even so, from time to time the close proximity of all that water would raise his anxiety suddenly, forcing him to focus carefully on his running and the ground beneath his feet to keep from fainting. There was no predicting which mornings he would struggle with the strange and persistent fear. He was relieved that as yet, the lessons of Master Ulmindos had consisted of lessons in the classroom about life at sea, but he knew that in Autumn Rise they would spend a fortnight together on the Southern Ocean, sailing one of the great ships of the Sulare fleet under Ulmindos's direction. How he would survive while on that ship, Joraiem could not imagine.

On his way into the Great Hall for breakfast that morning, Joraiem saw Wylla inside the open door talking to someone he could not see, though he could hear words being whispered just softly enough that he couldn't make them out. He paused outside, lingering in the morning sun without thinking, gazing at Wylla. As it dawned on him that he was staring, she looked toward the door and saw him standing there. A smile broke across her face as he stepped hesitantly inside.

As he did, he saw Rulalin standing against the near wall. The hushed words had stopped, and now Rulalin looked at Joraiem as he entered, then stepped away from the wall and walked quietly away.

"I'm sorry, Wylla, I didn't mean to intterupt anything."

"You didn't. It wasn't important," she said, the smile slipping from her face.

She turned and walked with him toward the tables for breakfast. "How was your morning run?"

"Good."

"When I was a girl, I used to love to run around and play games. Back then, I was actually pretty fast. I used to race anyone I could find who was willing."

"Did you lose interest as you grew older?"

"No, I just lost the time," she sighed, then smiled at him again. "There are lots of things you have to learn when you are the heir to the throne, so while my brothers spent their free time playing, I spent mine in lessons, always lessons."

Joraiem looked at her carefully. Despite the smile, he could see the sadness. He had never really considered before what Wylla's position might have required of her from her earliest years. She interacted with the others so naturally, so normally, it was easy to forget she would one day be a queen.

"Still," Wylla added quickly, "I don't want you to get the wrong idea. We are all called to service, and serving as queen of Enthanin will be a great privilege. Allfather has called me to this task, and He will equip me for it."

Joraiem continued to study her, and he saw now, beyond the sadness, resolution and confidence in Wylla's eyes. He smiled, "Would the queen like some breakfast?"

Wylla laughed, "My mother isn't here, but I'd love some."

After breakfast, Caan took them to their training ring.

The sun was still low in the eastern sky, but the day was already hot and the humid air was thick. Sweat slipped down Joraiem's chest and sides beneath his light shirt, and he wondered if it wouldn't be a good idea to remove it altogether as the twins had already done. Pedraal and Pedraan walked side by side not more than a span ahead, and their massive backs and broad shoulders glistened with sweat. Their now shoulder-length golden locks hung wet and matted. He thought it wise to wait, though, and see what Master Caan had in store for them. If the plans included exercises that involved Joraiem being thrown to the ground, he would leave his shirt on.

They filed into the grassy clearing and took their seats around the ring, waiting patiently and quietly. Master Caan, never quick to speak, always paced around the ring for as long as he deemed appropriate, and addressed his pupils only when he was ready. Elyas joked that he spent the time trying to devise new exercises to cause them all pain, and while the rest of them chuckled at the idea, they probably all suspected he might be right. Caan never let them do the same exercises and drills long enough for them to become comfortable and routine. "A warrior," Caan would say, "becomes skilled through constant drilling. He must practice again and again the same skills, the same moves, the same thrusts and motions and defenses, or they will not be second nature. I have six months to teach you skills it takes years to master. You will have to drill yourselves when you return home, for I do not have the time."

Caan taught them forms to commit to memory, male and female alike. These forms walked them through the essential motions of the skills they were learning and could be practiced whenever a student had twenty minutes of time to give them. Joraiem sometimes practiced his in the mornings after his run, and often in the evenings several of them would gather by the fountain of the Great Hall to go through them together, sometimes with an audience of young stewards from the Hall. For the most part, Joraiem picked them up quickly, though no one learned them as well or as quickly as Aljeron. One evening, Joraiem watched Aljeron work through the forms while Koshti sat calmly beside him. It may have been the red light of the sunset behind him, or the close proximity of the tiger, but it seemed to Joraiem at that moment that there was something of Koshti's feline grace in Aljeron's smooth but powerful movements.

This morning, however, Master Caan wasn't pacing. He stood patiently at the far side of the ring, his back to them, near the trees that encircled it on the western side. After a few minutes he turned and strode back into the middle of the ring. He called Aljeron, Rulalin, and Joraiem to join him. He grabbed three solid, wooden staffs, each about a span in length, and passed one to each of them.

"Take these, and wait. Don't worry about what to do with them. When the time is right, you'll know."

Joraiem looked at the others, puzzled. Rulalin, too, looked confused. Aljeron simply waited, expressionless. Koshti suddenly rose to his feet and stood facing the far side of the ring where Master Caan had been standing.

"Please ask Koshti to sit down, Aljeron," Caan said quietly from where he stood behind them. "I assure you, everything is all right."

Aljeron walked over to where Koshti stood, and leaning over, whispered in his ear. Koshti knelt down, but Joraiem could see he was far from relaxed.

His attention to the tiger was diverted by a remarkable appearance at the far end of the ring. Ambling in from between two great trees was an enormous bear, as tall as Joraiem even though down on all fours. The bear was mostly deep brown, though the fur on his head was largely grey, especially around the eyes and on top of his head. A huge wooden pole, perhaps a span and a half in length and easily as thick as one of Joraiem's legs, was strapped to the bear's back.

The bear stood upright after entering the ring, looming a good two spans high when stretched out at his full height. With one great paw he grabbed the bottom of the pole on his back, sliding it out of whatever held it to him in one quick fluid motion. "You had better all think fast and move faster," Joraiem heard Caan say, "because you have just met a superior foe. Unless you work together flawlessly, you will soon be in a world of trouble and pain!"

Joraiem scrambled to one side of the ring, Rulalin to the other. Aljeron stood warily opposite the Great Bear, who came toward them, moving both gracefully and speedily. Joraiem felt the adrenaline rush through him. There was no time to think about how they should coordinate their attack, just the instinctive impulse to slip behind the bear and strike when he couldn't possibly defend against them all at once.

They never got that opportunity. Just as the Great Bear moved toward the space they had left open for him, he quickly stepped to the side and, with a lightning-fast jab of the great pole, smashed Rulalin in the chest, knocking him through the air and onto his back. Joraiem heard more than saw the blow, for even as the loud crack echoed across the ring, he was closing in behind the Great Bear to strike him on the back. As he swung his own staff through the air, the Great Bear whirled its weapon in a sweeping arc and caught Joraiem in the side, pushing him laterally toward Aljeron, who had also been moving in. After being pushed almost a span through the air, Joraiem flew off the end of the pole and tumbled several times in the grass in the middle of the ring. When he picked himself up, he saw Rulalin kneeling, doubled over and gasping for air, and Aljeron sitting empty handed not far away, holding his left hand gingerly and looking in stunned amazement at his staff, which had been knocked across the ring into the branches of a tree.

The Great Bear stood calmly, motionless in the center of the ring. Though the pole he had used to vanquish them was perhaps a span and a half long, it didn't look so big in his enormous paw as he held it upright in front of his body. He leaned lackadaisically upon it, as though nothing of any significance had just taken place. He appeared about as taxed as if he'd just brushed a few flies away from his head.

As Joraiem slowly staggered to his feet, feeling the ache of his bruised side and ribs, Caan called Saegan, Darias, and Kelvan to come forward. Joraiem stepped out of the ring as quickly as he was able, taking a seat beside Aljeron. Rulalin joined them walking slowly and deliberately, trying hard, Joraiem thought, not to show how much pain he was in. But as he approached, Joraiem could hear him wheezing.

"You doing all right?" Aljeron asked quietly.

Rulalin nodded, not really looking in their direction. "Yeah," he said after a moment. "I'm just trying to catch my breath."

"He gave you a pretty stiff blow," Joraiem said. "I couldn't tell how hard Aljeron got it, though, because I was face down in the dirt."

Aljeron laughed at that, and even Rulalin allowed himself the slightest of smiles. Aljeron gazed across the ring at the Great Bear, still standing quietly as Caan distributed staffs to the next three. "He's every bit as remarkable as I would have expected," he said in admiration. "My father has met some Great Bear, but I've never seen one."

"Me neither," Joraiem said. "Both the Great Bear and the Voiceless seemed almost unreal to me as a boy, creatures of myth. The stories of the one were as hard to imagine as the stories of the other. When I saw a Malekim, though, the tales of their size and strength, not to mention the stories of their malice and cruelty—like the one you told, Aljeron—all of these became believable. It struck me that the Great Bear must be very great if in truth they really were the scourge of the Malekim. I don't doubt the claim now."

Saegan, Darias, and Kelvan had begun to approach the Great Bear. What happened took only a matter of seconds. As the three approached, Kelvan, who was on the far right, didn't even get a chance to raise his staff as the Great Bear swiftly swung his pole in a short arc, clipping Kelvan in the shoulder and tumbling him backward to the ground. Even as the Great Bear did this, he also prepared for the others, who were closing in from the opposite side. He adjusted the pole, holding it by one end, and swung it in a great arc that was meant to catch Saegan on the side and thrust him sideways toward Darias. Saegan somehow avoided the swinging pole by dropping almost completely to the ground as the pole passed above his head.

Seeing that he had missed his target, the Great Bear altered the trajectory of his swing so that he knocked Darias's staff from his hands. Stepping toward Darias, he thrust the pole forward and caught Darias in the stomach, doubling him over, then, with a stiff though not too terribly forceful tap on his back, knocked him down. Joraiem was amazed to notice that since the moment Saegan dodged his blow, the Great Bear hadn't taken his eyes off him. He dealt with Darias swiftly and effectively without even giving him his full attention. Now he stood with the pole extended in Saegan's direction, as the two circled each other warily.

Back on his feet with dirt all over his side and grass in his hair, Saegan moved in quickly and with determination, holding his staff defensively, perhaps hoping to deflect any sudden strikes. If the Great Bear had looked lackadaisical moments ago, he did not look so now, and Saegan did not evade him a second time. With speed and agility that made his previous moves look lethargic, the Great Bear stepped directly into Saegan's path and, gripping his pole firmly in the middle, struck

Saegan's staff and knocked it several spans away. Then, in a flash, the other end of the pole came swinging back hard in a downward motion that caught Saegan just behind his right knee, sweeping his leg out from underneath him. Saegan twirled in a sort of semi-circle as he fell hard into the grass. The Great Bear stepped to the side and again stood still.

"The Great Bear are remarkable, aren't they?" a voice said from beside Joraiem. Valzaan stood nearby, his hands resting on the carved King Falcon that graced the top of his staff.

"Master Valzaan," Joraiem said, surprised. "Welcome to the practice ring. What brings you here today?"

"I came to speak to Sarneth," Valzaan replied, directing his attention at Joraiem, Rulalin, and Aljeron. "I haven't seen him in a very long time."

"Sarneth?" Joraiem said, as all three of them stole a quick glance across the ring at the Great Bear.

"You know this Great Bear?" Aljeron added.

"Yes, I know him well. He is one of the few who still travels beyond the draals and holds commerce with the outside world. Sarneth may be our best hope for reconciliation between Great Bear and men, for he is honored as a lord among them, and his heart is grieved over the division that has torn us apart."

"Is his status due to his abilities as a warrior, or are all Great Bear as nimble and strong as he?" Rulalin asked.

Valzaan laughed before answering. "Sarneth is honored primarily for his wisdom. In human terms, all of the Great Bears are old, but he is old even by the Great Bears' reckoning. If anything, he is a step slower than the average Great Bear."

"If he's old and slow," Aljeron said, "I'd like to see a Great Bear in his prime."

"When roused in their wrath, they are terrible to behold. I have seen what they can do when pushed to it. Still, you have nothing to fear from them. I have never seen a Great Bear angry at any creature in Kirthanin that was not in the service of Malek."

"Even after Corindel?" Rulalin asked, doubtful.

"Yes, even after Corindel. If you had listened to what you have been told before, you would know that. They do not hate us, Rulalin, but they are slow to trust humans. Not being human, they never understood how Malek could have compelled Corindel's betrayal, for no Great Bear, under any circumstance, would have betrayed a draal. The idea that a friend could be turned into an enemy wasn't new to them, because they knew of Andunin's treachery. Corindel's betrayal, though, was more personal."

Caan summoned Pedraal, Pedraan, and Elyas to come forward and gave them also three staffs. Their exchange with Sarneth was brief. As large and strong as the twins were, the Great Bear stood twice as tall and wielded a weapon that the two of them together would have struggled to lift and swing. Their strength was no match for Sarneth, and lacking Saegan's reflexes, they could not evade his attack. Soon both they and Elyas, who barely did more than try to soften Sarneth's blow, were on the ground. Caan walked to the center of the ring and stood by Sarneth, summoning them all to come in.

"I want you all to meet our distinguished guest," Caan began. "This is Sarneth, and he has journeyed here from the Lindandraal, which lies just this side of the Arimaar Mountains, many leagues east and north of here. Sarneth does not always visit during the seventh-year gathering of the Novaana here in Sulare, so this is a treat for you."

"A painful treat," Pedraal said, grinning as he rubbed his right arm. The others laughed, even Sarneth, who had not to this point made a sound.

"If you had ever seen a Great Bear strike a serious blow, you would know that Sarneth was actually being gentle with you," Caan replied.

The men looked at one another, and Aljeron said, "I, for one, am grateful that you were gentle. I'd hate to feel your staff when you intend to harm. I'm Aljeron, and it is a pleasure to meet you, Master Sarneth."

Aljeron bowed slightly as he said this, but as he stood, Sarneth placed his massive paw gently on Aljeron's shoulder, and the Great Bear leaned over so that his head was only a little bit above Aljeron. "The pleasure is mine, Aljeron, and you do not need to call me Master. I am a humble servant of Allfather as are you. You were a worthy opponent."

"I was completely overmatched," Aljeron said, surprised.

"You are young and inexperienced in battle. I have known combat since my youth, long before you were born. You could not have been expected to be successful today, and yet you moved when you were told and approached with all the skill you had. Your courage makes up for whatever skills you lacked, making you a worthy opponent indeed."

"Courage? I didn't even get close to touching you."

"Courage is not measured by the success of the venture, but by that venture's size. For a warrior to do as his commander tells him without question and despite great odds is both honorable and courageous. I salute you, Aljeron, indeed, I salute you all."

Valzaan joined the group huddled around Sarneth. "Greetings, old friend," Valzaan said. "Allfather's blessing upon you and your draal forever."

Sarneth stepped forward and the ring parted to let him pass. He stopped before Valzaan and stooped onto one knee to lower his head to Valzaan's level. His respect for the prophet was clear. "Valzaan, it has been too long. I accept your greetings and return them, asking that Allfather would shine his favor upon you, that you who appeared with the dawn would continue in the Kirthanin sun. Sunset is coming, Valzaan, do you not feel it?"

"I do, Sarneth, I do." Valzaan reached out his hand and for a moment fumbled to find Sarneth's shoulder. It struck Joraiem that this was the first time he'd ever seen Valzaan's blindness evident in such a way. In fact, at times Joraiem had wondered if Valzaan really was blind, since he seemed so capable of doing all he needed without help.

Valzaan leaned in toward Sarneth, and for a long moment he talked quietly in his ear so that none of them could hear. They watched though, as Sarneth listened intently, from time to time nodding his head. Joraiem looked intently at Sarneth's eyes, which were deep brown with flecks of light grey. They seemed both kind and stern, sober and wise. Joraiem wondered what they had seen. He also wondered what he and the other Novaana must look like to Sarneth—large dolls perhaps, or Great Bear children without the fur.

Valzaan lifted his head suddenly and stepped away from Sarneth, facing the trees that lined the northeastern portion of the ring. Someone behind Joraiem started to speak, but Valzaan raised his hand to silence him. Sarneth stood to his full height and peered toward the trees as well, and Koshti darted out across the space toward them. He began to trot back and forth along the edge of the ring.

Then Joraiem felt it, an urgent, almost frantic sense of danger. The feeling pulsed and throbbed like panic, but without the sense of helplessness that panic brings. He felt the sweat that already lined his brow begin to trickle down his face and neck and chest. He scanned the faces he could see, including Aljeron's, and even though he couldn't have explained how, he knew they couldn't feel the same sensation. He immediately understood that what he felt was not natural. The experience was like *torrim redara*, which he had experienced first by the dragon tower and a few times since coming to Sulare. This, too, seemed to flow from the very core of his being, and yet, paradoxically, it also seemed to connect him with a presence and a power far greater than himself. Valzaan had said Joraiem would never fully get used to it, because it was the feeling of Allfather's presence as He worked in and through His servants. Joraiem felt that presence now, and it told him that Valzaan sensed it too. It was all Joraiem could do to calm himself as the pounding within worked itself into a frenzy.

Valzaan turned to the others and said clearly but softly, "Draw your weapons and draw close to one another, now! Form a circle, facing out."

Most of the men still held the staffs they had wielded against Sarneth, and a few even had knives. Quickly they formed a circle surrounding the women. Joraiem stepped over to Caan, who had his sword out and was focusing intently on the trees before him.

"Did I see your bow by the bench earlier?" Joraiem whispered.

Caan nodded, but didn't speak.

"May I use it?"

Again Caan nodded.

Joraiem darted across the open space to a bench some ten spans away, and as he stooped to pick the bow and quiver up out of the grass, a series of howls from the trees beyond chilled him. He ran quickly back to the group. "Black Wolves," he said.

"Yes," Valzaan answered.

"I thought Black Wolves preferred the night?" Aljeron asked.

"They do."

"Then what's going on?"

"I don't know."

The group became silent again, and Joraiem noticed a tug on his shirt from behind. He turned to see Bryar.

"I want your staff," she said.

"What?"

"If you're going to use that bow, I want your staff. I don't want to be defenseless when those wolves get here. Besides, I'm as good with it as most of you."

Joraiem looked at the determination in her eyes and then handed her the staff that had been lying at his feet. "Take it."

"Thanks."

She gripped it firmly, then stepped back into the circle. Joraiem watched her for a moment, but soon regretted it. The younger girls were huddled together, some of them crying, while Karalin, Mindarin, and Wylla tried to comfort them. Wylla looked up and tried to smile bravely at Joraiem. Joraiem's heart sank. If they failed to keep the wolves away, if he failed, the consequences would be horrific. He couldn't fail.

Several tense moments passed. No one spoke, and if anyone moved, it was only to nervously shift feet. The howling did not continue, and Elyas said hopefully, "Perhaps they've gone away."

"They're still coming," Joraiem said.

"They are almost upon us," Valzaan added at the exact same-moment.

The pulsating within Joraiem had peaked, and he felt himself readying the bow, expecting Black Wolves to emerge into the clearing at any moment. Seconds later Koshti dashed across the clearing just in time to meet an enormous Black Wolf as it broke into the open. The tiger leapt through the air upon the wolf, and that was the last Joraiem saw of that fight, for chaos broke out all around him.

To his left, Valzaan stepped forward with his staff raised high, the carved face of the windhover almost glowing. A Black Wolf leapt over a row of short bushes at the edge of the tree-line and started toward the prophet. Valzaan said something Joraiem did not understand, and a flash of light enveloped the clearing. The Black Wolf erupted into flame. It howled and shrieked as it continued forward a few steps before stumbling to the ground, a smoldering heap of flesh and fur.

On Joraiem's right, Sarneth faced two Black Wolves. His wooden pole twirled and flashed in his paws as he carefully held both at bay. Sarneth moved nimbly and struck quickly, stepping to his right and bringing the pole down with awesome speed and strength on one wolf's head. The cracking of the shattered skull echoed through the clearing, and the wolf fell into a crumpled, lifeless mass. Sarneth whirled smoothly to prevent the second Black Wolf from slipping past him.

The circle started to expand as pairs of men tried to keep the Black Wolves from penetrating it. Joraiem, arrow nocked and ready, quickly surveyed the clearing and grew alarmed. Near him, Pedraal and Pedraan worked to keep a couple wolves outside the circle, as did Aljeron and Rulalin, Saegan and Darias, Elyas and Kelvan, along with Caan and even Valzaan, who was wielding his staff defensively. Joraiem could see how easy it would be for a wolf still lurking in the trees to make a run at the women, still trying to huddle together in their center. Only Bryar guarded them, holding her staff, and she wasn't able to guard all sides.

At that moment, a Black Wolf jumped one of the benches near the outer edge of the clearing, dodged behind Darias on the one side and Rulalin on the other, and ran straight for the women. Joraiem held Caan's bow, wishing more than ever that it was Suruna, and took aim. The Black Wolf cut the distance to the women to just under five spans, and Joraiem fired the arrow. It hit the wolf in the neck just under its jaw and forced him sideways. As it fell, Bryar pounced, striking it repeatedly with the staff as she stomped on its wounded neck with her boot.

Quickly Joraiem grabbed another arrow, but he wasn't quick enough. A second Black Wolf entered his peripheral vision. Joraiem spun reflexively, his arms raised to deflect the leaping wolf, but as the creature jumped, Pedraal landed a stiff blow to it midair, knocking it onto the grass. As the creature rolled to regain his feet, Pedraan leapt on top of the wolf, grabbing the sides of its head just behind the jaw with his powerful hands. The wolf thrashed and snarled, but Pedraan hung on, smashing the wolf's head against the ground repeatedly until the body went limp.

"Thanks," Joraiem said, as he held his bow ready.

"Sure," Pedraan said, grinning as he looked around to see where he might be needed most. He twirled the staff like he was preparing for one of Caan's exercises instead of facing a life-or-death struggle with Black Wolves in the service of Malek.

Joraiem waited for the next attack, but none came. Few Black Wolves remained in the clearing, at least few that were alive. Many bodies lay on the ground, some bloody and at least one still smoking. Joraiem didn't relax, though, wondering how many more might still be lurking under cover of the trees.

As he turned to his left, he saw a pair of Black Wolves darting back into the trees. Koshti shot after them, his mouth bloody and his claws tearing up the grass. Aljeron dashed into the trees behind him.

"Aljeron, wait!" Joraiem called after him, but Aljeron did not wait. Joraiem started to follow, and the twins did too. "Stay with the women!" Joraiem yelled as he ran through the brush.

Faster and in better shape, Joraiem soon caught up to Aljeron. He fell into step with his friend and both plunged wildly through the trees, trusting the bond between Aljeron and Koshti to direct them through the dense wood. The branches hung low, obstructing their visibility. Joraiem's fear that they might be running blindly into a trap was replaced by his fear that they would impale themselves on a tree branch. Unless they emerged into open ground soon, one or both of them were going to get hurt.

A few moments later, they did emerge onto a broad, grassy

plain. In that open place, it was easy to spot Koshti's orange fur as he raced after the two black forms. Joraiem admired the power of the tiger as it ran with a speed Joraiem had never seen in any horse. It was soon apparent that Koshti would catch the pair, but Joraiem also knew he would only be able to take down one of the wolves.

Then Koshti did. He sprang forward onto the Black Wolf that was trailing just slightly, and his front claws locked onto the creature's back, forcing him to the ground. The wolf tried to roll out from underneath the tiger, but Koshti held him fast. He lifted his majestic head and opened his bloody mouth to roar, then buried his jaws in the wolf's neck.

The free wolf paused for just a moment and turned to look at his fallen friend, and Joraiem knew this would be the closest he would get. He stopped running and lifted the bow, arrow ready on the string. He took aim as quickly as he could and let the arrow fly. The arrow soared across the spans between them and struck the dirt just under the Black Wolf's head, sparking the creature's renewed flight.

"I missed!" Joraiem said.

"Of course you missed," Aljeron said, catching his breath. "That wolf must have been almost fifty spans away. Even you aren't that good."

"If I'd had Suruna," Joraiem said fiercely, "that wolf would be dead."

Aljeron looked at Joraiem. "I believe you, but there's nothing to be done now. He's gone. Let's get Koshti and get back to the others."

A half hour later, dragging the dead wolf behind them, Joraiem and Aljeron reached the combat ring. Joraiem did a quick head count and smiled with relief to see that all were alive and accounted for. Sarneth stood talking to Valzaan near the mound of carcasses, which the other men had built while they were gone. Kelvan sat upright in the grass next to Bryar, who held what appeared to be a cloak against his side as many of the other women hovered nearby. As it turned out, one of the creatures had ripped into his side with its claw. The cuts were deep, but Caan assured them Kelvan would recover. Caan himself was limping around the combat circle with a makeshift bandage wrapped around his calf. As Caan was driving his sword through the head of one Black Wolf, another sunk its teeth into the instructor's leg. The wolf paid for that bite with his life, as Caan had managed to free his sword and drive it down and backward through the creature's throat. The jaws of the dead wolf had needed to be pried off with the sword tip, but Caan swore that he was fine.

Koshti's dead wolf made eighteen, Valzaan told Joraiem and Aljeron as they added it to the pile of carcasses. Those eighteen, plus the one that had escaped, meant that at least nineteen Black Wolves had been in the clearing.

Pedraal asked the question on everyone's mind. "What were they doing here?"

"I don't know," Valzaan answered. "But it is clear they were after one or all of us. It cannot be a coincidence that we encountered a pack of Black Wolves on the road to Sulare, and now a pack has struck us here."

"If they meant to kill one or all of us," Saegan said, "surely they would have brought more. They couldn't have thought that nineteen would be enough to take a group of armed men, especially with a Great Bear and Valzaan the prophet among them."

"Had they come another day, they might not have found either Sarneth or me among you. In fact, had they come another day at a time when you were not armed and practicing here, they would have had little trouble in killing most or all of you. Allfather was watching over us today, and He deserves the thanks for our survival. Whatever their reason for coming, at least we can be grateful that the wounds received were not poisoned, and no one has been killed."

"I'm afraid that is not true," said someone from behind them all.

"Master Berin?" Valzaan said. All turned to face him. "What do you mean?"

"One of our stewards, Corlin, has been found dead, torn and mangled. I'd sent him down here with a message for Caan shortly before the howling began. I secured the Hall and armed my other men before coming to help you, and I found him on the way."

One of the women began crying softly.

"You bear no responsibility in the boy's death, Berin," Valzaan said. "Both of you were only doing your duty."

"That is of little comfort now," Berin answered bitterly. "And I shall need more than that to comfort his mother."

Master Berin walked silently through their midst and to the edge of the pile. The carcasses lay draped across one another, smoke from the one struck down by Valzaan still creeping out from somewhere deep in the stack. Master Berin gazed at them, his eyes cold and emotionless, and after a long moment, he spat on the pile and turned away. "I want a mountain of wood gathered immediately. If there are more of this kind anywhere in Sulare, I want them to smell the burning flesh of their brothers and see the flames that are devouring their bones."

Everyone but Kelvan dispersed to gather wood, but he paused to listen as Master Berin spoke to the prophet.

"They have brought death to Sulare, Valzaan," he began, his voice quiet but hard. "After almost a thousand years of peace in this place, they have brought death back."

"They have, and there is nothing we can do about it now. Even had they not killed the boy, I would have little doubt that the relative calm and peace of the Third Age is in jeopardy. Malek is stirring."

"What are you saying? Have you had a prophecy, a revelation?"

"No. No specific prophecy of this," Valzaan answered.

Joraiem breathed a sigh of relief, but too soon.

"Nevertheless," Valzaan added, "I feel in my bones that time is short. The Black Wolves have brought more than death to Sulare; they have done more than disturb the tranquility of this peaceful haven. As I listened to them come, I heard in their footfalls the sound of doom."

11

A LIGHT ON THE HORIZON

THE LIGHT THE FLAMES cast on the dark beach was fading, but the heat from the fire was still strong. Joraiem knew without looking at his companions what would still be on their exhausted and grieving faces, so he looked instead at the night sky above Sulare. Rarely had he gazed into the summer sky here and found it empty, but heavy clouds had rolled in off the Southern Ocean, covering the land as far as the eye could see. There was no moon, no stars, no light of any kind from the heavens. It looked like storm weather, but Joraiem, who usually had a good feel for rain before it came, could not sense it now.

He could feel the south wind that had brought the clouds still blowing the cooler ocean air over the beach. On any number of recent, stifling hot days, that breeze would have been a welcome change, but tonight it was an intruder, taking the edge off of the warmth they all so desperately sought.

After the attack, they had trudged wearily and silently back to the Great Hall, passing Falin and some of the stewards tearfully mourning over Corlin's shrouded body, which lay on a stone slab under an arbor. Though Falin withdrew from the crowd to enter the Great Hall with them, the other stewards did not look up. Joraiem heard one of the women from behind him start to sob again, but he didn't turn to see who it was. He didn't think it was Wylla, but he wasn't sure he could have handled turning to find her tearful.

Their dinner was silent, so silent that the splashing of the fountain, usually soothing and peaceful, sounded loud and unpleasant. Though he didn't feel like eating, the smell of warm stew brought Joraiem's appetite back, and he hungrily devoured it. When finished, he felt guilty, even though he knew it was irrational. The dead couldn't begrudge the living a full stomach, especially since they'd fought to prevent more from dying.

Valzaan and Sarneth withdrew to a smaller table some distance away. A great stone bench near the fountain had to be moved to accommodate Sarneth, and even then it looked hardly adequate to support his body. Soon Master Berin, along with Caan and Ulmindos, drifted over to join them. Joraiem couldn't hear what they were talking about, but the conversation was certainly animated. At one point, when the volume of their discourse rose high enough that their voices if not their words could be heard across the hall, Valzaan brought his staff down with a crack upon the paved floor and brought the conversation to a halt. He said something and the conversation continued, but without the same amount of shouting and demonstration.

When they finished, they led the young Novaana down to the beach where they had "tended the fire" their first night in Sulare, and where they had gathered many evenings since. Tonight, though, they went because they were exhausted but did not want to go to their beds to lie awake and wait for sleep. They craved each other's company, not simply out of a wish for security and safety, but because they didn't wish to be alone with the memories of the afternoon.

So Joraiem looked again toward the horizon and the night-time sky for a sign, anything that might signal an end to the day's waking nightmare. He sighed as he lowered his head. There was no light to be seen anywhere.

About a quarter of the way around the circle, Bryar watched over Kelvan, who'd fallen asleep beside the fire with his head in her lap. The wounds in his stomach weren't so bad he couldn't walk, but he moved slowly. Master Berin had encouraged him to stay in one of the rooms of the Great Hall where Falin and Merya could tend him, but Kelvan insisted on coming to the fire with the others. He'd come, at his own pace, with Bryar helping each step of the way.

Bryar stroked Kelvan's hair. Joraiem watched them, unable to remember the precise moment the two of them had stopped trying to keep their mutual affection a secret. Perhaps even they didn't know. Joraiem was not surprised that their love for one another had been too much to conceal in this place of bright summer skies and cool ocean breezes, and as he looked at them, he found himself thinking of his own parents. He scanned the circle, wondering if there were other hearts even now inclining toward one another. He hadn't noticed anything to suggest it, although the young cousins, Tarin and Valia, giggled more than usual any time Saegan was near. For his part, Saegan hardly seemed to notice either of them, or any of the women for that matter.

Joraiem realized that he had stopped scanning the circle and was now looking at Wylla, who sat on the other side of Kelvan. He thought he should look away but quickly realized he didn't want to. Wylla was so lovely, her bright eyes reflecting the embers of the fire and her long dark hair falling both before and behind her shoulders. She was leaning forward with her chin resting upon her hands, which lay on her knees.

Inside himself he heard a voice saying, "I love her," and he struggled to silence it. He argued with himself, reasoning that he didn't really, that the thought was merely a result of the day's emotional strain. And yet, Joraiem knew that this was not the case. The events of the day had in fact stripped away his pretense and efforts to avoid the truth: he loved Wylla, desperately.

He recognized the same denial of his love for Alina at work in himself now. He could see the same thoughts that led to the same evasions. There was no sense in lying to himself anymore, though. He loved Wylla. She was not only the most beautiful woman he'd ever seen, she was also kind and gentle, bright and cheerful. Her presence brought him joy, sheer joy, and when she wasn't around, his life felt heavier.

He had no idea what to do. He should speak to Rulalin, explain what had happened, but deep down he knew he could not. Rulalin would never be able to see Joraiem's love as anything short of betrayal. This would be a mess, perhaps a much bigger mess than he already knew. He was pretty sure that Wylla did not return Rulalin's interest. If Rulalin kept trying to force the issue, she would one day run out of gracious ways to emphasize her appreciation of Rulalin's *friendship*. Joraiem could tell that Wylla was hoping Rulalin would give up, but until she explicitly rejected him, he would surely cling to the hope that her feelings would one day change. When she finally did reject him, well, Joraiem shuddered to think about what that might mean to the cohesion of the group. That scenario did not take into account the possibility that Wylla might return Joraiem's affection for her. Wylla rejecting Rulalin would be unpleasant; if Wylla rejected Rulalin in favor of Joraiem, it could be ugly.

To love Wylla openly as Bryar and Kelvan loved each other would invite permanent division between Rulalin and Joraiem, among the group here, and possibly throughout their lives as leaders in the Assembly. The political consequences could be far-reaching. Rulalin would be an important figure as a representative of Fel Edorath, and Wylla would be queen of Enthanin. Even if Joraiem gave up his place in Suthanin to live with Wylla in Amaan Sul, as surely he would if she returned his love and they were married, it was possible that Rulalin would make life difficult for them for years to come.

Or Rulalin might get over it. Maybe after the question was finally settled he would be able to let it go. After all, though learning of Alina's engagement had been difficult, Joraiem had survived. Perhaps Rulalin would learn to love again, once freed of his attachment to Wylla. Joraiem looked from Wylla to Rulalin, who was sitting with legs crossed, also gazing into the fire. Joraiem considered the intensity in Rulalin's eyes, and he felt the fear and uncertainty return. He sighed. Rulalin wouldn't deal with losing Wylla well, that he knew.

Wylla's loveliness drew his gaze back to her. Looking on her brought him some comfort. This time, his love had not made itself known too late for him to do something about it. Still, though the situation with Alina had been bad, in many ways this felt worse.

These thoughts plus his weariness had almost reached the point where he was ready to excuse himself, but as Joraiem considered leaving, Aljeron broke the silence that had covered them like a shroud for more than an hour.

"Master Valzaan, you suggested earlier that what happened on our way to Sulare was connected to what happened today, but I can't make sense of it. I've been trying to, but I can't. To attack weary travelers sleeping beside the road in the darkness seems a bit different than attacking a group of armed men in broad daylight."

Valzaan continued to gaze into the fire. "If it's logic you're seeking, then you might as well stop. What is logical to us and what is logical to Malek or Malek's creatures may be very different things."

"Malek is skulking in his lair deep inside Agia Muldonai. Why do you speak of him?" Saegan said this with something of a low growl, as though just saying the name irritated him.

"I speak of him because he, and no other, commands the Black Wolves," Valzaan answered sharply. "The will of Malek led them here, of that you can be sure. And how do you know that Malek is 'skulking' in the depths of Agia Muldonai?"

Murmurs spread around the circle. Rulalin looked up and answered. "Malek does not leave the Mountain. The men of Fel Edorath in the west and many Enthanim in the east make sure of that. We have been vigilant in this for almost a thousand years!"

"Don't be naïve. You know as well as I do that Malekim and Black Wolves go to and from Agia Muldonai, both through the Forest of Gyrin to the south and through the wilderness of Nolthanin in the north. Do you really think that Malek has simply been sitting for a thousand years, waiting? No! I tell you it is not so! He was crippled physically when Alazare cast him from the Holy Mountain, but he is still powerful. If he desired, he could pass through our midst without our knowing."

A whimper escaped young Talia, and Wylla quickly tried to steady her, whispering in her ear. Valzaan shook his head and sighed. "Forgive me, I did not mean to frighten you, and I apologize to you, Saegan, and to you, Rulalin, for speaking sharply. I spoke out of heaviness of heart. I am frustrated. I didn't see the attack until the Black Wolves were upon us, and I can't see even now why they have come. It's all dark. There is nothing but darkness all around."

"You don't need to apologize to me, Master Valzaan," Saegan said. "I am not a child that I should pout over hard words, provided they are true. Do you really believe Malek moves freely about Kirthanin?"

"I did not mean to suggest that he is out, roaming Kirthanin as we sit here," Valzaan said, "but I do think it foolish to believe we somehow have him trapped in Agia Muldonai. If he remains hidden there, it is the result of his own choice and not our armies, as vigilant as they may be. Standing against Malek when he issues forth again will be hard enough without overestimating ourselves and underestimating him. I don't know for sure that he has left Agia Muldonai, but there have been times, a few times, when I have been sure that Malek was closer to me than to the Holy Mountain. I have no proof of this, but I believe it."

Joraiem asked the next question. "What about the Black Wolf that got away? Do you have any sense for what became of him?"

"I think he is gone," Valzaan answered, and Joraiem felt relieved. He had tried while they were burning the others to reach out for a sense of the escaped Black Wolf, but he had found nothing. "If there had been more nearby, they would have all come together," Valzaan continued. "I would guess that he has gone to report to whomever sent him about the failure of their mission, presuming that it was a failure."

"You mean he's gone back to Malek?" Mindarin asked, incredulously.

"His orders likely originated with Malek, but it is unlikely they came from him directly," Valzaan answered. "There are many creatures that do Malek's bidding, and there are many ways he can communicate with those under his command. I don't know where the wolf has gone, nor do I care. Malek chose to attack, and if he chooses to come again, that will also be his choice. We have no control over what he does."

Again, murmurs spread around the fire. Joraiem looked at Valzaan, who did not offer comfort or reassurance. It was Sarneth who helped to calm them with his low and steady voice. "What Valzaan means to say, I think, is that we need to do the job that lies before us, for it is our calling only to prepare for the dark day when it comes. We cannot choose what day it shall be. It is pointless to worry over those things we cannot control, but it is wisdom to prepare for those things we know are going to come."

"Well said, Sarneth," Valzaan said. "Your presence and your words do much to comfort me. I'm glad you are here tonight."

"And I'm glad you were here today," Pedraal added. "You were amazing against those Black Wolves."

Sarneth moved as though to reply when two things happened suddenly and simultaneously. First, Joraiem noticed a brilliant flash of light appear out over the waters of the Southern Ocean. It was as though an explosion of light somewhere beyond the horizon had suddenly occurred, and immediately the darkness that had just moments ago seemed overwhelming and impenetrable was now pierced by the sparkling rays that dominated the southern sky. Second, Joraiem felt himself sliding quickly, very quickly, into *torrim redara*. In his first experience the shift had occurred gradually; this time he blinked and knew at once that he had stepped out of time as he knew it. The others did not move, the breeze no longer whisked in off of the sea, and the flames of the fire stood still before him. Only Valzaan, across the circle, still moved.

Valzaan stood, his face turned toward the southern sky where the bright flash of light also hung frozen above the waters. "Joraiem," Valzaan said without turning, his voice firm but full of something close to wonder, "I need you to do exactly as I say."

"Yes, Master Valzaan," Joraiem answered, trying to sound calm but fearing that he was not being successful.

"It is time for another lesson in *torrim redara*, and you will need to follow my directions carefully. Understood?"

"Yes."

"Stand up."

Joraiem stood, but as he did, he felt a bit dizzy.

"Good," Valzaan said as Joraiem struggled to keep his balance. "What you are feeling is normal. Moving in *torrim tedara* is not so much difficult as unusual. The dizziness is something you'll get used to, but it never goes away. Now walk with me down to the water's edge."

Joraiem joined Valzaan just beyond the circle and walked toward the water's edge with him. When they were close enough to the water that the waves lapped at their bare feet, Valzaan stopped.

"When you feel yourself beginning to slip out of slow time, try to hold back the transition in your mind and return to your seat immediately. Real time will not allow you to step back into its flow in a different place than the place from which you left. If you are not where you were when you entered slow time, real time will pull you immediately and painfully back to that place. It is a jolt that the body does not appreciate, I assure you. Are you following me?"

"I think so," Joraiem said, looking back up the beach toward the still circle around the unmoving fire. He was not at all sure he did follow, nor did he know how he could hold the transition back, since in none of his excursions either into or out of slow time had he felt the least bit in control. Still, if he was in any real danger, he was sure that Valzaan would help him. Mostly sure, anyway.

"Now," Valzaan said, placing his hand on Joraiem's shoulder. "Look out over the water and tell me what you see."

"I see a brilliant light, flooding the whole horizon. It, it's like a fantastic explosion of light."

"Can you tell where it is coming from?"

"Not exactly," Joraiem said, straining as he looked. "Although, for some reason it doesn't seem to be from above the horizon, it looks as though it has come up out of the horizon, like some bright star suddenly rising out of the sea."

"It is as I feared."

"Feared? Isn't it something wonderful? The light has swept the gloom of night away!"

"Not all light brings hope."

"I don't understand."

Valzaan turned toward Joraiem, but extended his arm and staff out over the wave, pointing in the direction of the flash of light hanging suspended over the water. "The light that you see, you say it looks as though it is coming up from under the horizon, not like something shining down from above it. Correct?"

"Yes, it looks like it is shooting up from somewhere beyond the curvature of the horizon, like a flood erupting from the sea."

"I believe you," Valzaan said, turning back toward the water. "A ship coming home across the water appears to those who stand at a distance as though it is rising up out of the midst of the water itself. That is the nature of things. Light that comes from a distant place, a place so far away that it lies beyond our vision, appears as it approaches us as though it were coming up from out of the water, when in fact it is only shining outward across the water. Do you understand now?"

Joraiem was puzzled and looked back over the water. "You are saying that the light is coming from somewhere beyond our sight, somewhere over the horizon, but there is nothing out there but—" Joraiem suddenly stopped. He did see. If Valzaan was right, then this was something far more nightmarish than the appearance of the Black Wolves. "Can it be, Valzaan?"

"It would seem that it is, whether I thought it could be or not."

"But how? There is nothing on the Forbidden Isle anymore."

"So we thought."

They stood in silence, and Joraiem tried to comprehend

what this must mean. Something, or someone, was even now active on the Forbidden Isle, and this explosion of light must have been produced by some devilry at work there.

"Now I understand why Allfather has called me here," Valzaan whispered. "Malek has returned to the Forbidden Isle. Only he has the kind of power that could create a light visible this far away. Only he would dare to walk on that shore, to tread the long empty streets of Nal Gildoroth. This is grievous news." He turned to Joraiem, gripping his shoulder firml. "Joraiem, Allfather hasn't given me much time to teach you about your gifts. I don't know where all of this will go, but you may need to make a choice, and soon. It may be that you will have to choose between your companions here and training with me. I can't tell you which to choose, but there is much that I would show you. Come, let's return to the fire, I must tell the others. It would appear that there will be no real rest for us today."

They walked back to the fire, and Joraiem took his seat again in the sand beside the motionless fire. The strange light-headedness that swept over him was all the warning of the change that he had, and before he knew it, he had returned to real time.

All around him, startled gasps and cries were erupting as his companions stood and turned toward the water.

"What is it?"

"Where does it come from?"

"What does it mean?"

The shimmering light danced across the water, drawing them away from the fire and down the beach. They stared in stunned amazement at the strange and wondrous phenomena.

"I think I know the answer to most of your questions."

Valzaan's voice broke the trance, and they turned to look

at Valzaan, who stood a few steps behind them with Joraiem at his side.

Aljeron stepped forward, excited and curious. Joraiem could see in his eyes the same hopefulness that he himself had possessed when first he saw the light, something that seemed distant now. "Master Valzaan, what can you tell us of this mystery?"

"I can tell you that this light is not a portent of hope as you desire. You must know that first and know it absolutely. You must brace yourselves, for this is not good news to face after such a day."

They looked at one another, the excitement replaced by fear and grim expectation. "Tell us what needs to be said," Saegan growled as he stepped up beside Aljeron. "Whatever it is, it's best we know straight out."

Valzaan pointed his staff out over the water, as he had done in slow time. "The light comes from the Forbidden Isle."

Utter silence greeted that revelation. "There is little doubt that this means Malek has been there or is possibly there still," Valzaan said. "Whatever is going on, only his power could have created a light so clearly visible this far away."

"What does that mean?" Aljeron said, holding his voice steady, though Joraiem could tell it was not without effort.

"I don't know all that it means, but it means at least this much: You had all best go and get whatever sleep the night may still hold. At first light, we must gather in the Great Hall for an emergency council. If Malek is indeed at work on the Forbidden Isle, then we, standing here, are the closest to him of Allfather's servants and must bear the weight of decision over what to do."

"What can we do?" Wylla asked, holding her voice as calmly as Aljeron had managed to.

Valzaan shrugged and turned his back on the water, his figure now silhouetted by the light. "That is what we will meet to decide in the morning."

Wylla received Valzaan's calm and simple answer without any visible reaction. Slowly, the others around her began to slip silently back up the beach, but Wylla did not move with them. Instead, she stood looking at the water. Joraiem thought about walking down to comfort her, but as he started forward, he saw Rulalin step up to her and speak softly in her ear. Joraiem turned and walked back up the beach.

Sleep did not come right away for anyone, but eventually the even, deep breathing from across the room confirmed that Pedraal and Kelvan were asleep. A strong wind was gusting through the house, and suddenly a brilliant flash of light split the sky. This flash, though, was lightning, and it was followed by the low and distant rumble of thunder. Dense pellets of rain began to slap against the roof, and some fell on Joraiem through the south facing window. Soon, the rain was falling in torrents as streaks of lighting dropped with remarkable speed and brilliance upon the ocean waters in the distance. Though Joraiem had sensed no rain, the black clouds had indeed brought the storm they heralded. Was this also from the Forbidden Isle? Could this raging storm be the creation of Malek, a harbinger of things to come?

Joraiem did not know, and his intuition wasn't telling him anything. The only message he was receiving was the desperate plea of his aching body for sleep. He lay back, watching the light show. Gradually, the rhythmic pounding of the rain on the roof sent him to sleep, as the occasional raindrop splashed his exposed face.

The storm raged overhead, and the rain fell on Joraiem's bare chest. He wore no shirt, and his light pants were soaked and clinging to his legs. He was panting from the long run, and only then did he realize that he had stopped to catch his breath. Evrim stood beside him, almost doubled over. Joraiem had always known that his training would stand him in good stead one day, but he was nervous about his friend, who didn't look like he could keep up the pace much longer.

"You all right?"

Evrim nodded without straightening up. "Yeah," he said with a gasp.

"I don't think we should pause too long."

"I know. Almost ready."

Joraiem listened to the sound of the wind whipping through the branches above him. He couldn't hear the howls anymore. Could he and Evrim have finally given them the slip? He turned back to Evrim. "It's great to see you again. It's been too long."

Evrim finally looked up, grinning. "Likewise."

"And you were worried I wouldn't be back," Joraiem said, poking Evrim playfully on the shoulder.

"Guess I was wrong."

"Yeah you were, I—"

The piercing sound of a wolf's howl on the wind interrupted them, and Joraiem bounded away with Evrim following closely behind.

How long they had been running was hard for Joraiem to guess. His legs were unusually heavy. He would only be this tired if he had run for many miles. Exactly where and when the Black Wolves had picked up the chase also eluded his recollection. He didn't strain his memory too much, as losing his focus at this particular moment wouldn't have done him any good.

Soon Joraiem found the relatively dense woods giving way to an open field. He turned to look for Evrim but couldn't see him. Joraiem stopped on the edge of the field, trying to decide what to do. He hadn't heard any cries or a struggle, so he didn't think that Evrim had been caught, but where was he? Most likely they had simply been separated in the darkness. Perhaps Evrim hadn't been able to keep up and had taken a different way.

He wanted to go back to look for Evrim, but he knew this was foolish. Evrim could take care of himself, and turning back into the woods would probably lead Joraiem to the wolves instead of his friend. No, he needed to keep going. Whispering a prayer to Allfather for Evrim's safety, he started out across the wide plain.

As he did, Joraiem noticed a large, dark form running toward him at an angle from a distance on the right. He slowed to look, thinking that perhaps it might be Evrim, even though he didn't understand how his friend could have gotten that far away from him so quickly. It only took seconds to realize his mistake, and soon he was off again, this time flying as fast as his fatigued body could carry him. He hadn't seen any of the Voiceless in the woods, but if that dark shape wasn't a Malekim, he wasn't one of the Novaana. He had seen that steady stride before.

He tore across the plain, angling away from the trees and the Malekim. The rain had slowed considerably, but even so, the water dripped from his hair, his ears, his nose, his arms, his fingers—from everything. He was waterlogged. His legs grew heavier by the moment and his chest was on fire. He couldn't keep up this pace much longer.

At that moment, he spotted several glowing lights in the distance. He locked his eyes upon them and ran. He soon discovered that the lights came from a large ship anchored at the end of a long quay just ahead. Without looking back, he dashed across the beach and onto the dock. His feet echoed off the wooden slats as he raced to the end of the quay. A narrow gangway stretched up to the deck of the ship. His foot hit the bottom of the gangway, and he pulled up short.

The dark water between the ship and the dock surged and fell below him. The now gentle but steady rain made light splashing noises as it fed the Southern Ocean. The cry of the wolves in the dark drew his attention. He couldn't see either the Malekim or the Black Wolves, but he could sense their encroaching presence. He turned toward the ship again and tried not to look down.

Wylla appeared on the deck at the top of the gangway, holding a lantern and smiling at him. She motioned with her hand for him to come quickly. He looked down at the roiling waters. He was frozen where he stood.

An intense shuddering reverberated through the boards under his feet, and he knew without looking that the Malekim had come. Its solid footsteps echoed even louder than his own had, and soon he felt the malevolence of the creature almost within reach. Closing his eyes, Joraiem leapt up the gangway. He took a few rapid strides upward, and then felt a tremendous crack beneath his feet. The gangway shattered and gave way, and he was falling amid the shards into the cold, dark water.

Joraiem opened his eyes and looked at the clear blue sky. The storm from the previous night had passed, and he could tell from how warm the morning was already that this was going to be another hot day. He looked over and saw Pedraal, already dressed, preparing to step out of the house.

"Pedraal, where is Kelvan?"

"Master Berin and some of the stewards came for him at first light. They took him up to the Great Hall to examine his wounds."

"Are you heading there now?"

"Yes, Valzaan wanted us there first thing."

"Would you wait for me?"

"Sure," Pedraal said with a half smile, "provided you are quick and promise not to moan like you have been in your sleep."

Soon Joraiem was ready, and he stepped out of the house with Pedraal to walk up to the Great Hall. Several of the others were just ahead of them, and hurrying to catch up, Joraiem and Pedraal walked with them across the bridge. The beautiful gardens hadn't changed, but they seemed somehow less peaceful this morning. *How remarkable that the events of a single day could color so deeply how one sees the world.* Joraiem wondered what this day held for them.

As they neared the Great Hall, a voice called out for them to wait. It was Aljeron with Koshti, crossing the bridge. Behind him came Rulalin and Darias, trudging wearily with heads down. Joraiem thought they looked like he felt, tired and downhearted. Yesterday's exhilaration at having faced the enemy and defeated it had given way to mourning at the news of Corlin's death. If joy could turn so easily when only one was dead, and he not one of their own, what must it be like to stand shoulder-to-shoulder with friends, brothers, countrymen, and see scores if not hundreds fall at your side? If the death of a single steward hardly known to him could rob the victory of its savor, how could Joraiem ever find delight in conquest on the battlefield where the blood of many flowed? Monias had not discouraged him from playing at fighting as a boy, but he had from time to time tried to tell him that war was not as children envisioned it. It was harder, grimmer, colder, messier, and more horrific than he could imagine. Joraiem wondered if this was the last time he would see the face of battle.

As they entered the Hall, Joraiem's eyes were drawn to another lively discussion among the elders. At one end of the tables, Master Berin stood, gesturing demonstratively. Most of the gestures seemed to be aimed at Valzaan, who, as far as Joraiem could tell, sat impassively at the opposite end. On the side, sitting still and not saying a word, were Caan, Ulmindos, and Sarneth.

As they entered, Master Berin calmed himself, though he didn't turn to look at them as they approached. In the uncomfortable silence, they took their seats and waited. They waited until all had gathered, then Caan stood and broke the silence.

"There are important matters that need to be discussed here, but before we begin, it is important that I speak to some of the events of yesterday. While the fight in the practice ring was not the prettiest encounter I have witnessed, you all deserve commendation. You have learned well, and you held your ground like the men and women that you are. I am proud of you."

They looked at one another as Caan sat down. Joraiem saw pride as well as surprise on several faces. Rarely did Caan praise them, and never without pointing out weaknesses in their techniques, attitudes, or performance. Joraiem found a slight resurgence of the elation he thought had gone.

There was no time to dwell on Caan's words, however, for after a pause, Valzaan rose to his feet. Joraiem looked from the prophet to Master Berin, who was staring at the fountain, looking away from Valzaan and the others at the table.

"There is a decision to be made," Valzaan began.

Master Berin stood quickly, gazing with anger in his eyes down the length of the table. "The only one with the right to make that decision is me, and I have already spoken!" he said, slapping the table with his open palm so that the sound of it echoed across the Great Hall.

Joraiem glanced nervously at Valzaan. He had vivid memories of what befell Mindarin when she had challenged the prophet.

"I have heard what you have said," Valzaan answered calmly, speaking with no trace of anger; in fact, his voice seemed softer and more compassionate than Joraiem had ever heard it. "And I say again, that though you are right to assert your authority over Sulare, this is no longer a matter of concern only for you and for this place. Someone, almost surely

Malek himself has trespassed on the Forbidden Isle. All Kirthanin could be at risk. To decide what must be done about the threat is not your decision alone."

"These sons and daughters," Berin answered, motioning to them, "have been entrusted to me by their parents. They are here under my care, and I, not you, am answerable to the Assembly for their safety. I will not sit here and allow you to take them needlessly into danger. I will not allow more people under my care to die."

"Berin, you wrong yourself to take blame for the boy's death. Allfather and Allfather alone governs the destiny of men. You are not God that you should have known the thousand years of peace in Sulare would be broken yesterday. I myself am a prophet, and I did not foresee it. To fail to act appropriately today because of yesterday's sorrow would be folly, not wisdom."

"You call me a fool?"

"There is no man alive who has not played the fool at one time or another, so sit down and let me say what I need to say, or I will lose my patience with you!" Valzaan stood tall with both hands resting comfortably upon the windhover head of his wooden staff. Master Berin looked for a moment like he had something more to say, but he decided against it and sat down, again looking away from the table.

Valzaan continued. "There is a decision to be made. I believe what we saw last night was evidence of Malek's presence on the Forbidden Isle. We must decide what is to be done about it. Master Berin thinks we should send word to Cimaris Rul and wait for the Novaana of that city to confer with us before we make any decisions. I believe that there is no time and that we must sail for the Forbidden Isle at once."

The silence that followed Valzaan's words was total. Joraiem found his own heart racing. From his exchange with Valzaan in slow time to his own bizarre dream, he had somehow known that today they would decide whether to sail or stay. Aside from the fearful prospect of what might be waiting for them on the Forbidden Isle, the thought of boarding a ship and heading into the Southern Ocean was almost overwhelming.

Though he may have been alone in the latter of those fears, he was not alone in the former. Soon stirrings around the table led to whispers, and eventually Aljeron spoke for them all, addressing Valzaan. "You mean that you think we should go after Malek?"

"If he is still there when we arrive."

They looked at one another, and Aljeron asked the question they were all contemplating. "But how can we face him?"

"We would face him even as the men and Great Bear and dragons of Kirthanin have faced him in the past, as bravely and as ably as we can. But you have gone ahead of the story. Malek does not like to face an enemy unless he is surrounded by an army of his own, and it seems unlikely to me that he has brought a whole army with him from Agia Muldonai. Most likely, if he is there, he is there with only a few. Furthermore, if he was responsible for whatever we saw last night, then he will certainly be aware of the warning it sent us and may flee the Island before we ever arrive."

"Then why go?" Saegan asked.

"Because we must. It was during his exile on the Forbidden Isle that Malek created the Grendolai and, with Vulsutyr's help, the Malekim. If he is at work there again, I am afraid of what that might mean for us. We must go to find out all we can about what is happening and to stop it if possible. We must go because there is no time to lose and there is no one else. Every moment we delay gives him more time to slip away or to hide what he has done."

The magnitude of what Valzaan was suggesting was beginning to sink in. Leaving Sulare, traveling to the Forbidden

Isle, looking for Malek or signs of his handiwork—the prospect seemed surreal. Yesterday they had waked to another beautiful day together in the Summerland, the closest thing to paradise Kirthanin had to offer, a place like Avalione must have been in the beginning. Joraiem shuddered at the thought of what they would find if ever they reached that distant shore.

Master Berin turned and addressed them, "You see why I am opposed to this idea! I understand that there might be much to gain from investigating as quickly as possible, but there is also much to lose. I forbid any of you to go."

"You cannot forbid what Allfather wishes," Valzaan quickly answered, the volume in his voice rising. "Allfather spoke to me last night, and I have been commanded to go to the Forbidden Isle. I will go alone if need be, but Allfather told me to take those of you who would come. I will not force anyone who is not willing, but do not be naïve about Sulare's safety. Yesterday has proven that even here Malek will strike. If he is at large and at work in the world, then there is no place where you can go to be safe from him if he desires to find you. Decide what you will, but as for me, if Allfather commanded it, I would rather go into the depths of Agia Muldonai where all Malek's host lay waiting than to the furthermost corner of this world. Choose quickly, for if you will not come, I must seek passage another way."

They sat quietly, looking down. At last, Aljeron rose from his seat. "Though I respect Master Berin's authority as master over Sulare, I must submit myself to Allfather's greater authority. I will go with you, Valzaan. I offer you my sword, my allegiance, and my life, small comfort though those things may be."

"I, too, will come," Saegan added, also rising. Bryar was not far behind, echoing both his words and his determined tone.

Soon they were all on their feet, even the younger girls,

Nyan, Tarin, and Valia. Joraiem suspected that though not all were eager to go, none wanted to be left behind.

"Surely, Valzaan," Master Berin began quietly, "at least the women should be left here under my care. There is no need to take them into danger."

Bryar spoke up, angrily, "I am not a little girl to be told what I can and can't do, where I can and can't go. I will not be left."

"Allfather did not discriminate between the men and the women when He spoke to me, and I will not tell them they have to stay behind."

Wylla added, "Master Berin, it seems clear that to go is Allfather's will. If any of us go, surely we should all go. We have come to train together, to learn to trust one another. We must continue the training. That is more important than any of us individually, more important even than our lives."

With a sigh, Master Berin hung his head. "I had hoped to avoid this, but since I apparently cannot, I will do all I can to make sure it is done right. I cannot leave, especially after yesterday, but Ulmindos will prepare the ship that is to take you, and he will be your captain. Caan, you will also go with them on my behalf. I entrust their care to you."

"I also will come," Sarneth said rising from his seat to tower above them. "I am only one Great Bear, and against the might of Malek I have little to offer, but I will aid you if I can."

"I would have begged you to come," Valzaan answered, looking as though he were relieved. "It is settled then. At first light we sail."

The rest of that day they worked in the hot sun, preparing the *Evening Star* for its voyage. The *Evening Star* was Ulmindos's own vessel, the smallest and fastest of the ships that served Sulare. The dock where it was moored was an hour's walk from the Great Hall, west along the coast to the place where the great channel that ran around Sulare emptied into the Southern Ocean. The dock jutted out from the coast into the wide mouth of the channel, a small, protected harbor that could shelter perhaps ten such vessels. All day, they loaded carts with food, weapons, and supplies from the storehouses under the Great Hall and drove them down to the dock, placing them wherever Ulmindos directed.

Joraiem had convinced them that it would be much easier and more efficient to do the loading if they formed a chain along which the goods could be passed on board. Volunteering to do the legwork of unloading the carts and carrying each new item to the foot of the gangway, he managed to put off stepping foot on board the *Evening Star* all day. When the last load had been carried aboard, he listened to the others talking among themselves on deck, and he could picture them leaning against the side and looking out to sea as the late afternoon sun hung low above the water. He took the reins of one of the carts and began to drive it back toward the Great Hall. He knew that tomorrow he would have to step aboard the ship, but he was more than willing to wait until then.

After dropping off the cart, Joraiem walked down the broad avenue to the beach. He wanted to be alone for a while, and he knew that once they set sail in the morning, there would be few chances of that. The sun sat just above the water in the west, and the breeze that came in off the ocean had lost the hot edge that it had carried all day.

He stood by the water and stared, wondering what was out there. He wondered what they would find when they reached the Forbidden Isle, and he wondered how he would cope with spending all that time on the water. He had known that sooner or later he would have to set sail with the others, and now the time had come. His only hope was that he would be able to pass off any squeamishness or odd reactions as seasickness. Ulmindos had made a point of telling them that there was no predicting who would struggle with sailing, that even the strongest and bravest of men might have difficulty with the rolling of the waves. Still, Ulmindos was an experienced sailor who would no doubt be able to recognize what was and wasn't seasickness, and what's more, he couldn't guarantee that he wouldn't be wholly incapacitated once the ship left the dock.

As he stood there, mumbling a prayer to Allfather that he wouldn't make a fool of himself all the days they were at sea, he heard Wylla's voice. "Joraiem?"

He turned. She was standing there in a long white dress, her dark hair rustling slightly in the breeze, looking at him. She quickly added when she saw the surprise in his eyes, "Am I bothering you?"

"No, of course not."

"I came down to see the sunset and saw you here, so I thought I'd come talk to you."

"I'm glad."

Joraiem stood looking at Wylla for a moment as she stepped up beside him, then turned back toward the water, unsure of what to say and feeling embarrassed.

"I've been meaning to thank you for yesterday," Wylla started, mercifully ending the silence.

"What for?"

"For protecting us. When I saw that Black Wolf coming straight at us, I thought we were in trouble. But then, seemingly out of nowhere, your arrow struck him and down he fell. Thanks."

"You're welcome. When they first broke out of the trees, I was a little paralyzed as to which wolf I should target. My hesitation turned out to be a good thing, though, since I might not have had an arrow nocked and ready when I saw the wolf charging you."

"It was a good thing, even if awful close," Wylla answered. She looked up at him with a slight, mischievous smile, "Why did you let the wolf get so close? Were you having second thoughts about whether any of us were worth saving? Or did you just want to let us sweat a little?"

Joraiem blushed. "No, no. Of course not. It was the right thing to do."

"To wait?"

"Yes. Letting the wolf close the distance gave me a better shot."

"But if you had missed?"

Joraiem looked closely at Wylla, "If I had missed, at least one of you would be dead, and I would hate myself right now. Even so, it was the right decision."

"Why?" she said, curiously.

"Monias, my father, taught me how to use my bow—"

"He obviously taught you well."

"He did, and he taught me that when you are in a situation where an enemy or an animal confronts you at close quarters, you have only one shot. Since to miss is to face injury or death, a good bowman will hold that one shot until the last moment, to make sure it is the best shot he can take. Do you see?"

"You didn't think you could shoot at the wolf when it was further away and then shoot again if you missed?"

"No. So I decided that if I only had one shot with which to save your life, it would have to be a good one."

"Was it my life you thought you were saving?" Wylla asked softly.

Joraiem colored again. "I don't know who the wolf was aiming for. I meant all of you."

Wylla nodded. "Well, I am certainly glad that you were there and looking out for me, and all of us. I didn't really doubt you. I was just curious."

"Sure, I can understand why you'd wonder."

They stood together for a while, watching the setting sun fall across the water. Then Wylla delivered him again from the silence. "Are you nervous about tomorrow?"

"Yes. Are you?"

"I am. I never considered myself a coward, but I've had butterflies in my stomach all day. I wish it wasn't necessary."

"You're no coward. Anyone with any sense would be nervous about this trip."

"At least we'll get to spend some peaceful days on the ocean first," Wylla said, sounding happier. "I've been so looking forward to going out to sea with Ulmindos, and even though it's not quite the way I had envisioned it, I'm still excited about that."

Joraiem didn't say anything, and when he realized she had turned to look at him, he nodded slightly in reply.

"Aren't you looking forward to it? Watching the sun rise and set over the water, seeing the stars and moon reflected on the waves, working together by day and by night to sail the ship? I think it'll be a great adventure."

"Sure," Joraiem said awkwardly, "I'm sure it will be interesting."

"Interesting?" Wylla echoed, gazing carefully at him. He looked at her and soon realized his mistake. He must not have been hiding his true reaction as well as he thought, because she saw the concern in his face. He knew it from the way compassion suddenly spread across her own. "What is it? Why are you worried?"

Joraiem stumbled over his words. "I'm not really much of a sailor."

She watched him carefully, not satisfied. "Come on, Joraiem, tell me the truth. So what if you aren't much of a sailor? That wouldn't bother you. You pick up everything quickly. I've seen you learn weapons you've never held before as fast or faster than any of the others. I've heard the questions you ask Ulmindos when he's teaching. You know as much about the ocean as any of us. What's the real story?"

"I . . . " Joraiem thought for a moment about making something up, but looking at Wylla, he felt an urge to confide in her. "I'm afraid of large bodies of water."

"Did something happen to you?" she asked quietly.

"No, not that I remember, anyway. I've just always been afraid. Sometimes I grow dizzy or faint near them, and I don't just mean the ocean. I had difficulty crossing both the Barunaan and the channel that surrounds Sulare. I'm just afraid of the water. Sometimes, I even have bad dreams. . . ." His voice trailed off.

Wylla slipped her hands around Joraiem's arm and clasped it tight. "I'm sorry, Joraiem."

"Thanks."

"I'd like to help you if I can. Is there anything I can do?"

"Not that I know of. I'm glad that you know, though. I've been dreading trying to brave it alone."

"Well, you're not alone. I'll do anything I can to help. Do you think you'll be able to adjust, once we are underway?"

"I have no idea. That's what I was just wondering. I could be completely incapacitated."

"Why don't we tell the others, I'm sure they would understand—"

"No, Wylla, I don't want to. I'd like to see if I can manage first. If I can't, then I'll tell them whatever I have to."

"If you like," she said as she stepped in front of him, releasing his arm and now pointing one of her fingers in his chest, "but don't you go hiding how you're doing from me, understand? You've told me now, so you might as well let me share this burden with you, all right?"

"I will," Joraiem said, missing already the feel of her touch.

For a moment she stood there, beautiful, framed by the sunset and the ocean behind her. He felt an urge to take her in his arms and hold her close, but he held the urge in check.

"It's almost dark," she said after a few moments, stepping around him on the other side. "I should head back."

"Would you mind if I walked you back?"

"Not at all," she answered with a smile.

For a long while Rulalin remained seated under the branches of the dense tree that offered him shelter. Though the sun was now down and the mild summer evening was growing cool, it still felt comfortable where he was. The sun disappeared below the horizon, and gradually the stars and moon began to shine down from above. He rose to his feet and strolled across the beach to the edge of the water. He gazed out over it for a long time. The waves washed in around his feet, filling the pair of footprints he was standing beside, but he didn't look down at them. After a while, he turned from the water and headed slowly back up the beach.

BEYOND

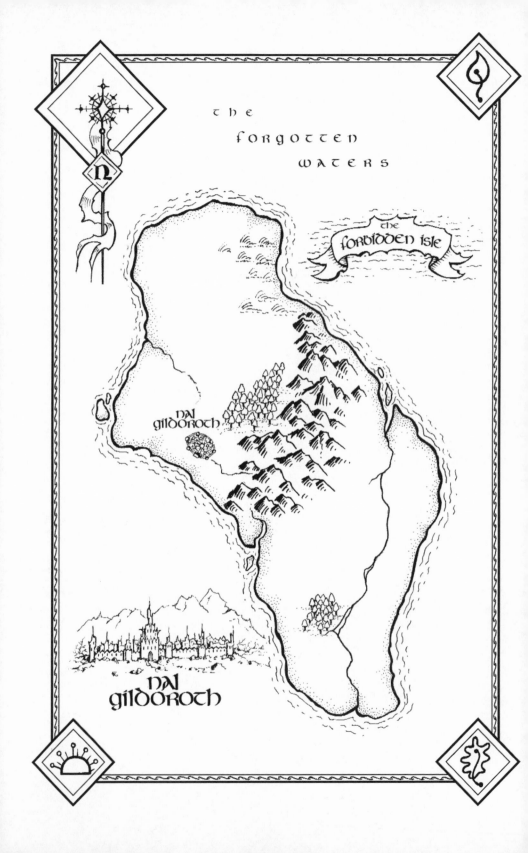

THE
FORGOTTEN
WATERS

THE FORBIDDEN ISLE

NAI GILDOROTH

NAI GILDOROTH

THE FORGOTTEN
WATERS

JORAIEM LEANED AGAINST THE side of the *Evening Star* as the
morning sun rose across the water in the east. The waves were
higher now then they had been at any point yesterday, their
first day away from Sulare, and he could feel the deck surge
and sink beneath his feet. He was slightly queasy and so rested
much of his weight upon the solid wooden rail beneath him,
but the churning inside was not nearly as severe as he'd expected, so he wasn't complaining.

In fact, though approaching and boarding the ship had
been difficult, once he'd actually set foot on board, he hadn't
felt very bad at all. Wylla had stationed herself nearby as they
cast off and monitored him closely, but he hadn't needed any
help and had been forced to solemnly swear before Allfather
that he wasn't just trying to tough out a bad situation. The
third or fourth time Joraiem made this claim, Wylla accepted

his protest, smiled warmly at him as she clasped his arm, and said, "I'm so glad," before slipping away to join some of the other women at the bow.

Joraiem remained behind in the stern, watching the shores of Sulare as they set out to sea. Nearby, a pair of Merrion, graceful and sleek, flew low above the water. Joraiem watched as they glided, their long white wings with the telltale pair of blue stripes on each, extended to their full measure. Then, one of them dove down into the water, and Joraiem strained to follow the white form swimming almost as gracefully just below the water's surface as it had flown above. Then, just as quickly as it had dropped into the sea, the bird shot out above the waves with a fish in its mouth, and both Merrion wheeled off north toward land.

The first day had gone well, so well that he was able to spend much of it consoling Saegan, who had not gotten his sea legs quite as quickly. He sat alone below deck most of the day, looking as pale as a winter's moon. Joraiem took pity on him, for he had envisioned a long and lonely voyage for himself and did not wish to abandon a friend to that same fate. Most of the others worked on deck in the warm sun with the ten or so crewmen that Ulmindos had brought with them (insisting that though the Novaana had come along well in their lessons, he could not entrust this voyage through the long forgotten waters to complete novices).

The day had passed quickly, and for the most part, their spirits were high. The silence that had hung about them as they prepared the *Evening Star* for voyage was gradually replaced by excitement as they watched the shores of Kirthanin slip below the horizon. They were going where few but the servants of Malek had gone before, and even if their ultimate destination was fearful enough to make them quake at the thought of it, they had many days of beautiful sailing ahead and were able, if barely, to push their fears away for the moment.

Now Joraiem stood on deck on the morning of their second day at sea, gazing at the majesty and wonder of the Southern Ocean. He had never expected to be able to enjoy such a view without fear and foreboding, but today he felt neither. Perhaps by going to sea, all those strange feelings and visions had been put to rest. Perhaps in facing his fear, he had conquered it. Perhaps he now gazed on the wide ocean a free man. Perhaps.

What worried him now was what to do about Rulalin. Standing beside Wylla on the beach in the twilight had been wonderful, and feeling her touch on his arm, intoxicating. Deep within a voice kept urging him to speak to her, to name his desire and seek her favor. Even when he tried to shut it out, the voice was there, whispering, *Don't wait too long and lose her as you lost Alina. Not again.*

He didn't think he could face that possibility. Reflecting on those wet, rainy nights between Dal Harat and Peris Mil, when the grey sogginess eerily reflected his own feelings, he knew he was lucky to have found Wylla. He hadn't thought he would ever find a reprieve from the sorrow of losing Alina. He hadn't ever expected to feel his heart soar and sing in the presence of another, and yet he knew with Wylla that he had found the object of his soul's delight. Her presence wrung from him a deeper passion than he had ever felt. It would be foolishness to turn away. Inexperience in matters of love had cost him his chance for happiness with Alina, but now he knew enough to understand the nature of his own feelings. If he lost Wylla, too, he would have only himself to blame.

Still, the problem of Rulalin had not been solved, and all the certainty in the world that he needed to speak to Wylla had not provided an answer to that dilemma. Joraiem had never before encountered a choice that appeared so right and so wrong at the same time.

"I will ask Aljeron," Joraiem said quietly and out loud.

That's the answer. Aljeron knows Rulalin and is a wise friend, trusted by us both. Perhaps he will see an answer where I cannot. At least I will no longer bear the weight of this quandary on my own. Just thinking about telling someone else comforted Joraiem.

"It's a beautiful morning, isn't it?"

Joraiem turned, surprised to see Aljeron beside him. The coincidence flustered him. "It is," he answered.

"I sometimes have to remind myself what serious business this is. Yesterday I enjoyed the wind and the waves, the ship and the sun so much that I kept losing track of where we were headed."

"It's a bit overwhelming, isn't it."

"Yeah, a bit," Aljeron laughed. "I've always thought myself a pretty hardy soul, up to about any challenge, but I never thought I'd be headed to the Forbidden Isle. Never."

"Do you think he'll be there?" Joraiem asked, unable to mention Malek's name on such a beautiful morning.

Aljeron shrugged. "Who knows? If he is, I don't think it will go well with us. He's already survived being cast from Avalione by Alazare in the First Age, the massive if failed attempt to conquer all Kirthanin at the close of the Second, and Corindel's assault on the Holy Mountain in the Third. What can we do?"

"I don't know, but it had to be us, didn't it? Even leaving as soon as we did, by the time we arrive it'll have been more than a week since we saw the light. It may already be too late to discover what happened. If we'd sent a message to Cimaris Rul or gone there ourselves, it would have taken more than twice as long. If anyone could look into things quickly, it had to be us. And don't forget Valzaan is with us. I suspect if anyone could stand face to face with him, it's Valzaan."

"True enough."

"And," Joraiem hastily added, "don't sell yourself short either. I'd say you're about as formidable as a man could be, especially with Koshti by your side."

"Don't be crazy," Aljeron laughed. "You're the most deadly of us all."

"Me?" Joraiem said incredulously.

"Yes, you! The way you use that bow, none of us would stand a chance against you unless we snuck up on you in your sleep."

"You're the one who's crazy. I'm more of a hunter than a warrior."

"Maybe a hunter is what we need. Warriors haven't had any success with Malek yet." The mention of the name sobered them.

"Koshti isn't dealing very well with the voyage," Aljeron said, changing the subject. "He keeps moaning in his corner below deck, and he hardly ate a thing all day yesterday. I hope he gets used to the ship soon. I'd feel a lot better about going ashore if I knew he was at full strength."

Joraiem wondered if it would be rude not to acknowledge Aljeron's comment and to launch right into his question. He didn't think Aljeron expected a response, so he didn't think he would mind. Besides, he needed to move while his resolve held. "Aljeron, can I tell you something?"

"Go ahead," Aljeron said, turning from the sea to look at him.

"I'm not sure where to begin," Joraiem started, but he halted mid-sentence as he noticed several of the others approaching along the rail, Wylla among them. Joraiem leaned in closer, "Could we talk later, when we have a free moment?" Joraiem asked.

"Of course. What about?"

"That'll have to wait," Joraiem said quickly, for the others were upon them.

"A secret, how exciting," Aljeron said with a grin.

Eventually, all of them were assembled on deck, expecting Ulmindos to come and put them to work as he had the day before. But, when Ulmindos was asked what he would have them do today, Joraiem was surprised to hear that their time was required elsewhere.

"What requires our time?" Mindarin asked, as shocked as the rest.

"You will see when Caan comes," Ulmindos answered.

"Caan," Rulalin said, almost under his breath. "Of course. We should have known he couldn't resist making the most of this opportunity to work us one last time."

Joraiem saw Aljeron give Rulalin a hard look, and if Rulalin had thought about taking his grim joke any further, he changed his mind and held his tongue. Joraiem knew Aljeron had taken Rulalin aside when they were loading the *Evening Star* and rebuked him for dropping phrases like "last voyage" and "certain death" into his gloomier-than-usual conversations with the others. They all knew what they were doing was dangerous, but their morale dipped with every despairing word. Rulalin had stopped talking altogether, perhaps doubtful that he could open his mouth without drawing Aljeron's ire, perhaps sulking because of the rebuke.

In any case, the look shut him up again, and he said no more about the situation. Even so, he'd said enough. They stood or sat quietly, awaiting Caan's arrival.

Caan did come, before long, his long hair hanging in half a dozen braids around his shoulders. He wore a thin white shirt and long grey pants with his sword dangling at his side. None of them had ever seen Caan without his sword, and so the sight was not wholly surprising, though at least the men had speculated the night before they sailed about whether he would wear it on board, since it seemed a reasonable assumption that no danger would befall them while on the *Evening Star*. But to no one's real surprise, he had boarded with it on and not been parted from it since.

Caan carried with him a long, dark bundle. Joraiem couldn't

tell what it was, but he could hear the sound of metallic objects jostling against one another inside the black cloth when
Caan set it down. He called them to take a seat with their
backs to the side of the ship, and they did.

Pulling a stool over beside the bundle, he sat down facing
them. "There is always so much to learn when a new group
comes, that it is hard to know what to teach first. Sitting here,
heading toward the Forbidden Isle, I regret not having had
this discussion sooner, though I know this situation was un-
foreseeable. Still, regrets are not always rational, even as they
are not always avoidable. Be that as it may, I will do my best to
make the most of the situation as it is, rather than regretting
what I cannot change. Aljeron, do you have your sword with
you?"

"It's down below," Aljeron answered, surprised.

"Bring it up, please. We'll wait."

Aljeron slipped below deck. Caan sat with his hands
clasped, his eyes staring over them into the clear sky above. Joraiem looked at the others, but between Rulalin's dark humor
and Caan's strange words, it was a glum group. Joraiem was
glad to see Aljeron return as quickly as he'd left, standing
about midway between the others and Caan.

"May I see your sword?" Caan asked, holding out his hand.

Aljeron, who never hesitated to obey the directives and re-
quests of their teachers, stood motionless. Joraiem leaned forward, trying to see more clearly what was happening in
Aljeron's face. From where he was sitting, he could see little
more in Aljeron's profile than the scars.

Caan stood, and Joraiem felt himself flinch. Caan had not
dealt gently with those who'd been slow to follow his orders,
and never had anyone simply not done what he'd asked. Joraiem braced himself for the consequences of Aljeron's hesitation, but there was no need. Caan stepped calmly beside
Aljeron, spoke quietly to him, and placed his hand on the

sheath of Aljeron's sword. Bowing his head at whatever it was that Caan said, Aljeron let go.

Caan drew the sword. The dark runes, just slightly lighter than the darker blade, glinted in the bright morning sun. As Joraiem watched Caan draw and hold the sword, he realized it was not unlike Caan's own blade.

"This is no ordinary sword," Caan said as he stepped closer to the others. "Who, besides Aljeron, can tell me why?"

Joraiem looked around but didn't speak. He had no idea. He was wondering if any of them did when Saegan spoke out. "Is it one of the Azmavarim?"

"It is, and what are the Azmavarim?"

Saegan continued, "The Azmavarim are the Firstblades, swords made during the First Age. They are the best swords that have ever been forged. My uncle has one, and he values it almost as highly as he values my cousins, maybe even more."

Saegan's joke, a rarity for him, broke the tension and several of them laughed. "That's right. The Firstblades, or Azmavarim in the language of the Mountain, were made near the end of the First Age. Most of them were made by the smithies of Andunin in the distant reaches of Nolthanin as he prepared to follow Malek. Some of them were made by Malek himself."

A hush fell on them, and they stared at the long dark blade. Their eyes were drawn to it and to the runes upon it. "Was Aljeron's sword made by Malek?" Elyas asked.

"I don't know, and I don't know if there is anyone who does. As Malek fled with Andunin and the Nolthanim to the ocean, many swords were recovered from the ensuing battles. Some were even employed by those who pursued Malek, and so his own weapons were turned against him. At the beginning of the Second Age, the best blacksmiths in Kirthanin studied the recovered Azmavarim and tried to replicate them, with varying degrees of success. Many fine swords were made, but none were ever as good as the Azmavarim themselves. The recovered Firstblades became precious family heirlooms, a truly valuable commodity."

"What makes them so special?" Darias asked.

"No one knows the secret to Malek's work. If they did, presumably, we could imitate it."

"I don't mean that, I mean, what can they do that makes them better than other swords?"

"They are stronger and sharper than other swords." Turning to Aljeron, Caan continued, "When did you get this?"

"My father gave it to me."

"When?"

"He gave it to me when I came of age, but he started teaching me how to use it when I returned to my home with Koshti, after the Malekim killed my cousin."

"Why then?"

"He told me a normal sword wasn't much good against a Malekim, but that if I carried this, I would be able to cut a Malekim's head right off." Caan handed the sword back to Aljeron, who added while he sheathed it, "He was right."

Caan looked at Aljeron, a little surprised, but soon his face was as impassive as ever. "That's right. A Firstblade wielded by a skillful hand will penetrate the thick hide of a Malekim like a sharp knife slices through a melon."

Drawing his own sword, Caan laid it on the sun-warmed wood of the deck, and like a mystic talisman it drew all eyes to it. "This is Kurveen, which means something like 'quick kill' in the language of the Mountain, though I've been told the translation is inexact. Most of the weapons were named by the men who carried them or who saw them used in battle, and no words yet existed to express the kind of conflict they were seeing, so the naming of the Azmavarim created a whole new vocabulary."

"Does your sword have a name, Aljeron?" Wylla asked.

"It is called Daaltaran."

When Aljeron did not go on, Mindarin prompted him with the question they all had. "Yes? That means?"

Aljeron looked up and gazed past them at the deep blue sky and bright morning sun that gleamed down upon the ocean waves. "It means, 'death comes to all.'"

"How cheery," Mindarin replied dryly.

"Did you expect the naming of swords to evoke cheery thoughts?" Valzaan asked as they turned to look at the prophet who had arrived unnoticed at the side of the ship. "They are a reminder of Malek's great treachery and the ruin that has been wrought on the peace that once existed in Kirthanin. Having said that, they may ultimately, and ironically, be of the utmost importance if we are to stand against Malek's third and final onslaught. We will all wish on that day, when the spawn of Malek issue forth from their deep hiding places beneath Agia Muldonai, that every Firstblade ever forged was held in the hand of a worthy Kirthanin warrior. What's more, depending on what we find on the Forbidden Isle, we may all be very grateful that both Kurveen and Daaltaran are in our midst and in capable hands. May both sing their battle songs well, and may many of Malek's children taste death at their edges."

"Indeed," Caan said. "The Azmavarim may help us to survive this journey and bring us back home again." He slipped Kurveen back into its sheath, lifted the bundle at his feet, and carried it closer to the group. Unfolding the cloth, he revealed four more long, dark hilts.

"More Azmavarim?" Saegan whispered in wonder.

"Yes, all that remain in the armory of Sulare. Once, when Sulare teemed with warriors from all over Kirthanin, there were more Azmavarim in Sulare than anywhere else in the world. This is not so now, but these four remain. Master Berin has sent them along, knowing . . ." Here Caan stopped.

". . . knowing he might never see them again." Valzaan finished Caan's thought. "It is all right, Caan. We must speak truthfully of the danger ahead. No man who sets out on any journey knows if he will ever return, regardless of how confident he may be of the road. How much more do we sail into the unknown, unaware of what waits but aware of our fragile mortality? And yet, even as I stand on this deck and face the new morning sun with the strong breeze at my back, I do not despair. Allfather has guided me into many dark places and safely out again, and that without the stout bodies and capable hands that go with me this time."

Walking through their midst, Valzaan continued, growing more animated. "Hear me, there are gathered among us many who will be great as this world accounts greatness. I sense it as clearly as I sense our calling to the Forbidden Isle. Perhaps it would be truer to say that there are here among us many who are already great, though their true greatness has yet to be revealed. Greatness is not something suddenly found like an unexpected treasure beside the road. No, greatness is a gift of Allfather, bestowed upon those who have been called to serve His purposes in time of need. This is just such an hour, unless I am very much mistaken, and I believe that before long we will see what some here are truly capable of."

Joraiem felt strangely comforted by these words, even though he would not necessarily have said before that moment that he was in need of comfort. He felt both awed and embarrassed, as he had felt as a boy when Monias would praise him for some task performed well. In fact, he suddenly realized that unless he was reading his own body wrong, he was blushing.

Caan eventually drew his attention back to the Azmavarim. "Master Berin sent these as well as some other things, which I have stored below, to aid us in our quest. Though the swords will be helpful, there are obviously not enough for all to carry one. So, this is what I have decided. These four will be carried by Saegan, Rulalin, Darias, and Elyas. My thinking behind this decision is simple. Aljeron does not need one, nor do I. For Pedraal and Pedraan, I have brought two ancient treasures of a different sort. One is a war hammer, so large that an average man would have trouble lifting it, much less wielding it. The other is a great two-handed battle-axe, again, too large to be of much use for most men. I am confident, though, that both Pedraal and Pedraan are strong enough to carry these weapons into battle and use them effectively. The battle-axe would sever a fair-sized tree if wielded by powerful enough hands, and the war hammer would crush even stone. There is more than one way to kill a Malekim, and even though they are not Azmavarim, they will do in the right hands.

"As for Joraiem, Suruna is his true weapon. He will have all the cyranic arrows he can carry, and may he fire with great speed and accuracy in our hour of need. Because of his wound, Kelvan will also carry a bow rather than a sword, and so will Bryar, for her skills will be of much help should we find ourselves in combat. The rest of the women will be given smaller arms to carry, but they will be needed in other capacities should we run into trouble, and they must be ready to serve in those ways."

Caan stood and paused for effect. "You have all seen that battle is gruesome, and if Malekim are involved next time, it will be worse. We will be relying upon you to do what needs to be done to support those who are fighting, or to tend them as may be needed."

When Caan finished, no one spoke or moved. If anyone was unhappy with the lot assigned to him, he didn't show it. For Joraiem's part, he was a little envious of those privileged to carry one of the Azmavarim, but he understood Caan's decision. He was most effective with Suruna. With a whole quiver of cyranic arrows, he knew he could single-handedly do a lot of damage to a whole company of Malekim before they were close enough to engage in battle.

"All right, then," Caan said. "We have five or six days to practice, and I intend to start now. Saegan, take one of the Azmavarim and distribute the other three as I have directed. I will work with you four as much as I can, but you are all to practice with Aljeron when I can't. There is no time to quibble about who is oldest or about being equals as Novaana. You aren't equals anymore. When I'm not around, Aljeron is in charge of the swordsman, and Saegan is his second. This is final," Caan added, looking directly at Rulalin.

Joraiem thought that Rulalin would be both angry and hurt at Caan's command, but if he was either, he didn't show it. Perhaps, Joraiem thought, Rulalin was honest enough with himself to know that while he was good, Aljeron and Saegan were simply the best swordsmen among them.

"Joraiem, you will be in charge of the archers. I will be counting on you to direct all archery engagements as needed. You are a better shot than I ever was, so I have nothing to teach you about how to use that bow.

"Pedraal and Pedraan, you will work with Sarneth for the remainder of the voyage. Though he carries neither a battle-axe nor a war hammer, he is best able to teach you how to wield them in combat. You will follow his command in battle. For now, though, come with me, and we will get you your new toys." Caan smiled as he finished, and so did the twins. It was clear that they weren't upset at being set apart from the others for this task.

Caan took a few steps, then stopped to turn around. "Remember, all of you. You have already faced battle and excelled. You are no longer novices or amateurs. Now you will be better equipped and better prepared. Whoever or whatever we may find on the Forbidden Isle, if anyone decides to exchange blows with us, they will find it costly."

At the end of the day, all were exhausted but had higher spirits than they had seen since the Black Wolf attack. Though they had worked under Caan's unflagging direction until their bodies ached and their hands could barely clench their weapons, in some odd way that full-body burn had translated into a morale boost. Joraiem, sitting with his back against a heavy wooden barrel in the middle of the deck, watched Valzaan speak with Caan and Ulmindos and wondered if they hadn't intended the new work regimen to have that very effect. They seemed looser and more relaxed themselves, and hope and good cheer marked their faces.

Evidently, the sense of mirth and merriment was palpable to more than just Joraiem, as several of the women sitting with heads together not five spans from where Joraiem rested began to whoop and howl with laughter. Joraiem could make out not only Tarin and Valia, Karalin and Calissa, but oddly enough, Wylla, too. This last realization took him a bit by surprise. It wasn't that she didn't like to laugh, but she was laughing so hard that tears were streaming down her cheeks.

Mindarin and Nyan went running over and knelt down beside them. Joraiem could hear Mindarin saying, "What? What?" over and over. It took a moment for any of them to be able to answer, but when Karalin eventually spoke, it was too soft for Joraiem to hear. It wasn't too soft for Nyan and Mindarin, however, both of whom were as amused as the others.

Only Bryar of all the women was content to remain outside the joke. She sat against the rail of the ship opposite from where Valzaan stood with Ulmindos and Caan, leaning against Kelvan. They sat together, smiling, perhaps at the spectacle of the hysterical girls in the center of the deck, perhaps at some shared jest of their own. Joraiem felt like an intruder, watching, and so turned back to the now quieter, giggling mass, looking again for Wylla's face.

Before he could find her, the ladies rose and began to sing as best they could amid their laughter as they danced in a circle together. The men sat speechless and inert, all save Elyas, who was never slow to seize an opportunity for silliness. He skipped from outside the circle and ducked between two of the ladies to step into their midst. He leapt and twirled and made faces as he pranced about among them. Soon, they were laughing even harder than they had been before, and only Elyas remained upright as they crumpled into heaps of two or three back on the deck.

"He's acting like a fool," Pedraan said to his brother, almost growling.

"Yes," Pedraal answered, "but he's surrounded by a host of women who think he's hilarious."

"Maybe, but I'd rather not be noticed by any of the women than be known to them as a clown."

Pedraal shrugged, "Leave him be, Pedraan. We need a clown about now. At least there is laughter in the air."

With his companions in the dance seated again, Elyas soon stopped, perhaps self-conscious at last, though clearly not too much. He took several bows and received much applause from the women. One of them called to him to sing one of his pointless ditties, and soon all of them were.

"All right, all right," he finally acquiesced, though Joraiem believed everyone there well knew that Elyas was about as reticent to display his "talent" as a peacock is hesitant to show his feathers. "I think I have just the right song for this fine romantic evening. Here it goes."

Darowin was a handsome lad
Who lived by the Kellisor Sea.
He went down for a swim
And while getting in
His heart was filled with glee.

"I love Larilea, a beauty she
I'll tell her my love in the morn.
She'll take my hand,
Wear my wedding band,
And our vows will soon be sworn."

And heading back to his warm fireside,
Darowin hummed a merry old tune.
He was filled with joy,
Such a happy boy,
Tomorrow couldn't come too soon.

But in the light of the next day's morn,
Darowin forgot his plan.
He went out to work
He ploughed in the dirt,
And spent all day on his land.

And lovely Larilea married someone else
And they were happy as could be.
They made a home,
Of their very own,
That sat by the Kellisor Sea.

"What was that?" Calissa asked. "That wasn't a happy song. Where's your sense of occasion?"

"Nonsense, Calissa," Mindarin interrupted. "It was happy enough for Larilea. Darowin just got what he deserved."

"Mindarin!" some of them replied, laughing. "You're shameless."

"Someone has to be," she retorted.

Things settled down after that, and though the ebullience dissipated somewhat, the distinct feel of relief mixed with optimism persisted. They talked in pairs and groups around the deck as the bright moon rose above the water. Brought back by Elyas's song to his own predicament, Joraiem took Aljeron aside when an opportunity presented itself.

"Do you mind if we finish our conversation now?" he asked.

"Not at all, I've been wondering what was on your mind."

"I need some advice."

"About what?"

"A girl."

"Ah, I see." Aljeron answered, nodding.

Joraiem looked at him carefully. He wondered if Aljeron would take him seriously, speaking of troubles of the heart as they sailed toward the Forbidden Isle. It seemed so incongruous to be having this conversation here, on this night, but there was no hint of amusement or mockery in Aljeron's manner. "You see? What do you mean?"

"I mean that I see. I have eyes after all. I wondered when this would come up."

"You mean you knew?" Joraiem asked, shocked. He knew that Rulalin had noticed the attention Wylla sometimes paid him, but he had thought that only Rulalin's keen senses where Wylla was concerned accounted for his suspicions. How could Aljeron know? He thought he had been careful to conceal even a hint of his feelings from the others.

"Know is a strong word. I didn't know, I suspected. I've seen the way you look at her when you think no one's looking, and I've also seen the way she looks at you. So what's the problem?"

"Don't you know that too?"

"Rulalin?"

"Of course. What am I to do, Aljeron?"

"Talk to him. What else is there to do?"

Joraiem laughed bitterly. "And what am I to say? Sorry, Rulalin, I'm in love with the girl of your dreams—do you mind if I steal her away?"

Aljeron didn't laugh. "Joraiem, stop torturing yourself. You haven't done anything wrong. First of all, as I understand it, Wylla has never told Rulalin she was interested in him. Second, you didn't set out to steal the girl of anyone's dreams, did you?"

"Of course not. I've tried everything I can think of to avoid this entirely."

"That's right. You've done nothing to be ashamed of, but to keep it that way, you'll need to talk to Rulalin. He's obviously told you his story, so you need to be honest with him. Rulalin can be difficult, I know, but he is a grown man. He'll learn to deal with it."

"I'm not so sure. I've seen the look in his eyes when he seems desperate about Wylla, and I fear he will not forgive."

"He is a funny one sometimes. Still, I think that the longer you wait, the harder it will be. My recommendation is that you tell him as soon as we get back. Until then, I wouldn't worry about it."

Joraiem weighed the advice a moment before conceding. "Good idea. If the expedition goes well, I won't have to worry about it for a couple weeks at least. If things don't go so well, then, I guess I won't have to worry about it at all."

Aljeron smiled this time. "Trust you to find an upside to the worst possible scenario."

They stood silently together for a few moments, looking out into the darkness, then Aljeron continued softly, "You are a lucky man, Joraiem. Wylla is quite a woman."

Joraiem looked at Aljeron, surprised. "Aljeron, you don't mean that, I mean, you aren't—"

"No, I'm not," Aljeron cut him off quickly. "At least, not seriously." He returned Joraiem's gaze. "Don't look so surprised, Joraiem. I said I had eyes, didn't I? Did you really think that you and Rulalin were the only two who had noticed that Wylla is beautiful? And wonderful? Any man would notice. I'm not made of stone, you know."

"Of course not," Joraiem fumbled for words. "I'm sorry, Aljeron. I've just been so preoccupied with Rulalin, I didn't stop to consider other possibilities."

"It's all right, don't worry about it."

"No, Aljeron, really, I don't mind if you want to speak to her first. I'll defer to you. It's not right for me to step in where—"

"Don't be an idiot," Aljeron snarled. "Didn't you hear what I said? I've seen the way *she* looks at *you*. She's never looked at me that way." He looked back out to sea, tracing the rough scars on his face. "Wylla and I have talked, of course, and she is always gracious. When we first arrived, I saw her kindness and tenderness toward me and thought that maybe, maybe she would look at me the way she looks at you, but she never did. I've seen her look at me with pity, but never with desire or love. I've seen that look of pity a hundred times, and I despise it."

"Aljeron . . ."

"I don't despise her, Joraiem, nor you," he added, turning back to face him. "You are like a brother to me, and I will stand beside you whatever comes. Know that, as surely as you know anything."

"Thanks, Aljeron. You're like a brother to me, too. I will stand beside you, and more importantly, I will follow wherever you lead. You are the best of us all, you know. Whatever lies out there, out beyond the horizon on the dark shores of the Forbidden Isle, I rest easier at night knowing you are with us."

"That's because where I go, Koshti goes."

"No, that isn't it. You were born to lead. If Valzaan is right, if Malek is at work on some dark design, if he is preparing even now for his final assault, then I have no doubt that it is for this time that Allfather has made you. I can feel it, Aljeron." And he did, Joraiem's heart burned within him. "You are Allfather's chosen instrument. Your destiny lies veiled from my eyes, but it is a great and noble calling, I know it."

Aljeron peered through the dark at Joraiem's strangely excited face. "You've been spending too much time around Valzaan," he said. "You're beginning to sound like a prophet."

Joraiem mumbled, stumbling over his words, "Sorry, I get carried away sometimes."

"Don't worry about it." Aljeron answered, putting his arm across Joraiem's shoulders. "Come on, if Caan intends to work us tomorrow like he did today, we'll need our sleep tonight."

Wylla remained where she was, sitting quietly in the shadows near Ulmindos's quarters in the stern. She watched Joraiem and Aljeron turn from where they had been talking and head toward the stairs that led down into the hold. How she wished she had been able to hear them, to hear him. Every movement of his was beautiful. From the moment she'd first seen him, standing beneath the snow trees, she'd thought he was beautiful. Her heart had raced when he had turned to speak to her, and she had seen how beautiful he really was. Each day brought the delight and agony of watching him, of being near him and conversing with him. She both prayed for and dreaded each day.

At first it had been terrible. For some reason, he seemed to avoid her. He'd look away when she'd smile or pretend never to have been looking in the first place. He'd be polite when conversing, but then he would find some reason to excuse himself. She had been completely at a loss.

But as their time in the Summerland had passed, she had begun to notice signs that this avoidance was not so much natural as forced. She had caught him gazing at her at times, occasionally so deeply that he did not immediately realize that she had noticed him. He would still excuse himself in awkward ways from their conversations, but not as quickly, and she had been able to see that often he wanted to linger. No, she believed now, at last, that he returned her feelings, but why had he not spoken of them to her? Why would he not ac-knowledge them and come forward? He might be beautiful, but he was very frustrating.

She stood and walked across the deck toward the place where he had been standing. She paused when she reached the spot and ran her hand against the smooth wooden rail that ran along the side of the ship. She loved to look at the moonlight dancing on the waves. She had always been drawn to bright things, beautiful things, but she loved moonlight best of all. Seeing it shine across the wide waters of the Southern Ocean, she understood why there had always been men and women in love with the sea. She wondered if there was anything on earth, other than perhaps Joraiem, as beautiful as a moonlit night on the ocean.

"Wylla?" she heard a voice behind her.

She turned, startled, and found Rulalin stepping toward her. "Oh, Rulalin."

"Hello, Wylla. Sorry I startled you. I came up to enjoy the cool night air a little longer and saw you walking here. I hope you don't mind."

"Of course not. I was just enjoying the beautiful night too."

"It is beautiful. Of course, anyplace where you are would be beautiful, Wylla."

Wylla blushed and turned away, embarrassed by his bold-ness. Perhaps he was too, because he quickly added, "Have you enjoyed the voyage so far? I mean, I know you were look-ing forward to our time at sea with Ulmindos. I was hoping the particular circumstances that led to our early departure hasn't overshadowed the pleasure of the voyage too much."

"They haven't, thank you," Wylla said as calmly as she could, but she felt tense and wary. "Despite our destination, I have enjoyed every moment. If Valzaan wasn't so sure that we had pressing business ahead, I should wish that we were lost at sea and unable to land anywhere for as long as we could survive on this ship. I have felt at times that I would be perfectly happy never to see the shore again."

Rulalin studied her face and nodded. Feeling even more uncomfortable, Wylla asked, "And you, Rulalin? Have you enjoyed the trip so far?"

"I have. I have been sailing on the Kellisor Sea, but never out on the Ocean. It is truly magnificent, something I shall not soon forget."

It was Wylla's turn to nod, but she remained silent, looking out across the water. Rulalin did not let the silence go for long, though, and soon he continued. "This night, it reminds me of another night, many years ago, in Amaan Sul with you. We sat beside the great reflecting pool at the palace, watching the fountain in the middle. From where we were, the moon hung just above the top of the water, and you said that the moon looked just like a great silver ball lifted into the sky by the fountain's spray. Do you remember?"

"Yes," Wylla answered softly, turning back to look at him. His tender gaze was heartbreaking. She had tried all those years ago, when Rulalin had first opened his heart to her, to discourage his affection. She had enjoyed his company, a pleasant diversion at a difficult time, but she had never thought of him as a love interest. She had hoped that the last eight years would have cooled his desire, but it had been pretty clear, even while they traveled together, that he remained interested. She had been careful not to wrongly encourage him; in fact, she tried to discourage any romantic thoughts on his part by emphasizing her appreciation of his friendship. "I do remember that night, and many others like it. It was a hard time, burying my father and trying to comfort my mother and the twins. I have often thought of how much I appreciated your company then. Even when our time together in Sulare is past and your business keeps you far away in Fel Edorath, even then I will remember with fondness those days. I thank you for your many kindnesses to me."

Rulalin acknowledged her words with a slight nod. Wylla hoped he would realize that if she harbored the same hopes for a future together, she would not speak so readily of their parting, but when he spoke again, it was clear he was undaunted. "Wylla, I don't know what might lie ahead, but whatever it is, there are things I need to say to you—"

"Rulalin," Wylla started to interrupt.

"No, please, I beg you, Wylla, just give me a moment. I'll be clear and quick, I promise."

Wylla swallowed, bracing. "All right."

"You may suspect what I'm going to say, but even if you do, please just hear me out. Once before, while we walked together on a grey afternoon through the streets of Amaan Sul, I tried to express my heart to you. It was poor timing, and I shouldn't have burdened you with my feelings then. I was captivated by your remarkable beauty and the dream of loving you that had filled my days and nights with hope. Wylla, I know I'm not perfect, but I am faithful and true and would gladly surrender my position in Fel Edorath to be your husband and serve as your consort when you are queen of Enthanin. I offer you all that I am, whatever may come, both now and in the future. I have loved you every moment of my life since first we met, and I will love you until I die. I'm asking you, here and now, if you think there is any way you could return that love?"

"Rulalin, I'm flattered, of course," Wylla said, trying to find the right words now that this was finally out in the open, "but we were so young when we met. How could you love me all these years when we were but children? We were only sixteen!"

"I know, don't you think I've thought of that? As I grew older and the love grew with me, I feared that I had created you in my mind, transformed you into something you weren't. I turned away women who loved me, including Mindarin, who still hasn't forgiven me. And all the way here, I was both excited and afraid, eager to see you but fearful I would find that I'd been wrong or that you'd changed. But I wasn't wrong, and you haven't changed. I knew immediately that you were not a figment of my imagination, but the fulfillment of my dreams."

Rulalin dropped down on a single knee beside her on the deck. "All I am and will ever be, I offer to you. Take my life and my heart, they are yours."

"Rulalin, please stand up. I can't accept what you offer. As I said, I will always treasure the memory of the days we spent together, as I will treasure my memories of our time here in Sulare, but I do not love you as you love me. I am sorry."

Rulalin didn't stand, but instead dropped onto both knees and virtually groveled on the deck before her. "Wylla, do not cast my love aside so lightly! I believe what you say is true, that you do not love me now, but that might change. I have spoken my desires to you, and I don't take them back. Don't answer, for now. Wait and see. Spend time with me. Let's talk more often. Perhaps when you understand how deeply and truly I love you, perhaps when you see me more clearly, perhaps then you will feel as I do."

"Rulalin, my feelings haven't changed, and they aren't going to." Wylla was exasperated. This had gone on long enough. "I know all hearts can be unpredictable, but I know mine well enough to say that it is not fair to you to hold out false hope. I like you, but I do not love you."

Rulalin slapped both hands violently on the wooden deck, startling Wylla, who stepped away. Rulalin sprang to his feet with his fists clenched and a wild, desperate look in his eyes. "Oh no, you don't love me, though I have only ever sought to be a friend to you, to love and support you." His voice rose, angry and trembling. "No indeed, but I've seen the way you look at Joraiem and his golden hair. He's just a boy, Wylla, who doesn't know the first thing about love. Has he told you of the girl he loves back home yet? No? He hasn't mentioned that? Maybe you should ask him before you give too much of your heart to him."

Wylla, after the initial shock of Rulalin's dramatic transformation, had grown increasingly outraged at his shameful display. When the diatribe zeroed in so quickly and directly on Joraiem, she could no longer control herself. She would not hear him disparaged, even if it was possible he might love another. "Don't you dare speak like this to me! You have no right. And what's more, Joraiem has never been anything but kind and gracious to me, and to you too for that matter. I've seen how you disrespect and ignore him. You're the one who is behaving like a boy."

Wylla turned to go, and Rulalin reached out and grabbed her arm. Pain shot down her weary arm, and with all her might she wrenched herself free from his grip. "How dare you touch me!" she exclaimed, standing up as tall as she could to glare in his face. "Don't ever lay a hand on me again, Rulalin. Not ever!"

She wheeled and started away across the dark, empty deck. Rulalin called once after her, "Wylla!" His voice more desperate than before, but she heard in it that he had gotten her message. She did not turn around.

2

SYNOKI

ON THE EVENING OF their seventh day at sea, the *Evening Star* entered a dense fog that completely enveloped the ship. Ulmindos brought the ship to a veritable crawl and stationed half of his crew as lookouts around the deck and up in the rigging. The mood at dinner was sober among the Novaana, as Caan and Valzaan kept their own counsel.

When they finished eating, Valzaan approached the circle and stood with Caan beside and a little behind him. "We are close. We should spot land tomorrow, if not tonight."

"How do you know we're close?"

"The voyage in good weather takes only about a week, but beyond this I feel it. The same way I felt it the night we saw the great flash of light from the beach. The same way I felt it the last time I was here."

"The last time!" Aljeron exclaimed. "You didn't say you'd been on the Forbidden Isle before!"

"No, I didn't. The memory is dark, like the place itself. I don't like to think of it."

The Novaana stared at one another, amazement resting on their faces. Aljeron knew it was his place to ask, if any of them were to, so he did. "Though the memory is dark, would you tell us about it? It might help us to prepare."

"I will not speak of it in detail. It was many years ago, near the dawn of the Third Age. Sulmandir had killed Vulsutyr, the Fire Giant, on the slopes of Agia Muldonai, then disappeared. The rest of the dragons, mourning their great father, had retreated to their mountain lairs, seldom to be seen after. Malek had also disappeared, into the vast, cavernous depths of Agia Muldonai. Men and Great Bear held councils to decide on a course of action, for Corindel had not yet laid assault to the Holy Mountain or betrayed the Great Bear.

"I came then to the Forbidden Isle, sent here by Allfather to explore the abandoned city of Nal Gildoroth. I was as disinclined then as I am now to set foot there, for the city where Malek, his followers, and the Vulstyrim dwelt is a foul place. The scent of evil was a stench that lay thick upon the whole land, like a shroud upon a decaying corpse. Even with almost a thousand years of fresh air blowing in off the Southern Ocean, I wouldn't be surprised if the scent remains."

Joraiem watched Valzaan stand, his eerie, white eyes wide open and fixed on the dense fog. "I had hoped," Valzaan continued, "when I departed this shore so long ago that I was leaving for the last time. I know that when the time comes, Allfather will make all things new, and Kirthanin will once again be the blessed land Allfather intended. In that day, even the Forbidden Isle will be made clean. I know this, but it is hard to hold onto that vision of the future when there is so much darkness ahead, and when I have no idea how long the night is going to last. It is hard to think of anything as we approach this land, except the misery that Malek and Vulsutyr and their creations have brought to us all.

"Nevertheless, Allfather brought me safely to and from the Forbidden Isle then, and He may do so again. We go because we have been called to go; the rest is up to Him. We will take what comes as it comes. There is nothing else we can do."

Before he disappeared into his quarters, Valzaan urged them all to make the most of the night and sleep while they still enjoyed the relative safety of the *Evening Star*. Most of them went below shortly thereafter, but Joraiem remained above, knowing that he wasn't ready for sleep.

Joraiem was not alone. Kelvan and Bryar walked quietly toward the stern and rested there together against the wall of the above-deck storage room. Joraiem sat down and watched them go and at first didn't notice the form in white gliding along the rail beside him. He looked up and found Wylla, her long dark hair hanging down upon her shoulders, wearing a long white summer dress, smiling gently down on him. Her beautiful eyes sparkled like the stars that the fog hid from view. Joraiem's heart trembled.

"Not sleepy yet?" she asked, stopping beside him.

"No. You neither?"

She shook her head. "Mind if I join you?"

He motioned to the deck beside him, patting it with his hand. "Not at all, please, join me." His voice sounded calmer than he would have expected.

"Thanks," she said, sitting down and folding her legs as she leaned back against the rail too. Her shoulder rubbed slightly against his as she settled in, as did her knee, which for a moment rested against his own leg. The feel of her so close was unnerving, a feeling made even worse when a sudden gust of wind blew wisps of her fragrant hair against his cheek. She rescued him, though, from total distraction by adjusting herself so that even though she was still close, there was no more contact. "Tell me about Dal Harat."

"Dal Harat? Why? Amaan Sul is a much more fascinating topic."

"Not to me," Wylla answered, wryly. "I am well versed in the daily life of Amaan Sul. Besides, you never talk about yourself."

"Maybe I don't have many stories to tell," Joraiem answered.

"Joraiem," Wylla said, putting her hand on his arm, "it would help me to face this dark night to hear you speak of home, of warm things, and of sunny days far away before all of this. Please? For me?"

"All right, if it would help," Joraiem began. "Dal Harat is a beautiful place, even if small. I didn't know until I reached Peris Mil how small it was, and I know from what I've heard that Peris Mil is to Amaan Sul as Dal Harat is to Peris Mil. You might ride through Dal Harat and almost miss the town itself. But that would be too bad, because what makes Dal Harat special are the people. They are wonderful, and I miss them."

"What makes them wonderful?"

"They're like family. We celebrate births and birthdays, engagements and weddings, all the events of our lives together. When trouble comes, or when death visits a family, we face it together. All the high and low points of my actual family have been shared with them."

"Tell me about your family—do you miss them a lot?"

"Yes, especially this past week. I keep finding myself talking to my dad in my sleep. It's hard not being able to discuss what we're doing with him. I want his guidance."

"What's his name?"

"Monias."

"What's Monias like?"

Joraiem shrugged. "He's wise, thoughtful, full of advice—

most of it welcome." Joraiem smiled. "I could use some now, that's for sure."

"And your mom?"

"Elsora. She's like my dad in some ways, only beautiful, more gentle, and not as intense. She's a good balance for him. They met here, in Sulare I mean. My mom grew up near Cimaris Rul, and like a lot of the far southern Suthanim, she has golden hair and brown skin from the warm climate."

"So they didn't know each other before?"

"No, not at all. They spent a lot of time together and married before they left for home. Monias says that he knew the moment he saw my mom that he wanted to marry her, but that it took him most of their time here to get the courage up to ask."

"Really? Interesting," Wylla said, and Joraiem, remembering to whom he was talking, blushed. "And do you have siblings?" she continued.

"My sister Kyril is seventeen, though she will be eighteen soon, and my brother Brenim is twelve."

"Your sister will come of age while you're gone?"

"Yes."

"That must be hard for you."

"It is. I may well return to find her engaged."

"You sound as though you expect it."

"I do. My best friend, Evrim, told me the day I left for Sulare of his intention to seek Kyril's hand and sought my blessing. I gave it."

"It was good of him to ask, but it still must be hard to know you'll miss the celebration."

"It is hard, but if ever I come home again, I will make sure they celebrate some more."

"And what else do you look forward to when you return?" Wylla asked quietly. "Are there others that you miss, aside from your family, and this friend, Evrim?"

Joraiem turned to study Wylla's face. "What do you mean? Do I have other friends?"

"You know," she said, hesitating, and Joraiem couldn't tell but it appeared as though she were blushing, "of the many wonderful young ladies of Dal Harat, is there anyone in particular waiting for you at home?"

"No."

"None? A handsome man like yourself in a small village? Surely there must be some woman there, pining away for the day your horse will bring you home."

"There is Aleta, who claims to have been in love with me since she was eleven years old."

"But you don't love her?"

"Love her? I'd like to throttle her."

"Is loving you such a serious offense as that?" Wylla asked.

Joraiem looked at her. There was no smirk on her face or mischief in her eyes. "No, it isn't loving me that I have against her."

"So there are no women in Dal Harat worthy of your love?" Wylla asked.

"I didn't say that."

Wylla waited.

Joraiem sighed. "Aleta has a twin sister, Alina. As difficult and repulsive as Aleta may be, Alina is the opposite. She's sweet and kind and was also in love with me, for a time. But, she's engaged to be married, if she isn't married already."

"What happened?"

"Nothing happened. I spent so much time and energy fending off Aleta, I didn't realize until just before I left how much I cared for Alina. I told her, but it was too late."

Joraiem watched Wylla stare down at the deck, her clasped hands trembling in her lap. "I'm sorry, Joraiem. You must miss her very much."

Joraiem smiled. Speaking of Alina had brought an image

of her clearly before his mind's eye. He smiled at the thought of her, in part because she seemed happy in his imagination, but mostly, because he saw with utter clarity that he was wholly free of his feelings for her. He saw her waving good-bye and turning to walk away, up the long central street in Dal Harat. "Don't be," he whispered. "I don't miss her so much any more."

Wylla looked at him then, and though he knew his affection for her must be shining in his eyes, he didn't look away. He felt as if he was really looking at her for the first time. She lowered her eyes and turned away, masking her face in the shadows. "Why not? I mean, you've only been away from home since the start of Spring Rise, right?"

"That's right. I left the first day of Spring Rise, so it's been just about four and a half months since I left."

"And she is already forgotten?" Wylla began, then added hastily, "I mean, it seems that though much has happened, that wasn't really so long ago."

Joraiem looked away, not sure how to respond. He had seen both relief and disbelief in her eyes, and he was torn. He had crossed the causeway to Sulare just over two months ago, almost as brokenhearted as when he had left Dal Harat. The pain had not begun to dissipate until the day he saw Wylla on the road and found the healing wonder of her presence. But how could he explain that to her? He had not planned to speak of this yet.

"Wylla, I don't want you to have the wrong idea," he began, but she took his hand and squeezed it tightly, interrupting him.

"Don't, Joraiem," she said, almost in tears. "I don't know what got into me. I was rude. Please don't say anything. I shouldn't have said that."

"Wylla," Joraiem said, holding tightly to her hand as she tried to retract it. "Don't worry. I want to tell you. All right?"

She nodded.

"The journey here was long and difficult. Especially those

first long days to Peris Mil through the spring rains. They were miserable. I found myself constantly seeking hope in some wild dream that maybe she would realize while I was gone that she really loved me and would break off her engagement. Every day, I carried sorrow in my heart. Every step of the way, she came with me, and I hoped that when I arrived here, I would find temporary distraction before I had to turn home again and face the loss. But, Allfather gave me a gift I was not looking for, beyond all hope and beyond the wildest dreams of my imagination. He gave me, beside the road and beneath the blossoms of the snow trees, my first glimpse of you."

Now some of Wylla's tears slipped down her cheeks, and she gently rested her head on Joraiem's shoulders. She slid her hands up his arm and clasped it tightly. "Oh Joraiem, you can't know how happy I am to hear you say that."

"Then you feel the same way?" he replied, softly.

"Of course," she answered, wiping the tears from her cheeks. "I've been trying to tell you as clearly as I could without being forward, silly boy."

"I had hoped, but I didn't want to presume."

"You wouldn't have had to presume if you had spoken to me before this. Why have you waited so long? Did you just need to be sure?"

"At first, perhaps. I needed time to realize it was all right. I felt I was betraying Alina, though of course that was ridiculous. There was nothing to betray except memories of regret. I also needed to be sure that what I felt for you was real and not some redirection of my spurned affection."

"And you know now that it isn't?"

"Yes. There's no doubt in me whatsoever that Alina's engagement, which seemed like a cruel twist of fate, was really Allfather's mercy. Though wounded, my heart was free when I saw you, totally free."

She squeezed his arm again. "I keep squeezing you, because I need to keep checking to see if this is really real. It's like a dream."

Joraiem placed his hand on Wylla's, and traced her slender, smooth fingers with his own. "It does feel like a dream, but it isn't. We are on the *Evening Star,* in the middle of the Southern Ocean, perhaps within hours of the Forbidden Isle."

"Oh don't speak of that. Tomorrow will come soon enough. I want to hold onto this feeling a little longer." She stood and, offering her hand to Joraiem, helped him up. "You know what's really out there?" she asked, gesturing out over the water into the fog.

"What?"

"The future, and whatever it holds, it can't be all bad if you're with me. I think I could face just about anything with you," she whispered as she gazed up into his eyes, and he felt them pulling him. They were as blue, as deep and as beautiful as the first day he had seen them, but this time they were shining for him. He slipped his fingers through her long black hair. It was smooth and silky. He leaned over her and very nearly, without thinking, kissed her, but he realized what he was about to do and held himself in check. He was embarrassed by what he had almost done, but there was no reproach on her face. In fact, she leaned in and rested her head against his chest. "Joraiem, I'm so happy. We can face tomorrow together. I'm so tired of hiding how I feel, and now I don't have to."

Joraiem felt a sudden stab of worry—Rulalin. He still hadn't spoken to him about any of this, and it wouldn't be right for Rulalin simply to look over in the morning and see Joraiem holding Wylla like he was Kelvan holding Bryar! "Wylla, I'm not sure we should tell anyone, just yet, I—"

"Why not?" Wylla asked, lifting her head up and looking at him closely.

Her voice was calm, but he heard a shift in her tone. He didn't know why, but he sensed he was in delicate territory. "Well, because there's something I should take care of first."

"What?"

"Wylla, I'm not the only man here who cares for you. I need to talk to someone and explain."

"You mean Rulalin," Wylla said, with an anger in her voice Joraiem had never heard before. "What do you have to explain to him?"

"Wylla, I don't understand why—"

"What? What do you have to explain to him?"

"About you, about us. I'm concerned about him and how he'll feel about this. I'm worried about how he'll react and how it might disrupt our time together as a group. He barely speaks to me as it is. I don't know what to do, but whatever it is, it may be a while before I can do it and before we can be open about this."

"You're concerned about him, about how he feels? What about me? What about how I feel? I've been pretty clear with Rulalin on numerous occasions about my lack of interest. What else do I have to do? How long do I have to be a prisoner to what he wants and how he feels? Can you tell me that?"

"I can't."

"No, I guess you can't." She didn't yell, but Joraiem could tell she was furious, and how much of that anger was directed at him wasn't exactly clear. He knew enough about women, though, to know it might not matter. If he stepped wrong now, she might direct it all at him. When she turned and stalked away, he hesitated for fear of unleashing a stronger rebuke than what he had already received, but he couldn't restrain himself entirely. He called after her.

"Wylla!" She disappeared from view. He ran his fingers through his hair. *Now what?*

After a brief and restless sleep, Joraiem was awakened by an excited voice exclaiming that land had been sighted. Dressing hastily, Joraiem joined the others on deck.

Land was indeed in view. No trace of the previous day's fog was left, and Joraiem smiled at the broad azure sky above the deep blue sea. Ahead lay the Forbidden Isle, the coastline stretching well out of view in either direction with mountains barely visible many leagues inland. Joraiem's first impression was surprise, surprise that the island looked so inviting. Its color was a rich green dotted with summer brown as far as his eye could see.

The normally quiet Kelvan voiced his thoughts out loud as they all stood staring. "It's . . . it's beautiful."

"Indeed it is," Valzaan answered. "It has always been so. Are you surprised?"

"Yes. I always imagined it a darker place."

"As well you should, for there is no place darker than this. Good and beauty are not the same thing. Evil that comes in pleasant packaging is nonetheless evil."

"My father used to make that point of Malek," Joraiem added, half to himself.

"Yes," Valzaan said, "Malek, before he was cast from the Mountain, was as handsome and beautiful as any living thing."

"Then why are Malek's creations so hideous?" asked Karalin, her voice wavering a little. Joraiem turned to see her clinging to Wylla's arm, perhaps for support for her bad ankle, perhaps just for support. Joraiem glanced at Wylla, but she did not look at him. Feeling annoyed, Joraiem turned back toward Valzaan.

"They are hideous because real beauty, though not necessarily evidence of goodness, is nevertheless the product of goodness—Allfather's goodness. The Grendolai, which Malek and Vulsutyr created together, were not only hideous, but hated the light and avoided it at all cost, roaming only in darkness. The Malekim and Black Wolves, though weaker and less formidable than the Grendolai, were improved at least in that respect. Nevertheless, they also were monstrous, as you have seen. The hand of Malek can do many things, but it cannot reproduce even the simplest beauty that Allfather bestowed on virtually all His creation. That is one of many reasons why Malek hates Allfather more now then he ever did before. That is one reason why Malek will never stop in his quest to conquer and rule Kirthanin. He hates the beauty Allfather has made. He hates his inability to replicate it. Most of all, he hates his own loss of it."

"Valzaan," Ulmindos called from behind them, and they all turned as he approached. "The water here is deep, and the *Evening Star's* keel lies high in the water. I should be able to get you perhaps a hundred spans from shore. We'll drop anchor there, and then we can begin to ferry everything ashore."

"Good, Ulmindos. Good. Take us as close as you can. It may be that we'll have to reboard swiftly, and the shorter the distance, the better."

Joraiem glanced around at the others, but most were looking again at the island, showing no reaction to Valzaan's words. They stood soberly, quietly, until Caan moved among them clapping his hands and summoning them to work. Work they did, bringing their supplies for the journey from the lower to upper deck as Ulmindos and his crew took the *Evening Star* in closer and closer to the Forbidden Isle. The ship turned gradually until it was running almost parallel to the island but still moving ever closer. Eventually they heard Ulmindos giving the command to drop anchor. Before long, they were sitting still not more than eighty spans from shore by Joraiem's reckoning.

The long boats were readied, and all three were launched, with all but Ulmindos and his crew aboard them. Two were full with eight passengers apiece, while the third carried only Aljeron, Joraiem, Saegan, and Koshti. Despite the bond between them, it had looked at first as though Aljeron might not get Koshti into the boat at all. He had coaxed and pleaded, petted and rubbed, but Koshti had remained resolute about not stepping onto the slightly swaying longboat that hung over the water just a few feet beyond the deck. Standing not far behind Aljeron, Joraiem looked over Koshti's head at the longboat, and as he did, he saw the rolling waves and suddenly felt sick. He closed his eyes, but it was still there. He felt the disappointment wash over him. *Not cured, after all.*

Finally, Aljeron must have whispered just the right thing into Koshti's ear, for he stepped gingerly aboard the longboat and lay down, curled up along the keel line, his head down. Aljeron quickly followed, sitting down on the bottom of the boat with him. Joraiem, holding his breath, managed to step out after them, and soon they were being lowered alongside the others. He took the oars in the stern and, following Saegan's lead, rowed toward the island.

It took only a quarter of an hour or so to reach the shore, and soon they had pulled the boats far enough in to unload everyone. The twins, following Caan's directions, immediately rowed back out to the *Evening Star* in order to load their longboat with food and water. They had only had room on this trip for their weapons, which Caan had insisted must come with them from the start. No one had argued.

As the twins headed back toward the *Evening Star*, they passed Sarneth swimming steadily through the clear blue water. A bit large for the longboats and not necessarily eager to be in one anyway, Sarneth had asked simply to be lowered into the water so he could swim ashore. An experienced swimmer and fisher of the big rivers of Kirthanin, the gently rolling waves headed in toward the Forbidden Isle were probably quite inviting to him. And so, as the twins rowed back out toward the ship, Joraiem watched Sarneth's head bob up and down as he swam through the water. Soon, Sarneth joined the others, his fur sleek with dripping salt water as he stood in the hot midmorning sun, basking in the heat, enjoying the feel of the smooth hot sand beneath his paws.

The beach on which they were standing was narrow, stretching inland perhaps twenty spans before ending at the foot of a bluff of perhaps a span or more in height. The sand wall ran as far as the beach did in either direction. Ulmindos speculated they had landed with the tide at its highest, so the boats shouldn't be dragged inland too far unless they wanted to risk having to push and pull them a long way to the water should they find themselves retreating in a hurry.

Nothing could be seen along the beach in either direction, so Caan motioned for them to get into a formation he had shown them on board. When Aljeron and Saegan had joined Caan and Valzaan in the front, with Joraiem about a step behind on the right, Suruna ready, and Bryar and Kelvan likewise ready on the left, they moved forward. The women moved silently behind them, with Rulalin, Elyas, Darias, and Sarneth following them. They stopped at the foot of the bluff, and Caan slowly ascended just far enough to be able to look over it, and after a few moments, he slid back down.

"I can see nothing but rolling grassland," he said to their relief. "Joraiem, Kelvan, Bryar, climb up and spread out along this ridge. If you see or hear anything, signal immediately then get back down on this beach and come find us. We will need you should an attack come, so don't do anything foolish."

Joraiem led the way up, finding only rolling grassland as Caan had said. The tall, coarse green grass was maybe half a span high, about at Joraiem's waist, though a little higher up on both Bryar and Kelvan. It stretched as far as he could see. He crouched in the grass and waited until the others were crouching beside him. "Bryar, I want you to stay here, closest to the others, while I head about fifty spans that way," he said, motioning to their left along the coastline they had approached from, "while Kelvan moves the other way about the same distance."

Bryar looked annoyed, and as soon as he stopped, she began. "You don't need to try to protect me. This is foolish. Kelvan is hurt and if anyone should stay close to the others, it's him."

"Bryar, Caan told you to follow my orders."

"I will, when they make sense or when we're in battle."

Joraiem considered her stubbornness, not really wanting to fight her anymore than he wanted to rescind his first official order. He finally acquiesced. "All right, but you will go the way I directed Kelvan to go. If we were noticed from the island as we approached, it would probably have been from the direction I'm heading, so be ready to get back to the others and protect the camp should you hear me signal. All right?"

They nodded. He watched Bryar take her leave of Kelvan with a smile as she slipped away in the opposite direction, and soon he was sliding stealthily through the tall grass along the ridge that separated the beautiful sea and warm sand from the most feared place in all the world.

Over an hour passed, and as Fifth Hour approached, the sun rose high overhead. The cool breeze, which had felt constant aboard the *Evening Star*, seemed to have disappeared entirely, and sweat flowed freely down Joraiem's body. Unlike in Sulare, the air here was humid, and the sweat did not quickly evaporate. Indeed, it poured down his face, some of it forming beads on his nose before dropping onto the ground below. Some slid down his sides, a waterfall of perspiration soaking his skin and tunic and making his periodic brushes with the tall grass all the more ticklish. He tried to keep his hands dry so he would be ready if danger came, but it was becoming impossible to find a dry place on his clothing to wipe them.

A rustle behind him and a flash of movement alerted him to Caan's presence. He was glad that Malekim were not known for being unusually stealthy, for had Caan been one of the Voiceless, Joraiem would have been in trouble.

"Come, we have things to decide," Caan said softly.

"No more lookout?"

"Not for the moment." Caan disappeared back the way he had come, and Joraiem followed swiftly. When he arrived back at the place on the beach where the others were gathered, he found Bryar and Kelvan already there, along with the twins back from the *Evening Star* with the supplies unloaded. The group sat in the shade of the sandbank in three short rows, with Sarneth resting in the sand just beyond them and Valzaan facing them, sitting on a rock. A windhover rested on Valzaan's shoulder—a familiar enough sight back in Sulare, but Joraiem hadn't noticed any hovering around Valzaan on board. He recalled now, however, that more than once he had caught glimpses of tiny brown flecks in the sky, flecks he had attributed to too many hours on deck in the hot sun. Perhaps one or more windhovers had indeed accompanied the voyage.

As Joraiem took a seat in the back row beside Darias, Valzaan began to speak. "We have a decision to make, and we must make it quickly. Ulmindos brought us in at a perfect spot. Nal Gildoroth is not more than two hours march from here, and if we go immediately, we can be there by early afternoon. That would afford us several hours to look for answers to our questions and return before nightfall. If Allfather blesses us, we might be able to end this day back on board the *Evening Star*, heading back out to sea."

An excited murmur ran through the group. The prospect of spending a night on the Forbidden Isle had been without doubt the most frightening prospect of all. The possibility that they could be on their way by nightfall began to push that fear far away.

"So what's the decision we need to make?" Rulalin asked. "Surely, if there wasn't more to it, we wouldn't need to even consider another way."

"Not knowing what we might find on our way there, or in the city itself, it is possible we might not be able to finish our task in time to make it back here by nightfall. That would leave us the unenviable options of passing a night in Nal Gildoroth, returning here only to have to make the trek again tomorrow morning, or finding our way back in darkness. It might be wise, to wait until first light and head out then."

As quickly as it had come, the elation faded. None of those scenarios involved getting away without spending a night here, and it seemed to Joraiem somehow impossible that they should have come all this way only to spend a single day walking to and from Nal Gildoroth. A wave of foreboding passed through him, along with a deep sense of urgency. He wanted to believe it was only his inner fear that made him shudder, but he knew deep down it was more than that.

"I say we go now," Seagan began. "What Valzaan says might be true even if we do wait for first light. If we cannot do what we have come to do in the several hours we have today, how do we know that four or five more hours tomorrow would make much difference? We may have to be here many days. Waiting until tomorrow would just make it one more. If we have to stay here a while, I'd like to know now. Let's get in there and see what's happening."

Nods of approval rippled down each of the lines. Valzaan looked at Caan, squatting nearby in the sand, who also nodded. "Very well then, it is what I would have advised had we been divided. Let's assemble our packs and be on our way."

The nine men, Valzaan and Kelvan excepted, took packs with food, water skins, and scant other supplies. Sarneth carried only his massive staff, strapped across his broad back. In a matter of moments, they were ready to go. They gathered in a circle around Valzaan. "Half a league down the coast, a dried river bed intersects this beach. We'll keep close to this bank all the way down, then turn inland along the riverbed. The riverbed will take us most of the way to Nal Gildoroth, but just shy of the city, we'll turn onto the main road that heads to the city gates. We are going in by the front door, something which very few but Malek, his spawn, and the Vulsutyrim themselves have ever done."

"Delightful," someone murmured from the back, and Valzaan and Caan started down the beach, leading them double file along the sandy bank on their left. Joraiem and Bryar followed, bows in hand.

They had not gone far when Valzaan halted the line. A hand from Caan, raised and clenched, a signal calling for silence, prevented any from asking why they'd stopped. Soon, Joraiem knew anyway. Something, or someone, was moving down the beach toward them. Caan pressed himself up against the sand wall, motioning for Joraiem to step up beside Valzaan, which he did. Kneeling, Joraiem drew a cyranic arrow and nocked it on Suruna. Whatever it was, it kept right on coming their way.

At first hard to make out in the bright sun against the backdrop of the light sand, the figure of a man gradually became clear, a man with ragged black hair, no shirt, and little but rags around his waist. He was lean and tan from the sun, his bare feet kicking up sand as he walked with a decided limp down the broad beach. There was nothing in his hands, and his tall frame was slight and sinewy.

"Point the bow down, Joraiem," Valzaan whispered, "but be ready."

Valzaan stepped out from the shade of the sandbank and toward the man who was now just twenty spans away. If the man paused or hesitated for even a moment it was imperceptible to Joraiem, who held tightly to Suruna, ready to bring the man down at even a hint of a threat to Valzaan. He trembled slightly, but not because he was nervous to be contemplating pointing Suruna at a man, but because he felt a pounding within him almost pushing him to put the arrow through the man's chest. The pounding, like a pulsating throb within, seemed to whisper *shoot, don't wait, shoot, don't wait.* He pushed the pounding out of his mind and trained his attention on the scene before him.

When the haggard man was just ten spans away, Valzaan addressed him at last. "Greetings, stranger," the prophet began calmly, even kindly, but with authority nonetheless. "I would greet you in Allfather's name and give you Allfather's blessing if you would but stop and introduce yourself. What is your name, and what brings you to this wild and fearful place?"

At Valzaan's words, the man recoiled, or so it seemed to Joraiem. A glint of anger or rage flashed through his eyes, though it could have as easily been fear.

The man's lips, dry and cracked, moved almost silently, and he, realizing only halfway into his sentence that no audible sound was coming out, stopped and started over. "I am Synoki," he said, shakily. "At least, that's what my name was before. I've not said it or heard it said now for several years. Synoki," he said again, forming the word, this time slowly, even reverently, "a name from another time and place."

"Synoki," Valzaan echoed him. "What are you doing here and in such a ragged state?"

Synoki looked past the prophet at the rest of them, still stretched out along the sand wall and covered by its shade. "I will gladly tell you, only please allow me to sit down in the shade."

Valzaan motioned to the shade and stepped aside as Synoki shuffled over in front of the group and sat carefully down, leaning against the cool sandy bank. He stretched as he sat and used his arms to position his right leg, which from the knee down was deformed and discolored. His right foot was also disfigured, the toes crooked and misshapen. Even so, the rest of his body was lean but strong, and despite the heavy presence of grey throughout his wild, black hair, he didn't look much older than they were.

"I grew up in Col Marena, a large port not far from Shalin Bel." Aljeron stirred at this mention of his hometown. "I was crippled in my youth by a fall, and so any thought I had of working the dock with my brothers soon disappeared. It is hard work loading and unloading the merchant ships of Werthanin, and a lame boy is not in high demand. So, I took to the sea as a sailor, and though again I was not of much use for the more physical work of a seaman, I was agile despite my deformity, possessed of superior arm strength and unusually gifted in ascending and navigating the rigging of a ship. Thus I earned my keep as a lookout and scout.

"It was not quite three years ago—I think, though I have to admit I've lost track of what time of year it is, exactly. We are in summer, now, I assume?"

"It is the twelfth day of Full Summer," Valzaan said, "in the year 959 of the Third Age."

"The twelfth day of Full Summer," Synoki echoed quietly, staring beyond them out to sea. "It was not quite Winter Rise, then, almost three years ago, and we had been delayed in Cimaris Rul. Even so, when finally we were ready to sail for home, our captain took us out to sea, confident that it was not yet late enough in the year for the winter winds and storms to bother us. Rarely has such a knowledgeable man of the sea been more wrong. Our third day out to sea, we were caught in a storm the likes of which I have never seen before. It blew us south for twelve straight days. We were totally lost, knowing only that we were farther from Kirthanin than any one of us had ever been before. Then, on the twelfth day, the storm stopped, but not before a series of enormous waves had all but swamped the boat. The crew baled all night and all the next day, but it was clear we were lost. In the early morning of the fourteenth day, we abandoned ship, each of us clinging to a separate piece of wood, the rowboats having been lost early in the storm.

"We were scattered to die alone, and as far as I know, I am the only member of the crew to survive. Perhaps in this, my upper body strength served me well. After three days on the open ocean, I was ready to die. It was all but impossible for me to grip the barrel I floated on any longer. As I finally let go, I began to sink beneath the waves in the pitch black of a moonless night. As I did, I felt my feet touch bottom. Invested with hope for the first time in days, I swam back to the surface, and in the dark stared in all directions until at last I could make out the shore of this very island. And, here I have been, ever since."

"Do you know where 'here' is?" Valzaan asked, as the rest of us gazed in renewed wonder at the stranger in our midst.

A wild light again glowed in Synoki's eyes as he looked at Valzaan. Again, Joraiem could not tell if it was anger or fear, though the latter seemed more likely. "I did not know at first, but after living only on the shore for several months, hoping that I might someday find another vessel passing by, I eventually left the shore altogether to more fully explore the island. It was Spring Rise, then, and I traversed much of this island before I first saw it. I had headed inland from the southern tip of the island, and this course took me high into the mountains that you can see from here when you climb the embankment. As I reached the top of a pass between two of the peaks, where the air is crisp and cold even on the hottest of summer days, I looked down into the distance and saw it. The abandoned city sprawled across the valley like a great dark cloud upon a mountain top. It was dark and ominous and all I needed to see. I watched it from the pass for weeks, just to make sure it was empty, before going down to see it for myself. I spent only one night in the city, and that was a mistake. It is a fearful place of dark shadows, and on the morning of the next day I left it and have not been back since. Yes, I may not have been the best student of history and geography as a boy, but I know where I am."

"And in all the time you've been here, have you not seen anyone or anything else?"

"Fish, I have seen and caught. They have kept me fed well, more or less. Some animals also live here, animals like rabbits or gophers that burrow in the dark earth and only come out at night. Some of these I have caught and eaten, but I prefer the fish."

"And that is all?"

Synoki glanced away nervously, his voice rising in pitch. "That is all I have seen, but I know that at times there have been other things here. Things I fear to name."

"What do you mean?" Valzaan pressed for answers gently.

"After swimming this morning, I ascended a large rock to sun myself and dry. It was from that rock that I caught a glimpse of your sail in the sun. I would not have believed it, and almost certainly I would not have dragged myself all this way down the beach in the hope of finding you, had I not seen a ship off this shore before."

"There has been another ship?"

"Ship or ships, I don't know. At least twice I've seen a great ship, perhaps twice the size of yours." Synoki motioned toward the *Evening Star*, still visible from where they were huddled. "The first time was more than a year after I came here. In the fading twilight, I saw the ship come along shore, and though my first impulse was to run and wave madly until I had attracted its attention, I didn't. Something held me back, and I was glad. As the ship drew alongside me, I could see on the deck a figure framed in the fading light of day, a figure so large that it could not but have been a creature of legend. I would have not believed it possible, except that in the city there is a great statue, which, though even larger, looked just like the creature. It was a giant, standing upon the great ship, scanning the shore where I was sitting. I did not dare move, for fear he would see me."

Caan looked from Synoki to Valzaan, "One of the Vulsutyrim," he said, with wonder in his voice. Valzaan nodded.

Synoki continued, "Since then, I have stuck only to secret ways, moving usually at night. In fact, it took me a long time to find you, because I dared not approach along the beach until I was sure that yours was not the same ship. I all but crawled through the high grass of the ridge until I was sure, at which point I dropped onto the beach, unable to bear waiting any longer. I had long since given up hope I would ever get off this island, but now you're here. I don't know why you've come, but can't we leave, at once? I would be away from this place once and for all, and though I have nothing, I would pay you in any way I can for passage aboard your vessel."

"You are welcome to leave with us when we go," Valzaan answered, "and there may be a way you can pay us, but we cannot leave until we have done what we have come to do."

"What is that?" Synoki asked, timidly.

"That," Valzaan began, "will be clear in time. For now, you need only decide if you are willing to return with us to the city of Nal Gildoroth for a second time."

Synoki's eyes grew wide. "Why? Why go there? What could you possibly want in that place?"

"Do you not know?" Valzaan asked. "If you have been here for almost three years, have you not seen or noticed anything unusual of late?"

"You speak of the light that appeared over the island nine days ago."

"*Over* the island? What do you mean?"

"I was sleeping in a small cave near the alcove where I

swam this morning, when a great flash of light and a rumble like the sound of much thunder echoed above. The earth shook and the ocean water beyond my cave sprayed high into the heavens. The light was blinding, and I cowered inside until it all had passed. When I crawled out, the light was fading above the island, rolling in waves in every direction. I don't know what it was."

"And that is all you know?"

"That is all I know. It is enough. I cannot remain here any longer. Can we not go?"

"We can, but not before we have entered the city. Will you come? Your familiarity with the island could prove useful, and your guidance would be ample payment for your passage with us."

Synoki, for the first time, scanned the group carefully. He seemed to notice Sarneth and Koshti for the first time, and his eyes went wide with wonder at the sight of Aljeron stroking Koshti's head as it rested in his lap. He also seemed to notice the women for the first time. He did not stare at them rudely, though it must have been a shock to see women after so many years alone. Looking back at Valzaan, he nodded slowly. "I will go with you to the city, since I do not have to go alone, but I hope we will not be long. It is an evil place."

"I hope so too," Valzaan agreed. "The sooner we get there, the sooner we can get back. First, let me introduce everyone."

One by one he introduced each of them to Synoki, starting with Caan, and Joraiem watched intently. Though all Synoki's reactions seemed to make sense given his situation—his timidity with the women, his skittishness before Sarneth, and his outright fear of Koshti, Joraiem still felt uncertain about the castaway. *What a dark place this is that even a poor wretch stranded here awakens fear and doubt in me.*

When they were finished, though, they quickly reassembled their line. Sixth Hour approached, and every moment

brought them closer to sunset. They set out again with a renewed sense of urgency. Joraiem sensed that the others felt
the same heightened alertness he did: If a ship with one of the
Vulsutyrim had been there before, anything might be waiting
for them in Nal Gildoroth.

3

NAL GILDOROTH

THEY MARCHED IN SILENCE, alert and ready, though for what Joraiem wasn't sure. The dried riverbed that took them away
from the bright, shining waters of the Southern Ocean, ever
closer to their destination, was not so deep as to prevent him
from seeing over the banks on either side. It was wide enough
for them to walk four or five abreast, which they did, while
keeping Caan's formation tight. Every so often, the tall grass
on either side of the riverbed would thin out, and he could see
out over the broad grassland in either direction. They had
been walking for almost two hours, and he hadn't seen a living thing stir.

That is, he had seen nothing except for the King Falcon
that had been resting on Valzaan's shoulder earlier in the day.
It had been following them, flying in swooping arcs and circles
far above. Though the bird was so high as to be barely per-
ceptible to the human eye, Joraiem had felt a growing awareness of its presence through the course of the day. Even when

he stared straight ahead, deliberately avoiding looking up into the sky, his mind's eye held a clear image of the bird, keeping them company high above. Though a little unnerving, it was not an unpleasant feeling. In fact, the windhover's company was somewhat comforting, for he took it to be a symbol for the unseen guidance and watchful eye of Allfather Himself.

Synoki had fallen into the formation, walking just to the side and slightly behind Valzaan, between the prophet and Caan. From time to time, Valzaan would lean over to listen quietly to Synoki say something, or on occasion, point in one direction or another, but the brief exchanges were inaudible to the others. The company was quiet too, and there was no need for Caan to enforce his mandate of total silence or to follow through on any of the threats (which he called "promises") to reprimand severely the slightest infraction of this command. Joraiem doubted that either the command or the "promises" had been necessary. It was inconceivable to him that anyone with even minimal understanding of where they were and where they were heading would even think to disrupt the eerie silence.

The two hours Valzaan had estimated the trip would last were all but gone when they spotted a low wooden bridge ahead. The bridge was solid if basic, with several thick, strong pieces of wood spanning the dried riverbed, resting upon three columns of solid, dark grey rock. What was remarkable about the bridge, which they approached from the side, was the thickness of the wood and the solidity of the columns. Joraiem had occasionally paid attention to the engineering works around Dal Harat, and so understood a little of the principles involved, and he knew that what he was looking at had been built to support an astonishing amount of weight. It stood to reason that this should be so, since the bridge maker had no doubt intended it to hold up under the heavy feet of the Vulsutyrim for generations, but until this moment, it had not occurred to Joraiem what that would require. Joraiem also realized, as they continued to approach the bridge, that all of Nal Gildoroth would be the same. He couldn't imagine the scale of an entire city made in such a way.

As they approached the bridge, Valzaan led them to the bank on the left-hand side of the riverbed, and when they were gathered, Caan scrambled up, followed closely by Joraiem, Bryar, and Kelvan. Joraiem stood shoulder to shoulder with Caan, facing down the road that stretched into the distance on the inland side, while Kelvan and Bryar quickly scrambled across the bridge to watch the road behind them on the coastal side. As Joraiem stood, an arrow nocked and ready, he gasped as he gazed ahead. Great dark walls towered above the road, not two hundred spans away, stretching an enormous distance on either side of the road. A broad open gate was only barely discernible, for the dark buildings within were the same color as the walls. Only the road, which continued inside the city in a lighter color, betrayed an opening in Nal Gildoroth's walls at all.

Quickly, the others scrambled up, and as they gathered round, Joraiem could feel the collective wonder. Still, no one broke the injunction against speech, and they reassembled into their tight formation to travel the short distance that remained. Joraiem could tell that the sight of Nal Gildoroth had even taken the edge off the confidence that Caan usually wore like a cloak. He, like the rest of them, could not help but be humbled by the sight.

As they approached the open gate, it was hard for Joraiem to concentrate on only one thing. On the one hand, he wanted to peer through the gate and into the city, but at the same time, he wanted to examine the masonry of these grim and daunting walls. They had at first reminded him of the dragon towers, but he saw as he approached that they were not really like that at all. Whereas the dragon towers had smooth, shaped stones carefully placed together in intricate interlocking patterns, these walls were made with massive stones, each one so large as to be easily a span high and a span wide. Indeed, as they approached the gate and saw a cross section of the wall, it became clear that the blocks were cubic, as the wall was easily a span thick. Joraiem could not imagine how heavy each individual block must be, or how even the first level could have been maneuvered into place, let alone hefted to heights of some twenty to twenty-five spans in the air. Where had the stones been quarried? How great and terrible were the hands that had brought them here? No wonder all Kirthanin save Sulmandir alone had trembled before Vulsutyr when the Fire Giant had walked the land at the end of the Second Age.

Caan halted the company under the archway to briefly confer with Valzaan, and the city within drew Joraiem's attention at last. The road that had approached the city in more or less of a straight line continued on a straight line within. Along either side stood a wide assortment of buildings, densely packing the space beside the road, so that side roads were surprisingly few. Some were extremely large, with doorways a span taller than Sarneth, perhaps three times the height of Joraiem. Others were no larger than the buildings that lined the streets of Peris Mil, and Joraiem wondered what a sight these streets must have been when giants and men strode along them side by side. And later, when first the Grendolai and then the Malekim were made, how then would the city streets have appeared in the afternoon of a Full Summer's day?

There was no time to consider the question, for Caan motioned them into a close huddle around Valzaan. Joraiem leaned in to listen. "We have traveled far to reach this place. Now it is time to do what we have come to do. Follow me into the city, and pray silently each one of you that Allfather both reveal what He has brought us to see, and that He would lead us back out of this place when He has done so. What comes next I cannot see, though I have tried, but I am as sure as I have ever been that in coming we have done as Allfather wished. Follow me, and do not be afraid. Allfather is Lord over both life and death, now and forevermore!" Valzaan turned and started into the city.

The loose dirt and dust of the road outside the city gave way once within to rough cobblestones of a light grey, or at least a grey that appeared light when compared to the near-black of the walls and buildings. At each crossroad, the company halted, as Caan waited for Valzaan to determine their path. Still no one spoke, or whispered, or even dared to breathe aloud. Every time they stopped, the party pressed up against the nearest wall, looking carefully in every direction before moving on, and at every intersection, Valzaan took them forward along the same, central road.

Joraiem did not know how long they traveled like this. He looked at the sun, still visible above the buildings of the city, and he knew that it was a little past Eighth Hour. The tall grass that had bobbed and rustled in the slight island wind beside the riverbed, and the warm sand that had filtered through his toes earlier that morning at the beach, seemed memories of a distant past. Despite the light and heat of a Full Summer afternoon, the darkness of the buildings and their shadows seemed to surround him. No wonder Synoki had never returned.

Joraiem looked ahead at Synoki, who walked beside Valzaan. He was looking around as they all were, taking in the city, but Joraiem could not read from his body language his reaction to being back inside Nal Gildoroth. He was bent over a bit, but no more than he had been as they walked along the dried riverbed. If he was afraid to be back, Joraiem could not see signs of it.

Joraiem looked straight up. The sky seemed strange to him. As he hadn't expected the Forbidden Isle to be beautiful, so he hadn't expected a bright sunny sky to be above Nal Gildoroth. Even in the sunlight, though, the city was ominous. He had never been in a town that lacked the bustling energy of life, let alone a city. The city was wholly barren, and the only thing that broke the silence, other than their own feet, was the sound of the wind, stronger than Joraiem remembered it outside the city gate, whistling through the city streets. The city was, dare he say it, clean. It seemed to him an odd word to use, to call Nal Gildoroth clean, but it did have the appearance of a place swept immaculate. There was no litter or garbage, none of the waste that human habitations and the course of ordinary life produced. Neither were there pleasant or appealing aromas drifting out of the windows and doorways. It was quite unnerving, to be surrounded with the work of many hands but to feel so completely the absence of life.

That was it. Nal Gildoroth was not so much clean as dead. The bareness was not the orderliness of a well-kept house, it was the emptiness of death. Bereft of life, the city was also bereft of the signs of life. He understood why the city had not felt right from the beginning. He had seen what he believed were faded markings above the city gate, and perhaps they were the remnants of letters or runes, but other than that, there had been no signs. Nowhere had they passed a door or house with words or numbers or even pictures to represent the nature of the building or occupation of its former inhabitants. Images from Peris Mil returned to him of the busy streets with its row on row of merchants advertising their wares. Here there was no such competition, and Joraiem wondered if there ever had been.

There were no signs, no pictures, no lights, no ornamentation of any kind on any of the buildings. What about inside? He wondered if exploration of any of the open doors they had passed would have turned up anything. Would there be tables, chairs, beds, and dressers? Would there be utensils and tools, pots and pans? What had the Vulsutyrim and men who followed Malek known when they packed their belongings to board the great ships? Had they known that win or lose, there would be no coming back? For the Malekim and Black Wolves, surely there was no consideration other than obeying their creator, but for the Vulsutyrim, it must have been different. They had walked these streets long before Malek had landed on these shores. Did they curse the hour of his coming? Or was it for them the fulfillment of their unspoken dreams? Did they ready their weapons and board their ships, eager for the battle to come, or did they weep over their departure as over an unwanted exile? And when Vulsutyr fell and they retreated with Malek into the tunnels and caves inside Agia Muldonai, did they whisper longingly among themselves for these now empty streets? When they slept at night, did they dream of their long-lost home?

Surely the men with Malek, the descendants of Andunin, had left this place eager to return to Kirthanin. They must have dreamed of a return to Nolthanin. Generations had passed with no more memory of Kirthanin than the stories of their elders, passed from father to son. Perhaps they had walked these streets as warily as Joraiem and the others now did.

Valzaan stopped, even though there was no intersection in sight. Caan, stooping low, darted ahead, then across the road to the building on the other side. He picked up what appeared to Joraiem to be a smooth, slightly discolored stick lying at the base of the wall. He returned and approached Synoki. "Did you bring this here?"

Synoki shook his head, "No."

Caan broke off some blackened flakes from the burnt end and watched them flutter gently through the nearly completely still air. He glanced at Valzaan and spoke quietly, "I can't tell you how long ago it was lit, but it isn't a thousand years old, I can guarantee you that."

Valzaan nodded. "No indeed, but how old is it? Nal Gildoroth has recently had visitors and may still have them. Walk carefully."

They kept moving forward, looking down side streets and into any open doorway they passed, but they did not stray from the main road. Eventually, they saw ahead in the distance the outline of an enormous statue. Its form was imposing, to say the least, as it towered above even the tallest of the buildings around them. The closer they drew, the bigger they realized it was. If the walls of the city were twenty-five spans, the figure was fifty, without a doubt the most gigantic statue Joraiem had ever seen.

It stood in the center of a large open circle, which Valzaan confirmed was the center of Nal Gildoroth. The statue was an image of Vulsutyr. The legs were thick and muscular, one in front of the other like he had just taken an easy stride. Though a broad cloth was carved around his middle, his chest and arms were bare, revealing more of his muscular body. His right arm was raised over his head, and his legendary flaming sword swooped upward in an arc, appearing to cut a fearful swath through the afternoon sky. His left fist was clenched by his side, and long stone locks of hair dangled upon his shoulders. Somehow, the sculptor had managed to capture the fiery intensity in his eyes for which he was legendary, and even as they stood some distance across the open circle, he seemed to be staring them down. *Still watching over his city, even from the grave,* Joraiem thought.

They halted, and as Valzaan contemplated his next move, the rest of them stood transfixed. They knew Vulsutyr had not been sculpted to scale. The Twelve, when they had walked the streets of Avalione in the First Age had possessed forms of great magnitude, but not like this. Vulsutyr had stood almost four spans high, head and shoulders above any of his children, or so the stories said. Even Sulmandir, when raised to his full height, was said to have been less than five spans. And yet, as they rested under the gaze of this stone giant, which had stood guard over this long-vacant city for almost a thousand years, it seemed almost possible that at any moment, Vulsutyr himself would step down from that pedestal and their doom would come.

But he didn't, and Valzaan soon led the group to the right of the open circle, following the line of buildings. They had gone perhaps halfway around the circle, so that from where they were they could look up at the left side of the statue and see the rippling muscle that flowed from the clenched fist up to the broad shoulder, when the prophet hesitated at a narrow side lane. As Joraiem peered down it, he hoped that they would pass it by. It was a dead end, unremarkable except for two towering open doors that admitted a slender shaft of light into a broad hall. Both the street and the open doorway were singularly uninviting. Joraiem's hopes of moving past were dashed, however, as Caan motioned them forward down the narrow lane, following Valzaan's determined lead.

The doorway was as wide as the alley itself, and easily tall enough for Sarneth to pass through it on his hind legs had he wanted to. Caan removed half a dozen torches from his back and quickly lit and distributed them. The group plunged ahead and in.

The hall inside was every bit as bare as the city. They moved in formation to the center of the room, and when they could still see nothing of any significance, Caan motioned to them to break into several smaller groups, which they did, searching in different directions. The search confirmed what Joraiem already suspected: The room was large and empty.

Furthermore, there were no doors leading into adjoining rooms, but only a great, open archway directly opposite the door they had entered. The group made its way to the opening and gazed through at a broad tunnel that descended as though down a ramp. The archway was as high and as wide as the doors through which they had entered. Anything narrow enough to fit through the alley outside and short enough to pass through the external door could also pass through this archway.

The tunnel descended steadily, apparently in a straight line, at least as far as the torches revealed. The walls of the hallway were smooth and also arched, but they did not appear to be made of stone, as the rest of the hall. Joraiem felt a chill as he imagined what might lie in the darkness, deep below Nal Gildoroth.

"What now?" Caan asked Valzaan quietly and calmly, but even so, his voice betrayed that the place unnerved him as well.

Valzaan closed his eyes and for several moments stood motionless, as though in a trance. The rest of them shifted uneasily, watching Valzaan, sometimes turning to survey the large dark hall around them. Joraiem saw some of them looking almost eagerly at the light shining in through the front door, as though being out in the streets of Nal Gildoroth was more desirable than being here. Eventually, Valzaan spoke, and when he did, his voice was steady and clear. "We, or at least some of us, must go down. Our answers lie below."

"Is it wise to split up?" Aljeron asked.

"It may prove wise to leave a few to stand watch, while most go down. Or, depending on what lies below, it may be wise to take as few into trouble as possible. In the end, it's unlikely we will know which is the wiser course of action until after we've taken one."

"Delightful," Rulalin said with a grimace.

"Whatever we decide," Valzaan continued, ignoring the remark, "I must go down."

"I will go down with you, prophet of Allfather," Sarneth said. "I do not fear the dark places of the earth, and in the dark, a Great Bear's prowess and vision may prove useful."

"Good, Sarneth, I am grateful. We will descend quickly and return as soon as we are able. I would ask that Caan, Aljeron, and Koshti accompany me, and if Joraiem would come too, then we will also have a bowman. The rest of you should remain, keeping watch over this tunnel and the outer door. Send a runner if trouble comes."

It was soon arranged, but not without a small change. After conferring together for a few moments, Caan called the others around while Valzaan spoke briefly with Synoki. Joraiem was close enough to catch the general drift of the exchange, and it became clear that Valzaan was directing Synoki to come too. Joraiem wondered at this at first, but he realized that ever since they had found Synoki on the beach, Valzaan had kept him close. Perhaps Valzaan felt a personal responsibility to watch over the stranger, or maybe the prophet just felt he should be watched.

Caan positioned Bryar and Kelvan along with Saegan and Rulalin by the door to the street. He stationed Pedraal and Pedraan on either side of the tunnel, each with a torch. The others took the opportunity to sit along the wall and rest their weary feet, even if only for a few moments. Soon, Caan and Aljeron, both with torches, led the way down into the tunnel.

Valzaan, Synoki, and Joraiem followed close behind, Joraiem with Suruna ready. Sarneth and Koshti came at the end, moving soundlessly. It was immensely comforting to have them along, and Joraiem thought that in the end, if he had to be in Nal Gildoroth, he was glad he was with the likes of Valzaan and Sarneth, even if it meant descending into darkness rather than remaining above in the light.

The hallway descended steadily, but the further they went, the steeper it became. The grade of the decline was soon so steep that it was difficult to keep an even pace. Joraiem found himself stepping a bit sideways, placing one foot cautiously past the other on an angle to avoid slipping on the smooth floor. The others were doing the same, and even so, from time to time one or another would stumble or accelerate unintentionally and have to lean back to avoid tumbling down into the darkness ahead. Joraiem felt compassion for Synoki, despite the questions surrounding him, who with his disfigurement was clearly struggling with the slope. He did not complain, and Joraiem was impressed with his quiet determination to keep up with the others and make his way down without help.

Fortunately, before the decline could become too severe to navigate, the tunnel emptied into a great open cavern. Here, far beyond any glimpse of light from above, there was total darkness. The torches were bright, though, and their flickering rays managed to illuminate the distant roof of the cavernous room. Joraiem had thought the Great Hall in Sulare was big, and it was, but this room was easily larger, though it was hard to judge how much so, since the torches could not expose the room's width. They paused, gazing around them in awe.

"We should keep going," Valzaan said as he stepped forward. The others followed, staying close together. The room opened up, and before long, they could not see any walls before or behind.

"Sarneth, will you be able to lead us back to this spot?" Caan asked as they walked.

"Yes."

"Good. If we have to retreat in a hurry, I'd hate to lose my way in here."

"Don't worry, Caan," Aljeron said. "Even if Sarneth were not able to, Koshti could. He does not lose scents. He could pick out our exact path and lead us back without fail."

Caan nodded, and they continued walking. The large chamber was, like the hall far above it, completely empty other than a few loose rocks that lay around on the floor. After several minutes, they began to see in the distance a wall, and it was not completely solid. A large opening, perhaps ten spans wide and half as many spans high, lay before them. They made their way toward that opening, and when they reached it, they peered through, again shaking their heads with wonder at what they saw.

Beyond the opening was another cavernous room, the roof at least as far above them as the last and the sides and far wall again beyond view. This room, however, was not completely empty. To their right, a large raised structure lay perhaps fifty spans away. Pausing a moment to peer ahead, they moved down the wall on their right to examine the object. It was a forge. They slowed and approached in silence.

"Take me to it," Valzaan said, turning to face Joraiem. Joraiem took the prophet's outstretched hand and led him to the forge. Valzaan reached out and ran his fingers over the hard, smooth exterior. "The picture takes shape before me. There is life in the forge. It has been used, and recently."

The others came up beside him, and soon they were marveling, not only at the forge, but at the tools stored on a smooth slab of rock beside it. As they stood, gazing, Synoki stepped over to the slab and picked up a mid-sized, dark hammer from the pile.

"What are you doing?" Aljeron asked, incredulous. "Don't you realize whose hammer that might be?"

"I do," Synoki answered, "but I have no weapon, and this hammer fits my hand well enough." He gripped the hammer tightly in his left hand, and sliding the fingers of his right along it, felt the smooth firmness of the shaft and head.

"There is no time to linger here," Valzaan said. "Let us quickly examine where this room leads, so that we may know if we have seen all we have been brought here to see."

They slid away from the forge, resuming their tight formation behind the flickering torchlight. Joraiem wiped his hand on his pant leg and renewed his grip on Suruna. The darkness before them parted little by little, and soon they were walking downhill again. The floor in the first large cavern had not exactly been level, but it hadn't had any definite slope in one direction or another. This floor, though, was noticeably and increasingly sloping down, away from the wall where the forge and the entrance to the other cavern lay.

It wasn't far before the sloping floor leveled out and changed color, stretching far across the cavern. It was odd, having sloped so steadily, to suddenly straighten out so completely, and as they approached the change in angle, Caan stopped, putting out both arms to either side to make sure they all stopped behind him. Stooping, he picked a small rock off the floor and rolled it down the final span between the silent men and the level floor. The rock rolled smoothly down, but instead of continuing out across the flat section, it disappeared beneath the surface of what they all saw now was dark, murky water.

"I'm not sure how close I would get," Caan said, when Aljeron started forward. Aljeron stopped, but Koshti slid cautiously down to the edge of the water and seemed to sniff at it for a moment. Raising his head, Koshti looked out across the placid surface, then began to walk agitatedly to and fro along the water's edge.

"Can anyone see a far side to this, this, lake?" Valzaan asked.

"No," Caan answered. "The water stretches as far as my eyes can see."

"If the ground beneath the water slopes at the same rate it has been," Joraiem began, "then the water on the far side must be incredibly deep. It would take an enormous amount to fill this place up. What would so much water be doing beneath the city, and where would it have come from?"

"The ocean," Sarneth said quietly.

"The ocean?" Aljeron answered, turning from the water to the Great Bear. "How could that be? We are many leagues from the water here, surely."

"Perhaps," Valzaan said, "but having approached Nal Gildoroth from the south and west, we didn't come by the most direct path possible. As the falcon flies, the westernmost part of the city might only be an hour's walk from the ocean, and who knows how far under the coast in caves and subterranean streams the water of the sea might flow. At any rate, Sarneth is most assuredly correct, however the water came to be here, for mixed in with the dank smell of stagnant water, there is the unmistakable hint of salt."

As soon as Valzaan had said it, Joraiem detected the trace of salt in the odor of the water. However, there wasn't time to contemplate the question further, for a deep growl from Koshti grabbed their attention. Aljeron sprang after him, and the others followed.

"What in the name of Allfather is this?" Aljeron murmured as he approached the place where Koshti stood. The others came up beside him, and Joraiem gasped. A massive pile of bones, perhaps five or six spans high, lay heaped just beyond the water's edge. The base of the pile stretched away from the water at least ten spans or more. Around the pile, bones and bone shards were spread as far as the eye could see. Joraiem looked uneasily from the bones to the others to the dark waters beside them. Suddenly, he felt quite sure that it would be foolish to remain so close to the water.

"I think we'd better step away," he said, unable to take his eyes off the expanse. As he spoke, and before any of the others could reply, a deep, resonant splash like the thundering sound of a boulder dropped from the ceiling of the cavern into the distant depths of the waters reverberated across the surface. Waves and ripples spread outward from some distant epicenter, beyond the glow of their torches.

At that moment, several things happened at once. Koshti turned from the bones to the water and began to roar as though turning to face an enemy in battle. Valzaan raised his staff above his head, and a bright flash burst from the head of the King Falcon engraved upon it, illuminating an enormous portion of the cavern for just a few seconds. In those few seconds, when the light was brightest, Joraiem noticed three things. First, he noticed that the pile of bones beside them was not the only one. Further down the waterline was another, perhaps even bigger, and around it stretched a hoard of bones perhaps waist-high as far as the eye could see. Second, he saw droplets splashing on the water all around him like drops of rain falling from the sky. Third, he saw, or thought he saw, a long dark form arc out over the water across the cavern and then slip beneath the dark surface of the pool.

"Sarneth," Valzaan called. "Lead the way back as quickly as you can! Whatever this room once was, it is now little more than a boneyard."

Sarneth led the way, running quickly on all fours. He was large but graceful, and as Koshti ran up beside him, Joraiem couldn't help but be envious of their powerful muscles and extra legs. Again what sounded like the sound of a boulder splashing in the water echoed from behind, though this time it didn't sound so far away, but he didn't dare pause to look over his shoulder. Rather, he ran as he hadn't run since his last workout along the beach in Sulare. The thought of that sunny, pleasant place seemed unreal here, where everything felt like darkness and death. He ran up alongside Sarneth on the other side, feeling his chest pound as they passed beneath the archway that led to the first cavern. Aljeron and Caan were a little behind him, and the torches threw his shadow across the dark floor.

Fortunately, the entrance to the long tunnel up to the surface of the city was not as far away as he thought, and they soon reached it, pausing just long enough to make sure they were all there. Valzaan's white hair was damp with sweat, and Synoki's limp was even more pronounced as he ran, but the long months fending for himself on the island had hardened his slender body, and though he glistened with sweat, he was not breathing with exceptional difficulty.

They began their ascent, and the steep grade at the bottom was frustrating. Though Joraiem had no idea what exactly they were running from, the prospect of being caught while scrambling up this slippery ramp to the world of light and hope was unpleasant. But again, it was not as far as Joraiem had thought it would be until the grade of the floor was not as severe and they could run quickly once more. After perhaps ten minutes ascending at a run the long hallway, the light of the upper world became visible through the wide opening that was gradually taking shape above. It seemed to Joraiem as he ran toward it, that the light was as glorious as the sun in the midday sky, and he longed for it like cool water on a hot summer's day.

The elation of reaching the upper hall was quickly replaced with a completely different kind of dread. Neither Pedraal nor Pedraan stood at their stations beside the archway, nor were there any others resting quietly against the cool walls of the chamber. Rather, they were standing in a tight knot in the middle of the room, heatedly discussing something. It didn't take Joraiem long to figure out what occupied them, for somewhere outside the sound of a deep, resonant horn echoed through the barren streets. Nal Gildoroth was not empty.

They started across the hall, and when they were noticed, the whole group moved en masse to join them. Fear was written on all of their faces, from the oldest to the youngest, but they remained quiet and controlled as Saegan stepped out to speak to Caan and Valzaan.

"We first heard the horn a few moments ago. We were just trying to figure out whether we should all go down to join you or send someone down to get you. Is there any chance that hallway leads somewhere safe, like under the walls and out of the city?"

"No," Valzaan said simply, and Joraiem shuddered at the idea of that dark shape gliding across the surface of the water being safe. "The only way out of here is back the way we came. If they haven't gotten between us and the gate, we might be able to outrun them. Come, quickly."

Again, they dropped into formation, and soon Joraiem found himself once again jogging at the head of the tight pack, Suruna in hand. Stepping out into the sunlight was momentarily blinding. Joraiem blinked several times, trying to adjust as quickly as possible so that he could take stock of what lay before them. Once his eyes had adjusted, he peered down the alley. He saw nothing, at least not in the portion of the square visible to him, and hope rose within. Perhaps the way would be clear, and they would slip out of Nal Gildoroth, make it back to the ship, and be back on board the *Evening Star* and out to sea before sunset.

With that hope he pressed forward at a steady gait, aware suddenly that he was just ahead of the others and was setting their pace. He glanced quickly over his head, to see how they were coping. He was drawn to Wylla, whose eyes were fixed steadily upon him. As he looked at her, he read in her face the fear they all felt, but also something more. There was regret, and she held his gaze steadily. Understanding without words passed between them. She was sorry they had argued, and he was sorry he had hurt her. He loved her, and she saw it. For a brief moment, a faint smile formed on her lips and in her eyes as they ran through the late afternoon.

He turned forward and gazed again at the large open square as they approached. With the sun lower in the sky than it had been when they first passed by, the giant statue of Vul-sutyr stood slightly darker and more ominous. Approaching the square and looking toward the street that would take them back to the gate, Joraiem suddenly stopped. A party of per-haps ten or so Malekim were moving across the far side of the square toward the same street. They were also running. More importantly, they had also just noticed that they were not alone.

Caan barked quick commands, bringing the men to the front and sending the women back down the alley a little way. Joraiem motioned for Bryar and Kelvan to join him along the wall of the nearest building on their right that faced the square and the now fast-approaching Malekim. Joraiem felt none of the hesitation he had felt in the clearing when the Black Wolves had come; rather, he felt a remarkable clarity of mind. In a single fluid motion he raised Suruna, aimed, and fired.

The arrow soared straight and true and struck the lead Malekim squarely in the chest. The Voiceless stumbled back with the impact, and swerved a few feet to the side before tum-bling headlong onto the ground. All this Joraiem saw, but only as he drew with astounding swiftness and fired again, hitting another Malekim, this time in the stomach. Twice more he fired and hit as the remainder of the Silent Ones closed the gap between themselves and the others. As Joraiem fired his final shot, he saw arrows from Bryar and Kelvan also strike home, and three more Malekim fell, just short of Sarneth, Koshti, and the waiting men.

Only five Malekim remained upright, and now they were too close for Joraiem to fire again. He drew another arrow and dropped back with Kelvan and Bryar to take down any Malekim that might break through and make a run at the women. But there would be no need. Their numbers having been cut more than in half, the remaining Malekim arrived wide-eyed and stunned by the swift death of their comrades. They never recovered from that feeling, for before they knew it, Sarneth had drawn himself up to his full height, and he wielded his tree-like staff with a fury that made Joraiem tremble. When the first blow struck the closest Silent One, the sound of bones shattering in his chest echoed across the square. The creature flew back several spans before it came to rest lifelessly in a crumpled heap. The next two to arrive fared little better, though managing to raise their short, dark swords in a vain attempt to block Sarneth's blows. In fact, as the second one fell, Joraiem noticed that he went down with his own blade embedded in his stomach. For a moment he lay quivering at Sarneth's feet, but a swift decisive jab from the end of the Great Bear's staff halted his misery immediately.

The last two were able to avoid the fury of the Great Bear, trying their luck with the men waiting on the other side of the street, but they were outnumbered, as Pedraal, Pedraan, Aljeron, Saegan, Rulalin, and Caan swarmed around them. A flurry of blows from all sides sliced through their hides, spilling their dark, thick blood.

Joraiem surveyed the scene. Half a dozen Malekim lay dead from cyranic arrows, another three had fallen by Sarneth's hands, and the last two had died at the hands of the other men. In a matter of moments they had wiped out eleven Malekim. A few months ago, when he and Evrim had pursued one, he would never have believed he could calmly take down four charging Voiceless. Caan had taught them well.

"Come," Valzaan called as he started across the square, "these may not be the only enemies we face. We must not wait."

They set off again across the square, jogging toward the street that would take them out. The sound of running feet echoed from directly across the square. As they reached the head of the street, Joraiem looked over his shoulder and saw in dismay another group of Malekim, with several Black Wolves around them, pouring out from another wide street on the opposite side of the square. They were not out yet.

They began to reform the line and as Joraiem motioned to Kelvan and Bryar, Caan stepped forward and grabbed Bryar by the collar, tugging her in close to him as he spoke calmly but very swiftly to her. "You must take the women out of the city and back to the ship."

"You can't send me away, I—"

"There is no time!" Caan all but shouted. "You must go now! I have no idea what is coming this way or how long we can hold them, nor do I know that the way out is completely safe. I need you to take them. Get back to the ship and tell Ulmindos what has happened. Go!"

Joraiem could see she wanted to speak, but seeing the determined command in Caan's eyes, she turned away with a look of helpless frustration, motioned to the women and began to run at a brisk jog back down the broad street that led to the gate. She did not look back. Knowing there was no time, Joraiem and the others turned away from them to face the approaching enemy.

The Black Wolves came first, far outpacing the half dozen or so Malekim behind them. As soon as they drew even with the statue of Vulsutyr, Joraiem drew Suruna and fired. Again his arrow struck home and the lead wolf dropped. Joraiem's whole body tingled and shuddered as he prepared to fire again. Caan had spoken of battle frenzy, when a warrior lost consciousness of self as his battle training and preparation took over his actions, and Joraiem felt something like that must be happening now. He watched the second arrow leave Suruna's string as if he were a mere bystander. A second wolf dropped. His body continued to move fluidly and with a speed he had never before experienced with a bow, and he knew somehow that if he tried to think through each separate action involved in drawing his arrows, nocking them, aiming, and firing, then he would surely lose this battle rhythm. He murmured a brief prayer to Allfather that his hands be steady and his aim be true and watched as another Black Wolf fell.

The wolves were upon them, and Joraiem jumped back from the front line as several leapt in nearby. He wanted to be ready for the Voiceless, but confusion reigned. Right before him, Daltaraan flashed through the air and a wolf howled as Aljeron's dark blade ripped through the creature's shoulder muscles and bones, severing the spinal chord and killing it instantly. Pedraan swung his mighty war hammer, catching a wolf in mid-leap, both smashing it and hurling its broken carcass against a nearby wall. Further down the line he saw Sarneth rise up to his full height as his staff thundered in a wide sweeping arc, and he saw Caan slashing one wolf while another managed to sink its jaws into his calf. The wolf had locked onto Caan's leg precisely where he had been bitten before. A flash of dark metal, and Synoki crushed the wolf's head, and the creature fell with bloody jaws to the ground. Caan staggered back, but there was no time to tend the wound, for the Malekim were right behind.

The first of them were there already, but Joraiem repositioned himself so that he had a shot at the last of them, and the arrow pierced a Silent One's neck. He had been in the act of raising his sword, and the short, curved blade flew through the air until it fell rattling on the dark stones of the square. The others were all engaged closely with his friends, so even though Joraiem had another arrow ready, there was nothing he could do but watch.

He looked at Rulalin, hard pressed to defend himself as the Malekim that had engaged him pressed furiously in. But Joraiem saw in Rulalin's eyes an equally intense fury as he wielded the Azmavarim that Caan had entrusted to him. For several moments he appeared to be purely on the defensive, fighting for little more than time or perhaps hope that someone else would come to his aid, but when he saw his opening, he drove the Firstblade into the Malekim's chest.

At the same moment, Synoki whirled from beside Caan to the very same Malekim and brought the hammer crashing down against the back of the Malekim's skull. The creature jerked forward on Rulalin's blade, as both Synoki and Rulalin made sure he was dead.

Then Joraiem saw why the Malekim were so rightfully feared. Though outnumbered with the wolves dead and dying, the Silent Ones that remained had taken advantage of the broken battle line and slipped in among them. With swords drawn, they whirled and struck with such speed and strength that for the moment, the momentum of the engagement had swung in their favor. Then a wave of light erupted from Valzaan's staff and the Malekim were momentarily blinded. Joraiem saw the tide turn again and watched both man and Great Bear struggle to conquer their ancient enemy. At first it looked as though it would proceed as before, for the first thing Joraiem saw was Sarneth smashing one of the Malekim with his staff. Next he saw Saegan's Azmavarim rammed almost to the hilt through the gut of another. The battle seemed to be over.

If only it had been.

Pedraal stepped in to finish the Malekim before him with his battle-axe, but the Malekim dodged it and with the back of his great arm sent Pedraal sprawling across the street. The Malekim spun, swinging viciously at the nearest target, which was a stunned Kelvan, armed with only his bow and caught off guard too close to the action. Ducking and trying to block the stroke with his bow, he was knocked off balance. The Malekim stepped in and over him, and with a single swing of his free claw, ripped Kelvan open from shoulder to hip.

It was the last thing the Malekim did, for its killing blow

was only just finished when a flying Koshti mauled him. The Malekim struggled at first, but Koshti's strong claws kept him pinned down. Koshti went right for his throat, and soon the Malekim also lay lifelessly on the street.

For a moment they all just stood, looking at the place where Kelvan had fallen. The last echo of battle died away, and the silence around them was eerie. Joraiem didn't feel able to move.

"There is no time for mourning," Caan said, pausing and stooping to tend his wound and looking over his shoulder at the open square. He ripped a long strip of cloth from the bottom of his shirt and tied it around his bloody leg, knotting it tightly over the open wound like a bandage. He gritted his teeth tightly as he rose and continued to speak, and Joraiem winced at the thought of the sting the sweaty bandage must have caused. "For now, we must take him up and go."

With that, their legs began to work again. Pedraal tossed his brother the battle-axe and in a second had Kelvan over his shoulder. Joraiem grabbed Kelvan's bow and closed around Pedraal with the others, and they stepped over and around the dead Malekim and continued their retreat.

They moved wordlessly down the street, watching and listening for any sign of more danger. Joraiem kept seeing Kelvan fall. It was as if death had come instantaneously, for he had dropped, not as an injured man or animal that has lost its strength to stand, but as an inanimate object like a rock or tree. Even from behind, the loss of spirit and life from the falling body had been all but visible.

He found his mind turning to Bryar. Reluctantly she had departed with the others, and when she found out, who could tell what she would do? Anger at the news was as likely as grief, and woe to the messenger who unleashed it! As he ran down the street, wondering about Bryar, Wylla's face appeared before him, beautiful and happy, smiling for him. Relief that he had not lost her rushed over him, and he looked around guiltily, as though worried someone might detect his feelings. He thought of Wylla on the deck of the *Evening Star* and also felt regret, regret that he had not taken advantage of the opportunity to speak more openly of his love. He regretted not having kissed her as she stood before him in the moonlight. She was right. Life was too short to worry about what someone else might think. He could have died in that fight just as easily as Kelvan, and then he would never have had a second chance for that kiss. As he ran, he vowed that at the first opportunity he would declare himself openly and clearly without hesitation or fear. He would unfold to Wylla the feelings of his heart without holding back, and he would ask her to marry him.

He felt peace come over him, and he put the issue out of his mind, focusing clearly upon the situation around him. Caan was favoring his strong leg, and so again Joraiem found himself up front, setting a quick pace. The others followed closely behind, and even Pedraal, bearing Kelvan's body, kept up.

But ahead, Joraiem saw something was wrong. The road from the gate had moved straight through the city, turning neither left nor right. Logically, then, the road out of the city should have done the same, but in the distance, the road appeared to end, not with the green and brown of the world beyond Nal Gildoroth, but at a high grey wall. He shook his head in disbelief. The great gates of the city were shut.

4

BEYOND REACH

THEY STOOD DUMBFOUNDED BEFORE the towering gate. Joraiem traced a line on the warm grey surface with his fingers as though he needed to feel the smooth stone to believe the truth.

"How can this be?" Caan asked, looking to Valzaan. For the first time, Joraiem saw Caan struggling for control of himself.

"Someone, or something, has closed the gate while we walked the streets of the city, or while we lingered in the hall," Saegan said quietly. "What else could it be?"

Fear struck Joraiem's heart. "Then where have the women gone? They couldn't have been far ahead of us."

"Unless the gate was open when they came and has been closed since," Valzaan spoke softly.

"Either way, they must be in great danger," Joraiem said, fearing for Wylla's life, as the implications of both scenarios struck him. "If the gate was closed when they arrived, then where are they? What's happened? If the gate was open, then whoever shut it may be outside with them. What do we do?"

"They're not inside the city," Sarneth answered, walking forward to stand beside the great gate. "I saw no sign of life either to the left or the right as we ran. I smelled no scent of trouble other than our own. They were neither accosted nor attacked on their way here."

"Indeed, they are beyond the gates," Valzaan echoed Sarneth's words, "and they are also in great peril, for I see in my mind's eye one of Vulsutyr's children, and I know that he walks his ancient home beyond this gate and that he is not alone. More of Malek's servants are with him, and if the women have not already been slain or captured, their time is short."

"We must follow at once!" Joraiem cried, and turning back to the door he threw his whole weight against it. Sarneth stepped up alongside him, leaning his massive shoulder beside him. Soon, Pedraal had put Kelvan down and all but Valzaan, who stood with eyes closed and hands raised, were grunting as they pushed against the gate. It felt like trying to push over a mountain, and as Joraiem strained with all his might, he despaired that the gate would even budge, much less open so they could all slide out. He shuddered to think of the strength of the Vulsutyrim if he had closed the gate alone.

But, even as he despaired, the gate suddenly slid forward a short way, though not far enough for daylight to appear through the crack, and they redoubled their efforts. Again it slid forward, and now there was an opening perhaps wide enough for Joraiem's fingers to pass through. His legs surged as he pushed, and he felt the others surge forward also. The gate slipped forward still more, and now it was wide enough for all but Sarneth to pass through. Some of the others began to relax but Joraiem called to them, "More! More!"

Again they pushed, but they had lost their momentum. *Not now,* Joraiem thought, *we are so close. Allfather, strengthen my hands for this task. I am your servant.* He felt a flood as of light flooding his body, and instantly the heaviness in his muscles was gone. He pushed with might he had never felt and did not naturally possess, and the gate swung forward almost half a span. He stood and whirled with excitement to Aljeron beside him, but hesitated when he saw the look in his eyes. Aljeron stared at him with wonder, and Joraiem looked away, afraid, as the flush of light and strength passed and the weariness of the day returned.

"Let us follow," he called as he sprang through the gate and began jogging down the road.

He had not run far before he was forced to stop. He was not a tracker like Evrim, but even he could see that the ground before him had a tale to tell. Human footprints were scattered all over the dusty road, interlaced with larger prints that were clearly those of many Malekim. But, more fearful than that, were the immense prints along the side of the road that must have been made by the giant. There had been a scuffle here, but there were no obvious signs of blood or injury, save only a single dark spoor of what appeared to be Malekim blood. Perhaps Bryar had gotten an arrow off before they were taken.

Taken where? The others were likewise examining the ground and Caan, having regained his composure, was talking in hushed tones with Valzaan. Joraiem slipped down the road a bit farther and followed the tracks. Eventually they straightened out, and the smaller human tracks kept to the middle of the road with the larger Malekim tracks in double file on the outer side. The Vulsutyrim appeared to have kept to the inside, perhaps leading the group or prodding them from behind, Joraiem could not tell. Whatever the situation, it was at least clear to Joraiem that the women were not dead, but they were moving at a quick pace. Turning to the others, he motioned them forward. "Come, they are moving quickly, straight along the road. We must run!"

The others fell in behind him, and they ran through the lengthening shadows of the late afternoon that was fast becoming evening. They crossed the solid bridge that spanned the dried riverbed, but Joraiem didn't even turn to look down the way they had come, for he was fixed on the tracks before him. He had made a vow that he would tell Wylla he loved her and ask for her hand in marriage, and if that meant he had to find and free her to do so, he would, at any cost.

They followed the road for more than half an hour, but they had no sight of those before them. Even in the broad, open flatlands through which they traveled, there was no sign. Joraiem knew that he was setting a good pace, but he feared that they had lost too much time at the gate and that the Vulsutyrim was pressing the women too fast. He slowed and fell in beside Caan.

"We're not going to catch them at this rate, but with Valzaan, Synoki, your wound, and Kelvan's body, I can't increase the pace. Let me run, Caan. Let me run so I can at least have a chance of gaining sight of them. I will wait for you when I have found something worthwhile."

Caan, straining as he ran on his injured leg, nodded slowly. "You have proven yourself today, Joraiem. Go, and do what seems best to you."

Joraiem nodded in return and began to accelerate, running as he did when tearing through the hills of Dal Harat on his own. "Joraiem," Aljeron called from behind. He glanced back, and there was Aljeron following at his shoulder, breathing hard. "Forgive me, but I can't let you go alone."

"Aljeron, I can't wait for you to keep up . . ."

"Not me. Koshti. Take him. He will help if you find yourself in need." Aljeron called Koshti, and signaling toward Joraiem, the tiger leapt away and soon ran with smooth, even strides beside him.

Koshti's grace and power inspired him, and he lengthened his stride, reaching deep within for all his strength. He knew that he was running at a pace he couldn't possibly sustain for long, at least at a pace he had never sustained for long before if ever he had obtained it in the first place. *A second time I ask today, Allfather, that you grant me strength. Give me strength like Koshti that I might run without weariness and follow without fainting.*

Again, he felt a flood of light and strength, as though he had emerged from a dark tunnel into bright sunlight. His steps quickened, and he knew Koshti had also lengthened his stride. On they ran, leaving the others far behind. He began to ascend a gently sloping hill, the crest of which was within view. Though not exceptionally high, he hoped that from its summit he might catch glimpse of those he pursued.

At last he reached the crest, and though the height yielded a clear vista, he did not see what he had expected. Stretched out not more than a hundred spans before him were the coast and the waters of the Southern Ocean. Already some distance out, three great boats rowed toward a massive ship. He could discern no face in particular, but in the hindmost boat was clearly the Vulsutyrim, for even from this distance, his gigantic proportions stood out. The women must have been huddled in the boats further out, but all he could see were some slight glimpses of color interspersed with the dark grey of their Malekim guards.

He slowed to a walk. There was no use in running now. When the others caught up to him, they would all have to run north along the beach to reach the *Evening Star,* for their only hope now lay in the nautical prowess of Ulmindos. The run through the sand would be enough to challenge even Joraiem, so he stopped to conserve his energy. He watched helplessly as each boat reached the dark vessel and was hooked, tied, and raised to the broad upper deck. Soon the ship was underway, and one more time that day he heard the deep, resonant tone of the horn. Then he understood. The giant had sounded those notes over the city. It had been the giant, and they had sent the women down the street, away from them and right into his waiting arms. He watched the ship tack along the coast as the others came up from behind to him at last. Reluctantly, he peeled his eyes from the great ship and turned away.

It took only a few moments to explain the situation, and soon they were running up the coast. Some had suggested cutting along the grassland instead of across the sand, but Synoki had urged them to forego that idea, since the route was crossed by several small divides and gorges as well as the dried riverbed. He thought the time they made up as they ran on the firm grassland would be more than lost in delays and detours. So, their course decided, they each ran as best they were able along the shore.

By the time they began that leg of their journey, the departing ship was far enough out to sea as to be out of sight, and now they looked no longer for it but for signs of their own vessel and the boats they would need to reach it. When they passed the entrance to the dried riverbed at last, they felt their strength renewed. Though weary beyond words, they ran on, and though the sun was now low in the western sky, they were encouraged that there might be just enough daylight left to get out to sea and follow the fleeing ship. *Ulmindos will find them,* Joraiem thought to himself, *for he is a master of the seas as no child or servant of Malek is or can be.*

"Look, the boats!" came a cry from not far behind Joraiem. He turned and saw Elyas, who was running ahead of Aljeron and Sarneth, with Rulalin, Saegan, and Pedraan close behind. Further back, Valzaan ran with more strength and grace than Joraiem would have expected, even if he was slower than the others. With him were Caan, his limp as pronounced as Synoki's, who was beside him, and last of all came Pedraal, with Kelvan dangling from his shoulder. Joraiem smiled at Elyas and turned back to look. He was heartened by the sight of the boats, which lay where they had been left earlier that day.

He was only briefly heartened, though, for out in the water, well beyond the boats, the *Evening Star* listed steeply to the port side, and only the very uppermost rail of the starboard side protruded above the water. The ship was swamped. Hope quickly slipped away, and at last Joraiem could not will himself to move any further. He slowed to a stumbling walk, then stopped altogether, dropping to his knees in the sand. The women were gone, taken by their enemy, and there was nothing he or any of them could do about it.

No one spoke, and for what seemed like a long time, Joraiem simply kneeled in the warm sand with his eyes closed. A procession of images flashed through his mind. He saw the Malekim and Black Wolves charging across the square, their eyes glinting with rage, full of hatred and cruelty. He saw the boats arriving at the ship, and the enormous bulk of the Vulsutyrim, wondrous and fearful all at once, even from so great a distance. And, swirling around among and behind these things was Wylla's face. How quickly her face had drawn his eyes as they had run down the narrow alley. How easily all other things but her beautiful face had faded away for that brief moment. How vivid, how lovely, and how real even now did the image of her face appear to him. And now he saw her as she had appeared in the moonlight aboard the *Evening Star,* happy and radiant and warm. He opened his eyes and stared back out to sea. She was gone. Where and why he could not fathom.

As his eyes adjusted to the fading daylight, he saw three ragged figures move in the high grass at the top of the embankment up the beach and to their right. He turned to face them with Suruna ready and an arrow aimed at their leader, but as soon as he had aimed carefully, he released his grip on the bowstring. It was Ulmindos and two of his crewmen, walking shakily toward them.

Joraiem stood as the others came up beside him. For a moment their sorrow over other things receded as they stared at the tattered appearance of their bruised and bleeding friends. Ulmindos, normally spry and full of vigor, walked as though he had aged a decade since they had seen him that morning, and his two sailors were likewise tentative on their feet.

"What has happened here?" Caan asked, limping forward and taking his friend's arm. They took a few steps toward the embankment, and he helped Ulmindos to sit so that they both might lean back and find support for their exhausted bodies. Valzaan joined them while the others dropped nearby in almost haphazard fashion. Joraiem knew it was not wise to so completely abandon their guard, for if they had been followed from the city, they would be defenseless against attack. He wasn't sure he cared.

"Little more than an hour after the company set out for Nal Gildoroth this morning, my lookout spotted a small party of Malekim moving across the grasslands. Of course, this sight drew our attention, and I summoned all hands to my side. At that point, I was worried not for our safety or for the *Evening Star,* but for the boats that had been left behind for your return.

"As we watched the shore, we did not notice the son of Vulsutyr, who was approaching under water from the south."

"The south? But we saw nothing," Aljeron said in wonder.

"Perhaps we had already turned up the riverbed and so missed him," Valzaan began, "though I am not inclined to think so. It is beginning to make sense. I think the Vulsutyrim was aware of our presence but hid from us that we might continue on to the city. Our presence must have been detected earlier in the morning, and once we were away from the ship, he decided to take care of it, thereby cutting off our escape. How foolish of me to think we could make it so far undetected!"

"However it happened," Ulmindos continued, "all I know is that by the time I noticed him, it was too late. I felt his giant hands grasp the keel in the stern of the ship under the water, and hand over hand he crawled under the boat to the prow where we were gathered. The crew was paralyzed with fear as they felt the vessel shake, and when he finally stood before them in the water, panic broke out. From his broad shoulders down he was immersed, but even with only his arms and head above water, that was enough. Before we could even think of trying to stop him, he had punched a massive hole through the side of the ship all the way into the hold. We began to take on water immediately. Most of the men panicked and jumped into the water to try for the shore, but everyone who did so died, as one by one he began to kill my men. Only the three of us escaped, and that by slipping down into the hold and huddling in the rising water there.

"We waited for almost two hours as the hold slowly filled, until very little air remained. For a long time it had been quiet and still, but I didn't trust the giant. We were forced at last, though, to go and see if it was safe. I took a deep breath and swam through the hole in the side and up to the surface. There was no sign either of the giant or the Malekim. Quickly, we headed for shore and moved inland up into the tall grass to wait and see if anyone would return. There we have been until this very moment. To tell you the truth, I was beginning to doubt that I would see any of you alive again. It appears that at least some of you have returned safely."

Valzaan, understanding the implied question, answered. "Yes, the women have been taken by the Vulsutyrim and some of the Voiceless, as I shall explain."

"And Kelvan?" Ulmindos asked, looking somberly at the body that lay on the sand with Pedraal watching over it.

"He fell in battle," Caan said, quietly.

"I will tell you our story briefly," Valzaan said, "for you should hear not only what happened, but also what we found, as should you all who did not descend with us deep below the city. Listen, for I must be brief, the sun is hanging low in the western sky and there is much yet we must do before dark if we are to pass the night here on the Forbidden Isle."

After explaining to Ulmindos about Synoki, how they had met him and how he had come to be there, he told of their journey to Nal Gildoroth. "We saw no one on our trip to the city, nor did we see anyone in the city. Allfather led us into the heart of the city, where I looked for the second time in my life upon the likeness of Vulsutyr, Father of the giants, wielder of the Flaming Sword. But we left the lifeless statue behind and passed down a side alley into a large hall, which was but the upper chamber of a more important discovery. Down below the city lay at least two vast chambers, and in one we found what I know Allfather brought us here to find. We saw a great forge, a forge where Malek had been at work."

The Novaana who hadn't seen the forge and Ulmindos looked stunned at the announcement. They had heard Valzaan say in Sulare that such might be the case, but deep down they had not wanted to believe it possible. To know now that Malek was not confined to his hiding place beneath the Holy Mountain was discomforting, to say the least.

"Are you sure Malek himself has been at work there?" Aljeron asked, more out of a desperate hope that Valzaan might only be mostly sure than out of any suspicion the prophet might be wholly mistaken.

"I do not know all things," Valzaan said. "I have missed things that were right before my face, for I am not granted sight of all I wish to see. I only see what is revealed, and as my hand touched the forge, I was granted a glimpse of his dread handiwork. It was terrible. I don't know what I saw or what to call it, but it was there, in the cavern with us."

"The thing in the water?" Joraiem said, the dread he had felt beside the water sweeping over him again.

"Yes. Most of the rest of that cavern is below water. In fact, it is little more than a vast holding tank for this thing that Malek has brought into the world. I no longer need to guess at the meaning of the light we saw flash across the sea nine days ago. We were witnessing the aftermath of the birth of another of Malek's foul creations."

The others were silent. Malek had brought forth yet something else to torment the world, and it lurked even now somewhere deep below the island. Joraiem began to wonder where the boundaries of this thing's domain lay, if indeed it had any boundaries at all.

"At any rate," Valzaan continued, "I did not realize immediately that the image that flashed through my mind was of a creature within that very room, and we continued to explore it unaware. Only after Koshti discovered an extensive bone heap did we realize the water was not a peaceful reservoir at all. We fled lest the thing devour us whole and spit our bones into that pile, and we did not stop running until we returned to the upper world. There we found danger at hand anyway, for as we emerged, I heard the horncall of the Vulsutyrim."

"You knew the horn had been sounded by a giant?" Joraiem asked.

"Yes."

"Then why didn't you tell us?"

"What good would it have done?" Valzaan answered. "I didn't know the Vulsutyrim was outside the city. Would it have been helpful to have named a foe that strikes overwhelming fear into the hearts of all but a dragon? There are some things that are better not to know until it is time. Thought, especially fear, is often the enemy of action. Besides, I hoped we might evade our enemy and slip away from the city unnoticed. I hoped I might not have to reveal the true extent of our peril until we were safely aboard the *Evening Star* and were slipping out to sea."

Valzaan told Ulmindos the rest of the story, describing the fighting in the city, the flight of the women, Kelvan's death, and finding the gate closed upon them. He finished with their pursuit of the women and the race up the beach toward the *Evening Star*. All stared forlorn at its wreck as he concluded, "I gather from your story, Ulmindos, that it is beyond repair."

"Given our situation, repair is for all intents and purposes an impossibility. The *Evening Star* will never sail from these shores again."

Again, disbelief and even despair swept over Joraiem. The full gravity of their situation flooded him. For the first time since they had reached the gate, he considered not only the ill fate of the abducted women, but theirs as well.

At that moment, Valzaan lifted his face to the sinking sun and gestured to the heavens. "Let no man surrender his heart to despair! Malek has used despair from the beginning, and perhaps above all else he uses it still. Allfather's mighty arm is long, and even if for a time the women have passed beyond our reach, we are not beyond His. I have seen Allfather do wondrous things, and I call you all to hold on to hope."

"You haven't been stuck here for three years," Synoki said in a soft, low, even distant voice.

"Say what you will," Valzaan replied, agitated, "but I am a prophet of Allfather, and I speak the truth."

"We will have plenty of time to consider our options later," Saegan said. "The pressing question is, what should we do now?"

"We must decide what to do about Kelvan and then leave

this place. If we are hunted after dark, the enemy will surely look here. So, let us do what needs to be done and then go."

"Aren't we going to bury him?" Elyas asked.

"Burial will take too much time," Caan said.

"Commit him to the sea," Ulmindos said quietly. "We cannot take the row boats with us, for they would only signal our new location. Let us lay him in one, then one or more of us could take him out beyond the surf where the water is deep, and commit him to the sea. There is no more peaceful resting place than beneath the waters of the deep."

They looked at Kelvan's still body, the blood that covered his chest now dry. His eyes were closed and his hair lay in clumps around him. Joraiem had seen death before, but the lifelessness of the body without the spirit still startled him. He could hear Monias's voice in his mind, "We are but dust. Without the spirit, we are but dust."

They rose to their feet, and Pedraal lifted Kelvan's body one last time and gently laid it in the nearest boat. Valzaan stood at the foot of the boat, and the others gathered round. They laid beside and around him what few personal possessions he had, except for Kelvan's bow and quiver, which one of Ulmindos's men picked up, and a sharp hunting knife, which Aljeron took. "This I will hold onto for Bryar," he said as he tucked its sheath into his belt.

Valzaan raised his arms above his head and turned his face again to the sky. "Allfather, we commend to you our fallen brother. He was your servant, and in your service he died. You give the spirit of life and in Your time You take it to Yourself again. Even so, we grieve. Send comfort to our mourning hearts and to all who will grieve when they learn of his passing. Keep him well until the restoration, until You fulfill Your promise to make all things new. So be it."

"So may it be," the others echoed.

Pedraal moved to get into the boat and take the oars, but

Sarneth came forward. "I will take him," he said, putting his great paw upon the side of the boat.

"I want to do it," Pedraal answered firmly.

"I will swim behind the boat and push it before me. It will be but a simple matter for me to do. Save your strength for what may come."

"I want to do it."

"There was nothing you could have done to save him, so you are not responsible for his death. You must not blame yourself. You are not Allfather. You cannot stand between your friends and their mortality. You cannot even do that for yourself. Let me take him. You carried him here. That is enough. Let the burden pass to me now."

Pedraal turned from the boat and Sarneth pushed it forward into the water. The tide was not too strong nor the waves too high, and before long the Great Bear and the boat were far past the visible remains of the *Evening Star*. The men watched until they couldn't see either anymore, then turned to discussing what to do next.

All agreed they should not stay on the coast, for other ships in the area might come looking in the night or in the morning. They also agreed that they should head north, as far away from the city as they could. Synoki said it had been some time since he had been to the northernmost tip of the island, but he believed there would be some reasonable places to camp that might afford shelter.

So, when Sarneth returned, they wasted no time assembling what supplies and gear they had left, and together they scrambled up the bank into the tall grassland. Looking back over his shoulder at the wreck of the *Evening Star*, it seemed to Joraiem incredible that it had been but a day since he had gazed at Wylla in the moonlight upon its deck. He turned from the ocean, but he couldn't turn from her image, and as he followed in the wake of the others, he wondered where she was and whether he would ever see her again.

They walked for perhaps an hour, until the sun was all but down. In the end, they stopped to camp where a small rock formation jutted up out of the level plain, providing a single wall and cover from at least one direction. Though no one was under any illusions about the degree of safety it afforded, they recognized it as the best they could do before nightfall. So, they made themselves comfortable at its base and divided into groups of three to keep lookout through the night. Caan, Ulmindos, and Sarneth kept the first watch, while Joraiem and the others tried to sleep. For Joraiem, at least, this proved to be futile, and he passed a restless time tossing and turning in the grass.

Joraiem gladly took the next watch with Saegan and Darias, and though they were spread out too far to talk to one another, it was comforting to look around the camp and see them sitting at their posts. *At least,* Joraiem thought, *I don't feel as alone as I do with my eyes closed.* He watched the surrounding fields of grass as intently as the moonlight allowed, but he saw nothing stirring. Their watch passed and they yielded their duty to Rulalin, Elyas, and Aljeron, and Joraiem was comforted that now Koshti, with his keen senses, was also keeping the watch. Joraiem returned almost reluctantly to his spot beside the cool rock and tried once more to sleep.

This time, his weary body would not be denied. It was a light sleep, from which he woke with a start several times. It was also a sleep of dreams, as scattered images continued to parade through his mind. After this had been going on for a while, he sat up and looked around. Several hours must have passed, for he could see that Pedraal, Pedraan, and Valzaan had taken over the watch. He lay back down, almost afraid to sleep again, but soon all such fears slipped away as he slept soundly and deeply at last.

He blinked as he looked around. He had just emerged from a dark place, but he could not see a door to where he had been. He was in the middle of a broad, open field, and behind him, rising into the sky like a dragon tower, stood the remarkable statue of Vulsutyr, gazing cruelly over the empty plain. Joraiem closed his eyes to feel the cool breeze that whispered through the grasslands sweep across his face, when a voice shook him out of his trance.

"You are growing, Joraiem."

He looked at Valzaan, seated on a stone before him. Neither the prophet nor the stone had been there a second ago. "What do you mean?"

"For one, you were close to seeing through the eyes of the windhover this afternoon. It may not be long now."

"Do you see through them?"

"Yes. My own eyes are useless to me, but Allfather has opened other doors to the world of sight. I am not a complete invalid."

"I had wondered. We all had, actually."

"I know."

"You said 'for one.' What else?"

"In the city, when you sought Allfather's power. Did you not feel his presence as you pushed the gate?"

"Yes, I felt it, and when I was running. It was both terrifying and exhilarating."

"Service to Allfather usually is, Joraiem, if not always."

"Do you think the others noticed?"

"Maybe. Some may have sensed something. Others may have seen signs. Sometimes, it shines in the eyes."

Joraiem blinked and Valzaan was gone. Again the plain was empty, but not for long. Out of the grass sprang countless Malekim. Joraiem drew Suruna, and in mere seconds arrows were flying from his bow in all directions. He could feel the rhythm of that afternoon return, and his fingers danced from quiver to bowstring as though guided by an intelligence other than his own. All around him the Malekim fell, and Joraiem heard himself laugh as the rest began to fall back and run away.

The laughter was short-lived, however, as the ground shook violently beneath his feet. He turned to face the stone giant, which had stepped down upon the earth from the pedestal and towered above him. He began to run as he realized it had not been from his arrows that the Malekim had fled. Instinctively he dodged to the left as a great stone sword smashed to the ground where he had been, leaving a deep rut in the field. He was running like the wind, but as he looked over his shoulder, he saw the giant cut the distance between them in half with a single stride. As fast as he was, there was no escaping this foe.

But, strangely, the killing blow didn't come, and when at last he dared to look behind again, the giant was gone. Instead, there rose into the sky the Great Hall of Sulare, pristine and glorious in the morning sun. The gardens surrounding it were especially beautiful in all the color of full bloom. Walking toward him, down the center of a gravel pathway, was Wylla.

He turned and began to run back, the soft grass beneath his feet giving way to the crunch of the smooth stones. When he reached her, he slipped his arms around her waist and lifted her off the ground, spinning recklessly around and around. He lost his balance and tumbled off of the path onto a small patch of well-manicured lawn. She fell beside him, laughing, and as he looked over at her, long wisps of dark black hair obscured her lovely eyes. He reached over and slid his fingers through her hair, uncovering her beautiful face.

"I thought I had lost you."

"You can never lose me, Joraiem."

"Never?"

"Never."

For some reason, that seemed like enough. He said no

more, but lay stroking her silky hair in the grass. "Are you tired?" she asked.

"Very."

She smiled, "Then rest."

She also lay still, but she began to hum a soothing lullaby that he hadn't heard for years. The pretty melody and the feel of her soft hair put him slowly to sleep. "Very," he heard himself saying again as darkness crept over him at last.

When Joraiem awoke, he felt worse than he had the night before. The little sleep he had been able to manage teased him with but a glimpse of the real rest his body craved. He found himself lying in the tall grass, wondering what he was getting up for anyway. They weren't going anywhere, at least not as far as he could see. Still, Monias had driven deep his lessons of duty, and despite his body's groans and complaints, he forced himself to sit up.

Few of the others were stirring. Pedraal and Pedraan, just off of their watch, stood at the far edge of the rock formation, looking south across the open plain. Valzaan stood with his back to the camp some distance north. Resting on Valzaan's loosely clinched fist was a windhover. It sat still, not far from the prophet's face, though what Valzaan was doing with the bird, Joraiem could not see. Then the King Falcon leapt from his hand and spiraled up into the sky.

Valzaan returned to the camp and called each one gently to awake and gather. This they did, and before long, they all sat sleepily together before the prophet. Joraiem leaned against the stone that had been their semi-shelter, and Darias came and sat beside him. He didn't speak to Joraiem, but it was clear he was afraid. The previous evening had allowed little time to contemplate the true desperation of their situation, but the night had yielded plenty of it. As Joraiem scanned the gathering, he found it unlikely many of them had thought of much else.

"I think we are alone on the island now," Valzaan began.

"Are you sure of this?" Caan replied over the spreading murmurs.

"Not completely. But, it is a strong feeling. I think those of the enemy that remain alive have fled with the Vulsutyrim. I don't think we are in any immediate danger."

"Hadn't we better be careful, just in case?" Elyas asked.

"Yes. It is always wise to take precautions, but I wanted you all to know that we seem, for the moment, to be safe."

"Safe, and trapped," Saegan said.

"For the moment," Valzaan answered. "But like I said yesterday, Allfather's arm is not too short to save, nor is his power too weak to deliver, even in desperate circumstances."

"What should we do in the meantime?" Aljeron began. "I find the prospect of sitting and waiting for deliverance to be almost unbearable."

"Waiting is part of life, Aljeron. After yesterday, I would think you might relish a rest. Should Allfather deliver us from this place, as I believe He will, you may soon miss the rest you have been granted here."

"Perhaps," Aljeron answered, quietly.

"I have no real desire to return to Nal Gildoroth," Joraiem began, "but should we go back to burn the Malekim and Black Wolves as is the custom?"

"It is good to honor the tradition, Joraiem, but there is no need to observe that custom here. There are no villagers or townsfolk around who might be unduly disturbed by their scattered carcasses, and more importantly, there is no concern here to keep the ground from defilement. The streets of Nal Gildoroth are already cursed, so let the foul creatures rot where they lie."

"Then what do you propose we do? Should we just sit here and wait?" It was Rulalin, this time, sounding as Aljeron had, impatient at the prospect of inactivity.

"No. I propose we hike due north, until we reach the northernmost tip of the island."

They looked at one another, surprised. "Why?" several asked at once.

"Who knows what day today is?"

"It is the thirteenth day of Full Summer," Ulmindos answered.

"Correct. Which means that in three days it will be Midsummer's Day. Though we are stranded here, far from the comfort of our own homes, I intend that we should keep the rites of Midsummer."

"I had forgotten Midsummer," Aljeron said quietly, shaking his head.

"You're not the only one," Pedraal chimed in.

"There is no shame in losing track of the time, especially given the events of the last ten days. But, as things have turned out, we now find ourselves wholly free to observe the rites. So, I say again, let us move to the northernmost point of the island, where we may build on the beach a suitable mound from which we can gaze out over the Southern Ocean toward Kirthanin and Agia Muldonai. We will not just wait. We will also worship."

They prepared a light breakfast and ate it somberly. The news that the Malekim were likely gone was not quite enough to take the edge off their plight. To come to the Forbidden Isle at all had been a major victory of the mind over fear, but to be stranded on the Forbidden Isle seemed too much to come to terms with.

Assembling their things didn't take long, as they had essentially just dropped everything and left it where it lay when they reached the rock formation the previous night. Joraiem noticed Aljeron approach Synoki, a small bundle in his hands. Some words were exchanged, quietly, and as Aljeron departed, Synoki took what turned out to be a spare shirt and pair of pants and put them on. They were a little large for him, and for some moments Synoki stared down at them, trying to get used to the feel of clean clothes again after so many years.

Joraiem looked back from Synoki to Aljeron and found him staring at Kelvan's knife before quickly tucking it into his belt again. Aside from Bryar, Joraiem thought, Kelvan's death must have been hardest on Aljeron. Since the Werthanim had left home, Aljeron had been their leader. Joraiem had noticed on the journey to Sulare how responsible Aljeron felt for them. That feeling had grown in Sulare, and Joraiem felt sure it now persisted even beyond the grave.

Joraiem mused as the group began to move off through the tall grass about how much things had changed since that day he left Peris Mil and found Koshti lying in the road. They had all changed since coming to Sulare, all grown. It was not that they had become adults, for they had not been children before their arrival. It was something else, something for which Joraiem had no words. Somewhere along the way, some secondary transition had been made, something unseen, un-noticed, and unheralded. Perhaps it had been triggered by the fight in the clearing with the Black Wolves, or perhaps that was just the day it had become clear. Whatever it was, they had changed. They had faced some twenty Malekim and more than half as many Black Wolves, and they had been victorious. Sulare had changed them, and as Joraiem felt the warm breeze at his back, he wondered how the Forbidden Isle would change them, now that they had moved beyond Sulare, be-yond the Summerland.

Joraiem had been so preoccupied that he had failed to no-tice Aljeron come up beside him. He probably wouldn't have noticed at all if Koshti's warm breath hadn't blown against his legs. He turned and nodded to Aljeron, who was already look-ing at him.

"I wanted to tell you, Joraiem, that I've never seen anyone handle a bow like that before. I knew you were good. We all knew that. When I first saw you shoot, I realized you were perhaps the best bowman I'd ever seen, though I thought maybe there were one or two men back home who might rival you. After yesterday? Well, I don't think there is anyone alive who could have fired as quickly and as accurately as you did. Maybe there's never been anyone that good."

Joraiem shrugged it off, embarrassed by the compliment. "It was just one of those battle frenzies Caan talks about."

"Maybe, but you couldn't see yourself the way I saw you. At first, like everyone else, I was watching the Malekim heading toward us. Then I saw an arrow hit the first one, a solid hit, even though they were way out of my range. Before I could really grasp how incredible it was that you had hit him at that distance, another arrow flew into my field of vision and another Malekim fell. I turned to see whether it had come from Bryar or Kelvan, but both were taking aim with their own bows, probably waiting until they were able to get a shot that they knew they could take. In the meantime, you had already nocked another arrow, aimed, and were firing a third time. I watched you then, start to finish, as you fired the fourth arrow, and I swear to you, my eyes had trouble following your movements they were so fast."

Joraiem just kept walking, eyes studying the ground, and Aljeron continued after a pause. "Look, I don't really know if anyone's ever fired a bow faster than that, but I do know this. No one died in that first attack because you ripped the Malekim apart before they ever got to us. It was hard to lose Kelvan the way we did. We were so close to getting out all right, everybody safe. But, as I look back, I know it could have been much, much worse."

"I did my part," Joraiem said. "We all did. Allfather blessed my hands, that's all."

"That Allfather blessed you yesterday, I don't doubt. There is, though, another thing I don't understand. At the gate, just after we had managed to open it wide enough for all of us to get through, you looked at me, and your eyes were, well, different. I thought I saw something like the reflection of a flame of fire in them. It was strange."

"Perhaps the sun was playing tricks with your eyes, or perhaps the light from outside the city reflected oddly in mine when it streamed in through the opening in the gates."

"I don't think so. You turned from the gate and looked right at me, and I saw what I saw clearly. It wasn't an odd glow or indefinable light. I saw a pretty definite image of flame, and I think I've seen something like it before."

"Yeah?" Joraiem trembled a little bit.

"Haven't you?"

"I've seen what you've described."

"Joraiem, how can you be so casual about this? You need to ask him about it. Surely he can tell you what it means."

"There's no need to bother him about this now."

"Look, I'll do it if it would be easier. I don't mind. I can take him aside at some point on the way, or when we get there, and just tell him what I've seen in you both."

Joraiem turned to him. "No. Promise me you won't say a word to him about this. I will talk to Valzaan when I'm ready, all right?"

"All right. I won't say anything."

They walked together in silence for a while. Joraiem was in turmoil. He had been trying to get used to this idea that he was some kind of prophet, but it was a lot to swallow. The previous day's events and his dream had only added to the struggle, and now he realized clearly for the first time that it would be increasingly difficult to keep the truth from his friends. He wanted to tell Aljeron, to entrust his secret to him, but he didn't know what to say.

"Aljeron, I can't say I know exactly what happened yesterday, because I don't. What I do know, is that what happened yesterday wasn't completely out of the blue. There have been other things, other strange things." Joraiem looked around them to make sure no one was walking close enough to hear what he was saying, then continued. "Now probably isn't the best time to explain it all, but I will talk to Valzaan when I feel the time is right. After I do, I would like to talk about it with you, when I'm ready. All I can say now, is that yesterday, Allfather answered my prayers."

"Well," Aljeron answered, "we're going to be here for who knows how long. If I can help, even if just by listening, you know I will."

"I know. Thanks."

They walked until well past noon, when they halted for a drink. They didn't eat lunch, though, as they had agreed together that two small meals a day would have to be sufficient to make their scant supplies last as long as possible. As it was, they were fairly sure that between ten days and two weeks of food was all they had.

Not long before dusk, they caught a glimpse of the waters of the Southern Ocean, and though Joraiem knew that seeing the water brought them no closer to crossing it, he felt a certain comfort in the realization that home lay in that direction, beyond these shores. The idea of home brought images of Dal Harat flooding over him. He wondered if his father was watching the same sunset, smoking his pipe behind the house. He was probably pondering Midsummer and had likely kept the family at the table long after dinner, praying for the humility of the people of Dal Harat as the rites approached. Elsora might even be busy in the kitchen making food for the feast that followed the rites, or maybe she was just brushing Kyril's hair or telling Brenim a story. Of course, Joraiem realized, it was entirely possible that Evrim was sitting with the family, doing with them whatever it was they were all doing. Evrim moved slowly, but it had been long enough since he left that surely Evrim had spoken to Monias by now. He smiled at the thought of Evrim sitting at his place at the table. Brenim had always admired Evrim, and having him around the place all the time would be exciting for him. Elsora would be happy because Kyril would be happy. Even Monias would like it. While he would take seriously his duty to examine his only daughter's prospective husband, he would also enjoy having another man around in Joraiem's absence. One of the hardest things for Monias about Joraiem's trip to Sulare was that there were many things Monias cherished doing with his oldest son that Brenim just wasn't ready for. With Evrim there, at least some of those things wouldn't be lost entirely.

As they reached the edge of the beach, which was even with the grasslands at this end of the island, the images of home slipped away. They were replaced by his more immediate surroundings, which included not only sand, stretching in both directions as far as the eye could see, but large rocks jutting out of the shallow waters here and there. Suddenly, he felt very sad. He would have liked very much to be at that table, with the others, but home was a long, long way away.

5

MIDSUMMER

WYLLA STARED INTO THE darkness, listening to the sound of whimpering across the room. Silently she called out to Allfather again, begging Him for strength for them all, strength for whatever lay ahead. *Keep us strong,* she mumbled over and over again. She knew that half of them were already desperately close to breaking, if they were not already broken. Tarin and Valia had done little more than cry since their capture. They cried as the Malekim prodded them along the road, they cried in the row boats, and they cried when they were locked down below. Calissa and Nyan, the two Suthanim, had not shown such visible disturbance, but she knew they were not doing well. They huddled together, saying nothing, doing little more than stare blankly ahead of them. They were fragile, very fragile, and even the tiniest blow would shatter them.

Fortunately, the other half were doing better, some even better than she could have hoped. Bryar, of course, she had expected to be strong. Though she had been typically quiet since their capture, Wylla knew that if anything, she was furious, not distraught. Wylla had seen clearly the fiery defiance in Bryar's eyes when Caan gave her the order to lead the rest of them out of the city. Though she had obeyed, it had been manifestly against her wishes. She was not the retreating kind. Whether she was now furious at Caan for the command or with herself for her inability to carry it out and keep them safe, Wylla couldn't tell. What was clear, was that Bryar was too angry to speak.

What was more remarkable, was the strength both Karalin and Mindarin had shown. She had known Mindarin to be strong-willed, but she had not imagined her to be so calm and capable under such duress. Mindarin had been used to saying whatever she wanted, and what control she exercised over her own tongue seemed to take visible effort. From this Wylla had concluded that Mindarin was mostly bluster. Since their capture, however, she had proven to be quite resilient. She had been constant in her gentle attempts to support and encourage Calissa and Nyan, as well as Tarin and Valia.

The awkwardness between Mindarin and Wylla remained. Mindarin had not been overtly cruel or even cold to her, but there was an obvious difference between the way Mindarin dealt with Wylla and the way she dealt with other women. She had always been polite, indeed, even more polite with her than the rest. None of her dry wit had been directed Wylla's way, for which she had been glad, thinking initially that perhaps this was a sign of respect. Wylla understood, however, that though Mindarin's words were sometimes biting, there was a certain amount of fondness in Mindarin's relations with the other women that was absent in her formal dealings with Wylla.

Wylla shifted on the damp, hard floorboards. She turned her thoughts to Karalin, shrugging off thoughts of her relationship with Mindarin. Karalin, like Mindarin, had surprised

Wylla with her resolve and resilience, having also adopted a maternal role toward the others. After more than two months of lingering in the background of everyone's affairs in Sulare, Karalin—second in age only to Wylla—was emerging now as a leader. When Mindarin huddled quietly with Calissa and Nyan, Karalin tended Tarin and Valia, and when Mindarin switched her attention to the cousins, Karalin picked up with the Suthanim. Karalin had even been bold enough to sit silently beside Bryar, even when Bryar had exuded the desire to be left alone. Karalin's gentle persistence, though, had broken through Bryar's stubborn isolation, and eventually she had been accepted enough for Bryar to fall asleep with her head in Karalin's lap.

Wylla smiled as she thought again of her poor judgment. Because of Karalin's physical deformity and her slight frame, Wylla had thought of her as frail, even weak, but she had shown herself to be anything but that. Even in the dreadful march from the gates of Nal Gildoroth to the boats, Karalin had shown her strength. Pressed beyond all imaginable human limits to run as with wings, Karalin had not only kept up, but she had found strength to encourage the others to keep going.

Thinking of the awful moments between the city and the shore brought everything back. She had fled Nal Gildoroth, afraid not for themselves but for those they were leaving behind. Her last glimpse of the men had been of them bracing for a fresh onslaught from Black Wolves and Malekim. The women had run half-heartedly, eager to leave the dark city but reluctant to abandon their friends and brothers. She was sure none had considered that their own demise might lie ahead.

And then they had reached the gates, dashing through them with a sudden burst of energy. It had been like stepping from night into morning, from shadow into light. The sight of the dirt road and tall grass blowing in the wind brought hope back, until two dozen Malekim sprang upon them from beside the gates. Then a Vulsutyrim had stepped out from against the outside of the city wall where he had been quietly waiting.

Wylla knew that if she lived until the restoration of all things, she would never forget that sight. The giant had towered over them, a full three spans high, thick as well as tall, his stout legs like massive pillars or huge tree trunks. His exposed legs, arms, chest, and back were powerful, muscular, and tanned from long hours in the sun. Hair some shade of light black or perhaps brown, hung loosely down his back. But his eyes more than anything else had drawn her gaze, for they had struck her as deep and intense but not necessarily cruel. He was formidable, but he did not strike her as an unfeeling animal, as the Black Wolves did.

The Malekim were indeed but animals as far as Wylla was concerned. Up close they were even uglier than she had imagined. Their grey hides were thick and coarse, like the hides of the lumbering water beasts that lived peacefully in the shallows of the Kellisor Sea. Most were a span and three or four hands tall, though some were shorter. Their hair was black and thin, hanging limply from their rough scalps, and their eyes were black and empty. Looking into them was like looking into a starless night.

Of course, these observations had not come to her so completely in that brief moment when they emerged from the city. There had been too much confusion then. Before any of the rest of them could react, Mindarin had pulled her knife to stab the Malekim closest to her, only to be sent sprawling by the back of his arm. Bryar, unable to get an arrow ready, had managed to duck under the arm of the Malekim and plunge her knife into his foot. The blade barely punctured the Malekim's hide before Bryar was held fast in his arms, but slight traces of black blood in the dirt showed that she had done some damage.

Then the Vulsutyrim had walked through their midst, stepping past them toward the gates. With a massive groan he heaved first one of the gates and then the other shut. The grunt that emerged from his mouth was startling, both because of its contrast with the total silence of the Voiceless, but also because of the clear articulation in it. Wylla didn't know why this should surprise her. She had known that Vulsutyr's children were not animals, and so should have expected language, but she was startled nonetheless.

Soon their hands were bound, and they were running like the wind. Fear kept them going as their captors drove them along the long, smooth road. When they had finally reached the shore, exhausted, they had been dumped like sacks of grain into the bottom of two long rowboats, at least three times the size of the boats they had landed in earlier that day. Soon, they were being lifted to the deck of the waiting ship, and once the Vulsutyrim was there, he forced them below.

They had stayed in the cramped storage area the rest of that day and through the whole of that long night. Wylla had slept some, but she hadn't slept long. The sound of footsteps moving above through the night kept her awake and wondering. She wondered what had become of the men. She wondered why they had been taken rather than killed and where they were now headed. She wondered if she would ever see Joraiem again.

When the thought of Joraiem did not start her sobbing like the women around her, she held tightly to the last clear glimpse she had of him, leading them all up the alley toward the open square of Nal Gildoroth. She had regretted her angry words to him on the *Evening Star,* and she had seen that there was no resentment in his eyes when he looked at her. She had seen that there was peace between them, and she had seen how much he loved her. If Joraiem was alive, he would come after her.

The next morning, about Fourth Hour, the door above them had opened and the deep, resonant voice of the Vulsutyrim called them to come up. On deck, the giant motioned to the women to sit in a line against the starboard rail of the ship. Then, a Malekim had moved down the line, handing out chunks of hard bread, which they devoured. After they finished, another Malekim went back down the line giving drinks of tepid water with a large ladle.

It was during this that Wylla had first noticed the tension between the Malekim and the Vulsutyrim. When one of the girls, leaning forward to drink, lost her balance and fell, knocking the ladle out of the Malekim's hand and hitting it on the legs, another Malekim had jumped forward and roughly thrown her back against the rail. At this, the giant, who had been watching from the middle of the deck, stepped forward and smashed the Malekim sideways across the deck. The creature flew several spans before hitting the deck hard and sliding several more, and the other Malekim scampered out of the giant's reach. The giant followed this with some angry words for all the Silent Ones in a language Wylla didn't know. Then, he had stooped before them on one knee.

"They will be more careful next time, but you must be more careful too."

His tone was firm and authoritative, neither kind nor sympathetic. Wylla didn't doubt that what he said was true, for the other Malekim continued to cower in the giant's presence. She knew it would be wise to heed his warning to them as well.

They were not above deck long before being sent back down below. Two more times that day they were allowed up for perhaps a quarter of an hour, and each time they went through the same feeding ritual. Then they were locked below for another night. The cracks around the door above them did not allow much light, but now Wylla thought that they were perceptibly lighter than they had been. Maybe it was morning at last.

She sat up and rubbed the arm she had been resting upon. Not two days had passed since they'd been taken, but it felt like they'd been in this dark and unbearable place for a week. She listened to the whimpering and wondered how long it would be until she was reduced to tears. *Keep me strong,* she prayed again. With their teachers gone, with Aljeron gone, she knew it was up to her as the eldest to hold them together. She just didn't know if she could.

After his watch on the second night, Joraiem slept much better than he had the first. He suspected they all did. All around him his companions slept like the dead. No fearful images disturbed him and no odd dreams intruded. When he awoke, the sun was well above the horizon, and he felt the pleasant warmth of a Full Summer morning.

That morning there was more chatter as they ate, as the plan for the day called for them to construct a mound for the rites of Midsummer, a purpose that helped to distract them for the moment from their desperate situation. They were aware of course that nothing had changed: they were still stranded and the women were still held captive by the enemy, at least as far as they knew. Even so, they gladly and wholeheartedly threw their energy into the task at hand, glad to have something to occupy their minds and exercise their bodies.

So it was that midmorning found them hard at work preparing the foundation of the mound. They rounded up several slabs of stone from the coastline, and using them, they pushed great heaps of sand together to begin constructing the mound. At first, as they started piling the sand up, the base was somewhat square, maybe a span along each side. However, as the day progressed and they began to build upwards, the spill from the rising elevation of the mound created gentle slopes that pushed those boundaries outward in a circular manner, until the diameter of the base eventually became two or three spans.

By late afternoon, the mound was taller than any but Sarneth, and now the construction progressed slowly as it was harder to move sand to the top, lacking as they did any good instruments for the job. Eventually, though, they succeeded in raising the height to about a span and a half, managing to keep the sand packed solidly so that the Elder, whom Joraiem realized would almost certainly be Valzaan, would have no difficulty ascending to the top on Midsummer's Day.

As they sat for supper on the fourteenth day of Full Summer, the sense of accomplishment they felt gave them ease for the first time in days. They talked and laughed, forgetting for a time the sorrow of recent days. Joraiem watched the men around the small fire they had built on the beach, their first such fire since coming to the Forbidden Isle, and then he turned to Valzaan. The prophet did not participate in the conversation, but sat quietly, as though meditating. Joraiem wondered if Valzaan had known that even the preparation for the Midsummer rite would have such a healing effect on them all. All his words since their disheartening discovery of the sunken *Evening Star* had focused on pointing the men to Allfather for encouragement and hope. What the men had been either unable or unwilling to do through sheer strength of will, Valzaan had helped them to do by putting their hands to work. As their bodies had turned to the simple task of raising the mound, so their minds and spirits had been raised toward what the mound represented and the One for whom it was built.

That night, as the sun was going down for the third time since their arrival, Joraiem slipped a little distance down the shore, away from the others. He sat on a smooth rock well away from the water's edge, not really wanting to be anywhere near the waterline. There was too much else going on to face old fears and old problems. His thoughts, a mishmash of memories and images swirling relentlessly through his mind, were interrupted by Koshti jumping onto the rock behind him, brushing up against his back. The soft feel of his fur tickled, even through his thin tunic, and Joraiem turned to see what the tiger was doing. As he did, he saw Aljeron not far behind.

"Am I disturbing you?"

"Not really. I was lost in thought, but I'm happy for the distraction. I've decided that I think too much."

"What do you mean?"

"Just that. I think too much."

Aljeron sat down beside him, and eventually Koshti lay down behind them both. "Your thoughtfulness is one of your best qualities. Why regret it?"

"Thoughtfulness? If you mean being considerate, well that is a good thing, and if I am a thoughtful person at all then my parents have taught me well. But, that isn't what I meant. I think too much, not of other people, but of everything. I analyze up and down and back and forth, and then one more time for good measure. I turn things over and over in my mind, and that's the problem."

"I still think you're being too hard on yourself. We need careful thinkers. I know that when you speak, you've thought carefully. That's a good thing."

"I'm not explaining myself very well," Joraiem said, scanning the coast. "Before I left for Sulare, I realized that I cared very deeply for a woman in Dal Harat. It's a long story, but for a number of reasons, I had not seen or allowed myself to see the true nature of my feelings before. As I prepared to leave, I went to see her, filled with relief that I could see myself clearly at last. But, it was all for naught. Though she had indeed cared for me once, she was at that point promised to another.

"During the long weeks on the road to Sulare, I had a lot of time to try and understand what had happened. One thing was clear: If I had spoken sooner, I wouldn't have been too late. I tried to figure out why I hadn't, but I didn't know. I was of age. She was of age. The answer, I think, is that I did not speak because I had to make everything more complex than it was. I had loved her. She had loved me. That should have been enough. That is enough for most and has been enough since the beginning of time. But not for me. No, I had to worry about what her twin sister would think, a woman who had plagued me since childhood. I had to worry about allowing myself to feel deeply for someone before going to Sulare. I had to worry about what I would say, how I would say it, and what she would think, and I had to put a thousand hurdles and obstacles in the way of my own happiness."

Joraiem ran his fingers through his thick blond hair, scratching his head as he looked away from the water. Though he no longer missed Alina, he still felt the sting of his mistakes. "The thing is, Aljeron, none of that would matter, if I had just learned from my mistake. The wise are not those who make no mistakes. The wise are those who heed the lessons of their mistakes and never make them again. I am a fool, for what have I done? I have made the same mistake again. I knew, soon after coming to Sulare, that I cared for Wylla. What's more, I saw, though I could not believe it, that she cared for me. For me, Aljeron, for me! All this I saw. All this I knew. So again I ask, what more was there? What more did I need? Was this not all that mattered? Was this not enough? Was I not prepared now to avoid my prior mistake?

"Of course not. I did the exact same thing again. I delayed and pondered and fretted. I worried about Rulalin and how he would feel. I worried about telling Monias that I would not be coming back to live in Dal Harat. I worried about disappointing my best friend, Evrim, after promising him that his fears of my permanent departure were vain. I worried about causing disunity to our group and Kirthanin, as though my love for Wylla could derail the peace of the world!

"What a fool I've been! I was able to tell her that last night on the *Evening Star* that I cared for her, but even then, I couldn't really open up. I could not, or would not, give her the only thing she wanted, a full and true accounting of myself. And now she's gone, Aljeron. I've lost her, and I may never get another chance to do it right."

"Maybe you do think too much, Joraiem. You are torturing yourself needlessly. The plan to wait seemed like wisdom a few days ago. As far as we knew, there were only two possible outcomes of our journey here. We would be successful and live, or we would fail and die. No one foresaw what actually happened. How could you have known? Leave behind your regret and focus on getting her back. Focus instead on vengeance against those who have taken her and the others!" Aljeron's eyes glinted, and Joraiem saw again in them the look he had seen by the fire when they camped beside Elnin Wood.

"Hear, hear," another voice sounded from the deepening darkness beside them. They both turned, surprised, to see Rulalin coming closer.

"Rulalin," Aljeron said, agitation in his voice. "I didn't expect eavesdropping from you."

"My apologies for intruding, but I wasn't eavesdropping, at least not intentionally. I decided to go walking along the beach and as I came this way, I saw the two of you here. I'm sorry if I've interrupted a personal conversation."

"You have," Aljeron said, showing more restraint this time, but still not warm. "What have you heard?"

"Only that the two of you, like me, are struggling to sit patiently here while our friends are out there, in need of us now more than ever!" As Rulalin spoke, he waved his hand emphatically toward the Southern Ocean. Then, dramatically, he stepped toward them and addressed Joraiem directly. "Come, Joraiem, enough is enough. It is foolishness for us to carry on like this. We both love Wylla, do we not? There is no point denying it. Can we not lay aside our differences now? Of all the people here, could anyone desire their rescue and safe return more than the two of us? Let us vow, you and I, to let nothing on the earth or in the sky, nothing that walks or crawls or swims or flies, nothing that is or will be, nothing at all come between us and our task—to save Wylla and the others from their captors. Let us vow that should our quest take us to Agia Muldonai and Malek himself, that we will not stop nor turn aside until she is safe or we are dead. Will you vow? When she is safe, when they all are, we can deal with what is between us. Will you be my brother in this?"

Joraiem stood, surprised but also grateful for Rulalin's invitation, and answered, "I will vow, for I have always mourned the distance between us. I will go with you wherever this road leads, and I will do whatever this quest requires. I will not turn aside until she is safe and sound. In this, and in all things, I will be your brother."

Rulalin clasped Joraiem's hand and shook it, echoing, "And I will be yours, and we will not rest until she is safe. So be it?"

"So may it be. May Allfather hear and know that this is our vow."

Standing, Aljeron took their hands into his own. "I am a witness to this vow. Let there be peace among us. We are brothers, and I will go with you both to see the women safely home. I will not turn aside to the right or to the left until the deed is done or I am dead. So be it?"

"So may it be," the others answered.

For a moment they stood, silently, hands joined together. At last, they each stepped back, but Aljeron placed his big hands on each of their shoulders. "We are sworn, and our path is clear. We will follow the Vulsutyrim, wherever he goes, as long as the women are with him. Sulare will not see our return, nor Dal Harat, nor Fel Edorath nor Shalin Bel, unless we first find and free our lost companions. To this vow we will be true. Agreed?"

"Agreed." They turned and headed together back toward the fire. Joraiem looked up into the clear night sky and felt relief inside. It felt good to be at peace with Rulalin again, even if only for a time, but even so he wondered how long it could really last.

As the men ate breakfast the following morning, Ulmindos addressed Valzaan. "Since we've finished the mound and have a day before Midsummer, I'd like to take my men and any others willing to come back to the *Evening Star*. Since we think there won't be any attacks, it should be safe, and who knows what we may be able to salvage? I'd like some good swimmers and strong backs, in case Allfather blesses our expedition."

Before long, almost everyone, even Synoki, had agreed to go, many commenting that anything would be better than sitting around all day. They all seemed eager, except Valzaan, who said he'd enjoy some time to think, Caan, who was still nursing his tender leg, and Joraiem.

"Aren't you coming?" Pedraan asked Joraiem.

"I've never been much of a swimmer," Joraiem answered, blushing.

"That's all right, we'll still—"

"I'm sure Joraiem knows his own mind," Aljeron interrupted Pedraan. "Maybe he just wants some time alone with our beloved teachers. He has a genuine interest in learning, you know." Aljeron winked at Joraiem as he gave Pedraan a playful shove.

"Who would want to sit around on a beautiful day like today?" Pedraan shrugged and turned away. Joraiem nodded to Aljeron, grateful, as he also turned to leave.

During the morning, Joraiem did not have an opportunity to talk to Caan and Valzaan, who begged his pardon as soon as the others had gone and withdrew a short distance to talk. Joraiem found a comfortable place in the shorter grass on the edge of the beach and lay back in the warm morning sun. He tried to remember the last time he had been able simply to pass a morning lounging in soft summer grass. It was a rare treat, regardless of his surroundings and the circumstances. Before he knew it, he had fallen asleep.

"Joraiem?" A voice spoke to him from close by.

He strained to open his eyes, but the bright midday sun compelled him to blink. It was several moments before he could open his eyes and focus. Valzaan was sitting nearby, cross-legged in the grass, his green robe bunched up around his knees. He looked very comfortable, and Joraiem wondered how long he had been there.

"Yes, Valzaan?"

"There are questions you would like to ask me."

"There are." Joraiem hesitated, half-expecting Valzaan to begin answering them, since he seemed already aware of what was on his mind. But, the prophet didn't speak and so he began. "Before I met you, I saw you in my dreams. Were you really there, or was it some kind of premonition or vision that Allfather gave me, to prepare me to meet you?"

"A little of both, perhaps. You didn't know it, but you summoned me to those dreams."

"I summoned you?"

"It may be easier to think of it as Allfather summoning me through you. You were not aware you were doing it, but as you hone the gifts that go along with being a prophet, you will in time be able to summon me consciously. Even so, while you summoned me, it was something Allfather arranged to prepare you to meet me."

"And three nights ago, after Nal Gildoroth? Did I imagine that?"

"No. You did not summon me then, but I came to you in your dream because I knew you needed me. That was an important day for you. In addition to beginning to see for yourself how I use the windhovers, you began to experience some of what Allfather can work through you. You felt the peace of His presence as He guided your hand in combat. You felt the strength of His hand as He helped you to push open the gate—something you could not have done without Him, you know. You felt His strength again as you pursued the Vulsutyrim and the women. Have you ever felt that way before?"

Joraiem started to shake his head slowly and say no, but stopped. "Well, yes, actually, though not to that extent. There have been times while running, or while working, when I have felt a strange and unexpected exhilaration come upon me. Are you saying they are connected?"

"I would not be surprised. You *are* a prophet, Joraiem, hard as it may be to believe or accept. It is entirely likely that you have been marked for service since childhood. I wouldn't be surprised if over time, you began to see more and more evidence of its workings early in your life."

Joraiem pulled up some of the grass beside him, letting the wind blow the blades into the sea of grass behind him. "I have wrestled with this, but I believe you, Valzaan. You know that, don't you?"

"Yes."

"What I need is help understanding what it means to be a prophet. I need help understanding the implications and consequences of this. I mean, you told me that Allfather has called me, that He has set me aside, but for what? You are Allfather's prophet. What more is needed? What am I supposed to do? Why does He need me?"

"Allfather needs no one, really," Valzaan answered. "All

things exist because He is. Without Him there is nothing. He has always been and will always be. He could not cease to exist, but if somehow He did, then so also would all things. Even Malek knows that. Malek never really believed he could destroy Allfather, nor was that his intent. In his pride and folly, having ruled Kirthanin with the other Titans since the dawn of time, he believed that he could seize control of Kirthanin, wrest mastery of this world from his brothers. He knew he was the most powerful of them all, the most powerful of all Allfather's created beings. Somehow, from this, he came to believe that if he could assert his power over Kirthanin, his victory would forever frustrate Allfather's plan and will for this world, since Allfather had entrusted it to the Twelve. What he could not see, or would not, was that Allfather's plans are never frustrated. Why he could not see this, I don't know, but Allfather will accomplish what He intends, which is why we must never despair, no matter how dark the world becomes.

"But even though Malek is much on my mind, he was not the focus of your question. Allfather does not so much need me, or need you, as He has chosen to use us to accomplish His purposes. We are blessed, as indeed are all Allfather's servants, great and small, for we have a part to play in Allfather's plan of restoration. Agia Muldonai will not always be a lair for evil creatures and their evil master, but it will be cleansed and restored. The rites of Midsummer are not the product of the foolish wishes of desperate men, but they are the celebration of the sure promises of Allfather."

Joraiem shivered. "But what does any of that have to do with me? I am of all the Novaana, one of the least. My family is respected but by no means important. My home is a small village, not a great city. Can you not tell me, more exactly, what it is I've been called to?"

Valzaan reached over and set his hand on Joraiem's leg. "I'm sorry, Joraiem, but I can't. From the first moment Allfather made me aware of you, I have asked Him that very question. I have high hopes, Joraiem, but no answers. I have long waited for a promised one, a prophet whose service will be essential to Malek's ultimate defeat and the cleansing of Avalione and the Holy Mountain. I have hoped before and been disappointed as other prophets have come, but all for different purposes. There have been no other prophets for hundreds of years, and now, at last, another has come. What does it mean, you ask. I ask too and have received no answer—not yet. But, we will not stop asking, you and I. We will continue to do what Allfather sets before us to do, and in time, all questions will be answered, one way or another."

Joraiem's shiver had become a tremble, and he could not speak. Valzaan spoke of things beyond his capacity to understand and hinted at a future beyond his ability to imagine. A prophet he might be, but Valzaan spoke of someone who would be more than that, a child of destiny, created by Allfather for a high and holy purpose. Joraiem could not be that person.

Valzaan, aware that enough had been said for the present, went on to speak of other things, and time slipped quickly away as the afternoon grew late. Caan eventually joined them in the grass, and early evening came. The rumbling in Joraiem's stomach and the position of the sun told him the supper hour was upon them, and then, from down the beach, the others appeared.

They were coming in something of a straight line, dragging something large and white. As they drew closer, Joraiem realized that they had placed salvaged goods on a large piece of the main sail from the *Evening Star,* and they were pulling the load down the beach, back to the others. They pulled it all up to the edge of the fire pit they'd dug the previous day and sank wearily into the sand.

Ulmindos reported the story of their day. They had found

the sail first, ripped somehow from the main mast of the *Evening Star,* mostly aground and partially in the water. Ulmindos didn't know how, but he thought it might prove helpful to them. Ulmindos, then, with Sarneth, had swum out to the wreck, and after taking a few dives, had found the hole in the side. After some time, they had returned with a large, sealed barrel. As it turned out, no fewer than six sealed barrels of water had survived the ship's sinking, along with a barrel of salted meat and another of hard bread.

"I have lived the equivalent of many lifetimes," Valzaan said with a smile, "but I still marvel at Allfather's faithfulness to provide what is needed. Tomorrow is Midsummer, and when we break our fast, we are supposed to feast. Now we can!"

"Is that really wise?" Elyas asked, before turning red when he realized what he had said and to whom he had said it.

"It is always wise to celebrate the feasts of Allfather in the manner He has prescribed. Even the poorest farmer or villager knows there is a time to rejoice, to feast extravagantly. To honor Allfather in this way is not imprudent, it is beautiful. It is faithful, and it is right."

Elyas, relieved that Valzaan had chosen to overlook the impudence of his question, nodded vigorously in agreement, and Ulmindos continued, explaining why they had retrieved certain other items: some pieces of board, rope, and other smaller odds and ends. When he was finished, Caan asked, "And Synoki? What of him? Why has he not returned with you?"

"I'm sorry, Caan," Ulmindos answered, "that slipped my mind. When we had gathered what there was to gather, Synoki approached me about heading back to the alcove which hides the small cave where he has sheltered during his stay here. He said there were a couple items, not terribly important but personal, which he had left there. He asked if he might be allowed to go on to that place, pass tonight there, then return tomorrow. I didn't see the harm, so I told him to go."

"He will miss the rites of Midsummer," Caan said.

"He has missed many, during his sojourn," Ulmindos replied.

"It is all right," Valzaan answered. "What is done is done. He will return when he will return. We will not worry about it now. What we should do, is eat. We should eat and go to bed. Tomorrow, when we celebrate the rite, I will serve as the Elder, though it has been long since I have done so in a formal capacity. I should warn you that my prayers will not be short and my intercession will be long and detailed. I will not come down because your knees are weak or your stomachs are growling. So, I recommend that you eat well tonight. I also recommend that you sleep well. Ask for stamina in the morning. You will need it."

Heeding Valzaan's admonition, they prepared their dinner and ate, each man somewhat preoccupied with memories of Midsummer from their own homes. Many stories were told of the rite as it had been performed in their own homes, whether large or small. For some of them, their fathers served as the Elder for the rite. Joraiem thought of Monias, who was not the Elder in Dal Harat but probably would be soon. The current Elder was very old, and it was likely that Monias would be chosen by the village to succeed him.

It was an odd thought, to imagine Monias ascending the mound in the village square, but even odder, Joraiem thought, was the possibility that many years from now, he might be called upon to do it. He looked around the fireside at the other men with him. It was very possible that any or all of them might one day serve as Elder. For his part, he would observe Valzaan carefully the following day. After all, despite the prophet's protests, Joraiem suspected that in the morning he would see the role of Elder served as it should be by one who had followed Allfather longer than all living memory save Valzaan's own could recall.

The men arose before dawn, and dressing in total silence, they observed the prescribed fast from words even as they observed the fast from food. There would be time for talking and eating later. For now, full concentration on the Elder and the mound was required.

The morning was not bright and clear, as all their other mornings on the island had begun. Instead, the sky was overcast as low-hanging clouds covered both sea and land. Even so, they gathered in a semi-circle on the inland part of the mound, facing the mound and the Southern Ocean beyond it, and far beyond the eyes of men, the mainland of Kirthanin and Agia Muldonai hundreds of leagues to the north. They stood, two rows deep, surrounding the mound with heads erect, gazing both at and beyond it. Joraiem's mind strayed to Dal Harat, where he had observed this ritual every year of his life, and he saw in his mind's eye the whole village gathered southwest of the mound, even as they were, silently gazing straight ahead.

From some distance behind them, Valzaan called out, and from wherever they had each one of them gone in their heads, the men snapped back to the present and listened to the words of the Elder.

"Far away, Allfather, far away. We are cut off from the Holy Mountain and the healing waters of the Crystal Fountain. We are wanderers in the world, estranged from home and living in shadow. Avalione lies empty, stained with blood and closed to all living creatures. Agia Muldonai is infested with evil and from its bowels Malek spews forth wickedness into the world.

"Where is peace, Allfather, where is peace? For you made the world in peace and established harmony between the earth and the sky, between the forest and the field, between the mountains and the plain, between the sea and the shore. Once, all living things knew and understood their place in the fabric of life, before it was rent from top to bottom. In tatters it is and has been. How long it shall be, only You can say.

"What shall we do, Allfather, what shall we do? The sin of Andunin stains us all, for we are the children of a bent and twisted race. Though we curse his treachery, we are but flesh and bones and are not without blemish. Though we denounce Andunin's choice, we know it might have been ours, his shame and punishment with it. We know that we have sinned in other ways and share responsibility for the land's need of atonement.

"This is our lament. This is our grief. This is our shame, our sorrow, and our sin. We cry out to you, Allfather, and ask that you forgive. Hear us we pray."

"Hear us!" the men cried together.

"We also pray, Allfather, that you would restore peace. We ask that you would bring about the restoration that you have promised. We long for it, eagerly desiring the day when it will be, when all things will be made new. We long for the day when Malek will be no more, thrown down for a second and final time. We long for the end of evil and the death of death. We long for the day when the waters of the fountain will flow again, cleansing the streets of the city and tumbling down the Holy Mountain. We long for the restoration of life and the peace of Allfather and ask that you will hear our prayer."

"Hear us!"

Silence followed as Valzaan walked through their midst to the foot of the mound. He was dressed in his usual green robe with white sash, but today he also carried the water skin for the ritual. At the foot of the mound he paused and turned to face them.

"You have heard the lament?"

"We have heard."

"You have heard the prayer?"

"We have heard."

"You have agreed in your hearts?"

"We have agreed."

"You have come in humility?

"So have we come."

"You have come in repentance?"

"So have we come."

"You have come in hope for forgiveness?

"So have we come."

"So have you come, and may Allfather hear your prayers and bless the work of your hands. So be it."

"So may it be."

Valzaan then turned to the mound, and with short, steady steps, climbed to the top. When he reached the peak, he lay the water skin down beside him, and facing the north, knelt down. All of them likewise dropped to their knees and bowed their heads. Joraiem knelt in absolute stillness, reflecting as Monias had taught him to do, on Allfather's goodness and his own failures. The reflection moved him, as it usually did, to meditate upon the glory of what would be when the restoration came and their current struggles were no more. Memories of Monias and images of restoration that had been deeply planted in him since childhood swirled in his mind.

How long he meditated this way, Joraiem did not know. Hours passed, for when Valzaan finally spoke from on top of the mound, Joraiem opened his eyes and saw that the sun was well overhead. Even so, he was glad the day was still overcast, since adjusting to the light again was difficult enough without the full force of day. Gradually, though, the mound and the figure of the prophet upon it became clear. Valzaan was no longer kneeling, facing north, for he had stood and turned around. He stood with hands raised high above his head and face directed above, though Joraiem had no idea what the Prophet was seeing in his mind if he was seeing anything at all.

Valzaan broke the hours of silence. "The promises of Allfather are sure. What He has spoken, He will do. This is so and always has been so. Allfather has spoken of the future of this world. His words are truth and His purposes are certain. Is this not so?"

"It is so."

"Evil shall be destroyed. So be it?"

"So may it be."

"Malek shall be cast down and punished. So be it?"

"So may it be."

"Peace and life shall be restored. So be it?"

"So may it be."

"Allfather shall make all things new. So be it?"

"So may it be."

"Allfather shall cleanse the Crystal Fountain. So be it?"

"So may it be."

As Valzaan spoke and the men answered, he dipped the skin and poured a steady stream of water on top of the mound. Some of the water trickled down over the edge while much simply soaked into the thirsty sand.

"Allfather shall cleanse Avalione. So be it?"

"So may it be."

A second time Valzaan poured the water, this time more rapidly, and more splashed over the sides of the mound.

"Allfather shall cleanse Agia Muldonai. It shall be cleansed forevermore, as indeed all Kirthanin shall be cleansed. Never again will sword and spear be raised in war, for even they will be made anew, and all implements of war shall be made implements of peace, and no one will dare to harm or destroy on all His Holy Mountain. So be it?"

"So may it be."

With this, Valzaan poured the last of the water out in a gush upon the mound, and it flowed down the channels and rivulets formed by the other outpourings. Joraiem and the others watched the water flow and silently stood as Valzaan descended.

"The rite is complete, and now we may break our fasts. Let us speak freely to one another and feast the goodness of All-father, for we have been reminded that though the clouds are coming, indeed, some are already here, all is not dark nor is all lost. Allfather has not abandoned us and will not."

They followed Valzaan to the place where their evening fire had been, and soon they had the fire going strong. As some of them cooked and prepared the food, Joraiem sat with Aljeron, whispering together about the morning.

"Can you believe we just observed Midsummer with Valzaan? *The* Valzaan, legendary prophet, serving as Elder?" Joraiem asked with awe.

"It is remarkable." Aljeron nodded. "What did you think?"

"Much of it sounded similar to the words our Elder speaks in Dal Harat, of course, but not all of it. And even the parts where exactly the same words were used, where exactly the same things take place, felt different. I felt almost like we were standing at the foot of Agia Muldonai itself. I know it sounds odd, but I kept having this feeling that Valzaan was speaking right from Avalione. Isn't that crazy? I've never even seen Agia Muldonai, let alone Avalione, but I could feel the Mountain and feel the city and feel the Fountain. I knew as he spoke that they would be clean again. I knew with utter certainty. Didn't you?"

"Well, I'm not sure I could put it that strongly, but I felt something."

"Yes, and here, of all places. The thought of observing Midsummer on the Forbidden Isle! We just enacted the ritual of cleansing in a place that some don't even believe will be healed in the restoration, if it is allowed to survive at all."

"True." Aljeron nodded. "And yet even here, so far from our homes and so far from the Mountain, we felt Allfather's presence strongly and saw the hope of the future so clearly. It is amazing."

"It is enough to make me ashamed that I haven't dared to trust Valzaan that we will leave this place as he has suggested."

"I know. As we prayed, I found myself seeking forgiveness for my doubt, did you?"

"Many times," Joraiem answered. "I still can't imagine how help will find us in time, but is that any harder to imagine than Malek's final defeat? Is it harder to imagine than the cleansing of the Holy Mountain and the restoration of life and peace?"

Aljeron shook his head. "No, of course not. But those things have been an article of faith since long before we were born. They are not nearly so immediate and so personal as our current plight, not that this changes your logic. But I think it is harder to believe that Allfather will intervene in our immediate difficulties, even if it would be by far the lesser miracle."

"You're right, but let us not doubt Allfather's ability to save any longer. I will gladly feast with such a hope, right alongside the more glorious hope of what is ultimately to come at the end of the Age."

And feast they did. As they encircled the fire, they talked and laughed and sang, and Joraiem wondered if the rocks of this shore had ever heard such sounds. He didn't know if the Vulsutyrim had sung before Malek came, but he felt somehow quite sure that even if they had, they had ceased after. He looked around as they celebrated. Their faces reflected a confidence and happiness that had been absent since the Black Wolves attacked Sulare. For a brief moment, Joraiem felt as though they had gone back to that first wonderful evening when they tended the fire together.

Long after they had stopped eating, they sat and talked as the sun went down and darkness descended upon the Forbidden Isle. As they sat, Ulmindos slowly rose and stepped away from the fire, facing the ocean.

"What is it?" Caan asked, as the others grew quiet.

"Gather your things. A storm is coming."

The younger men looked at one another uneasily. Joraiem tried to listen to and feel for the wind, and indeed there seemed to be a cool change coming. It was so infinitesimal that he would not possibly have noticed it without being told it was there. The men separated and soon had dragged all their possessions together to one side of the fire. Ulmindos, with several of the others, took the sail and covered them.

"Already of use," he said as they did. "The storm may not hit for many hours. When it does, gather under the sail. There should be plenty of room for us all. Between now and then, though, we would do well to anchor the edges with large rocks. We have some strength among us, but not enough to hold down a large sail in a larger storm!"

They worked together for an hour or so, until almost the entire seaside perimeter of the sail was covered with the largest rocks they could move, many of them the very rocks they had used to build the mound. That done, they were all well and truly ready for bed, including Synoki, who had returned in time to help with the sail. Some went ahead and crawled under the sail. Joraiem saw the sense of this, but the wind coming in off of the ocean was now brisk and cool, and though it promised fiercer things to come, he found it refreshing.

Even as he curled up, not far from the sail in the short grass, he thought how uncomfortable it would have been to be below deck on the *Evening Star* if a big storm hit. He sat up. Wylla. She was out there, somewhere. Even had the Malekim and giant made terrific time, they could not have reached Suthanin yet. She had to be out there, perhaps even now in the storm. He lay back down, for the horizon held no comfort, and he prayed as he began to drift off to sleep that she was and would be, all right.

6

AFTER THE STORM

COOL SPLASHES FROM RAINDROPS hitting his face wakened Joraiem from a restless sleep full of unpleasant images. He remembered only that the dreams had been troubled and so happily turned his attention from them to the situation at hand.

A brilliant flash of lightning appeared out over the ocean, slashing across the sky horizontally through the deep black clouds that covered both land and sea. The flash was quickly followed by a dramatic rumble of echoing thunder. Ulmindos's storm was indeed upon them, and Joraiem rose to his feet and scampered the short distance to the sail. All the others were already there, and after a quick search, he located an open place beside Pedraal or Pedraan—in the storm he couldn't tell which.

"Come on in, sleepyhead," the twin greeted him over the wind of the storm. "The rest of us have been huddled here for almost half an hour, ever since the first big peals of thunder. You must sleep like the dead to have only now awakened."

"I wasn't sleeping," Joraiem retorted. "I was just enjoying the display. I'm not afraid of a little thunder like the rest of you."

The twin laughed as Joraiem slid in and ducked his head under the piece of sail. Aside from the occasional cough, the men were largely silent as they sheltered together. The rain fell rapidly now, and it pelted the sail above them unflaggingly for a long time. The wind blew hard and long, but they had been thorough in anchoring the sail, going so far as to bury the windward edge in the sand before placing the heavy rocks on top of it. For all its fury, the storm left them basically safe and sheltered as it raged above. Eventually, Joraiem fell asleep again, and despite the tumultuous forces unleashed around him, this time he had happier dreams.

When he woke in the morning, the storm had passed and so had the clouds. The sun hung low in the east, and as he slipped out from under the sail, he was glad for its warmth. He was wet, soaked in fact. The sail had done its job of keeping the rain off, but so much had fallen that small streams had formed along the shoreline, flowing down the slope of the sands and back into the Ocean. Some of those streams had flowed right under the sail and through their midst, and Joraiem shook with the soggy chill of it.

Several of the others emerged from under the sail at that moment, each of them soaked and sandy like Joraiem. Without speaking and almost without thinking, they started sleepily down toward the water to wash off. Joraiem watched for a moment, hesitant to join them, but feeling the gritty, wet sand all over his body, decided it was worth the potential discomfort and followed anyway.

As he walked, he pulled his shirt off as the others had done and, shaking it out while he walked, he managed to keep his doubts at bay until his feet touched the water. As they did, he felt the sickening queasiness slide over him, and he almost stopped. For some reason, this morning he was unwilling to be deterred. He waded in after the others. He didn't feel sad or upset, or even especially weary, he just wasn't willing to be afraid today. He was soon in over his waist, and the water rising and falling around him felt good. He dipped his shirt repeatedly under the waves, careful to wring it out each time. The queasiness didn't go away, but he found he was managing to distance himself from the feeling. He squatted down and let the water swirl around his head and hair. He ran his hand through his blond hair again and again, trying to get all the sand out. When he felt he was as clean as he was going to get, he started back in toward shore.

All were awake by the time he returned. They set about pulling the sail back to retrieve their belongings, but they decided to leave the ocean-side buried and weighted, in case such a shelter should be needed again.

A fire was out of the question as everything they had or could find was soaking wet, so they breakfasted on cold, damp bread, and Joraiem was glad he had eaten his fill the night before, because he couldn't stomach more than a few mouthfuls. After breakfast, he moved higher up into the grass and spread his shirt out to dry as he sat watching the clear blue sky above them. He couldn't have explained the feeling rationally, but as he gazed up and down the shore, he felt peace all around them. They had grown more relaxed here each day, but there was something qualitatively different about this morning. Perhaps it was the continuing relief of having moved toward reconciliation with Rulalin, or perhaps it was the afterglow of their Midsummer celebration. Or maybe it was the simple calm that only comes after one has passed through a big storm and opens his eyes on the other side to a bright, warm, sunny day. Whatever it was, he felt renewed. He felt energetic even, and suddenly he wanted to sit no longer. He stood and stretched his arms and legs as he walked back toward the beach. He turned east along the shore, in a direction he hadn't yet explored, and his walk slowly shifted into a jog. He made his way closer to the water where the sand was wet and firm, but he kept as far away from the water's edge as he could. The queasiness did not return, and he accelerated from a jog into a run. He realized that it must have been a strange sight to the others, to see him running barefoot along the beach away from them without explanation, but he didn't care. His legs ached to be used, and it felt good to run.

Joraiem returned to a fascinating sight. Aljeron was in the shallow water with Synoki and Rulalin, holding a long, slender stick with a sharp knife lashed to the end. Joraiem walked closer to get a better look. They were standing quietly, completely still, studying the waters carefully. After several minutes, Aljeron slowly began to raise the crude spear and thrust it quickly into the water. He withdrew it, empty, and smacked the water with his hand in frustration. He handed the spear to Rulalin and started in toward shore. When he didn't turn back, Rulalin and Synoki turned their attention back to the water.

Aljeron scowled as he emerged from the water onto the sand a few spans away from where Joraiem was. He looked back at the men still in the water, then at Joraiem, who stood sweaty and breathing deeply. He shook his head back and forth. "Fishing with a knife tied to a stick. Ridiculous. I don't care what he says about how he survived on this island, it can't be done."

"Has he not caught any himself yet?"

"He hasn't tried. Synoki said he'd be happy to go with us and explain how to do it, but he wasn't especially eager to do it himself. He said that he'd spent more hours than he cared to recall that way over the last three years, so he wasn't interested in doing it any more unless it was really necessary."

"Sounds reasonable to me," Joraiem said, and he looked carefully out at their strange guest again. His current impression of Synoki was that the castaway had been alone too long. The man always responded promptly when addressed and seemed willing to do what was asked of him, he had certainly been willing to stand beside them as they faced the Black Wolves and Malekim in Nal Gildoroth. That in itself had been no small feat and had earned him a fair amount of respect. And yet, he often seemed absent while among them, as though having been alone for so long he couldn't quite disengage from himself enough to interact with anyone fully. He seldom spoke and rarely looked any of them in the eye. When he did, it was not for long, and he was almost fidgety any time he was the object of direct attention in front of the others. He stayed nearby enough but often to the side by himself. It was odd, Joraiem thought, but then again, it was impossible for Joraiem to imagine what being shipwrecked alone on the Forbidden Isle would have done to him. It was probably a miracle that he was alive at all.

Joraiem turned to Aljeron, who still looked frustrated with the whole failed fishing venture. Joraiem realized he'd never seen Aljeron this irritated, but neither had he seen Aljeron fail at anything. "Come on, Aljeron, at least you didn't stab yourself in the foot or cut off any of your toes. Let's go sit in the grass."

"Thanks for the consolation," Aljeron smiled and started up the beach. Joraiem looked back out at the water at Synoki with Rulalin. He suddenly felt an itch to go get Suruna, but it passed as he turned to follow Aljeron. As they crossed onto the grassland, Koshti came jogging up beside them from the place where he had been resting, and the three of them sat in the sun.

The day passed lazily, as the Midsummer rites and storm overnight had left them drained. Rulalin proved Aljeron wrong. When he and Synoki eventually came in from the water, Rulalin came holding two large, sleek, silver fish. Everyone gathered round, impressed, and congratulated him on his success, but when Joraiem tried to compliment him, Rulalin turned away, saying he had to clean the fish. Joraiem watched Rulalin prepare the fish to cook, confused, but he soon pushed the awkward moment from his mind.

After they had eaten, Saegan put forward a simple question, "Isn't it time we began to talk about how we're going to get off this island?"

Most eyes turned to Valzaan, who understood that the question, though not overtly addressed to him, had nevertheless been intended for him. "What do you have in mind, Saegan?"

Saegan shrugged. "I don't know, but I know we need to talk about it. I'm all for believing that Allfather can deliver us, but maybe there's more we can do to cooperate with that deliverance than just sit here."

"We always want to believe there is more we can do, do we not? You are right that Allfather usually works in and through the actions of his people, but there are times when there is nothing to be done but wait. The key is being able to recognize those times. I believe this is such a time. Do you disagree?"

Joraiem listened, fascinated. He was surprised that it was progressing as peaceably as it was, since he could sense that Saegan was frustrated. But, he was also impressed by Saegan's self-control, because he would not allow that frustration to take the form of any kind of disrespect for Valzaan.

"I don't know if there are any good options, but we do have three boats intact, even if the *Evening Star* is beyond repair."

"You can't be suggesting we try to cross the Southern Ocean in our landing boats," Ulmindos interjected strongly. "It would be suicide. The ocean would swallow us up."

Saegan shook his head impatiently while Ulmindos talked, quickly responding, "I don't mean that we should try to row for it. But maybe we could salvage more boards from the *Evening Star* and lash them together with ropes to make one larger vessel. Maybe we could build some kind of sea craft with the sail here and take a shot. What other choice do we have? Should we just assume that Master Berin will eventually miss us and send out a rescue crew?"

"Is that such a crazy assumption?" Aljeron asked. "More help would have been sent if any had been available. If we don't return, then Master Berin will get help and send it; he'll probably even come himself."

"And when will that be? We took provisions for more than two weeks because we didn't know how long we'd be gone, and now most of them are lying at the bottom of the Southern Ocean. How long before he decides help needs to come? How long from that point until he is able to find help willing to come to the Forbidden Isle after a missing ship? Who would be brave enough to go to a place from which even Valzaan did not return?"

This last point struck home. Joraiem had himself assumed that it would be only a matter of time, if quite a bit of it, before help was sent to find out what had happened to them. He had worried about what might become of Wylla while they waited, but he hadn't really considered the possibility that help might not come at all.

Saegan continued, continuing to focus his gaze on Valzaan. "At any rate, wherever that giant and those Malekim are heading with the women, it won't take them forever to get there. If we don't get off this island soon, we're not going to catch them. They've already been underway for five days, and if their ship makes good time, they could be arriving in Kirthanin soon. My idea might be risky, but isn't it better than sitting here while they are hauled off who knows where?"

"Peace, Saegan," Valzaan said. "There are many things which may yet be, but none of these change what already is. The materials we have cannot possibly yield a seaworthy craft, no matter how hard we worked on it. Whatever we set out in, even if we did get out into the wide open sea, would be smashed to bits by even moderately high waves, not to mention what a storm like last night's would do to us in such a vessel. Any attempt to get off this island under our own power would require that we build a real boat, and that is beyond our capabilities and resources at this point.

"However," Valzaan continued, "you should know that when I said Allfather could deliver us, I did not mean that we should do nothing to help accelerate our rescue."

"What do you mean?" This time Aljeron asked the question.

"I mean that I agree completely with Saegan. I realized immediately that we could not afford to simply sit and wait until Master Berin realized we had been gone too long, and so I have sent for help."

"What?" several of them said, echoing each other.

"The windhover!" Joraiem exclaimed, turning red as several of the others turned to look at him. "The morning after we left Nal Gildoroth, I saw you with a windhover. I couldn't see clearly what you were doing from where I was, but it looked almost like you were whispering to the bird. I thought that was crazy, but you were, weren't you?"

Valzaan smiled. "I have sent news of our predicament. How long it will take for help to come, I cannot say, but all we can do is wait. I can't even promise the windhover will make it to the mainland. He did not fly all the way here without rest, for several times he rested with me on board the *Evening Star*. Still, he knows our plight and is willing to risk his own life to try to make Suthanin."

A few of the others tried to get more information out of Valzaan—how he communicated with the windhover, who would be able to receive such a message, where and to whom he had sent it, but he wouldn't say more. "You know enough," he repeated patiently to the few bold enough to continue prying.

The news had encouraged them, though, and emboldened by Valzaan's good mood, Saegan asked another question that silenced the gathering. "If we have done all that we can do for the time being, then at least we could pass the time continuing our lessons. Perhaps you would be willing to tell us a story of our history, Valzaan, and if Sulare was not the place to hear of Corindel, then surely the Forbidden Isle is just such a place. Can we not hear it now?"

Valzaan looked to Sarneth, who nodded. "All right," Valzaan said. "It is not easy to tell, but you should know the truth of it."

"With Malek's retreat into Agia Muldonai came its corruption, which had been prophesied long before, though no one could have foreseen the form that corruption would take. The defilement, accompanied by the withdrawal of the remaining dragons from the worries and concerns of the world, confirmed that the Second Age had passed. The Third Age began with much hope and much despair, for the words of Allfather pointed forward to momentous events, both wondrous and terrible. A third great assault on Kirthanin was assured, one that would surpass both that had preceded it in terror and tumult, a prospect that still causes the wise to tremble.

"And yet Allfather has also promised that the Age will end with the cleansing of the Holy Mountain. It will be followed, as you know from the prophecies, by the beginning of an age of peace and restoration like that which existed before Malek's temptation and Andunin's betrayal. Malek will be destroyed once and for all, and the three-fold movement of the ages will be finally complete. As the First Age ended with

Malek's first attempt at mastery over Kirthanin and the clearing of the Mountain, and as the Second ended with his second attempt and the corruption of the Mountain, so the Third will end with his final attack and then the Mountain's cleansing. This is of course a day we all eagerly desire, though its morning will dawn only on the other side of Kirthanin's darkest night.

"And so the Third Age began, with all Kirthanin once more adapting to a great change. They had learned in the Second Age to live without the protection and guidance of the Titans, even as they had learned to live with the menace of Malek as he dwelt here, on the Forbidden Isle. At the onset of the Third Age, they had to learn to live without the protection and guidance of the dragons, and the encroaching menace of Malek in the Holy Mountain. The full peace of the First Age had given way to the distant fear of the Second and again to the constant struggle of the Third, though many in Kirthanin have not had to maintain the unceasing vigilance of guarding the Mountain and so are not fully aware of the price that has been paid." Valzaan nodded to Rulalin as he paused. "Some here know that price firsthand.

"Corindel also knew that price. He was born in the fiftieth year of the Third Age to Arindel, king of Enthanin. He was eldest and heir to the throne. Corindel excelled in every possible way, his prowess in the art of war unmatched by any, and by his twentieth birthday he was captain of the Enthanim who kept the watch on the eastern side of the Mountain.

"In those days, all routes out of the Mountain were guarded save for the northern side, which faced the long-empty land of Nolthanin. Both the east and the west were guarded by men, and the southern side of the mountain was guarded by the Great Bear of the Gyrindraal, for in those days the Forest of Gyrin was not the dread and fearful place it is now. The only way out of the mountain led north, and no one cared if Malek went north, for geography and strategic outposts along the northern borders of Enthanin and Werthanin made invasion from Nolthanin unlikely.

"While ultimately this was a good thing, to have the net drawn so tightly around Agia Muldonai put a lot of pressure on the Werthanim and Enthanim. The Malekim did not understand the secret ways of the Forest and feared the Great Bear almost as much as they feared their master, and so they would gladly face hordes of men before they would venture into Gyrin. From time to time the defenses and resolve of the Enthanim were tested by incursions of Black Wolves and Malekim, and Corindel had many opportunities to prove his courage, valor, vigor, and zeal.

"But with his successes came pride, and deep within Corindel there began to grow a hope, a dangerous hope that should never have been. Corindel knew the prophesies; he knew that with Andunin's betrayal and the clearing of the Mountain, Allfather had forbidden man, Great Bear, and even the dragons to set foot on the slopes of Agia Muldonai. No servant of Allfather's had ever dared to violate that law, and had Corindel respected the sweep and scope of it, perhaps he would not have yielded to the promptings that pressed him from within.

"He dreamed of driving Malek from the Mountain. He dreamed of leading an army of men and Great Bear up the slopes of Agia Muldonai, where he intended to find entrance to Malek's lair, even if he had to ascend to the gates of Avalione itself to do so. He dreamed of purging the evil from the Mountain and putting to the sword every last creature of Malek that resided there.

"He called the Assembly to Amaan Sul and announced his intention, sending ripples of fear and excitement through the Novaana. The exploits of Corindel were known, and many whispered among themselves that perhaps Allfather had sent

Corindel to deliver them from Malek's grip. Many others, though, called for verification that this dream was indeed from Allfather and demanded that nothing be done before a prophet of Allfather should be consulted. So, a messenger was sent for me, and I was summoned to appear before the Assembly, for with the advent of the Third Age I had succeeded Erevir as first among the prophets of Allfather.

"I arrived on the fourth day after Corindel's hope had first been spoken, and I was alarmed to find how deeply rooted it had already become in the hearts of so many. I sat in the Assembly and listened as Corindel described his desire, though I already knew it as well as he, for Allfather had granted me in a dream to behold the vision even as Corindel imagined it day after day and night after night. When he finished, the Assembly fell silent as I arose and strode into the midst of the gathered Novaana, seated in traditional circle of unity.

" 'The strength and valor of Corindel's heart is great,' I told them, 'and Allfather is pleased with his zeal for Avalione and for the Holy Mountain. Their corruption and blight rises before Allfather's throne every day, and He despises the stain of evil that mars His world. The longing that you possess, Corindel, for an end to Malek and Malek's deeds is shared by every true follower of Allfather. Were this desire from Him, then it would be reprehensible for any able-bodied soldier in the world not to follow you now up the Mountain, never to return until the quest be complete.

" 'But this vision is not from Allfather. He has not rescinded His command to refrain from approaching its slopes. Though Malek transgresses this command as He has transgressed many of Allfather's commands, this is not warrant for you or any of us to disobey also. Allfather has already decreed that Agia Muldonai will be cleansed in due time, when He shall raise up one who is but a child in the eyes of the world to lead the faithful back onto the Mountain and through the gates of

Avalione. This chosen one will break the power of Malek, but he will not do so through use of the sword. This was declared and proclaimed long ago as the word of Allfather. It has not changed, as indeed no word of Allfather can change.

" 'Corindel, turn from this plan. It is a vain hope that finds its root in what Allfather has forbidden, no matter how noble your intent or admirable your goal. Malek will not be defeated in this way. He cannot. This is not the time. This is not the way. So says Allfather.'

"My words were enough to convince the Assembly to abandon the plan, and Corindel appeared to accept my word as Allfather's clear direction. But he did not abandon his hope, and for the next ten years he worked quietly within Enthanin to win the allegiance of all the officers of the Enthanim. By the ninety-eighth year of the Third Age, he knew that he had come as near achieving his goal as he would ever come, and he sent a messenger to the Council of Great Bear who sat over the Gyrindraal, soliciting their aid. The Great Bear were aware of Allfather's commands and my prophecy, and they would not come. Corindel was disappointed, but he would not be deterred, and on the first day of Summer Rise, he did what had not been done since the clearing of the Mountain. In violation of his own father's command and Allfather's revealed will, he dared to ascend the Holy Mountain.

"The soldiers who were left behind as a rear guard, and the people who lived within sight of the Mountain, watched each day for a sign. For ten days they could see and hear nothing. 'Perhaps Corindel has found passageway into the Mountain and Malek's domain, or perhaps the Mountain has opened up and swallowed them all,' they began to say. Every day the rumors grew. No one worked during the day, and some could be found sitting silently in the dark all night, just staring at the dark shape looming before them.

"When morning brought the eleventh day, though, Enthanin woke to the sign it had sought, and it was awesome. Clouds like dark smoke surrounded and obscured the Mountain. All that was visible were flashes of brilliant light like streaks of lightning running both up and down the sides of the Mountain. Booming sounds like peals of thunder rolled across the land, and the children hid in fear inside their homes while trembling adults prayed to Allfather for mercy. All who lived within sight of the Mountain that terrible day wondered if the end of all things had finally come.

"The day passed, and the light and roar continued all through the night. No one, in all the land, slept. I myself sat through the night in agony, for a sense of dread had overwhelmed me from the moment the dawn had broken. I could not name or explain it, and when I sleep at night, sometimes I feel it still. But, the morning of the twelfth day dawned to reveal the Mountain as it had always been. People again looked for a sign of the previous day's outcome, but they found none. Once more they waited, but few now hoped for good news. All feared that none who had ascended the Mountain would return.

"They were wrong. A couple of days later, the first of a tattered remnant began to trickle off Agia Muldonai and back into Enthanin. They drifted, sometimes in pairs, but often alone, across the western marches of Enthanin. They walked straight ahead without speaking, even when addressed by friends or loved ones who came across them on their way, and they would never, for any reason, turn back west toward the Mountain. In this way the few that survived, perhaps one for every five that followed Corindel, made their way as far as Amaan Sul. There Arindel grieved over his missing son, for Corindel was not among these stragglers, and all questions of his fate addressed to the survivors were met with the same eerie silence and blank stares. He also grieved over the destruction that had befallen his rebellious army and shut down the normal commerce of the city, bringing his people out to round up the wandering men. They were found and herded into hastily constructed camps and hospitals where the wives and mothers of the city tended them as their own. For six days this work went on, until the countryside had been scoured and every survivor placed under care, and Arindel himself moved among them, helping where needed, always searching for Corindel or some sign of him.

"I myself remember the camps clearly, especially at night. A restless sleep would come at last to the men, but even in sleep they could not find peace, for all wrestled with night terrors. Their screams were shrill and piercing, and only the strongest of Amaan Sul's men and women volunteered to work the camps after dark.

"With the army of Enthanin largely decimated, the officers who had refused to go with Corindel scrambled to assemble and train others, fearing that Malek might take advantage of this turn of events to come out of the Mountain. Enthanin braced for attack, but the attack never came, at least not in the form expected.

"Eventually, the remnant who had walked down off the Mountain began to speak again. Their first words were invariably names, names of parents and wives and children, names of towns and villages and cities. They slowly emerged from the fog that had shrouded them, and over time they gained both clarity of mind and courage of heart to speak of what had happened. All accounts of the first ten days on the mountain were roughly the same. They had followed their officers, who followed Corindel, carefully, determinedly, exploring the side of the Mountain and looking for an entrance to Malek's halls. Eventually, their search took them around the northern side of Agia Muldonai, and it was there, on the eleventh day, that the terror overcame them.

"Here all accounts became confused, each man telling a

slightly different story. Dawn on that fateful day had not brought light to the men on the Mountain, for the clouds hovered low and thick, encompassing everything and practically blinding them. In darkness they groped across dirt and rock, and in the darkness evil moved in their midst, bringing death and defeat. Corindel's army was shattered without ever engaging in anything that might be called a battle.

"As that day went on, a day that seemed a lifetime to all who recalled it, the storm that thundered and flashed around them somehow worked its way into their minds. Every man testified to a growing confusion, a darkness of soul that seeped inside them and drove them in terror, crawling down the Mountain on all fours. In the grip of this darkness they had wandered and been found, until at last it left them as imperceptibly as it had come.

"Some believed the weather and confusion had been sent by Allfather as punishment for their pride and disregard of His word through me. Others said that these things had been the work of Malek, some devilry unleashed from the Mountain itself. For me, I am not sure that they weren't both right. It may well have been that Malek did bring forth some great evil that day, and it may also be that Allfather allowed them to face the consequences of their folly without aid or deliverance in their time of need.

"Whatever the explanation, Corindel was not found among those who survived, and he was assumed to have died on the slopes of Agia Muldonai. Arindel held a service in which he begged Allfather's mercy on his son's soul, and upon Enthanin, that the country might not be held accountable for Corindel's sin. Those who had supported Corindel stood side by side with those who had opposed him. Except for the humility and contrition of Arindel, things might have ended differently for Enthanin.

"But Corindel was not dead, as we all believed. Where he

was during the months that followed, many have speculated, but no one really knows. All that we know for sure is that more than six months later, in Full Winter, Corindel was found wandering in the Forest of Gyrin, haggard, unkempt, and apparently not in his right mind. He was found by Great Bear from the Gyrindraal, and because they believed Corindel to be on the verge of death, they did what the Great Bear never do. They brought this outsider into the heart of the Gyrindraal, to the clan's secret dwelling places in the draal itself, hidden in the seemingly impassible depths of the Gyrin.

"They fed and clothed him and observed his strange behavior and restless sleep. They tended his physical needs and found many scars, which may have indicated that he had been tortured. They dispatched messengers to Amaan Sul to inform Arindel that his son had been found and that he would be brought to Amaan Sul if he survived, as soon as he was able to travel. During the second night of his stay among them, however, Corindel vanished. No Great Bear then or since believes that Corindel could have escaped from the most heavily guarded draal in Kirthanin without aid from Malek. What gift or spell or ability he had been given, no one knows. But the following night, an army of Malekim and Vulsutyrim passed into the Forest of Gyrin with Corindel at its head, leading them along once secret paths. With the Vulsutyrim among them, they overwhelmed the Great Bear patrols. Though the Great Bear fought desperately to save the Gyrindraal, the giants destroyed it and slaughtered its inhabitants.

"The whole Gyrin clan was all but wiped out. A handful of Great Bear on patrol in the outer reaches of the Gyrin survived, as did the two messengers sent to Arindel, who returned several days later to find their home in ruins. Among the ruins they found the other Great Bear who had survived, and it was from them that they learned the story, for some had arrived not long after the attack and heard the truth of it from the mouths of the dying. Corindel had not only served as guide, but he had fought against the Great Bear, his strong hands wielding a sword that gleamed in the starlight.

"Corindel was never seen by mortal eye again, for he disappeared as he had come, returning through the wintry night into the depths of Agia Muldonai. The Great Bear who survived departed from the Forest of Gyrin, leaving it unprotected and the southern slopes of Agia Muldonai unwatched. They passed into Lindan Wood in Suthanin, joining the Lindandraal and becoming in time part of that clan. With them went word of Corindel's betrayal, and the Great Bear withdrew from their dealings with men. Though they knew that even Arindel vehemently condemned the actions of his son, they believed men could no longer be trusted, for Corindel had been well known as a valiant and zealous enemy of Malek. His fierce hatred of Malek and Malek's corruption of the Holy Mountain had never been doubted or debated. The Great Bear knew then just how weak the hearts of men are, often unable or unwilling to be faithful to what they believed. Whatever Malek had done to secure Corindel's allegiance, whether by torture, threat, or temptation, no Great Bear could understand. For a Great Bear, nothing could explain Corindel's actions, for there is nothing a Great Bear could face that would drive them to knowingly betray a draal. The less men knew of them and their doings, they concluded, the better.

"And so the world changed again, and the last great hope of men in their already desperate need to stand against Malek was lost. The Great Bear, like the dragons before them, all but disappeared from the world of men. Some, like Sarneth here, come among human society from time to time, but it is rare, and there are many places in Kirthanin where the Great Bear, like the Golden Dragon himself, would seem to be little more than legend, the stuff of stories told by fathers to children around the hearth.

"Corindel's betrayal is remembered as the second great betrayal of men, and there are those who see it as even worse than Andunin's. While there is no doubt that Andunin's betrayal was wrapped up in the greatest calamity Kirthanin has ever seen, Corindel's act seemed to reveal an even deeper wickedness. While Andunin might have been deceived about the depth of Malek's treachery, Corindel knew these things full well. While Andunin might have had doubts about the will of Allfather for Kirthanin as his once-trusted counselor Malek twisted the truth, Corindel heard the voice of Allfather clearly through me, His prophet. I told Corindel that he was not to go up the Mountain, that it was not destined to be reclaimed that way. I told Corindel that the sword, which was Malek's creation to do Malek's will, could never be the instrument of Malek's defeat. The prophecies and I were clear about this, though he may not have wanted to see the truth.

"Corindel's betrayal is thus instructive for us in many ways. First and foremost, we know that to do Allfather's will, we must pursue Allfather's purposes in the manner He has prescribed. We also learn what we should have learned from Andunin himself, that even the great are vulnerable to temptation, for the heart of man is easily corrupted when he takes his eyes off of Allfather.

"Let us learn the lessons well, for failure to embrace them has cost us dearly. Although Corindel is undoubtedly long since in the grave and generations of men have come and gone in the centuries since, some among the Great Bear know the story of the Gyrindraal's destruction almost firsthand. In his youth, Sarneth's grandfather served as messenger of the Gyrindraal, and on that fateful night, he was himself leagues away, on his way to Amaan Sul with news that Arindel's lost son had been found."

The amazed men in the circle turned to Sarneth, who had listened like the rest of them, motionless as Valzaan talked. "It remains an evil memory for our family," he whispered in his deep, resonant voice. "But," he continued, looking up, "I have long since forgiven the race of men, though it was not easy and there are still some who have not. I also know that while what Valzaan says about the hearts of men is true, the rift between us must be mended, for we will all suffer the fate of the Gyrindraal if we do not first find peace among ourselves. Malek seeks ever to divide, for in our division we are weak, and he is already far too strong for us to allow ourselves to be further weakened."

Valzaan sighed. "It is true, very true, and though you and I and many others know the wisdom of it, there are many among the clans who are not yet ready to hear what you are saying, though there are some who are."

"Yes," Sarneth answered. "Some cannot see, or will not. But, I am not such a minority in this as I once was, and I believe that perhaps change is coming, for even in the Lindandraal, resistance to alliances between Great Bear and men is not as strong as it once was. Change often comes slowly among us, but it does come."

The creaking sound of hinges woke Wylla from her sleep. She was momentarily disoriented, but soon she had her bearings and was searching the blackness to see what was going on. She found the opening she was looking for, since the darkness on the other side was not so deep and a few stars twinkled in the distance above. Catching even a quick glimpse of the stars was encouraging, for she hadn't seen stars since the night before their arrival at the Forbidden Isle.

She watched the opening carefully while sitting up, but nothing happened, and so she lay back down where she could keep her eye on it more comfortably. Something unusual must be going on, for their captors hadn't ever awakened them before dawn.

"What's going on, Wylla?" Karalin whispered from nearby in the dark.

"I don't know," Wylla answered, maintaining her watch. Karalin didn't speak again, and if any of the others were awake, which she suspected they were, they kept quiet. She slid one arm beneath her head and went back over the voyage, as she had gotten in the habit of doing each morning when she woke up. She didn't know how long they were going to be captive or where they were headed, but she wanted to be able to give a thorough reckoning of it all if she did ever get away— or was rescued.

They had been taken on the twelfth day of Full Summer, in the afternoon. The days since had all followed the same pattern: up on deck three times a day for food and water, and down below the remainder of the day and all night. After four nights on the ship, it had been Midsummer. Wylla had tried to help the girls keep the rites as best they could, at least by gathering them together to pray to Allfather while they huddled in the hold, but obvious barriers prevented them from doing more. Fasting had been impossible, for it would have been unwise to refuse the ladle proffered by the Malekim. Feasting had likewise been impossible, for the evening feeding was the same as all the others, at least in terms of food offered. Aside from that, the evening feed had been quite a bit different, actually. First of all, it came earlier than on previous evenings, for it was barely late afternoon, and when the women had arrived above deck they had seen why. The clouds in the western sky were ominous and the winds extraordinary, and all about them the Malekim were bracing for a storm.

The women had been fed in the usual no-nonsense manner, if more quickly than before. Then, they were hastily put back down below, and not long after, the ship was in the midst of the storm. It had been ferocious, and the ship rocked wildly until the sun went down. Again the women huddled together as best they could for comfort, but the constant, dramatic rolling made them sick until they couldn't be sick any more. They passed their fifth night on board the ship with hardly any sleep.

Sometime in the night, the storm broke, or else the ship left it behind. When the morning light eventually followed, they were all happier than usual to be allowed up into the daylight. The warm sun on their faces, much more than their meager rations, was the food they desired. The cool summer morning and light blue sky above gave strength to their bodies, and as they returned to the hold, they each one managed to sleep all morning until they were again awakened for the midday meal.

If Wylla's accounting was correct, today would be the eighteenth day of Full Summer. If the ship had been maintaining a course for the Kirthanin mainland, something Wylla had tried to verify in the few moments she spent each day on deck, then surely they were almost there.

She sat up again, still looking up through the open hatchway. Perhaps that was it. Maybe they had arrived at their destination. Perhaps this was the end of their voyage. Even as she thought this, the silhouette of the giant's large head filled the opening, and his commanding voice spoke softly into the dark hold, "All of you, come up quietly, now."

All around her the others stood, not with the drowsiness of waking from sleep, but with the soreness of having spent a long night on hard wood. Wylla sent them up in the usual order, with Bryar leading the way. She came up after them, last, and took her place beside them as the giant closed the hatch behind her.

He guided them to the side of the boat and assembled them there, facing him. He spoke again, even quieter than before, but still with clear command, "It is imperative that you listen carefully and do as I say. The Malekim have not harmed you to this point because I instructed them not to. However, if any of you tries to escape or call out for attention or aid, they will kill that woman instantly. That also, I have instructed them. Do you understand?"

The women nodded. "Good," the giant continued. "Now you will all need to be bound. From now on, we travel only at night. You will not be gagged, but if we do have any trouble, the offender will be killed and the rest of you will be most unhappy with our method of keeping you quiet."

The Vulsutyrim walked away and soon they were surrounded by Malekim who tied their hands and feet together. Wylla could feel the cords cutting into her wrists and ankles and knew that at least some of the giant's warning had been unnecessary; she could not have gotten loose if she had tried.

Eventually they were placed in the landing ships that had been used to ferry them off of the Forbidden Isle and forced to lay along the keel on the bottom. When many Malekim had joined them in the boats, the ships were lowered into the water. Quietly, ever so quietly, the Malekim rowed toward what Wylla now felt certain must be the southern coast of Kirthanin, their oar strokes strong and sure despite their stealth.

Wylla gazed at the clear nighttime sky. Mixed emotions swirled inside. Yes, they were captive and in what was certainly a dire position, but the landing boats were taking her toward home. Going to the Forbidden Isle had been full of fear and foreboding, but she had never expected that she would return to Suthanin with the same emotions. It was a bittersweet homecoming.

Even so, she found comfort in the peaceful evening and beautiful stars above. The water lapped persistently against the side of the landing boat, which gently moved up and down as it surmounted each wave. How many nights in the past had she gazed up at these same stars, even in difficulty and distress, and found the same comfort? She felt certain that this circumstance, too, was not without hope. Joraiem and the *Evening Star* could not be far behind.

Eventually, the Malekim hopped out of the boats and drew them up on the beach. Wylla and the others were deposited in the sand, where they lay under the watchful guard of the Malekim. Soon, perhaps thirty or more Malekim were assembled on the shore, along with the giant, and they were ready to be on their way.

Wylla was lifted up in the air and thrown over the shoulder of one of the Voiceless, and there she hung for about an hour as the whole lot of them ran soundlessly through the darkness. Once in a while, as she hung upside down, she caught a passing and confused glimpse of what lay ahead. The Vulsutyrim ran at the head of the party, accompanied by a handful of Black Wolves.

This last observation confused Wylla a bit, for she hadn't seen or heard any Black Wolves on board. Wherever they had landed, Black Wolves nearby must have met up with them or picked up their scent. Perhaps their arrival had been expected.

After an hour of bouncing around like this, the Malekim stopped. The women were set down, only to be picked up again immediately, Wylla assumed, by another group of Malekim ready to take their turn. Off they ran again, once more running for perhaps an hour. This time, though, when they stopped, it was not to change places in the bearing of burdens. Apparently they were stopping for the day. The women were dropped in a clump against the side of what appeared to be a small hill, for with her feet and hands bound, Wylla's ability to look behind and above her was limited. Not far away, the giant grunted softly as he strained to move a large stone block, which, as it turned out, covered the entrance to a large hollowed out room inside the hill. The Malekim carried the women inside and as far back from the entrance as possible, and the Vulsutyrim entered after them, pulling the stone slab back into place as he did.

The women sat quietly together, and Wylla considered their situation. It appeared as though their life was going to be much the same as it had been on the ship. They would spend their days in darkness and their nights hanging upside down as their captors ran through the twilight.

When Wylla woke later in the day, she started going through her morning ritual, marking the events of her captivity in her mind. She did this until she realized that it was not really morning, but evening, late evening of the eighteenth day of Full Summer. She had slept most of the day, and from the sounds of the women breathing lightly beside her, most if not all of them were still asleep. She lay in the darkness and listened.

The sound of voices across the room startled. Other than their own voices, of course, there had been almost total silence since their capture. The Malekim could not speak or make sounds of any kinds with their mouths, and the giant rarely talked. Now, though, she was indeed hearing not one, but two voices floating to her across the room. She strained to hear them, and eventually began to make out the words.

The first voice she could make out was the giant's, "Whether it makes sense or not, it is what he told me to do, so I did it."

"I can see that," answered the second voice, which was soft and edged with arrogance and contempt. The timbre of this voice held something indescribably loathsome in it. She despised it instantly.

There was silence for a few moments, then the giant continued. "I don't know what you are going to do, Tashmiren, but I am going to finish the job I was given."

"As well you should, Ulutyr, but I certainly hope that what

you have told me is true. It will not go well with you if you have lied to me."

"You question me about telling the truth, Tashmiren?" the giant answered gruffly, and Wylla could hear the agitation in his voice. "I do not lie. The others that were with these are still on the island. I holed their ship before we left, and there is no way they could have repaired it and followed us. Even if they had the right materials, it would be impossible for them to extricate the wreckage from the water without help. When you get there you'll see for yourself. Only be careful. If they have not starved to death on the island by then, you may actually have to do some work yourself to kill them. He said there were powerful men among them."

Wylla's heart sank. The ship had been scuttled. Joraiem and Valzaan and the others were not following them at all. There was no help coming, no one between them and their destination—which she could only guess was Agia Muldonai itself—who knew they had been taken.

"How touching of you to be concerned for me, Ulutyr," the one called Tashmiren replied. "But don't worry too much. I'm sure he is watching them carefully, and I will not go unprepared. I will take a few of your brothers with me, and if they fail me, he will deal with them, won't he?"

There was silence for a moment from the far side of the room, and Wylla suddenly wished she could see the two speakers. She wanted to see what it looked like for a giant to bite his tongue, and even more than that, she wanted to see who or what would have such audacity to address one of the Vulsutyrim this way.

Instead her thoughts fled from this dark place across the wide sea, back to the Forbidden Isle. She tried to picture Joraiem standing on the beach, looking out over the sea after her. She wanted to warn him, for if what Ulutyr said was right, then they were stranded. *Beware, Joraiem, beware. They are coming.*

7

ELIANDIR

As the men sat around the morning fire on the eighteenth, eating their breakfast, their mood was almost as somber as it had been the night after the women's capture a week before. This time, though, their concerns were for Caan, whose wounded leg had become infected.

"I should have known I couldn't get away with it twice," he had half-heartedly joked.

As Joraiem looked back over the last couple of days, he recalled that even though Caan had helped to build the mound, he had not been as actively involved as the rest. Likewise, his decision to stay behind and talk to Valzaan rather than to go on the salvage mission to the *Evening Star* could also be explained, but Joraiem saw it now as the result of Caan's growing awareness that his leg was deteriorating. Yesterday, Caan had barely moved the whole day, and when he did try to walk, it was with great pain and difficulty. Joraiem was humbled to see Caan, who had embodied strength and health, laid low in this way.

And so this morning, as they had gathered around the fire, Caan and Valzaan had informed them about the seriousness of the situation. The infection was growing steadily worse, and there wasn't much under their current circumstances that could be done about it. Caan would need to get help before too long, but without any prospects for an imminent departure, the group was faced with yet another reason why every moment spent trapped on this island was wasted time. Joraiem looked around at the water and the beach and the grassland and felt all over again the helplessness of the circumstance. Caan, though just over a span away, was like the women— beyond his reach and beyond his aid.

After they had eaten, Joraiem approached Valzaan as he sat on the beach, his legs folded under him and his staff with the finely carved windhover on top cradled in his lap. "Valzaan? Will Caan die if we do not get off this island soon?"

"Yes, Joraiem, he will."

"How long do you think he has?"

"I don't know. Ten days, perhaps."

Joraiem could figure out the math. If it took about a week to sail between the Forbidden Isle and Sulare, then they would need to leave within the next few days. That also meant, though, that a ship would not arrive in time unless it had departed the Kirthanin mainland almost immediately after their visit to Nal Gildoroth. Joraiem didn't know how fast or how far a windhover could fly, or how long it would take a message sent by bird to reach understanding ears, or how long after that it would be before a rescue party could be sent, but it seemed to him that the situation was bleak indeed.

"Can you not do anything?" Joraiem asked quietly. "I mean, as a prophet, can you not summon healing or something from Allfather?"

"I have healed seemingly incurable diseases and apparently fatal wounds before, Joraiem, but I cannot summon such power at will. You will come to realize, as your understanding of both yourself and Allfather grows, that while you will develop some control over the gifts you have been given, ultimate control is really His. Not every prayer of mine for strength to destroy evil or power to work good has been answered the way I have wanted, and I have learned through this to wait upon Him. Sometimes I hold the power of life and death in my hand, but authority over life and death is His alone. Caan may die of his wound, even as Kelvan died. Of course, he may not. I haven't given up hope and neither should you. Help may yet come in time, or Allfather may answer our prayers for healing. Either way, Caan's life remains in His hands, as do all of ours—including the women, wherever they may be."

The day passed slowly, for they were all melancholy. They drifted up and down the beach, sometimes into the water and sometimes away from it. Any pursuit that they had contrived to give purpose to their days no longer seemed appealing, for the vanity of the contrivance had been exposed by the gravity of Caan's situation.

Morning became afternoon, and Joraiem's stomach rumbled faintly even though his body was largely used to the new schedule that included meals only in the morning and evening. For a moment he allowed himself to dream of the Summerland, where lunch was always just a notch below a feast, but knowing that allowing the thought of food couldn't possibly do him any good or satisfy the gnawing hunger in the back of his mind, he put the memory away. The afternoon was hot and the air humid. It was oppressive and stifling. There was no breeze coming in off the water, an oddity that irked rather than perplexed him. He was sick of waiting, sick of this place, and most of all, he was sick of worrying about Wylla. He wanted to be able to focus on pursuit, not dream of it.

At that moment, Joraiem saw something that was as beautiful as the new dawn to a man who has prayed for morning. A flash of gold appeared in the sky out over the water, reflecting dazzling light in all directions. The golden speck grew larger with remarkable rapidity and dropped lower over the water, until Joraiem could see clearly the grand and glorious silhouette of a dragon approaching, like history or legend suddenly springing to life.

Even at a distance, Joraiem could make out the large box-like object that the dragon carried in his talons. He knew enough of the past to know that the dragons had regularly transported the Titans, and occasionally even men, in carriages of the sky called garrion. As the dragon grew nearer, he could see more details of what he could only conclude was itself a garrion, a large chamber hanging between his rear claws, long and enclosed, dark with flecks and streaks of silver.

The men around him gradually realized what was happening and turned to face the majestic creature as he approached, each one standing transfixed where he was. The dragon came closer, his mighty wings creating their own wind as they beat rhythmically over the water. And then, all of a sudden, he passed right over them, the garrion perhaps four or five spans above their heads. They turned in unison to follow his flight inland. He swooped up and wheeled to the right in a long, steady arc, turning in large circles at first and then in smaller ones as he gradually slowed and descended. The dragon gently set the garrion down in the grassland not far from them, and like a bird gracefully coming to rest in a tree or bush, he landed not far from it.

Joraiem stood, gazing in awe at the dragon as he first stretched his wings to their full wingspan, then retracted them until they were folded against the side of his brilliant, gilded body. He had been told that no dragon save Sulmandir himself was entirely golden, that all Sulmandir's children bore hues of blue, green, or red, but he could not see any shades of these colors on this dragon. He knew that Sulmandir was dead, or at least, he knew that all believed him dead, but he wondered now if this could not be him, back from the grave or wherever he had been hiding all these years.

Joraiem's reverie was interrupted by the sight of Valzaan, walking quickly across the grass toward the dragon, motioning to them all to follow. Though he knew that dragons were good, true servants of Allfather, Joraiem trembled as he started forward. He had heard tales of the power and might of dragons since he was a boy, and he could not help but shake as he approached this one, every bit as impressive as he had imagined.

He fell in behind Valzaan with the others as they walked to the waiting creature, who sat motionless on the grass. He looked beside him at Aljeron and Koshti, who had come up on his right, and whispered, "Can you believe this is happening?"

Aljeron shook his head in response. "It is like a dream."

"You don't think it could be"—he hesitated—"Sulmandir himself, do you?" Joraiem asked.

"I don't know what to think," was all Aljeron said at first, adding a moment later, "I think I would believe just about anything at this point."

They stopped some three or four spans from the dragon, and Valzaan, still standing well in front of the rest, addressed him. "Eliandir, I welcome you in the name of Allfather."

The dragon seemed to snort and, lowering its head to a place roughly level with Valzaan's, the dragon spoke. Its voice was like thunder, and Joraiem heard in it the echo of ages past. "Prophet, in the name of Allfather you have summoned and greeted me, and in Allfather's name have I come. Many years has it been since I last left my lair, and many more since I have borne the weight of a garrion; indeed, since before the War of Division. I was reluctant to come, to meddle again in the affairs of men, but I heard in your summons the sound of a greater voice and have thus obeyed. Tell me, prophet, why have you awakened me?"

The dragon's great head, as large as half of Valzaan's body, was surprisingly inexpressive given the passion in the creature's voice. Eliandir's eyes were deep, like bottomless wells of light, and Joraiem peered into them, feeling the power and vitality of the magnificent beast. They were not like the empty, lifeless eyes of the Malekim, nor were they like the wary, searching eyes of men. They were at once filled with power and peace, majesty and love, intertwined in pools of light, and Joraiem could not imagine how Valzaan could stand face to face and eye to eye with them.

"I have summoned you, Eliandir, because you alone can give us hope. I was in Sulare just over two weeks ago with these others here, and we were attacked by a pack of Black Wolves. That night, as we mourned a young man slain in the attack, we witnessed a great flash of light across the sea. Allfather called us here, and we have obeyed and found evidence that Malek has been at work."

At the mention of Malek's name, the dragon stomped one of his front claws, and the ground shook. Synoki, who stood nearby, stumbled backward into Pedraan, almost knocking the big man down. The dragon reared his head and let out what Joraiem could only describe as a roar, a great cry that pierced him to the bone. His golden eyes glowed as with fire, and he leaned in closer to Valzaan. "What is this to me? If the Master of the Forge is at work again, it is no longer my concern!"

"It is the concern of all who serve Allfather, Eliandir."

"It was—until the War of Division, caused by the pettiness of men, brought ruin and destruction on us all."

"We have argued this point before, and I have not summoned you to argue it again, for I know that despite your protests, deep down you know that before peace can be restored to Kirthanin, there will come a day when all of us must stand together against Malek once more. Even the dragons who remain will have to come forth from their lairs and stand, for in that day the land will shake and the sea will roil and the very mountains in which you sleep will tremble. You may distance yourself from men, but you are not free to ignore the work of Malek!"

"Perhaps one day it will be as you say, but is this such a day, that you should disturb my rest with news that isn't news? Of course the Son of Betrayal is at work, did we not know that he would be even as he always has been? Why did you send for me and this garrion? What burden do you expect me to bear for you?"

"I called you because we were attacked, and though we killed many Silent Ones and Black Wolves, the women who were with us were taken captive by many Malekim, who sailed a week ago for Kirthanin, leaving us stranded here because our boat has been scuttled. We need you to take us back, or they are lost."

"I am sorry to hear of your misfortune, but griefs greater than this have come and gone in the wider world without need of me. You have not spoken all!"

"No I haven't, Eliandir. I have summoned you, not only because we need your strength and speed, but also because we need your power. The Malekim that fled with our friends were not alone. They were being led by one of Vulsutyr's children, and he is a foe beyond our strength."

This time, Eliandir did not stomp or cry out, but Joraiem could see fury glistening in his eyes as he stared silently at Valzaan. "I will carry you back to Kirthanin as you have asked, and I will go with you. But, I go only to kill the son of Vulsutyr. When he is dead, I will return home."

"So be it, Eliandir. We can ask no more of you. Indeed, were you willing only to take us back, we would still be in your debt. When will you be ready to take us?"

"I will rest, and we will leave at first light tomorrow. If all goes well, we will reach the mainland well after sunset. I will take you under cover of darkness to a place where no one will mark our coming."

"Go then, and rest well. We leave at dawn."

Eliandir leapt into the air and his great wings beat furiously as he moved upward in the reverse order of his arrival, with small, slow circles that became ever wider, ever swifter until he was high above them, speeding inland. Joraiem stood with the others and watched him glide away, a golden glimmer against the pale blue sky.

As Eliandir disappeared into the distance, Valzaan started across the grass toward the garrion that the dragon had deposited there. Joraiem and the others followed. Even on closer inspection the garrion looked much like a large box, though clearly it had once been a richly decorated and elaborately carved box. It was made of wood, though the bar that rose from its middle in a large "T" appeared to be some kind of metal. The corners were rounded smooth, and intricate patterns were carved along the top, sides and edges. It looked as though it had once been very beautiful, and Valzaan suggested that it might have been gilded with gold as well as silver, though only silver remained upon it in small scratched and worn patches.

Valzaan opened a large pair of double doors on one of the sides and stepped inside. The garrion was at least a span and a half wide, while running about two and a half spans long. The floor was long and smooth, with the ceiling another span and a half high. Both the walls and ceiling bore traces of carved figures and images long since eroded and hard to make out clearly. As Joraiem looked more closely at them, he thought he saw many of dragons in flight, and he wondered who had crafted this garrion. It might have been men of course, but his body tingled at the possibility one of the Twelve had done the work. Tall, slender window slats ran vertically from chest height to the top of the garrion, allowing fresh air to flow through in flight, and Joraiem imagined that if Eliandir flew fast enough to reach Kirthanin in a single day, the wind might well howl through the open windows.

"How old do you think this is?" Pedraal asked Valzaan, and Joraiem turned to hear the prophet's answer.

Valzaan stood inside, running his fingers along the smooth interior wall, and he seemed to shrug his shoulders. "I would guess that this was built during the First Age."

"You mean this might have been used to carry one of the Twelve in human form?" Aljeron followed, incredulously.

"Perhaps. Though in those days, there were many garrion, and many of the Novaana had them built for transport to the Assembly. Who built and used this garrion, I really couldn't say."

"Can you imagine that?" Elyas said, excitedly. "Arriving at the Assembly carried by a dragon!"

"I'm sure that it was a very comfortable mode of transport, but surely this garrion wasn't used to carry fourteen men, a tiger and a Great Bear," Rulalin said, looking around him, "and that is what we have here. How are we all going to fit?"

"It will be cramped," Valzaan replied, "but we will fit. Necessity demands it. There is no other way off this island, and we will leave no one behind."

Valzaan stepped out of the garrion, and a couple at a time, they each stepped in, examining the room that would be their home the following day, delighted at the prospect of getting off the island, but wondering exactly how cramped it was going to be. Soon, they had all taken a good look inside and out, and slowly the group started to make its way back toward the beach as afternoon moved toward evening, and time for the evening meal approached.

As they walked, Joraiem caught up to Valzaan, and though he tried to be discreet, he knew that the others were listening,

"Who was that, Valzaan? I thought Sulmandir's children were supposed to be partially green, or red, or blue. I couldn't see anything but gold. He wasn't, I mean, he couldn't have been . . ."

"No," Valzaan said, "he wasn't. His name is Eliandir, as I said, and he is a red dragon. It is hard at first to see color in one of Sulmandir's children, especially if you don't know where to look. When you see them in the sky, you will sometimes be able to discern a hue of something else in the golden reflection that shines off their scales, and in that slight hue of green or red or blue you have your answer. If you see a dragon close up, the easiest place to tell is to look at the talons of his claw. The soft skin under the talons is the clearest place where his color is displayed."

Preparations for supper were lively, as the prospect of their departure in the morning had invigorated them. They talked among themselves of the image of the dragon in flight, and they tried to describe what it must feel like to hang suspended from his claws in the air as he flew high above the sea. They wondered if the garrion rocked much in flight, and if it did, if there would be a sort of air sickness that accompanied travel in this way.

Joraiem listened to the discussion, but he didn't worry about the possibilities. He had greatly feared the voyage over here, but his fears had proved unfounded. It was interesting to hear some of the others worrying about some of the same issues as they prepared to travel by garrion. He would not worry, for surely if he could survive seven days on a ship, he could handle a single day in a garrion.

His thoughts turned to Wylla, and for the first time in days, he began to hope again that he might be able to find her. Wherever she was, they would be coming after her, and with the help of a dragon, the most powerful creature in Kirthanin. The giant no longer seemed so intimidating, for the odds had been evened a bit. At least, Joraiem thought, while they might still be outnumbered, and while they might still have a hard pursuit ahead, when they eventually did find the women, he knew who he would bet on when Eliandir and the Vulsutyrim came to blows.

Joraiem wondered what had become of Kelvan's body. Most likely the boat in which they had laid him had capsized not long after Sarneth took it out to sea, but if by some strange quirk of chance it hadn't, then surely the storm a few days ago would have smashed it to pieces. That meant that Kelvan's remains had long since sunk, waterlogged, to the ocean's floor, or had perhaps become food for some creature of the deep.

As that thought crossed Joraiem's mind, he felt a sudden chill as a dark and sinister image flashed before him. He seemed to see a massive, shadowy form swimming along the ocean floor, two great eyes peering out of an enormous head. In his mind's eye the body lacked precise definition, except that it was easily two or three times the size of Eliandir. It was like a fast moving shadow from a cloud, gliding across the sand. In the vision the creature swam toward the place where Kelvan's body had come to rest and then swept over and past it. When it had gone, the body had disappeared too. The ripples and waves on the ocean's surface alone bore witness to the passing of this thing below.

Joraiem knew without knowing how that he was seeing the creature they had found below Nal Gildoroth. He shivered at the thought that it might be swimming free in the Southern Ocean, but he thought the vision was a fabrication of his active imagination. There were other more likely fates for Kelvan's body than to be swallowed up by some mysterious sea creature that as far as Joraiem knew had no access to the sea, and so Joraiem pushed the strange and troubling images from his mind.

He walked back to the fire, where most of the men were

still sitting, talking, and sat near Valzaan, who was warming himself with his back to the Southern Ocean. "Valzaan," Joraiem began, "where do you think Eliandir went?"

"He went to find a place to sleep."

"Why not stay with us?"

"Dragons sleep as far above sea level as possible. That is why they make their homes in the mountain heights and why the dragon towers were built during the First Age."

"So he's flown off to those mountains we saw beyond Nal Gildoroth?"

"Yes. He will find a place high up in their peaks and sleep. When morning comes, he will be back for us, and we would be wise to be ready!"

A small cinder popped out of the fire and landed in the sand near Joraiem's feet, and he flipped some sand over it before continuing. "Do all dragons hate men as much as Eliandir?"

"Eliandir doesn't hate men. Nor do the other dragons."

"Well, he certainly doesn't seem very friendly."

Valzaan laughed. "No, I guess he doesn't. Still, even if he loved you dearly, he wouldn't come across as friendly. Dragons are dragons. They are not soft in word or deed and never will be. You'll get used to their way in time."

Valzaan paused and sighed, lifting his face from the fire and turning it in the direction Eliandir had flown away in that morning. "No, the dragons do not hate men, but great distance has grown between the races over time."

"Like the Great Bear?"

"Yes and no. Like the bear, the dragons are wary of human actions and motives. They remember the betrayal of Andunin, and as I'm sure you picked up, the War of Division. It was the War of Division that opened the door for Malek's invasion from the Forbidden Isle, and it was Malek's invasion that brought Vulsutyr. The dragons believe that the folly of men in the War of Division led, if indirectly, to the showdown between Sulmandir and Vulsutyr, and though Sulmandir killed the Fire Giant, it came at a high price. The Golden Dragon flew north from the Holy Mountain, greatly wounded, and was never seen in the skies of Kirthanin again. The dragons have lost their great father, and they hold mankind largely responsible.

"But it is not so simple as that. The dragons felt a responsibility for men that the Great Bear never felt. When Malek's Rebellion destroyed the Council of Twelve, the dragons assumed the role of protectors for Kirthanin. The War of Division drew their patrols from the Suthanin coast and their attention from the Forbidden Isle. When the Malekim came, they could not drive Malek back or keep him from taking Agia Muldonai. For these things they feel responsible. They feel that they failed Kirthanin in its moment of need. With Sulmandir and many of their number dead after Malek's invasion, the remainder gradually retreated into their mountain lairs, believing their time was past. I believe that this is not the case, and that the dragons still have an important role to play before all is said and done, but what that role will be, the prophecies do not say."

"I would never have guessed Eliandir felt guilty; he seemed angry."

"It is hard enough to read the true emotions of a man, Joraiem. Anger may hide shame or guilt, even when the speaker doesn't know it. It is even harder to read a dragon. They are wonderful and majestic creatures, but they are also fierce. They were made by Allfather with a fire inside that none of his other creations possesses. It is hard to explain, but it is this fire within that makes a dragon a dragon. A man cannot understand, for a man is not a dragon.

"Perhaps I could explain it best by comparing dragons to Great Bear. Great Bear are by nature steady and quiet. Every Great Bear I have known is like this; it is part of their makeup.

Often, men who meet Great Bear detect this quality and make the mistake of believing that they are gentle, even weak. You have seen Sarneth in combat; do you think that would be a fair depiction of him?"

"Certainly not. He is a fearful and ferocious enemy."

"Indeed, all Great Bear are, as many Malekim learned when they fought for control of Kirthanin at the end of the Second Age and pressed into the woods and forests to find and destroy the draals. There are few things more savage in this world than a clan of Great Bear stirred to defend their homes. No Malekim ever made it within sight of any of the draals, not before Corindel anyway.

"Likewise, it is easy to believe upon meeting a dragon that dragons are by nature distant and savage, incapable of love and affection, at least for anything that isn't also a dragon. However, this conclusion would be as misguided as the opposite conclusion about the Great Bear."

Joraiem nodded hesitantly. He recalled Eliandir's brief exchange with Valzaan and wasn't convinced, though he knew Valzaan would not mislead him.

Glancing at Synoki, who sat on the other side of the fire, near but separate from the men, Joraiem again felt uneasiness reverberating inside him. "Valzaan," he added softly, "I keep having these strange feelings of mistrust and suspicion about Synoki."

"Why strange? Is it not natural to mistrust what you don't know? We found him here, of all places, and even if the story he told us is true, there is much we don't know about him."

"You think his story might not be true?"

"I think many people do not tell their true story, especially to people they do not know."

Valzaan doesn't seem concerned; I'm overreacting, Joraiem thought. Even so, as he looked back through the dancing firelight at the man, he felt the wariness again within.

Joraiem was ready and waiting, as were all the others. All unnecessary supplies had been winnowed and stashed on the beach, though it was difficult to give up supplies salvaged from the *Evening Star.* But room was at a premium in the garrion, and they could pick up supplies on the mainland.

Eliandir arrived with the dawn, and his approach and landing were as spectacular as they had been the night before. Joraiem thought as he watched that it was truly a wonder to find such grace and beauty in a creature so mighty and so powerful. It was like watching Sarneth move with his giant staff, smooth and fluid, or like watching a stallion run, the surge of power and strength thrown into a sequence of movement as natural as water cascading over rocks. He couldn't imagine what it would be like to fly, but he was excited to think that he was about to find out.

They waited by the garrion as Valzaan conversed with Eliandir about their plan for after the crossing. They would head straight for Kirthanin, a little east of Sulare and inland, near the southern end of the Arimaar Mountains. There was a mid-sized town there called Derrion Wel. There they would acquire the necessary supplies, and then move north along the western side of the mountains. Though they didn't know the exact route of the enemy, Valzaan didn't think there were many options. Farms and small towns covered the gap between the Elnin and Lindan Woods, and the coastland east of the Arimaar Mountains and south of the Kalamin River saw too much trade by ship to be safe. Surely, Valzaan argued, they would want to get off the open sea as soon as possible, and though the route along the Arimaar Mountains was circuitous, there was little between the mountains and Lindan Wood to stand in the way of their progress north. From there, it would be a straight shot across the open plains of central Suthanin east of the Kellisor Sea, a crossing of the Kalamin, and then the southeastern reaches of the Forest of Gyrin would be within easy reach. The road was long but led through largely empty lands with few obstacles. Without any better ideas, the group agreed to follow Valzaan's instinct.

Joraiem looked around him one last time as he climbed into the garrion. He had walked on the Forbidden Isle, and for the moment at least, it looked like he was going to live to tell about it. He knew that if he lived long enough to bounce a son or daughter on his knee, this was going to be one story good enough to tell them many times over. Hopefully, it would end with the rescue of the women, and if Allfather smiled on him, that son or daughter would call one of those rescued, "Mother."

Inside the garrion, the situation was not as cramped as Joraiem had expected. Sarneth sat with legs crossed in one of the corners, and Caan lay next to him along the end of the garrion, resting his back against Sarneth for support. There was room enough, though barely, for the other thirteen and Koshti to stand or sit, provided they didn't try to stretch their legs. Valzaan came in last and pulled the double doors shut. Slits of light from the slender windows crisscrossed the garrion, but it felt very dark after so much time in the open air under the summer sun. *Strange,* Joraiem thought, *to associate the Forbidden Isle with light and going home with darkness.*

There was little time for Joraiem to wax philosophical, for Eliandir's great claws grasped the bar above them as they were ripped off the ground into the air. Joraiem had no idea how much they all weighed, fourteen men and a Great Bear, perhaps as much as 250 stone all together, and he had wondered if Eliandir would struggle to lift them off the ground and fly with them. His question was answered immediately as they rose rapidly and swung out in ever widening circles before finally speeding away north over the ocean.

The flight in the garrion was every bit as remarkable as Joraiem had imagined it would be. The first challenge was to get used to moving at such a great speed. Even the fastest horse Joraiem had ever ridden couldn't compare to the feeling of being pulled beneath Eliandir. Over time, though, Joraiem's body gradually adjusted to this smooth movement and enjoyed the ride in the garrion more easily, though things got tricky again when he tried to stand up to catch a glimpse of the outer world through the windows.

Aljeron was the first to try this, and Joraiem realized it must be hard if he struggled, for Aljeron's balance was exceptional. He stumbled in his first attempt and fell across both twins, who grunted and laughed as they shoved Aljeron off while he apologized profusely. The second time, he leaned heavily against a nearby wall and snaked his way up it slowly. Eventually, he achieved a more or less upright position, but when he looked out the window he stumbled again. Joraiem couldn't see what happened exactly, for one moment the wind rushing through the windows of the garrion started whipping Aljeron's hair madly around and then Aljeron was bent over, clutching at the wall for support. Slowly, he raised his head again, planting both hands firmly against the wall. He peered out through the windows again, and this time, did not fall.

For several moments he stared intently out the windows, which were high enough up that he had to stand on his toes to look down. It was the looking down that was the problem, though, for not only were they very, very high in the air, but the water below seemed to be itself moving at great speeds, Aljeron explained, now that they had adjusted to the motion of the garrion and no longer felt so keenly its movement. Of course, the others were eager to have a look, and one by one, sometimes on their own and sometimes with the help of others on the floor, they each stood to take their turn looking out the window.

The view was like nothing Joraiem had ever experienced. The wind through the windows alone was exhilarating. He could have closed his eyes and let the wind blow past his face like that for days. He stood there, soaking it in, memorizing the feeling, knowing that when he was lucky, it would come back to him in dreams. Then, he looked out, and he understood what Aljeron had meant. The clouds seemed strikingly close, but they did not appear to be moving as fast as the ocean below. Distant flashes of white that Joraiem guessed were whitecaps sped away and out of sight. Peering out and up, he could see one of Eliandir's extended wings moving rhythmically up and down, and beyond the wing, thick white clouds. The wind was constant, but when the great wings came down, he could feel the wind surge even more forcefully.

The whole day passed like this, with the men sitting quietly on the floor, one or two standing and stretching from time to time to look out the windows and feel their feet beneath them again. Eventually the sun crept higher and higher up the sides of the garrion until there was no light save for a general orange glow that faintly illuminated them before disappearing all together. They sat quietly as the darkness grew deeper, and still Eliandir flew on.

Well after dark, they noticed Eliandir banking in a long curving arc to the east, and when this arc sent them through several wide circles, they knew that this was not a change of direction but preparation for landing. The circles became smaller and smaller and then, almost abruptly, they felt the garrion touch ground. It was an odd sensation, having been moving at such speeds all day, suddenly to be motionless. Though Joraiem's body continued to feel as though it were soaring through the sky, he rose to his feet, eager to step onto Kirthanin soil again.

Out they tumbled, and Joraiem stood stretching awkwardly and rubbing sleepy eyes. The moon and stars illuminated most of their surroundings. They were in something of a depression in what appeared to be relatively open grassland. Joraiem could make out large, looming shadows that he knew must be the Arimaar Mountains, and he wondered as he gazed at them if Wylla and the others were indeed somewhere out there.

When Caan had been lifted out of the garrion and Sarneth had extricated himself, Eliandir lifted the transport back off the ground and, after cycling up into the sky, was soon gone in the direction of the mountains. Valzaan did not allow them to stand and stare for long, though. He quickly organized them into a camp and pressed them to sleep. In the morning they would have to walk to Derrion Wel, a good half day's journey away.

Joraiem did not have to be told a second time to try to sleep, for his body was sore and exhausted as though he had been running all day, rather than sitting. He yawned as he stretched out in the soft, cool grass, and that night, for the first time in his life, he dreamed that he was flying.

The morning came too quickly for Joraiem. When Valzaan woke him, he felt groggy and more weary than when he had lain down in the first place. The sun was not yet above the horizon, but already several of the others were on their feet preparing for the journey. He forced himself to join them, willing his body to shake off the sleepiness. *There will be plenty of time for sleep after we have her back,* he thought as he slipped on his small pack and grabbed Suruna and his quiver.

They set out at a quick pace through the tall summer grass, with Aljeron, Pedraal, and Pedraan taking turns carrying Caan carefully over their respective shoulders. Caan disliked the situation, not so much because it was less than comfortable to be draped over someone's shoulder, but because he knew he was slowing them down. Even so, they kept their pace relatively brisk.

Early in the afternoon, perhaps Seventh Hour, they spotted Derrion Wel in the distance. They were approaching it from the southeast and so altered their course to intercept the road heading toward the town's southern entrance.

Derrion Wel was not quite the size of Peris Mil, but it still easily dwarfed Dal Harat. A number of people were out and about as they entered the town, and they might have passed more or less unnoticed if not for Sarneth. The appearance of a Great Bear was not completely unheard of in this place south of Lindan Wood, but it was very rare. Certainly, a Great Bear had not entered the town as part of a larger human company, at least not in living memory. For that matter, as the people of Derrion Wel took a closer look, the strange appearance of the humans alone was just about enough to cause a stir. Most immediately there was Koshti, walking next to Aljeron, who with his imposing stature and scarred face must have been a startling sight, especially as he was carrying Caan. There were also the twins, large and bearing battle-axe and war hammer. The others carried swords and bows and arrows, walking armed in a place where few ever openly displayed weaponry except while hunting. And, of course, there was Valzaan, whose appearance was striking and memorable, even if it never occurred to the people of Derrion Wel that they were looking at *the* Valzaan. The normal trade and commerce ground to a halt, and people stopped and stared as the group moved along the middle of the central street toward the center of the town.

Caan directed them to an inn called The Quiet Glade, and they slipped inside. A middle-aged man with a thick mustache but no beard met them just inside the door as they entered. He was tall and strong with a glimmer in his eye that suggested a rascal to Joraiem, though not a scoundrel.

but isn't this a sight. A pack of handsome young lads in the company of a Great Bear and one of them toting Master Caan like a sack of grain. What is going on in the world outside Derrion Wel?"

"A fair question," Valzaan responded. "Many things, both for good and for ill have beset us on our road, and we would be obliged if you could spare some time and aid."

"He'll spare it, or when I'm better I'll be back to teach him the meaning of proper courtesy," Caan grunted from the seat on the floor where Aljeron had placed him.

"My name is Master Dreyling," the innkeeper said, taking a closer look at Valzaan, "and I am at your service. Tell me what you need."

Master Dreyling was true to his word, and without asking questions that might have been awkward or at least complex to answer, he began setting about making all the arrangements he could to meet their needs. Within half an hour, half a dozen town boys were scuttling about Derrion Wel on errands for the inn, and as life outside The Quiet Glade remained more or less at a standstill, they had little difficulty finding merchants ready to fill the orders and make delivery. By late in the afternoon, everything Valzaan had requested had been gathered. There were two strong horses and a large cart, whose owner had agreed to allow both his animals and cart to make the trek from Derrion Wel to Sulare, though he himself could not spare the time to drive it. So, Ulmindos was going to go, taking Caan and the two sailors back. Caan objected, wanting to seek aid in Derrion Wel and then, once cured and rested, follow the others in pursuit of the women, but it didn't take Valzaan long to convince him that this would not work. They were going to be moving as quickly as the terrain allowed, and by the time he could ride, it would be too late, one way or the other. It would be better for him and for them to get what aid he could in Derrion Wel, then head back to Sulare with the others.

Ten additional horses were secured, eight for the remaining Novaana, one for Valzaan, and one for Synoki. At first, Valzaan suggested Synoki go with Ulmindos and the others to

Sulare, but Synoki rejected this idea. He didn't have much to say, save that they had rescued him and he would stay with them until they had rescued the women. Besides, he added, his own home was north and west in Werthanin, and though that wasn't exactly where they were headed, he reasoned that at least Agia Muldonai was in that direction.

By dinnertime, the ten were outfitted with all the food they could pack on the horses and all the supplies they thought they would need. All this Master Dreyling provided for them, based solely on Caan's promise that Master Berin would send payment from Sulare if Master Dreyling would but send a bill with them. In the morning the two groups would part ways, but that evening they shared one last meal before retiring for what they all hoped would be a restful night's sleep.

Joraiem looked around him at the open beach, and as far as he could see, there was nothing but sand and sea. The large ocean waves rolled in one after the other in the relentless procession that had marked the meeting of sea and shore for a hundred generations. Joraiem bent over and picked up a large handful of fine, cool sand, and he let it slip gradually from his hand. The sand felt soothing as it slid through the cracks of his fingers and fell in a steady flow, lightly pelting his feet and ankles. *There is so much beauty in the ocean and the beach. It is such a shame that I have never really been able to enjoy them.*

The rolling crash of thunder disturbed his ruminations and Joraiem looked up, surprised to see how quickly the sky had been filled with gray clouds. The wind had changed too, for now it blew much harder and on the breeze Joraiem could smell the clear scent of a storm.

And then, just like that, it was there. The rain fell thick and heavy, as if poured out of giant buckets, and Joraiem was drenched. His wet blond hair clung to his head and neck, and his waterlogged clothes hung droopily from his body like randomly attached weights. Joraiem looked around him for shelter, but there was none. He retreated to the grass and huddled with his head between his knees as the storm continued to blow.

He didn't know how long he was there. Perhaps he had fallen asleep in the middle of the storm, but when he woke, the rain had stopped. He stood and was surprised to find his wet clothes were almost completely dry and the beach had disappeared. Before him lay a road like the road that ran from his house to Dal Harat, and snow covered it and the surrounding open country.

The sound of people singing reached his ears, coming from the road to his right. In the distance he could see a small group of people in a tight formation walking his way. The song was pretty, though sad and mournful. The small group drew nearer, and though Joraiem stood clearly in sight, none of them turned to look as they walked, face and eyes straight ahead.

Joraiem felt a cold chill ripple through his body. He noticed two things at just about the same moment. First, the group of people were carrying something draped in black and lying on a smooth board, and second, he knew the faces he was now seeing clearly. Monias was up front, and beside him little Brenim, who appeared to have sprouted at least a hand since he had left Dal Harat. Evrim walked somberly beside him on the right. Behind these three walked Kyril and Elsora, and both his mother and sister wept quietly as they sang. Along the sides of the body walked some of the other villagers of Dal Harat, along with some of the Novaana from Sulare. Aljeron was there, Koshti too, and Pedraal and Pedraan. More women from the village followed the men, and behind them came Wylla, arm in arm with Alina.

When Joraiem saw this last pair, he was taken aback. He blinked and peered at them again. They were still there. By this point, the procession was moving past him, and as it did, he started to run forward through the snow toward the strange group. He called out to them, softly at first, then more loudly. They didn't seem to hear him.

Just as he drew near to Wylla and Alina, a brilliant flash of light exploded all around him and Joraiem fell to the ground. When he was able at last to open his eyes, he was no longer in the snow, and the sad, peculiar group of his family and friends were nowhere to be seen. He brushed off some grass as he stood in the middle of a vast, open plain, looking around him again. He saw a man was walking straight toward him.

As he drew nearer, Joraiem thought to himself how much this man both did and did not look like Valzaan. His hair was long and wavy, though it was not white at all but a sandy blond. His face was young, bearing no wrinkles or signs of age. And, most of all, his sky-blue eyes were not unseeing, but radiated light as he approached.

"Do you see how it shall be?" the man asked with a voice that rang with the music of dancing.

"I don't know what I see."

The man nodded, gently, placing his arm around Joraiem's shoulders. "That's all right. It is enough, for now, simply that you see."

They began walking together through the broad field, and the stranger walked with his arm around Joraiem. "Allfather's will is a mystery to all but Himself. Even the Twelve never knew it all. So for every servant of Allfather's, trust in the One you serve is essential. Joraiem, you are important to Allfather's plan, though it may not be in a way that any expects or foresees."

"How will I know what to do?"

"Even now, Joraiem, Allfather is guiding your steps. You will know. Only do not be afraid. Though pain and suffering await you, they are both an end and a beginning. For when the time is come, behold, Allfather will make all things new!"

The man threw his arms high above his head into the air, and as the man's voice echoed across the plain, the brilliant flash of light that had knocked Joraiem down before exploded around them again. He fell to the ground, and all around him was darkness.

8

BY DAY AND
BY NIGHT

JORAIEM SAT IN HIS room in The Quiet Glade and pondered the curious dream. It remained with him so vividly that he found it difficult to dismiss it as a confused jumble of hopes and fears. The man with the bright blue eyes was especially hard to forget, and his words rang in Joraiem's ears: "Allfather will make all things new!" He would have to ask Valzaan about it.

The ten travelers gathered in the common room in the half-light of morning before the sun was up, and rather than sitting to eat breakfast, they took large hunks of bread and cheese and wrapped them in cloth to eat as they rode. Ulmindos and Caan came out to see them off, Caan leaning on Ulmindos as they stood by the stable. When they were mounted and ready, Caan motioned them closer.

"I wanted you all to know that whatever waits for you out there, you're ready. Though I have treated you as boys at times, you are men. I'd like to take credit for that, but you were men when you came to me, just in need of a little honing. Even so, remember that just because none of your Sulare instructors goes with you , you are not free to do as you please. You are still under Master Berin's authority, though you will go further from the Summerland with each passing day. Ulmindos and I have entrusted that authority to Valzaan and Sarneth. I'm sure you will heed them closely anyway, but know that I will hold you accountable if you do not. So, be sure that you obey, and don't think this leg of mine will be injured forever!"

They bid Caan farewell, and set out through the quiet streets of Derrion Wel. A few buildings were already lit, though not many, and the occasional early riser out and about paused to watch the strange procession pass, ten men on horses accompanied by a Great Bear and a large tiger. They passed through the town's north gate and pressed the horses to a gallop as Koshti and Sarneth ran in the grass beside them. After so many days of idleness on the island, Joraiem felt good to be moving with purpose again, and he spurred his horse toward the front to join Aljeron and Rulalin.

They rode hard all day, pausing only to provide rest and water for the horses, who labored to run in the summer heat. It was the twenty-first day of Full Summer, and while Joraiem imagined that hotter spells than this came in these southern climes this time of year, it was hot enough. Despite the heat and pace, Koshti and Sarneth seemed to be doing all right. That Koshti was able to keep up with them did not surprise Joraiem. He had never seen Koshti weary in all the weeks he traveled with Aljeron and the other Werthanim on their way to Sulare. Sarneth's ability to keep the pace and show no signs of weariness was more impressive. Joraiem knew that over short distances Sarneth could move very quickly. Still, he hadn't expected to find him able to run at this speed for so long, his frame full and solid, not so long and lean as Koshti's. And yet, every time they started forward again, Sarneth's huge form would shadow the leaders as he ran many spans out in the grass with Koshti, where they wouldn't spook the horses.

And so they ran, from dawn to midday and from midday to evening. Twelfth Hour came and went, and since the summer days were long, they rode on into First Watch, as long as there was enough sun to see their way forward.

When they finally stopped for the evening, Joraiem's body ached as he slid from his horse. It had been months since he had been in the saddle. He had pushed the discomfort from his mind all day, but he could feel the soreness vividly now and knew he would pay for his sudden and sustained return. He tried to console himself that in a few days he would be used to it again, but at present that was little consolation.

They devoured a hastily prepared supper in silence, and Joraiem gazed east at the Arimaar Mountains that had been their constant companion on the ride. The mountains lay a day or two's ride east of Derrion Wel, and according to Valzaan, the road would keep that distance fairly constant for the first few days north of town. On the third or fourth day, he explained, the road would bring them closer to the mountains, at a place where the range curved inland just a bit before trailing off in a northeasterly direction. There, where the road brought them almost within reach of the mountains themselves, they would meet Eliandir again and figure out from there what to do about trying to pick up the trail of the giant and the Malekim. It seemed like a simple enough plan, except that Joraiem couldn't help wondering what they would do if they found Eliandir but no trace of the women and their captors. There was no telling how much of a head start Malek's servants had, and the world was wide.

Completely exhausted, most of the others lay down for sleep soon after eating. When Joraiem could hear some of them snoring, he slipped around the fire to the place where Valzaan sat. "Valzaan," he said, "may I ask you something?"

"Yes."

"Last night, I had a strange dream—" Joraiem began, but before he could continue, Valzaan waved the end of his staff between them, and Joraiem felt the pull of *torrim redara*. The flames of the fire stopped flickering and the sound of crickets and escalating snores in the summer night disappeared.

"The dreams of a prophet are often just dreams," Valzaan said, remaining seated, "strange and unfathomable workings of both mind and heart. But it seemed prudent to discuss yours here in case this one is not."

"How did you do that?" Joraiem asked, still marveling at how Valzaan had so quickly and easily pulled him into slow time.

"I will show you that and many other things, when we have time. What were you saying about a dream?"

Joraiem walked him through the whole thing, and Valzaan did not say a word. He sat there chewing on a long blade of grass. The chewing stopped, though, when Joraiem came to the last part of the dream. The description of the man in the field and his words to Joraiem were of obvious importance to Valzaan. He questioned Joraiem carefully at length on the man's exact appearance, garments, sound and tone of voice, as well as mannerisms of movement and speech. All that Joraiem could remember he told Valzaan, until at last the prophet was quiet.

"What do you make of it, Valzaan?"

"I'm not sure." He started chewing again.

"But you have an idea," Joraiem answered. "All those questions, you must have asked them for a reason."

Valzaan sighed. "I think I have an idea of who you were talking to at the end of your dream, but in the end, I am not certain."

Joraiem nodded. "I understand your hesitation, but I'd still like to know what you think. I'm willing to accept the uncertainty."

"The first part of the dream could mean anything. It might be a vision of things to come; it might not be. Certainly the last part of the dream would suggest it is. But it is confusing, as visions often are. It could be a premonition of a death, or it might not be. If it is about death, the death might be symbolic rather than physical. Maybe a loss or change or parting. I don't know. You couldn't see the face of the body being carried, so I can only conclude that if this was a vision given you by Allfather, you weren't meant to see all.

"The last part of the dream or vision, though, that is a different matter. I think I know the name of the figure you saw, but I don't know how it could be."

"Why?"

"Because he is dead."

"Dead?"

"Yes, he died at the end of the First Age at Malek's own hand."

"What?" Joraiem asked incredulously. "I don't understand."

"The figure you are describing sounds to me like one of the Twelve, Balimere the Beautiful to be precise. He was the most beloved of the Titans. He died in Avalione before Alazare cast Malek from the Mountain."

"I have heard of Balimere, of course, but it could not have been him in my dream, could it?"

"I would have thought not, but as I have told you before, I do not know or see all. Many faithful servants of Allfather have died, and while their bodies await restoration, where do their spirits go? Where do the dead await the renewal of all things? With Allfather, I presume. So, I don't know why this would be impossible. The faithful Titans served Allfather in the body and may serve Him even now apart from it. If Allfather were to send Balimere into your dreams and visions, to speak His words, that is His decision. He does as He pleases.

"Or, of course, I could be wrong entirely. The man in your dream might not be Balimere. The similarities might be coincidental, and I might be looking too hard for Allfather's hand on you and meaning in your dreams. That is why I said I don't know." Valzaan sighed again. "Rarely have I sought direction and answers for so long with so little guidance."

"But you said you were mostly sure it was Balimere?"

"Yes, mostly sure. But mostly sure, in the end, is a far cry from certainty."

"What do you think I should do?"

Valzaan turned to Joraiem, and his empty, white eyes rested upon him. "There is nothing to do except what we are doing. I am sorry that I have so few answers for you, my boy. Though I spoke in frustration just now, I can see the hand of Allfather on you and on what you do. I can see the possibilities of greatness and great things. But all these things are just shadows, pieces of what is and will be. What those shadows point to, that is still beyond me. So, let us press on and trust that we know enough to do what is before us. Beyond that, we will have to go back to Allfather for more wisdom. I am sorry that I have nothing else to tell you."

"You don't need to be sorry, Valzaan. Without you, I'd know nothing of Allfather's hand on me. You have told me what you know, and it is comforting in a way to know that even you don't understand fully."

Valzaan nodded and waved his staff again between them, and Joraiem felt himself sliding back into real time. The sound of the summer night filled his ears again, and he felt the crackling warmth of the fire at his back. He put his hand gently on Valzaan's shoulder as a quiet thanks for his time and stood to go back to his place on the other side of the camp.

The dream was more mysterious now than ever, but Joraiem was learning the patience of living with mystery.

Wylla massaged her sore shoulder as she lay in the grass. The Malekim carrying her had dropped her none too gently when they had stopped a little while ago, and she knew that once they started moving again, she wouldn't be able to do anything about the ache.

This break, though, was already longer than any they had been granted before. This was their fourth night on the move since leaving the cave where Ulutyr had met with the mysterious Tashmiren, which meant that unless Wylla had lost track somewhere since Nal Gildoroth, it must be the twenty-first day of Full Summer. She had not been able to get a look at the man who had spoken so arrogantly to Ulutyr, but she had seen his silhouette as he slipped away before dawn and knew he was but a man.

She had to force herself to put Joraiem out of her mind, as the men would have to fend for themselves against Tashmiren and whomever else might go with him to the Forbidden Isle. She felt helpless, but that was a feeling she was getting used to. There was nothing she could do for them. Her immediate concern was the well-being of the seven women with her, four of whom, though marginally better than they were ten days ago, were still emotionally delicate. And, to make matters worse, though she had known now for three whole days that rescue was not coming and that they were going to have to escape on their own if they were ever to get away, she hadn't been able to come up with a feasible plan.

Even now, as they lay in the grass in the open night, not tied or bound in any way, she could see no possibility of escape, as they were encircled by a solid ring of Malekim. But what were they doing, stopping for so long? They had never stopped for longer than it took to swallow a few gulps of water, to be transferred to another carrier, and to be off. But they had lain in the grass for perhaps a quarter of an hour now.

Mindarin leaned in closely to whisper in Wylla's ear. The Voiceless didn't seem to care at all how or where the women moved, but they reacted violently to any sound they deemed unnecessary. How violently could still be seen in the cut above Karalin's ear, where she was struck by one of the Malekim when she tried to soothe Tarin and Valia with a gentle song. None of them had made that mistake again, but Mindarin was in many ways the boldest.

"Why the stop?" was all she said, and Wylla shrugged slightly in response. Mindarin continued, "Should we try to run?"

Wylla turned and looked Mindarin in the eye, shaking her head.

"This may be our opportunity! We've never stopped like this before, so what if we don't stop like this again?"

"I don't know, but it can't be done *now*."

Mindarin turned away frustrated. Wylla didn't blame her, because she only showed the frustration they all felt. There had to be some way, some opening that they could exploit, but she had no idea what it could be or what it might look like if it came.

She sat up quietly, still rubbing her shoulder as the circle around them opened to allow Ulutyr in and then closed again once he was inside. He knelt beside them and stooped so that he wasn't much more than a few hands taller than the tallest Malekim. He lifted his right hand to his mouth and placed one of his fingers up against his lips, motioning to them all to be silent. The whole circle of Malekim sat down silently, making no more noise than a leaf gently floating to the ground from its place among the branches of the tree.

For another quarter of an hour or more they sat, absolutely quiet and absolutely still. Ulutyr knelt beside them, but his face was uplifted and his eyes searched the night sky systematically. Eventually he stood and motioned to the Malekim, who hopped up instantly and had the women back on their shoulders in a matter of seconds. After such a nice stretch on the ground, it felt particularly cruel to Wylla to be returned to her now familiar traveling position, but she tried to be grateful for the break. The reason for it was still a mystery, but from time to time, as she hung upside down, she too turned her eyes to the starry sky and searched it for a sign of anything that might give her hope. Her old friend, the moon, continued through his cycles above her, but she did not find in him the comfort she once did. No, she looked for something else. Ulutyr had been looking for, and perhaps even hiding from, something in the sky.

On the third day out of Derrion Wel, the men reached the place where the road and the Arimaar Mountains seemed about to touch before the mountains turned east. They moved off the road and headed for the foot of the nearest mountain, where they planned to camp. As the others prepared the fire and the supper, Valzaan set out with his staff in one hand and a windhover circling above him and began to ascend the lower part of the mountain. He had made it clear that it would be best if he went alone. He was accustomed already to moving in darkness, so the coming night would make no difference to him as he navigated the lower slopes on his way to meet with Eliandir.

The others stayed behind, but could not rest. They sat around the fire, talking softly among themselves and keeping always an eye or two on the mountain beside them and the sky above. None of them had seen any sign of Eliandir since their return from the Forbidden Isle, and having found like Joraiem his greeting none too friendly, most wondered if they would ever see the dragon again. Joraiem, though, did not doubt Eliandir's word. He didn't believe Eliandir would fail to return, unless something or someone prevented it.

Deep into the night, Joraiem awoke to the sound of Valzaan returning to the camp. He did not remember falling asleep. The darkness around him seemed to be fading, and he didn't believe that morning could be far away. All around him, sleepy figures sat up, as though stirred by Valzaan's return, and soon they were gathered around the prophet.

"Did he come?" Aljeron asked.

"Yes, we spoke a few hours ago."

"And?" Rulalin asked hastily as Valzaan paused.

"And fortunately we have chosen rightly. Eliandir spotted the Vulsutyrim and the others a few nights ago, not far north of where we are right now, which means they have a lead on us of perhaps three days."

"And the women?" Joraiem asked, hesitantly. "Did he see them?"

"He wasn't able to make out the details of the group very clearly. He saw first only that a large group of creatures was moving very quickly northward along the foothills of the Arimaar Mountains. He says that he sensed almost immediately the presence of one of Vulsutyr's children, but he also believes that the Vulsutyrim sensed him, for the group quickly took shelter in a small copse of trees. Eliandir circled above for a while, but they did not move again, and so he turned away. So, no, he didn't actually see any of the women with them, but this is good news. We know now that we have guessed correctly, and so we can press forward with all speed. We also know that they are only three days ahead of us, so there is some hope that we may be able to overtake them before they can cross the Kalamin River and make their way into the Gyrin Forest."

"We will not stop there if we still follow behind," Rulalin

said softly. "We will plunge after them into Gyrin itself if need be."

"I hope it won't come to that," Valzaan said simply.

"Look," Elyas began, "I know that we all want to find the women safe and unharmed. But how do we know they are still alive? We just keep assuming they're fine, and I keep worrying that we will catch up with the giant and the Malekim only to find them dead."

His voice trembled as he finished, and a hushed silence fell over them. Of course, Joraiem thought, they had all thought many times that their pursuit might prove futile, but what else could they do?

"We can't turn back now, Elyas," said Rulalin, as if reading Joraiem's thoughts. "There is nothing else we can do."

"I don't want to turn back. I was just making a point since no one else has brought it up."

"It's a fair question," Valzaan said, cutting off a few of the others. "We don't really know for sure that they live. And yet I think it is more than just wishful thinking that leads us to believe your sister and the others are still alive. After all, if the enemy had wished to kill the women, why bother taking them alive in the first place?"

Several of the others nodded, and Aljeron added, "Not only were they captured alive, but we could find almost no trace of blood outside the gate where they were taken. They were captured with care."

"That's what raises the real question," Saegan offered quietly. "Why take them at all?"

"The women are all Novaana, like we are," Pedraal began. "They are all important in one way or another, like our sister, the heir to the Enthanin throne. Perhaps we were lured out to the island as a trap. Maybe that is why the Black Wolves attacked."

"The Black Wolves came to kill, not capture," Saegan said

firmly. "Whatever brought them to Sulare, I doubt it was kidnapping."

"It is a mystery," Valzaan said, chewing on a long, dry piece of grass. "Why would creatures of Malek twice try to kill us if they had a clear plan to abduct almost half of our party? And why set up such an elaborate plan, travel all the way to the Forbidden Isle, to lure us into a trap? I am not convinced.

"I believed from the first that Malek had his own agenda on the Forbidden Isle, independent of us. I believe we were attacked because we arrived before his mission was complete and before his servants, or at least some of them, could get away. I'm not sure the attack in Sulare was connected to what happened in Nal Gildoroth, unless it was meant as a distraction, to keep us busy while he did his work, and even that seems unlikely.

"I wonder if we are looking for the answer to the question in the wrong place. Maybe the women were not spared outside Nal Gildoroth because of something different about them. Maybe they were spared because of something different about their captors."

"I don't understand," Aljeron said, looking confused.

"Well, what was different about those who captured them?"

"There was a large group of Malekim and a Vulsutyrim—"

"Yes," Valzaan echoed, "a Vulsutyrim."

"The giant?" Joraiem asked, incredulously. "What about him?"

"What about him? Perhaps he ordered their capture rather than their killing. Perhaps he stayed the murderous hands of the Silent Ones. Perhaps he keeps them alive even now."

"But why?" Aljeron asked. "Why would the giant care if they were alive or dead? If they didn't go to the Forbidden Isle to take them, why burden themselves with the women at all? Why not leave their corpses behind?"

"Maybe for the same reason you wouldn't slaughter a

group of women you found wandering outside Shalin Bel, Al-jeron," Valzaan retorted.

"Me? But I'm not a servant of Malek's. What similarity can you draw between that creature and me?"

"I can draw this similarity, Aljeron: Despite the long allegiance between the sons of Vulsutyr and Malek, the giant is still a creature made by Allfather. Remember that. Malek and Vulsutyr made the Grendolai, and then Malek made the Malekim and bred the Black Wolves, but Vulsutyr and his children were not Malek's creation. That is the difference. The Black Wolves and Malekim were made to kill and destroy. To work the will of Malek is all they know. The Vulsutyrim are different. They serve Malek, but no matter how long they are bound in his service, there will always be a part of them that reflects their Creator. I cannot say for sure, but it may be that the women are alive today because the giant would not kill a group of women on their own. It may be that had we rushed out of the gate with them, we might not have been so fortunate. It may be that while he is our chief obstacle to retrieving them safely, he is also the one who has kept the Malekim from slitting their throats. Many times have I seen a sequence of events, each one appearing worse than those that came before, and only later have I seen that there was mercy in each and every one. Only later have I seen Allfather's hand in the timing of every step. Perhaps such a pattern is at work here as well."

"Mercy is a strange name for what that Malekim did to your young companion back in Nal Gildoroth, Prophet," Synoki said softly.

"Don't be a fool!" Valzaan said sharply, thumping the ground with the bottom of his staff in agitation. "I didn't say that everything tragic is really mercy. I know well enough that there is real evil in the world, and that there are purposes at work in Kirthanin that are not those of Allfather. That does not change the fact that Allfather is at work, weaving the tap-

494   BEYOND

estry of time. He is the Master Weaver, and though his handiwork stretches out before us always, we are not able to see the entirety of His designs. So it is, and so it has always been.

"Now, enough talk. Our path forward is clear. Let us prepare to ride, for we have still many days before us if we are to make up the gap that separates us from the enemy."

For ten days they rode north, hard, barely pausing at all during the day and stopping at night as much for the health of their horses as for their own need. On the evening of the third day of Summer Wane, they stopped within sight of the Arimaar Mountains to the east.

The difference this time was that Lindan Wood was now almost equally as close on the western side of the road. For the past few days, the Wood had loomed thick and dark in the distance, and now they could easily reach its border with but a short ride off of the road. The immense trees rising above the horizon reminded Joraiem of the group's brief passage through the Elnin Wood on their way to Sulare in the spring. It seemed to him now a distant memory of happier days.

They set up camp and ate in silence. Though no one spoke of it, Joraiem sensed they were weary and disheartened. Each day as they rode, they had looked for signs left by those they pursued. Though Joraiem was not especially good at tracking, Saegan was—as he was good at everything—but the best among them was probably Darias, who said it was a gift he'd received from his father and grandfather. A few times during those ten days, they had indeed found signs that the giant and the Malekim had passed that way, but invariably the tracks were several days old, indicating that the gap between them remained, despite their haste. The most recent find had been that very morning, and Darias's estimate was three days, the same gap Eliandir had suggested ten days ago.

It was almost unbearable to consider that in almost two

weeks of riding they hadn't made up any ground. Once they passed beyond the northern end of Lindan Wood and the Arimaar Mountains, the terrain was easy and the ground wide open. Those they pursued would no longer be hemmed in by the trees and mountains. Valzaan questioned whether they, faced with a long run through the open plain, would even stop until they were safely inside Gyrin.

As they stared gloomily into the faintly glowing embers of their fire, a dark form passed quickly above them, and Joraiem looked up to see Eliandir arcing out over the land between the road and wood. He passed overhead a few more times before landing near their fire.

They were quickly on their feet and right behind Valzaan as he walked to the dragon. "Eliandir, what news tonight?"

"There is none. That's what's wrong. I found them again last night, and they are still three days before you, running from dusk till dawn without showing any signs of slowing their pace. Unless something changes, and soon, we will not catch up to them before they are in the open plains."

"Your report confirms our fears," Valzaan said. "Perhaps, though we rejected the idea before, there is now no other choice but to use the garrion again, though it will mean leaving the horses behind and facing the foe without them."

Eliandir snorted. "The flight over the Southern Ocean with the garrion exhausted me, Prophet. I have only recently felt my full strength return. If we use the garrion again, for all of you, then I may not be at full strength when we face the child of Vulsutyr."

"There are four less of us this time, Eliandir," Valzaan replied.

"That is better, but still, I will be weary. Don't forget that I have long been resting inside my lair, and every night since our return I have flown up and down the length of the Arimaar range. Even dragons need sleep."

"There is another way," Sarneth said, drawing all eyes. "The road ahead maintains its course between the mountains and Lindan Wood before turning due west as it curves around the northern end of the forest. Instead of following the road, I could lead you on a shortcut through Lindan. If we move quickly enough, we could cut the distance almost in half and be waiting for them as they emerge into the open plain. If everything goes as planned, Eliandir would not need to weary himself further, and even we might be able to get a little rest before we had to fight."

"Sarneth," Valzaan said as he turned to the Great Bear. "A shortcut through Lindan Wood would not truly be short unless you led along the secret ways. You know the law prohibits this, and even you cannot disregard it."

"I know the law," Sarneth said, and Joraiem thought he heard a slight growl, though perhaps he was mistaken, for the Great Bear continued peaceably. "I will need to seek and receive permission, but that is not impossible as only a foolish society holds blindly to laws when situations arise for which those laws were not intended. The intention of the law is to make sure the mistake made with Corindel is never repeated, that outsiders are not brought in and shown too much. Our intention is not so much to go in as to go through, and the clan never interferes with those who move in and through the wood unless they go where they should not be. The way will be complicated enough, and I doubt that you would be able to retrace our steps once we are through. What's more, I will not show you the way to the draal."

"What do you then suggest?"

"I suggest that when the sun rises, you follow me to the edge of the wood. We will find a patrol of Great Bear, and I will relay the urgency of our need to the draal by messenger. We will continue north along the perimeter of the wood until we receive word from the elders of the clan. If our request is granted, we will cut through the northeastern portion of Lindan Wood and hopefully find ourselves ahead of the enemy. If our request is denied, we can still use the garrion if that is our only choice."

"It is not without risk, Sarneth. If we lose a few days this way, then there will be even less time for Eliandir to rest."

"I did not say that it was without risk, only that it was another way."

"Valzaan, I say we take the chance," Pedraal interjected. "If it works, then maybe we can all rest. I think we could use it. I know I could. What's more, I am reluctant to leave the horses behind. They may prove helpful when we face the Silent Ones. If we cannot pass through the wood, then we can still use the garrion, and if Eliandir is willing, we can go all the way to the Kalamin River. There aren't many places close to the Kellisor Sea and Gyrin Forest where it is passable, and we might even be able to recruit some men to help us patrol the crossings. Additional swords are the only things we could use as much as rest at this point."

"All right then," Valzaan said, "it is settled. We will try the wood first, but let us pray that the draal has compassion. Any delay at this point could be catastrophic."

"I will. I will monitor the eastern edge of the wood, and if I do not find you returning to the road in the next four or five days, I will look for you on the northern edge."

The next morning they followed Sarneth's measured pace as he led them north and west toward the edge of Lindan Wood. It was still early when they came alongside it and Sarneth began to run north along the border. Joraiem watched the Great Bear ahead of them, running with his head cocked just slightly to his left, watching the trees. Then, suddenly, he turned and plunged into the forest.

The rest of them followed, though their horses needed a

bit of coaxing. Still, Sarneth did not slow down as he led them deeper and deeper into the wood. The path he took seemed anything but a path. There were no swaths of open ground before or behind, and yet, as Sarneth zigzagged among the trees, they always had plenty of room to ride two or three abreast behind him.

Joraiem tried to figure out the secret of the pathway, how it worked, how to know which way to turn and when, but he couldn't. He watched Sarneth run ahead, left, straight, right, straight, left, then left again, back straight, right, left, a little doubling back, and then back straight again. He looked back over his shoulder and could see no hint of a trail, and yet they had neither slowed nor been forced to dodge any trees. In fact, when they stopped a few hours later for lunch, again Joraiem couldn't see any path at all, only a partially open clearing in the midst of the trees. He dismounted in total confusion, shaking his head.

"Did you follow any of that?" Aljeron asked.

"Not at all," Joraiem answered. "I wouldn't have the slightest idea how to get back to the edge of the wood on my own."

"It was like magic," Aljeron whispered, the wonder showing in his voice. "The road we followed through Elnin was just that, a road. It was wide and clear and you could see some distance behind and before. This, well, this was a road too, each little piece connected to the next, but it was as if the trees had been planted or spaced deliberately to create a design that only the Great Bear can see. If this is one of the secret ways Valzaan and Sarneth were talking about, I think their secret will be plenty safe."

Joraiem looked up at the thick, full canopy of leaves above them. Some of the trees around him were the enormous size of the trees they had seen in Elnin Wood. Others were small enough that a man could put his arms around them, but all were tall, and the foliage above was many, many spans above even Sarneth's head. Though it wasn't as dark as a cave or room without windows, there was a perpetual feeling of dusk about them. The sun, though Joraiem knew it had been out and shining brightly when they entered the wood, was totally obscured, so he could not use it to try to guess their location or direction. "Aljeron, do you even have a general idea of the direction in which the Arimaar Mountains lie?"

"Sure," Aljeron answered, turning around slightly. "It would be due east, that way." Aljeron pointed behind them.

"You think that we are facing west, and that going that way would take us east?" Joraiem asked, frowning a little.

"Sure, don't you?"

"No. I thought we had turned back north. So, I thought that the road we were on would be running more or less parallel to where we stand. That way," Joraiem pointed out more or less at a right angle from where they stood.

Aljeron grinned. "This should be easy enough to settle. We'll ask Sarneth what direction we are facing. If he says west, then I win. If he says north, then you win. All right?"

"Sure, but what will I win? Because we're not facing west."

"I'll win the satisfaction of knowing I was right, because we're not facing north."

Aljeron and Joraiem walked past the others to Sarneth. "Sarneth, excuse us, but would you mind telling us what direction we are facing now?"

The Great Bear looked down at Aljeron, and it seemed to Joraiem that something resembling a smile crossed his face. "You are facing east. The edge of the wood and the road we were on lies straight ahead as the falcon flies, though it would be difficult for anyone to maintain such a straight line if they wanted to get out by going that way."

Joraiem could see in Aljeron's face the perplexity that must have been showing in his own, so without saying anything, he turned and started back to their horses. They sat and ate, enjoying the rest and shade. For the first time since Joraiem could remember, they were able to take their noonday meal without squinting or shielding their eyes.

There wasn't much of a chance to eat in peace, though, for not long into the meal, both Sarneth and Koshti rose and stood alert. Sarneth turned to Aljeron and said, "It is only a patrol of my people, Aljeron."

Aljeron motioned to Koshti, and the tiger crouched down beside him, remaining alert. Seconds later, a Great Bear wielding a staff appeared before them. A second appeared to their right and a third to their left, and turning around quickly confirmed Joraiem's suspicion that a fourth had entered the small clearing behind them.

Sarneth addressed the Great Bear who had appeared first. "Arintol, greetings, and welcome within our circle."

The Great Bear called Arintol considered Sarneth carefully, even cautiously, but replied in an even tone. "I accept your welcome, Sarneth. Many days have you sojourned away from the draal, and strange is the manner of your return. Valzaan of course is known and honored among us, but these others are unknown to me. Why have you returned in this way, and who are these that you lead in places they should not be?"

"Call the others to join our circle as well, for I will tell you our tale. It is long, though, and I would have you comfortable for its hearing. When you have heard, then you may judge for yourself what I have done."

Arintol motioned to the others, and they came and sat before Sarneth. Sarneth then proceeded to tell the whole story, beginning with the attack in Sulare by the Black Wolves. Though he did not elaborate unnecessarily, it was a long tale and took some time. Throughout the story, as Sarneth told it, Joraiem watched the impassive faces of the other Great Bear. Ever so gradually and slightly, signs of wonder and incredulity began to show, and when Sarneth eventually came to the description of their flight in the garrion high above the Southern Ocean, their amazement was unmistakable. Not surprisingly, when he ended the story they were speechless, so Sarneth persisted, making overt his implied request.

"Arintol, I know that I have brought outsiders within the wood and along one of the secret ways, but I have given Valzaan and Eliandir my word that our request would at least by heard by the elders of the clan. Would you take word of our presence to the draal, and so return to us an answer, whether we may pass through by the secret ways to the northern edge of the Wood?"

Arintol looked from Sarneth and the rest to the other Great Bear with him. "We will consider your request."

The four Great Bear withdrew into the trees, and Joraiem and the others awaited their reply anxiously. They didn't have to wait long, for soon Arintol and two of the Great Bear were back.

"Kuurgan has been dispatched to the clan leaders. He will relate your tale and request to the first patrol he finds, and so the message shall be relayed from messenger to messenger until the elders in the draal know of your story and need. Margan, Lorineth, and I will accompany you as you proceed along your way. Perhaps those who will be unhappy with your presumption, despite your reasons, will be mollified when they know that while you awaited word, you were accompanied by a patrol of the draal."

Sarneth bowed slightly to Arintol. "Your decision is both gracious and wise, and we will be happy to have you as our companions. Again, I welcome you to our circle."

Brief introductions were made, and though Joraiem could tell which of the Great Bear was Arintol, he was not sure as they prepared to move on that he would be able to distinguish between Margan and Lorineth. Even so, they mounted again, and with four Great Bear now before them, they continued their ride through Lindan Wood.

That night they camped and ate supper as usual around the fire, and this time, Valzaan engaged the other Great Bear in discussions of the draal that Joraiem did not understand. Soon after dinner, as their talk continued into the night, Joraiem lay back and closed his eyes to sleep.

He did not sleep right away, but was conscious of a feeling like flying. A whirling darkness inside his head left him a little giddy, but he tried to focus and concentrate. Eventually, he understood what was happening inside him.

He was looking through the eyes of a windhover, and he was seeing the dark world outside the forest. In fact, as he was increasingly able to focus his own eyes to see what the bird was seeing, he realized that the windhover was circling in the nighttime sky above the wood. The tops of tall trees stretched in every direction as far as he could see.

Joraiem decided to try and switch his focus. He imagined searching for another windhover, somewhere further away, and before he realized it, he was looking through another set of eyes. At first, the switch made him dizzy, but again he focused, and soon he was seeing a different setting. This King Falcon was high above the road between the mountains and wood. He searched the ground through its eyes, then tried to imagine another, perhaps further north along the road.

For several moments, he moved in and out of the eyes of various windhovers. Each time, their searching eyes revealed the same thing, silence and stillness beneath the nighttime sky. Joraiem, though, was enjoying the novelty of the experience, and he began to switch more and more quickly.

Then, suddenly, he stopped. The present windhover was not looking down at a peaceful, sleeping countryside. Not far below was a large and quickly moving group of dark shapes and forms. He focused as well as he could and tried with his mind to instruct the bird to move closer, which it did. As it swooped lower, he could make out the enormous form of the

Vulsutyrim running with long powerful strides along the road. Behind him ran the Malekim, formed in rough columns perhaps five across and ten deep. Joraiem double-checked the numbers, because he only remembered half that number boarding the ship on the Forbidden Isle.

In the middle of the pack, a handful of Malekim carried what looked like bundles over their shoulders. He tried to look more closely but, when he could not see what he was looking for, once more urged the windhover to fly closer. Again, the bird responded, and he felt the bird dip and accelerate, and he hoped that it would not fly too close or put itself in any immediate danger. But as it flew low, perhaps just three or four spans above the Malekim, he finally saw what he had been looking for. One of the women, draped over the shoulder of the Malekim, turned her face to peer up into the dark sky. She had long, beautiful black hair that swept along the ground as the creature ran, and Joraiem strained to see her until the arc of the windhover's flight path took him out of sight.

Joraiem sat up suddenly, and rose to his feet so quickly that the blood rushed to his head and he felt a little dizzy. The others turned their attention to him, and the conversation between Valzaan and the Great Bear came to a halt.

"They're alive. The women, they're alive!"

9

AMBUSH IN THE NIGHT

JORAIEM REALIZED AS HE looked at the stunned faces of his companions that he was not at all prepared to explain his sudden outburst. He wasn't really interested in telling the others he had just been gazing through the eyes of a falcon many leagues to the northeast, and he had never really talked with Valzaan about whether he should keep his calling a secret. What's more, Valzaan himself had never bothered to explain to the group that he could see through the eyes of the windhovers, and Joraiem didn't know if the prophet would appreciate him blurting out what he had just been doing. So his elation turned to humiliation and embarrassment as he struggled for something fitting to say.

"Joraiem, what do you mean?" Aljeron asked, sitting up sleepily from where he had been dozing off nearby. He looked intently at his friend's wild and impassioned face.

"I, I'm sorry everyone," Joraiem began awkwardly. He looked at Valzaan to gauge the prophet's reaction to the situation, but the blank look on the prophet's face didn't speak of anger or annoyance or anything, though for a moment, he appeared to Joraiem almost to be bemused. "I must have been having a dream, a very vivid dream. I thought I could see the Malekim carrying the women, and they were alive, that's all I meant."

"We've already established that the women are alive," Pedraan said, then added sarcastically, "but thanks for the big announcement."

Valzaan, moving through their midst from the place where he had been talking with Sarneth and the other Great Bear, followed Pedraan's words quickly. "Dreams can often reveal much to those who know how to read them. Tell me, Joraiem, what exactly did you see?"

The prophet stood before him, and Joraiem knew he was serious. He had, Joraiem believed, guessed at the truth of the matter and wanted to know exactly what Joraiem had seen of the enemy.

"Well, I was looking down on the road as it ran north between Lindan Wood and the Arimaar Mountains, and I saw the giant running with perhaps fifty Malekim behind him—"

"Fifty?" Aljeron echoed, incredulous. "Didn't you say you only saw about twenty rowing out to the ship on the Forbidden Isle?"

"There may have been more already on board, or they may have been joined by more somewhere along the way," Valzaan answered. "Go on."

"As I watched them run, I was gradually able to make out several Malekim carrying the women draped over their shoulders. It looked uncomfortable, but they were all there, and from what I could see, alive."

"Good, any confirmation of our hopes and suspicions is

welcome, even if in the form of a dream," Valzaan said, turning to the others. "Do not be daunted by the possibility that so many Malekim may be waiting for us. We are few, but we are not weak. You have already shown your ability to defeat two waves of Malekim in Nal Gildoroth, and you did not have the aid of Eliandir then. Though he will be engaged with the Vulsutyrim when we find them, do not underestimate the amount of fear a dragon can create among the Voiceless. As long as the women are alive and in need of rescue, and as long as we are alive to rescue them, there is hope!"

Valzaan moved back through their midst to the Great Bear, and as that conversation resumed, Joraiem settled back, immensely grateful for Valzaan's help in an awkward situation. He would have to remember to thank him in the morning.

"Was it really a dream?" Aljeron asked softly from nearby in the darkness.

Joraiem hesitated. "I don't know, Aljeron. I saw them, as clearly as the nighttime sky would allow. What that means and how it worked, I guess I don't really know."

Joraiem knew Aljeron wanted to ask more, or at least to say more, but he left it at that. At that moment, Joraiem realized just how much he had come to appreciate Aljeron as a friend. He understood when it was time to speak, and when it was time to be quiet. That, from Joraiem's perspective, was a pretty rare and precious quality. Joraiem made another mental note to express his thanks in the morning and closed his eyes.

For two days they continued their journey, Arintol, Sarneth, and the other two Great Bear leading them as they rode on through the mysterious ways of Lindan Wood. On the evening of the sixth day of Summer Wane, their third night in the wood, they camped again, with still no word from the draal granting or denying the completion of their journey. Joraiem wondered how far they had gone and if word might not ultimately come too late to be much good. What would the clan do if Sarneth's request was denied and yet the closest way out was the northern edge of the wood? Surely they wouldn't be made to go back the way they had come. That would not only be pointless, it would only prolong their time within Lindan and make more likely—though Joraiem was quite sure more likely still meant all but impossible—the possibility that someone in the group would figure out the key to the secret ways. Perhaps Sarneth had known all this and was banking on the likelihood that by the time a decision could be made and communicated, their goal would have been reached.

Whatever Sarneth knew or assumed, he seemed completely relaxed, sitting with Arintol, Margan, and Lorineth around the fire as twilight approached. Looking at the four Great Bear, Joraiem felt a pang of sorrow. Once, he realized, men and Great Bear had moved freely if not frequently among one another. How much was lost to the world of men now that the Great Bear were no longer known openly to them? How much could be regained if those ties could be mended and restored? It was hard to imagine much commerce of ideas or trade had ever transpired between men and dragons, but surely the relationship between men and Great Bear had been more mutually beneficial, though Joraiem could not think off hand of much Sarneth could learn from him or his people.

A large, dark form moving in the half-light beneath the trees drew Joraiem's attention. He studied the surrounding trees carefully, and though he could not make out anything in particular, he knew they were being watched. He picked up his bow and motioned to Aljeron, who was still eating his dinner. Aljeron seemed to understand the look in Joraiem's eyes and quickly but stealthily picked up Daaltaran, sliding the blade from the scabbard.

The four Great Bear were all standing now, their conversation over. Soon, everyone in the camp had stopped eating, talking, or doing anything but watching the shadowy trees.

"All of you, put your weapons down," Sarneth said softly but firmly. "You are surrounded by my people. They mean you no harm, and we must not greet them armed."

Joraiem set Suruna down, and Aljeron sheathed Daaltaran. They stood, still a little uneasy at the prospect of being surrounded by soldiers they couldn't see. Then, though he noticed no sudden or swift movements, Great Bear were everywhere. They filled every gap between every tree in every direction.

"Kuurgan," Arintol spoke now, "welcome within the light of our circle. What news do you bring from the draal that you come with so many of our people?"

Kuurgan stepped forward and made a quick, smooth gesture with one of his front paws. "The elders of the Lindandraal send word to you, Sarneth, that they have received your message, and I am sent back with greetings and welcome for your companions, especially to Valzaan, who is highly honored among us. Prophet, welcome to Lindan Wood." Kuurgan bowed his head slightly with these words.

Valzaan, bowing in reply, answered, "I am honored by your kind words and the favorable reception of the elders."

"Your story has been told," Kuurgan continued, "and your request has been considered. For many hours the elders met within the council chambers of the draal to consider what you ask. They have decided to grant your request. Though the law forbids the giving of passage to outsiders through the secret ways of Lindan Wood, the law was intended to protect the clan by protecting the draal, not to prevent acts of mercy that do not endanger us or to thwart the purposes of those who hate and oppose Malek. Pass through Lindan Wood with the blessing of the clan."

"Thank you, Kuurgan," Valzaan replied, "and thank the elders for us."

"I will, Prophet, but I will not see them again for a while, for they have sent me and these with me to accompany you."

"You are to escort us through the Wood?" Valzaan asked, his voice betraying a rare note of surprise.

"And beyond, if need be. We have been sent to help you destroy the Silent Ones who hold your friends."

Joraiem looked at Aljeron, who looked back, joy mingling with the surprise on his face. "Unbelievable," Aljeron whispered.

Joraiem just nodded. Soon, the Great Bear were gathered in the circle, and Joraiem counted three times to make sure he had it right. Kuurgan had brought thirty Great Bear with him, so with Sarneth, Arintol, Margan, and Lorineth, there were thirty-five total. Thirty-five Great Bear! He no longer cared that he had seen fifty Malekim through the eyes of the windhover. What were fifty Malekim if you had thirty-five Great Bear? What were a hundred Malekim for that matter?

He looked at the others, and he could see his hope reflected in their eyes. They, too, knew what this meant. The real question now was could they catch them, for with Eliandir to fight the Vulsutyrim, they would be able to handle the rest.

That night, the camp was truly merry. Valzaan introduced each of the Novaana and Synoki to the Great Bear, and Sarneth introduced the Great Bear to the Novaana, though Joraiem didn't even bother trying to keep track of their names. It had taken him two days to figure out which of the original four was Margan and which Lorineth, and he was under no illusions that he would be able to distinguish thirty-one more, especially when they were introduced by firelight.

The next day, they set out, eager for the day's ride, and the company of Great Bear divided into two groups, one running before them, and one after. All that day and all the next they ran, from just before dawn to just after sunset. And then, on the evening of their fifth day in Lindan Wood, the eighth day of Summer Wane, they reached the edge of the open plains.

They stopped at the tree line and gazed out over the wide-open space. It appeared both vast and empty after five days in Lindan. What's more, the Arimaar Mountains were not before them, though the northern tip of the range could be seen to the east. Rulalin and Aljeron stood beside Joraiem, and Rulalin looked north and west. "Agia Muldonai lies that way, beyond the Kalamin River and the Gyrin Forest, though hopefully our road ends here. I hope we don't have to take this any further. I'm tired of riding from dawn to dusk. I'm ready to end this."

"How will we know?" Joraiem asked.

"Eliandir, I guess," Aljeron answered, shrugging his shoulders.

"If he finds us," Rulalin added.

"He'll find us," Aljeron said.

"He'll come," Joraiem agreed, "and then we'll know if we ride on, or take our stand here." Joraiem looked around them at the Great Bear which surrounded them. "Either way, we will make the Malekim pay for Kelvan, and for taking the women."

Aljeron turned to Joraiem, his scarred face all smile as he stroked Koshti's soft fur. "Oh we'll make them pay, all right. Don't worry about that. We'll hear the heartscream of many Silent Ones before this is over. We'll soak the ground with their blood and burn what remains of their foul carcasses until nothing is left of them but the stains and the stench. That I promise you."

That night they did not build a fire. Sarneth and Valzaan agreed that the giant and Malekim had likely not passed this way yet, and they could not risk announcing by fire and smoke their presence should the enemy come in the night. So they established a watch along the tree line before them and waited.

"What if the giant and the others do come tonight," Elyas had asked earlier in the evening, "and we don't know where Eliandir is?"

"Then we will kill him ourselves," Rulalin answered. "We have thirty-five Great Bear, ten men, and a tiger. He can't kill us all."

"By himself, it is unlikely," Valzaan added. "But don't underestimate what the son of Vulsutyr is capable of, especially if he has the aid of fifty Malekim. The sons of Vulsutyr are not brutes or beasts, all might and no mind. They are cunning, strong almost beyond comprehension, and as fierce as a dragon in battle. Even Eliandir knows better than to take victory for granted, and we would do well to give the giant the same respect."

"Then what are we to do if they come?" Aljeron asked. "Do we just watch them run past and start chasing them all over?"

"I didn't say that we couldn't fight without Eliandir, I was simply making the point that the worst thing you can do on the eve of battle is assume you will win. Even if they do come tonight, Eliandir will likely be close at hand. Yes, I expect that before this night is through, we will see Eliandir again, one way or another."

"How do you know?" Pedraal asked.

"Have you forgotten the windhovers?" Pedraan said, giving his brother a smack on the head. "Think!"

"Yes, I have sent word of our location. He will be here."

And he was. In the middle of the night, as Joraiem lay half asleep, half watching with the others the open land beneath the quarter moon, Eliandir's swift, shining form glided down from the sky and landed by the edge of the forest. The men and Great Bear, roused from their sleepy watches by the dragon's arrival, followed Valzaan out to the red dragon.

"Your numbers have grown in your journey through Lindan Wood," Eliandir rumbled as he bent over to speak to them. "That is good, for the numbers of your enemy have grown too. Until recently, there had been but thirty Malekim with the Son of Vulsutyr, but a few nights ago that number doubled to almost sixty. Then, last night, more joined them. I would guess that some seventy-five or eighty Voiceless run now behind the Vulsutyrim."

"Seventy-five or eighty!" Valzaan exclaimed. "I would not have guessed so many Malekim would be moving together so far from Agia Muldonai. Malek has become far more active abroad than I had imagined."

"Of course he is active, Prophet," Eliandir answered. "His dark and twisted heart couldn't possibly remain at rest. He doesn't know what rest is. Evil doesn't sleep."

"How long before they reach us here?" Valzaan asked.

"Tomorrow night. Tonight they will camp one last time near the Arimaar Mountains. It is the last shelter they will find during daylight until they reach the Kalamin. It is my guess that when the sun sets, they will set out along the edge of Lindan and will not rest or sleep even by daylight. They know that they are being watched. The Vulsutyrim is aware of me, I am sure of it. He watches the skies carefully, even though he no longer tries to hide from me. He knows his great hope now is speed and likely thinks that if he passes beyond my realm, I will let him go."

Valzaan nodded thoughtfully. "When they set out from the mountains, there can be no rest between here and the Kalamin. I am torn. If we wait, it would take them most of the first night to get this far from the mountains, and they would likely be growing at least somewhat weary. By the same token, think how weary they would be if we allowed them to pass by and then followed them on the way, taking them the following day. Still, both options are risky. They may shadow the wood as long as it doesn't take them too far out of their way, since the edge of the forest offers some shelter in case things should go awry. They may not. If they are planning to run without stopping, they may head more openly out into the plains right away, and we may miss them in the dark if we stay this far away.

"It would be a mistake to stay," Sarneth said firmly. "They could pass and we might never know. Even if we did know, if we gave them too wide a berth, we might never catch them. We were not able to close the gap before, and it would be foolish to assume they will fatigue more quickly than we. At first light, we should move east along the trees. There are places all along the perimeter of Lindan Wood that would be suitable for ambush. When we agree upon one, we can camp there until they come. We have come a long way already, and we are as weary as we are going to be. One more day of light travel won't make much difference. It is time to bring this to conclusion."

Aljeron was nodding and he quickly surveyed the faces of the other men near him. "I agree. I think we all do. We're ready. I don't think any of us could bear to let them past and then have to take to the road again. We'll do what we need to do, here and now. We'll go wherever you want us to go tomorrow, however far, so that we are in the best possible place to intercept them, but we don't want to wait any longer."

Valzaan stood silently, listening. "Then we're agreed. Tonight we will sleep. At dawn, we move east."

Midmorning found them already several hours east of the place where they had spent the night. Joraiem had slept soundly and well, a gift from Allfather, for surely this was going to be one of the longest days of his life. Though he knew this was what battles must normally be like—two armies marching toward one another, perhaps even camping within sight or sound of one another—it still seemed odd to be planning for it as you would plan an outing with friends or a birthday party or a wedding. The Black Wolves in Sulare had come upon them without warning, and they had defended themselves as they must. Likewise, in Nal Gildoroth, they had done only what was needed to protect themselves and get out alive. Today felt fundamentally different. They were maneuvering to find the best possible spot for ambush, so that in the night they could fall upon their enemy and destroy them utterly, without parley and without quarter.

It wasn't that Joraiem believed Malekim deserved mercy of any kind, or that he had any misgivings about killing them. He knew that they would not hesitate to kill him, nor would they ever consider a parley if it was offered. Surrender was not a possibility. They would fight until they won or they were dead; it was really that simple. Still, there was something odd about scheduling a battle, about the certain knowledge that on this day, after the sun went down, there was going to be a life and death struggle somewhere on these beautiful plains, not far from the peaceful shade of these grand and mighty trees.

Joraiem looked around him, closed his eyes, and breathed deeply. It was a splendid summer day. High above, branches of trees swayed in the slight breeze, which rustled the large green leaves and swept the thick green grass nearby in a southerly direction. When he strayed just half a span to his left, he was riding in the morning sun, already hot though well before midday. It was the ninth day of Summer Wane, and it was going to be a hot one. Still, the warming glow of the morning light on his face and arms was welcome. It felt good to ride in the sun again, even if the brightness made him squint and the heat made him sweat. They were small nuisances, and on a day like today, they served as simple reminders that he was alive.

If not for the large company of Great Bear accompanying them, Joraiem might have been able to imagine this as a simple riding expedition, out for a tour through some of Kirthanin's less frequented climes. He tried to imagine what was going through his companions' heads. None of them were any more experienced with psychological preparation for battle than he was. Were they reviewing Caan's combat lessons, trying to remember everything he had said about the nature of battle and the keys to combat? Were they visualizing themselves wielding their weapons, cutting down Malekim or crushing them with battle-axe or war hammer? Perhaps they were reliving their brief engagements in Nal Gildoroth, trying to remember how it felt to have no time to think or ruminate, only time to draw, defend, and react.

Maybe they were thinking about anything else, anything at all, anything that might take their minds away from what was coming. Though Joraiem was not able to put the coming battle completely out of mind, it was his own desire. It would be time soon enough to draw Suruna, to take his stand against the Silent Ones and the giant, to rescue Wylla from their hands, should Allfather grant his wish. For now, he just wanted to think about something else.

He was most successful when his thoughts turned homeward. Perhaps it was the summer sun and wide expanse of green grass that drew him back to so many summer days spent running in the rolling green hills near Dal Harat. Perhaps it was the realization that for the second time in his life, he was hunting a Malekim, this time many Malekim, and that this very day, before he slept again, he was going to have to kill again. This time, Evrim wasn't with him, and Joraiem couldn't help but wish he was. He wanted the encouragement of Evrim's silent but steadying presence. He wanted the familiarity of a friendship that was as old as he was.

He wondered if Kyril was promised to Evrim yet. Surely Monias had agreed to the suit, if Kyril wanted it as Evrim believed she did. The family was probably preparing for the wedding even now. Elsora would be planning a feast for the whole village, and Monias would be working on his speech. He always labored over having just the right words to say on big occasions. And probably, they all assumed Joraiem was frolicking in Sulare, enjoying the lessons, training, and leisure of the Summerland. Wouldn't they be surprised when they learned what he had really been doing!

For his mother's sake, at least, it was good she didn't know yet. She had worried enough when he played with friends as a boy. This would be one of those things only safe to tell her after it was over. Joraiem wouldn't have minded, however, being able to pick his father's brain before evening came. It would be good to know what he would do on a day like today. Joraiem was sure he would have good advice, and even if the advice wasn't that good, Monias's advice usually came with a good story, and he could use the distraction.

His thoughts drifted back to Wylla. She had seemed alive and in good health when he had seen her through the eyes of the windhover. Still, he couldn't imagine what a wearying thing it must be to have been held captive by a host of Malekim and a giant for almost a month. He hoped it hadn't changed her too much, that the unpleasant if not evil memories would go away. He meant to help her replace them with happy memories as soon as she would let him. He would help her any way he could, and he would start helping her tonight.

The more Joraiem thought of Wylla, the more he ached for the day to pass. If they were weary of the chase, how much more were the women weary of their flight? Wherever they were right now, they must be dreading the setting of the sun. They must be dreading another night's travel on the shoulders of their captors, bouncing up and down with every step and aching with every league. They probably didn't know that the leg of the journey they would soon begin would continue without rest or sleep until they were beyond the Kalamin and possibly beyond hope of rescue at all. They must have known, though, that with each passing day, their hope of rescue grew slimmer, for the further north they moved and the closer they came to the Holy Mountain, the closer they came to Malek.

Joraiem pressed his horse on, determined. *It must be tonight. Whatever it takes, we must rescue them here and now. We are running out of time. Soon there will be no tomorrow. It must be tonight.*

Though the days were getting shorter, daylight still lasted well into First Watch. Valzaan insisted they find their place a few hours before dark. "We will have to fight in the dark," he said, "but we should see the ground on which we will fight in daylight. We will pick the ground, and we must use it to our advantage."

And so, about the Eleventh Hour, with the sun still hanging well above the trees and plains in the west, the Great Bear stopped, conferred, and approached Valzaan. "This is it, Valzaan," Sarneth said. "The tree line here is dense so that we can hide within it, but not too dense that we won't be able to rush out quickly. The downward slope of the ground is smooth for many leagues. Our visibility will be excellent, even with just the stars and quarter moon. If they pass anywhere remotely close to us—and they must—we will see them. Unless they intend to head due north toward the more populous plains of Suthanin, which would defy all common sense, they must come this way. This is our place."

And so they stopped. The men tethered their horses several trees deep inside Lindan, hoping the horses would be well rested when the enemy came. Together they stood with the Great Bear, looking out beyond the trees and surveying the wide plains. Sarneth was right; it was an ideal spot. Not only did the ground slope gently and evenly down, away from the wood, but just east of them the tree line dipped south sharply, so that from where they were, they could survey the whole corridor between the curving northern tip of the Arimaar Mountains and Lindan Wood. The Vulsutyrim and Malekim approaching from that direction would be visible for some time before they even arrived at the place where the ambush would be waiting.

Sarneth and Valzaan led them out of the trees. As the last rays of daylight slanted across the horizon, Sarneth, Arintol, and Valzaan walked together across the sloping ground, talking and pointing. Joraiem wondered what they were saying, but he knew better than to ask. Valzaan would tell them when he was ready. He turned instead to walk with Aljeron and Rulalin. "What do you think, Aljeron? Is this a good place to kill some Malekim?"

"Any place is good for that."

"I meant, is this a good place for our ambush?"

Aljeron shrugged. "I suppose so. I just wish we didn't have to. I wish we could sit here, right here, weapons drawn, waiting. I don't want to come rushing out of the trees under cover of darkness and attack them from behind or the side. I want them to come over that rise there, and I want them to see me here waiting, with Daaltaran and Koshti, waiting to kill them."

Joraiem understood the deep and burning hatred Aljeron felt for the Malekim, but he still found it fascinating that his friend, who was really quite gentle most of the time, carried it around ever smoldering within. What must it be like to live like that?

"We're going to be attacking a superior number of Malekim who, along with a giant, are holding some of our own hostage. There's still plenty of courage required, and no loss of honor for the ambush we're laying."

"I know," Aljeron answered. "I just don't like it."

"Well, I don't care how we do it, I just want to do it soon. I can't stand this waiting," Rulalin said. He drew his sword. "My sword is ready to sing its battle song."

"And mine will sing too."

"The sun is going down," Joraiem said. "If Eliandir is right, it won't be long."

They turned and walked behind the others to the tree line. Valzaan and Sarneth were moving up and down it, examining the views and placement of specific trees. Eventually, they summoned everyone together.

"Let us make sure we are all clear on our roles tonight," Valzaan said. "If you have any questions, ask as we go. All right?"

There were general nods of agreement and some growls of assent from the stone-faced Great Bear. Joraiem felt again deep gratitude for their presence. He couldn't imagine sitting here in the twilight with just the other men, Sarneth, and Koshti, waiting for seventy-five or eighty Malekim.

Valzaan continued. "We wait for Eliandir. None of us moves until he comes. This is imperative. Our goal is not just to win the battle, but to rescue the women. The women are alive, but their lives will be in danger almost as soon as the battle begins. Don't think for a moment that the enemy will just let them go. If they have a chance, they will kill them all.

"So our first objective is to get the women. That's why we wait for Eliandir. He will draw the giant away from the Malekim, and in so doing will cause confusion in their ranks. We must take advantage of that confusion. We can't give the Malekim time to realize what is happening, time to think about anything other than saving their own ugly hides. They must from that first, critical moment be fully and totally engaged in the struggle of survival, the only force that can override all their prior instructions and loyalties.

"So when the giant is drawn away from the Malekim and panic sets in, it will be time for us to strike. This is what we want. Sarneth?"

Sarneth stepped forward. "The first attack will come from us," he said, motioning to the other Great Bear, who nodded silently among themselves in reply. "The Malekim are our ancient enemy, and the best way to exploit the dragon's disruption will be for us to fall upon them immediately."

"What about us?" Aljeron began, cutting Sarneth off.

"I have only said we will begin the fight," Sarneth said. "We will move in two groups. I will lead half of our number here on the eastern part of our line, attacking their left as they turn to face us. Arintol will lead the other half in an arc, to come around from the west, attacking their right. If Allfather smiles upon us, they will divide themselves as they turn to meet us, some to face me and the rest to face Arintol.

"Now, when you see this division, you will ride as swiftly as you can into that crack and cut through their midst. In all likelihood, you will find the women there, probably under a light guard. You must kill that guard as quickly as possible, and then you must take the women onto your horses and keep going! Do not turn around and bring them back this way. However the battle goes, the safest place for you will be straight ahead. We will try to keep the Malekim so busy they cannot follow. If we fail, then you must flee until you are beyond their reach. Kel Imlaris is several days to a week in that direction, south of the Kalamin River, and even if the worst happens, you should be able to outrun them and gain safety that way. Again, if Allfather wills it and all goes as planned, you won't have to. You will be able to watch from a distance and return when we have finished."

"I will not just ride on while the battle rages behind me," Aljeron said, barely concealing his scorn. "I have not crossed the Southern Ocean and ridden half the length of Suthanin to let others fight my battle for me."

"No, you haven't," Valzaan replied. "You have come to rescue your friends, and that is precisely what you will do. If Caan were here he would join you. A good soldier never puts himself above the objective he is fighting for. You must humble yourself to perform your duty. And don't be too sure you will have such an easy time of it. Once the Malekim realize what you are there to do, they may just as easily disengage from the Great Bear and surround you. It may be a very bloody path you forge to lead the women to freedom after all."

"May Allfather shine his favor upon me," Aljeron growled under his breath.

Valzaan and Sarneth reviewed the plan again, positioning the groups accordingly. Sarneth chose a detachment of Great Bear and settled them along the eastern edge of their line, and they all disappeared into the undergrowth of the wood to keep watch over the ever darkening plains.

Likewise, Arintol settled the other half of the Great Bear along the western edge of their line, and they too sat down to watch. Valzaan gathered the men between the two companies of Great Bear, making sure that their horses were ready to be mounted at a moment's notice. When he was finished, he pulled Joraiem aside.

"Joraiem, I know you are eager to rescue the women."

"I am."

"Yes, you have your own particular reason, I know."

Joraiem stared, open-mouthed. "How?"

Valzaan smiled. "I am old and blind, not dead. Anyway, you must understand now, before the battle comes, that I may need you. You are the only archer we have left, and if I need you, you will have to let the others go and do what I tell you. Do you understand?"

Joraiem's heart sank. He had not been any happier than Aljeron about the prospect that they might be only tangential to the real work of the battle, but he had at least been glad that they would take charge of rescuing the women. He didn't like the thought of Wylla not finding him there for her when the time came.

"Joraiem?" Valzaan repeated. "Do you understand?"

"Yes, I will do what you need me to do."

Valzaan patted him on the shoulder. "Good. I hope there

will be no need to deviate from the plan. But, I wanted you to be ready, just in case."

Joraiem joined the other men, now sitting cross-legged in a semi-circle, the open side facing the now almost completely dark tree line.

"What did Valzaan want?" Aljeron asked.

"He wanted me to be ready to go with him if necessary, if things don't go according to plan."

"Lucky devil," Pedraal said. "You may actually get to fight then."

Joraiem hoped the dark hid his grimace. "I am coming with you unless something goes wrong," he answered evenly. "And if something goes wrong, I'm not sure any of us will be lucky."

"So what are we going to do now?" Mindarin asked, leaning over to whisper in Wylla's ear in the darkness.

Wylla shrugged and whispered back, "I don't know."

She had never spoken more truly. If the idea of escape had been daunting before, it was overwhelming now. It had been bad enough to watch the number of Malekim running with them swell to more than double. And now this.

She felt like giving up. The feeling surprised her a bit, but she didn't think she had the strength to fight it. It felt like the only rational thing to do. She had known all along they might not ever get away—she was not a fool. And yet, she had never believed she would be broken, but that was the only word that described what she felt.

"Wylla," Bryar spoke. "We can't give up now."

"Why not?"

"Because if we give up, we will die. You saw what we saw tonight."

"That's why I give up."

"No, not that," Mindarin jumped in again. "The mountains. We've reached the end of them. If we are headed to Agia

Muldonai, the plains remain between us and the Kalamin River. We're running out of time."

"And what do you suggest?" Wylla said sharply, sorry instantly for the edge in her voice. The hopelessness of their situation wasn't Mindarin's fault. She was only trying to hold despair at bay.

"I don't know," Mindarin's answer came back softly. Wylla looked at her, surprised that the woman had returned a gentle reply. She almost regretted they wouldn't have a chance in better circumstances to try to forge the friendship that had eluded them in Sulare.

"Neither do I," Bryar echoed, "but we can't give up, not now. There will be time enough in the Forest of Gyrin or in the caverns of Malek beneath the Holy Mountain for despair, but not yet."

Movement across the dark room silenced them, but not before Wylla managed to muster a nod, acquiescing to Bryar. Wylla realized as they turned away and lay down again, that despite their own remarkable strength, it had somehow been imperative to them that she not give up.

She felt dishonest. What good did it do to give them false hope? She had given up. This morning they had stopped as usual, shortly before dawn, and Ulutyr had led them into the foothills of what must have been the very northern tip of the Arimaar Mountain range. As the Malekim had dropped them to the ground, a feeling that despite the painful jolt was always a blessed relief, a deep voice greeted them from within the cave. Wylla looked up, her mind scrambling to put the voice in context, and saw him. At first she thought he could have been Ulutyr's twin, except for the scruffy beard and bushy eyebrows. Eventually, she realized that he was also a little shorter than Ulutyr, and his hair was laced with gray. Of course, none of that really mattered. Only one thing did, and Wylla resigned herself to it now: If escape had been impossible with one Vulsutyrim, it would surely be impossible with two.

10

WHAT WORDS CANNOT SAY

JORAIEM CROUCHED IN THE darkness. The sunlight had left them more than an hour ago, and the small talk that held back the nervousness had disappeared with the light. Gone were the jokes about how much their fathers had omitted when preparing them for the Summerland. Gone were the discussions of what they would do first when they returned to Sulare with the women. Gone were the speculations about what Caan was doing right now, even as they waited for the enemy. All of this was replaced by watchfulness. They didn't stir, didn't speak, and hardly even breathed.

As they waited, the minutes seeming like hours, a sudden movement nearby attracted their attention. Valzaan rose rapidly, staggering a little bit before steadying himself with his staff. For a long moment, he simply stood, seeming to gaze straight ahead. Then he mumbled something to himself, something that sounded a lot like, "It can't be."

Valzaan started off through the darkness toward the position where Sarneth waited with his company of Great Bear. Joraiem turned to Aljeron. "Did you hear that?" he whispered.

"I think so. Did he say, 'It can't be?' "

"I think he did."

"What do you think that means?"

"I don't know, but it doesn't sound good."

The others crowded in around them, at least as close as they could get with Koshti lying beside Aljeron. "What's going on? What is Valzaan doing?"

"We don't know," Aljeron answered. "Just wait."

Valzaan soon returned, moving swiftly past them toward Arintol. They watched his dim silhouette motioning as he spoke with the Great Bear captain, and they watched Arintol gather the Great Bear around him as Valzaan headed back their way.

"What's going on?" several asked at once.

"I will tell you if you give me a chance," Valzaan said impatiently. "The plan has not changed. You will wait until the Great Bear fall upon the Malekim before you drive through them like a wedge after the women. However, you should know that there are two Vulsutyrim traveling with the women."

"Two!"

"Just keep your posts and stick to the plan. Leave the giants to Eliandir and to me. It won't be long now."

A quiet but heated discussion broke out among them, and Valzaan grabbed Joraiem's tunic, pulling him a little distance away from the others. "This is precisely the kind of thing I meant when I talked to you earlier. I'm sorry, Joraiem, but I will need you with me tonight, you and your bow."

Joraiem's heart sank again. "All right. What am I to do?"

"Stay close to me and do as I say. Unless we are going to ask Eliandir to fight two Vulsutyrim alone, we will have to help him as we can, and the only weapon we have that can aid him is Suruna. I will need you in a position where you can shoot for their eyes. I will try to keep you at a safe distance, but it will be very dangerous. Do you understand?"

Joraiem nodded. "I will do what I need to do."

Valzaan placed his hands on Joraiem's shoulders. "Good. I have not said so before, Joraiem, but Allfather's hand upon you is not all that sets you apart. You are an admirable young man, and I'm not the only one who thinks so."

Joraiem blushed, for Valzaan had said this last with a smirk. He knew Valzaan was probably just trying to help him keep his mind off what he was about to have to do, but it was embarrassing all the same.

Joraiem returned to the others, who had regained their composure and renewed their vigil. He looked at them, sitting on the ground before their horses, watching him. He knew he needed to go with Valzaan, but he didn't want to.

"It's all right, Joraiem," Aljeron said, looking up as he stroked Koshti's fur. "You have to go."

"I do."

"We know. You're a great bowman, Joraiem. If anyone can help Eliandir tonight, it's you. Even if Caan were here, it would be you they needed."

"I'd rather go with you."

"We'll be fine. We'll tell you all about it after."

Joraiem nodded and turned away to join Valzaan. He sat beside the Prophet and ran his fingers lightly along the long smooth surface of Suruna's front edge, settling in to wait.

He didn't have long to wait. No more than half an hour later, a Great Bear runner informed Valzaan and Joraiem that the enemy had been spotted fifty spans beyond the edge of Lindan, running quickly westward. It was too soon to move, so they sat and waited, and now it was almost more than Joraiem could bear. He strained his eyes through the darkness, trying to see those they had come to fight. At last he could, and the sight was remarkable.

The Vulsutyrim ran shoulder to shoulder before the rest, their enormous figures towering above the earth. Seeing the one off the coast of the Forbidden Isle hadn't prepared Joraiem for how enormous they were close up, and if Valzaan's plan worked, he would be seeing them much closer up still.

Behind them, in the gloom, ran what seemed to be a dark herd of Malekim. Though dwarfed by the Vulsutyrim, they were still large and fearful as they ran, wave after wave. Joraiem wiped sweat from his brow, slung his quiver over his shoulder and drew an arrow. He nocked it on the bowstring and prepared to run behind Valzaan.

The Vulsutyrim and Malekim were now almost level with their hidden positions. Joraiem didn't have to strain his eyes to see them anymore. Valzaan began to move quickly westward through the trees, behind Arintol and his Great Bear. Joraiem followed. If he was going to be able to use Suruna, Valzaan would have to keep him ahead of the giants until Eliandir came.

Suddenly, with a roar that split the still evening air, a great flash of light and heat erupted before them, not far beyond the tree line. Eliandir had come. In the afterglow of his own flame, the great dragon swept down over the enemy, and as Joraiem watched, awestruck, the two Vulsutyrim stopped and drew their weapons.

As quickly as Eliandir had come, he disappeared, and as Joraiem's eyes adjusted to the sudden return of darkness, he studied the giants. The one closest to them had a great curved sword, the blade easily two spans long. The other giant, who was bearded, wielded a double-headed axe, the shaft of which was almost as long as the giant was tall. The Vulsutyrim whirled the cruel weapon in an arc above his head, no doubt a defense against another low pass from Eliandir.

There was no defense against Eliandir in mid-flight, however, and the next explosion of heat and flame was not for effect. It poured from Eliandir's mouth as he swooped down just spans above the plain between the wood and the enemy, and the giants and Malekim had to flatten themselves against the ground to avoid being burnt alive.

Eliandir circled wide to the west, where he landed some twenty-five spans away. Raising himself instantly to his full height, he fully extended his great golden wings and blew fire a third time from his mouth. As it gusted across the open field, Joraiem could see that the initial stage of the plan had worked. The Malekim stood or lay rooted to the ground while the Vulsutyrim moved toward Eliandir, instinctively splitting up to approach the dragon from two sides.

Swiftly and silently both groups of Great Bear rushed from the wood, their dark forms all but unnoticed by the Malekim, who were engrossed by the unfolding events. Joraiem watched the first wave of Great Bear crash into the Malekim and crush the bodies of dozens before they even knew they were in danger.

"Come," Valzaan whispered urgently. "Eliandir's advantage of surprise has already been neutralized. We must move quickly!"

Joraiem would later wonder about many things in the procession of events that followed, not the least of which was how Valzaan could move so quickly through the trees. Whatever sense or gift from Allfather compensated for his lack of vision, Joraiem wished he had some of the same. Joraiem tripped and stumbled twice over roots and even crashed painfully through a wild bramble bush that stripped gashes in his bare arms, but Valzaan seemed always to be steady and sure and three steps ahead.

Part of his problem was that he was trying to watch the battle as he ran. The Vulsutyrim were still arcing north and south to divide Eliandir's attention, but steady flurries of flame in both directions held them at bay for the moment. Still, Joraiem could see that Eliandir was maneuvering almost purely on the defensive now, and the giants were growing bolder between the fiery bursts.

At last, Valzaan reached the place he was looking for, and Joraiem followed the prophet into the open. They now ran even more quickly, down the slope, still in a northwestern direction. They were well west of the colossal combatants now, and Joraiem hoped that the attentions of the nearest Vulsutyrim was well and truly fixed on Eliandir. If he had turned away from the dragon at that point, just ten of his great strides would have brought him and his sword upon them.

When they were level with Eliandir, some twenty spans directly behind him, Valzaan dropped to his knees in the high grass. The dragon's great wings were still extended, though not completely, and his powerful tail was writhing like a massive golden serpent a couple spans off the ground. Flame continued to burst from his jaws at regular intervals, as the giants began to close in.

"Which is your better shot?"

Joraiem looked at the one south of Eliandir, with his back to the forest. He was moving in at an angle, his shoulder turned just enough that his face was almost obscured from them. Joraiem looked at the other, still twirling the long shaft of his ax, and he realized his front was much more exposed.

"The bearded one, north of Eliandir."

"Take aim. I'm going to light things up, and when I do, take your shot."

Before Joraiem could ask what Valzaan meant, the prophet raised his staff above his head and a wave of searing white light swept outward and upward like a vast dome above the whole field, bathing it in the piercing light. Joraiem squinted, struggling to adjust, worrying that he would lose his shot. He needn't have worried, though, for somehow Valzaan had managed to make the brightness fade around them, even while the wave of light intensified as it swept across the grass. The Vulsutyrim whirled his axe blindly, overwhelmed by the flash of light. Joraiem aimed, and his arrow flew.

As Joraiem was nocking a second arrow, the field of battle was rent by a terrific howl from the Vulsutyrim. He had dropped his ax as one of his hands grabbed wildly for the shaft buried in his neck. Eliandir leapt into the air and fell upon the giant with a great pounce, his front claws ripping into its flesh. Joraiem turned away.

"The other!" Valzaan called.

Joraiem turned to see the second giant, now largely recovered from the blinding flash, running enraged at Eliandir. Joraiem raised Suruna, tried to gauge the giant's range and speed, and fired. Again the arrow's flight was true, and though Joraiem had no hope of bringing the giant down, the arrow buried itself deep in his shoulder.

This time there was no howl, for Eliandir had turned, and the giant knew that the smallest lapse at this moment would bring death. With his sword in his right hand, he faced Eliandir warily. For a moment, the two ancient foes circled, as if taking measure of one another. With a slight dip of his head, Eliandir sent flame licking out across the grass at his enemy. The giant, anticipating this attack, quickly ducked and rolled on his good shoulder, coming up a few steps closer to Eliandir, swinging his sword desperately at the dragon. Eliandir swept his left wing out to meet the blow and blocked the giant's arm before he could finish his swing. Then, faster almost than Joraiem's eye could follow it, Eliandir's tail whipped around the other direction, smashing the giant on his wounded shoulder.

The Vulsutyrim was down, but he didn't stay down. Though Eliandir pounced again, the wounded giant somehow managed to evade him. He started to rise, and Joraiem fired again. The arrow landed with a sharp thud in the middle of the giant's back. This time, furious, the giant howled mightily, his wounded but free arm flailing behind him as he tried to grasp the protruding shaft in his back.

He swung around to face Joraiem and Valzaan, as though he had forgotten the dragon, but he didn't start toward them. Instead, he just stared as though trying to see who or what had twice wounded him. And then, as though suddenly aware again that his true danger was on the other side, he started to turn back, sword raised.

He never got a chance to use it, however, for as he turned, Eliandir's razor-sharp claw tore him open across the chest. A second strike from Eliandir's other claw ripped through the soft flesh of his neck, and the giant tottered for a couple of seconds before falling dead as a stone into the grass, his sword dropping softly beside him.

Eliandir reared up to his full height, and raising his head to the moon and stars, blew another great streak of flame into the nighttime sky. He stretched his wings out and up until they were raised as far above his head as they would go. Then, as suddenly as his demonstrative celebration had begun, it was over. Silently and swiftly, Eliandir leapt into the sky, circled quickly overhead, and flew back in the direction of the others.

As Eliandir flew away, Joraiem turned to Valzaan. The prophet was still, leaning on his long, sturdy staff. Both the King Falcon carved on top of it and Valzaan himself appeared to be gazing at him, looking very much alike at that moment, except for the wide smile on the prophet's face.

"Remarkable," was all that Valzaan said at first, his head shaking a little bit. "And you thought a few months ago that tracking and killing a Malekim would be the big accomplishment of your life. You have a gift, Joraiem, and only Allfather knows how you are going to use it."

Joraiem shrugged, embarrassed. "There wasn't anything spectacular about what I did tonight—"

"Nonsense, boy, nonsense," Valzaan cut in demonstratively, even waving the staff before Joraiem's face. "It is not humility to deny the wonder of what Allfather has accomplished through you. Few, if any, could have stood here without cowering in fear. Even fewer could have made the shot you made from this distance, perhaps thirty spans away, putting that arrow right into the giant's neck. Even had it been midday, it would have been a difficult shot. Your next two shots were also masterful. You were like a dog nipping at his heels, or a bird swooping in to peck a bit of flesh before swooping off again. You kept him off balance and left him wide open for Eliandir too. Your instinct and timing were flawless."

Joraiem did not answer but looked across the field through the moonlight, which in the aftermath of Valzaan's brilliant display appeared fainter than it had before. The bodies of both Vulsutyrim lay motionless where they had fallen, their enormous forms protruding well above the grass that rose to Joraiem's knees and lower thighs. Joraiem shuddered. Even though they had been his enemy since that day Wylla and the others were taken in Nal Gildoroth, he had no desire to see what was left of their corpses. After what Eliandir had done to them, he knew a bog of blood must have formed in the depressions created by their fallen bodies. Joraiem had seen enough of death and battle to haunt his dreams for years to come. He had no wish to see more.

"Come," Valzaan said to him, placing his hand gently on Joraiem's arm. "Let's go and see what has become of the others."

Valzaan started to run at a smooth, even pace, across the field, and much to Joraiem's relief, he navigated a path between the fallen giants that was far from both. Joraiem ran behind him, watching only Valzaan as he ran. When the bodies had been left behind, he allowed himself to look beyond the prophet and to take in the wider horizon.

He hadn't known quite what to expect, but he hadn't imagined to find what he did: the complete absence of battle. He had no idea how much time had passed since the battle began. Perhaps it had been a quarter of an hour, maybe more. He didn't really know. And yet, however much time it had been, it had been enough for the Great Bear to do their part as well, for while a large number of Great Bear moved around the battlefield, he couldn't see a single Malekim on its feet. Nor could he see any of the Novaana.

Eliandir was not here as he had expected. The vast number of fallen Malekim, covering the field in scattered clumps, made for a grim sight, but he did not feel the same compunction viewing their death and demise as he had with the Vulsutyrim's.

"Valzaan and Joraiem," Arintol said as he approached them under the dim moonlight. "It is good to see you both. The sons of Vulsutyr are dead?"

"Yes," Valzaan replied simply.

"We thought they must be when Eliandir circled overhead twice a moment ago," Arintol replied.

"Where has he gone?" Joraiem asked.

"He headed off north and east," Arintol answered, "presumably to find your companions."

"Things here seem to have gone well," Valzaan added. "What tale do you have to tell, Arintol?"

"Malek's children were caught off guard as we had hoped. I would say that fully thirty Silent Ones died before one of them lifted a weapon. We drove them asunder, and the few caught in the middle were cut down by the men on horseback and the tiger. There was a brief and furious resurgence, but with fewer than fifty Malekim still alive, they were hopelessly overmatched. Whether falling back before us or flying in vain directly at us, their fate was the same."

"Any casualties?" Valzaan asked.

"Yes, five Great Bear, of whom two have returned to the Maker. Three lie wounded, though they will probably survive, and one man."

"Who?" Joraiem asked, fearing the answer as he added, "Is he dead?"

"It is the one you call Rulalin, and no, he is not dead, though his wound is serious."

"Where is he?"

Arintol pointed through the darkness. "You will find Sarneth watching over him."

Joraiem ran across the battlefield, sometimes leaping over the body of a fallen Malekim, sometimes having to go around a place where they had fallen two and three high. He came across a few Great Bear moving around the field as he went, but as soon as he was close enough to know that none of them was Sarneth, he kept going. At last he found Sarneth, and also Rulalin.

Sarneth was sitting in the high grass, his back to Joraiem, but even from where he was, Joraiem could see Rulalin's head resting in Sarneth's lap. His body was still, and in the darkness, Joraiem could not make out immediately the wound. He approached slowly, wondering what he would find.

Joraiem could hear Rulalin's breathing, both labored and raspy. His eyes were shut, but even through the darkness, Joraiem could see his eyelids twitching rapidly. As he stooped to kneel beside him, he could see at last, the long blood-soaked line that stretched across Rulalin's chest. Sarneth looked up from where he was sitting and nodded at Joraiem.

"How is he?" Joraiem asked, leaning over to whisper in Sarneth's ear.

"Holding on. He's awake. Go ahead and speak to him.

He'll be glad for the distraction, I'm sure. We've given him something for the pain that will make him sleepy, but it takes time to work."

Joraiem settled into the grass beside Rulalin and gently took his bloody hand in his own, "Rulalin," he said, leaning over him. "It's me, Joraiem."

Rulalin's eyes fluttered open, and after a moment he was able to focus on Joraiem. "Looks like you survived the giants."

"I did. I was at a safe distance the whole time. You were the one in real danger."

Rulalin coughed as he tried to speak. "Easy, Rulalin," Joraiem said. "Take your time."

"I wouldn't have been in danger if I hadn't been so slow. We flew out of the woods, Joraiem. You should have seen it. Koshti led the way across the plain. He was like a streaking flash of orange and black fur in the moonlight, a fury of fur if you will." Rulalin laughed at his joke and started to cough some more.

"Aljeron flew behind him across the ground between us and the Malekim like a madman, Daaltaran raised above his head. You should have seen him cutting and hacking at the Voiceless. I'll tell you, Joraiem, after coming all this way, it felt good to ride into battle. We swept through them and into an open space in the middle, where we found the women huddled on the ground under a guard of four or five Malekim. Koshti was upon the guard before they knew it, and both twins dropped from their horses, battle-axe and war hammer wreaking havoc. When the guards were dead, we set about freeing the women. I dismounted with Aljeron to help the twins, and in no time, just about every horse was doubled up and ready to go. I was the last to remount, and just as I was going to, I saw Mindarin slipping sideways off of my horse. Instead of mounting, I stepped over to help her back up, and when I did, she screamed.

"I turned and there was a Malekim. He sliced me open with a nasty looking dagger. I stumbled back, into the side of the horse, trying to raise my Azmavarim, but my chest was on fire and I couldn't, I just couldn't. Then, also out of nowhere, Synoki stepped his horse between me and the creature, and all I saw was that hammer from Nal Gildoroth flashing down. What happened after that I don't remember.

"When I woke up, Sarneth was here and the others were gone. He told me a small group of Great Bear had reached us just as Synoki killed the Malekim. Synoki rode off with one of the women behind him, I can't remember which, and Mindarin followed."

"Reluctantly," Sarneth added. "I am told my brothers who were guarding Rulalin had to growl at her to drive her away. Rulalin was in no shape to ride, and our main thought at that moment was to make sure the women were safe while we finished what we'd come to do."

"Sarneth, now even you understand how stubborn that woman can be." Rulalin turned to Joraiem, "How ironic, after all our history, in the middle of all that confusion, that Mindarin ended up on my horse! I was afraid she would be the death of me!"

"You aren't going to die," Joraiem said, though he was not at all sure he was speaking the truth. "You'll live to tell this story a thousand times to your children and grandchildren."

"Children and grandchildren," Rulalin echoed weakly, turning away with his eyes closed. Joraiem heard the pain in his voice and suspected it was not just the wound he was hearing.

"Hold on, Rulalin," Joraiem said, squeezing his hand as he leaned over him. "You've done what you came to do. Hold on."

"That's right," Rulalin answered, opening his eyes again to look at Joraiem. "We've done it. We've fulfilled our vows. She's safe, Joraiem. I saw one of her brothers pull her up onto his horse. It doesn't matter what happens now. She's safe."

Joraiem could see it, Pedraal or Pedraan reaching down with his huge hand to pull Wylla up onto horseback. He could see her long black hair sweeping back and forth in the moonlight as she came to rest on the horse. He could see them riding off into the darkness, to safety. He suppressed for a moment the joy of the thought and bent his attention to Rulalin. "It does matter what happens now. Your life matters, which is why you must live. Whatever the future holds for you, for me, for any of us, you must not give up. Hold on."

Rulalin nodded slightly, but he didn't speak again. His eyes flickered shut, but they didn't seem to twitch and flutter as much as they had before. He seemed more peaceful. "Don't worry," Sarneth said. "This is not death but sleep that you see. The medicine is working now. Whether he ultimately has the strength to survive this wound, Joraiem, I don't know, but he isn't going to die now. Not here."

Joraiem stared at Rulalin's face as he set his hand down gently. His chest rose and fell rhythmically, his breathing came more smoothly, and Joraiem knew he was in a deep sleep. He hoped that wherever he went in his dreams, it would be bright and warm and peaceful.

He stood to stretch his legs and noticed that Valzaan was standing behind him. "Is there anything you could—"

"We will do all we can, Joraiem. His life is in Allfather's hands."

Joraiem nodded. That was the answer he expected, but he had needed to ask. He looked away from Valzaan and stared north and west into the dark plains, wondering where the others were and if they were already on their way back with Eliandir. He had time and opportunity now to let himself feel excited. So many days waiting to see Wylla again, and now the moment was almost here. He couldn't believe that at any moment she would come riding over the horizon and back into his life.

He suddenly felt nervous. He had promised himself over and over that he would never again be separated from Wylla, that as soon as he saw her he would declare himself and seek her hand in marriage. It was just about time to act upon those intentions, and he realized that despite the events of the past month, the prospect of speaking plainly and boldly to the woman he loved still overwhelmed him. Even so, he knew he had to do it. He had promised himself he would, and he owed it to Wylla to be forthright.

With nothing on the horizon, he turned back and saw over Valzaan's shoulder the gathering of Great Bear in the distance. They were standing front to back in a circle, their enormous paws resting on each other's shoulders. They began to sing. It was a deep, rich, resonant song, and it sounded almost as though they were singing of and to and with the earth itself. It was melodious and sad and slow. Valzaan turned in their direction and bowed his head slightly to the top of his staff. Joraiem looked back to ask Sarneth what was going on, but the Great Bear's eyes were closed and his lips moved soundlessly. Joraiem stepped over to Valzaan and whispered softly, "What is it?"

"They are singing the song of the dead. They are mourning the passing of their brothers."

"It is a sad song, but beautiful."

"It is, for it is not a hopeless grief. The Great Bear know that the prophecies have promised that Allfather will make all things new. They grieve, but they do so knowing they will see their loved ones again, in time."

"It is comforting," Joraiem answered, looking back over his shoulder at the place where Rulalin lay. "Valzaan, is all of life like this? Sorrow and joy, interwoven, intermingled? We win the battle but not without loss. Wylla returns tonight and we will be reunited, but Rulalin may die for his efforts to save her. Even if he lives, he may never forgive me for winning her heart. Is there no moment in this world of pure and unalloyed happiness?"

"There are some that are close."

"But not many, and none complete?"

"Not yet. There will come a day when we will know what joy really is, joy that is not mixed with sorrow and sadness. But that day is not yet, Joraiem. Not yet."

"I can't wait for that day," Joraiem said softly.

"Neither can I."

Joraiem waited by Valzaan's side as the Great Bear sang their song of mourning, and when they were finished, he sat down beside Sarneth to await the return of the others. Behind him, he could hear the Great Bear going about the work of gathering the fallen Malekim into mounds to be burned. Joraiem grimaced as he thought of the smell. He recalled the noxious odor of the burning Malekim on that distant beach as he had stood with Monias and Evrim, and he couldn't imagine that smell multiplied by eighty.

The sound of pounding hooves in the distance came to him before he could actually see the approaching riders. It was a welcome sound of thunder, echoing across the broad grassland. Soon, the horses and their riders appeared, and he rose to greet them. He could feel the vibrations of their footfalls beneath his feet, and it was to him the most welcome feeling in the world.

Koshti appeared first, leaping into view, still showing the energy and excitement of battle. Even though the enemy was gone, Joraiem thought he could still see in his bounding the heart of a cat on the hunt. Aljeron rode behind him, looking as though he was still hopeful for an occasion to put Daaltaran to use.

Joraiem, who had been walking toward them almost without willing it, like an insect drawn to the light of a torch, called out a greeting to Aljeron. "Welcome, it is good to see you."

Aljeron all but leapt from his horse, leaving Karalin behind. He grabbed Joraiem by the shoulders and shook him like a wayward boy. "Back from felling giants, eh? What was it like?"

"Remarkable, watching Eliandir do his work that is. My part was easy. Stand at a safe distance and pelt the Vulsutyrim with arrows."

"You make it sound easy. You probably put an arrow through an opening the size of a keyhole from fifty spans away. I know you, Joraiem. I'll have to get the real story from Valzaan."

Joraiem realized Eliandir had not returned. "Eliandir, did he not come to you?"

"He did," Aljeron answered, sounding puzzled. "He told us that the battle was over. That's why we have returned. We thought he was flying back ahead of us. Is he not here?"

"No."

Aljeron turned and surveyed the distant, dark outline of the Arimaar Mountains. "Gone already, then. Well, he said he was coming to kill the Vulsutyrim. I guess he's done what he came for. Still, I should have liked to thank him. It's a shame we won't see him again."

"Oh, you never know about dragons," Valzaan said, coming up behind Joraiem. "They come and go as they please. He may be back yet."

The others had come up around them, and Joraiem was peering at the twins, trying to figure out which of them had Wylla. They were both so broad, though, that he couldn't see who was riding with either of them. The others started to dismount. Aljeron helped Karalin down, and Saegan lowered Valia. Elyas and his sister, Bryar, hopped down, as did Darias and his sister, Calissa. Synoki lowered Nyan before dismounting himself, and Mindarin dropped from Rulalin's horse, which she had been riding alone. Finally, Pedraal dismounted with Tarin, and Pedraan got down with Wylla.

Joraiem felt his trembling legs start to move as he glided through the darkness past the others. Barely had Wylla's feet touched the ground when she was swept up off it again by Joraiem, taking her into his arms. He clutched her tightly and felt the joy of her response as she clung to him with all her might. Her hair fell all around his face, and it felt better than a warm summer's breeze. "At last," he said, his voice a hushed whisper on the brink of tears.

"Yes, at last," came the reply from Wylla, her face buried in his shoulder. He could feel her shaking, and he set her down. She did not let go. She stood hanging onto him as though she would fall if she let him go. "All this time, waiting for you to come," she said at last, when she was able to look up into his face. "I thought of a thousand things I would say to you when you came, but I can't remember any of them."

"That's all right, you don't need to say anything."

She leaned in against his chest and nodded her head. "You're right. There are some things words cannot say."

He stood and held her, tears of happiness falling from his eyes. He knew the others were standing all around them, but he didn't care. What did that matter now? She was safe and in his arms.

A quiet voice broke the spell. "Where is Rulalin? Do you know, Joraiem?" It was Mindarin, and it took a moment for Joraiem to realize what she had said.

Gently, Joraiem released his hold on Wylla, and opening his eyes, he found that the others were doing an admirable job of not staring. Mindarin stood nearby, as though she understood all too clearly what she was interrupting and hated to do it. Joraiem looked at her own tear-streaked face, and letting go of Wylla, said, "Come, I'll take you too him."

Joraiem led them to the place not ten spans away where Rulalin lay sleeping. His head was still in Sarneth's lap, and his breathing remained peaceful and even. They stood, gazing down in silence.

"He was wounded trying to help me."

"It wasn't your fault," Wylla said quietly, putting her arm around Mindarin.

Mindarin shook her head as the tears started again. "If I hadn't slipped, he would be all right. And I've been so horrible to him for so long."

"Mindarin," Joraiem began, "I talked with him before he went to sleep. He was glad he could help you, and he would do it again. He doesn't blame you."

Mindarin sobbed a little, then stooped beside him. She stroked his hair gently and whispered quietly into his ears. What she said, Joraiem could not hear, but when she was done she stood and wiped her tears from her eyes. "I will stay with him until he is well. I'm going to will him to live, if I can."

Wylla leaned over and gave Mindarin a hug. "If anyone can do it, you can."

Mindarin smiled and hung on to Wylla. "Thank you. Thank you for everything. You held us together. Now go on. Don't stand here with me. You have some catching up to do."

The two of them let go, looked at each other, and laughed. Joraiem smiled. He had seen the coolness between them before, of course, had understood at least some of the reasons for it, and now felt greatly relieved. If what they had been through together had helped them to overcome their problems, then maybe there was hope for him and Rulalin.

There was no time now to contemplate such things, however, for as soon as Wylla and Mindarin had parted, Valzaan was there, gathering them all together. "I know we are all weary, and before long there will be time for sleep. Before long, you will be able to return to the Summerland and enjoy the rest that can be found there. But, right now, we have one last job to do. The bodies of the Malekim must be disposed of.

Ladies, this is not something you need take part in. You have seen enough of them over the past several weeks, but I will need to borrow the men."

"You can borrow me too," Bryar said coldly. "I'd like to burn them myself."

Joraiem pulled Wylla aside as the others started off behind Valzaan. "Does she know?"

Wylla nodded. "She hasn't spoken until now. She hasn't cried, hasn't yelled, hasn't done anything."

"It probably hasn't really hit her yet," Joraiem said. "She's just been rescued, but what a hollow victory. I can't imagine how she must feel. If we'd caught up to you, and you hadn't been all right, Wylla, I don't know what I would have done."

"I know. I almost couldn't breathe until I saw you standing there in front of us."

"Wylla, there are a lot of things I want to say to you."

"I know, and there are a lot of things I want to say to you too, but you should go help the others. We'll talk later."

Joraiem paused. Part of him was glad for the reprieve, but he didn't want to put it off any longer. He wanted to say what he had to say and be done with it. But what would he do then, propose to her and go off to dispose of the bodies? Maybe she was right. He could go do what needed to be done and then tell her. She wasn't going anywhere. "All right," he said, pulling her close, "but before we leave this place, I will say what I have to say."

"Good. I want to hear it." She smiled as he pulled himself away and turned to go.

The sun was rising over the Arimaar Mountains. They had worked all night to build two great mounds. With a little help from Valzaan and his staff, two large fires had been ignited beneath the pyres, and the Great Bear had joined in the traditional ritual chant:

Child of Malek, born in flame,
Return to the fire from whence you came.
Return to the darkness, return to the earth,
You have no part in the second birth.

With the ritual completed and the fires at full blaze, the men and Great Bear retreated to the edge of the Lindan to watch from a distance.

The smell was every bit as unpleasant as Joraiem had expected, but fortunately a strong breeze was blowing out of the south and they were spared the full measure of the stench. As they sat under the eaves of the wood, Elyas asked, "Why aren't we burning the Vulsutyrim?"

Joraiem answered, "Valzaan says they aren't creatures of Malek and that the burning is not required for them. Leaving their bodies unburied is punishment enough. The birds will eat their flesh and gnaw their bones."

Wylla, sitting beside Joraiem and resting her head on his shoulders sat up at this and looked at Joraiem. "Would you take me to the place where they lie? I'd like to see Ulutyr one more time."

"Ulutyr?"

"Yes, he is the giant who captured us on the Forbidden Isle."

"Why do you want to see him?"

Wylla shrugged. "I think he's the reason we're still alive. The Malekim would have killed us long before now."

Joraiem gazed out over the plain in the direction of the fallen Vulsutyrim. "Eliandir wasn't gentle when he killed them. I'm not sure you want to see this."

By this point, though, Wylla was on her feet. "I do want to see it, actually. I've seen some grim things, recently. I think I can handle this."

Joraiem saw the determination in her face and acquiesced. "All right, I don't think I want to see it, but I'll take you."

He took her hand, something he had done a few times during the night, and they started across the field together. Behind them, Joraiem heard Aljeron say softly and sharply, "Where do you think you're going?" He almost turned to see if Aljeron had been talking to him, but he heard Elyas reply, "I want to see the Vulsutyrim up close too. Why can't I go?"

"Sit down," Aljeron hissed. "Do I have to spell it out for you?"

They heard no more behind them, and when Joraiem looked at Wylla, he saw that she was blushing, but with a smile on her face. They walked across the field, and except for the burning pyres and the awful smell, it was a beautiful morning. The sky was a radiant blue with just a few thin wisps of white cloud in the distance. The bright summer sun shone down upon them, radiating warmth. They walked quietly, almost reverently. They were going to a grave.

Joraiem was beginning to wonder if he had missed his way, if perhaps he had been turned around in the darkness of the night and not realized where he had been, when Wylla's gasp alerted him to the body lying in the distance. They approached, slowly, and Joraiem realized they were looking at the body of the beardless one who had wielded the curved sword. Wylla approached cautiously, circling around the other side to get a look at the giant's face. Joraiem followed her, only half able to make himself look at the decimated body.

Suddenly Wylla cried out and turned away from the Vulsutyrim, into Joraiem's arms, her hand over her mouth. "What is it?" he asked. "Is this the one?"

She nodded. "It's Ulutyr. His eyes, they're open. They were looking at me."

Joraiem looked over her shoulder. Sure enough, the giant's face was turned to the side and his dead eyes were wide open and staring through the tall grass. Hopefully, Joraiem thought as he looked at the gaping wound in the giant's neck,

Wylla had only seen the staring eyes. "His eyes are open, Wylla, but he isn't staring at you."

Wylla started to turn around, but Joraiem held on to her. She looked up at him. "Wylla, don't look again, please? You've seen what you came to see. Whatever he might have done for you, you don't want to remember him this way."

"No." She hesitated. "I don't."

They started back slowly through the grass. "Joraiem," Wylla said as they walked. "I know he was the enemy. You did what you had to do. You know I know that, right?"

Joraiem looked at her. She was gazing at him. "I know you do," he said. He knew, but he hadn't known until that moment that he wanted to hear her say it. He hadn't stopped to consider that she might sympathize with the giant, even though Valzaan had said the Vulsutyrim might be the only reason the women were alive. He shook his head. How complicated life was.

As they walked, facing the rising sun and feeling its warmth, Wylla slipped her arm in Joraiem's. "I don't ever want to let you go again, Joraiem Andira," she said softly, almost wistfully.

"Nor I you," Joraiem said, stopping in the middle of the field and stopping her. She looked up at him, a little startled. He felt his heart racing. This was the moment. He had to speak. "Wylla, every moment of the last month, every single moment, I have prayed that I would find you again, and that I would have a chance to say this. I love you. I love you more than I ever thought possible. I love you so much I don't even know if I can tell you properly." Joraiem wiped sweat off of his forehead. He was babbling, and he didn't want to babble. "I know this is sudden, but I want to be completely clear. I want to marry you, as soon as possible. I want to be your husband if you will have me. I want to—"

Wylla threw her arms around his neck. "Have you! Of

course I'll have you, silly. Why do you think I got so angry with you on the *Evening Star?*" She stepped back from him and wiped tears from her eyes. "I'm sorry about that, by the way."

"You don't need to be sorry about anything."

She hugged him tighter. "You know what marrying me means."

"Yes."

"You're willing to leave Dal Harat?"

"Yes, for you I'm willing."

"Joraiem, I am so happy." She held onto him for a long moment, then stepped back, her eyes glistening. "When?"

"Whenever you like."

"How about as soon as we get back to Sulare?"

"I can't think of a better time or place."

She threw herself against him again, and for a second time, he picked her up off her feet and held her close.

11

SUMMER'S END

RETURNING HAND IN HAND to the edge of Lindan Wood, Joraiem and Wylla found the others gathered around Valzaan.
Rulalin, awake now, was lying in the shade with his head in
Mindarin's lap, who stroked his hair. If Joraiem had not ridden with them to Sulare, he would not have believed how
much like mortal enemies they were only a few months before. Perhaps the baiting and ill will would return if Rulalin
survived and normalcy returned, but Joraiem suspected the
old grievances had herein been laid aside for good. Synoki
also sat beside them, almost as though watching over him.

It wasn't hard for Joraiem and Wylla to pick up the thread
of the broader discussion, which revolved around the one
question no one had given much thought to—what to do now,
in particular, where to go. Some of them were halfway home
and more, but it was only the tenth day of Summer Wane, and
their time in Sulare was not supposed to end until the last day
of Full Autumn. Many of them were not expected back until

the end of Winter Rise or Full Winter. And yet, by Valzaan's estimation, assuming that passage back through Lindan Wood was not an option now that their mission was complete, they were probably a month away from Sulare, even if they rode at a good pace. This prospect was not especially appealing to anyone. Taking the voyage to the Forbidden Isle into account, they had been traveling now for more than a month. The prospect of traveling for another, only to have to turn around so quickly and head back onto the road, was almost more than some of them could bear.

And yet, they all seemed to recognize that the larger vision for their time at Sulare could not be abandoned. They had come to the Summerland for many reasons. One of them was to learn to trust and love one another, and though the crisis had forced that to happen in many ways, they all agreed it would be good to spend time together in more settled circumstances as they had in Spring Wane and Summer Rise. Further, they knew that Master Berin would be eager for them to resume their studies.

Also of issue were some lesser questions. What should they do about Rulalin? It was not at all clear that even with rest and good care he would live, and he was certainly not in any shape to be making the long journey to Sulare. Whatever they were going to do, they were going to have to figure out what would be best for him and do it soon. Beyond that, there was the question of Synoki. He had come willingly from Derrion Wel, but now the women had been rescued and he was still a long way from his Werthanin home.

All this was being discussed when Joraiem and Wylla rejoined the others, and Joraiem was torn. He didn't want to ride all the way back to Sulare just to turn around a few months later and set out on the road any more than anyone else did. At the same time, he had daydreamed of marrying Wylla in the Summerland, as his father had married his mother, and of spending their first few months as husband and wife in that enchanted place. He felt robbed of his chance to enjoy the glory and wonder of the Summerland and wanted to go back.

His heart began to sink as some of the others discussed a possible compromise. What if they neither go home nor return to the Summerland? Instead, they suggested, they should go somewhere close by. Kel Imlaris, east of the Arimaar Mountains, for instance, or even Amaan Sul, north of them above the Kalamin River. It was even suggested that message could be sent to Master Berin and that he might be willing to go to the place where they ended up and continue their training there.

This was enthusiastically received by some, though those who lived not far from Sulare didn't like the idea of going further north or east all that much since they would have a long road home when it was finished, and they would be expected home shortly after the start of Autumn Wane. To this it was suggested that everyone could go when they needed to, that the usual workings of time in the Summerland had perhaps been abrogated by recent events.

"Do you think so?" asked Valzaan, who had been uncharacteristically quiet. "I keep hearing talk of what is practical or convenient, but I haven't heard anyone refer to the directives of the Assembly, which stipulate that your time in Sulare is supposed to last from the first day of Spring Wane until the last day of Full Autumn. Isn't that really the issue, whether the law that brought you to Sulare still applies?"

"We know what the law says, but obviously things have changed," Saegan answered.

"Have they?" Valzaan inquired.

"Of course. After all, the specifics of the law weren't important when you saw the light over the Southern Ocean. It didn't matter that we were supposed to be in Sulare then. We boarded the ship and headed off to do what Allfather was calling us to do, regardless of the Assembly's command. Does that not matter anymore?"

"It is true, the specific call of Allfather overrode the directive of the Assembly, and I doubt that any member of the Novaana would say it shouldn't have. But we are not talking now about the call of Allfather for you to go to Kel Imlaris or Amaan Sul. As far as I know, there is no specific reason why the law should not be heeded, other than inconvenience."

"What of Rulalin?" Mindarin asked.

"That is a separate question that will need to be answered regardless of where we go," Valzaan answered. "Though shorter, the trip to Amaan Sul or Kel Imlaris could be just as difficult for him."

"And Synoki?" Aljeron asked.

"Don't let me be a problem," Synoki said, entering the discussion for the first time. "Though I have long been away from home, I can find my way back from here."

Silence descended upon them and hope returned to Joraiem. The sooner they started out for Sulare, the sooner he and Wylla could be wed. As that thought was passing through his mind, Wylla squeezed his hand and called out, "Look!"

Joraiem turned, as did the others, to look out over the sunny grassland. There, sweeping low over the still burning pyres and trees was Eliandir, circling them in a wide but narrowing arc. "There he is," Wylla added. "I've never seen a dragon in daylight. Isn't he beautiful?"

"He is," Joraiem answered.

"And," Aljeron added, "perhaps he is the answer to our dilemma. Look, he has the garrion again!"

Except for Mindarin and Rulalin, the Novaana poured out from the edge of the wood to the place where Eliandir had landed.

"Prophet," Eliandir began in his magnificent voice, "you

have been busy since my departure in the night. The stench of Malek's children was evident ten leagues away. However, though unpleasant, it is not entirely without happy associations."

"You have returned with the garrion, Eliandir. Do I dare to hope that this means you are available to provide one last service?"

"I am grateful to you and to your bowman for your help in the night with the children of Vulsutyr. I thought I might repay you by taking you where you need to go."

Aljeron thumped Joraiem on the back, and Wylla squeezed the hand she was holding. Joraiem blushed as several of the others smiled his way.

"You are not in our debt, Eliandir, but we would be grateful if you could take us to Sulare."

"I can and will, but we should go soon. I might be able to have you there by sundown if we leave now. Can you all fit?"

"Yes, we should be able to," Valzaan answered, thinking out loud. "We will be adding the eight women, but we won't be carrying Synoki, Caan, Ulmindos, his two sailors or Sarneth."

"No Sarneth?" some of them echoed.

"I am home now," Sarneth answered from behind them, "and my purpose for traveling to Sulare has been served already."

Several tears and hugs followed. There were many exchanges of thanks, of well wishes, and of hopes to meet again some day. At last they decided there was no point waiting any longer. The Great Bear could attend to the horses and the disposal of the Malekim, and Synoki was just as eager to start his journey home. They loaded him and his horse with all their leftover supplies, and after taking a moment to speak with Rulalin before he left, he started across the open grassland.

"It's strange," Joraiem said, "even after all he went through with us, even endangering his life, I just never found myself at ease with him."

"I know what you mean," Aljeron answered. "I guess it just shows how strong and how wrong first impressions can be."

"I guess it does." Joraiem watched Synoki go and wondered what life would be like for him now that he was back from his long sojourn on the Forbidden Isle. Where would he go and what would he do? Slowly, Synoki disappeared into the horizon, and it was time for the rest of them to go.

They lifted Rulalin into the garrion first, and Mindarin sat in the corner as Rulalin lay stretched out along one of the walls. The others climbed in and took a seat. It was crowded, like before, but there were no complaints. The men were talking about getting to fly again, and the women were excited about the prospect of doing it at all.

Joraiem and Wylla came in just about last and sat side by side against the door when Sarneth closed it behind them. Eliandir wasted no time in getting away, and soon they felt the garrion rising off the ground. They circled in ever-widening arcs until they were high above the battlefield and Lindan Wood, and soon they were speeding south toward Sulare. It felt to Joraiem like going home.

It must have taken longer than Eliandir expected, because it was well after dark when they arrived. The slanted rays of sunset slipping from the west through the slat windows had long since disappeared when Eliandir began to circle downward. Joraiem found his heart beating madly as he moved to undo the interior latch. He opened the door and stepped out into the cool night air and fresh ocean smell of the Summerland. The soft moonlight illuminated the gardens and grounds of the area surrounding the Great Hall. Eliandir had set them down on the wide avenue leading from the bridge to the front door of the Great Hall.

The others filed out silently, beaming. It was a curious moment of sheer happiness and sober reflection. They had journeyed so far and been through so much since their departure from this hallowed ground, and now they had returned beyond all hope and against great odds.

Joraiem turned to Wylla and drew her close as he put an arm around her shoulder. "We're back," he whispered.

She didn't answer verbally but smiled as she ran her hand across his chest and leaned upon his shoulder in reply. It was answer enough.

As they gazed at the freshly rediscovered beauty of Sulare and deeply inhaled the clean, fresh air, a burst of light flooded them from the Great Hall where one of the front doors had just swung open. Three figures stood silhouetted in the light, Master Berin, Ulmindos, and Caan, who leaned on a thick staff like a walking stick. Master Berin started out down the wide avenue with Ulmindos and Caan close behind.

"You are back," he said at last as he reached Tarin and Valia first, clasping them tightly to himself. "Caan and Ulmindos told me about the garrion and Eliandir, but I almost couldn't believe it. Now I have seen both with my own eyes. Eliandir, noble son of your noble father, welcome to Sulare. You are most welcome here."

Eliandir dipped his head slightly, answering, "Thank you, but I am bound tonight for home. My journey is over, and the mountains call to me."

"We are ever in your debt," Valzaan said, "and may Allfather guard your wings and guide your flight. Go in peace."

Eliandir's head dipped slightly again, but this time he said nothing as he leapt into the air and circled once, twice, then took up the garrion. With a parting cry from the dark sky above, a cry that pierced the quiet stillness of the night air and gave them shivers, Eliandir glided away west in the direction of Derrion Wel and the Arimaar Mountains.

"Well," Master Berin said at last. "Let's not stand around out here. Come in and eat. I want to hear all about your adventures since leaving Derrion Wel."

"First we must make arrangement for Rulalin," Valzaan said, motioning to the place where Rulalin reclined on the grass. "He needs attention before we do anything else."

Master Berin walked to Rulalin, stooped over him and made a cursory examination of the wound, now bandaged with the bloody remains of the shirt he was wearing when he received it. "I'm sorry, Valzaan," Master Berin said gently as he stood again. "I didn't see the boy at first. We will take him to Falin and Merya's."

Master Berin sent Aljeron with Ulmindos to get a stretcher from the storerooms below the Great Hall. He held Joraiem back to help Aljeron when he returned and sent the others inside to wait for a late dinner.

"Master Berin, if you will allow me," Mindarin said, lingering, "I'd like to go with Rulalin."

"There's no need, Mindarin. He'll be well taken care of, I assure you."

"I'm sure he will, but I'd like to go with him all the same."

Master Berin considered this. "Why don't you come with us so you know where he'll be, but return with us when we come back. He will need rest and you could use some supper. All right?"

Mindarin nodded, and soon Aljeron returned with the stretcher. They started off with Rulalin around the side of the Great Hall, winding through the grounds to the more densely cultivated and seldom visited northern side. Master Berin brought them through a small gap in a long, tall hedge, then to a gate that swung open on a narrow path that wound slightly downhill to a couple of large houses. One of them, Joraiem knew, was Master Berin's. The brightly lit house on their right was where Falin and Merya lived. Merya answered the door in her night clothes, holding a large lamp. When she saw them bearing Rulalin on a stretcher, she asked no questions but ushered them in, giving directions to them all, including

Valzaan and Master Berin. In about ten minutes, she had Rulalin's wound clean and freshly dressed, and Rulalin himself sleeping peacefully in a quiet room.

"See what I mean?" Master Berin said as he turned smiling to Mindarin as they made their way back to the Great Hall. "Rulalin is in good hands."

She nodded. "Still, I would like to visit him in the morning."

"I will speak to Merya for you."

When they entered the Great Hall, they found the others seated around a few of the bigger tables pushed together on the far side of the fountain. Joraiem took the seat beside Wylla and relaxed immediately. The food had just arrived, and they helped themselves to roasted lamb, a large assortment of fruits and vegetables, and lots of fresh bread. Memories of his first night in the Great Hall washed over him, but he was tired and hungry, and his growling stomach prompted him to join the feast. At first, they talked little and ate much, but eventually, as plates were emptied a second and third time, most sat back from the table and stretched out in more comfortable positions as Master Berin called for an accounting of their adventures since sending Caan back to Sulare.

Valzaan told most of the men's story, and Wylla was called upon by the women to tell theirs, but from time to time others chimed in. When it was time at last to narrate the previous night's battle, Aljeron told of the charge through the middle of the Malekim, and everyone asked Joraiem to speak of the battle with the Vulsutyrim. Joraiem was hesitant and embarrassed, but with a little aid from Valzaan, he made it through. Eventually, all had been told, and they sat in silence, wondering at it all.

"It is a remarkable story of an amazing journey," Master Berin reflected. "If only young Kelvan could have lived," he added quietly.

Bryar began to cry. Mindarin, who was beside her, put her

arm around her, and Bryar buried her face in her shoulder. Joraiem looked at Wylla, who seemed sad for Bryar's sake but also relieved that she was crying at last. Perhaps she had needed the warmth and safety of Sulare to do it.

Master Berin continued. "I've sent a messenger to Kelvan's family, and if Allfather is merciful to Rulalin, that will hopefully be the last message like it that I ever have to send. It is the first time that one of the Novaana entrusted to the care of Sulare has died during the six months they were meant to be here. I know the voyage was necessary, but it is a terrible thing all the same.

"Valzaan," he continued, "Caan's report about the Forbidden Isle was alarming. The Assembly will need a full report of Malek's presence and work there. Perhaps it is time to patrol the Southern Ocean again, to make additional travel to and from the Forbidden Isle difficult. Either way, I am curious of what you make of it all."

"I don't know what to make of it, save that there can be no doubt Malek was there. What he was doing there is unclear, but I would guess he is preparing for his third great assault. Whether we have discovered his work and presence there in time to thwart his plans, we may never know. In the end, I am satisfied we have done what we were summoned there to do. All we can do now is take the matter before the Assembly to see what the collective wisdom of Kirthanin decides to do, if Malek gives us a chance to do anything."

Master Berin nodded. "Well, there is still much to say and much to do, but I suppose it would be wise to get some rest. Malek's work and will is out of our hands."

"Master Berin," Joraiem said as the group rose to their feet. "Before we go, there is one more thing that should be said."

Master Berin looked at Joraiem in surprise. "Yes?"

"Wylla and I have an announcement." He looked at Wylla,

and she smiled, nodding for him to go on. "We'd like to get married, and we were hoping you and Valzaan wouldn't mind overseeing the ceremony, since we'd like to get married in Sulare."

Several mouths dropped open around the table, and Aljeron laughed out loud. Master Berin, when he was fully recovered, looked at Joraiem and said, "You really are Monias's son, aren't you?" Then he smiled. "I'd be delighted to do my part, and Sulare has seen a few weddings in its time, so the request is not as unusual as it might appear. Though," he added, "I'm not sure we've had any involving the royal family of Enthanin. This will be quite an honor."

Valzaan also nodded. "I would be happy to participate."

"When were you thinking you'd like the wedding to take place?" Master Berin asked.

"We were thinking a week from today," Wylla said, "on the seventeenth day of Summer Wane."

"A week from today it is. Any other announcements?" he asked, scanning the room.

When there was no answer to his question, he added, "All right, then perhaps now we can all go to bed. I think we've had enough surprises and excitement for one day."

They rose from the table, and the other Novaana gathered around Joraiem and Wylla to congratulate them. Pedraal and Pedraan almost crushed Joraiem with two monstrous bear hugs. Even Bryar gave Wylla a long hug, crying softly as she did, and Joraiem knew it must have been a costly sacrifice to offer her goodwill so freely to them both.

Everyone walked back out into the open and down the long, wide avenue. The sky was clear and they could see a thousand stars in the sky above. When they reached the place where the women usually turned off to go to their lodgings, no one wanted to go. They had worked so hard to be reunited. At last, though, Mindarin and Karalin said good night, and one by one the women started down the path that led to the small houses they had shared before. Likewise, the men started back down the wide avenue, and Joraiem lingered to say good night to Wylla. He hugged her tight and whispered into her ear, "Just one week, then we'll be together."

"One week," she answered, looking up at him.

"I love you."

"I love you too."

Then he kissed her. Her lips were soft and warm and all he knew was that he didn't want to let her go.

"It's about time," she said playfully when she had gotten her breath back.

"Sorry, I'm a little slow."

"That's all right. It was worth the wait."

"Good."

She squeezed his hands and stepped back off the avenue. "I should go."

"I should too."

"Joraiem," she added. "Thanks for never giving up."

"You're welcome, but I don't need to be thanked. I did what I had to do, that's all."

"Thanks all the same."

"Wylla?" Joraiem said as she turned to go.

"Yes?"

"There is something else."

She walked back toward him. "What is it?"

"Well, it's a little bit awkward," he began, searching for his words.

"Go ahead, say it," she said, looking concerned now.

"All right. I don't know how to say this except to, except to just say it. Valzaan says I'm a prophet."

Her eyebrows rose but she didn't say anything.

"And I think he's right. Before I ever met him, I dreamed of him, and he spoke to me. We spoke with each other in the dreams. Then, when I did meet him, something strange happened. The world around us seemed to stop, but we could move and speak normally. Valzaan called it *torrim redara,* or slow time. That night on the beach, when we saw the light coming across the Southern Ocean, well, Valzaan and I talked about it for a while before we all walked down to the waterside."

"But, I was there, nothing happened."

"I know. Everyone seems to freeze to me and to Valzaan, but they don't notice. I think, if I knew better what I was doing, I could slip into slow time right now, come back in a little while, and you wouldn't notice."

"That's crazy."

"I know, but it happened. And then, in Nal Gildoroth, I felt Allfather's power in me with Suruna when we were attacked, at the city gate, and when I ran behind you and the others to find out what had happened to you. Finally, in Lindan Wood the other day, I saw through the eyes of a windhover like Valzaan does."

"What? Valzaan looks through the eyes of windhovers?"

"Yes," Joraiem said nervously, "but I don't know if I was supposed to tell you that. Keep it between us, all right?"

"Sure," she said. "I should have known, you know, because there are times when it's really hard to believe he's blind. I figured Allfather helped him compensate, but I never imagined this."

"I know, and the other night I did it too. I saw through several until I found one flying over the giant and the Malekim, then I willed the bird to fly in closer, and it did. I saw you, Wylla, hanging over the shoulder of one of the Voiceless. That was how I knew you were all right."

"Amazing," Wylla whispered under her breath.

"Anyway, I say all of this because you should know now. You asked me if I understood what it meant for me to marry you, and I think I do. I will have to leave my family and Dal Harat to go to Amaan Sul. That is the cost to me, but I don't know what price you might have to pay if you marry me. Valzaan says Allfather has called me, but I don't know to what yet."

Wylla moved closer to Joraiem and took his hands in hers. "Joraiem Andira, I have already told you that I love you. It may surprise me that you're a prophet, that you've been set apart for some special purpose, but it doesn't surprise me that you're special. You are different, and that is one reason why I love you. I wouldn't turn away from you for this, whatever this means. I want to be there for you and discover with you what Allfather wants from you. I'm sure that whatever lies ahead, I can handle it if you can. That's what all married people do, share the future together. There's no reason why you can't marry just because you're a prophet, is there?"

Joraiem shrugged his shoulders. "Not as far as I know. Valzaan seemed to know about us before tonight, and he never told me it couldn't work."

"Then don't worry about it. I'm going to marry you as planned, and we'll deal with what comes together, all right?"

"It's more than all right. It's a dream come true."

"I agree," she said, standing up on her toes to kiss him. "Now I'll say good night again, not just because I'm tired, but because I want the seventeenth day of Summer Wane to come as quickly as possible."

"Good night." Joraiem watched her walk away down the path from the avenue. Turning at last back toward the Southern Ocean and the men's houses further down the road, he whistled softly as he walked away.

The next day they were afforded the rare pleasure of doing absolutely nothing all day. They strolled into the Great Hall at all hours of the morning, depending on when they finally awoke, and between breakfast and lunch there was a steady stream of takers for fresh fruit and bread and sparkling cold water. Not for the first time, Joraiem sat back at his seat beside the great fountain and wondered if there were any other place in Kirthanin like this.

The day passed lazily and that evening, the tables were again full to overflowing, and they ate and listened to music being played by some of the stewards of the hall. The sounds of songs and laughter were almost as restorative as the good night's sleep. It was as though a long dark nightmare had ended, and they had been thrust back into a sunny and joyous reality.

Of course, the absence of Kelvan and Rulalin was a reminder that this was not entirely true. Bryar had not cried again, but neither had she returned to the hardened coldness that had covered her like a shroud since her rescue. She sat just outside the circle with a sadness in her countenance that drew them all one or two at a time to sit with her. As Joraiem watched the procession of both men and women silently slip over to her to put a hand on her shoulder or offer to get her another drink, he thought that this was precisely the type of union among the Novaana that the Assembly intended. Whatever Malek had been doing on the Forbidden Isle, and whatever purpose Ulutyr had in mind when he took the women, they had not managed to foil the fundamental goal of their coming. Surely their mutual trials and sufferings would so unite them that the Novaana would never again be divided in their lifetime. Surely they would carry this solidarity with them, wherever they went from here, and they would be as strong as the times called them to be, together.

Almost as subdued as Bryar was Mindarin. Though Falin had insisted at breakfast that Merya would brook no visitors, Mindarin had slipped out midmorning to see him, and when she did not return until well into lunchtime, they knew she had been successful. What exactly she had found and what

Merya might have said, she kept to herself, for when they inquired after Rulalin, she would say nothing.

The days after their arrival and before the wedding returned more to the pattern of days before their departure for the Forbidden Isle. In the mornings, after breakfast, they would gather for Master Berin's lessons. He continued to instruct them in the history and politics of Kirthanin, trying to make up the ground he had lost. Still, they found him increasingly more willing to speak of the War of Division and the alienation of the dragons and Great Bear. At times, Master Berin caught himself explaining certain things they had witnessed firsthand, and he would stop short and blush and say something like, "But of course, you already know that, don't you?"

In the afternoons, they continued to split time with Ulmindos and Caan. Ulmindos spent the week using the voyage to the Forbidden Isle as a teaching tool. He laid out charts of the Southern Ocean and even a map of the Forbidden Isle made many, many years ago. He showed them the route they had taken, what constellations they had used to navigate, what the most likely routes between Kirthanin and the Forbidden Isle would be, should Malek seek to go back. "He must know by now if he didn't know from the beginning that he was discovered," Ulmindos said one day. "There is no turning back for him, and there can be no rest for us."

Their time with Caan took on a very different nature. He stopped taking them down to the practice ring to work on combat skills and weapons training. It wasn't, he insisted, that they had nothing else to learn. There is always more to learn about the art of combat, he repeated often, for despite some highly complimentary remarks their first afternoon together again about what they had achieved while away, he soon returned to the Caan of old, a teacher among his pupils. He insisted that the change in focus would have happened anyway,

564   BEYOND

that he always took the last three months to discuss larger issues of battle strategy: how to choose the ground for a battle, how to arrange your troops, how to recognize when it is time to stand and fight and when it is time to pick another day, and so on. They talked about smaller engagements Caan had seen firsthand near the Mountain, and they also talked about some of the famous battles of the past. They even analyzed what they had done well and what perhaps could have been improved in their encounters with the enemy in Nal Gildoroth and above Lindan Wood. All in all, Caan had concluded that given their numbers and lack of options, they had handled those situations about as well as they could have, though he stressed that alternatives always appear in hindsight. "We must learn the lessons of our past," he said, "if we are to be better soldiers in the future."

And so life gradually slipped into a routine again. But the new routine was tainted with shadow. Rulalin had not returned, and his condition was serious. His absence was a constant reminder of the mark Malek had put on their sojourn, and of the reality of Malek's presence and power in their world. Even so, they embraced the return to a routine full of productive purpose.

But the routine had hardly been set when they broke wholly from it the day before the wedding. That afternoon, Caan announced there would be no lesson, and they worked together to prepare the Great Hall for the feast that would follow the wedding, which Joraiem and Wylla had agreed should take place outside in the gardens, where the bright yellow vines on the towering walls had budded, and large, bright blossoms of white and blue now covered the Great Hall.

That evening, when hundreds of golden lamp stands had been set up and the Great Hall had been strewn with flower chains, they sat around the fountain and celebrated the approaching union. Several of the women paid tribute to Wylla, and several of the men likewise either toasted or roasted Joraiem, though even when teasing him, their comments were full of respect and affection. Mindarin's brief but touching tribute to Wylla moved most of them to tears, mainly because each recognized that a divide had been bridged. When everyone else had spoken, Aljeron, who had laughed and interjected from time to time but not yet risen, finally stood to speak.

"I guess I'm still not sure what I want to say tonight, but there isn't any way to procrastinate further. I look back at the day I met Joraiem, just outside of Peris Mil, and I thank Allfather for the little inconveniences of life. Had one of the many inns in the town been willing to give Koshti shelter, I wouldn't have been sitting beside the road when Joraiem came along, and it's possible we wouldn't have met until we arrived here. That would have been too bad, because traveling together gave me a privilege most of you didn't have. We all know Joraiem is a lucky man to have won Wylla's heart, but I think Wylla is lucky too. When our time here is through, they'll be going home together. While we may travel the same road for a while, all together, depending on the route they take, at some point our roads will diverge. At some point, we're going to have to say good-bye. As difficult as these past few weeks have been, and as much as we've probably all dreamed of home at one time or another, I don't really want to say good-bye to any of you, especially you, Joraiem. You've become as good a friend as I have in this world."

Aljeron stopped speaking. The room grew silent. A few of them were looking around, not wanting to think about the inevitability of separation. Joraiem stood and walked into the middle of the circle, to the place where Aljeron stood, paused as Aljeron looked up, then threw his arms around him.

"We are heartened by your good wishes, not just Aljeron's, but all of yours," Joraiem said as Aljeron sat down. "Though farewells must come, fortunately, it isn't time yet. Wylla and I look forward to spending the first two and a half months of our life together right here with you, our friends. I know I speak for her when I say, we wouldn't want it any other way, and when we do return to Amaan Sul, we'll always have a room open and a fire ready for any of you who may be passing through. You are like family."

The assembly lingered a few moments more but soon dispersed, and Joraiem soon found himself back in one of the little houses, preparing for bed. At first, as he lay down and looked up through the large open window into the clear nighttime sky, Joraiem thought sleep would be impossible, but Allfather was merciful, and before he knew it, he was opening his eyes to the first rays of the early morning sun. He looked up to see Pedraal and Pedraan standing over him, smiling down with rascally grins. "We're glad to see you awake on your own, because we would have hated to have been forced to wake you." They looked at each other and laughed before reaching down and hauling him up out of bed.

Pedraal continued, "Today, you become our brother, though as far as we're concerned, you were our brother before, but today it is sort of official, if you follow. So we thought we'd look after you to make sure you don't mess up—after all, no one knows Wylla better than we do."

"Thanks, I think," Joraiem said sleepily as they handed him his clothes. Soon, Aljeron had also joined them, and with the constant "advice" that flowed from the three of them, it was a wonder that Joraiem was ever dressed and ready to head up to the Great Hall. In the end, he left the twins behind arguing over whether or not carrying a weapon of some sort to the ceremony that evening would make him a more "manly" groom.

Breakfast was a quiet affair, as none of the women were there. They had insisted on taking their breakfast and lunch apart from the men, and they had further solemnly charged the men to keep Joraiem away from the women's quarters at all costs. The men had consented, and Joraiem had voluntarily promised not to stray that way, but they had looked at him dubiously, as though he was almost certain to try it.

The morning passed quietly as the men ate and swam in the pools beneath the fountain. In the late afternoon, they all returned to their houses and changed into their best pants and tunics. Then, at the appointed hour, they walked together up to the Great Hall and around the side.

Wylla was even more beautiful than Joraiem had imagined she would be. From somewhere, the women had acquired a gorgeous, long white summer dress. It fit Wylla perfectly, and she stood before him with her lovely dark hair pulled up on top of her head with a garland of summer blossoms around it, the dress shimmering in the early evening sunlight. Her long slender arms hung down before her, and she held a simple bouquet of small white flowers. Her beautiful eyes were concentrated fully on Joraiem as the men approached, and he trembled to behold her.

Behind her, both Master Berin and Valzaan were waiting. Valzaan was wearing his customary long green robe with a clean white sash, and Master Berin was colorfully dressed with a bright blue robe with a golden pattern carefully worked up and down and around it. They both smiled in greeting as Joraiem took his place beside Wylla. Pedraal and Pedraan stood one on either side, and the others fell in behind them in a shallow semi-circle so they could better hear the proceedings.

Joraiem was not nearly as nervous as he had imagined he would be, and he found himself able both to focus on Wylla and to enjoy the simple service as it proceeded. Wylla also seemed to be relaxed, and she beamed with a satisfied smile from beginning to end.

At last Valzaan stepped forward with a long golden cord, and taking a small knife, cut the cord into roughly equal sections. The first section he took to Joraiem, and stretching out his bare left arm, wrapped the cord around his upper arm twice before tying the loose ends off. The other section he took to Wylla's bare left arm, and he wrapped the cord around her upper arm three times before tying the loose ends off.

"Today, Joraiem Andira and Wylla Someris, you are bound together. Even as the golden cord was once one, so are the two of you one. Even as the golden cord has been bound to each of you, so you are bound to each other. Remember, more than your friends and siblings bear witness to this union. Allfather Himself watches over us, and ultimately it is He who has bound and will continue to bind you together. Take this binding to heart, and let nothing in this world come between you, so long as the Maker gives you breath and life. Now may you go from this place, not two but one, called to serve Allfather and each other, and may Allfather's rich and abundant blessings go with you, wherever you may go."

With that the others showered them with flower petals and gave them hugs and kisses for so long that Wylla and Joraiem finally had to encourage them all to head inside where the food and music and festivities awaited.

The night was a blur, full of eating and drinking, singing and dancing. And, as if the wedding was not good news enough, Merya came into the Great Hall late in the evening and whispered something to Master Berin, who all but jumped up and down where he stood. He turned to the others and announced that Rulalin had turned a corner, and that while his recovery would still take time, his life seemed no longer in doubt.

The Great Hall erupted. Mindarin sank into a chair and sobbed as the women hugged one another and the men shouted for joy. Joraiem slipped his arm around Wylla and pulled her close. He thought as he hugged her, how good it was that she was now his wife, and that they would celebrate all their mutual joys together.

At last, in the late hours of the night, Master Berin grabbed a lamp and led Joraiem and Wylla to the front door of the Great Hall. The others waved from beside the fountain. "Now," he said as he pushed the door open and led them out into the night. "While it is true that you have come like the others to Sulare to build unity with your peers, the two of you are to forget about all that for the next two weeks, do you understand? We don't want to hear from you, or see you, or even think about you until the first day of Autumn Rise. We've prepared a lovely, comfortable house on the far western side of Sulare with all you could possibly need or ask for, and a steward will drop off fresh fruit and milk and bread each morning outside in a little box that is there for that purpose. If you really must leave the house, then by all means go west or south and away from here, all right?"

"All right," Joraiem answered, blushing a little.

They followed Master Berin through the side roads and smaller paths of the western reaches of Sulare. Houses once full of sailors and their families and those who had patrolled the southern coast of Kirthanin a thousand years before now stood empty and open, inhabited only by the warm evening breeze. Finally, Master Berin brought them to a lovely house, where two candles burned on the frame on either side of the front door, and he bid them goodnight.

"Master Berin," Joraiem called.

"Yes?"

"Thanks."

Master Berin smiled, waved, and turned away in the darkness. When he had passed out of sight, Joraiem kissed Wylla and opened the door.

When Wylla and Joraiem rejoined the others in Autumn Rise, they quickly returned to the old routine, with a few exceptions. Rulalin returned as well, though not fully at first. He started by coming for breakfast and the morning sessions with Master Berin, then Merya would whisk him away after lunch for the rest of the day. Eventually, she let him stay from breakfast to supper, but she enforced strictly an early bedtime and would march him back to his room then no matter what was happening or how demonstrative his protest.

But the day did come, near the end of Autumn Rise, when Rulalin was finally released to live and eat with the others and to participate as much as he could in all the activities of their final month in Sulare. The second night after his return, they were all down at the beach, and when Rulalin removed his shirt to swim with the others, several of them gasped at his scar. It was thick and stretched from side to side across his entire chest, right below his breast line. It was a wicked looking wound, and even most of the men, who talked of the scar like it was a trophy to be cherished, didn't have the stomach to look at it for long.

It became apparent, pretty quickly, that this was not the only wound Rulalin carried. If Joraiem had hoped their earlier quest had helped them to put the issue of Wylla behind them, he was mistaken. The alliance and seeming good will of the vow made upon the distant shore of the Forbidden Isle was gone. To be fair, Rulalin did not treat either of them poorly, he just didn't treat them any way at all. Except for a mumbled congratulations the first time he saw them after his own return, he never spoke to them except to be polite. He avoided both completely. He was never anywhere to be found when they bid the others good night, and he never sat near them at meals.

Though disappointed, Joraiem was helped by Wylla to put it in perspective. As she said to him often, they had both known this would be hard on Rulalin, and a distant silence wasn't the end of the world. It was going to take him a while to get used to their marriage, and that probably wouldn't happen until he was back in Fel Edorath. They could not have reasonably expected openness and friendliness from him, neither being hallmarks of Rulalin's personality anyway.

Autumn Rise gave way to Full Autumn, and eventually Midautumn arrived too. The Novaana observed the rites of Midautumn together, and at the feast that followed, the men found themselves going over in detail their memories of the rites of Midsummer celebrated on the Forbidden Isle. That it had been a whole season ago seemed as hard to believe as the fact that they had built a mound and worshipped Allfather in that place.

"I know it is an unpleasant topic," Master Berin said as they prepared to retire, "but it is probably a good idea that we talk about your departure, since that day is coming soon."

There were some groans from the assembled Novaana, but they stood patiently and quietly, waiting for Master Berin to continue. "I want to encourage you, if possible, to extend your Sulare experience by traveling together. I know that for some of you, the most direct way home would mean traveling alone, but perhaps you don't need to take the most direct way home. Autumn Wane can be very beautiful in Suthanin, and a detour might be enjoyable. Besides, I was here when most if not all of your parents came, and I know for a fact that not all of them went straight home. You might even find, when you get back, that they never really expected you to."

"What's more," Valzaan said, "larger groups might better withstand trouble, should trouble come. We have enjoyed a season of peace since our return, but I have an uneasy heart and fear the storm clouds are gathering. We should not take our current peace for granted."

There were murmurs among them as they headed out into the evening. Just before the bridge, Joraiem pulled Wylla aside and whispered something in her ear. She smiled and nodded. Joraiem called to Aljeron, who came over with Koshti.

"What is it?" Aljeron asked.

"Well," Joraiem started, "Wylla and I were wondering if you would mind if we traveled with you for a while on your way home. Were you planning on going back the way we came?"

Aljeron gazed at them. "Yes, I was, and of course I'd love you to come along, but how far do you mean? Your most direct way to Amaan Sul would take you through the gap between Elnin Wood and Lindan Wood. Did you mean to come further than that?"

"Yes, we're not going to Amaan Sul."

"What do you mean?"

"We're going to Dal Harat first, and we wanted to know if you wanted to come too, though it is a bit out of your way."

"Going to Dal Harat?" was all Aljeron managed to say.

"Wylla wants to meet my family and see my home. You are welcome to come too. After our visit, we'll have to head back to Peris Mil, and you could find passage to Werthanin somewhere along the southern shore of the Kellisor Sea. That is, if you are willing to go that far out of your way."

Aljeron smiled. "I'd love to. It would be great. I'll send word home ahead of me with Mindarin or Bryar and Elyas." He suddenly grew serious. "Of course, you might not really want a third party around all that time. Wouldn't you like to be alone with your family, Joraiem?"

"We aren't going alone, Pedraal and Pedraan are coming too. So what's one more?"

"Actually," another voice spoke from behind them, and they turned to see Valzaan coming down the walk from the Great Hall, "I was going to ask you the very same question."

"What question?"

"Whether one more would matter all that much to you. It appears that our roads lie in the same direction a little while longer. Would you mind another traveling companion?" Valzaan asked, his unblinking eyes looking directly at Joraiem.

"We'd be delighted to have you," Wylla said, her face beaming and reaching out to clasp Valzaan by the hand. "It will hardly be like we've left at all with you and Aljeron along. Don't you think so, Joraiem?"

"Absolutely."

"Good," Valzaan answered, "then it is decided. I assume we will travel with all of the Werthanim at least as far as Peris Mil, that is, unless they have made other travel arrangements. It'll be like old times."

Four days before they were set to leave, Rulalin pulled Joraiem aside as they were leaving the Great Hall for bed. Before Joraiem could say anything, Rulalin had blurted out his request, "I was hoping I could talk to you in the morning, before I leave."

"What do you mean? Aren't you leaving on the last day of Full Autumn?"

"No, I've talked with Master Berin, and he's given me permission to leave early.

"Oh," Joraiem said, "I'm sorry to hear that."

"Anyway, since I won't be traveling with you, I hoped you and I could talk in the morning. There are things that should be said."

Joraiem nodded. "All right, I had hoped we'd be able to talk."

"Good. Then how about before breakfast? I'll meet you where the avenue from the Great Hall empties out onto the beach, all right?"

"Sure, when?"

"I'll head down at first light. Meet me when you're ready."

With that, Rulalin turned and walked quickly away. Joraiem watched him go and joined Wylla, who was waiting by the front door of the Great Hall for him. She found it difficult to share Joraiem's enthusiasm for the meeting.

"I just wouldn't be too sure he wants reconciliation, that's all," she finally said when Joraiem pressed for her objection.

"Well, even if he wants to berate me or yell at me, I think I should give him that chance. Maybe if he gets it out, we can put this behind us."

"Maybe."

Joraiem took a morning run over some winding paths past the combat ring, where they had met Sarneth months before, and when he reached the beach, he turned west until he reached the place where the avenue emptied out onto it. Rulalin was waiting as promised. He held the reins of his horse, which was saddled and ready for the long journey back to Fel Edorath.

Joraiem jogged up to the place where Rulalin was standing. "Do you mind if we walk?" Rulalin asked.

"Sure," Joraiem said, a little short of breath. "I like to walk a little bit after a run anyway."

They started along the beach, but Rulalin didn't speak, and Joraiem waited, thinking it best to give Rulalin space until he was ready. Eventually, Rulalin stopped, somewhat abruptly, and turned to Joraiem.

"Joraiem, I want to ask you a question. It might sound odd, but it is very important."

"Go ahead."

Rulalin glanced out over the ocean but turned back to Joraiem. "If the only way you could be happy with Wylla, was to kill me, would you do it?"

Joraiem looked with horror at Rulalin. "What are you talking about?"

"I said the question was strange, just answer it."

"Why?"

"Because it's important."

"Of course not, Rulalin. You're my friend. At least you were, and I want you to be my friend still. I would never hurt you."

"Even if killing me was the only way that you and Wylla could be happy?"

"That's absurd. Your death has nothing to do with our happiness."

"Whether it does or doesn't isn't the point. Just imagine you had to choose between killing me and having a happy life with Wylla. What would you do?"

"This is crazy," Joraiem said and started to turn away.

"Joraiem!" Rulalin called, and Joraiem turned back. "I just want you to think it through and give me an honest answer."

Joraiem stood, staring at Rulalin as he walked closer. Slowly, Rulalin lifted his hand to Joraiem and extended a long, narrow dagger, handle first. "Take it."

"No," Joraiem said.

"Just hold it."

Joraiem took it in his hand. "Now," Rulalin repeated, quietly. "The question is, if you had to choose between my life and your mutual happiness with Wylla, what would you do?"

Joraiem looked down at the dagger, then back at Rulalin. "Rulalin, I could never kill you, for any reason."

Joraiem turned the dagger around and handed it back to Rulalin, handle first. Rulalin took it reluctantly. "Now," Joraiem sighed, feeling suddenly very sad. "Are we through with this foolishness?"

"Yes," Rulalin said softly. "You know, Joraiem, if I had Wylla, I don't think I would have said the same thing."

Joraiem looked into Rulalin's eyes, studying them, and for the first time since this bizarre conversation had begun, he wondered how hypothetical the question had been.

"Wylla is everything," Rulalin continued. "If I had her, I would do anything to keep her. Not having her, well, it makes me wonder if life is worth living. If you had said you'd be willing to kill me, I wouldn't have resisted, you know. I almost hoped you would."

"Rulalin, this is crazy."

"Maybe so, Joraiem, maybe so, but, I've been over this a thousand times. It always comes back to the same two things. Now that you've married Wylla, I have two choices. I can't go on living knowing she's with someone else, even if that person is you. I like you, but I can't. So either I have to die, or you do."

Suddenly, Joraiem saw the odd look in Rulalin's eyes flare up, and before he could move or block the blow, Rulalin had thrust the dagger into his chest. He gasped at the feeling of fire as the dagger sank deep. Rulalin stepped quickly in toward Joraiem and pushed the dagger still deeper, making sure the wound would be fatal. He grabbed Joraiem's shoulder and pulled Joraiem in onto the blade, whispering, "I'm sorry."

Joraiem's legs buckled, and he dropped to his knees in the sand. The pain in his chest was overwhelming, and he felt weakly for the handle of the dagger. He found it, but it took all his remaining strength to remove it. He looked up, but Rulalin was already gone. In the distance, a dark figure was mounting a horse and hurrying away. Joraiem's mind raced. He looked down at the blood oozing through his fingers, dropping onto the sand.

He closed his eyes, searching for something, but he wasn't sure what. Suddenly, he could see the broad avenue leading up from the Southern Ocean to the Great Hall. About midway along it, Valzaan was on horseback, flying like the wind toward the beach. He could hear the prophet's voice, as though speaking directly into his mind.

"Joraiem, hold on, I'm coming."

"Valzaan?"

"I'm coming. Hold on!"

"Too late," Joraiem whispered, as he lay down on his side in the sand. The sand was warm and pleasant to his face. The fire in his chest wasn't so bad when he lay down, and he almost felt he could sleep here, just for a little while.

"No! Hold on! You must hold on, Joraiem!" the voice in his head called, loudly and persistently.

Joraiem looked down from the sky at Valzaan, who had almost reached the beach. "Valzaan, you will have to tell her good-bye for me. Will you do that?"

"Hold on until I come, then you can tell her yourself many years from now."

"Tell her I love her," Joraiem said, and his eyes fluttered open. The waves from the ocean were rolling in rhythmically, and the sound was very soothing. *Sleep, just for a little while.* He closed his eyes.

EPILOGUE

KOSHTI JOGGED ALONG BESIDE Aljeron, his powerful legs padding softly through the snow that lay both on and beside the road, about two hands deep. Now that it was early evening, the temperature had fallen substantially. The cold spell of the past two weeks was unusual, even for Winter Rise, and none of the snow that had fallen a week ago had melted. So, yet again, they pushed the horses on through it as they had for days. Still, the villagers had indicated it wasn't far now to the Andiras' home, and Aljeron hoped their long journey would soon be over.

Turning to the carefully wrapped bundle draped over the horse that Joraiem had ridden to Sulare, he thought that the cold weather had been in a sense, a blessing. Two months on the road with Joraiem's body could have been difficult in warm weather, but thankfully, the cold had kept the odor reasonable. It was hard enough as it was, having to bring his friend home to his parents like this, without worrying about that.

Thinking of facing Joraiem's father and the rest of the family with the news put Aljeron in a foul mood again. He wished again they had been successful in preventing Rulalin from escaping Sulare. He wished that even when they had failed to cut him off before reaching the causeway, that Master Berin would have allowed him to organize a search party. He wouldn't have stopped until Rulalin was tied over his horse, dead or alive.

But Master Berin had probably foreseen that Rulalin would have come back dead if he came back at all, so he had insisted that Aljeron do this instead. He had argued that eventually, Rulalin would be found, and that this murder was a matter for the Assembly, not personal revenge. It was a matter for public justice, and the Novaana of Kirthanin would have to deal with it. Aljeron had reluctantly agreed, but most nights on the road he had prayed they would stumble across Rulalin on the way. He had prayed Rulalin would try to fight him, so that he would have no choice but to show him with Daaltaran that death does indeed come to all.

But he hadn't been so lucky, and now here they were. He had arrived in Dal Harat with the others about midmorning, and they waited outside the village with Koshti and Joraiem's body while he found out where they were to go. When he was sure of the way to the Andiras' home, he rejoined Koshti, Valzaan, the twins, and Wylla and headed out along the road that would take them finally to their destination, so that he could tell a man he had never met that his son was dead.

Wylla rode quietly behind Valzaan and Aljeron. She stared out over the frozen, barren landscape, but her mind slid regularly between the white snow and the sandy beach of Sulare. Increasingly, when she was fatigued on the road, she found herself slipping back into the Summerland, sometimes with Joraiem, sometimes without. She was there without him now, and she relived yet again that painful morning. A commotion of confused stories had come to her near the Great Hall that

Joraiem was hurt on the beach, and she had raced down the long avenue as fast as she could run. Some of the other women had gone with her, helping her to keep going when she had stumbled and fallen in the sand. When she had finally reached him, he was already dead, his face looking peaceful despite the bloody and brutal way in which he had died. She had fallen to the sand beside him, cradled his head in her hands, and wept.

The image faded from her mind as she heard Pedraal repeat his question, "Are you all right?"

She nodded, "Yes, just a little tired."

He looked concerned. "I know we've been on the road a long time, but this isn't like you. I've never seen you this fatigued."

"I'm all right, Pedraal. Don't worry about me," she tried to reassure him with a smile, but he didn't look convinced.

"Anyway, we're there," he said as he pointed up along the road.

She looked at the warm, cozy house that she saw ahead. How she had dreamed of coming to this place with Joraiem, though of course none of those dreams had been like this.

"At least," she whispered to herself as Pedraal turned forward again, "I haven't lost him completely." She looked down at the front of her cloak at the slight bulge in her stomach. None of the others had noticed it yet, so she wondered if she was only imagining that the change was visible, but she knew she wasn't imagining the whole thing. "I'm not making you up, little one, that I know," she whispered again. "I may miss him terribly, but I'm not crazy."

Looking up, she saw Aljeron looking back at her. She smiled back as they turned up a short side avenue, leading to the house. She rubbed her stomach gently, soothingly, and hummed a lullaby softly to herself.

Where is the hot summer wind that rustles the grass?
　　The warm dry sand that burrows into your toes?
　　The glistening dew on the delicate rose?
They've fled like the dragons into the golden past.
　　They hide in the mountains and under the sea,
　　Afraid of the future and what it will be.

—From "Summer's End," a poem by an unknown
Suthanim poet, written early in the Third Age.

The End
of the First Book of
The Binding of the Blade

GLOSSARY

Aelwyn Elathien (ALE-win el-ATHE-ee-un): Novaana of Werthanin, Mindarin's younger sister.

Agia Muldonai (ah-GEE-uh MUL-doe-nye): The Holy Mountain. Agia Muldonai was the ancient home of the Titans, who lived in Avalione, the city nestled high upon the mountain between its twin peaks. Agia Muldonai has been under Malek's control since the end of the Second Age, when he invaded Kirthanin from his home in exile on the Forbidden Isle.

Alazare (AL-uh-zair): The Titan who cast Malek from Agia Muldonai at the end of the First Age when Malek's Rebellion failed. Severely injured in his battle with Malek, Alazare passed from the stage of Kirthanin history and was never seen again.

Aleta Tomian (uh-LEE-tuh toe-MY-an): Alina's twin, who has a crush on Joraiem in Dal Harat.

Alina Tomian (uh-LEE-nuh toe-MY-an): Aleta's twin.

Aljeron Balinor (AL-jer-on BALL-ih-nore): Novaana of Werthanin (Shalin Bel), travels with his battle brother Koshti.

Allfather: Creator of Kirthanin, who gave control of Kirthanin's day-to-day affairs to the Council of Twelve. To accomplish this task, He gave great power to each of these Titans. Since the time of Malek's Rebellion, Allfather has continued to speak to His creation through prophets who remind Kirthanin of Allfather's sovereign rule.

Andunin (an-DOO-nin): The Nolthanim man chosen by Malek at the Rebellion to be king over mankind.

Arimaar Mountains (AIR-ih-mar): Suthanin's longest range, which runs between Lindan Wood and the eastern coast of Suthanin.

Arindel (AIR-in-del): Corindel's father, king of Enthanin near the beginning of the Third Age.

Assembly: The official gathering of all Kirthanin Novaana who are appointed to represent their family and region.

Autumn Rise: See Seasons.

Autumn Wane: See Seasons.

Avalione (av-uh-lee-OWN): Blessed city and home of the Crystal Fountain. It rests between the peaks of Agia Muldonai and was once the home of the Titans. Like the rest of Agia Muldonai, the city was declared off limits by Allfather at the beginning of the Second Age.

Azaruul butterflies (AZ-uh-rule): Green luminescent butterflies.

Azmavarim (az-MAV-uh-rim): Also known as Firstblades, these swords were forged during the First Age by Andunin and his followers.

Balimere (BALL-ih-mere): Also called Balimere the Beautiful. The most beloved of all the Titans to the lesser creatures of Kirthanin. It is said that when Allfather restores Kirthanin, Balimere will be the first of the faithful Titans to be resurrected.

Barunaan River (buh-RUE-nun): Major north-south river between Kellisor Sea and the Southern Ocean.

Berin: Master of Sulare.

Black Wolves: Creatures created by Malek during his exile on the Forbidden Isle.

Brenim Andira (BREN-im an-DEER-uh): Novaana of Suthanin (Dal Harat), Joraiem's younger brother.

Bryar (BRY-er): Novaana of Werthanin, Elyas's older sister.

Caan (KAHN): Combat instructor for the Novaana in Sulare.

Calendar: There are ninety-one days in every season, making the year 364 days. The midseason feast days are not numbered and instead are known only by their name (Midsummer, Midautumn, etc.). They fall between the fifteenth and sixteenth day of each season. These days are "outside of time" in part as a tribute to the timelessness of Allfather; they also look forward to the time when all things will be made new.

Calissa (kuh-LISS-uh): Novaana of Suthanin (Kel Imlarin), Darias's sister.

Cimaris Rul (sim-AHR-iss RULE): Town at the mouth of the Barunaan River where it pours into the Southern Ocean.

Col Marena (KOLE muh-REEN-uh): Port near Shalin Bel.

Corindel (KORE-in-del): Enthanim royal who attempted to drive Malek from Agia Muldonai and betrayed the Great Bear at the beginning of the Third Age.

Council of Twelve: The twelve Titans to whom Allfather entrusted the care of Kirthanin. The Council dwelt in Avalione on Agia Muldonai, but frequently they would clothe themselves in human form and travel throughout the land. The greatest of these was Malek, whose Rebellion ultimately brought about the destruction of the Twelve.

Crystal Fountain: Believed to be the fountainhead of all Kirthanin waters, this fountain once flowed in the center of Avalione.

cyranis (sir-AN-iss): A poison of remarkable potency that can kill most living things almost instantly if it gets into the bloodstream. Consequently, the cyranic arrow—the head of which is coated in cyranis—is one of few weapons that the people of Kirthanin trust against the Malekim.

Daaltaran (doll-TARE-an): Aljeron's sword, a Firstblade whose name means "death comes to all."

Dal Harat (DOLL HARE-at): Village in western Suthanin, Joraiem Andira's home.

Darias (DARE-ee-us): Novaana of Suthanin (Kel Imlarin), Calissa's brother.

Derrion Wel (DARE-ee-un WELL): Town in southeastern Suthanin.

draal (DRAWL): A tight-knit community of Great Bear.

dragon tower: These ancient structures were built in the First Age as homes away from home for dragons who naturally live in the high places of Kirthanin's mountains and prefer to sleep high above the ground.

dragons: One of the three great races of Kirthanin. All dragons are descended from the golden dragon, Sulmandir, the first creation of Allfather after the Titans. All dragons appear at first glance to be golden, but none except Sulmandir are entirely golden. Three dragon lines exist, marked by their distinct coloring: red, blue, and green.

Eliandir (el-ee-AN-deer): A red dragon.

Elnin Wood (EL-nin): Suthanin forest south of Vol Tumian.

Elnindraal (EL-nin-drawl): The draal of Great Bear living in Suthanin's Elnin Wood.

Elsora Andira (el-SORE-uh an-DEER-uh): Novaana of Suthanin (Dal Harat), Joraiem's mother.

Elyas (eh-LIE-us): Novaana of Werthanin, Bryar's younger brother.

Enthanin (EN-than-in): Kirthanin's eastern country. Residents are Enthanim.

Erevir (AIR-uh-veer): Major prophet of Allfather in the Second Age.

Evrim Minluan (EV-rim MIN-loo-in): Joraiem's best friend in Dal Harat.

Fall Rise: See Seasons.

Fire Giant: See Vulsutyr.

First Age: The age of peace and harmony that preceded Malek's Rebellion. Not only did peace govern the affairs of men in the First Age, but the three great races of men, dragons, and Great Bear coexisted then in harmony. Any date given which refers to the First Age will be followed by the letters FA.

Firstblade: See Azmavarim.

Forbidden Isle: After Malek's failed Rebellion at the end of the First Age, he was driven from Kirthanin and took refuge on the Forbidden Isle, home of Vulsutyr, the Fire Giant.

Forest of Gyrin (GEAR-in): Forest south of Agia Muldonai.

Full Autumn: See Seasons.

Full Spring: See Seasons.

Full Summer: See Seasons.

Full Winter: See Seasons.

Garek Elathien (GAIR-ick el-ATH-ee-un): Novaana of Werthanin, Mindarin's father

garrion (GARE-ee-un): Mode of transport common in the First Age used by the Titans and some Novaana. Garrions came in many shapes and sizes, but they all functioned similarly: A dragon would pick up the garrion with his talons as he flew.

giants: See Vulsutyrim.

Great Bear: One of the three great races of Kirthanin. These magnificent creatures commonly stand two spans high and are ferocious fighters when need calls. Nevertheless, they are known for their great wisdom and gentleness.

Grendolai (GREN-doe-lie): Rumored to have been the joint creation of Malek and Vulsutyr, these terrifying creatures were reportedly used to attack the Dragon Towers when Malek invaded Kirthanin from the Forbidden Isle. They have not been seen since, and some believe their existence is wholly legendary.

gyre: A manmade dragon den built on top of a dragon tower.

Gyrindraal (GEAR-in-drawl): Clan of Great Bear inhabiting the Forest of Gyrin south of Agia Muldonai.

hour: See time.

Invasion, the: Malek's second attempt to conquer Kirthanin.

Joraiem Andira (jore-EYE-em an-DEER-uh): Novaana of Suthanin (Dal Harat).

Karalin (CARE-uh-lin): Novaana from Enthanin (near Amaan Sul), crippled left ankle.

Kellisor Sea (KELL-ih-sore): The great internal sea of Kirthanin that lies directly south of Agia Muldonai.

Kelvan (KEL-vin): Novaana from Werthanin.

King Falcon: See windhover.

Kiraseth (KEER-uh-seth): Father of the Great Bear.

Kirthanin (KEER-than-in): The world in which the story takes place. Kirthanin comprises four countries on a single continent. Each country is defined by its geographic relationship to Agia Muldonai.

Kiruan River (KEER-oo-an): Marks the boundary of Werthanin and Nolthanin.

Koshti (KOSH-tee): Aljeron's tiger, battle brother.

Kurveen (kur-VEEN): Caan's sword, a Firstblade whose name means "quick kill."

Kyril Andira (KEER-il an-DEER-uh): Novaana of Suthanin (Dal Harat), Joraiem's younger sister.

Lindan Wood (LIN-duhn): Forest in eastern Suthanin, just west of the Arimaar Mountains.

Lindandraal (LIN-duhn-drawl): Clan of Great Bear that resides west of the Arimaar Mountains in Lindan Wood.

Malek (MAH-leck): The greatest of Titans whose betrayal brought death to his Titan brothers and ruin to Kirthanin. Since the end of the Second Age and his second failed attempt to conquer all Kirthanin, he has ruled over Agia Muldonai and the surrounding area.

Malekim (MALL-uh-keem): Also known as Malek's Children, the Silent Ones, and the Voiceless. These creatures were first seen when Malek invaded Kirthanin at the end of the Second Age from the Forbidden Isle. A typical Malekim stands from a span and a third to a span and a half high and has a smooth thick grey hide. "Malekim" is both a singular and a plural term.

Marella Someris (muh-REL-uh so-MAIR-iss): Novaana and Queen of Enthanin, widow of Pedrone, Wylla's mother.

Margan (MAHR-gun): patrol bear of Lindandraal.

Merrion (MAIR-ee-un): White sea birds with blue stripes on their wings that can swim short distances underwater in pursuit of fish.

Mindarin Orlene (MIN-dar-in ore-LEAN): Novaana of Werthanin, Aelwyn's older sister.

Monias Andira (moe-NYE-us an-DEER-uh): Novaana of Suthanin (Dal Harat), Joraiem's father.

Mound: Central feature in the midseason rituals that focus on Agia Muldonai's need for cleansing.

Nal Gildoroth (NAL GIL-dore-oth): Solitary city on the Forbidden Isle.

Nol Rumar (KNOLL RUE-mar): small village in the north central plains of Werthanin.

Nolthanin (KNOLL-than-in): Kirthanin's northern country, largely in ruin during the Third Age.

Novaana (no-VAHN-uh): The nobility of human society in Kirthanin who at first governed human affairs under the direction of the Titans but have since adapted to autonomous control. Every seven years the Novaana between the ages of eighteen and twenty-five as of the first day of Spring Rise were to assemble from the first day of Spring Wane until the first day of Fall Wane. Sulare is commonly referred to as the Summerland. "Novaana" is both a singular and a plural term.

Nyan (NYE-un): Novaana of Suthanin (Cimaris Rul).

Pedraal Someris (PAY-drawl so-MAIR-iss): Novaana of Enthanin (Amaan Sul), Wylla's younger brother, Pedraan's older twin.

Pedraan Someris (PAY-drahn so-MAIR-iss): Novaana of Enthanin (Amaan Sul), Wylla's younger brother, Pedraal's younger twin.

Pedrone Someris (PAY-drone so-MAIR-iss): Last king of Enthanin, deceased.

Peris Mil (PARE-iss MILL): Town south of Kellisor Sea on the Barunaan River.

Rucaran the Great (RUE-car-en): Father of the Black Wolves.

Rulalin Tarasir (rue-LAH-lin TARE-us-ear): Novaana of Werthanin (Fel Edorath), who loves Wylla Someris.

Ruun Harak (RUNE HARE-ack): A spear given to Andunin by Malek.

Saegan (SIGH-gan): Novaana of Enthanin (Tol Emuna).

Sarneth (SAHR-neth): A lord among Great Bear, one of the few to still hold commerce with men.

seasons: As a largely agrarian world, Kirthanin follows a calendar that revolves around the four seasons. Each season is subdivided into three distinct periods, each of which contains thirty days. For example, the first thirty days of Summer are known as Summer Rise, the middle thirty days as Full Summer, and the last thirty as Summer Wane.

Second Age: The period that followed Malek's Rebellion and preceded his return to Kirthanin. The Second Age was largely a time of peace until a massive civil war devastated Kirthanin's defenses and opened the door for Malek's second attempt at total conquest. Any date given which refers to the Second Age will be followed by the letters SA.

Shalin Bel (SHALL-in BELL): Large city of Werthanin.

Silent One: See Malekim.

slow time: See torrim redara.

span: The most common form of measurement in Kirthanin. Its origin is forgotten but it could refer to the length of a man. A span is approximately 10 hands or what we would call 6 feet.

Spring Rise: See seasons.

Spring Wane: See seasons.

Sulare (sue-LAHR-ee): Also known as the Sumerland. At the beginning of the Third Age the Assembly decreed that Sulare, a retreat at the southern tip of Kirthanin, would be the place where every seven years all Novaana between the ages of eighteen and twenty-five were to assemble from the first day of Spring Wane until the first day of Fall Wane.

Sulmandir (sul-man-DEER): Also known as Father of the Dragons and the Golden Dragon. He is the most magnificent of all Allfather's creations besides the Titans. After many of his children died during Malek's invasion of Kirthanin at the end of the Second Age, Sulmandir disappeared.

Summer Rise: See Seasons.

Summer Wane: See Seasons.

Summerland: Sulare.

Suruna (suh-RUE-nuh): Joraiem Andira's bow, previously his father's, whose name means "sure one."

Suthanin (SUE-than-in): The largest of Kirthanin's four countries, occupying the southern third of the continent. Ruled by a loose council of Navaana. Residents are Suthanim.

Synoki (sin-OH-kee): A castaway on the Forbidden Isle.

Tal Kuvarin (TAL KOO-var-in): Novaana friend of Monias in Peris Mil.

Tarin (TARE-in): Novaana of Enthanin, Valia's cousin.

Tarlin (TAHR-lin): Andunin's son.

Third Age: The present age, which began with the fall and occupation of Agia Muldonai by Malek.

time: Time in Kirthanin is reckoned differently during the day and the night. Daytime is divided into twelve Hours. First

Hour begins at what we would call 7 A.M. and Twelfth Hour ends at what we would call 7 P.M. Nighttime is divided into four watches, each three hours long. So First Watch runs from 7 P.M. to 10 P.M. and so on through the night until First Hour.

Titans: Those first created by Allfather who were given the authority to rule Kirthanin on Allfather's behalf. Their great power was used to do many remarkable things before Malek's rebellion ruined them.

torrim redara (TORE-eem ruh-DAR-uh): Prophetic state of being temporarily outside of time.

Ulmindos (ul-MIN-doss): High captain of the ships of Sulare.

Ulutyr (OO-loo-teer): Vulsutyrim captor of the women on the Forbidden Isle.

Valia (vuh-LEE-uh): Novaana of Enthanin, Tarin's cousin.

Valzaan (val-ZAHN): The blind prophet of Allfather.

Voiceless: See Malekim.

Vol Tumian (VAHL TOO-my-an): Village along the Barunaan River between Peris Mil and Cimaris Rul.

Vulsutyr (VUL-sue-teer): Also known as Father of the Giants and the Fire Giant. Vulsutyr ruled the Forbidden Isle and gave shelter to Malek when he fled Kirthanin. At first he was but little more than a distant host, but Malek eventually seduced Vulsutyr to help him plan and prepare for his invasion of Kirthanin. This giant was killed by Sulmandir at the end of the Second Age.

Vulsutyrim (vul-sue-TER-eem): Name for all descendants of Vulsutyr; both a singular and a plural.

War of Division: Civil war that weakened Kirthanin's defenses against Malek at the end of the Second Age.

Water Stones: Stone formations created by the upward thrust of water released from the great deep at the creation of the world.

Werthanin (WARE-than-in): Kirthanin's western country. Residents are Werthanim.

windhover: Small brown falcons that are seen as "holy" birds in some areas of Kirthanin because of some stories that associate them with Agia Muldonai.

Winter Rise: See Seasons.

Winter Wane: See Seasons.

Wylla Someris (WILL-uh so-MAIR-iss): Princess Novaana of Enthanin (Amaan Sul), future queen.

ABOUT THE AUTHOR

L. B. Graham was born in Baltimore, Maryland, in 1971. He loved school so much that he never left, transitioning seamlessly between life as a student and life as a teacher. He and his wife Jo now live in St. Louis. They would like one day to have a house by the sea, which he wants to call "The Grey Havens." His wife is Australian, which he thinks is appropriate since his grandfather was Australian and his father was born in Melbourne. The fact that he has these Australian connections and that his father grew up in Ethiopia all make him think he is more international than he really is. He went to Wheaton College outside of Chicago, where Billy Graham went, but they aren't related. He likes sports of all varieties, especially basketball and lacrosse. His biggest sports achievement was scoring 7 goals in a lacrosse game when he was a junior in college (a 10–6 win against Illinois State). He and his wife have two beautiful children, Tom and Ella, who love books, which pleases him immensely.